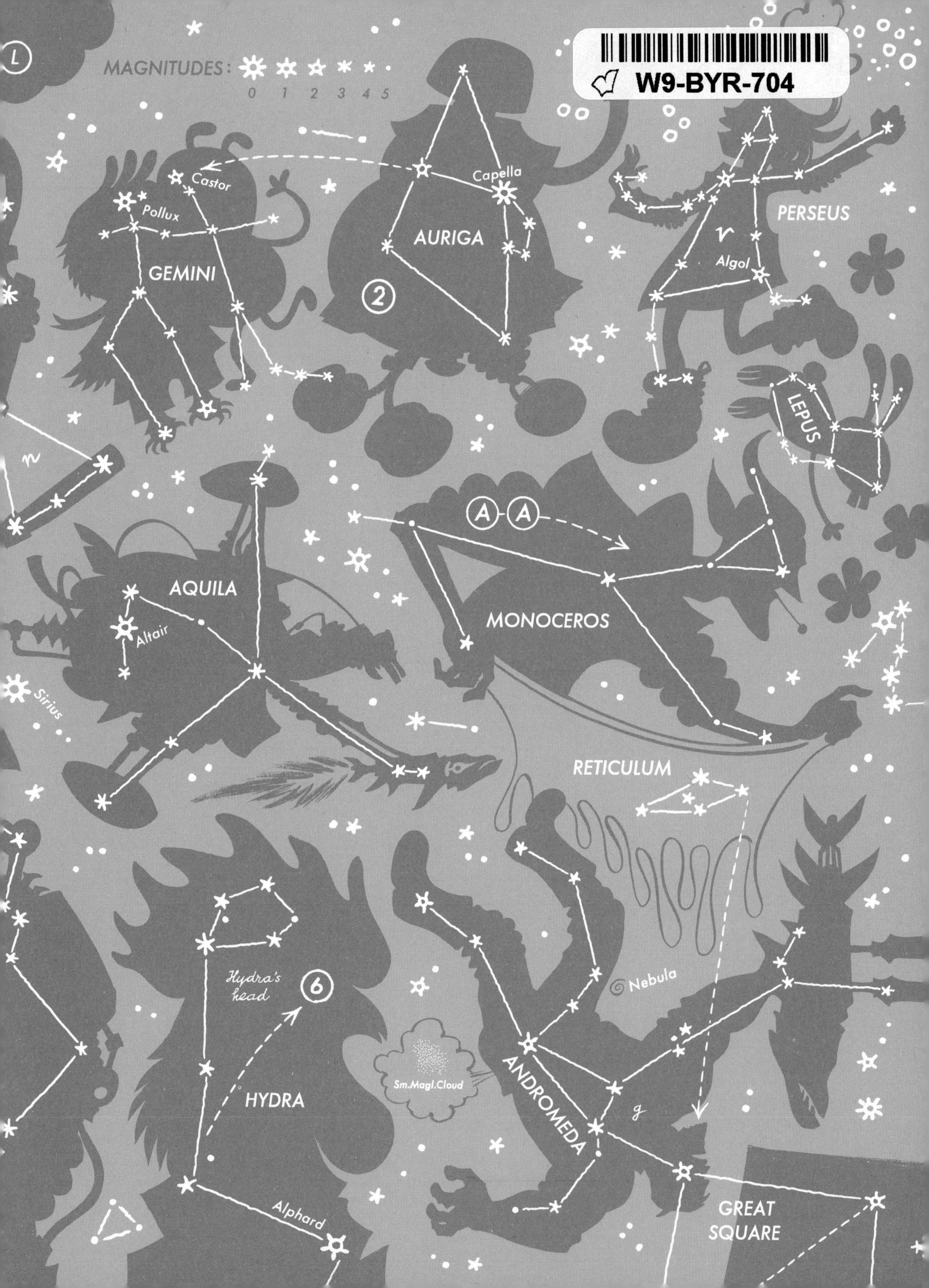
L
MAGNITUDES: 0 1 2 3 4 5
Castor
Pollux
GEMINI
Capella
AURIGA
2
PERSEUS
Algol
LEPUS
A-A
AQUILA
Altair
Sirius
MONOCEROS
RETICULUM
Hydra's head
6
Nebula
Sm.Magl.Cloud
HYDRA
ANDROMEDA
Alphard
GREAT SQUARE

SPACE DUMPLINS

CRAIG THOMPSON
WITH COLOR BY DAVE STEWART

graphix

AN IMPRINT OF

■ SCHOLASTIC

"They had dumplings, too; small, but substantial, symmetrically globular, and INDESTRUCTIBLE DUMPLINGS."

MOBY-DICK
BY HERMAN MELVILLE

All rights reserved. Published by Graphix, an imprint of Scholastic Inc., *Publishers since 1920.* SCHOLASTIC, GRAPHIX, and associated logos are trademarks and/or registered trademarks of Scholastic Inc.

The publisher does not have any control over and does not assume any responsibility for author or third-party websites or their content.

Library of Congress Control Number Available

ISBN 978-0-545-56541-7 (hardcover)
ISBN 978-0-545-56543-1 (paperback)

10 9 8 7 6 5 4 3 2 1   15 16 17 18 19

Printed in China   38
First edition, September 2015
Edited by David Saylor & Adam Rau
Color by Dave Stewart
Book design by Craig Thompson & Phil Falco
Creative Director: David Saylor

STAR MAP

GYROMETER

NAVIGATION

SW

MAGNITUDES • ★ ✴ ✺ ✹ ❈

01

GIMME SHELL-TARR

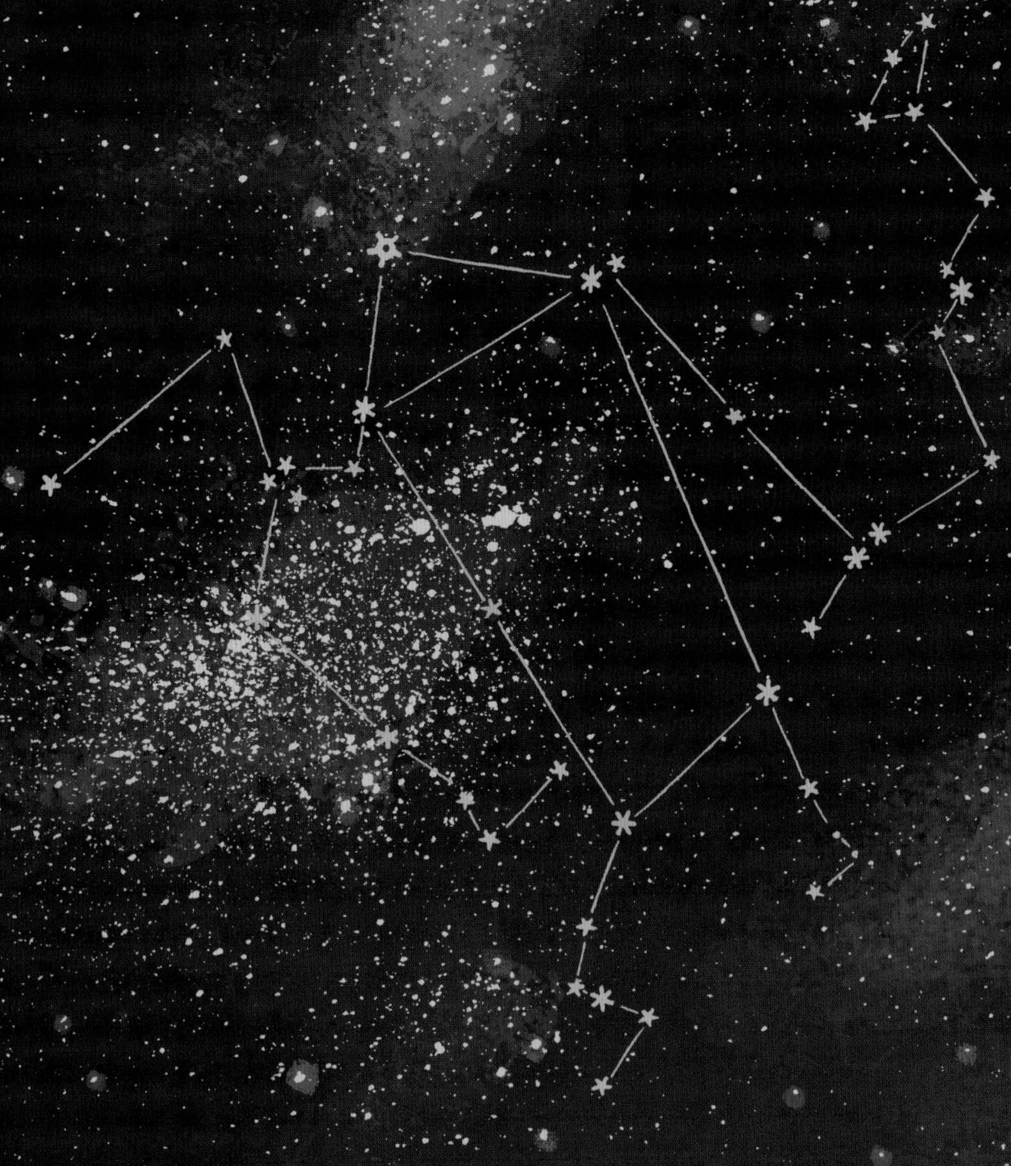

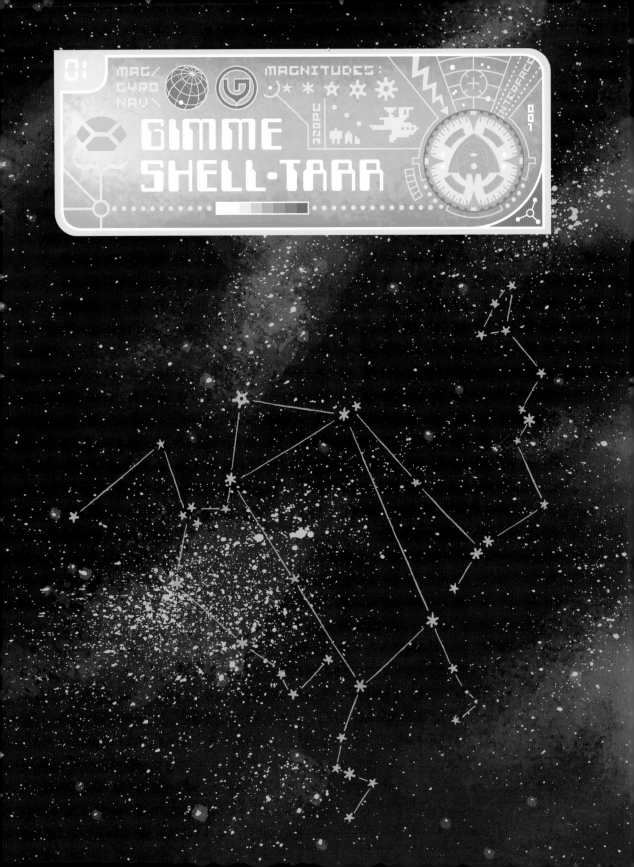

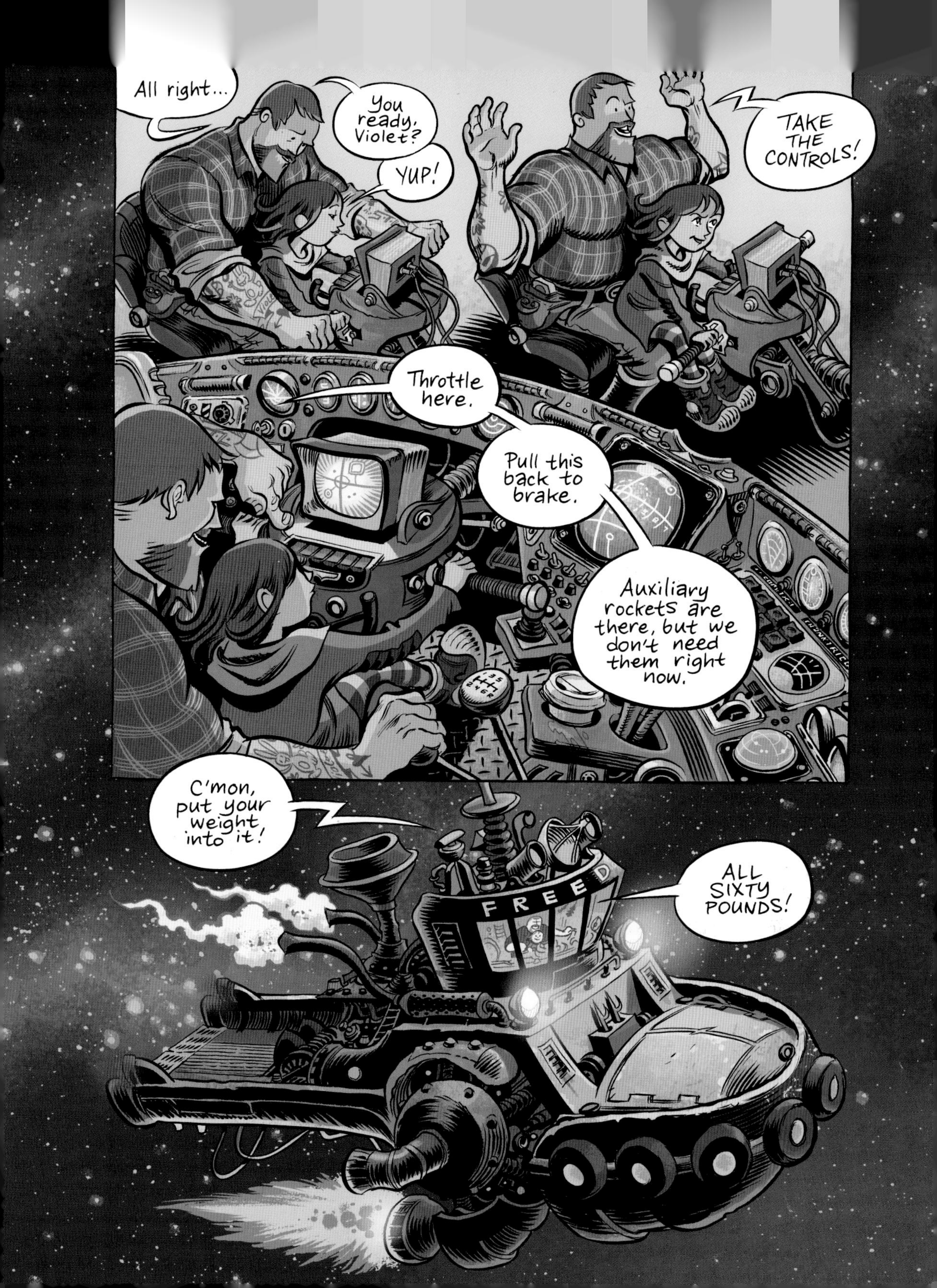
All right...
You ready, Violet?
YUP!
TAKE THE CONTROLS!
Throttle here.
Pull this back to brake.
Auxiliary rockets are there, but we don't need them right now.
C'mon, put your weight into it!
ALL SIXTY POUNDS!
FREED

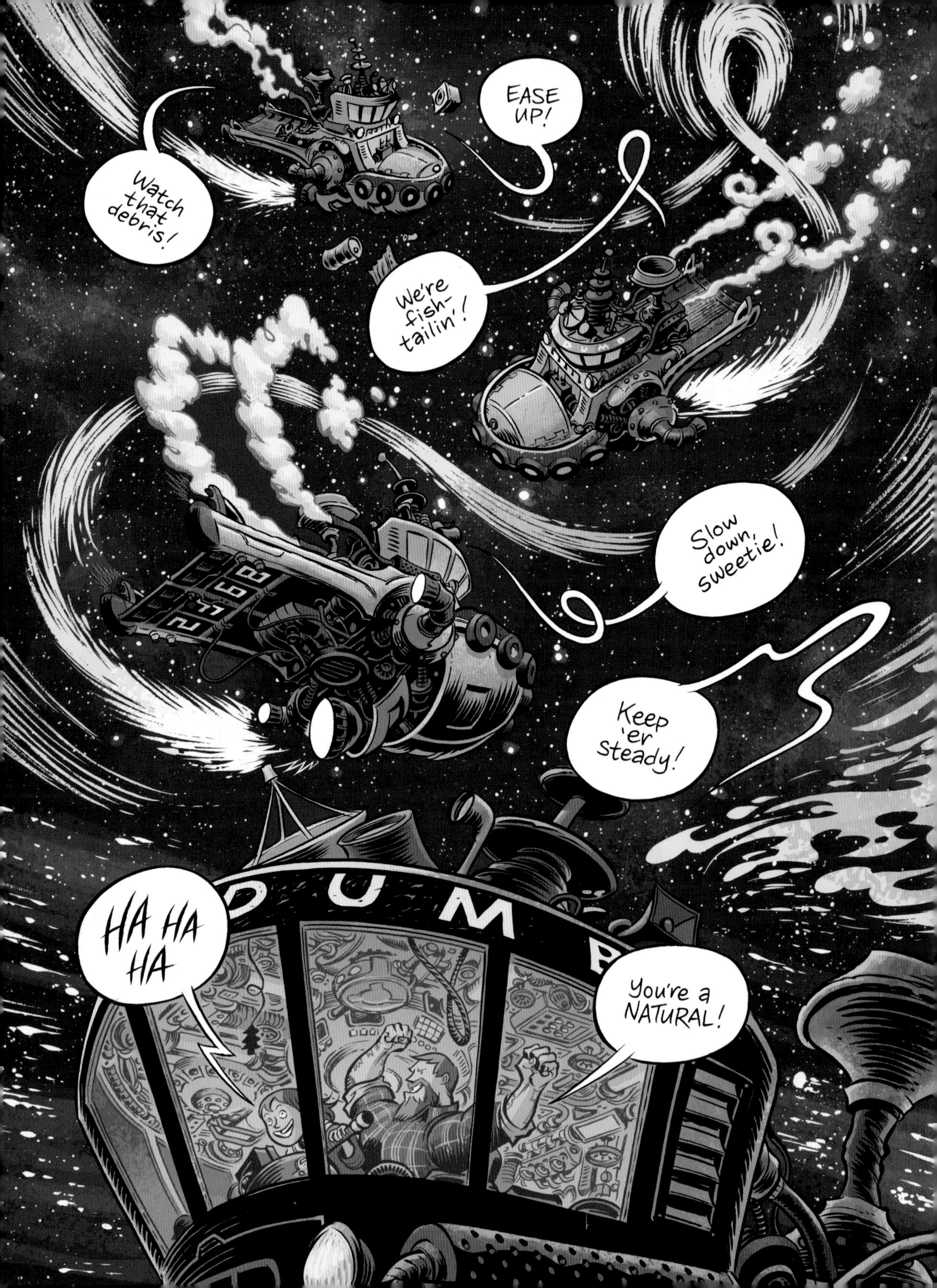
Watch that debris!
EASE UP!
We're fish-tailin'!
Slow down, sweetie!
Keep 'er steady!
HA HA HA
You're a NATURAL!

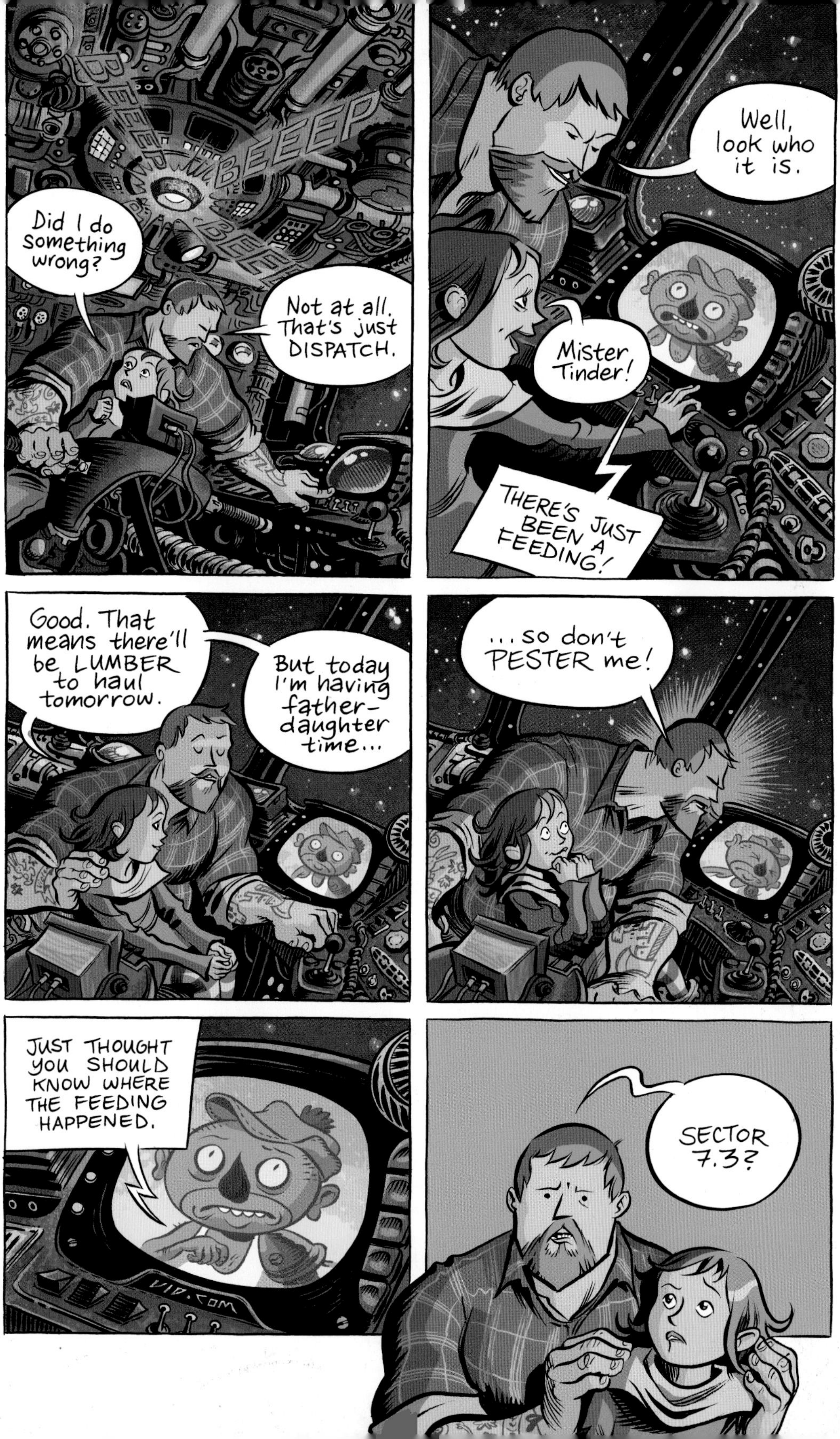
BEEEP BEEEP BEEP
Did I do something wrong?
Not at all. That's just DISPATCH.
Well, look who it is.
Mister Tinder!
THERE'S JUST BEEN A FEEDING!
Good. That means there'll be LUMBER to haul tomorrow.
But today I'm having father-daughter time...
...so don't PESTER me!
JUST THOUGHT YOU SHOULD KNOW WHERE THE FEEDING HAPPENED.
VID.COM
SECTOR 7.3?

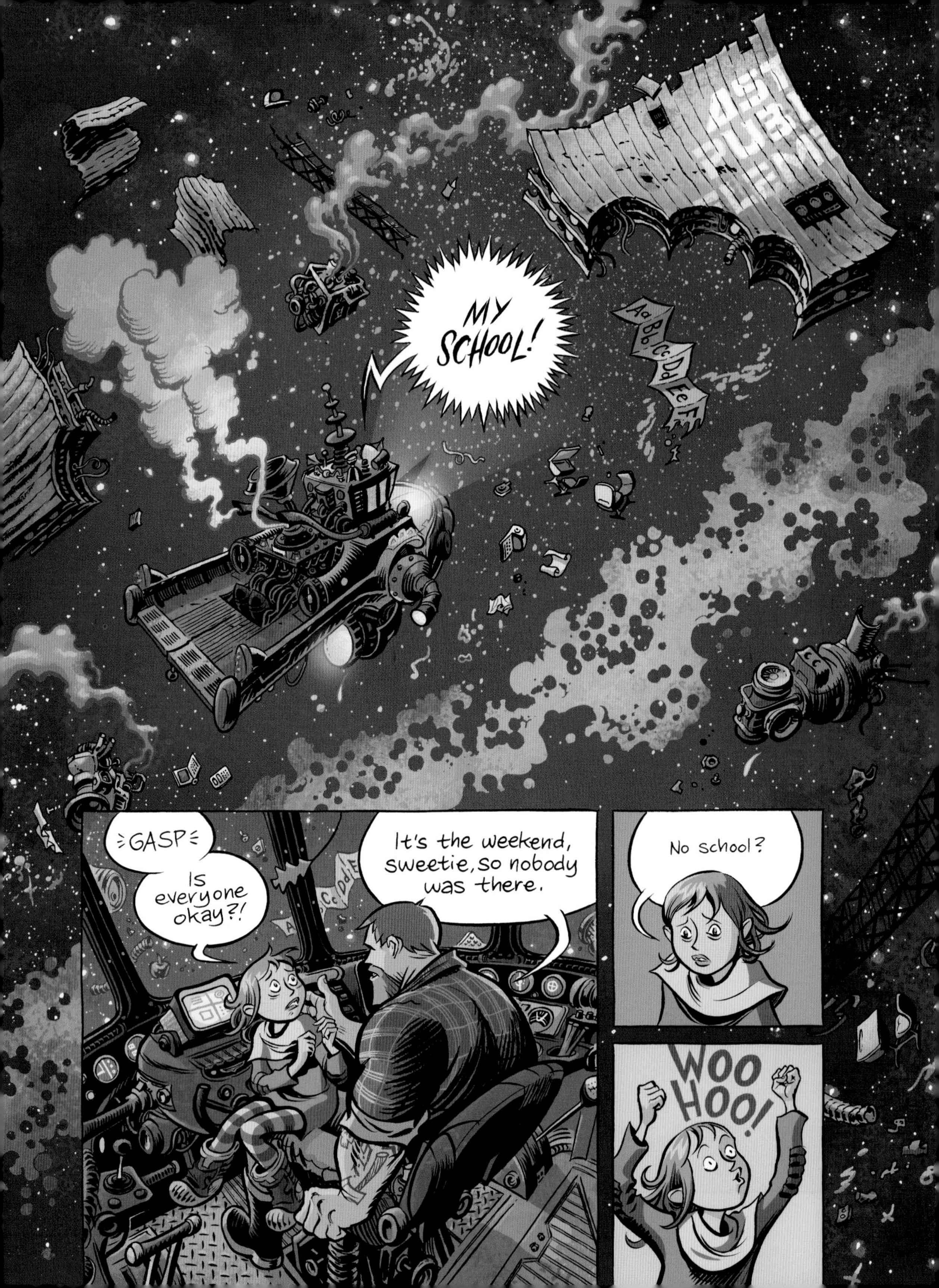
MY SCHOOL!
GASP
Is everyone okay?!
It's the weekend, sweetie, so nobody was there.
No school?
WOO HOO!

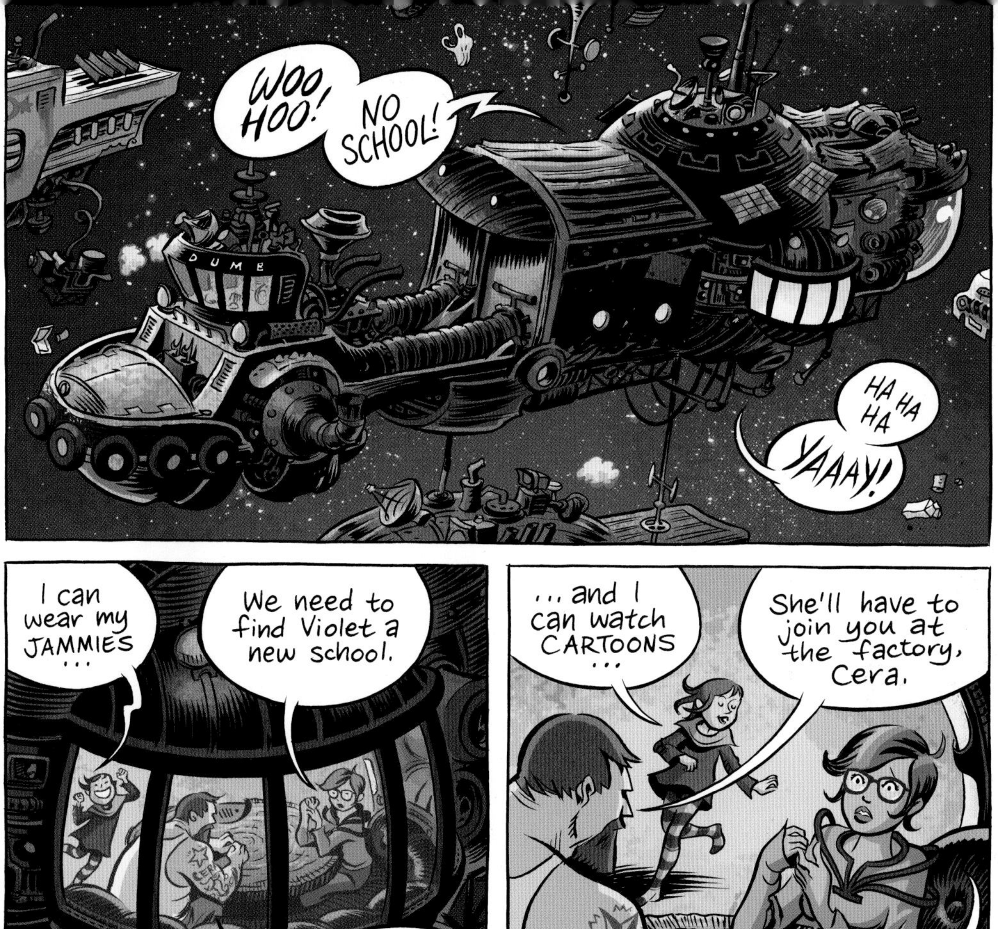
DUMB
WOO HOO!
NO SCHOOL!
HA HA HA
YAAAY!
I can wear my JAMMIES ...
We need to find Violet a new school.
Can't tomorrow. It's harvesting time.
... and I can watch CARTOONS ...
She'll have to join you at the factory, Cera.
But, Gar...
I want to go to Daddy's work!
DADDY'S WORK IS TOO DANGEROUS!

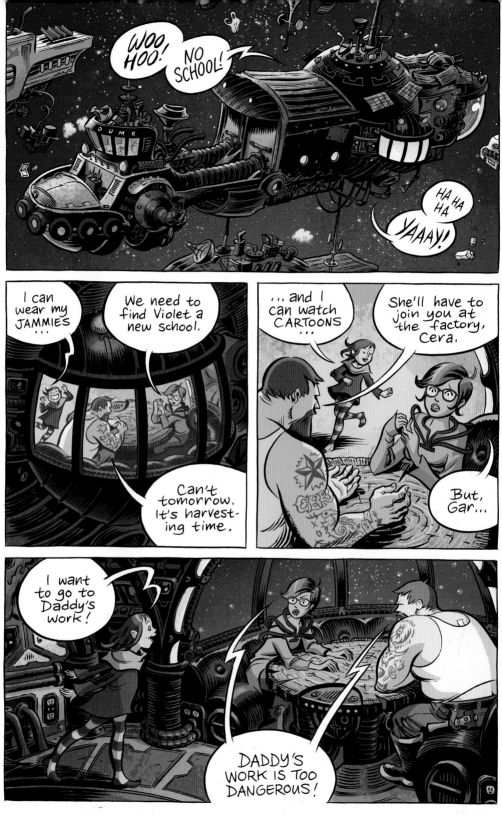

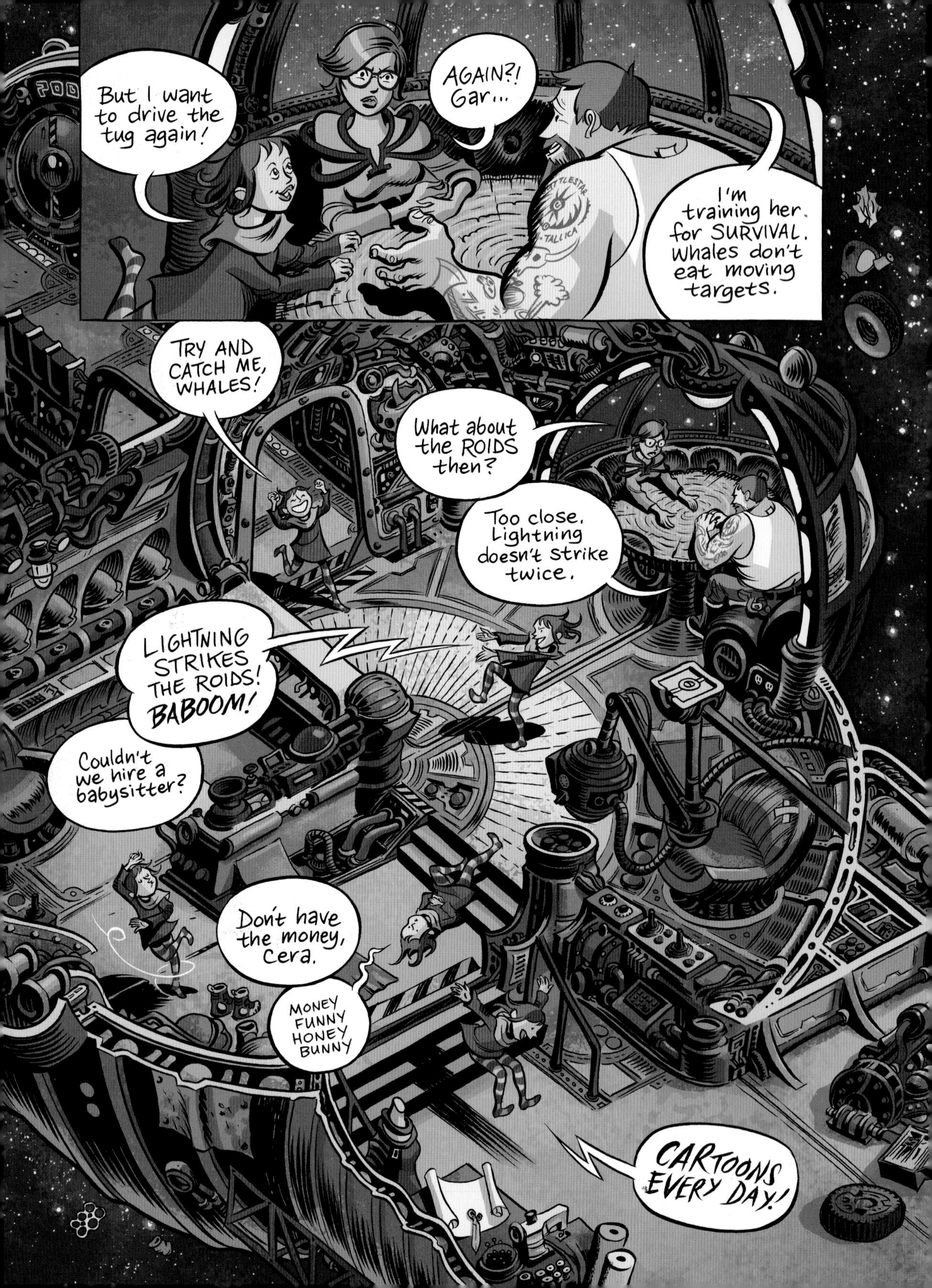
But I want to drive the tug again!
AGAIN?! Gar...
I'm training her for SURVIVAL. Whales don't eat moving targets.
TRY AND CATCH ME, WHALES!
What about the ROIDS then?
Too close. Lightning doesn't strike twice.
LIGHTNING STRIKES THE ROIDS! BABOOM!
Couldn't we hire a babysitter?
Don't have the money, Cera.
MONEY FUNNY HONEY BUNNY
CARTOONS EVERY DAY!

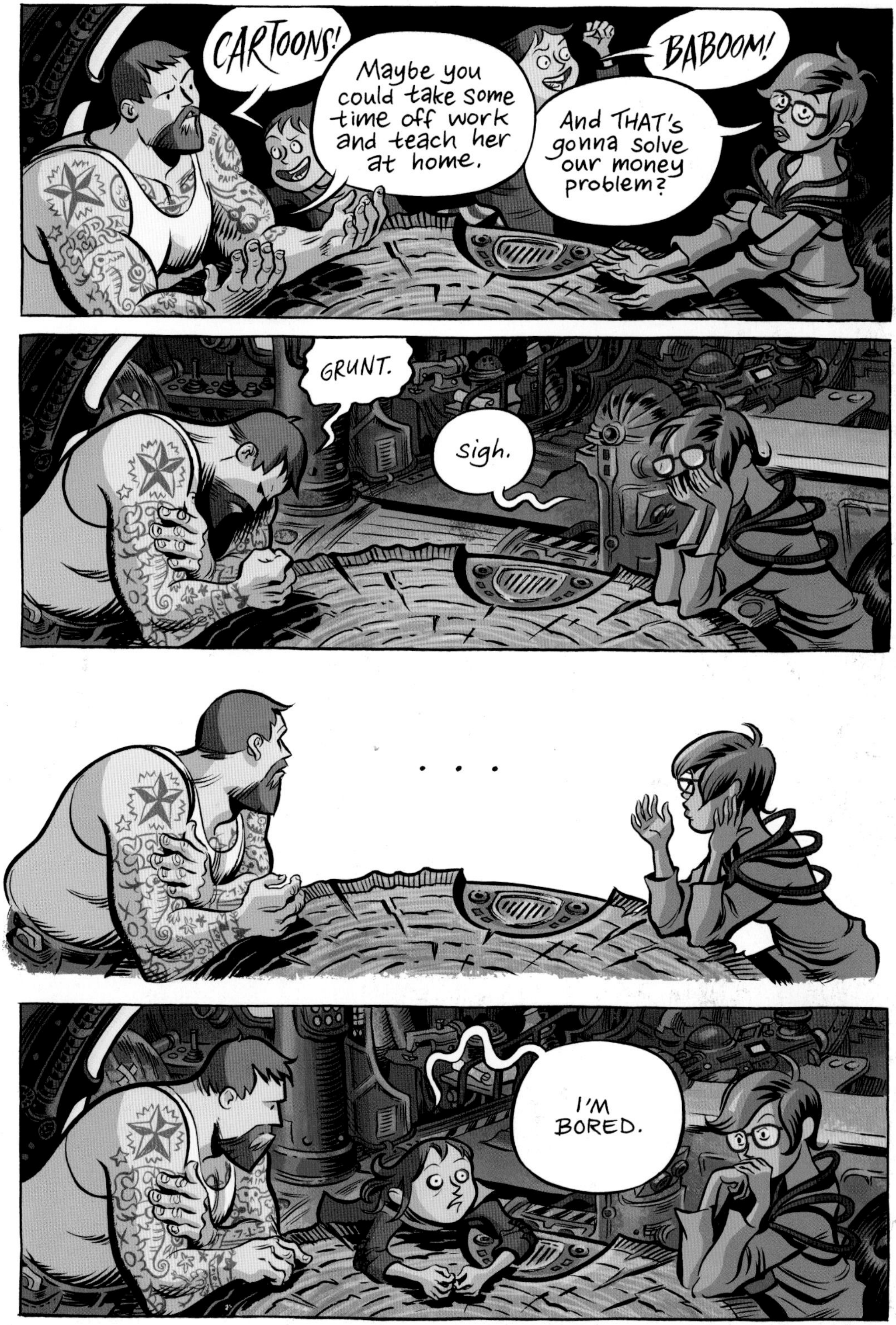
CARTOONS!
Maybe you could take some time off work and teach her at home.
BABOOM!
And THAT's gonna solve our money problem?
GRUNT.
sigh.
. . .
I'M BORED.

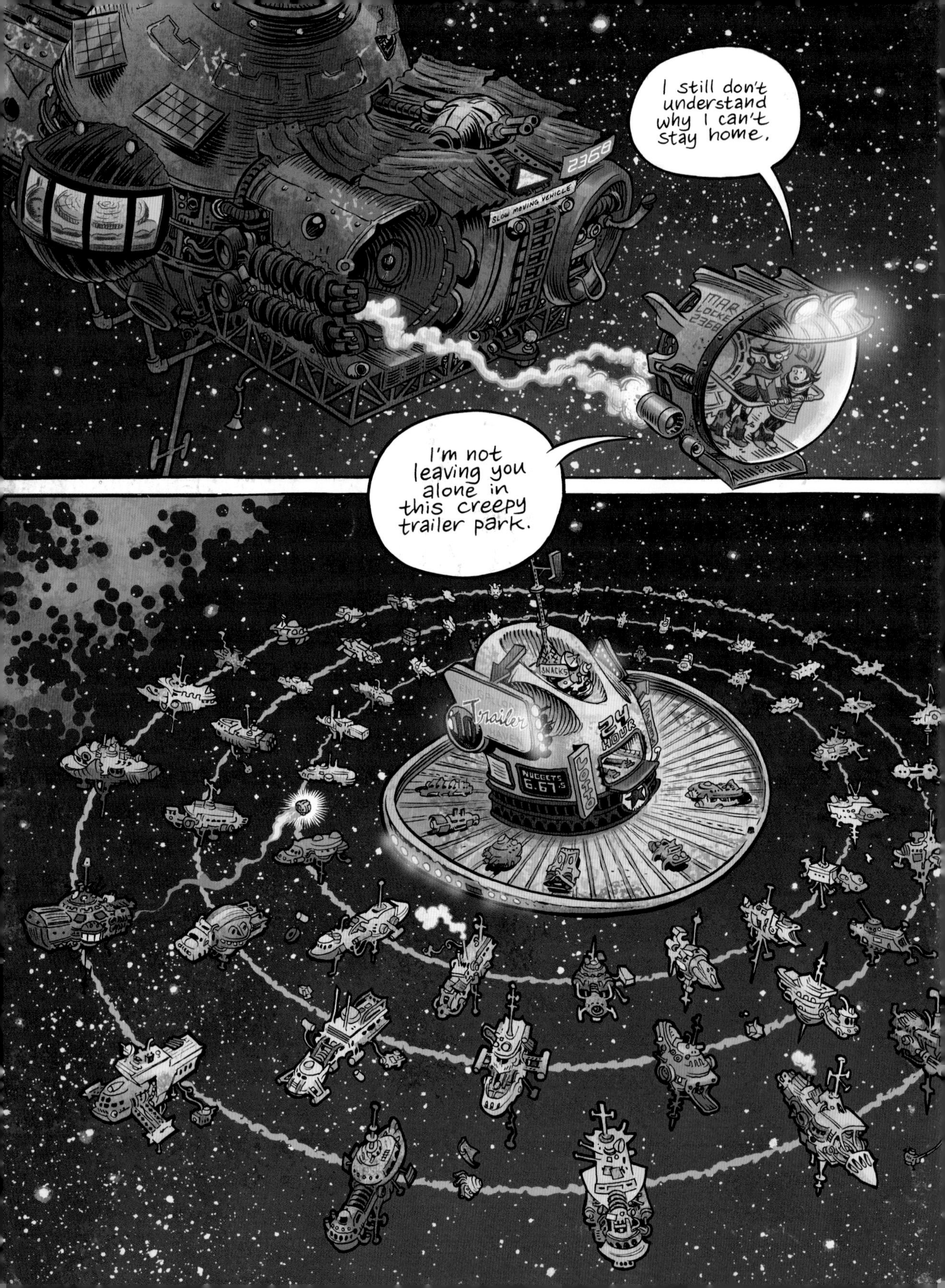
I still don't understand why I can't stay home.
I'm not leaving you alone in this creepy trailer park.
2368
SLOW MOVING VEHICLE
SNACKS
Trailer
24 HOUR
NUGGETS 6.67's

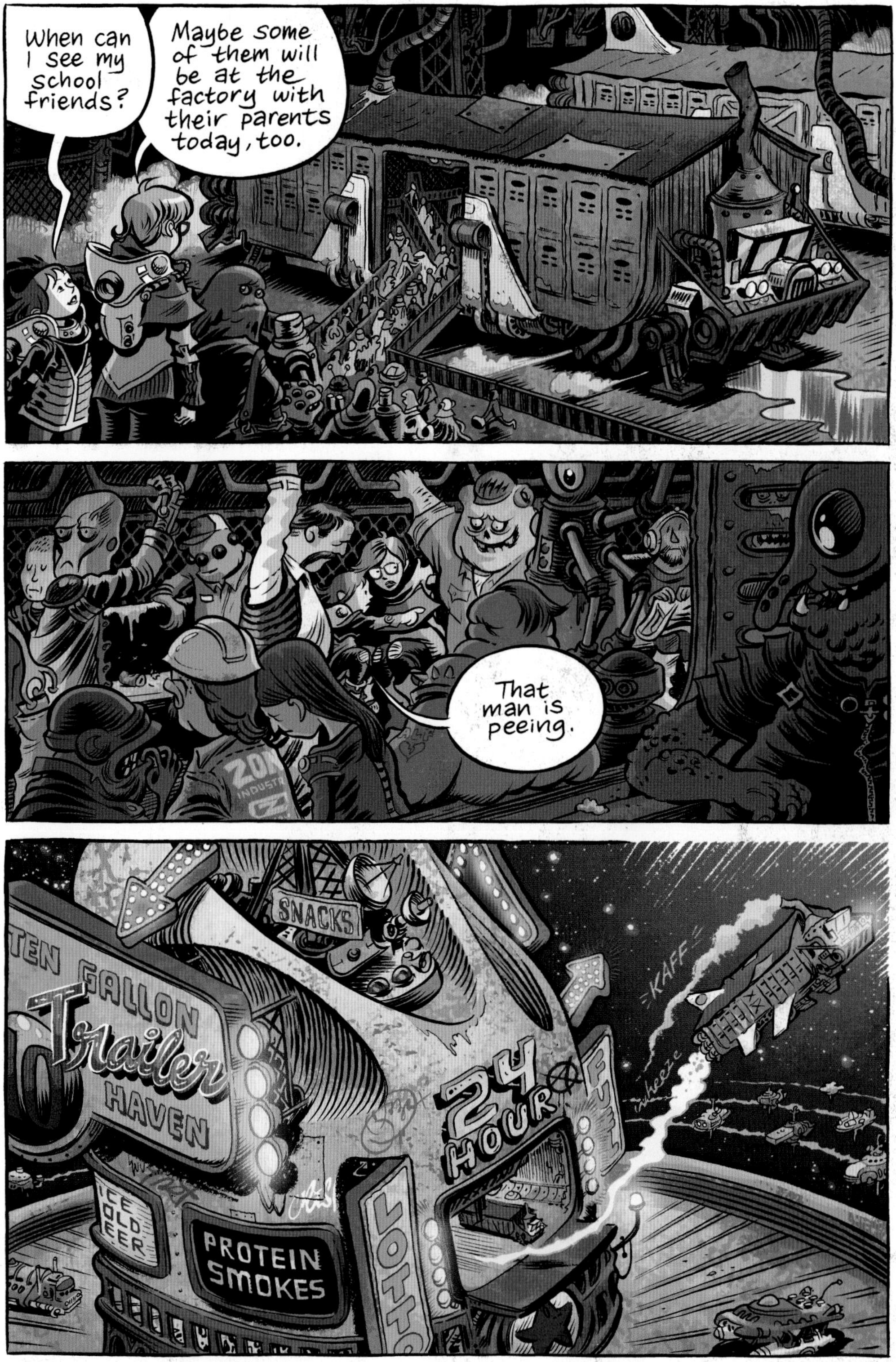
When can I see my school friends?
Maybe some of them will be at the factory with their parents today, too.
10
That man is peeing.
ZON INDUSTR
SNACKS
TEN GALLON
Trailer
HAVEN
24 HOUR
FUEL
LOTTO
PROTEIN SMOKES
ICE OLD EER
KAFF
wheeze

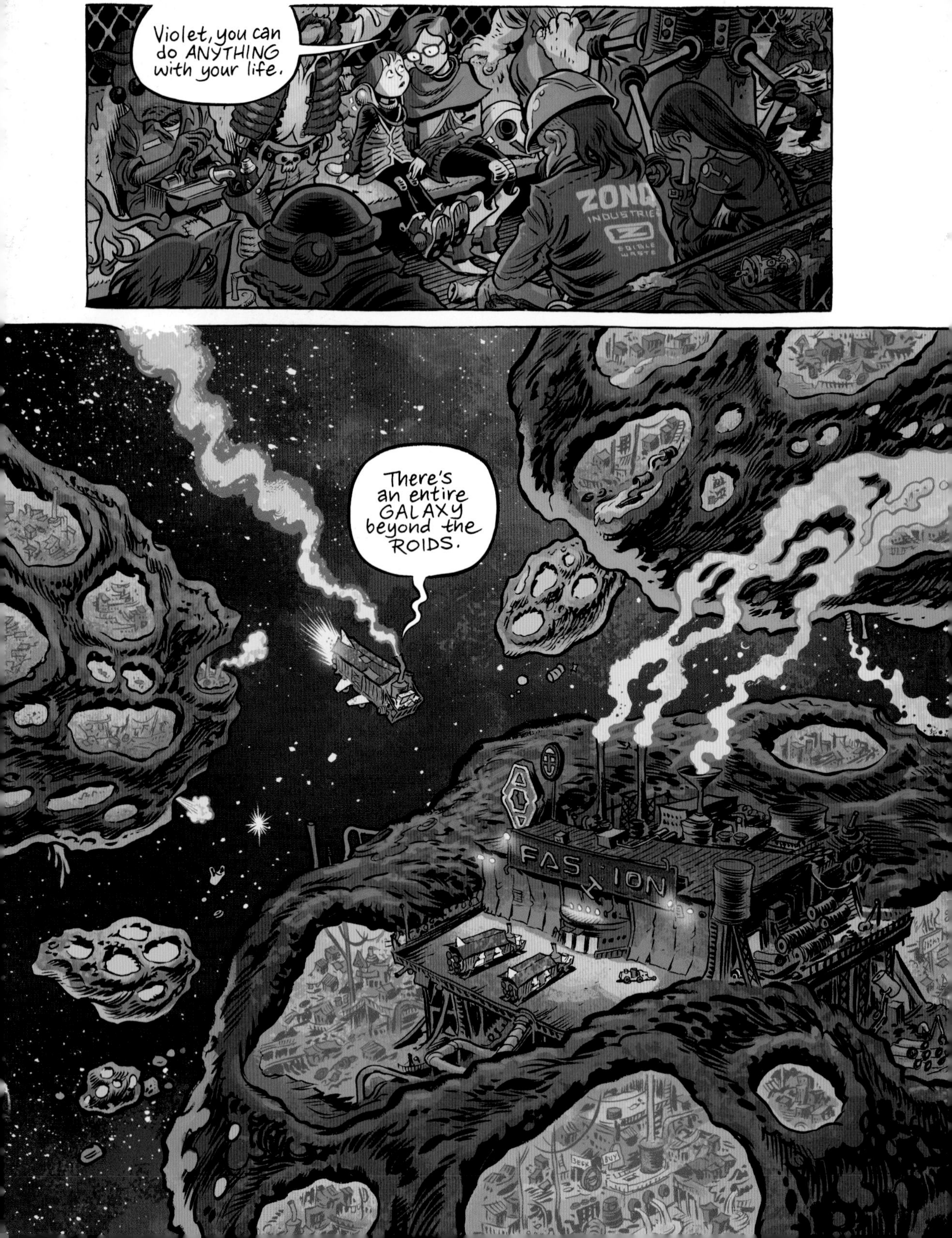
Violet, you can do ANYTHING with your life.
ZONQ
INDUSTRIES
EDIBLE WASTE
There's an entire GALAXY beyond the ROIDS.

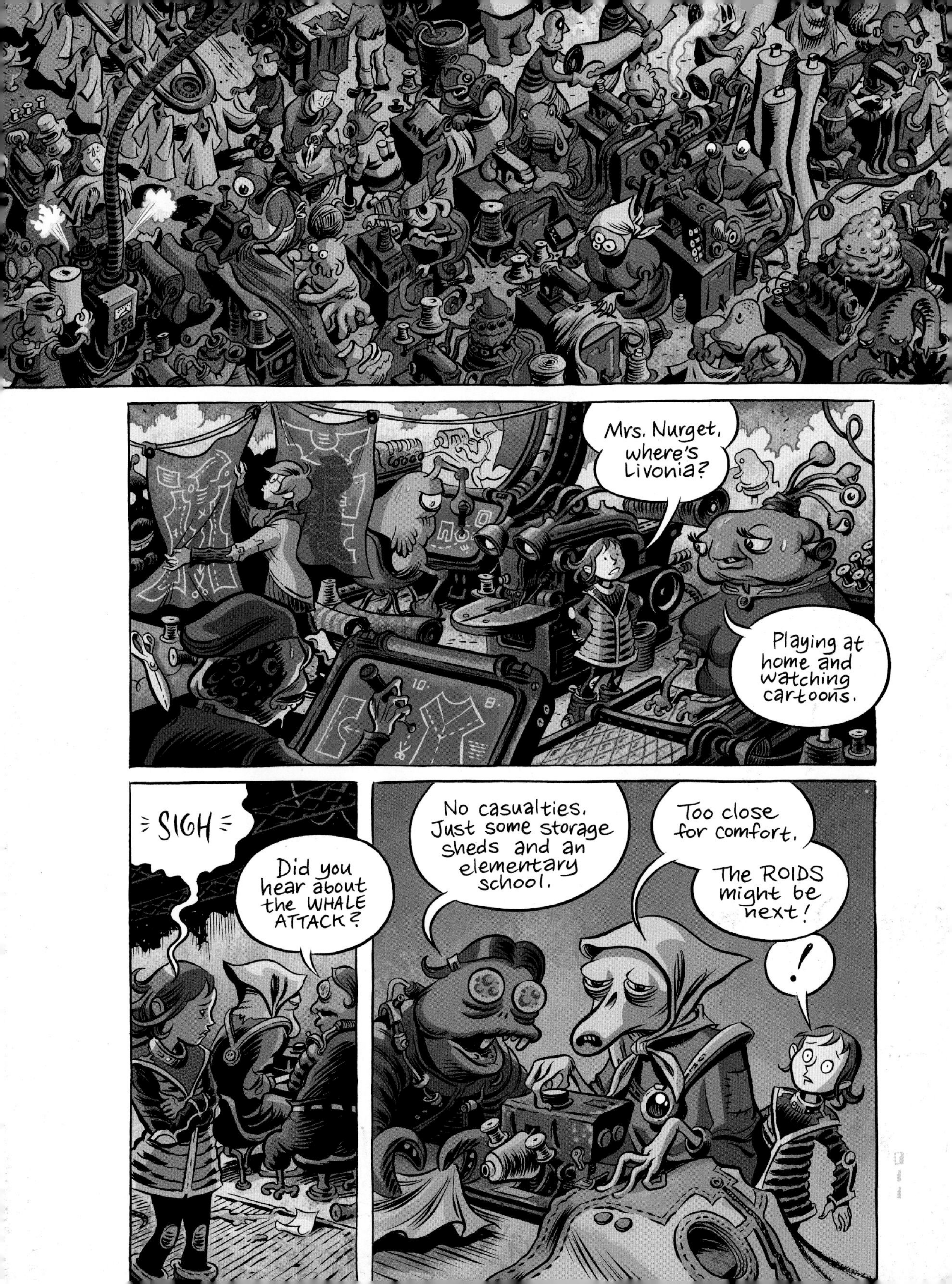
Mrs. Nurget, where's Livonia?
Playing at home and watching cartoons.
SIGH
Did you hear about the WHALE ATTACK?
No casualties. Just some storage sheds and an elementary school.
Too close for comfort.
The ROIDS might be next!
!

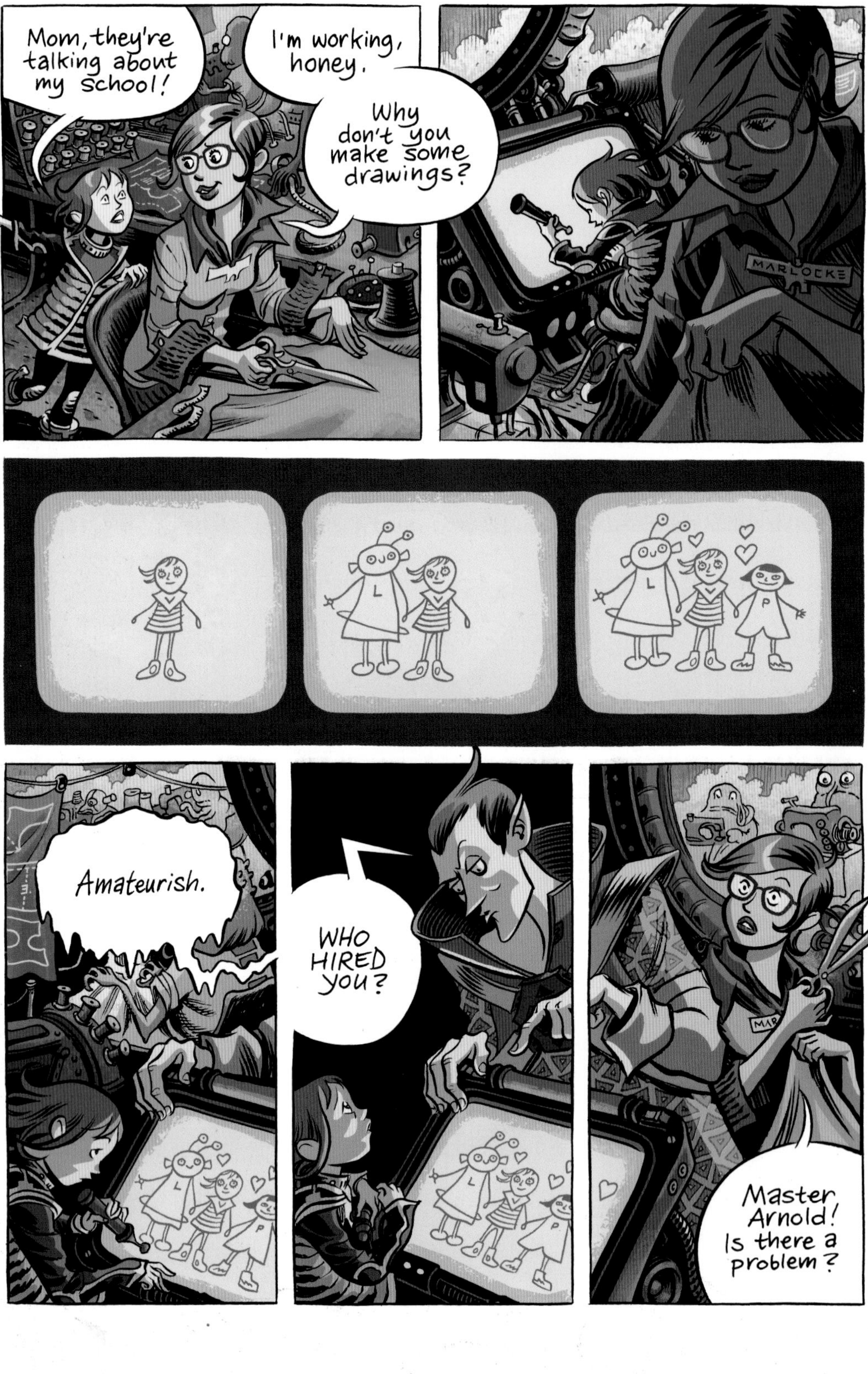
Mom, they're talking about my school!
I'm working, honey.
Why don't you make some drawings?
MARLOCKE
Amateurish.
WHO HIRED YOU?
Master Arnold! Is there a problem?

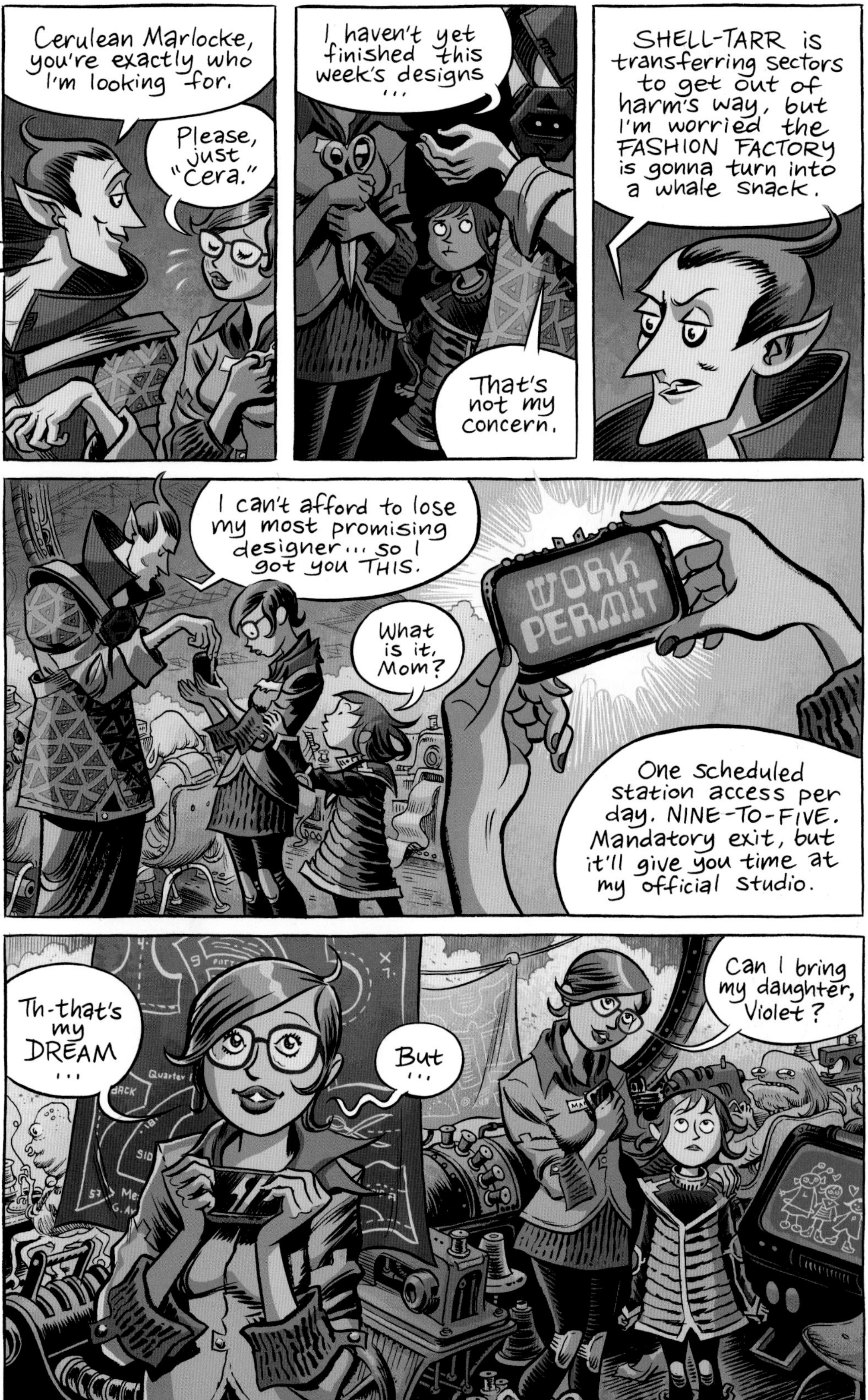
Cerulean Marlocke, you're exactly who I'm looking for.
Please, just "Cera."
I haven't yet finished this week's designs ...
That's not my concern.
SHELL-TARR is transferring sectors to get out of harm's way, but I'm worried the FASHION FACTORY is gonna turn into a whale snack.
I can't afford to lose my most promising designer... so I got you THIS.
WORK PERMIT
What is it, Mom?
One scheduled station access per day. NINE-TO-FIVE. Mandatory exit, but it'll give you time at my official studio.
Th-that's my DREAM ...
But ...
Can I bring my daughter, Violet?

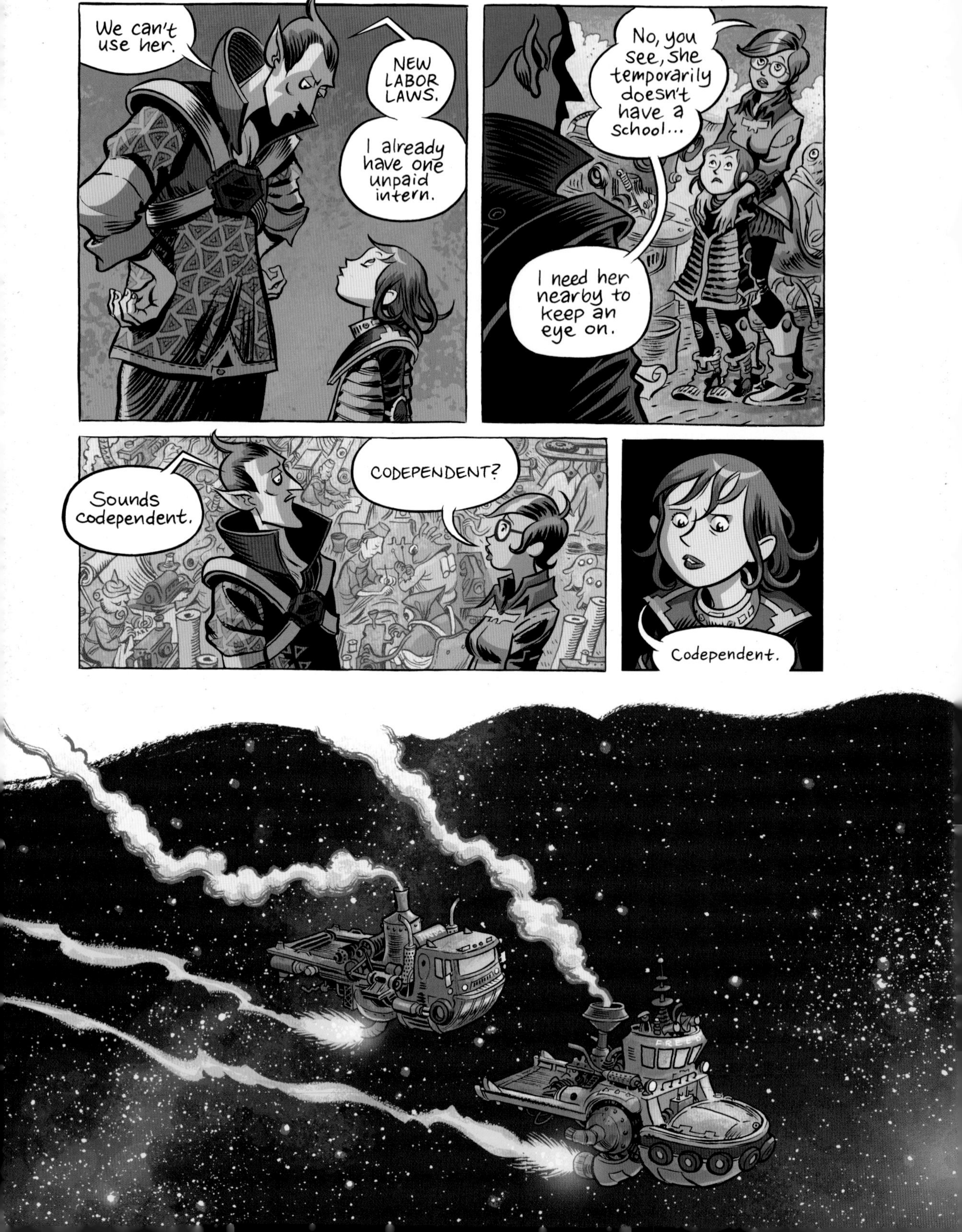
We can't use her.
NEW LABOR LAWS.
I already have one unpaid intern.
No, you see, she temporarily doesn't have a school...
I need her nearby to keep an eye on.
Sounds codependent.
CODEPENDENT?
Codependent.

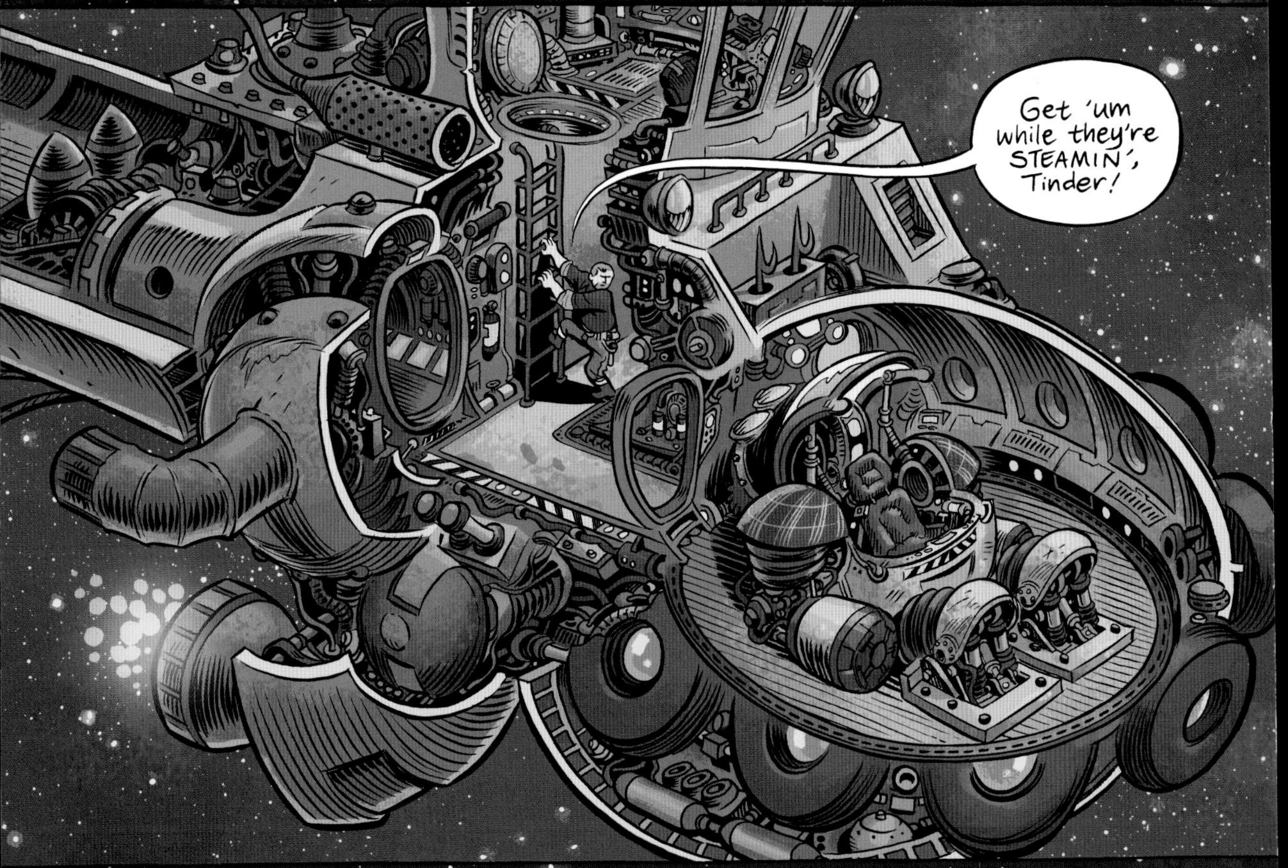
Get 'um while they're STEAMIN', Tinder!

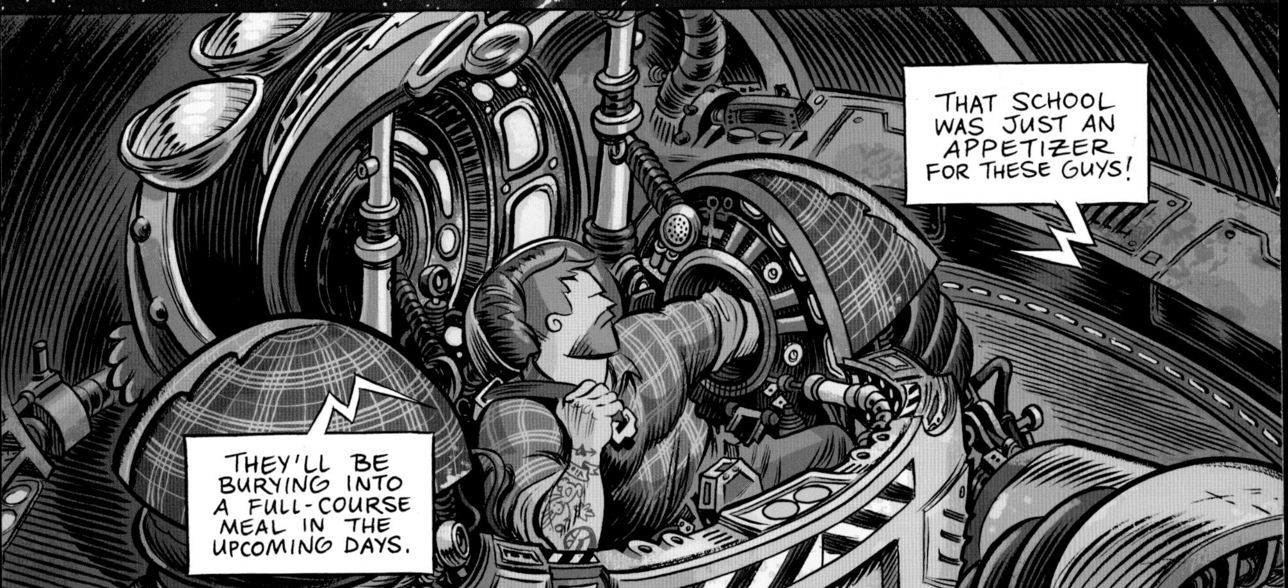
THAT SCHOOL WAS JUST AN APPETIZER FOR THESE GUYS!
THEY'LL BE BURYING INTO A FULL-COURSE MEAL IN THE UPCOMING DAYS.

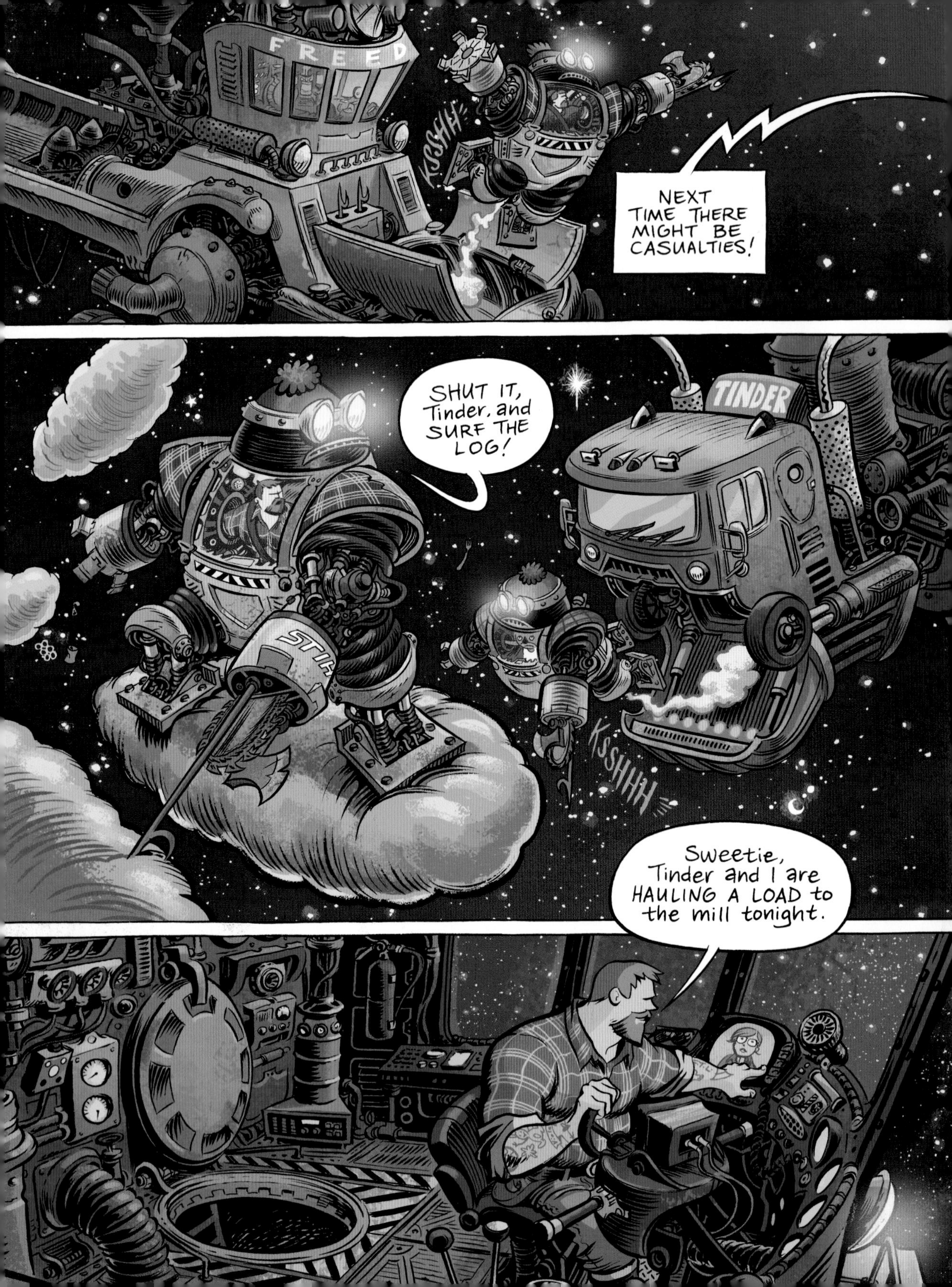
FREED
KSSHH
NEXT TIME THERE MIGHT BE CASUALTIES!
SHUT IT, Tinder, and SURF THE LOG!
TINDER
STIH
KSSHHH
Sweetie, Tinder and I are HAULING A LOAD to the mill tonight.

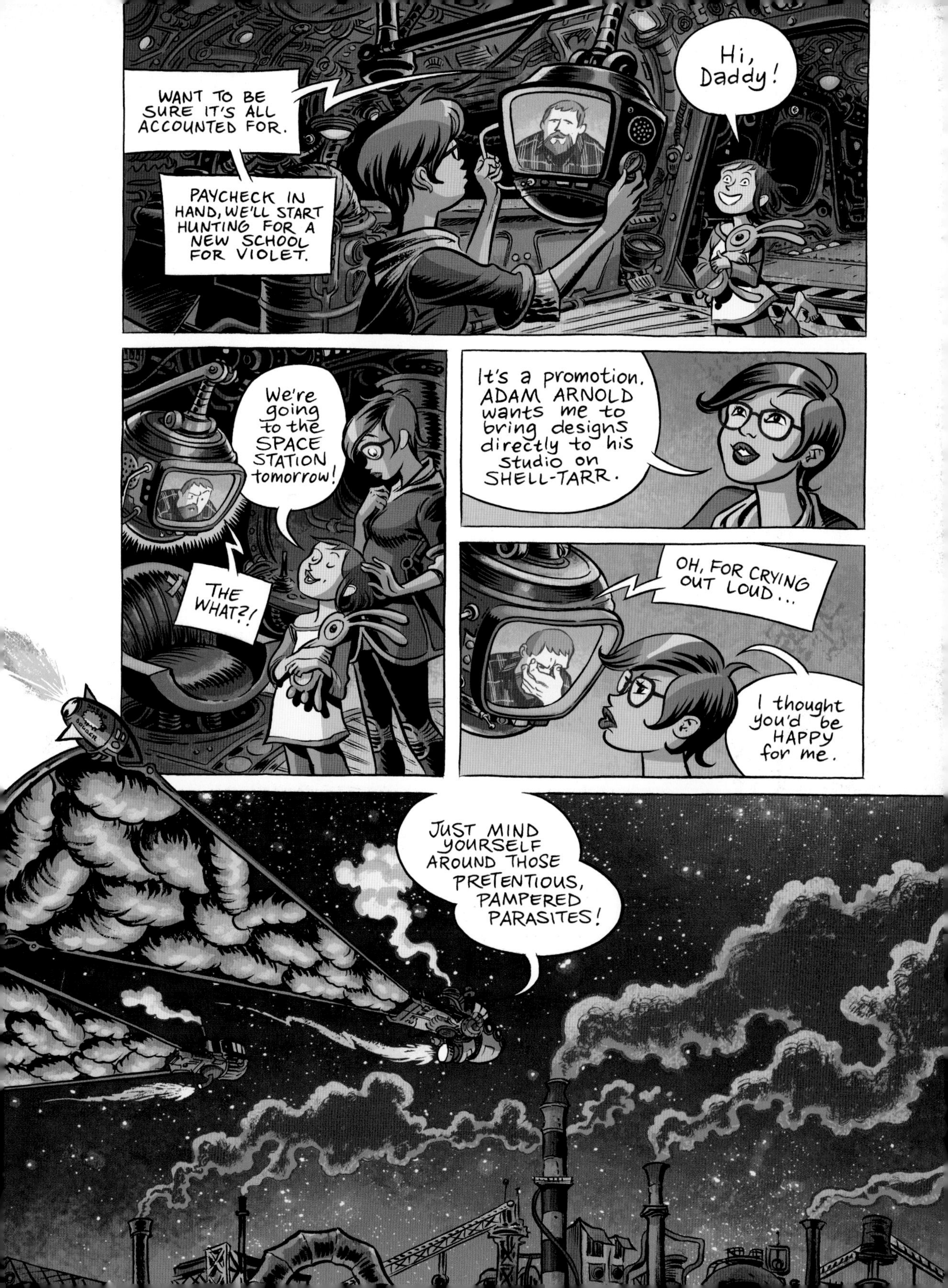
WANT TO BE SURE IT'S ALL ACCOUNTED FOR.
PAYCHECK IN HAND, WE'LL START HUNTING FOR A NEW SCHOOL FOR VIOLET.
Hi, Daddy!
We're going to the SPACE STATION tomorrow!
THE WHAT?!
It's a promotion. ADAM ARNOLD wants me to bring designs directly to his studio on SHELL-TARR.
OH, FOR CRYING OUT LOUD...
I thought you'd be HAPPY for me.
JUST MIND YOURSELF AROUND THOSE PRETENTIOUS, PAMPERED PARASITES!

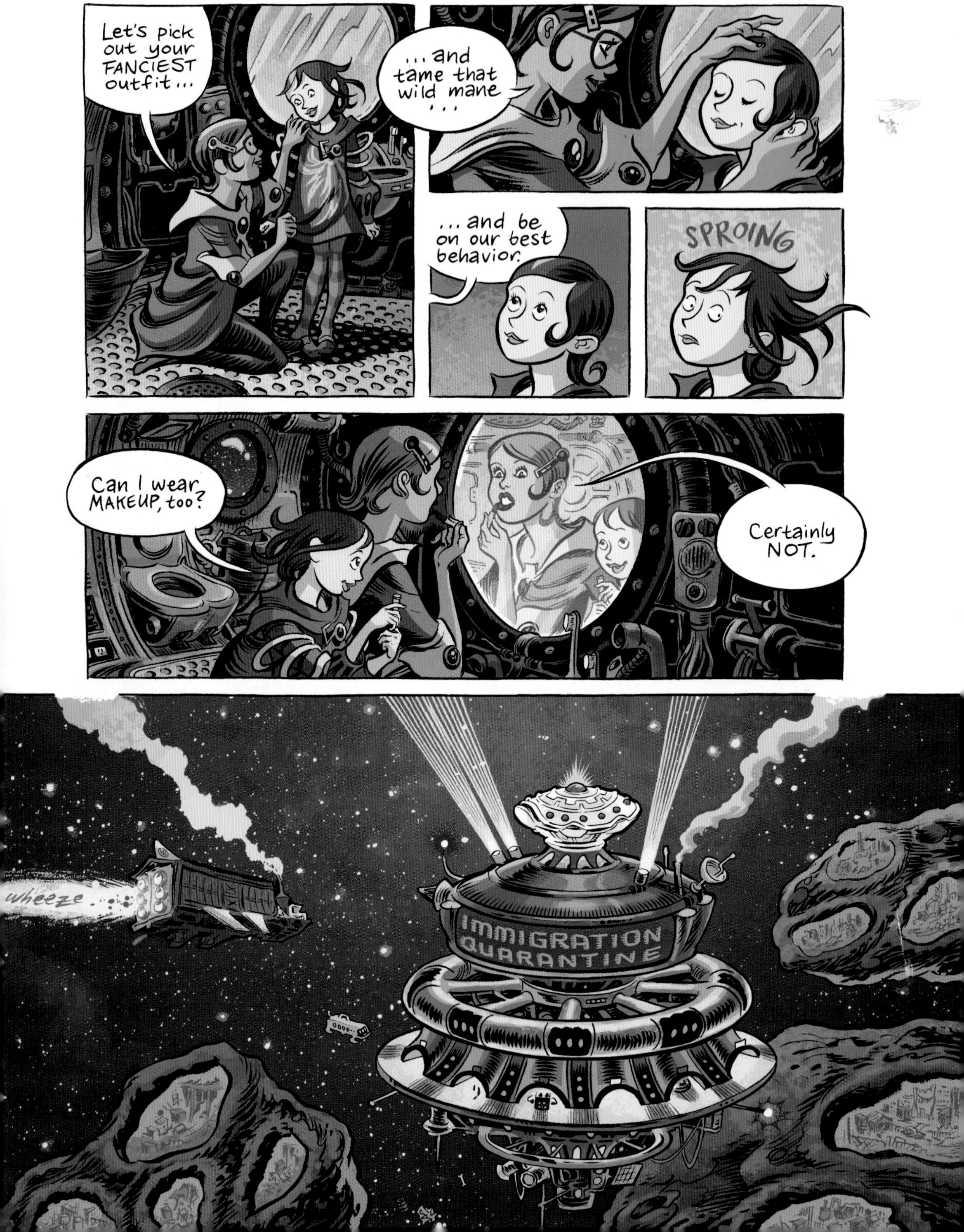
Let's pick out your FANCIEST outfit...
...and tame that wild mane...
...and be on our best behavior.
SPROING
Can I wear MAKEUP, too?
Certainly NOT.
wheeze
IMMIGRATION QUARANTINE

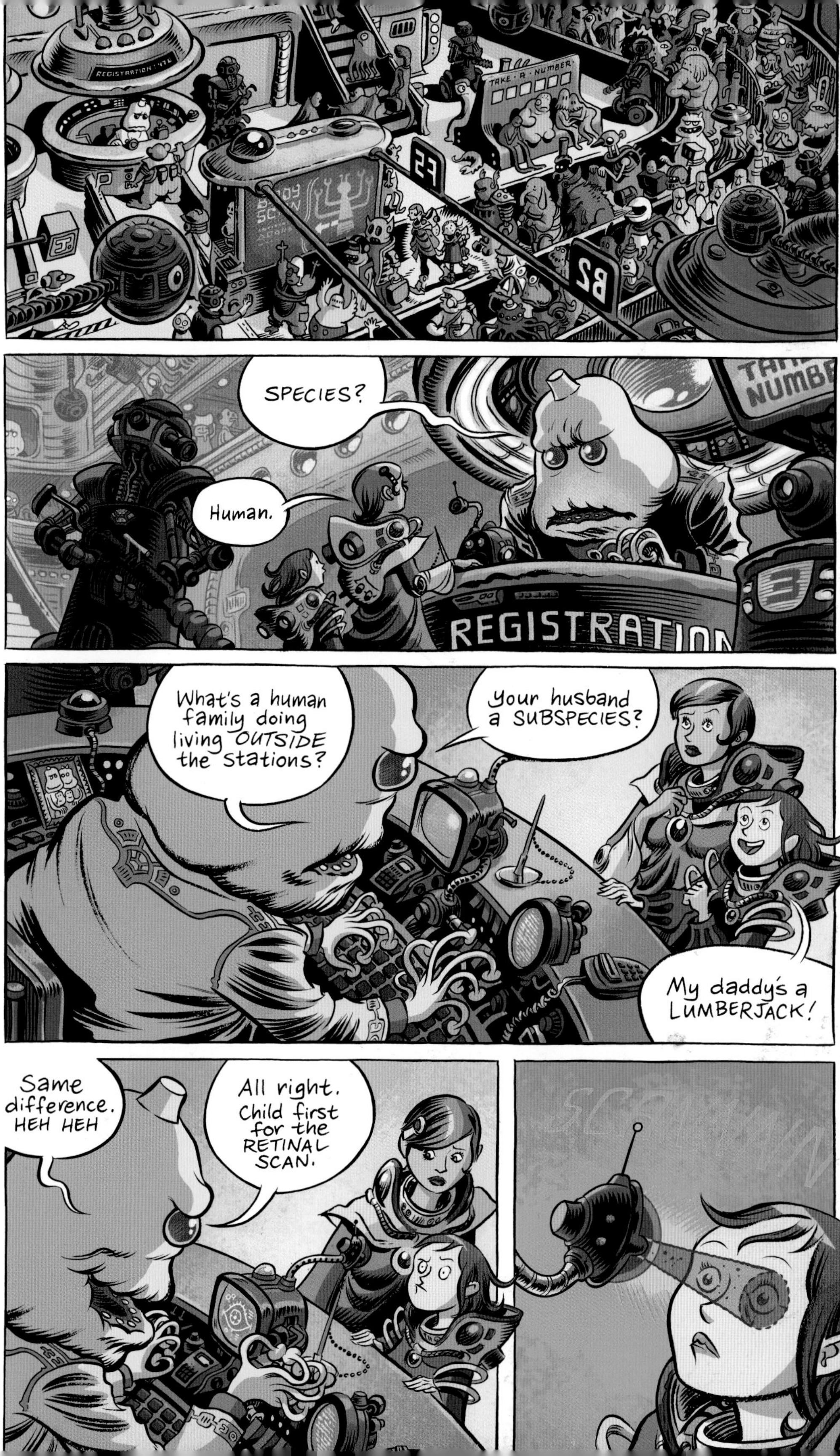
REGISTRATION
TAKE A NUMBER
BODY SCAN
SPECIES?
Human.
REGISTRATION
What's a human family doing living OUTSIDE the stations?
Your husband a SUBSPECIES?
My daddy's a LUMBERJACK!
Same difference. HEH HEH
All right. Child first for the RETINAL SCAN.
SCNNNN

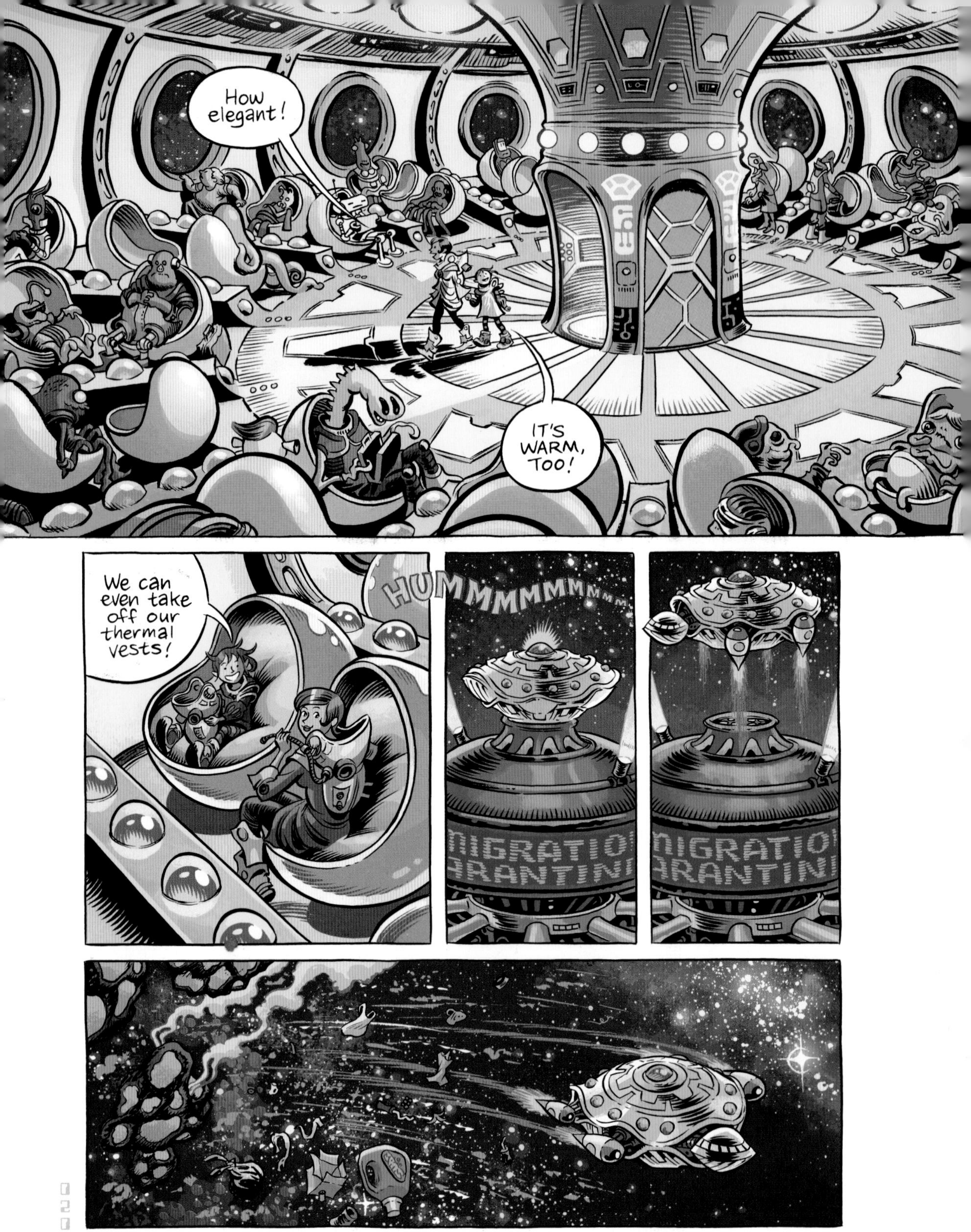
How elegant!
IT'S WARM, TOO!
We can even take off our thermal vests!
HUMMMMMMMMM
MIGRATIO
ARANTINI
MIGRATIO
ARANTINI

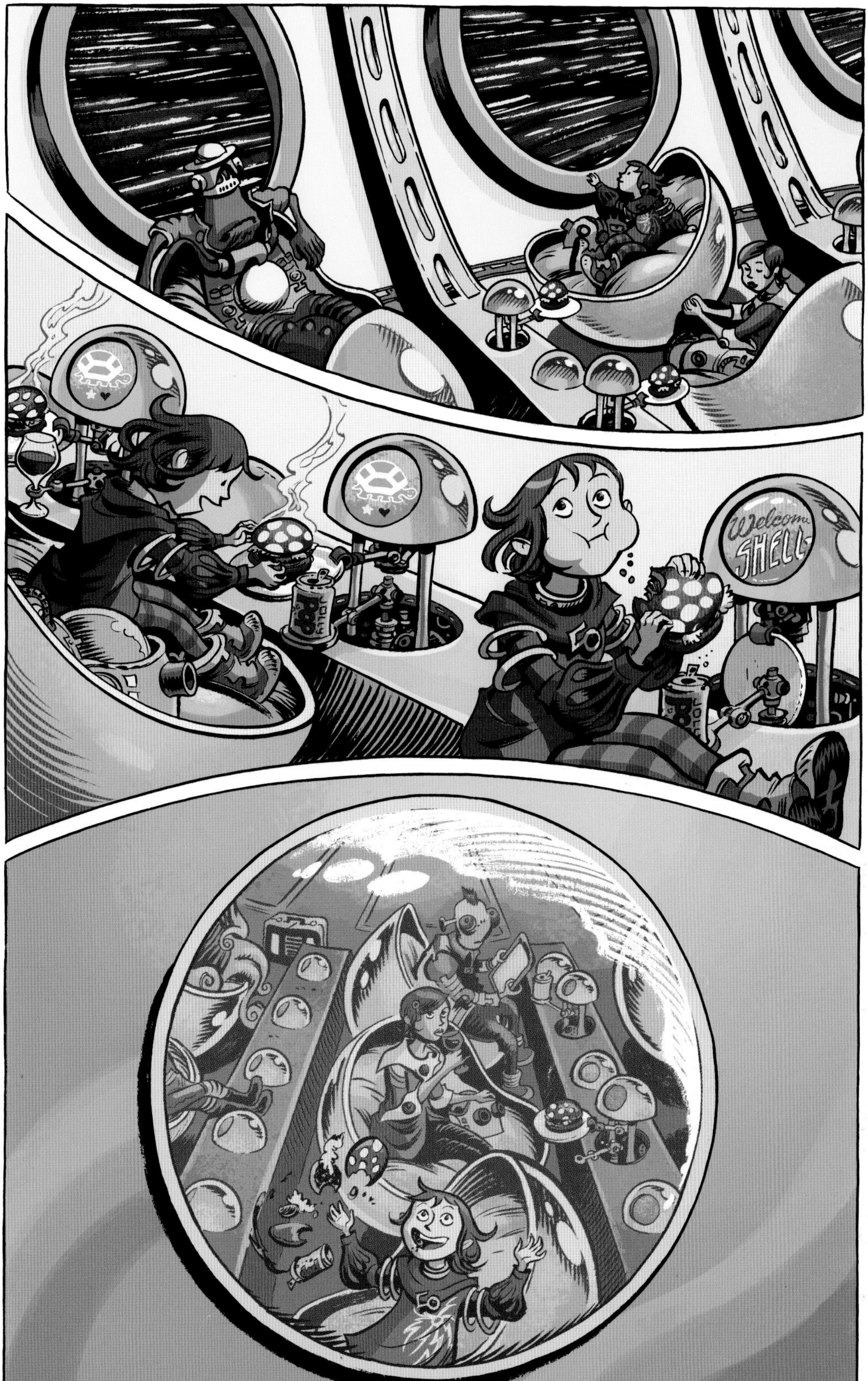
Welcome
SHELL

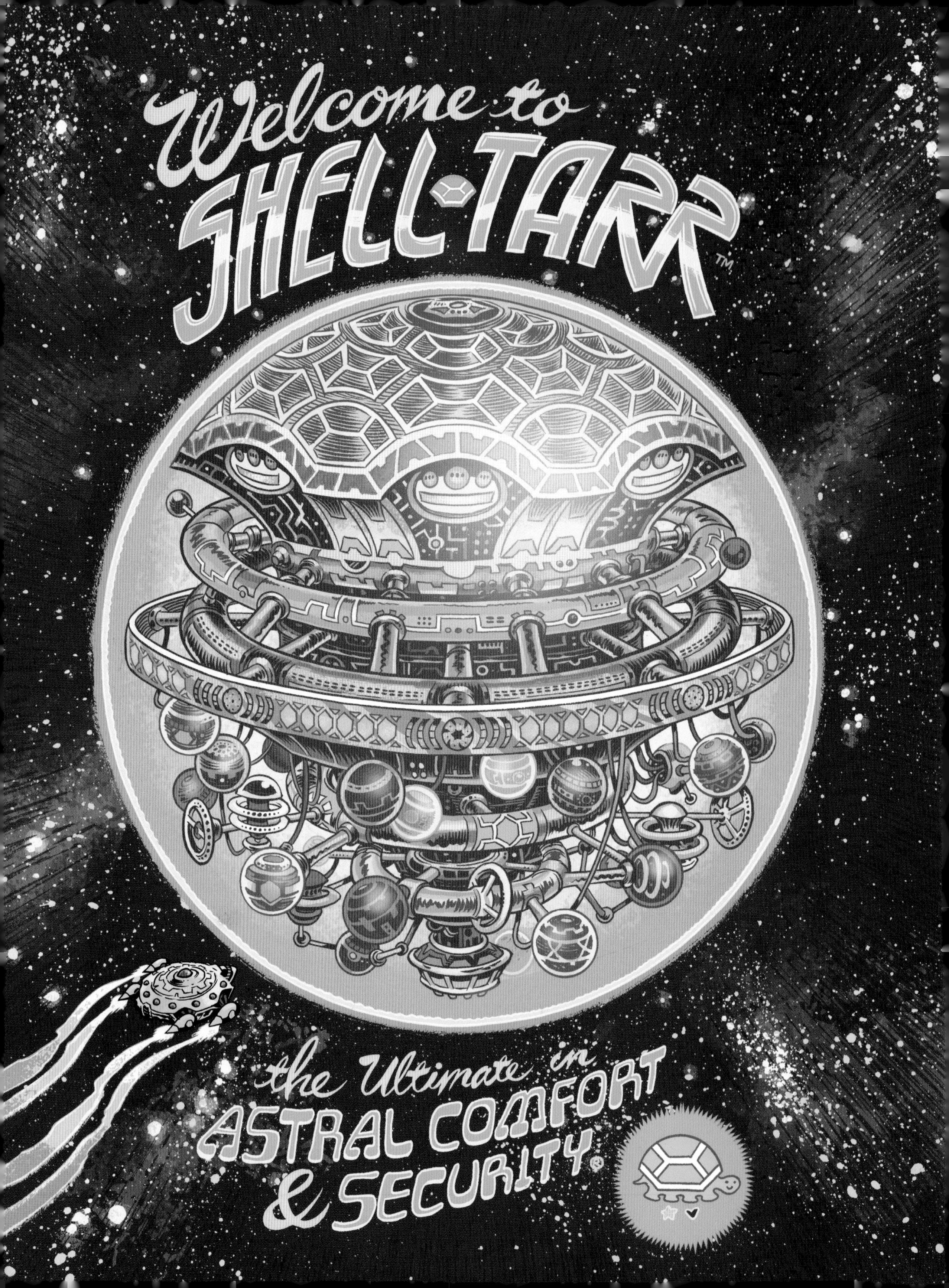
Welcome to
SHELL-TARR™
the Ultimate in
ASTRAL COMFORT
& SECURITY®

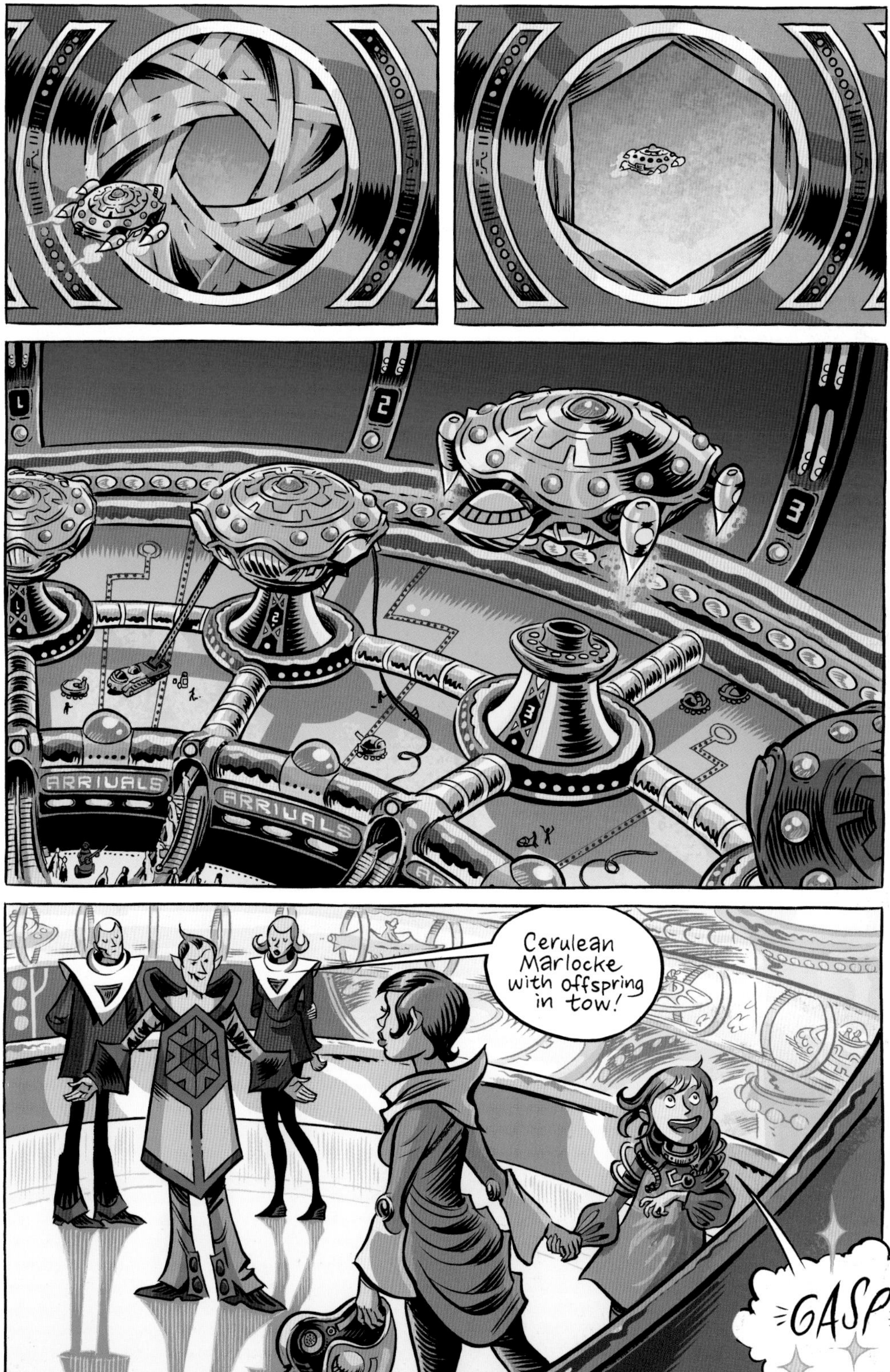
1
2
3
ARRIVALS
ARRIVALS
Cerulean Marlocke with offspring in tow!
GASP

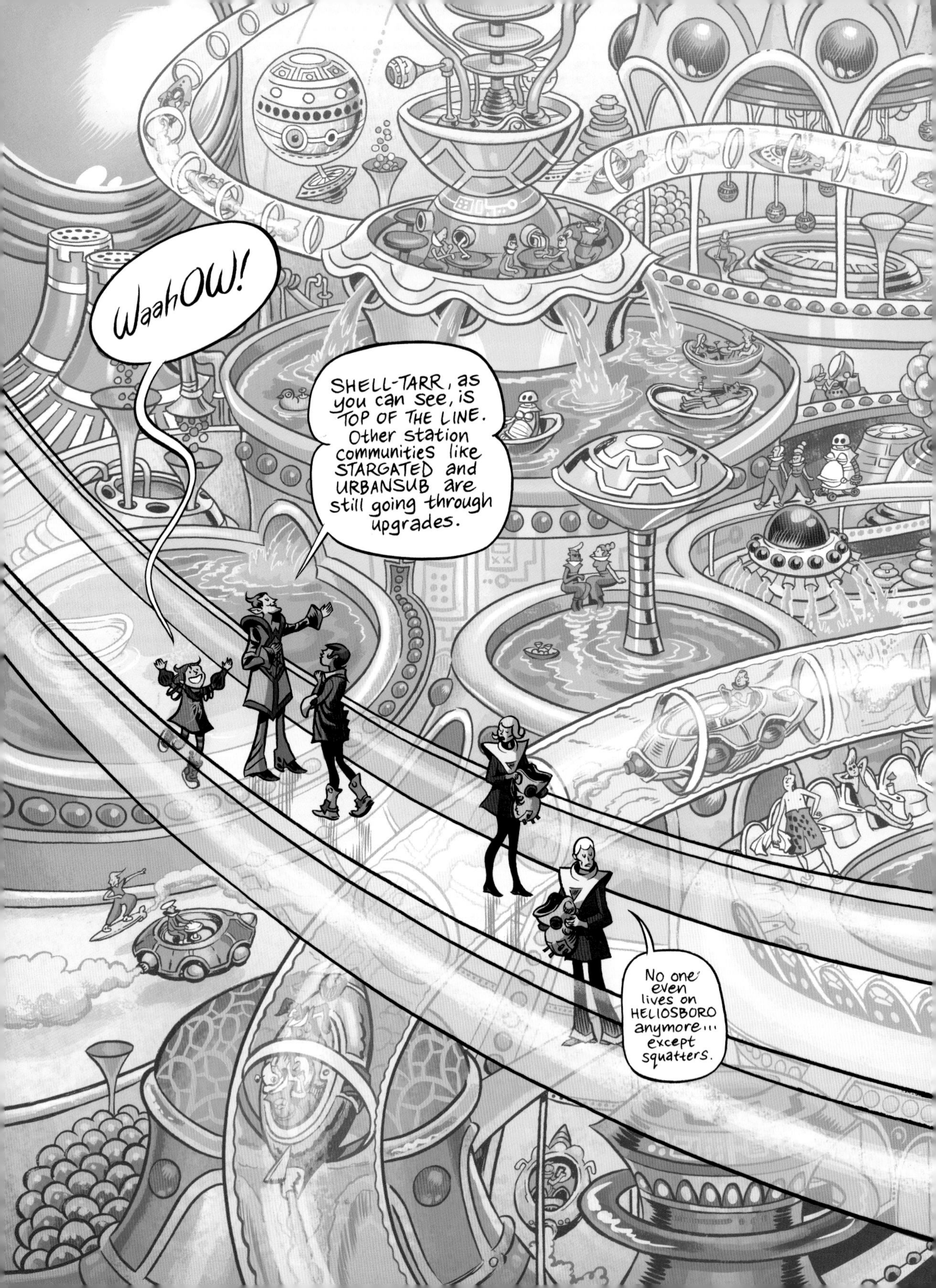
WaahOW!
SHELL-TARR, as you can see, is TOP OF THE LINE. Other station communities like STARGATED and URBANSUB are still going through upgrades.
No one even lives on HELIOSBORO anymore... except squatters.

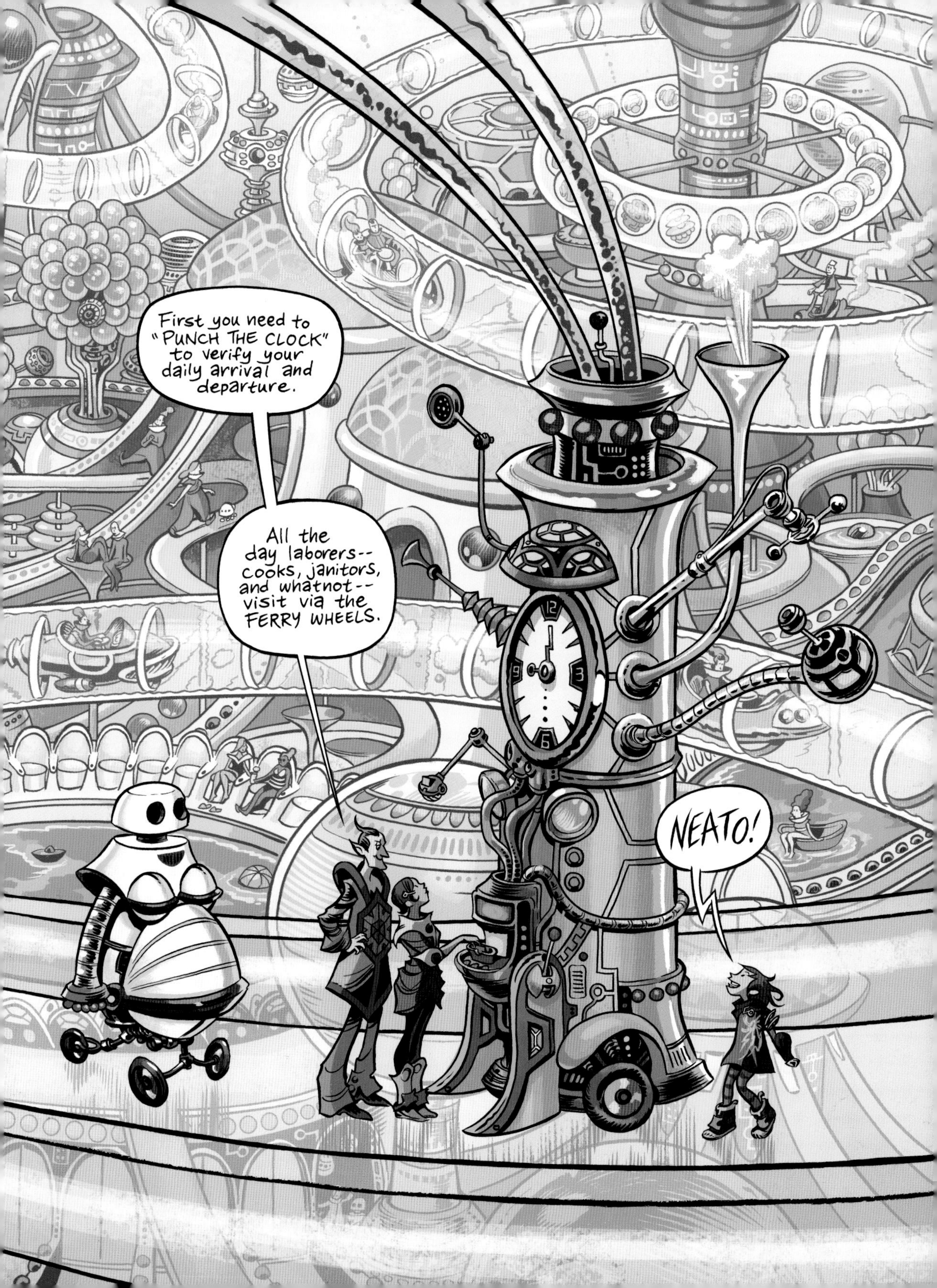
First you need to "PUNCH THE CLOCK" to verify your daily arrival and departure.
All the day laborers--cooks, janitors, and whatnot--visit via the FERRY WHEELS.
NEATO!

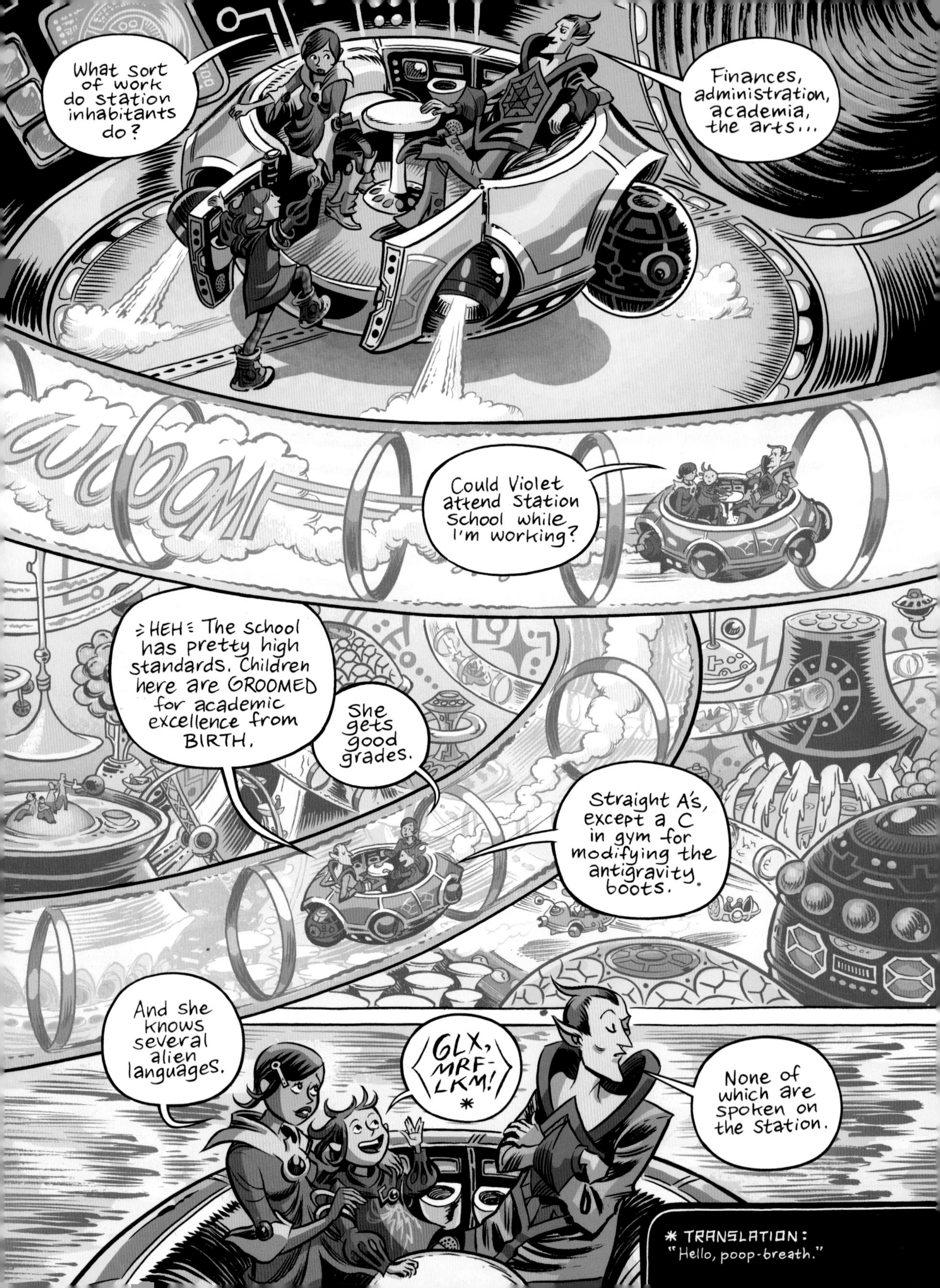
What sort of work do station inhabitants do?
Finances, administration, academia, the arts...
WOOOM
Could Violet attend Station School while I'm working?
HEH The school has pretty high standards. Children here are GROOMED for academic excellence from BIRTH.
She gets good grades.
Straight A's, except a C in gym for modifying the antigravity boots.
And she knows several alien languages.
GLX, MRF-LKM! *
None of which are spoken on the Station.
* TRANSLATION: "Hello, poop-breath."

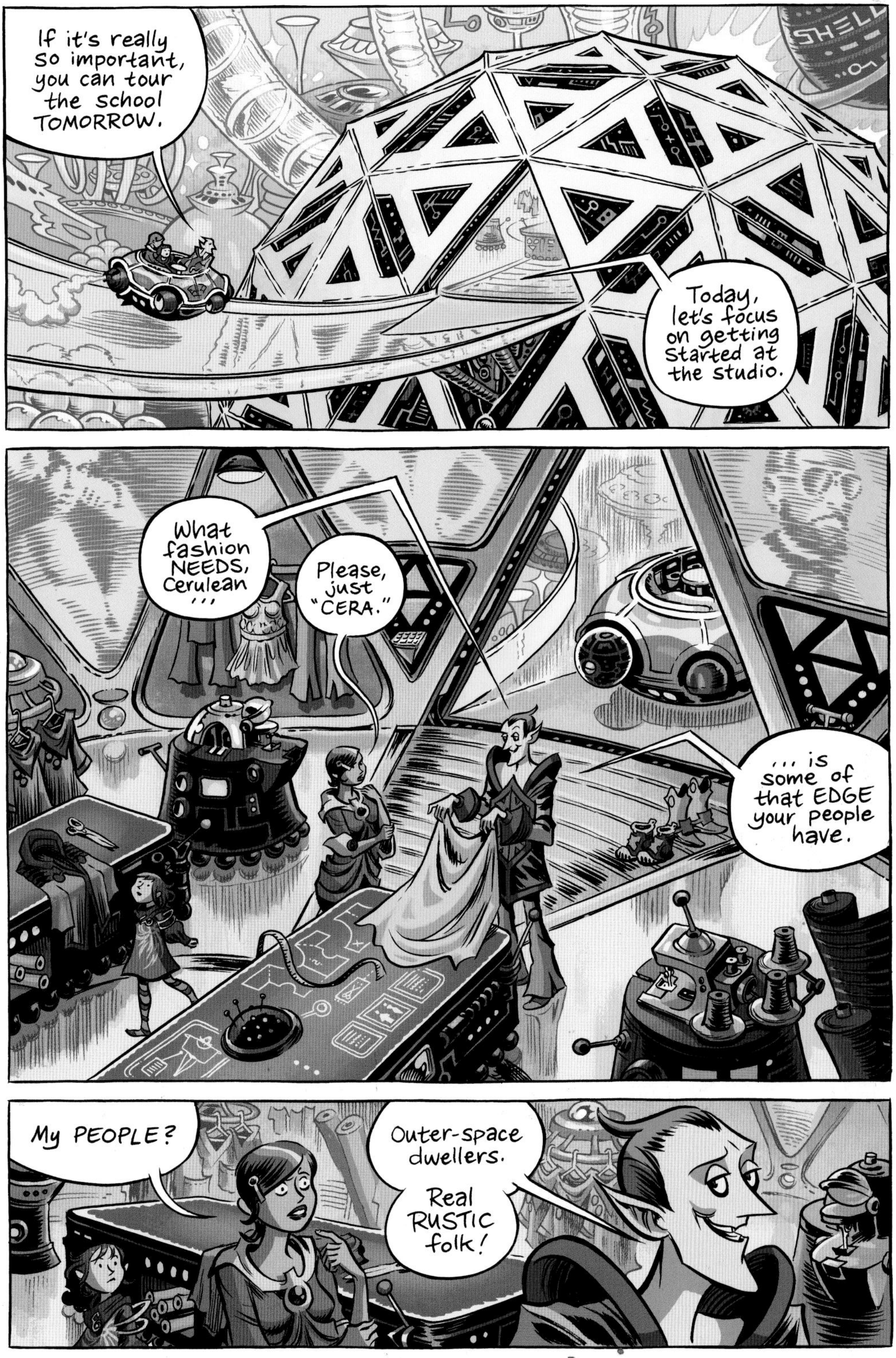
If it's really so important, you can tour the school TOMORROW.
Today, let's focus on getting started at the studio.
What fashion NEEDS, Cerulean ...
Please, just "CERA."
... is some of that EDGE your people have.
My PEOPLE?
Outer-space dwellers.
Real RUSTIC folk!

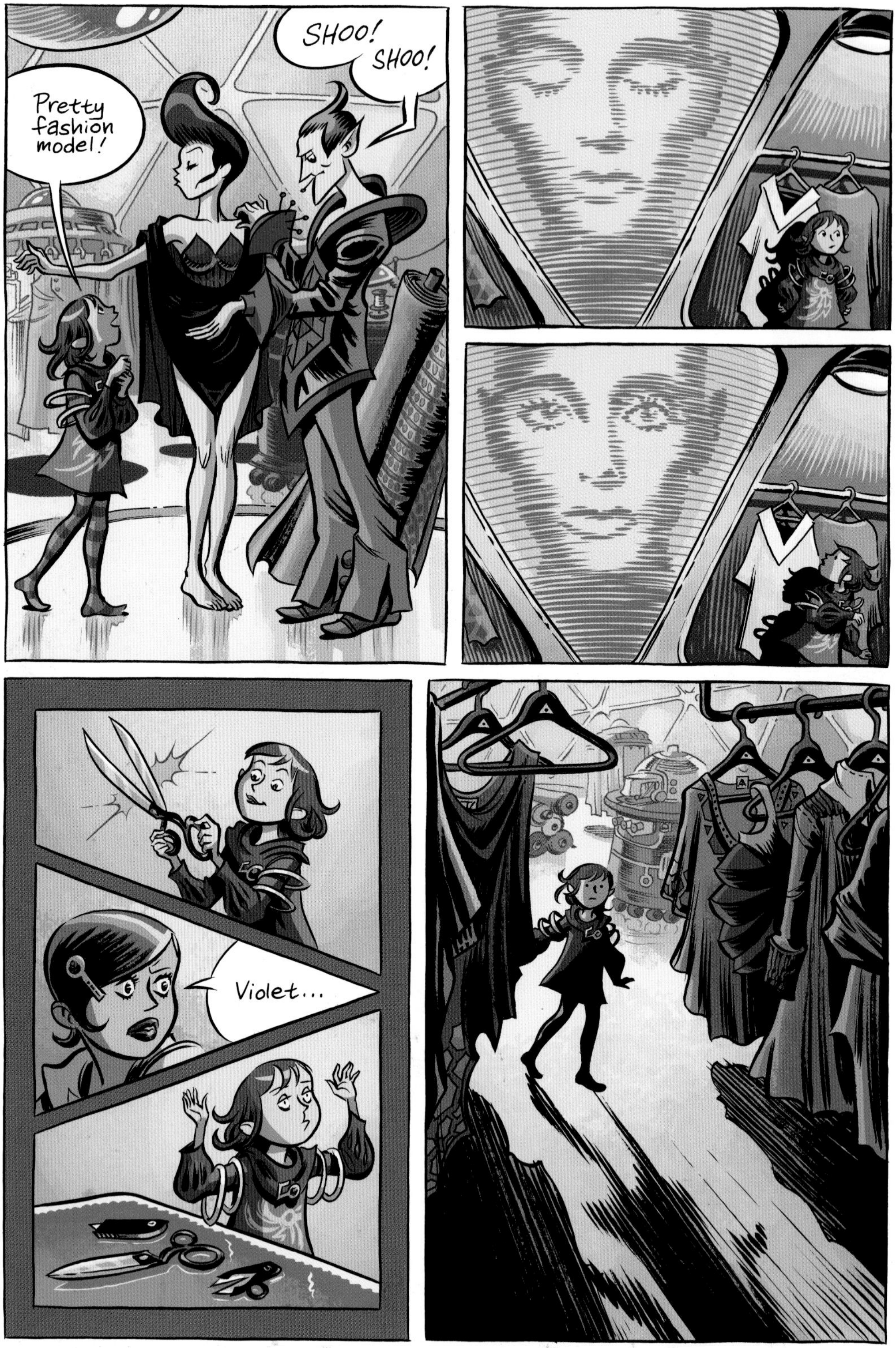
Pretty fashion model!
SHOO! SHOO!
Violet...

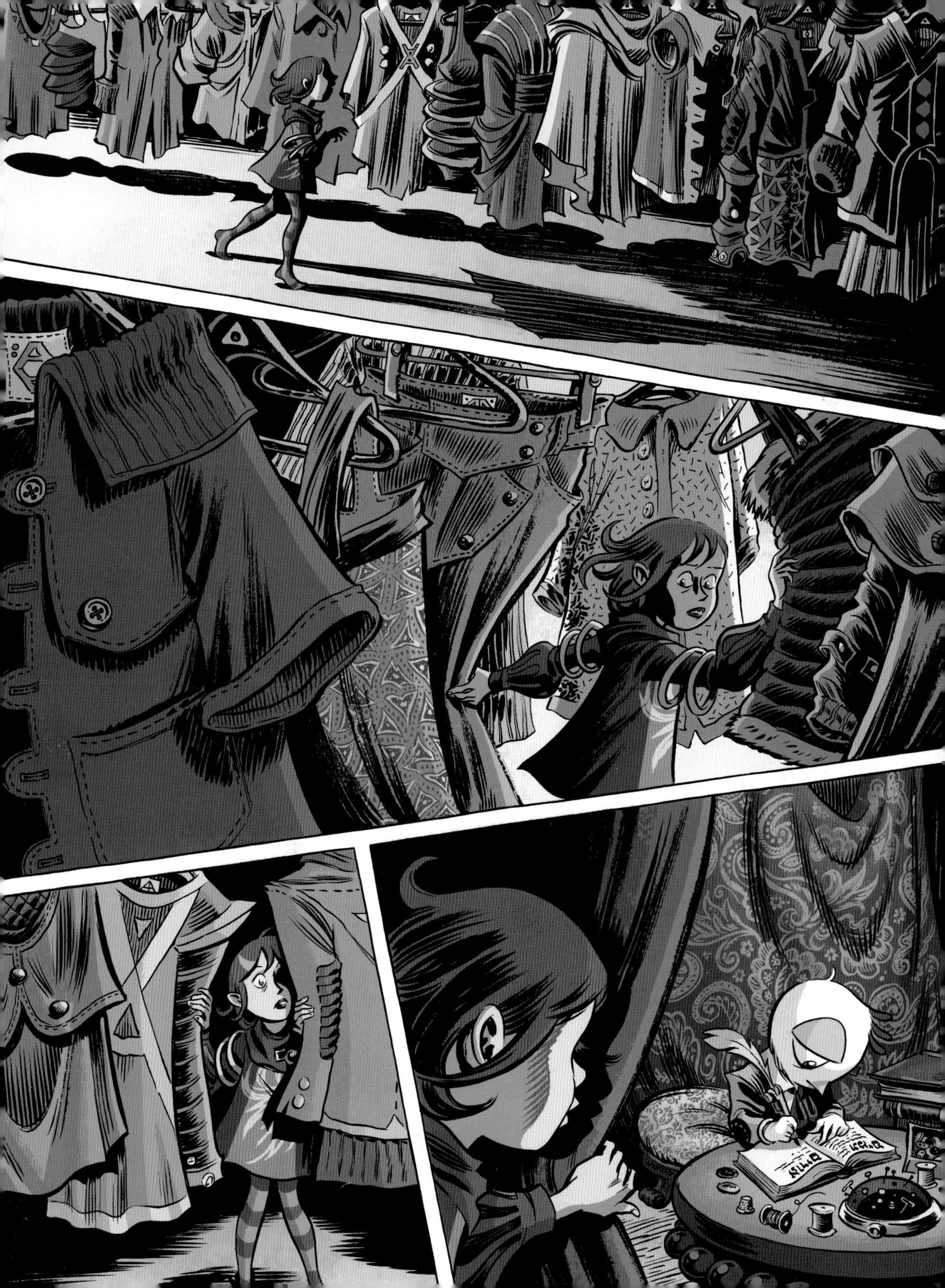

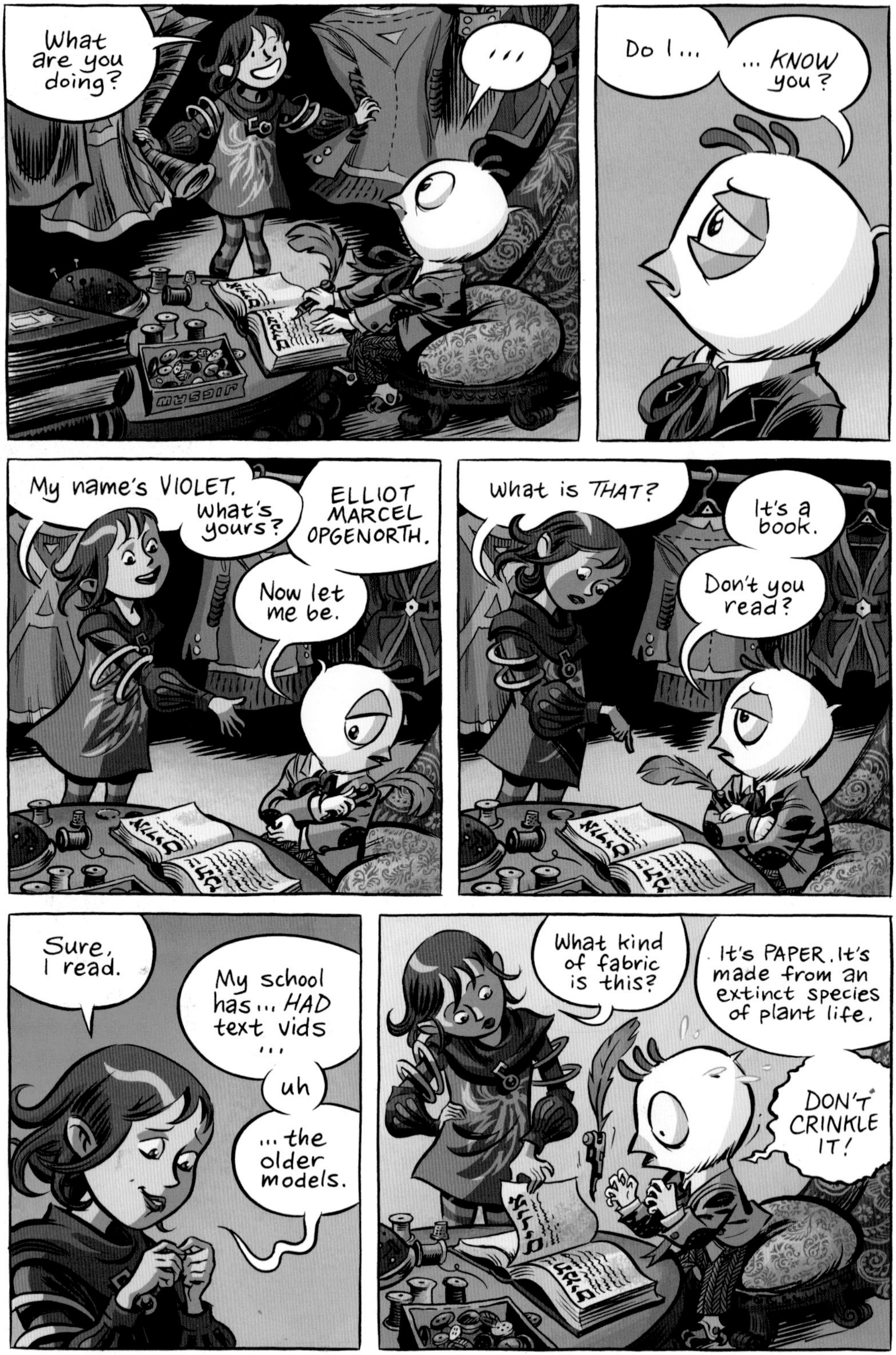
What are you doing?
...
JIGSAW
Do I...
... KNOW you?
My name's VIOLET. What's yours?
ELLIOT MARCEL OPGENORTH.
Now let me be.
What is THAT?
It's a book.
Don't you read?
Sure, I read.
My school has... HAD text vids ...
uh
... the older models.
What kind of fabric is this?
It's PAPER. It's made from an extinct species of plant life.
DON'T CRINKLE IT!

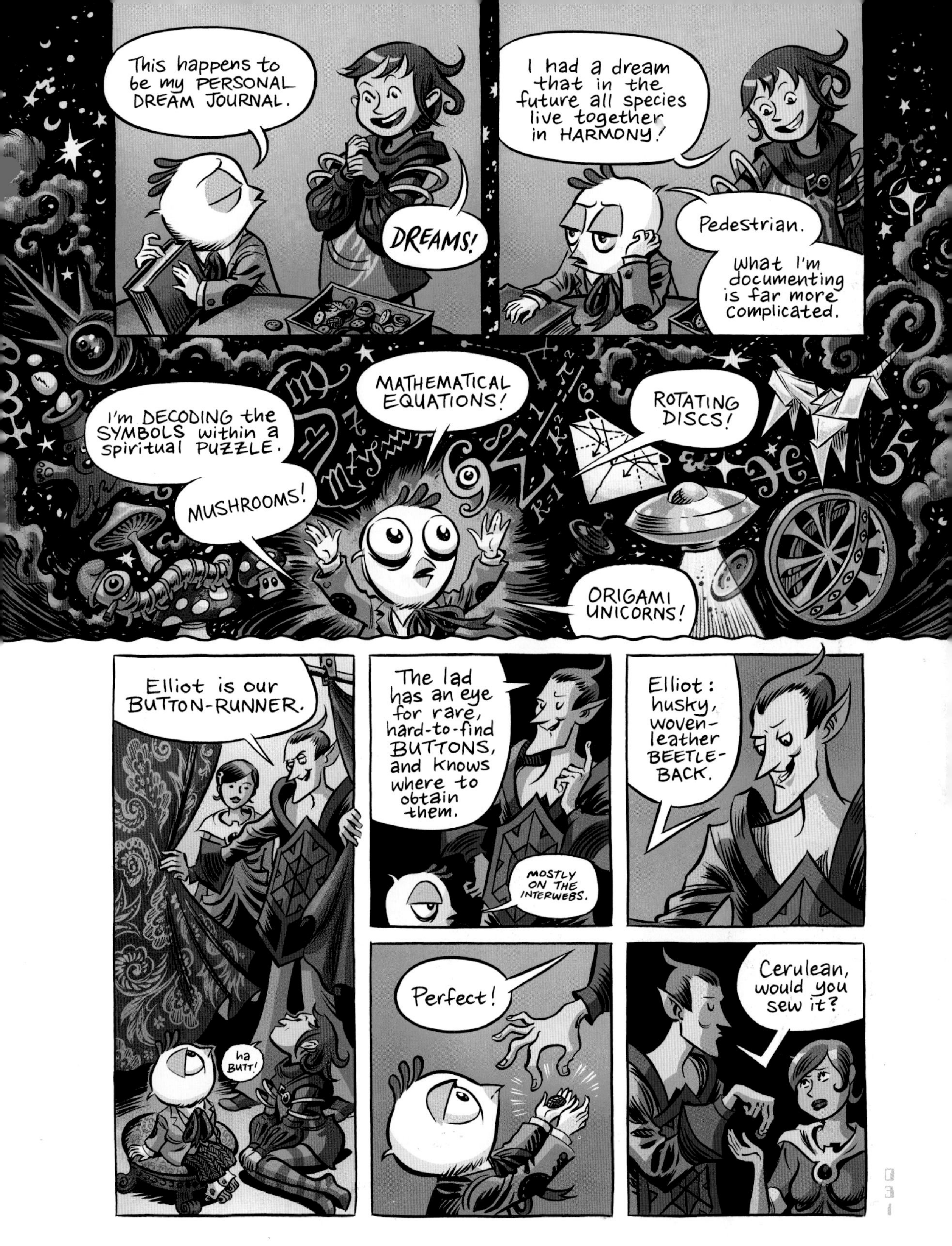
This happens to be my PERSONAL DREAM JOURNAL.
DREAMS!
I had a dream that in the future all species live together in HARMONY!
Pedestrian.
What I'm documenting is far more complicated.
I'm DECODING the SYMBOLS within a spiritual PUZZLE.
MATHEMATICAL EQUATIONS!
ROTATING DISCS!
MUSHROOMS!
ORIGAMI UNICORNS!
Elliot is our BUTTON-RUNNER.
ha BUTT!
The lad has an eye for rare, hard-to-find BUTTONS, and knows where to obtain them.
MOSTLY ON THE INTERWEBS.
Elliot: husky, woven-leather BEETLE-BACK.
Perfect!
Cerulean, would you sew it?

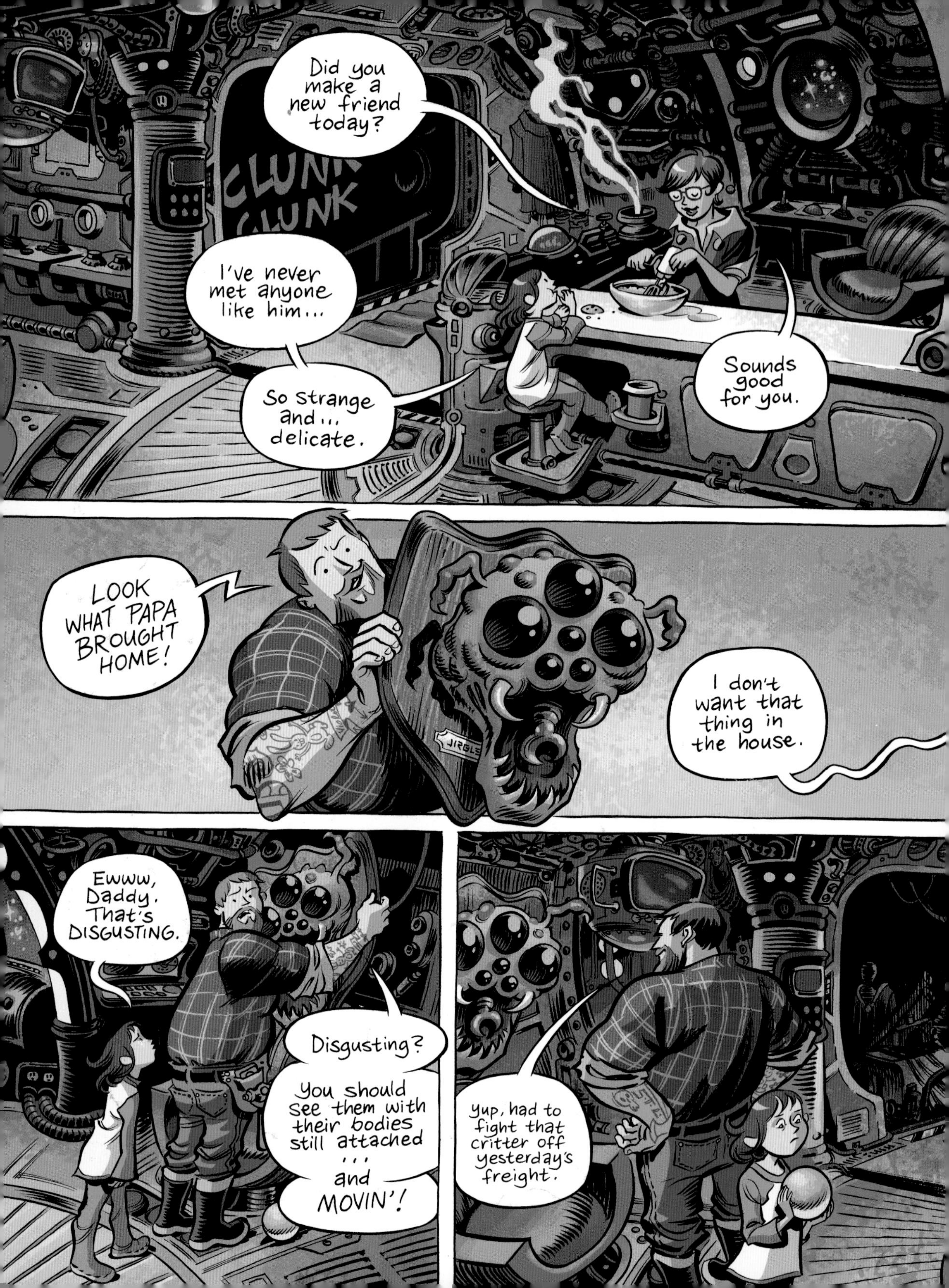
CLUNK CLUNK
Did you make a new friend today?
I've never met anyone like him...
So strange and... delicate.
Sounds good for you.
LOOK WHAT PAPA BROUGHT HOME!
I don't want that thing in the house.
Ewww, Daddy. That's DISGUSTING.
Disgusting?
You should see them with their bodies still attached ... and MOVIN'!
Yup, had to fight that critter off yesterday's freight.

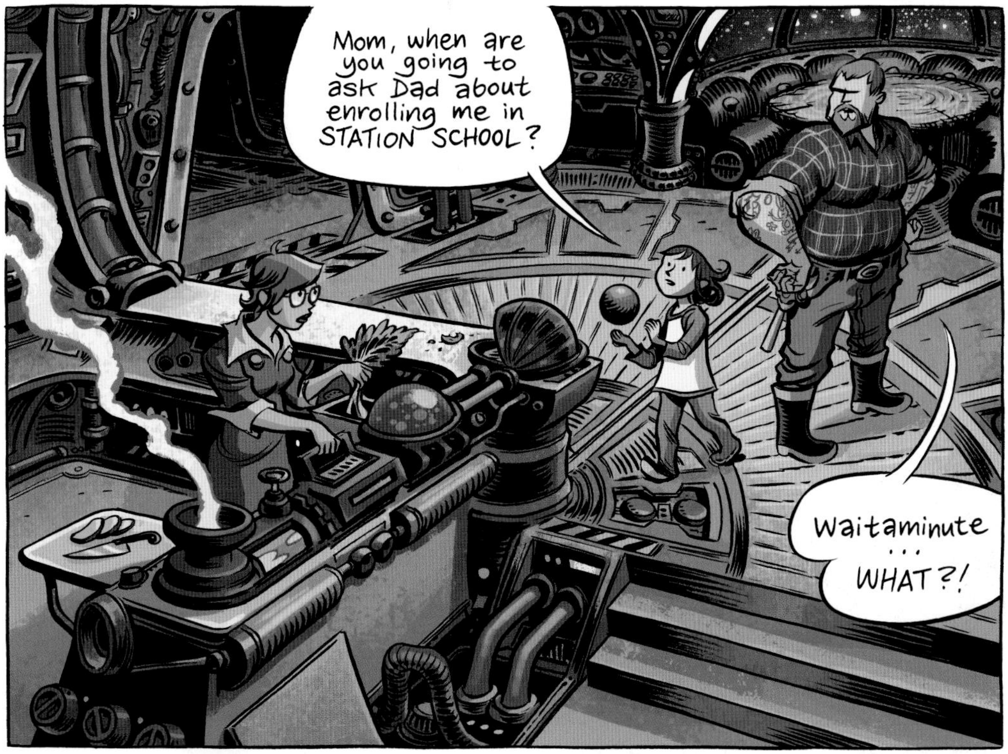
Mom, when are you going to ask Dad about enrolling me in STATION SCHOOL?
Waitaminute . . . WHAT?!

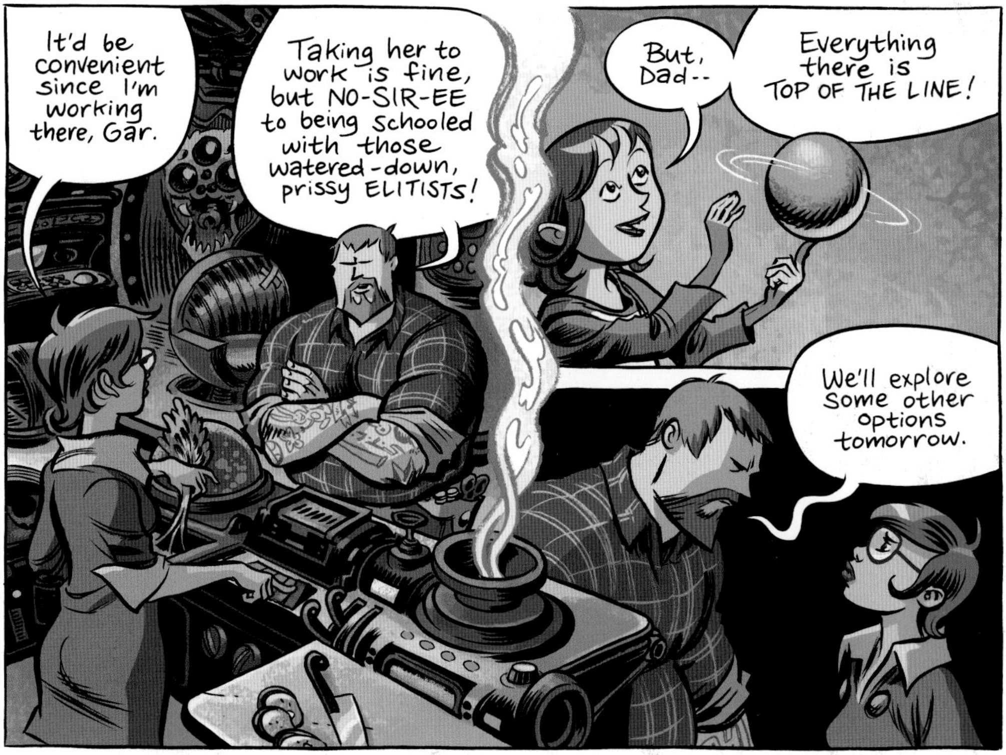
It'd be convenient since I'm working there, Gar.
Taking her to work is fine, but NO-SIR-EE to being schooled with those watered-down, prissy ELITISTS!
But, Dad--
Everything there is TOP OF THE LINE!
We'll explore some other options tomorrow.

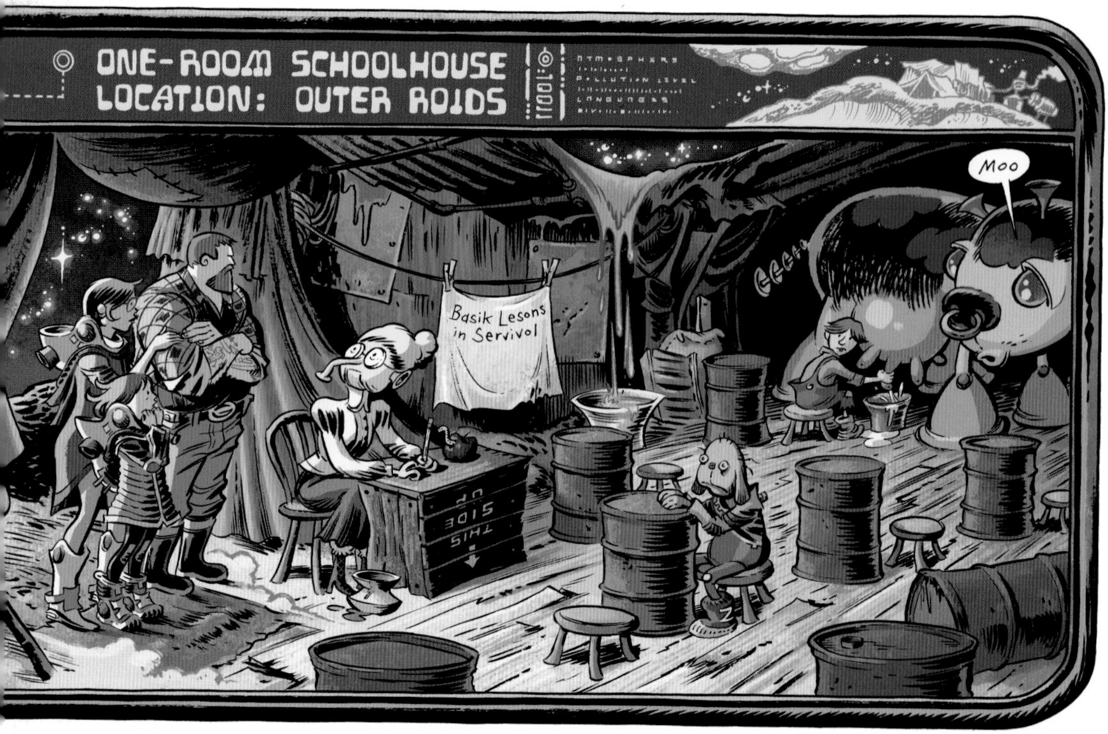
ONE-ROOM SCHOOLHOUSE
LOCATION: OUTER ROIDS
ATMOSPHERE
POLLUTION LEVEL
LANGUAGES
Moo
Basik Lesons in Servivol
THIS SIDE UP

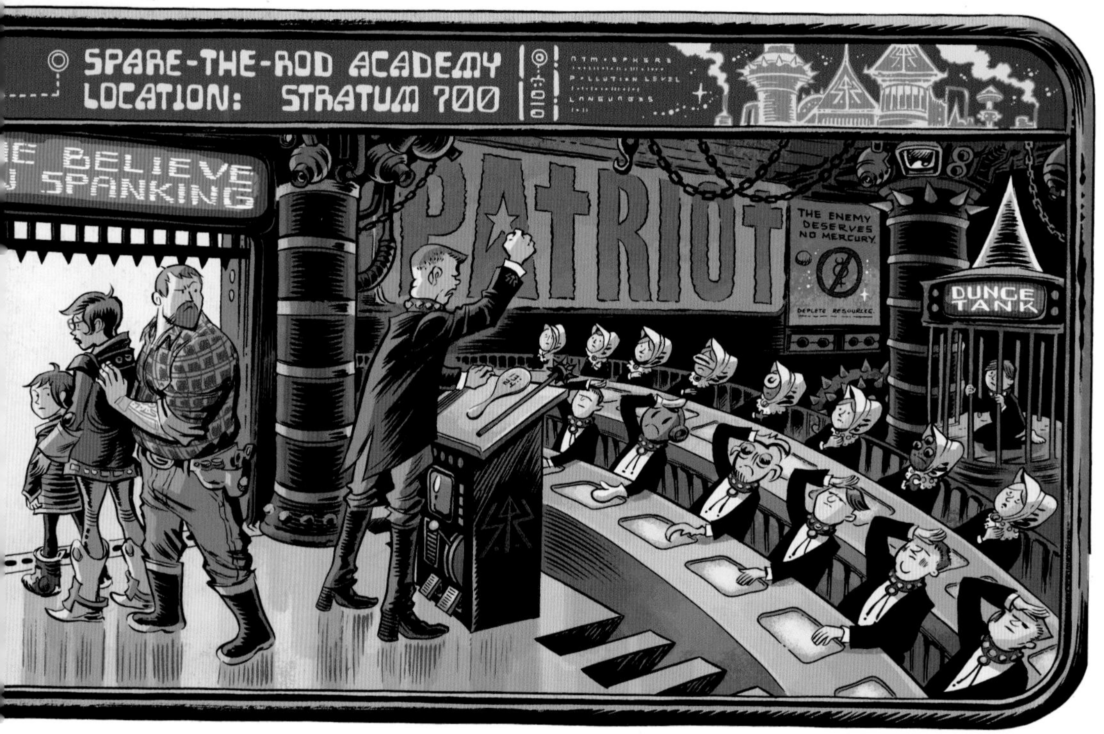
SPARE-THE-ROD ACADEMY
LOCATION: STRATUM 700
ATMOSPHERE
POLLUTION LEVEL
LANGUAGES
E BELIEVE
SPANKING
PATRIOT
THE ENEMY DESERVES NO MERCURY.
DEPLETE RESOURCES.
DUNGE TANK

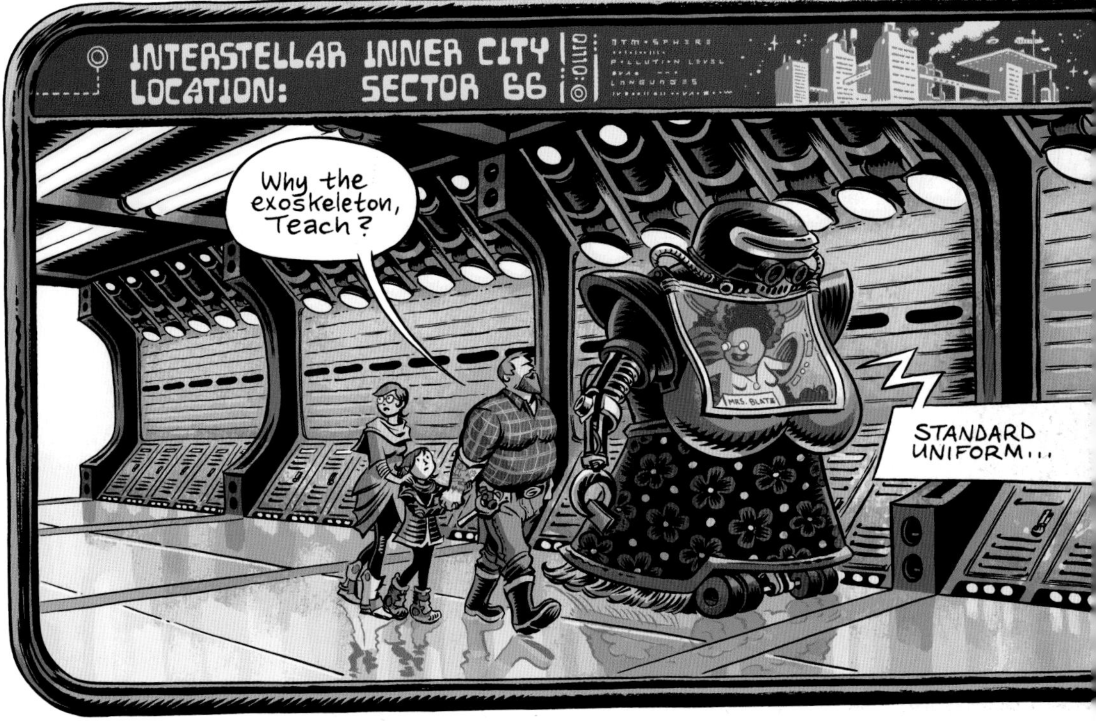
INTERSTELLAR INNER CITY
LOCATION: SECTOR 66
Why the exoskeleton, Teach?
STANDARD UNIFORM...
MRS. BLATZ

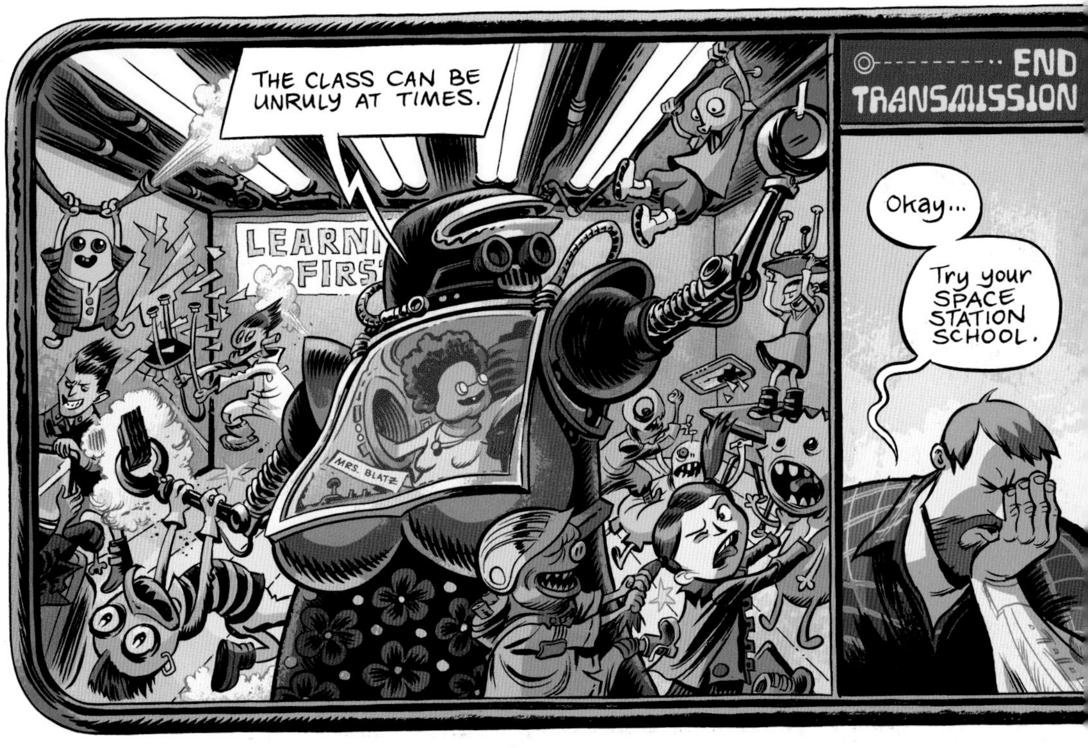
THE CLASS CAN BE UNRULY AT TIMES.
LEARNI
FIRS
MRS. BLATZ
END TRANSMISSION
Okay...
Try your SPACE STATION SCHOOL.

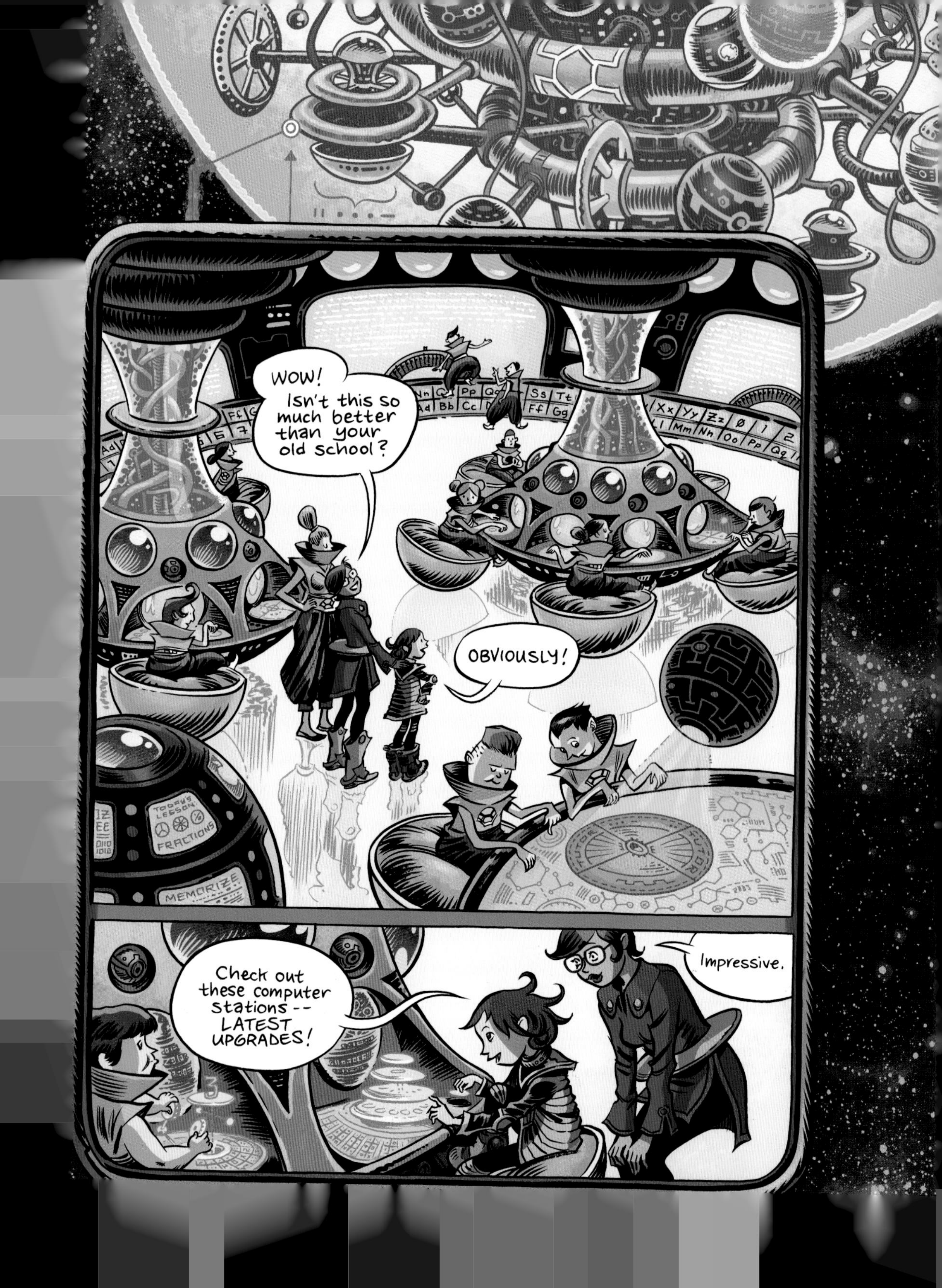
WOW! Isn't this so much better than your old school?
OBVIOUSLY!
TODAY'S LESSON: FRACTIONS
MEMORIZE
TUTOR
Check out these computer stations -- LATEST UPGRADES!
Impressive.

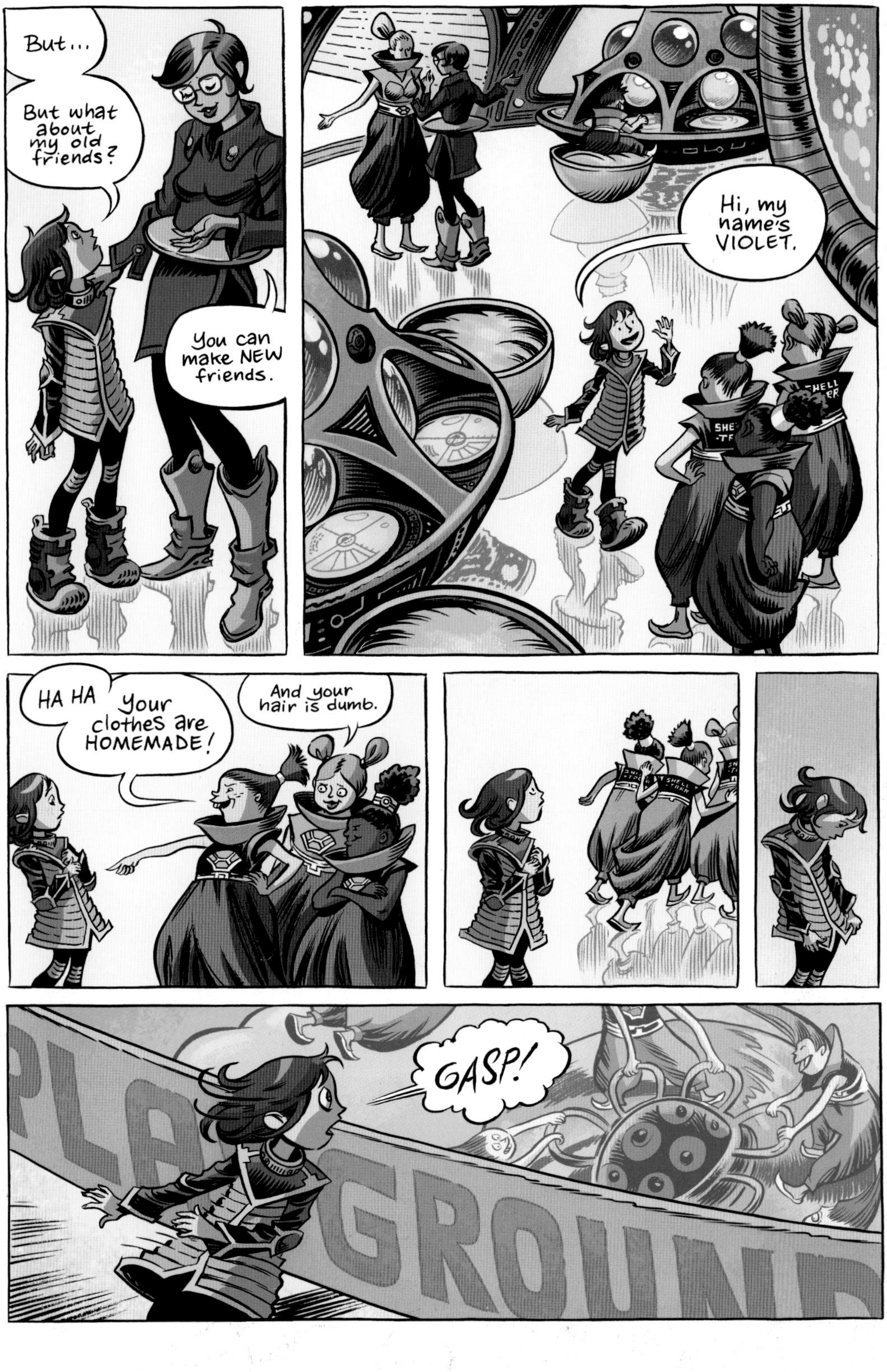
But...
But what about my old friends?
You can make NEW friends.
Hi, my name's VIOLET.
HA HA
Your clothes are HOMEMADE!
And your hair is dumb.
GASP!
PLA
GROUN

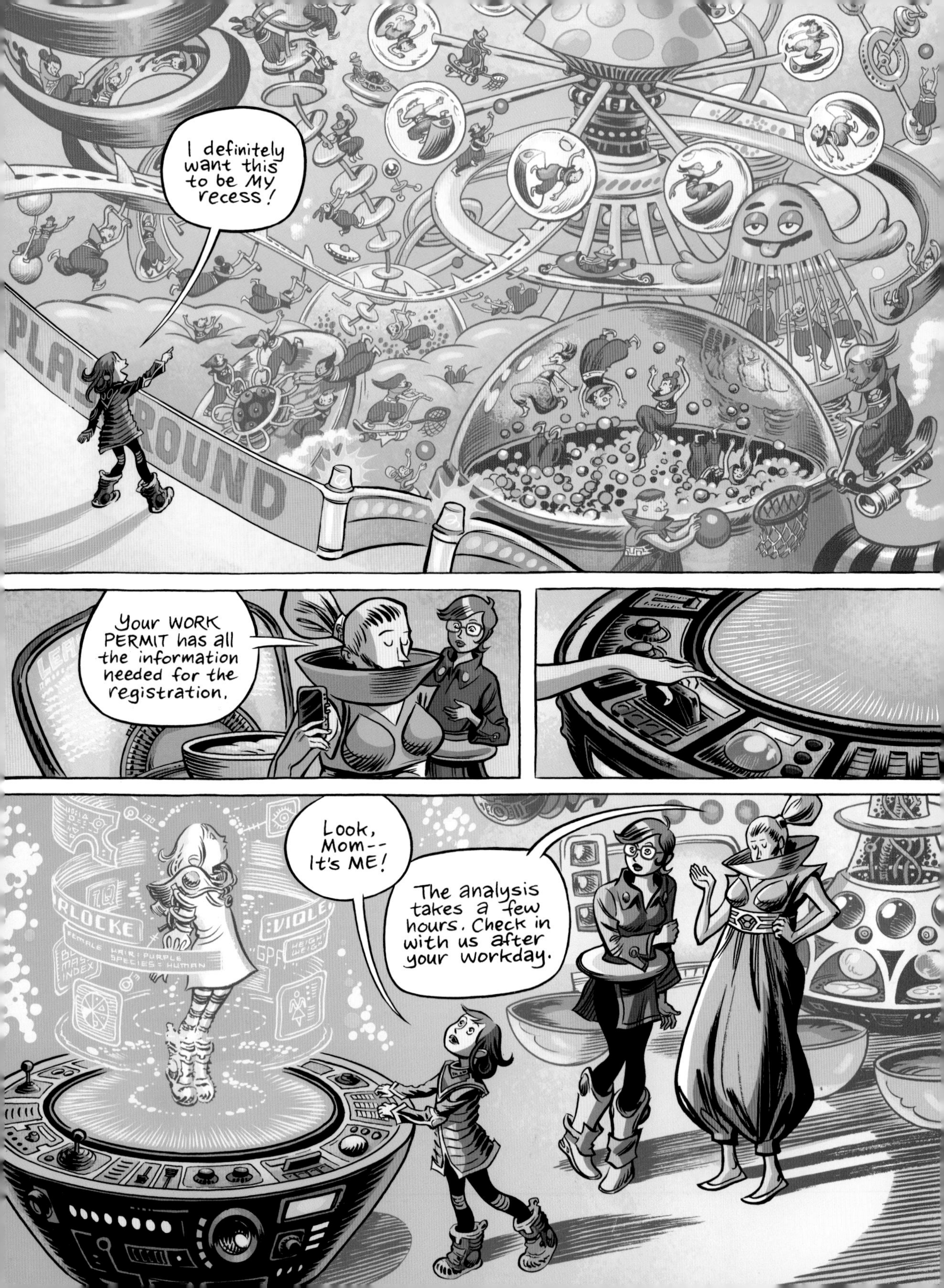
I definitely want this to be MY recess!
PLAY
ROUND
Your WORK PERMIT has all the information needed for the registration.
Look, Mom-- It's ME!
The analysis takes a few hours. Check in with us after your workday.
RLOCKE
VIOLE
IQ
FEMALE HAIR: PURPLE
SPECIES: HUMAN
GPA

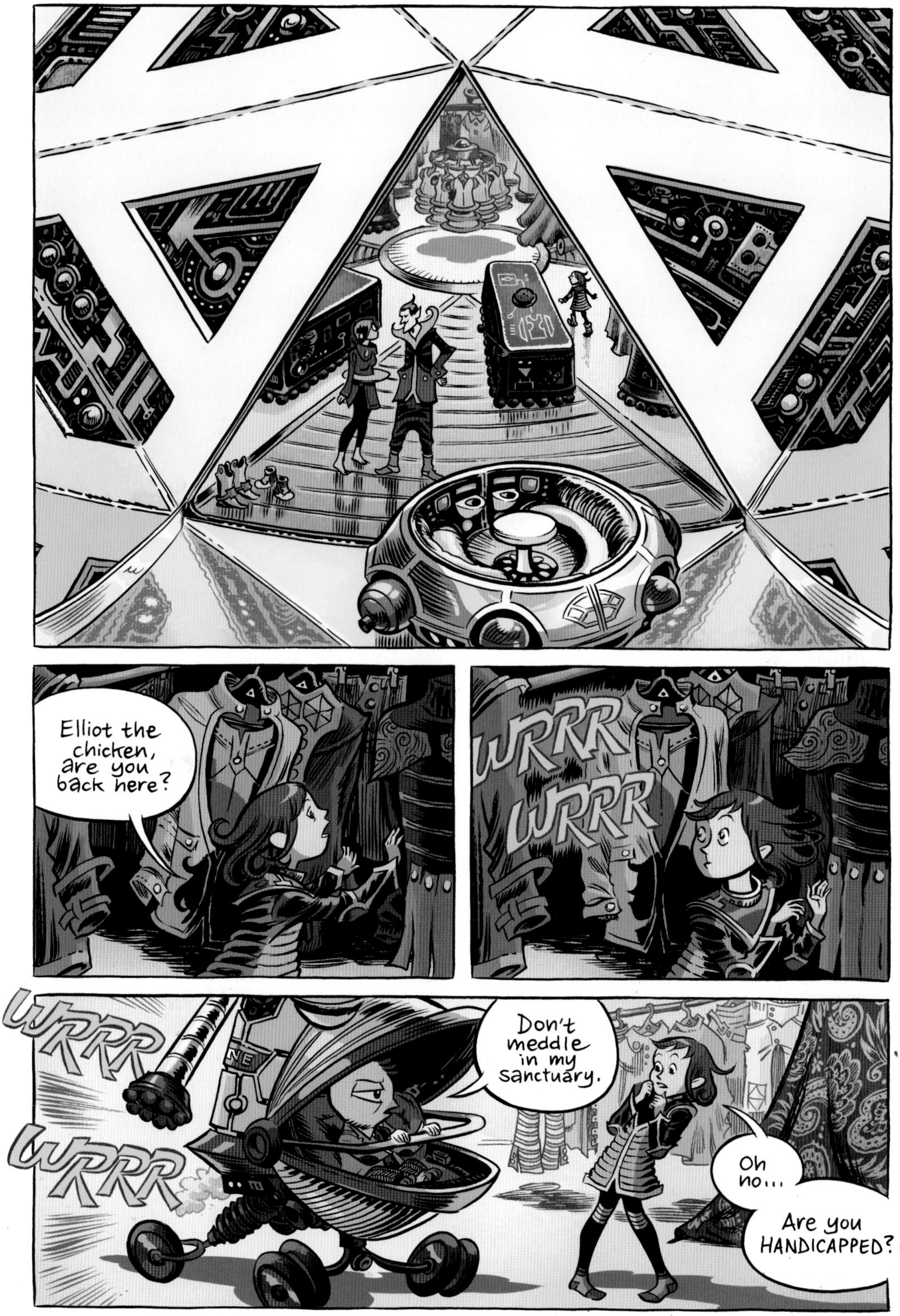
Elliot the chicken, are you back here?
WRRR WRRR
WRRR
WRRR
Don't meddle in my sanctuary.
Oh no...
Are you HANDICAPPED?

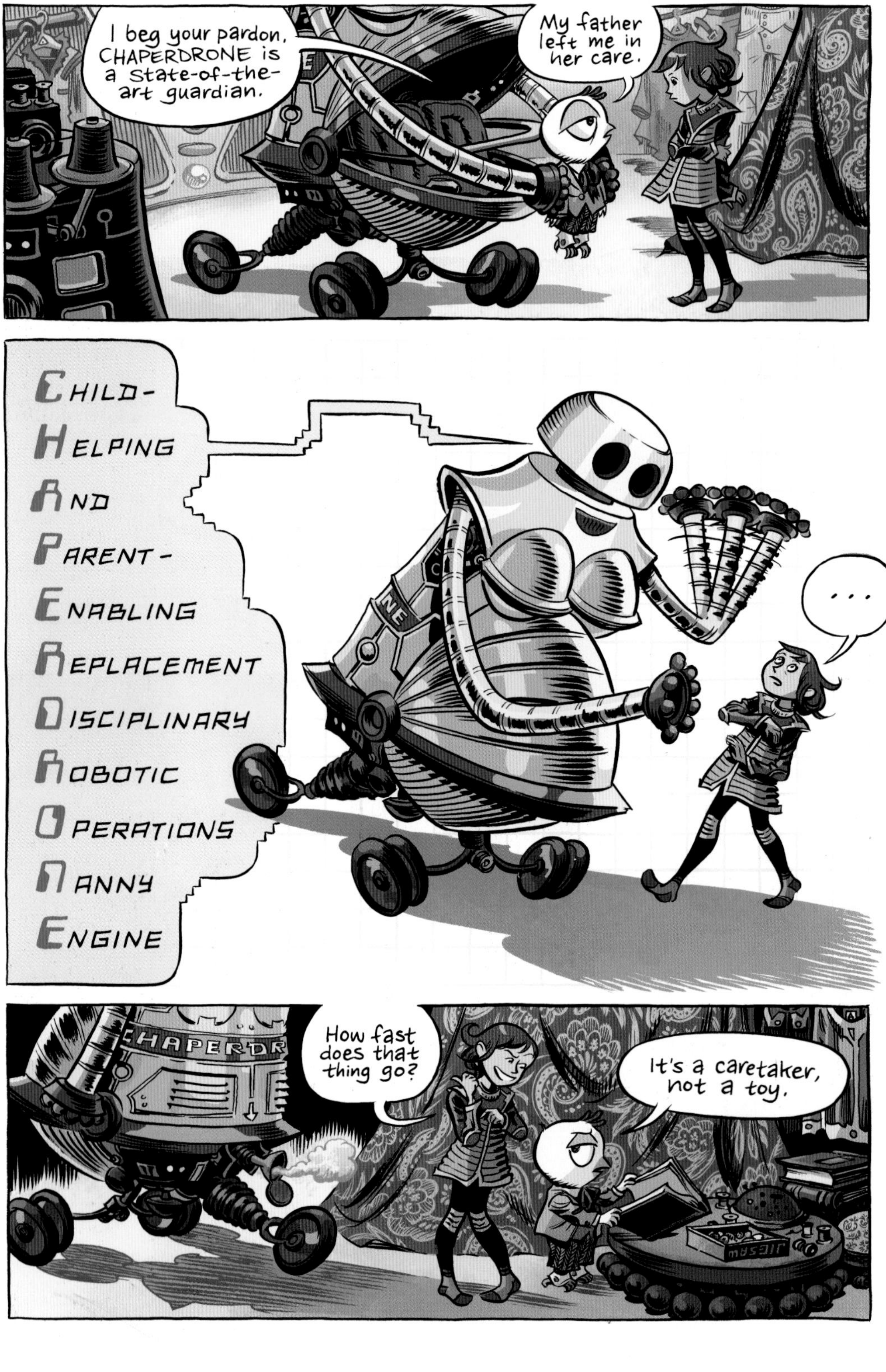
I beg your pardon, CHAPERDRONE is a state-of-the-art guardian.
My father left me in her care.
CHILD-
HELPING
AND
PARENT-
ENABLING
REPLACEMENT
DISCIPLINARY
ROBOTIC
OPERATIONS
NANNY
ENGINE
...
CHAPERDR
How fast does that thing go?
It's a caretaker, not a toy.

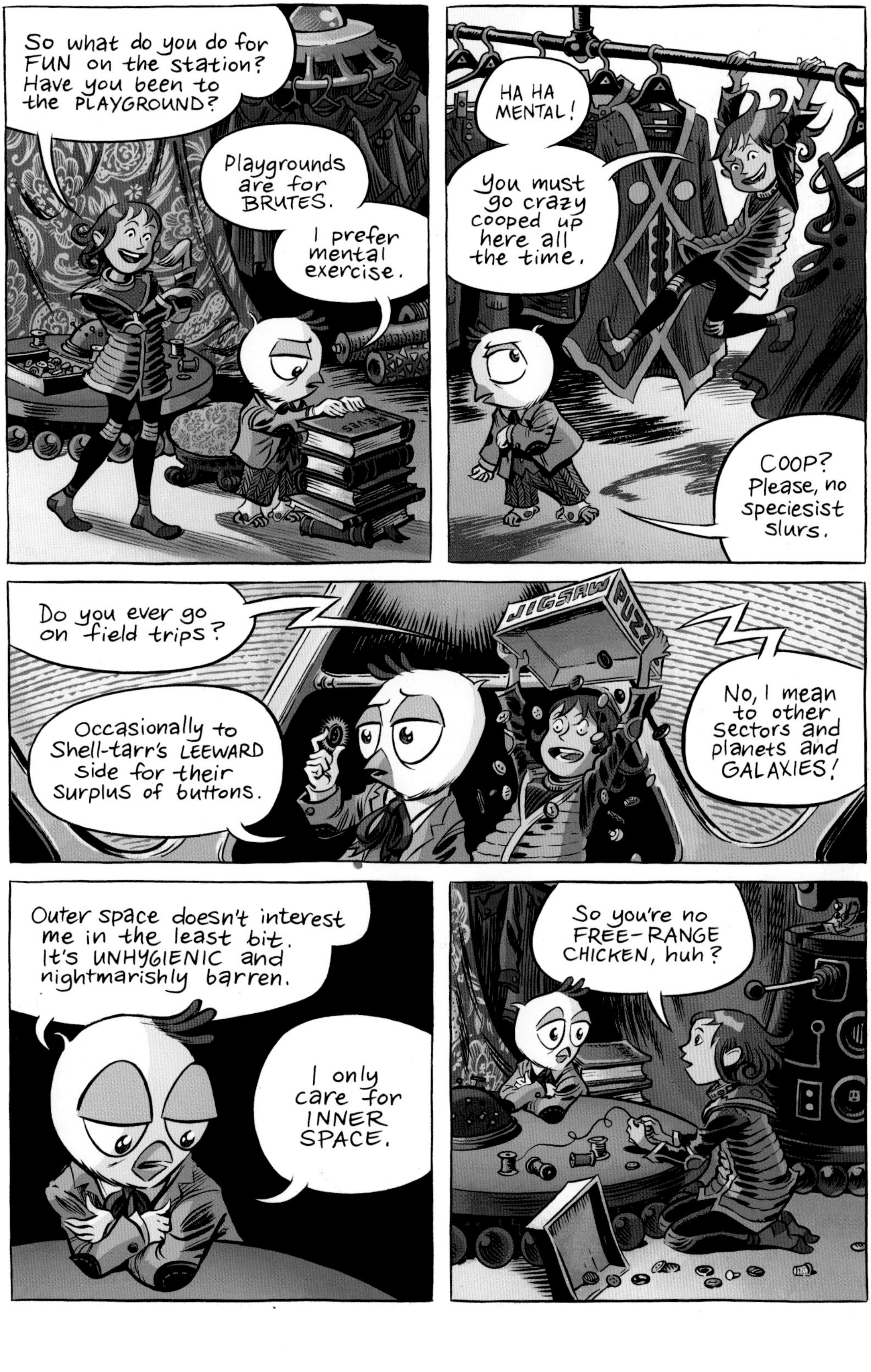
So what do you do for FUN on the station? Have you been to the PLAYGROUND?
Playgrounds are for BRUTES.
I prefer mental exercise.
HA HA MENTAL!
You must go crazy cooped up here all the time.
COOP? Please, no speciesist slurs.
Do you ever go on field trips?
JIGSAW PUZZ
Occasionally to Shell-tarr's LEEWARD side for their surplus of buttons.
No, I mean to other sectors and planets and GALAXIES!
Outer space doesn't interest me in the least bit. It's UNHYGIENIC and nightmarishly barren.
I only care for INNER SPACE.
So you're no FREE-RANGE CHICKEN, huh?

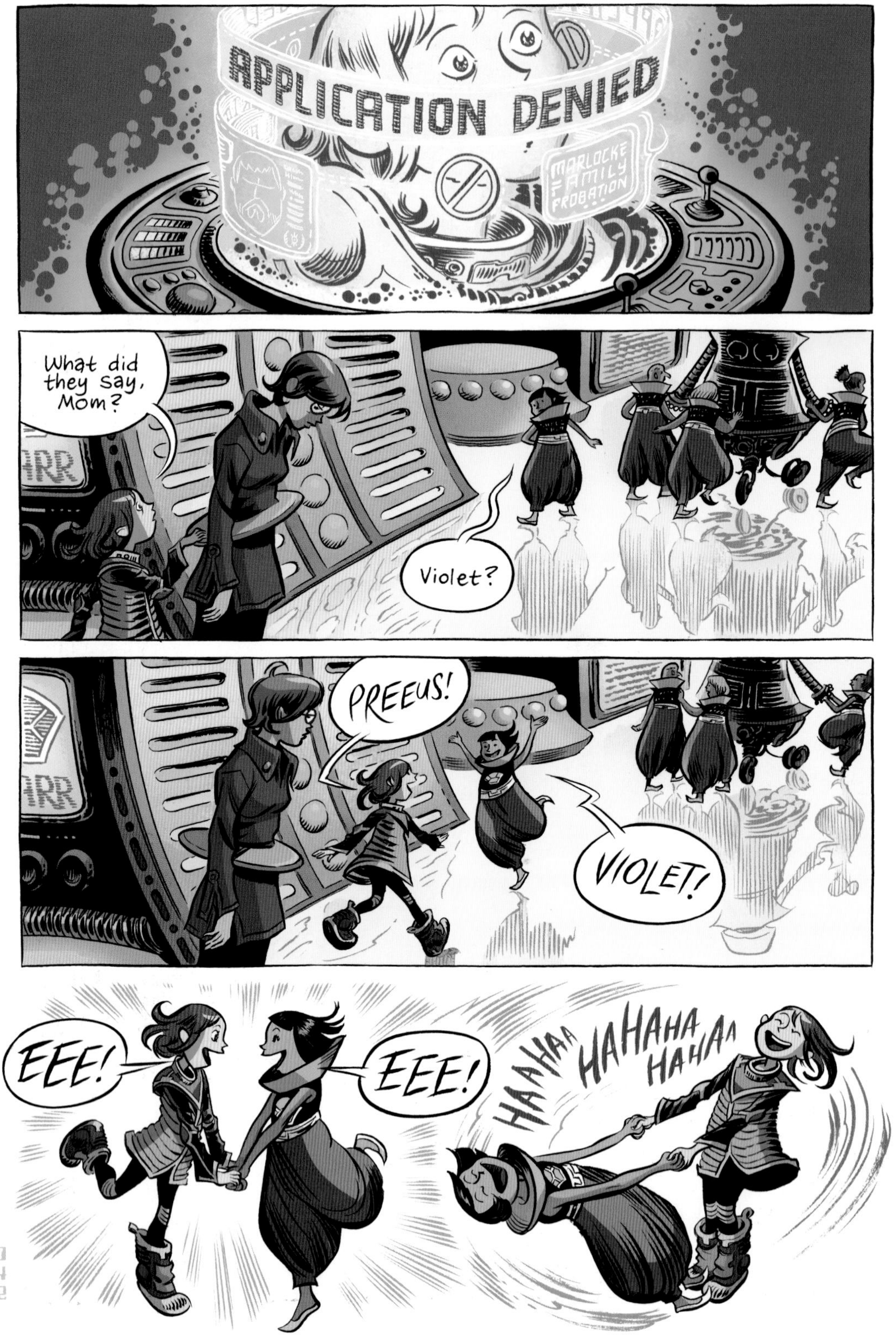
APPLICATION DENIED
MARLOCKE FAMILY PROBATION
What did they say, Mom?
Violet?
PREEUS!
VIOLET!
EEE!
EEE!
HAHAHA HAHAHA HAHAA

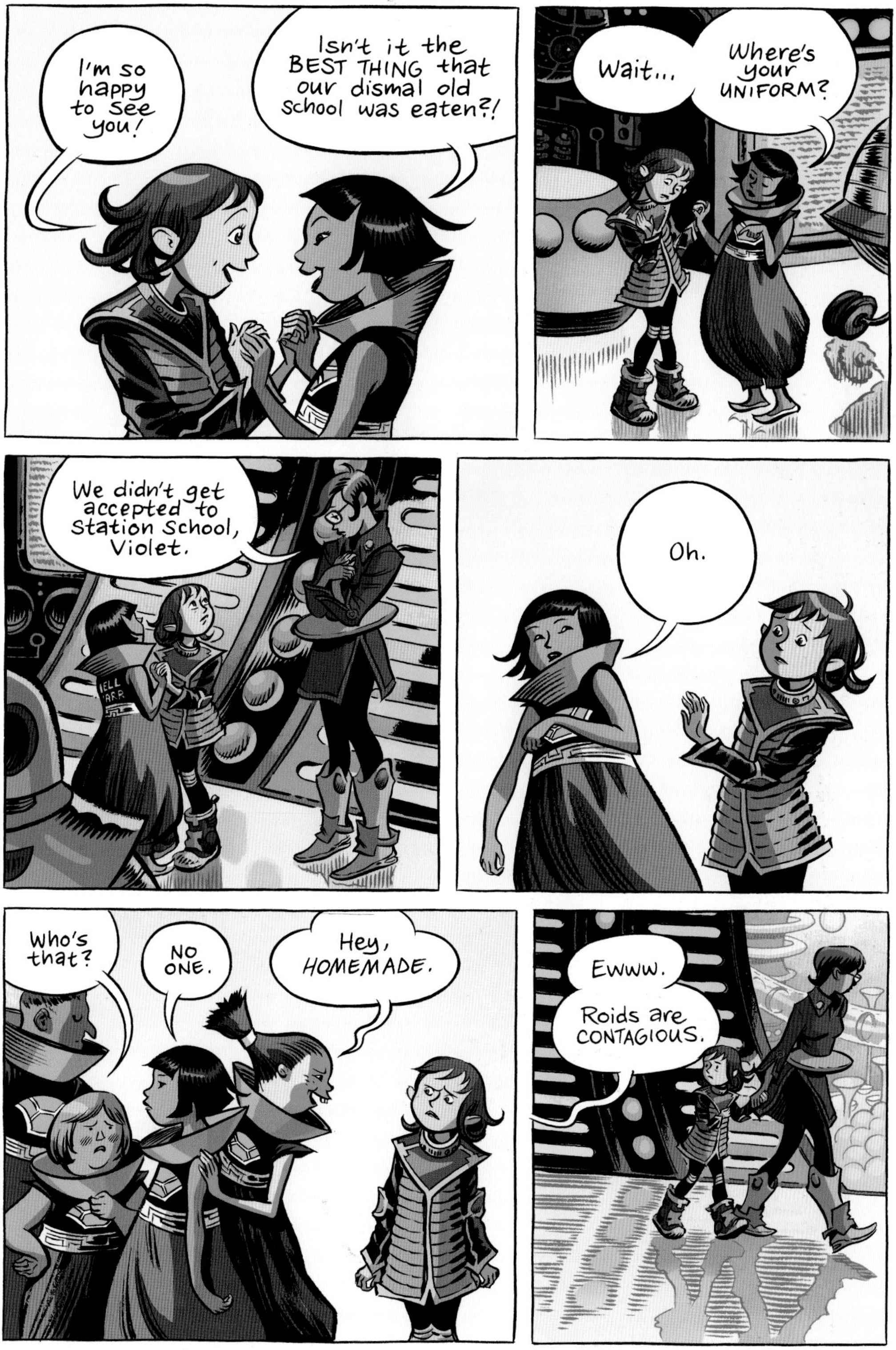
I'm so happy to see you!
Isn't it the BEST THING that our dismal old school was eaten?!
Wait...
Where's your UNIFORM?
We didn't get accepted to Station School, Violet.
Oh.
Who's that?
NO ONE.
Hey, HOMEMADE.
Ewww.
Roids are CONTAGIOUS.

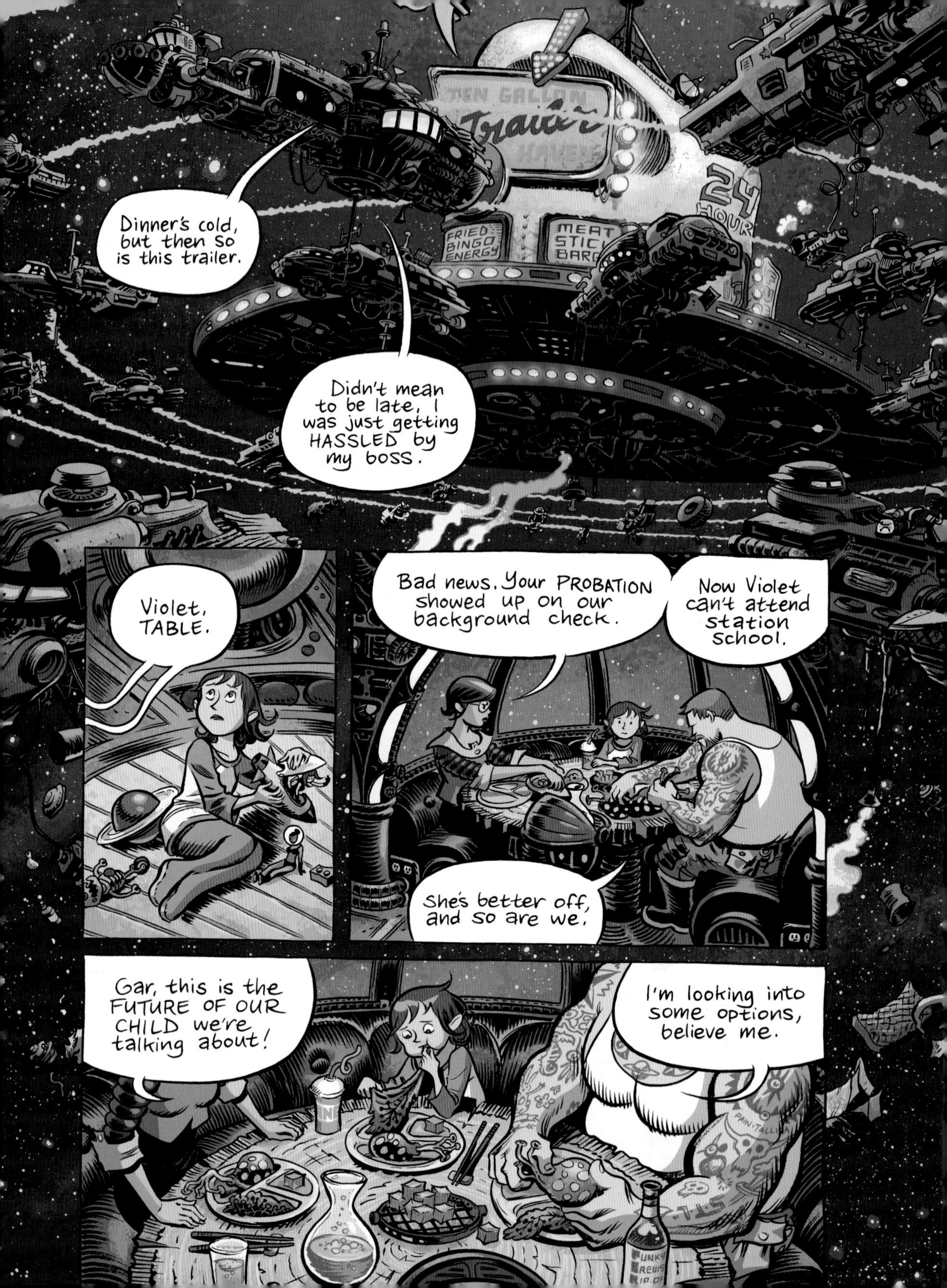
TEN GALLON
Trailer
HAVEN
24 HOUR
FRIED BINGO ENERGY
MEAT STICK BARG
Dinner's cold, but then so is this trailer.
Didn't mean to be late, I was just getting HASSLED by my boss.
Violet, TABLE.
Bad news. Your PROBATION showed up on our background check.
Now Violet can't attend station school.
She's better off, and so are we.
Gar, this is the FUTURE OF OUR CHILD we're talking about!
I'm looking into some options, believe me.

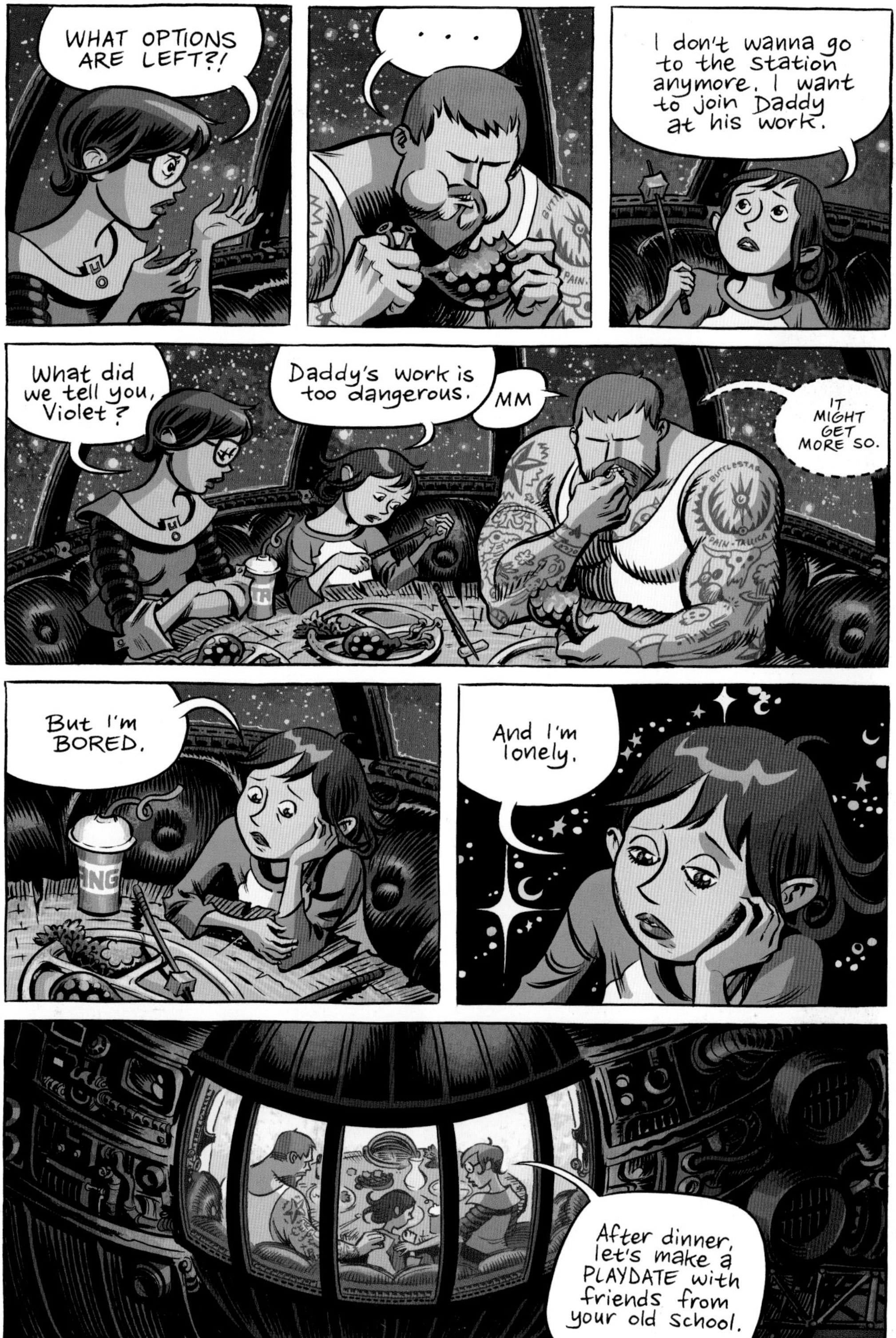
WHAT OPTIONS ARE LEFT?!
. . .
I don't wanna go to the station anymore. I want to join Daddy at his work.
What did we tell you, Violet?
Daddy's work is too dangerous.
MM
IT MIGHT GET MORE SO.
But I'm BORED.
And I'm lonely.
After dinner, let's make a PLAYDATE with friends from your old school.

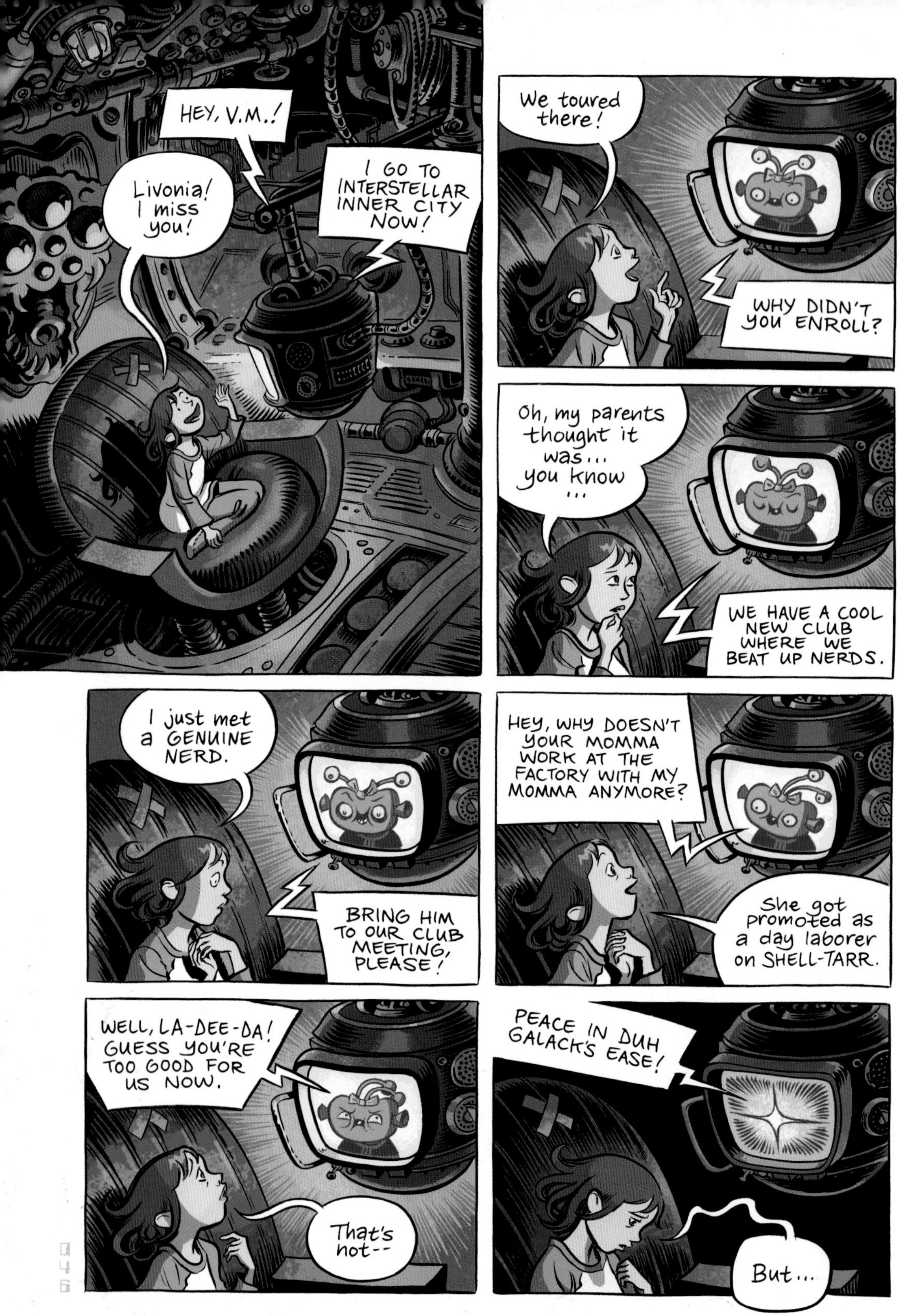
HEY, V.M.!
Livonia! I miss you!
I GO TO INTERSTELLAR INNER CITY NOW!
We toured there!
WHY DIDN'T YOU ENROLL?
Oh, my parents thought it was... you know ...
WE HAVE A COOL NEW CLUB WHERE WE BEAT UP NERDS.
I just met a GENUINE NERD.
BRING HIM TO OUR CLUB MEETING, PLEASE!
HEY, WHY DOESN'T YOUR MOMMA WORK AT THE FACTORY WITH MY MOMMA ANYMORE?
She got promoted as a day laborer on SHELL-TARR.
WELL, LA-DEE-DA! GUESS YOU'RE TOO GOOD FOR US NOW.
That's not--
PEACE IN DUH GALACK'S EASE!
But...

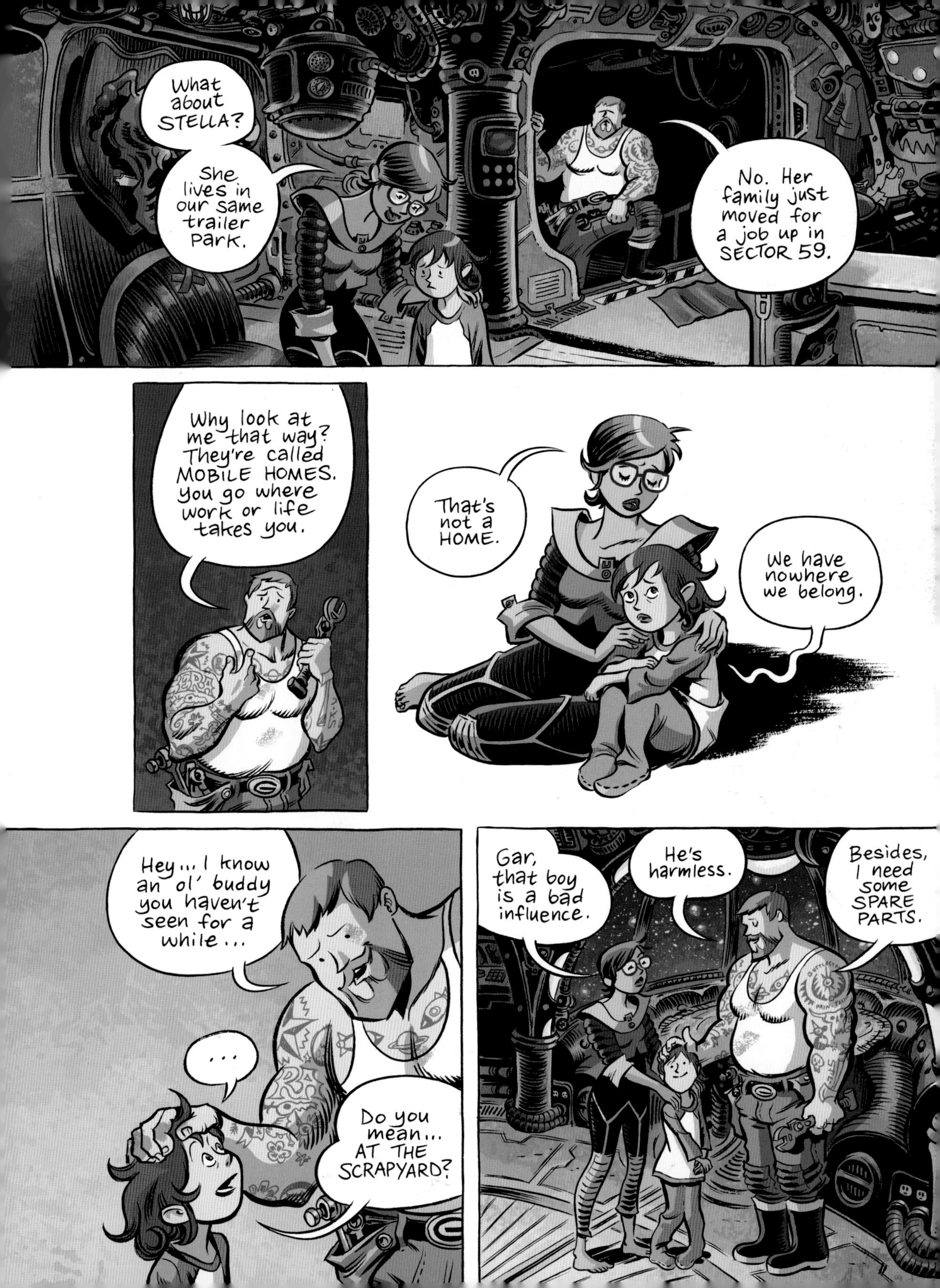
What about STELLA?
She lives in our same trailer park.
No. Her family just moved for a job up in SECTOR 59.
Why look at me that way? They're called MOBILE HOMES. You go where work or life takes you.
That's not a HOME.
We have nowhere we belong.
Hey... I know an ol' buddy you haven't seen for a while...
...
Do you mean... AT THE SCRAPYARD?
Gar, that boy is a bad influence.
He's harmless.
Besides, I need some SPARE PARTS.

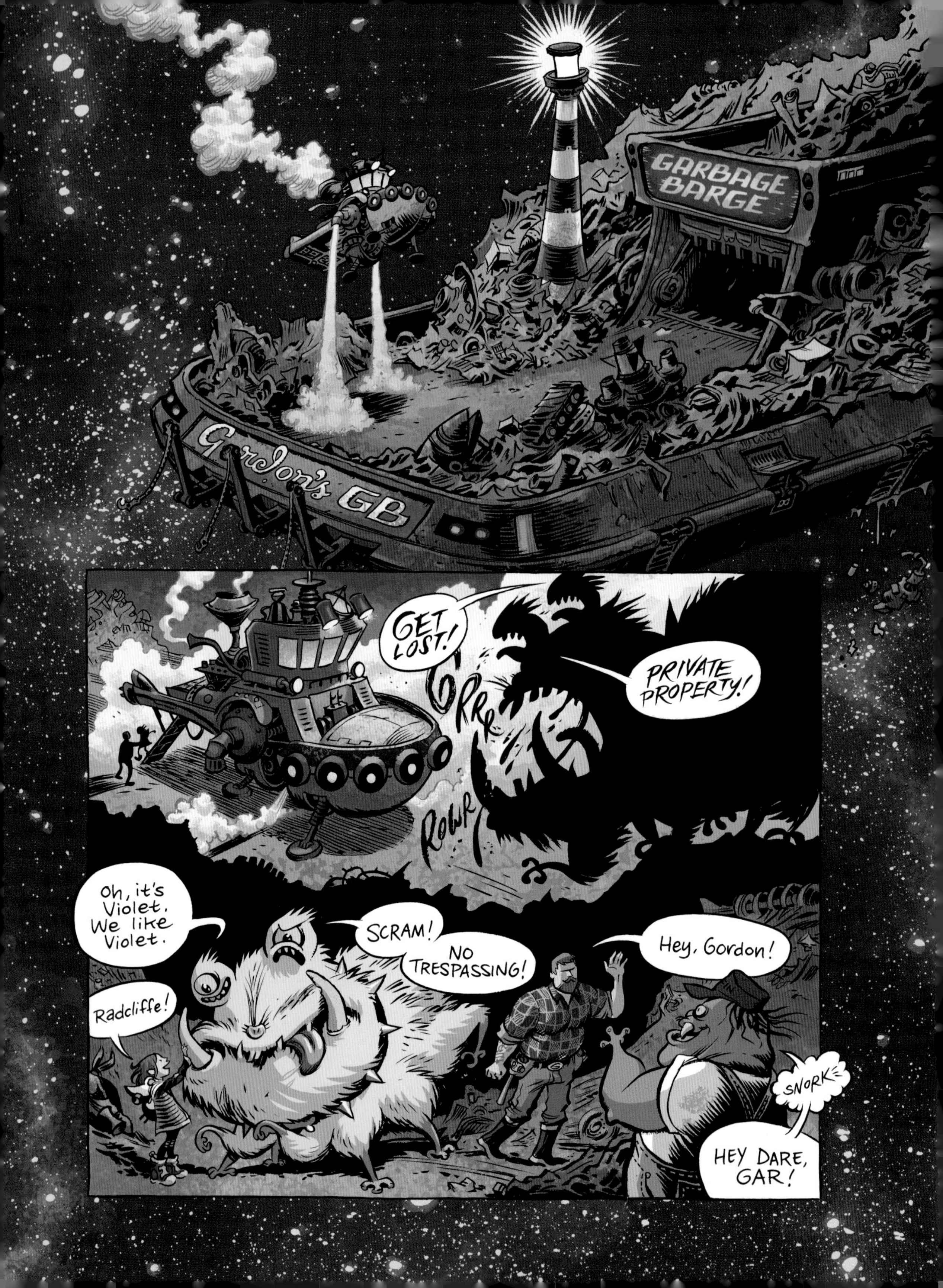
GARBAGE BARGE
Gordon's GB
GET LOST!
PRIVATE PROPERTY!
ROWR
Oh, it's Violet. We like Violet.
SCRAM!
NO TRESPASSING!
Radcliffe!
Hey, Gordon!
SNORK
HEY DARE, GAR!

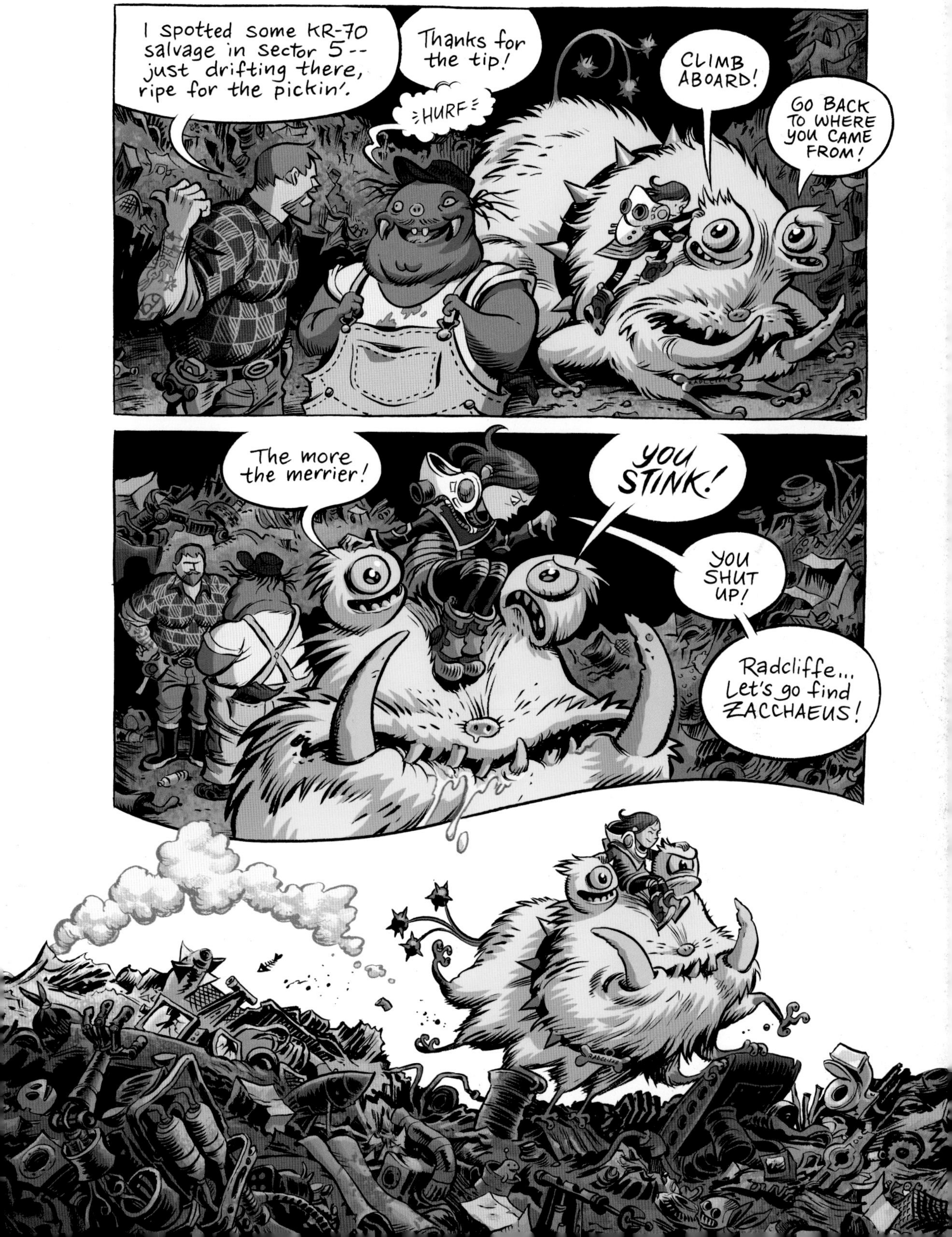
I spotted some KR-70 salvage in sector 5 -- just drifting there, ripe for the pickin'.
Thanks for the tip!
HURF
CLIMB ABOARD!
GO BACK TO WHERE YOU CAME FROM!
The more the merrier!
YOU STINK!
YOU SHUT UP!
Radcliffe... Let's go find ZACCHAEUS!

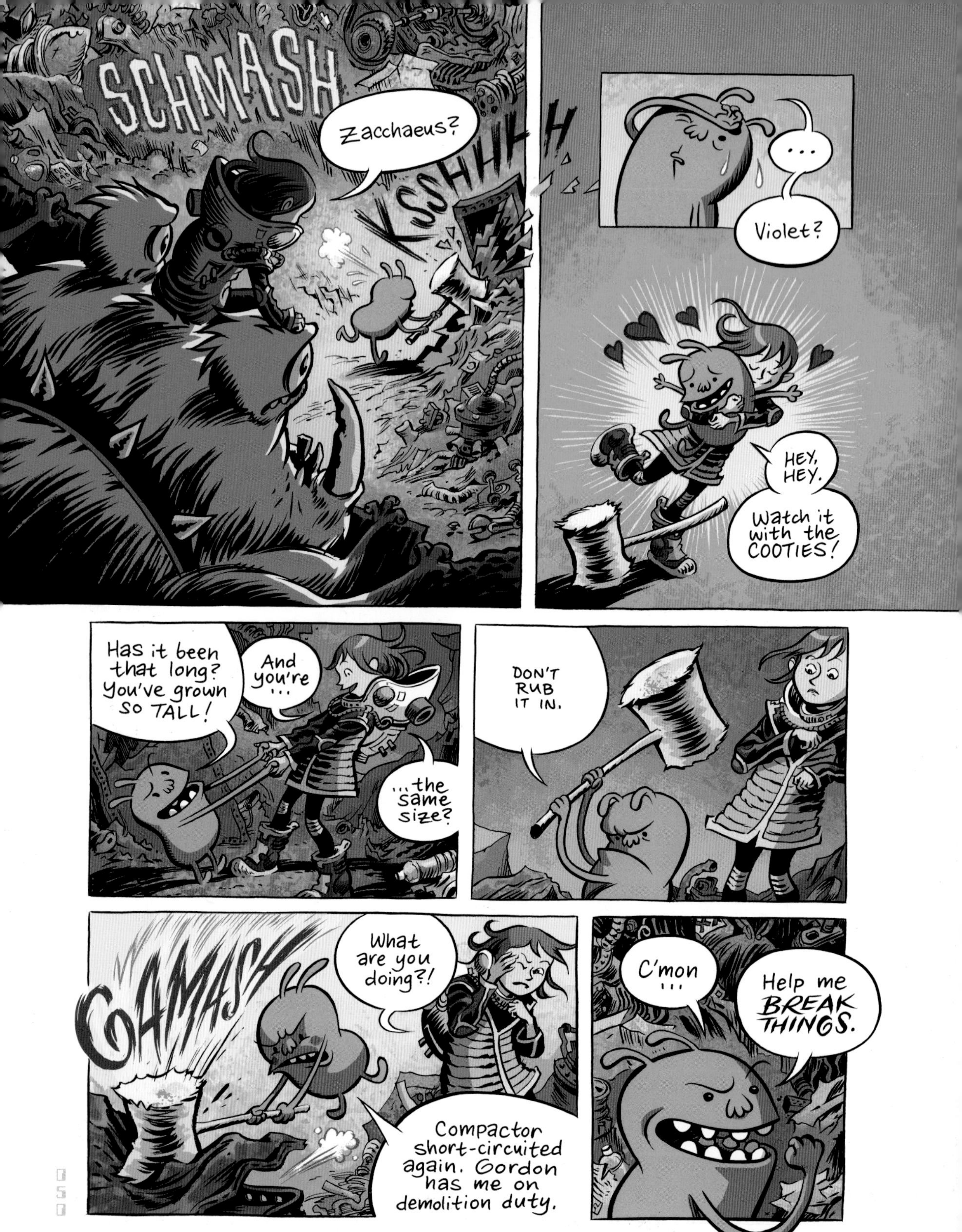
SCHMASH
Zacchaeus?
KSSHHHH
...
Violet?
HEY, HEY.
Watch it with the COOTIES!
Has it been that long? You've grown SO TALL!
And you're ...
...the same size?
DON'T RUB IT IN.
GAMASH
What are you doing?!
Compactor short-circuited again. Gordon has me on demolition duty.
C'mon ...
Help me BREAK THINGS.

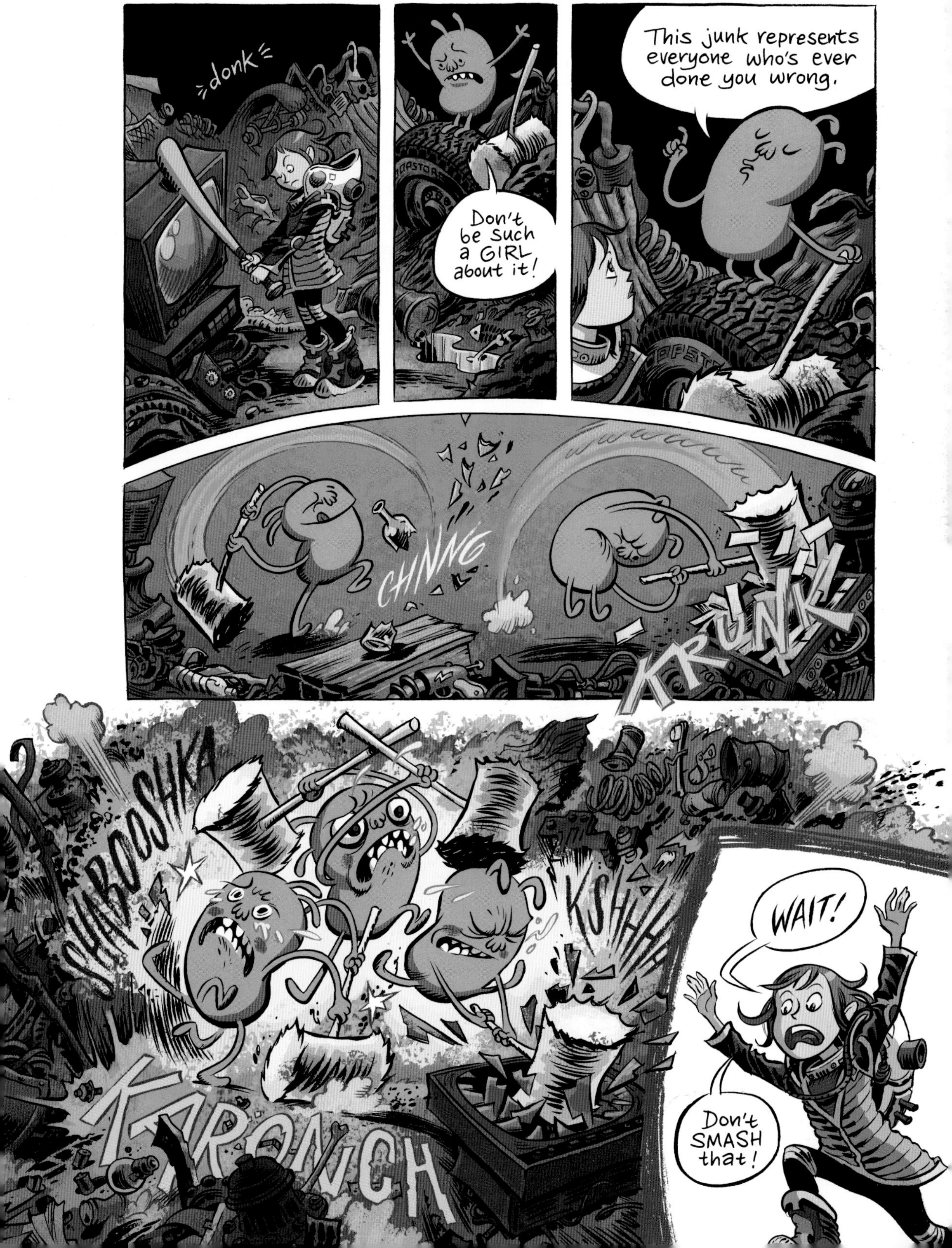

donk
Don't be such a GIRL about it!
This junk represents everyone who's ever done you wrong.
CHINNG
KRUNK
SHABOOSHKA
KSHHH
KARONCH
WAIT!
Don't SMASH that!

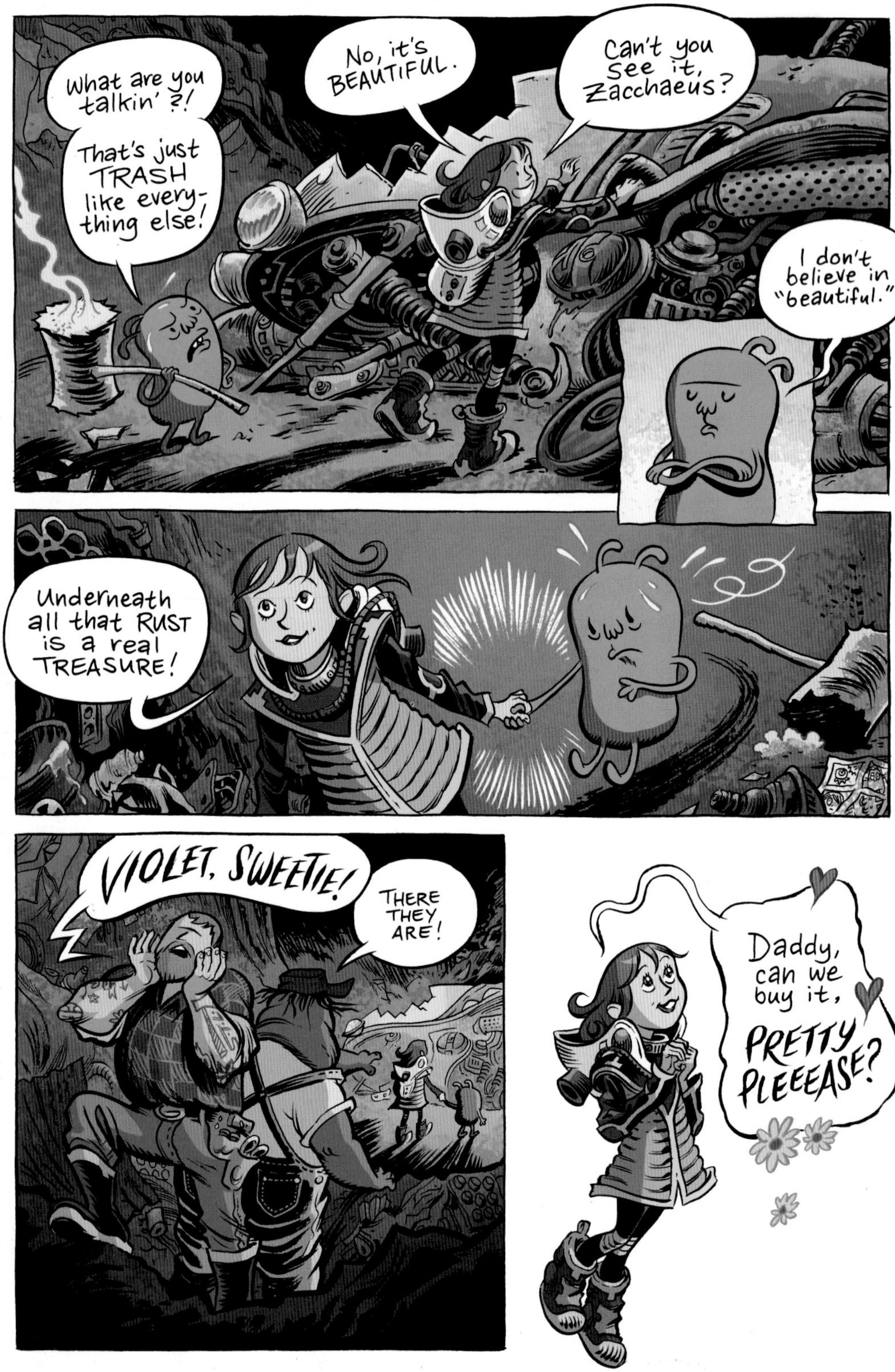
What are you talkin' ?!
That's just TRASH like every-thing else!
No, it's BEAUTIFUL.
Can't you see it, Zacchaeus?
I don't believe in "beautiful."
Underneath all that RUST is a real TREASURE!
VIOLET, SWEETIE!
THERE THEY ARE!
Daddy, can we buy it, PRETTY PLEEEASE?

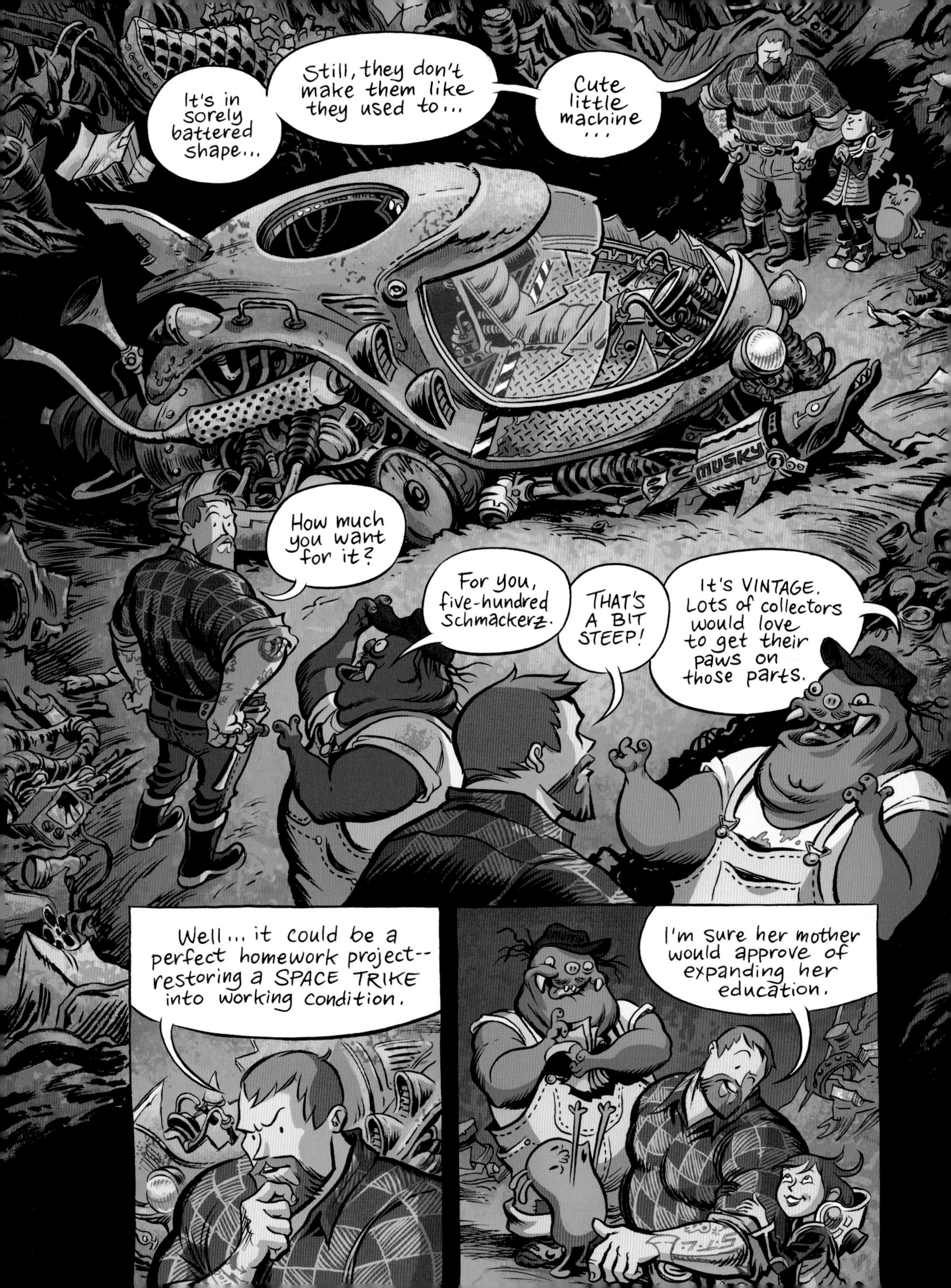
It's in sorely battered shape...
Still, they don't make them like they used to...
Cute little machine . . .
How much you want for it?
For you, five-hundred Schmackerz.
THAT'S A BIT STEEP!
It's VINTAGE. Lots of collectors would love to get their paws on those parts.
MUSKY
Well... it could be a perfect homework project-- restoring a SPACE TRIKE into working condition.
I'm sure her mother would approve of expanding her education.

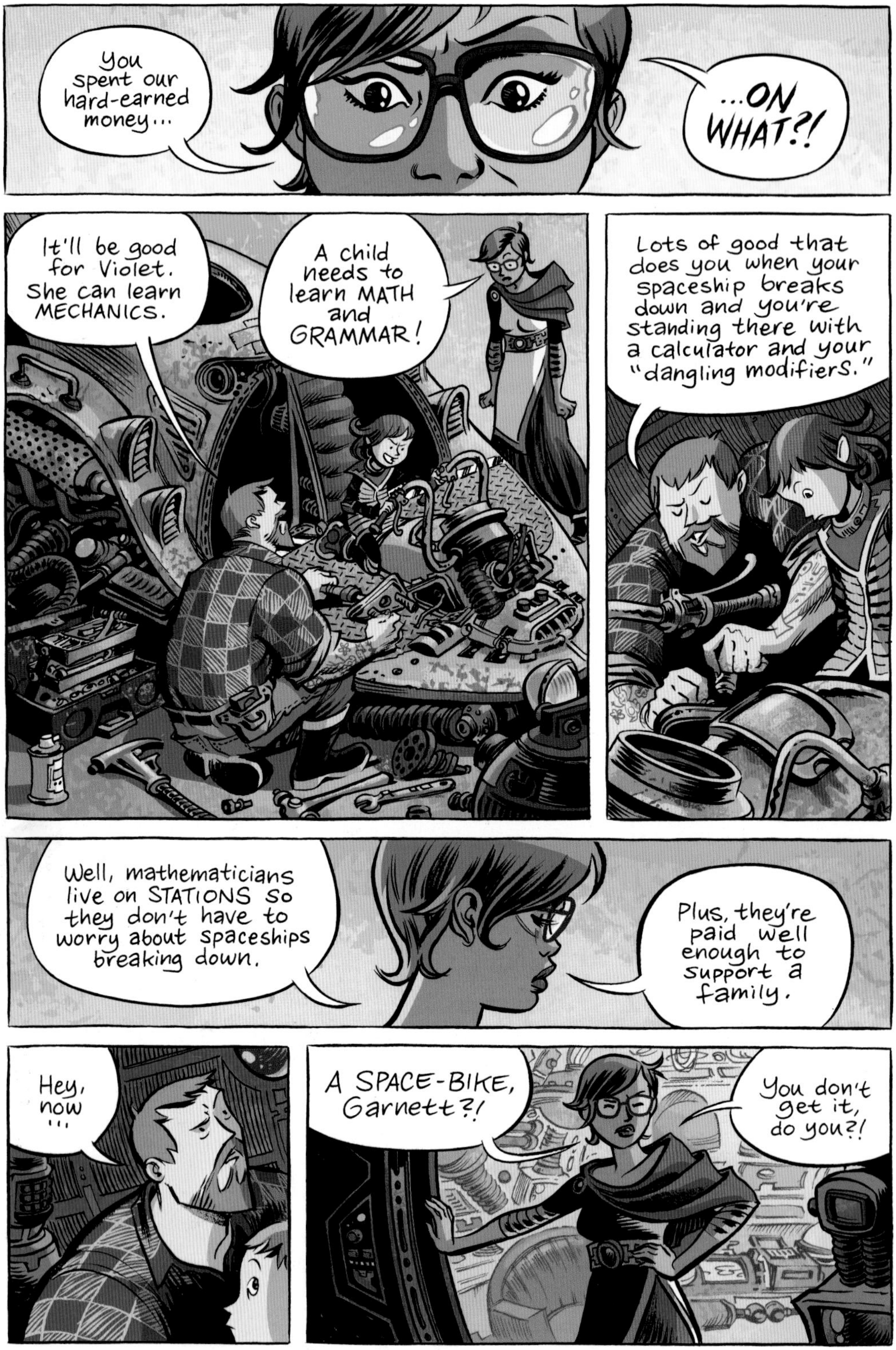
You spent our hard-earned money...
...ON WHAT?!
It'll be good for Violet. She can learn MECHANICS.
A child needs to learn MATH and GRAMMAR!
Lots of good that does you when your spaceship breaks down and you're standing there with a calculator and your "dangling modifiers."
Well, mathematicians live on STATIONS so they don't have to worry about spaceships breaking down.
Plus, they're paid well enough to support a family.
Hey, now ...
A SPACE-BIKE, Garnett?!
You don't get it, do you?!

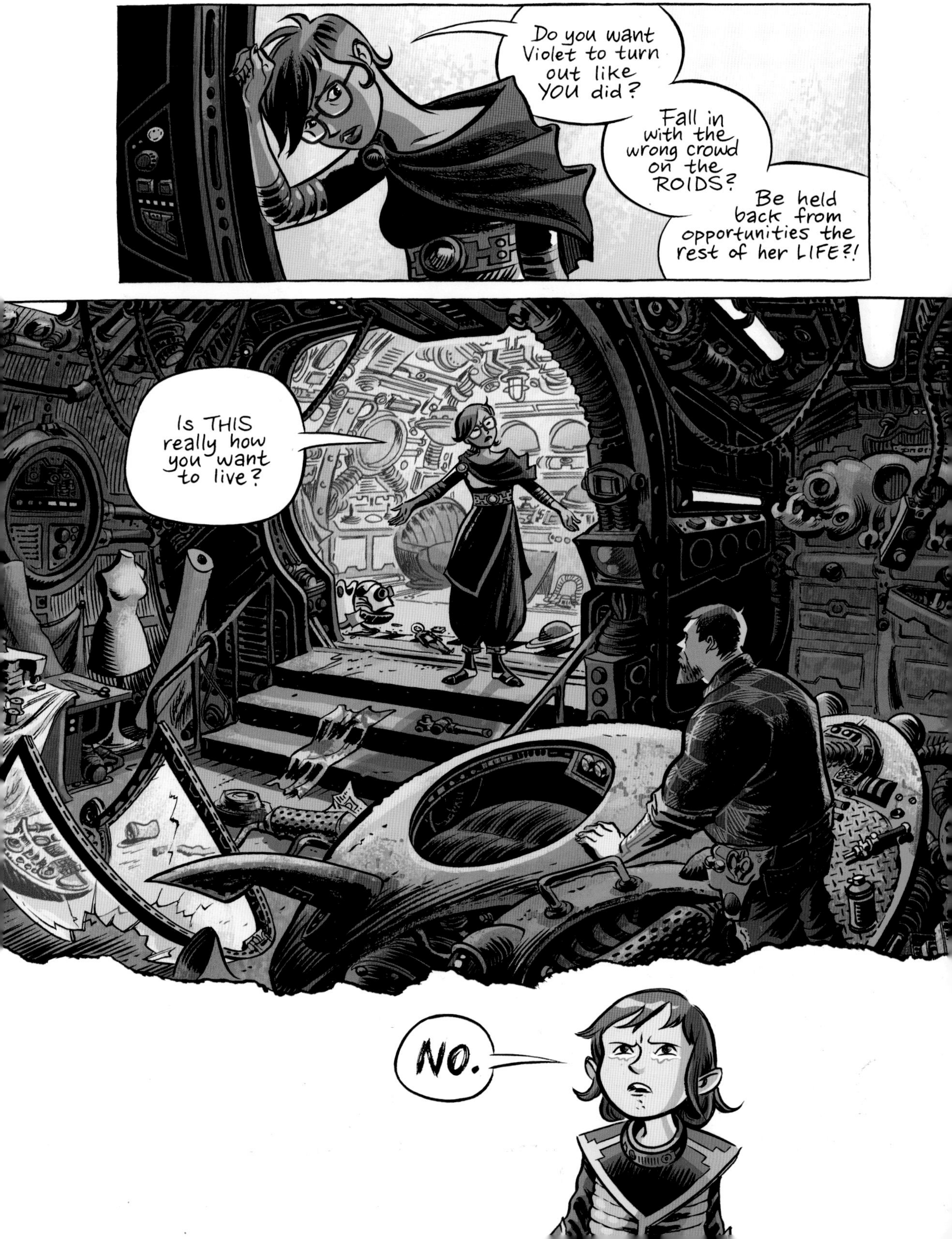
Do you want Violet to turn out like YOU did?
Fall in with the wrong crowd on the ROIDS?
Be held back from opportunities the rest of her LIFE?!
Is THIS really how you want to live?
NO.

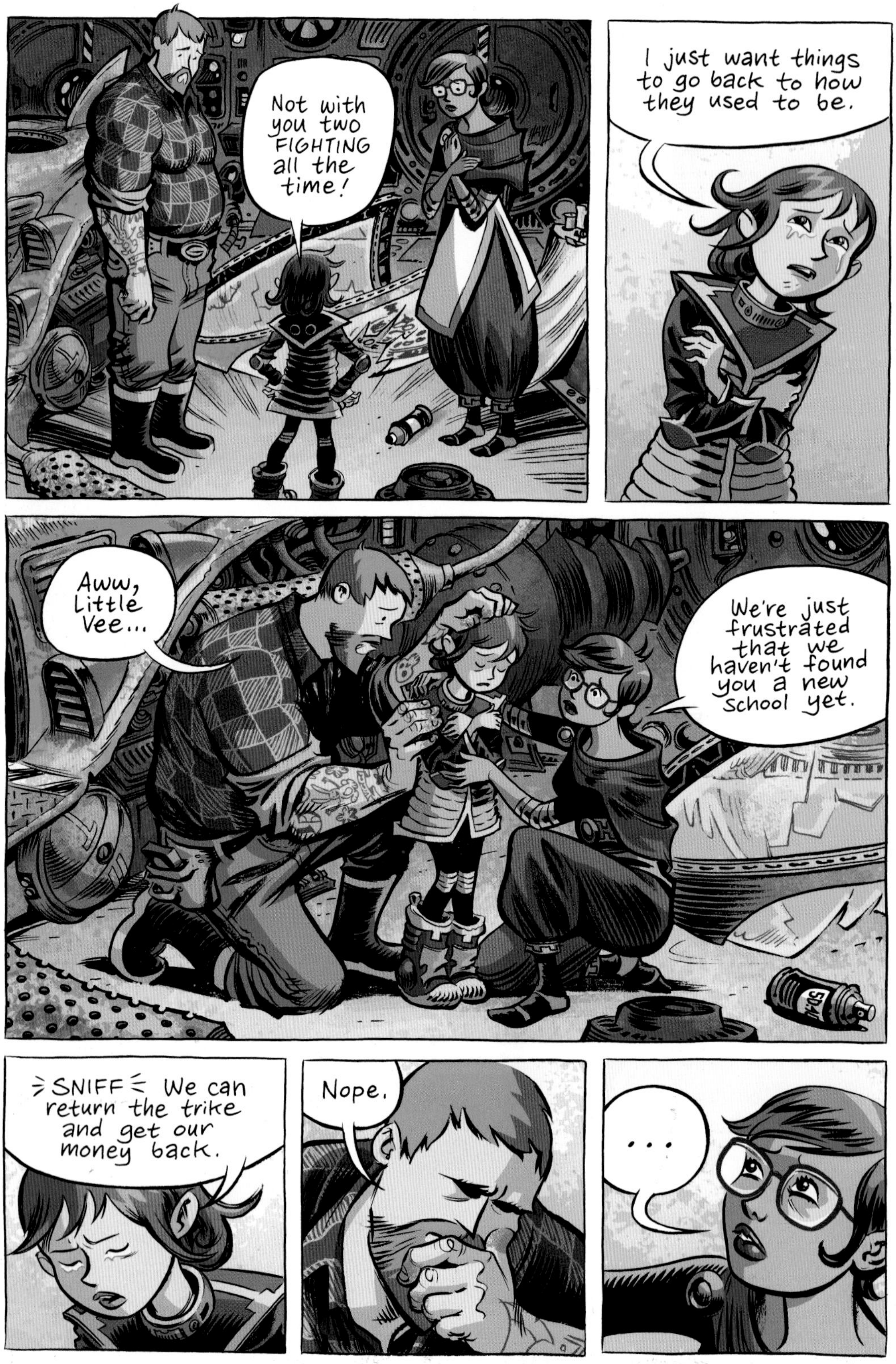
Not with you two FIGHTING all the time!
I just want things to go back to how they used to be.
Aww, Little Vee...
We're just frustrated that we haven't found you a new school yet.
SNIFF We can return the trike and get our money back.
Nope.
...

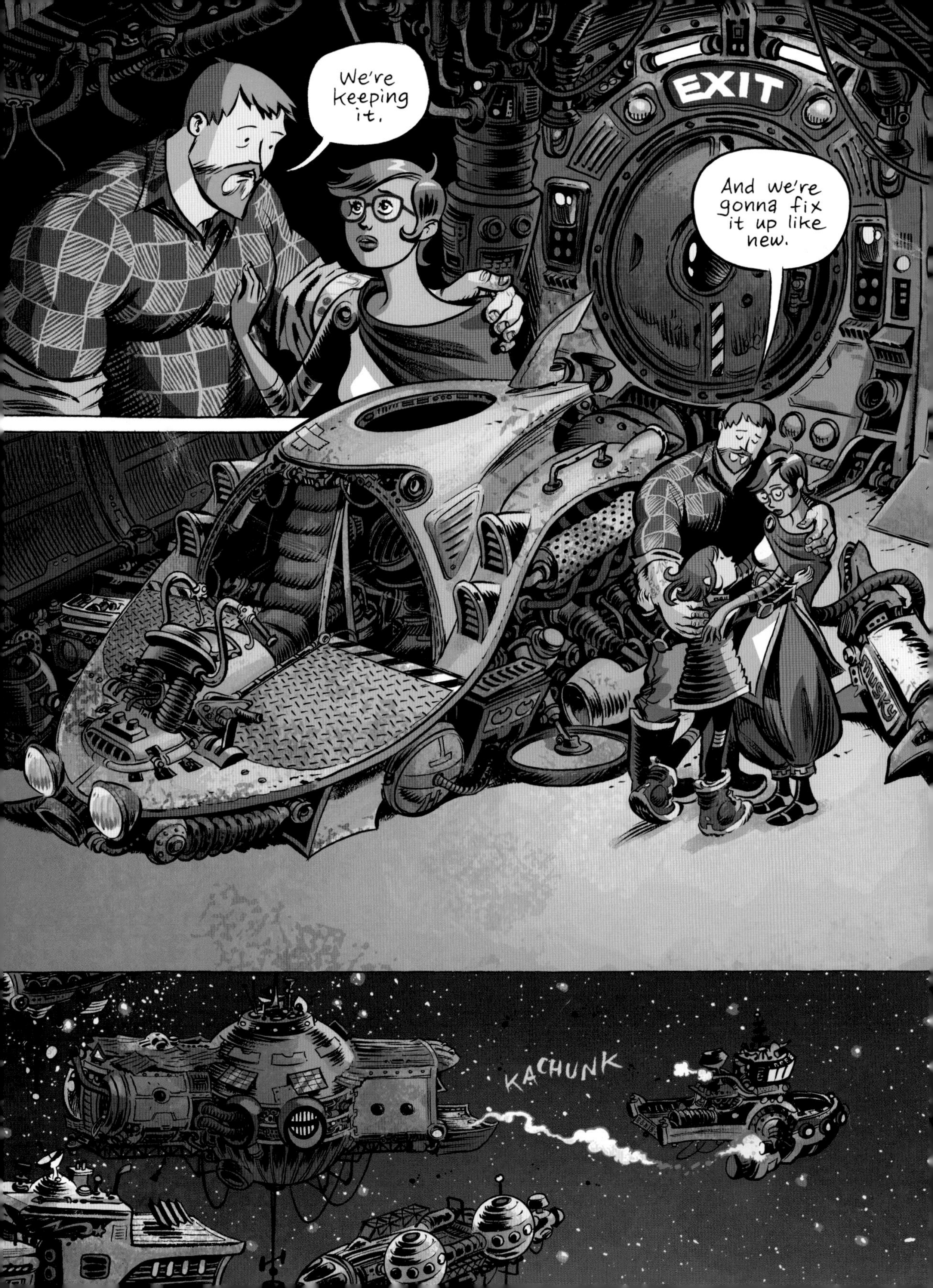
We're keeping it.
And we're gonna fix it up like new.
EXIT
MUSKY
KACHUNK

02

MAG/
GYRO
NAV

MAGNITUDES:

MISSING
COMPONENT

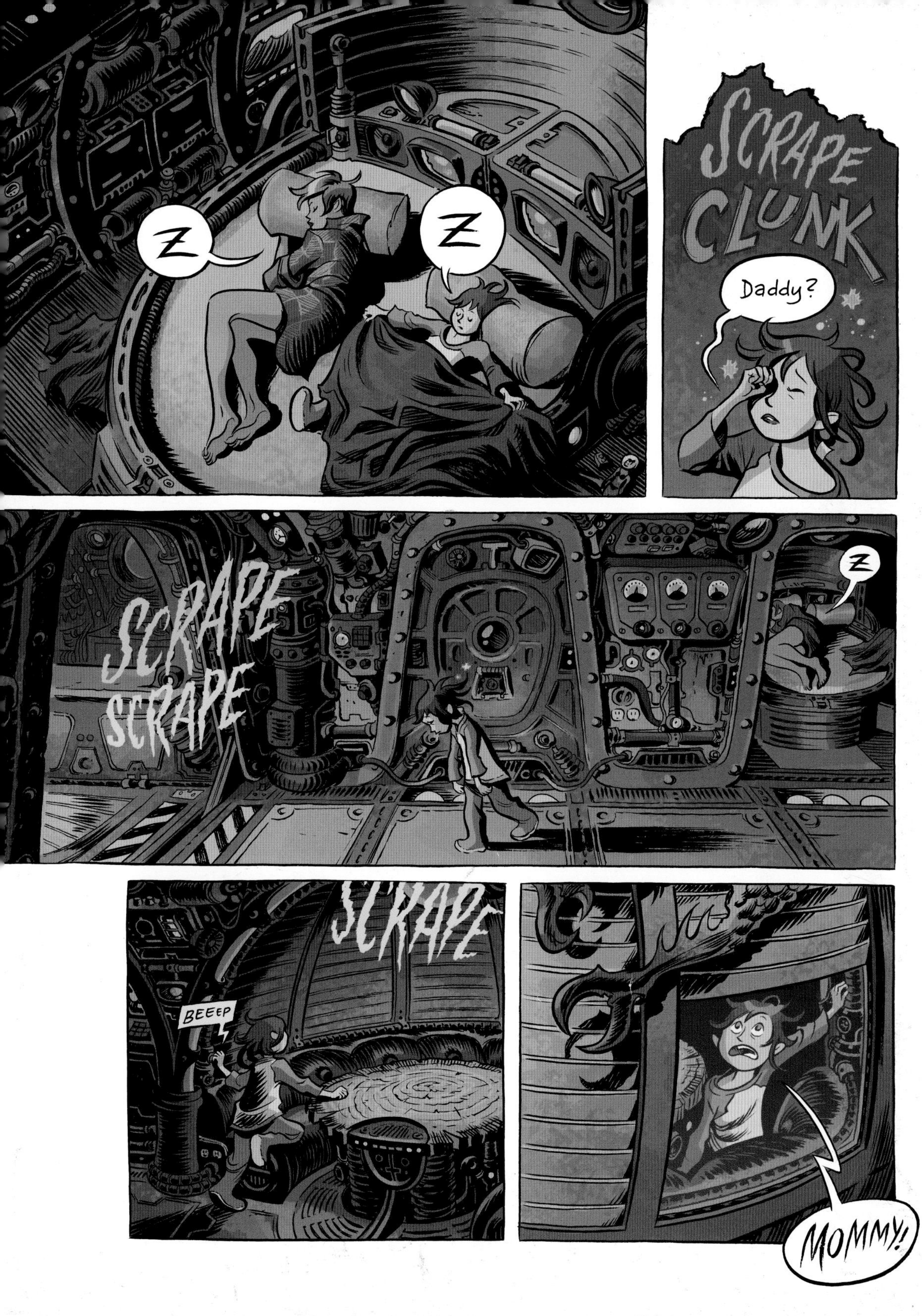
Z
Z
SCRAPE
CLUNK
Daddy?
SCRAPE
SCRAPE
Z
SCRAPE
BEEEP
MOMMY!

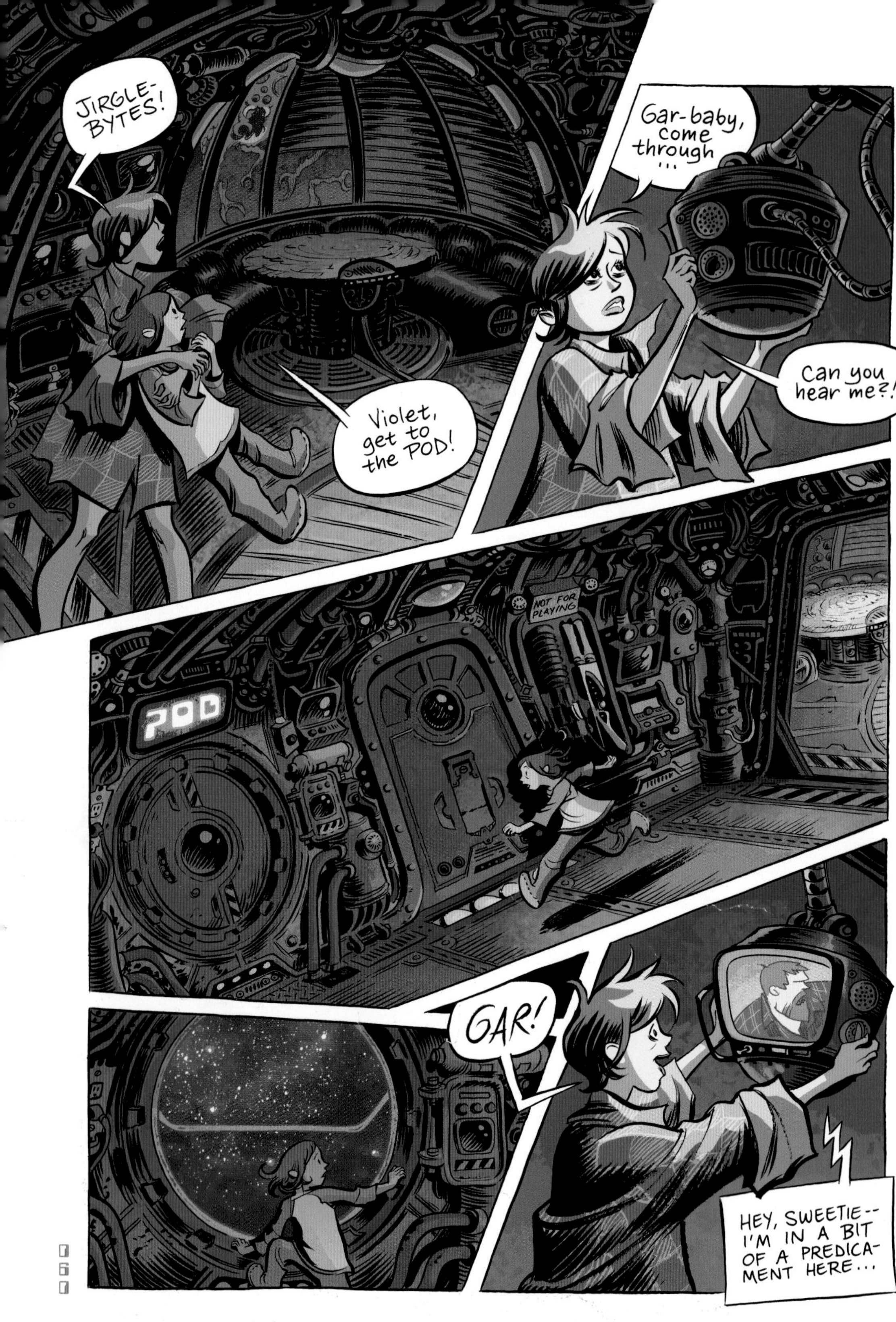
JIRGLE-BYTES!
Violet, get to the POD!
Gar-baby, come through ...
Can you hear me?!
NOT FOR PLAYING
POD
GAR!
HEY, SWEETIE-- I'M IN A BIT OF A PREDICAMENT HERE...

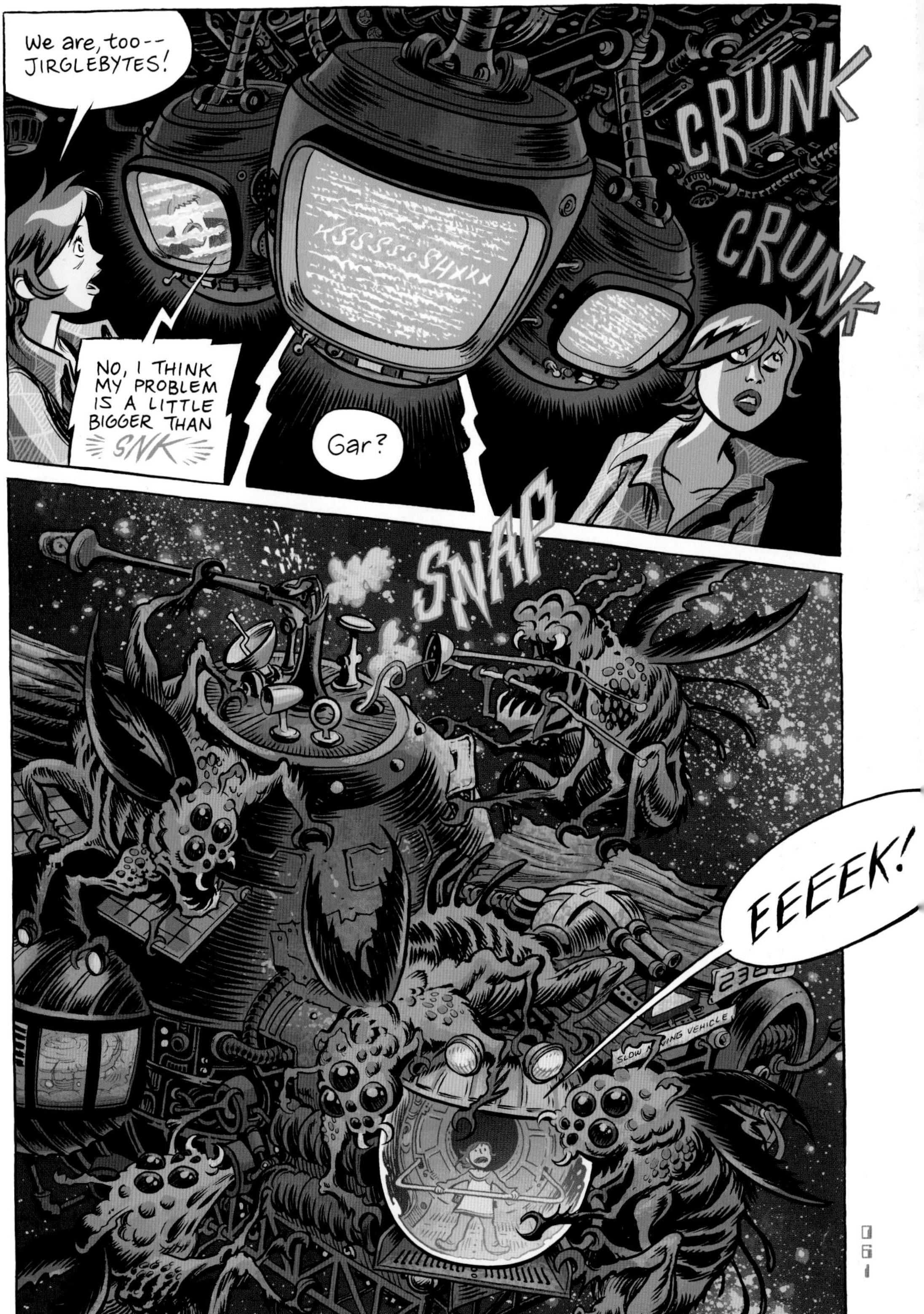
We are, too--
JIRGLEBYTES!
CRUNK
CRUNK
KSSSSSSHXXX
NO, I THINK MY PROBLEM IS A LITTLE BIGGER THAN SNK
Gar?
SNAP
EEEEK!

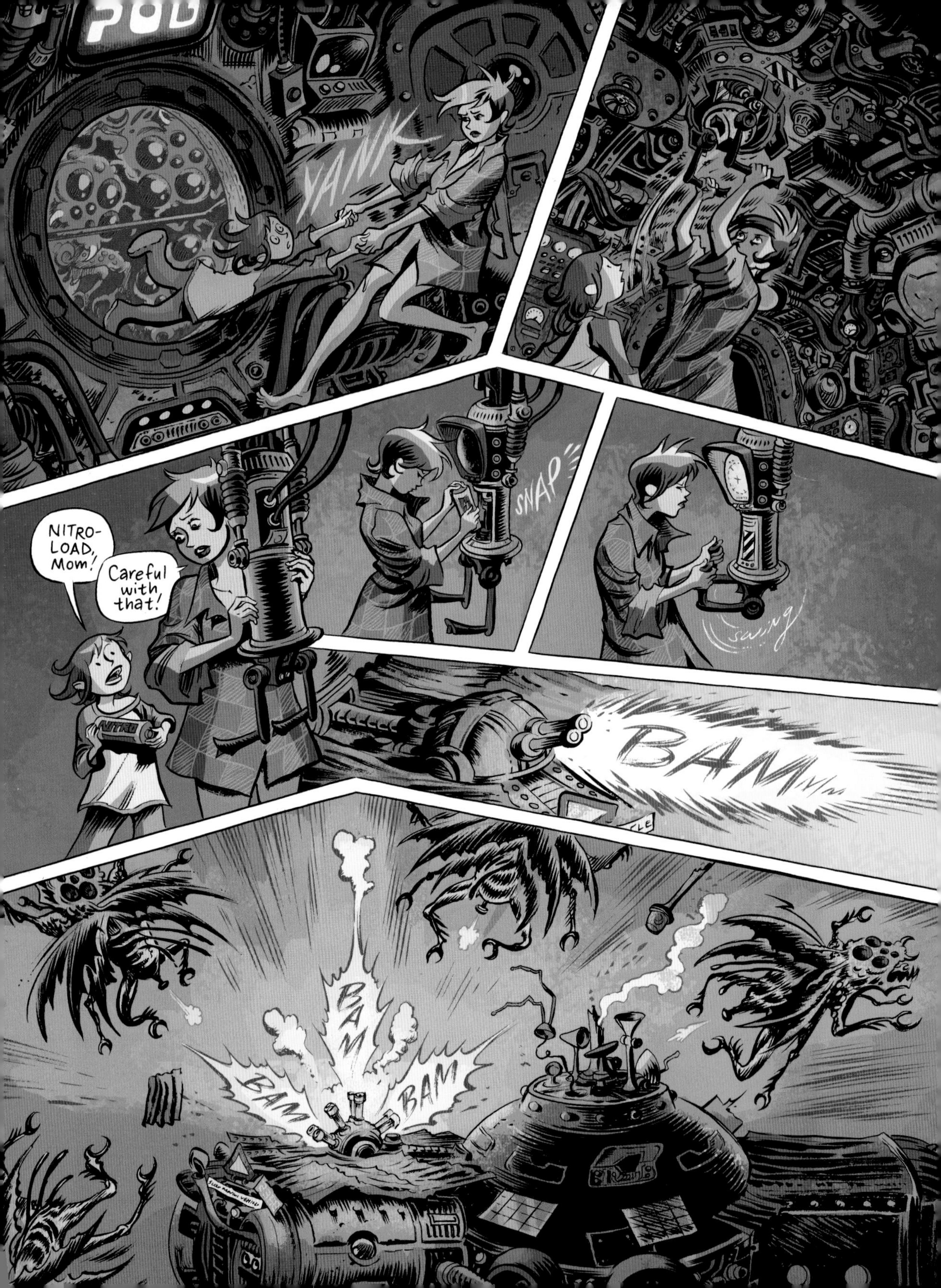
POD
YANK
NITRO-LOAD, Mom!
Careful with that!
NITRO
SNAP
swing
BAM
BAM
BAM
BAM
BAM

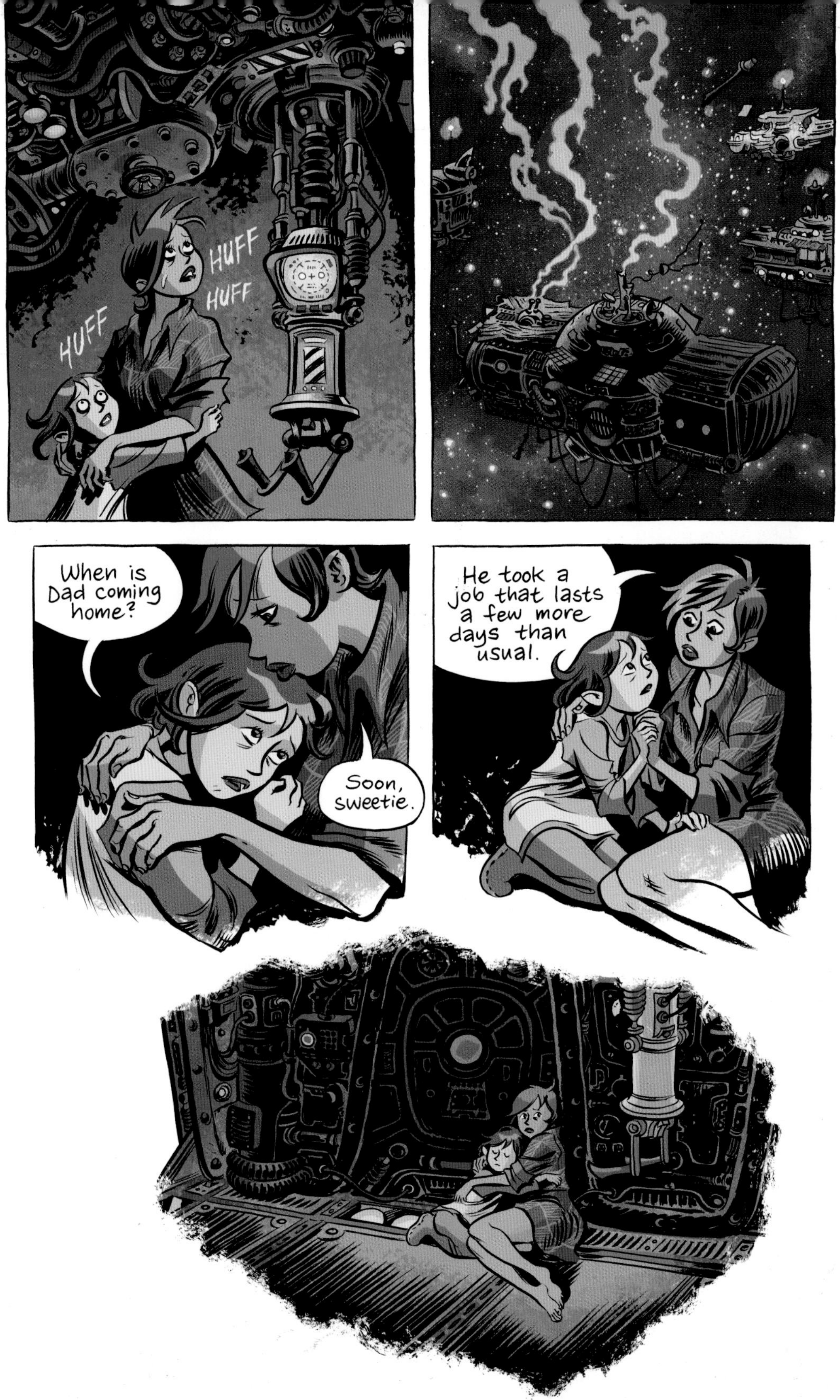
HUFF
HUFF
HUFF
When is Dad coming home?
Soon, sweetie.
He took a job that lasts a few more days than usual.

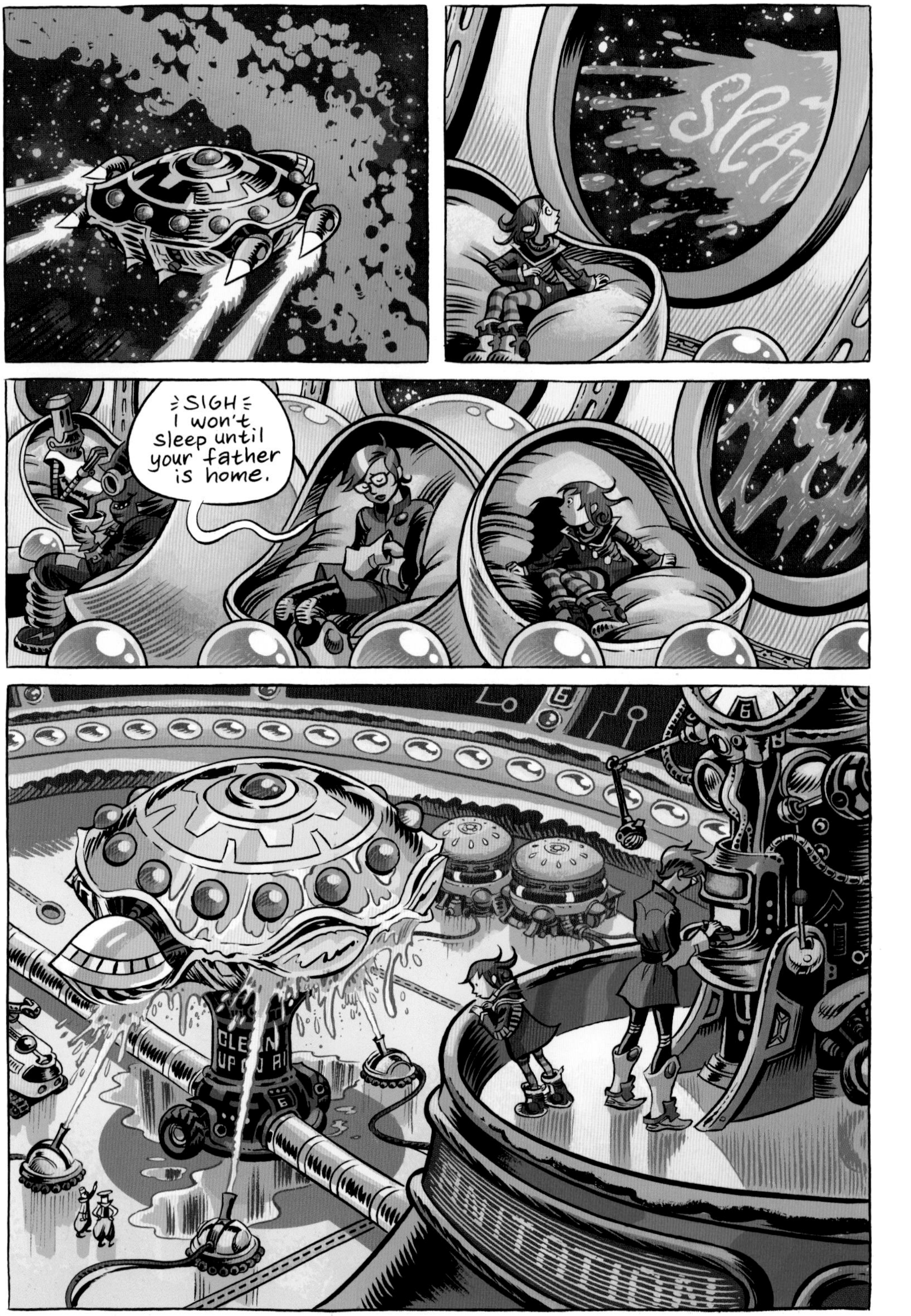
SIGH
I won't sleep until your father is home.

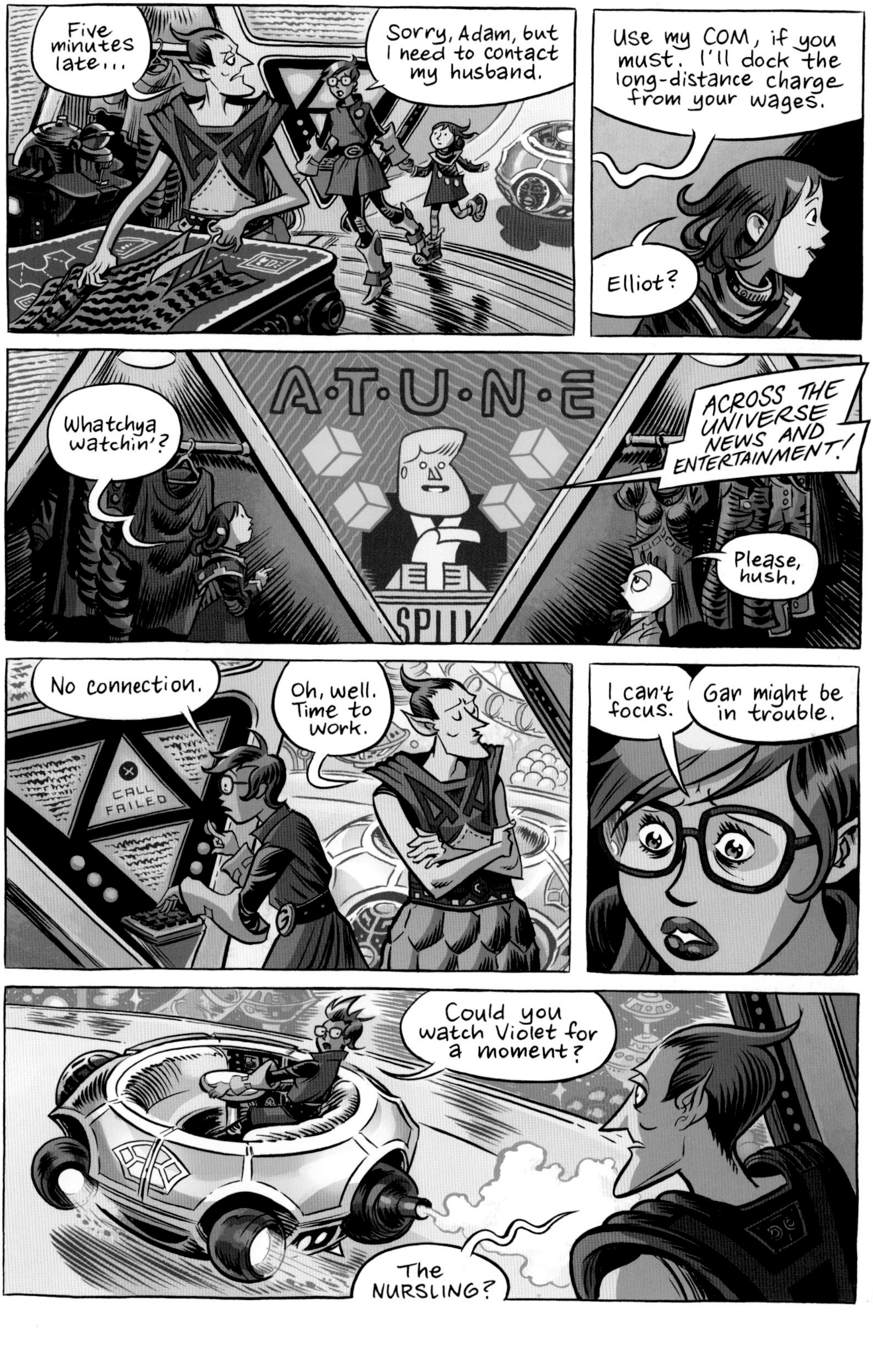
Five minutes late...
Sorry, Adam, but I need to contact my husband.
Use my COM, if you must. I'll dock the long-distance charge from your wages.
Elliot?
A·T·U·N·E
Whatchya watchin'?
ACROSS THE UNIVERSE NEWS AND ENTERTAINMENT!
Please, hush.
No connection.
CALL FAILED
Oh, well. Time to work.
I can't focus.
Gar might be in trouble.
Could you watch Violet for a moment?
The NURSLING?

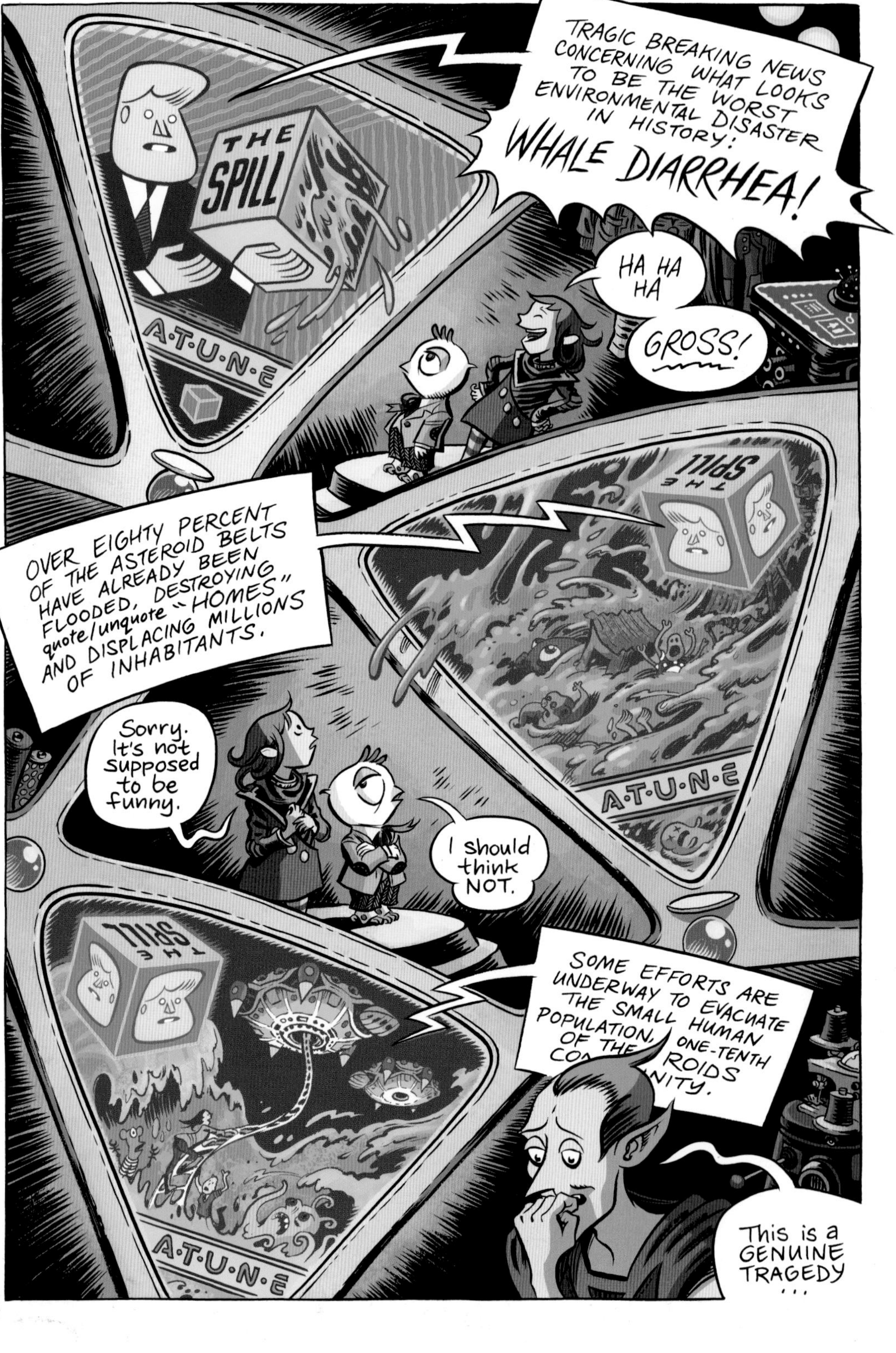
THE SPILL
A·T·U·N·E
TRAGIC BREAKING NEWS CONCERNING WHAT LOOKS TO BE THE WORST ENVIRONMENTAL DISASTER IN HISTORY: WHALE DIARRHEA!
HA HA HA
GROSS!
OVER EIGHTY PERCENT OF THE ASTEROID BELTS HAVE ALREADY BEEN FLOODED, DESTROYING quote/unquote "HOMES" AND DISPLACING MILLIONS OF INHABITANTS.
THE SPILL
A·T·U·N·E
Sorry. It's not supposed to be funny.
I should think NOT.
THE SPILL
A·T·U·N·E
SOME EFFORTS ARE UNDERWAY TO EVACUATE THE SMALL HUMAN POPULATION, ONE-TENTH OF THE ROIDS CO NITY.
This is a GENUINE TRAGEDY ...

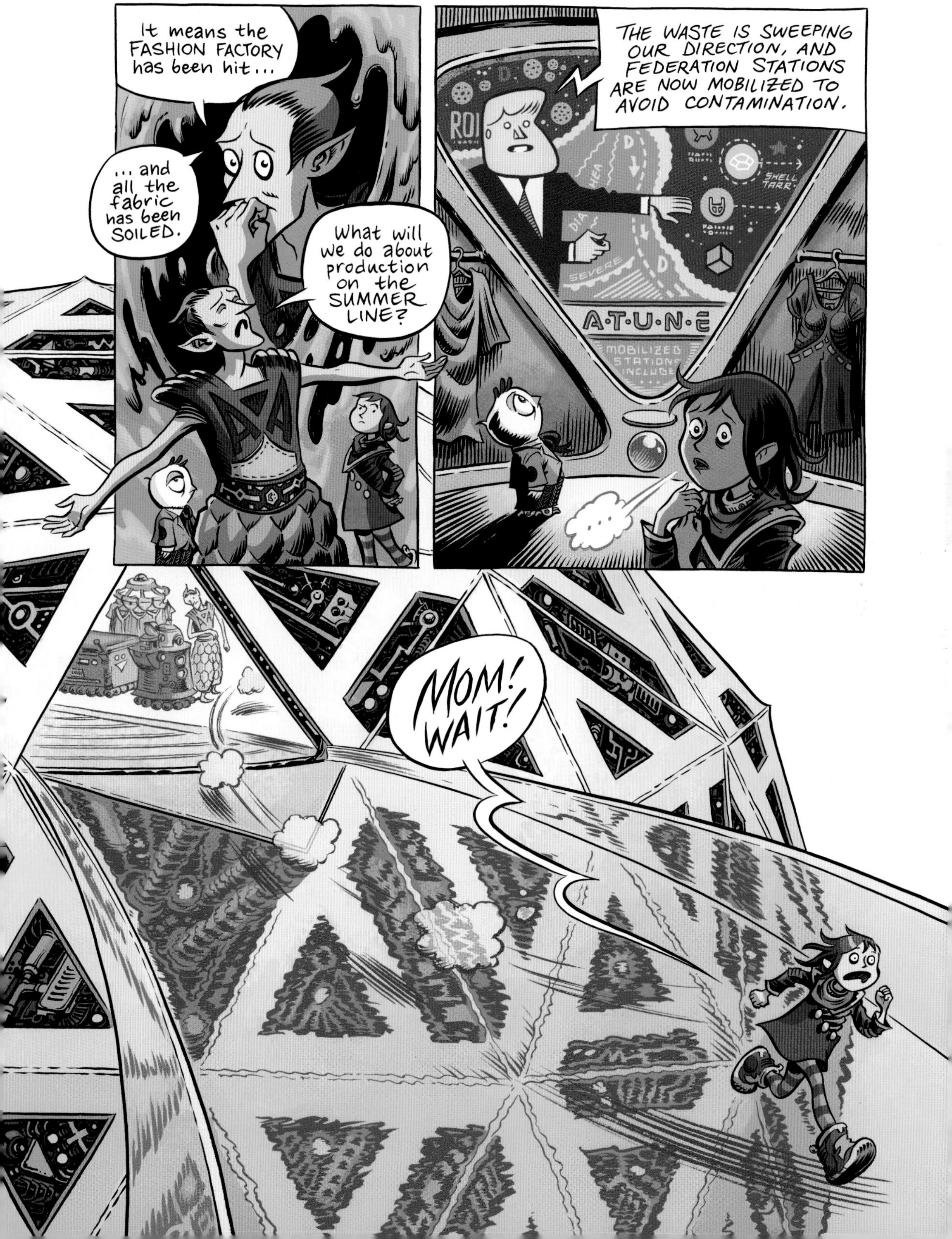

It means the FASHION FACTORY has been hit...
... and all the fabric has been SOILED.
What will we do about production on the SUMMER LINE?
THE WASTE IS SWEEPING OUR DIRECTION, AND FEDERATION STATIONS ARE NOW MOBILIZED TO AVOID CONTAMINATION.
A·T·U·N·E
MOBILIZED STATIONS INCLUDE
SEVERE
SHELL TARR
MOM! WAIT!

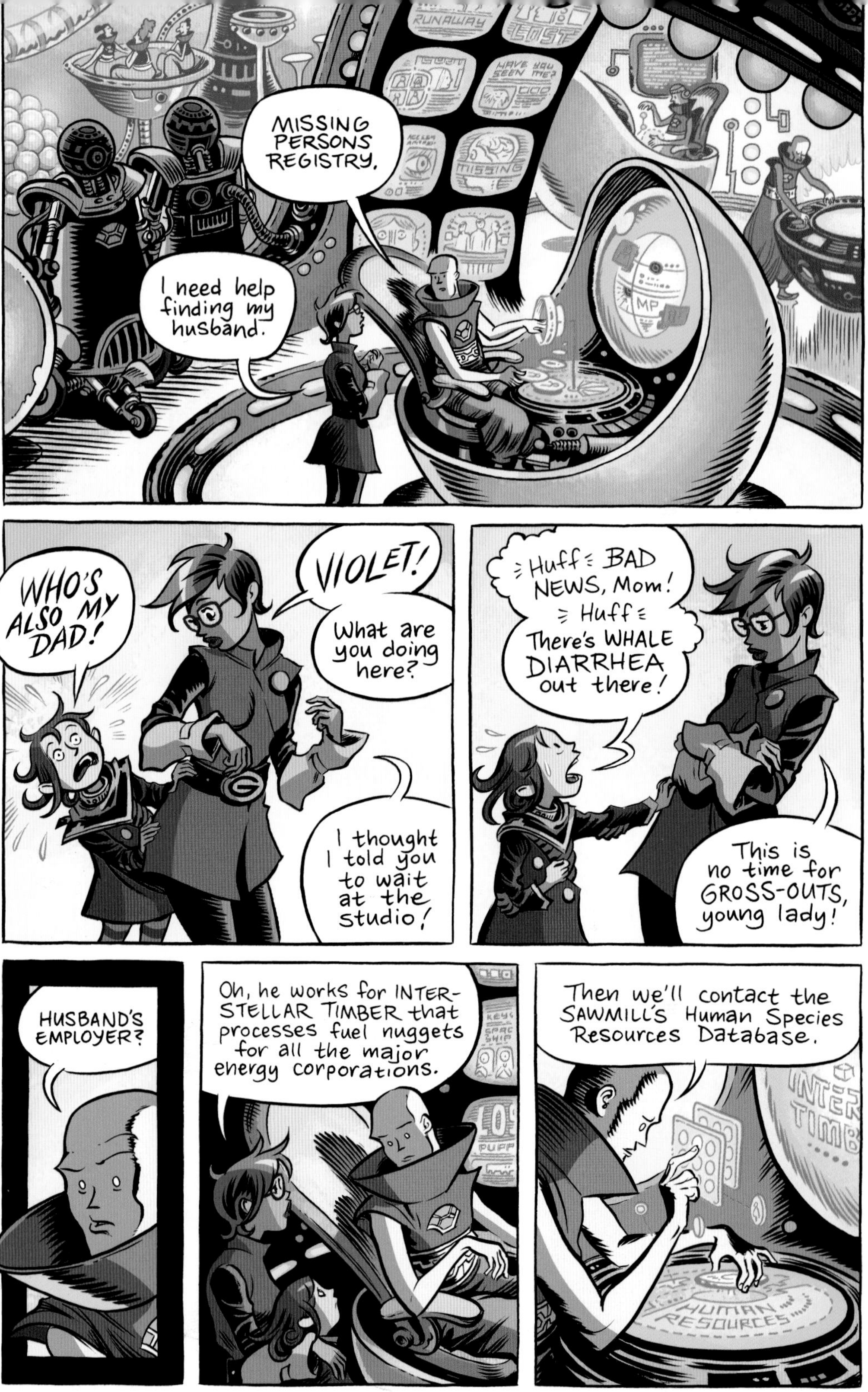
RUNAWAY
LOST
HAVE YOU SEEN ME?
MISSING
MISSING PERSONS REGISTRY.
I need help finding my husband.
MP
WHO'S ALSO MY DAD!
VIOLET!
What are you doing here?
I thought I told you to wait at the studio!
Huff BAD NEWS, Mom! Huff There's WHALE DIARRHEA out there!
This is no time for GROSS-OUTS, young lady!
HUSBAND'S EMPLOYER?
Oh, he works for INTERSTELLAR TIMBER that processes fuel nuggets for all the major energy corporations.
Then we'll contact the SAWMILL'S Human Species Resources Database.
HUMAN RESOURCES

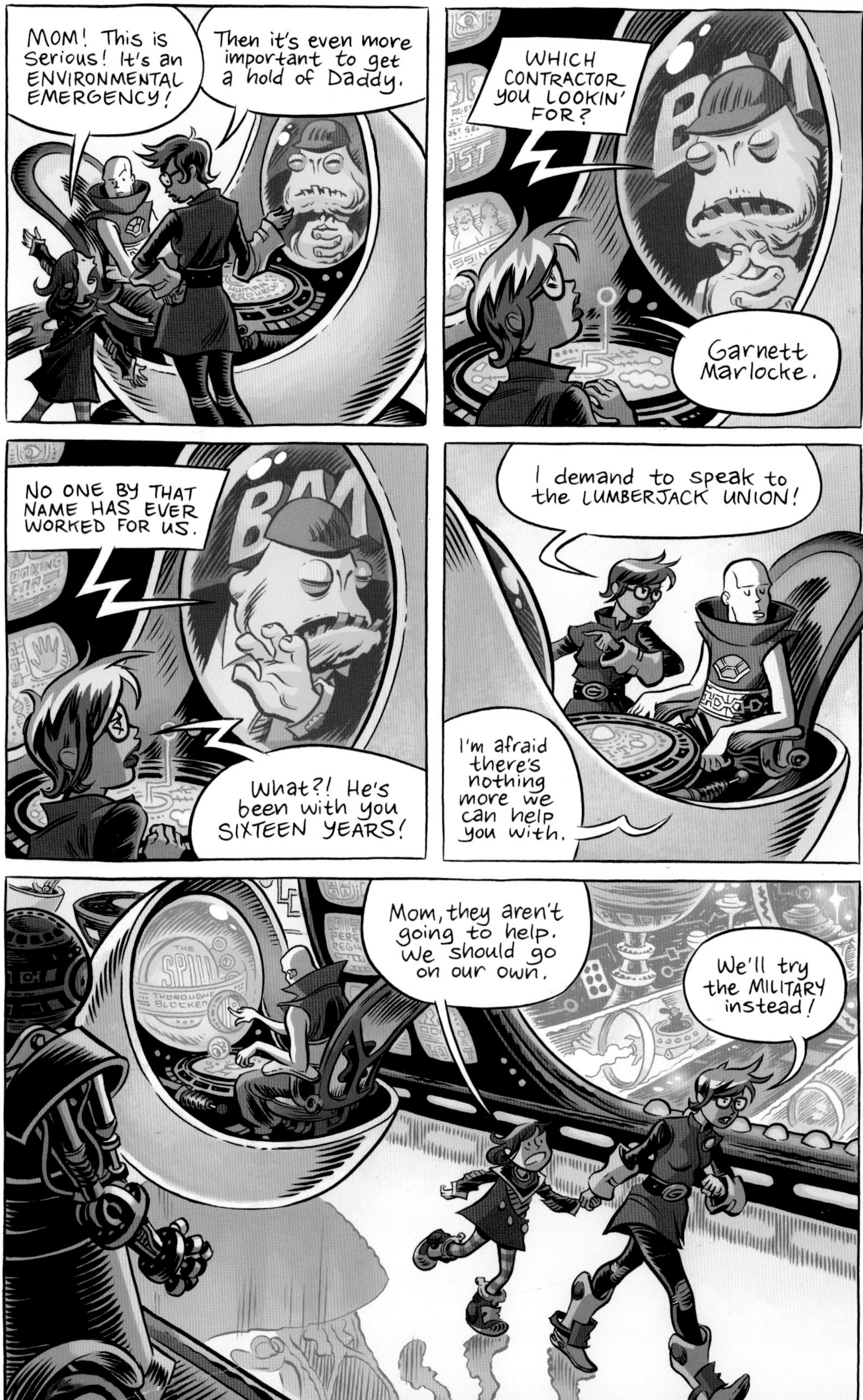
MOM! This is Serious! It's an ENVIRONMENTAL EMERGENCY!
Then it's even more important to get a hold of Daddy.
WHICH CONTRACTOR YOU LOOKIN' FOR?
Garnett Marlocke.
NO ONE BY THAT NAME HAS EVER WORKED FOR US.
What?! He's been with you SIXTEEN YEARS!
I demand to speak to the LUMBERJACK UNION!
I'm afraid there's nothing more we can help you with.
Mom, they aren't going to help. We should go on our own.
We'll try the MILITARY instead!

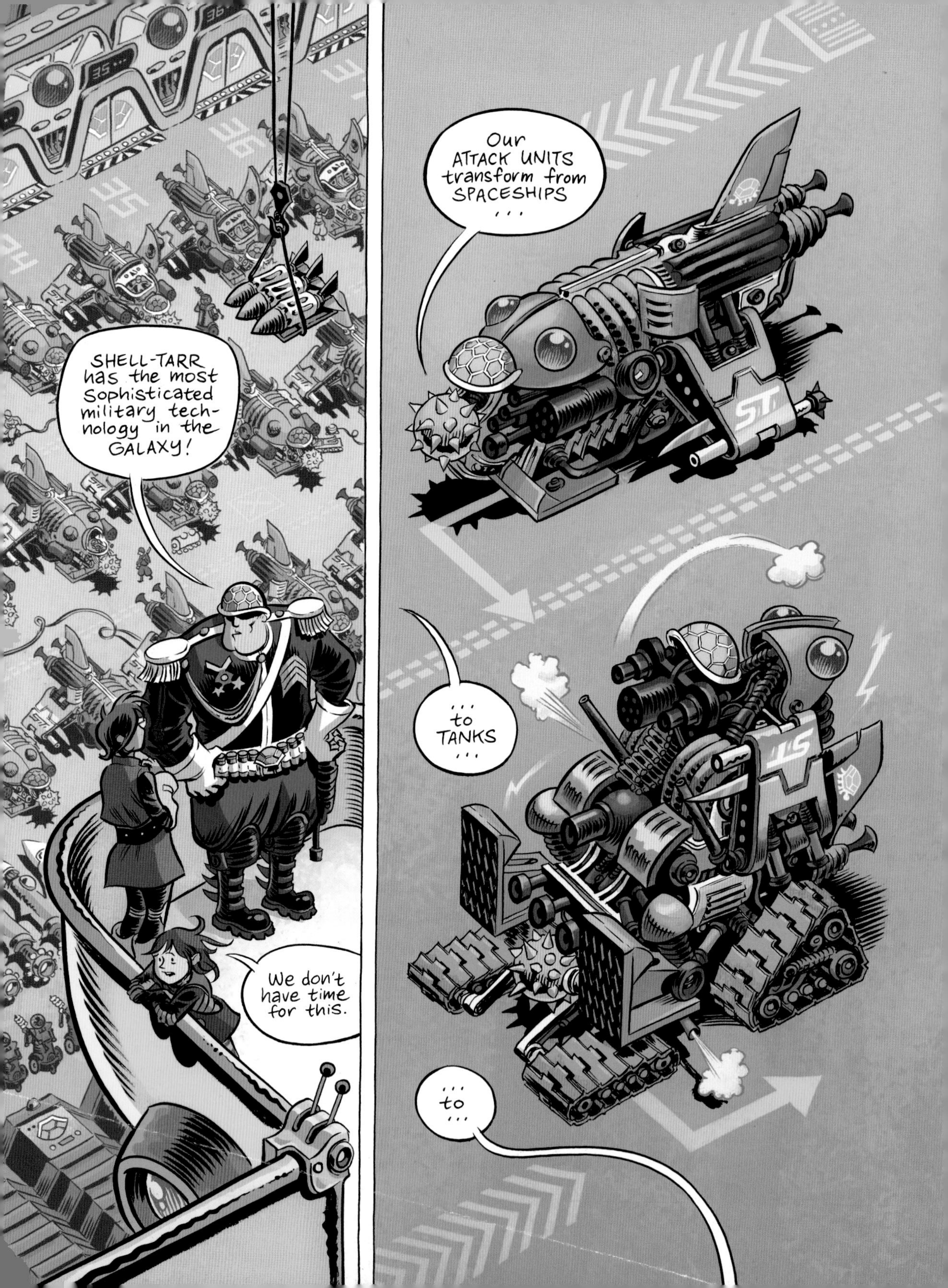
SHELL-TARR has the most sophisticated military tech-nology in the GALAXY!
We don't have time for this.
Our ATTACK UNITS transform from SPACESHIPS ...
... to TANKS ...
... to ...

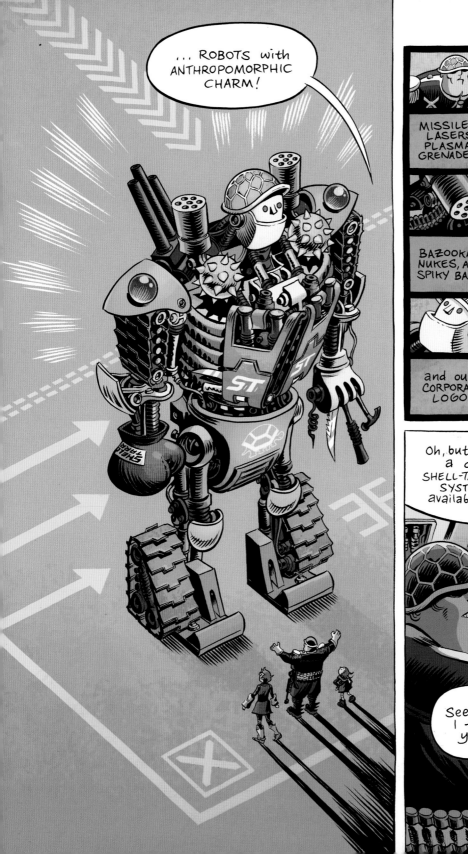

... ROBOTS with ANTHROPOMORPHIC CHARM!

They're loaded up with:

MISSILES, LASERS, PLASMA-GRENADES,

FLAME-THROWERS, HOWITZERS, BLUDGEONS,

BAZOOKAS, NUKES, AND SPIKY BALLS.

Then decorated with a friendly face,

and our CORPORATE LOGO.

Oh, but you're simply a day laborer. SHELL-TARR'S DEFENSE SYSTEM is only available to CITIZENS.

But...

See, Mom. I told you!

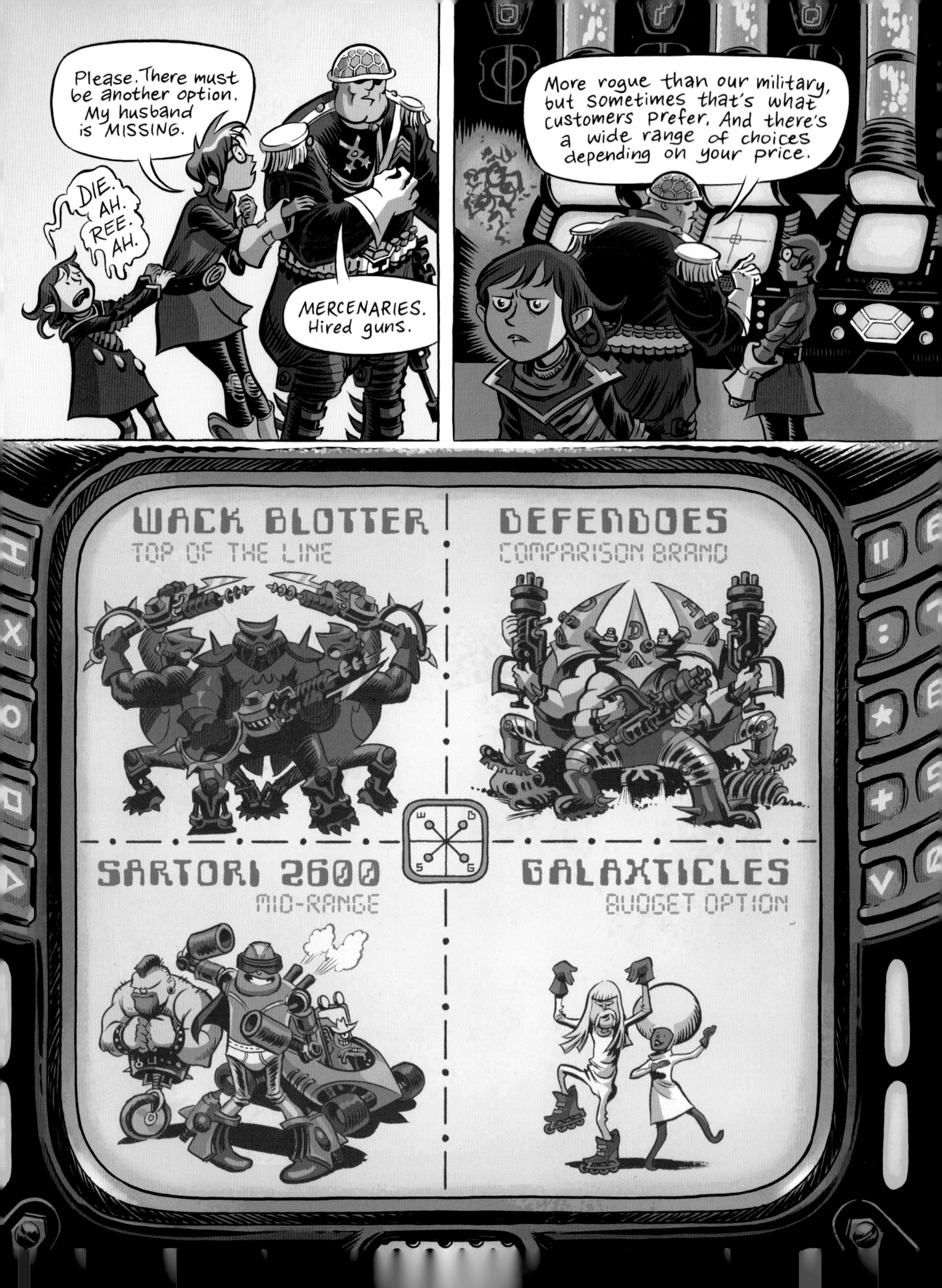
Please. There must be another option. My husband is MISSING.
DIE. AH. REE. AH.
MERCENARIES. Hired guns.
More rogue than our military, but sometimes that's what customers prefer. And there's a wide range of choices depending on your price.
WACK BLOTTER
TOP OF THE LINE
DEFENDOES
COMPARISON BRAND
SARTORI 2600
MID-RANGE
GALAXTICLES
BUDGET OPTION

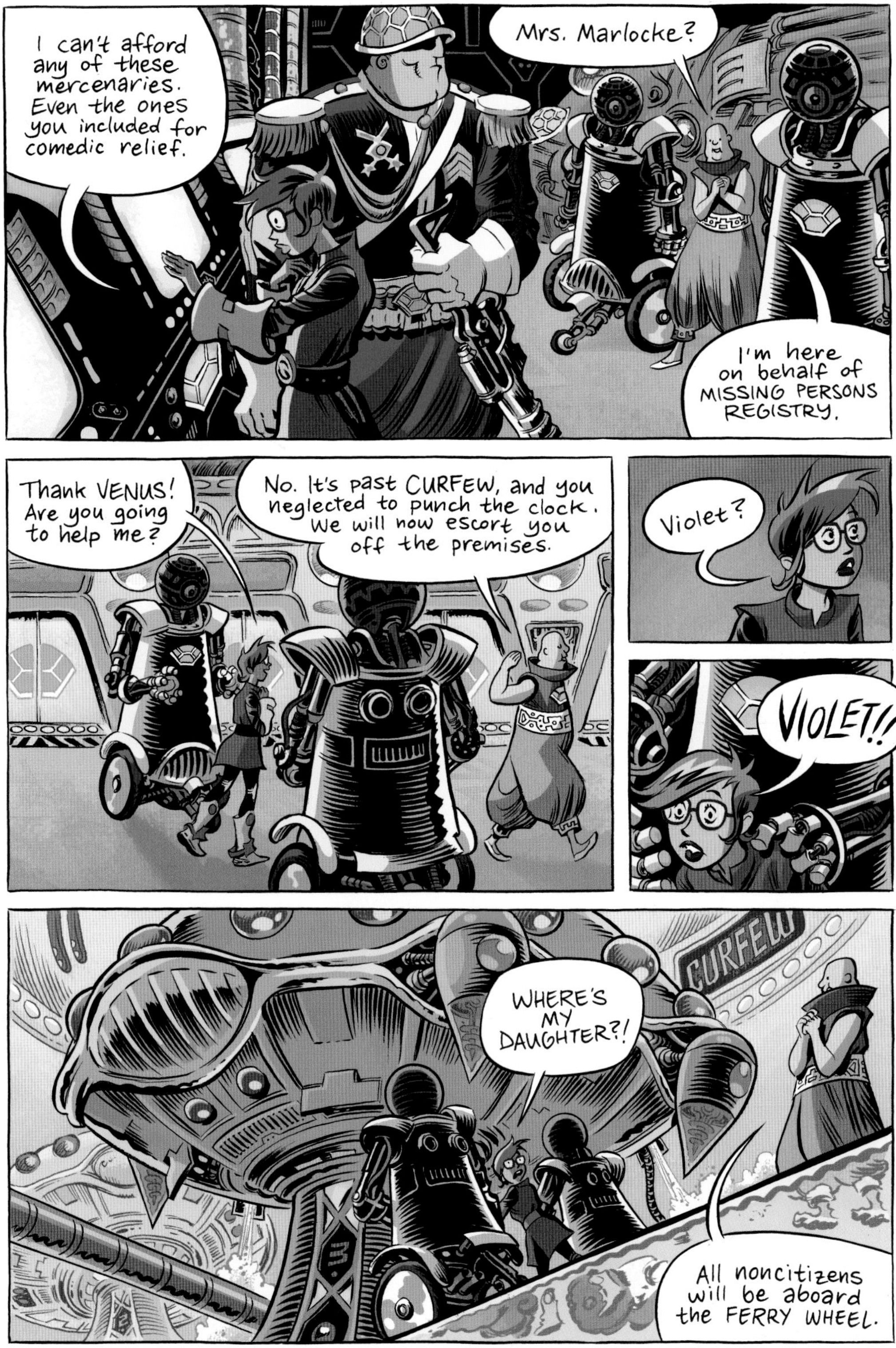
I can't afford any of these mercenaries. Even the ones you included for comedic relief.
Mrs. Marlocke?
I'm here on behalf of MISSING PERSONS REGISTRY.
Thank VENUS! Are you going to help me?
No. It's past CURFEW, and you neglected to punch the clock. We will now escort you off the premises.
Violet?
VIOLET!!
CURFEW
WHERE'S MY DAUGHTER?!
All noncitizens will be aboard the FERRY WHEEL.

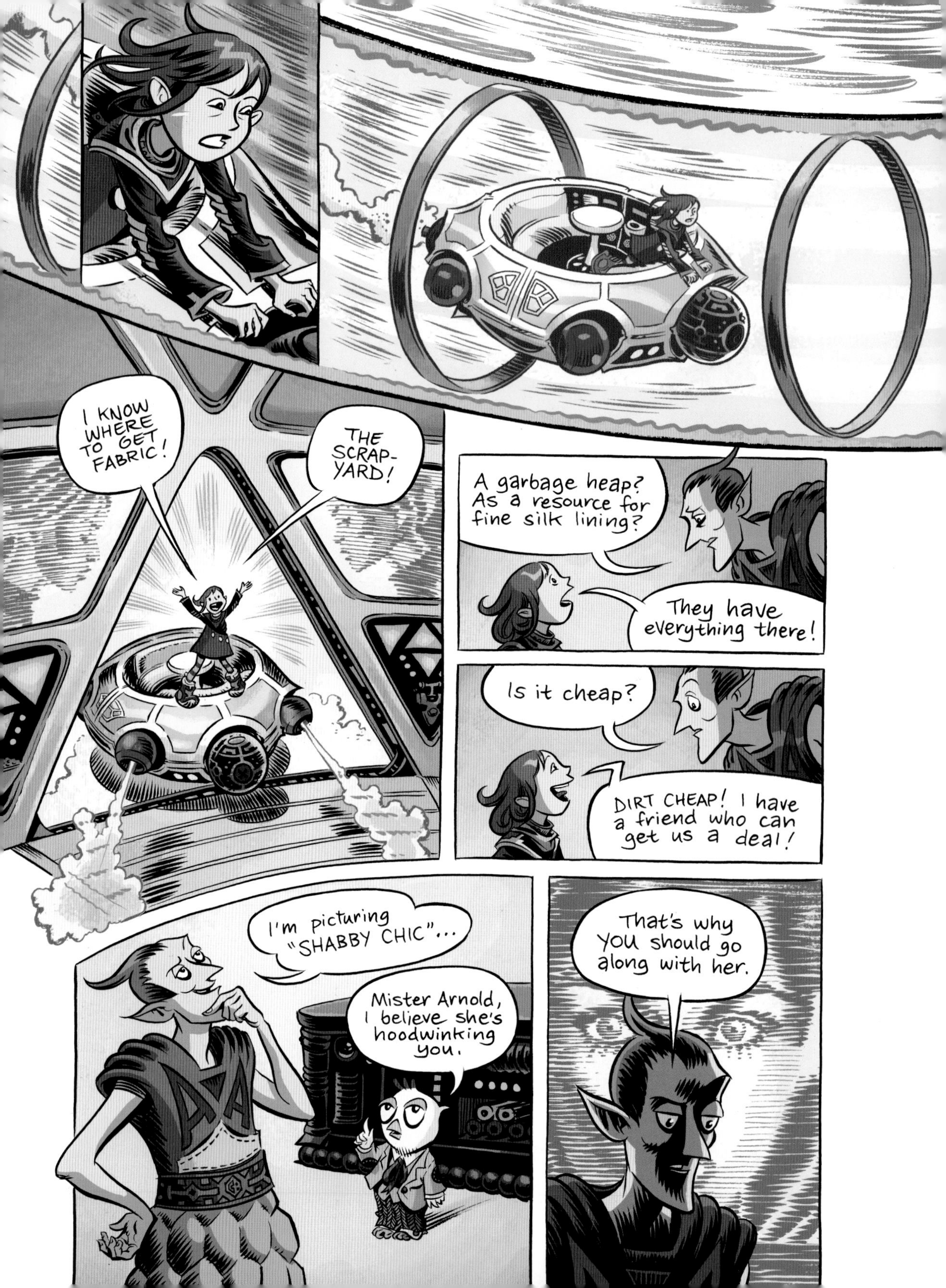
I KNOW WHERE TO GET FABRIC!
THE SCRAP-YARD!
A garbage heap? As a resource for fine silk lining?
They have everything there!
Is it cheap?
DIRT CHEAP! I have a friend who can get us a deal!
I'm picturing "SHABBY CHIC"...
Mister Arnold, I believe she's hoodwinking you.
That's why YOU should go along with her.

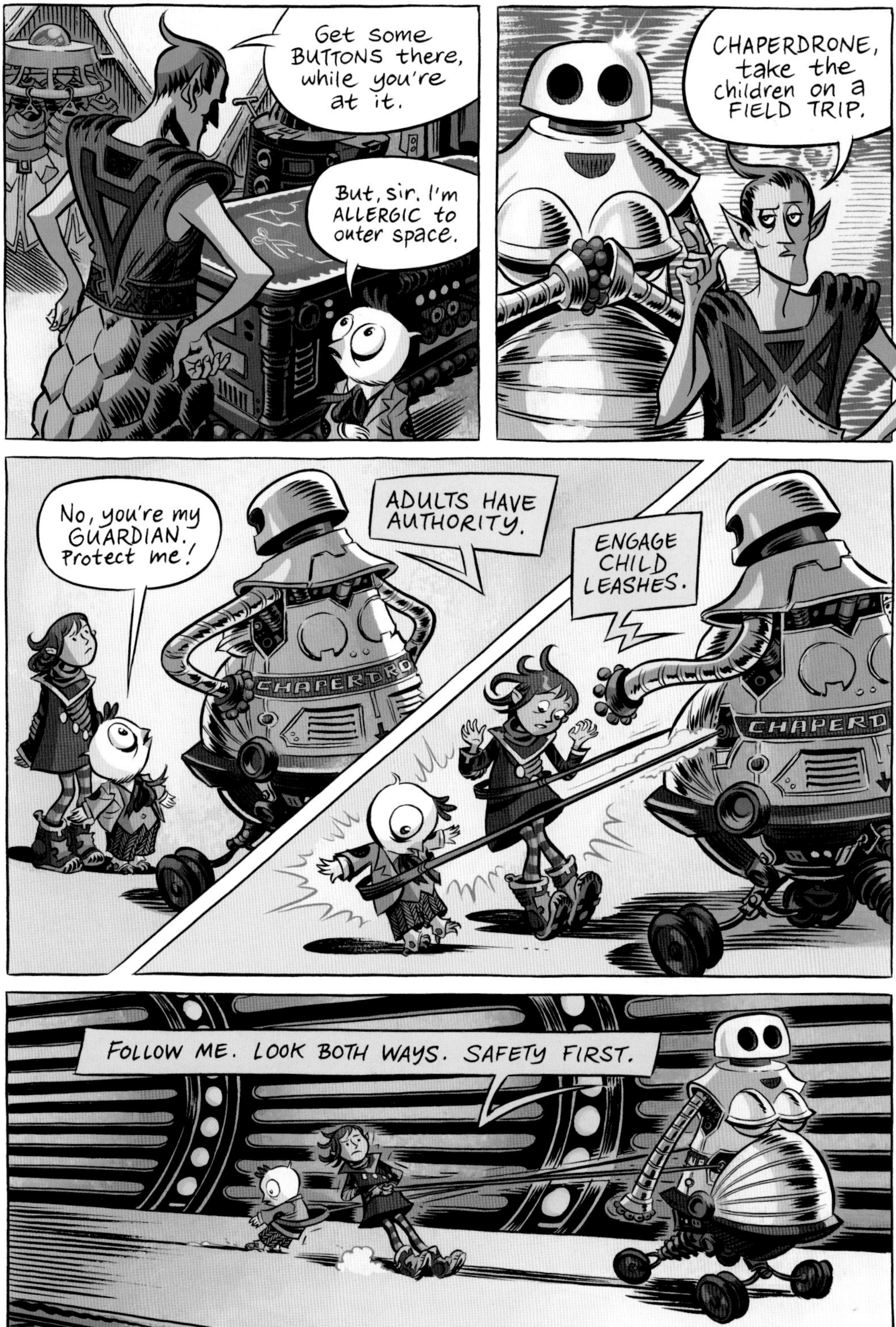

Get some BUTTONS there, while you're at it.
But, sir, I'm ALLERGIC to outer space.
CHAPERDRONE, take the children on a FIELD TRIP.
No, you're my GUARDIAN. Protect me!
ADULTS HAVE AUTHORITY.
CHAPERDRO
ENGAGE CHILD LEASHES.
CHAPERD
FOLLOW ME. LOOK BOTH WAYS. SAFETY FIRST.

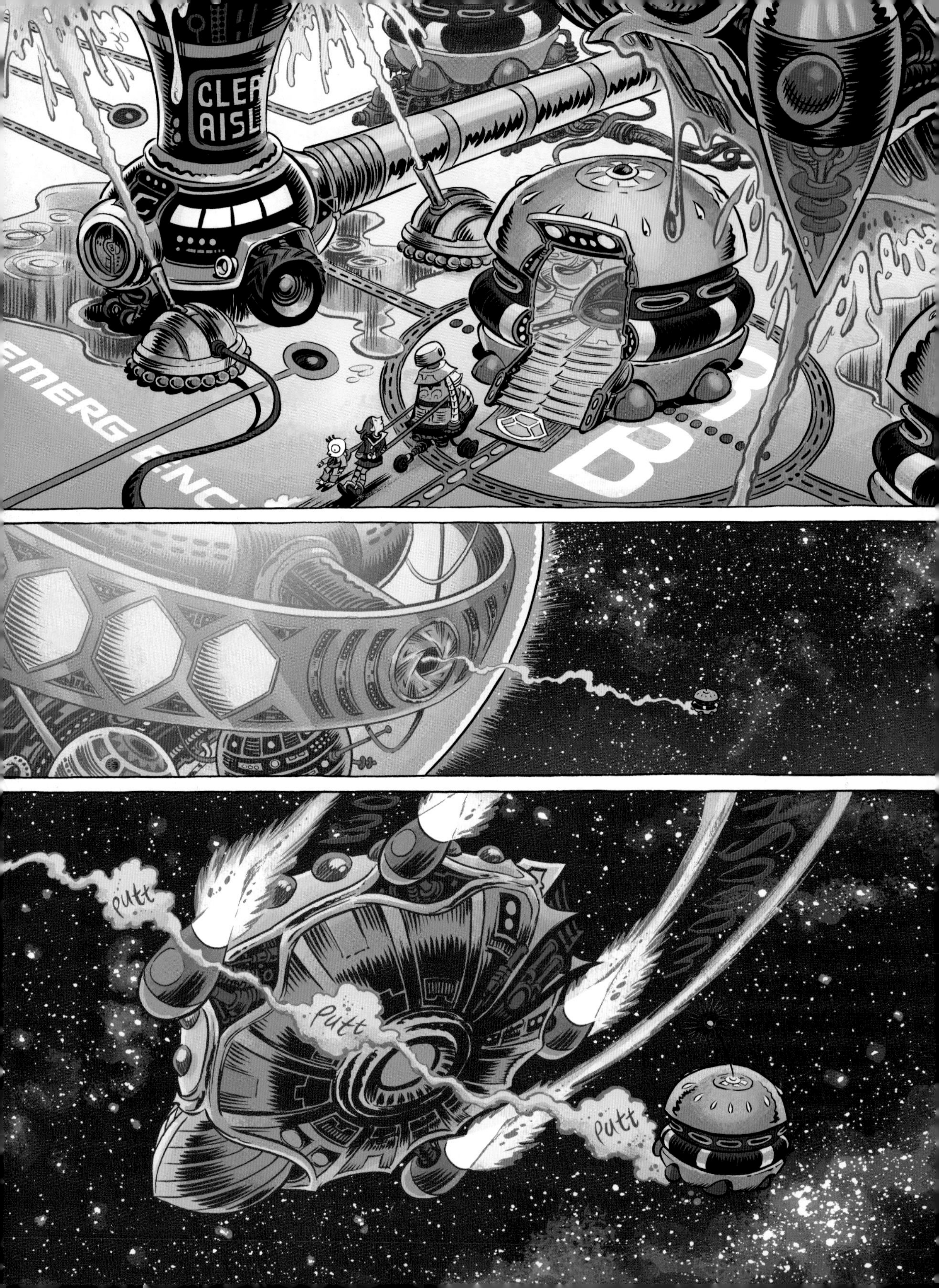
CLEA
AISL
EMERG
B
putt
putt
putt

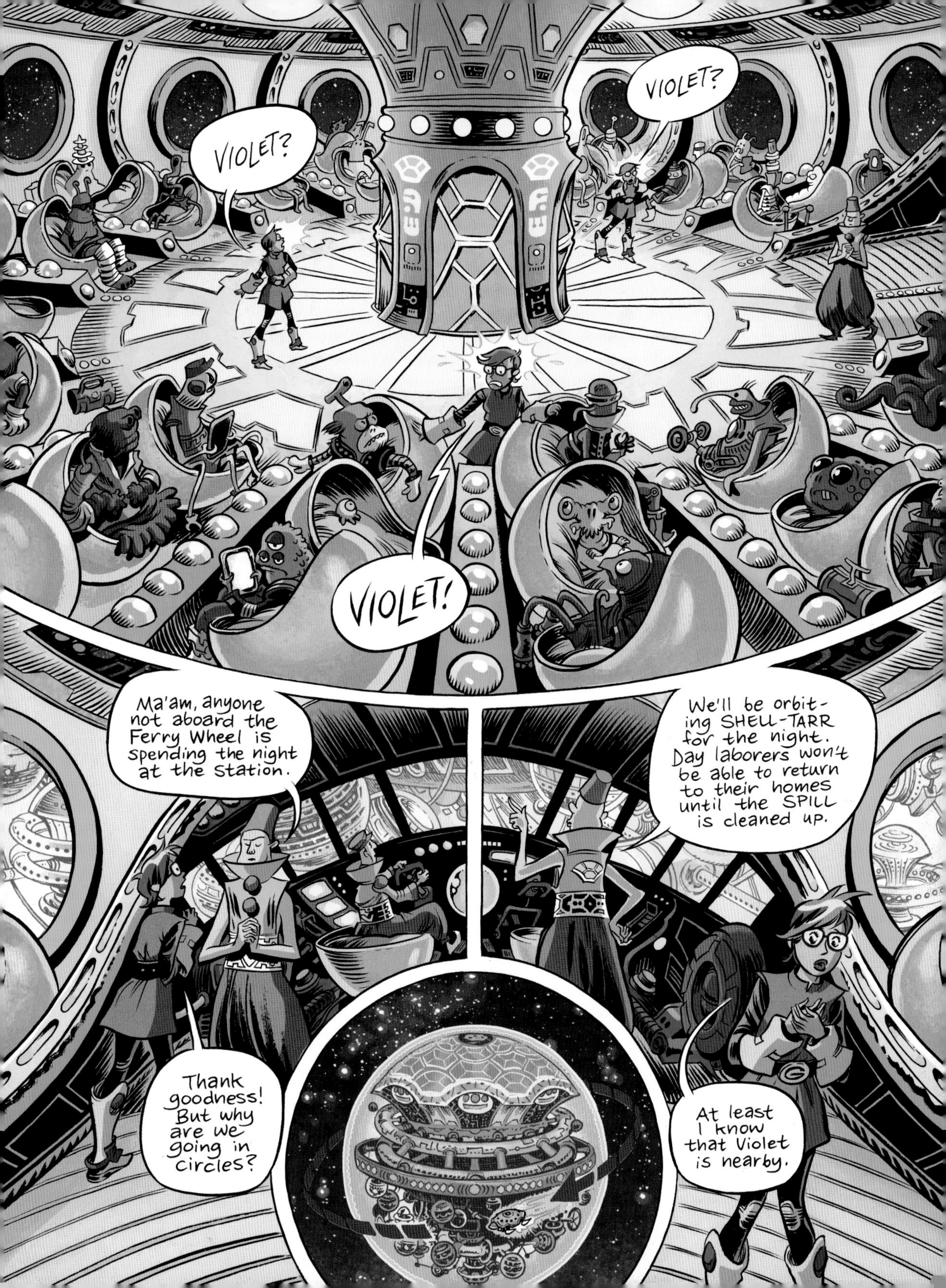
VIOLET?
VIOLET?
VIOLET!
Ma'am, anyone not aboard the Ferry Wheel is spending the night at the station.
We'll be orbiting SHELL-TARR for the night. Day laborers won't be able to return to their homes until the SPILL is cleaned up.
Thank goodness! But why are we going in circles?
At least I know that Violet is nearby.

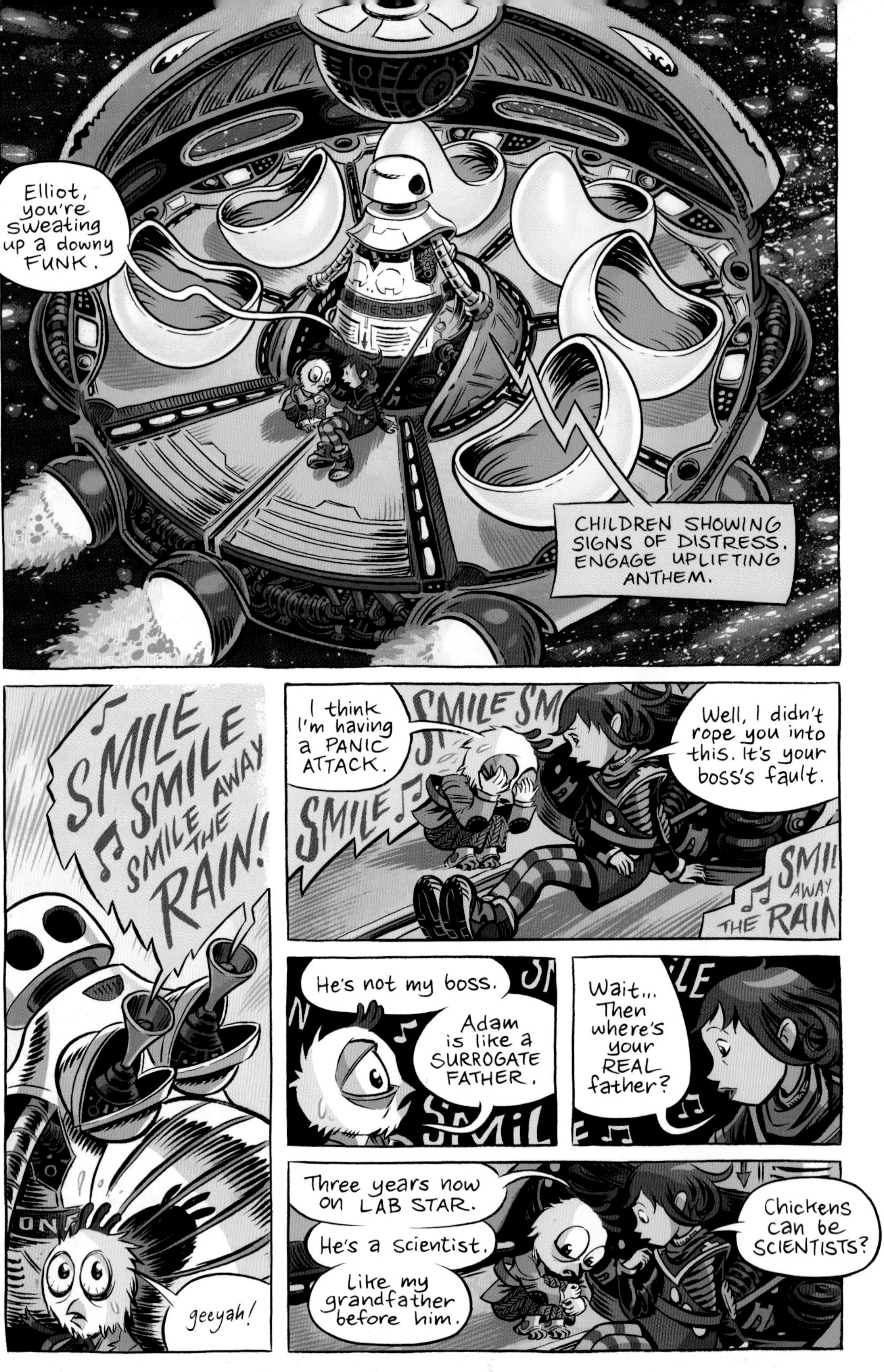
Elliot, you're sweating up a downy FUNK.
CHILDREN SHOWING SIGNS OF DISTRESS. ENGAGE UPLIFTING ANTHEM.
SMILE SMILE SMILE AWAY THE RAIN!
geeyah!
I think I'm having a PANIC ATTACK.
Well, I didn't rope you into this. It's your boss's fault.
SMILE
SMILE AWAY THE RAIN
He's not my boss.
Adam is like a SURROGATE FATHER.
Wait... Then where's your REAL father?
Three years now on LAB STAR.
He's a scientist.
Like my grandfather before him.
Chickens can be SCIENTISTS?

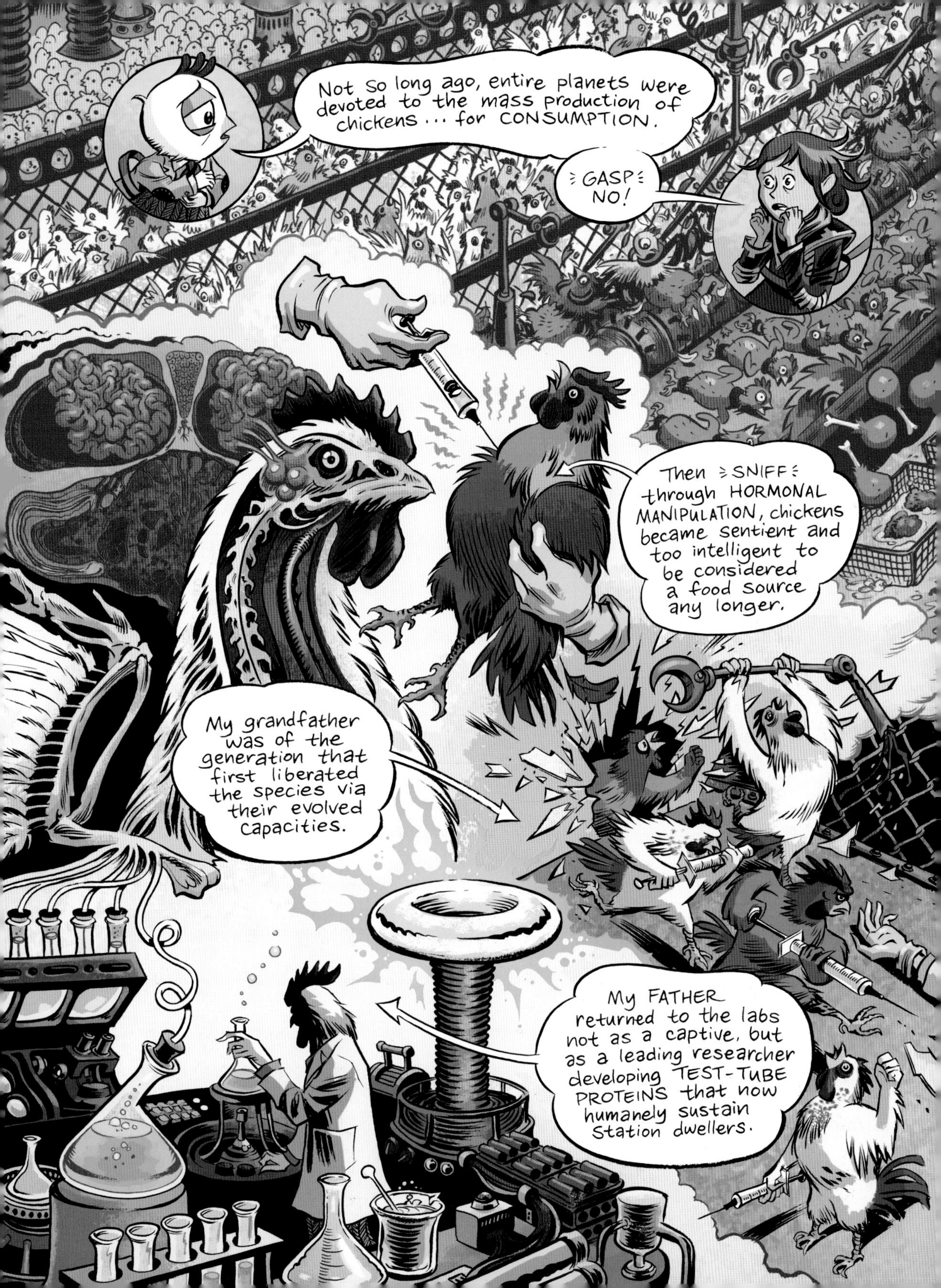

Not so long ago, entire planets were devoted to the mass production of chickens ... for CONSUMPTION.
GASP NO!
Then SNIFF through HORMONAL MANIPULATION, chickens became sentient and too intelligent to be considered a food source any longer.
My grandfather was of the generation that first liberated the species via their evolved capacities.
My FATHER returned to the labs not as a captive, but as a leading researcher developing TEST-TUBE PROTEINS that now humanely sustain Station dwellers.

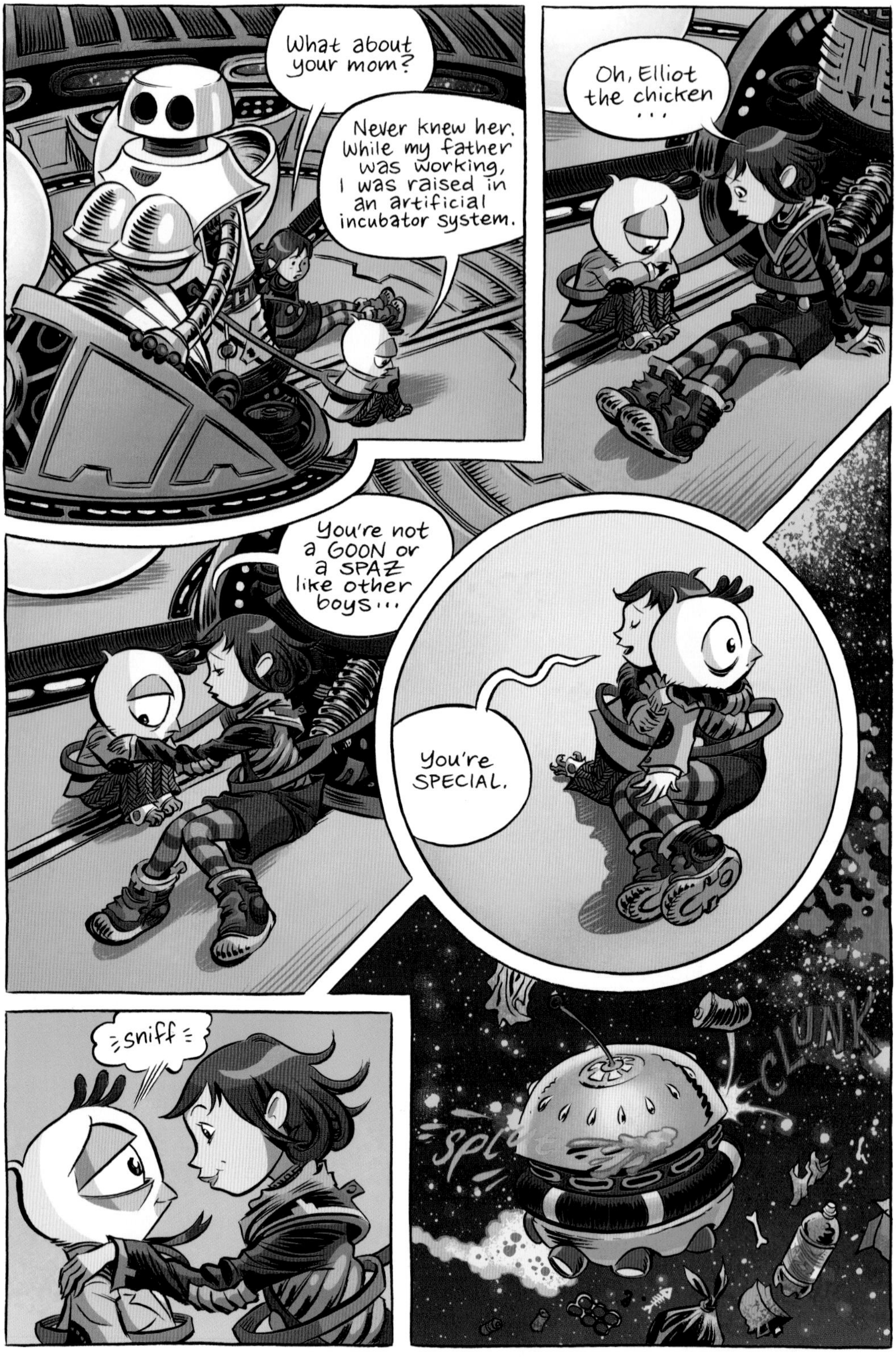
What about your mom?
Never knew her. While my father was working, I was raised in an artificial incubator system.
Oh, Elliot the chicken . . .
You're not a GOON or a SPAZ like other boys . . .
You're SPECIAL.
sniff
CLUNK

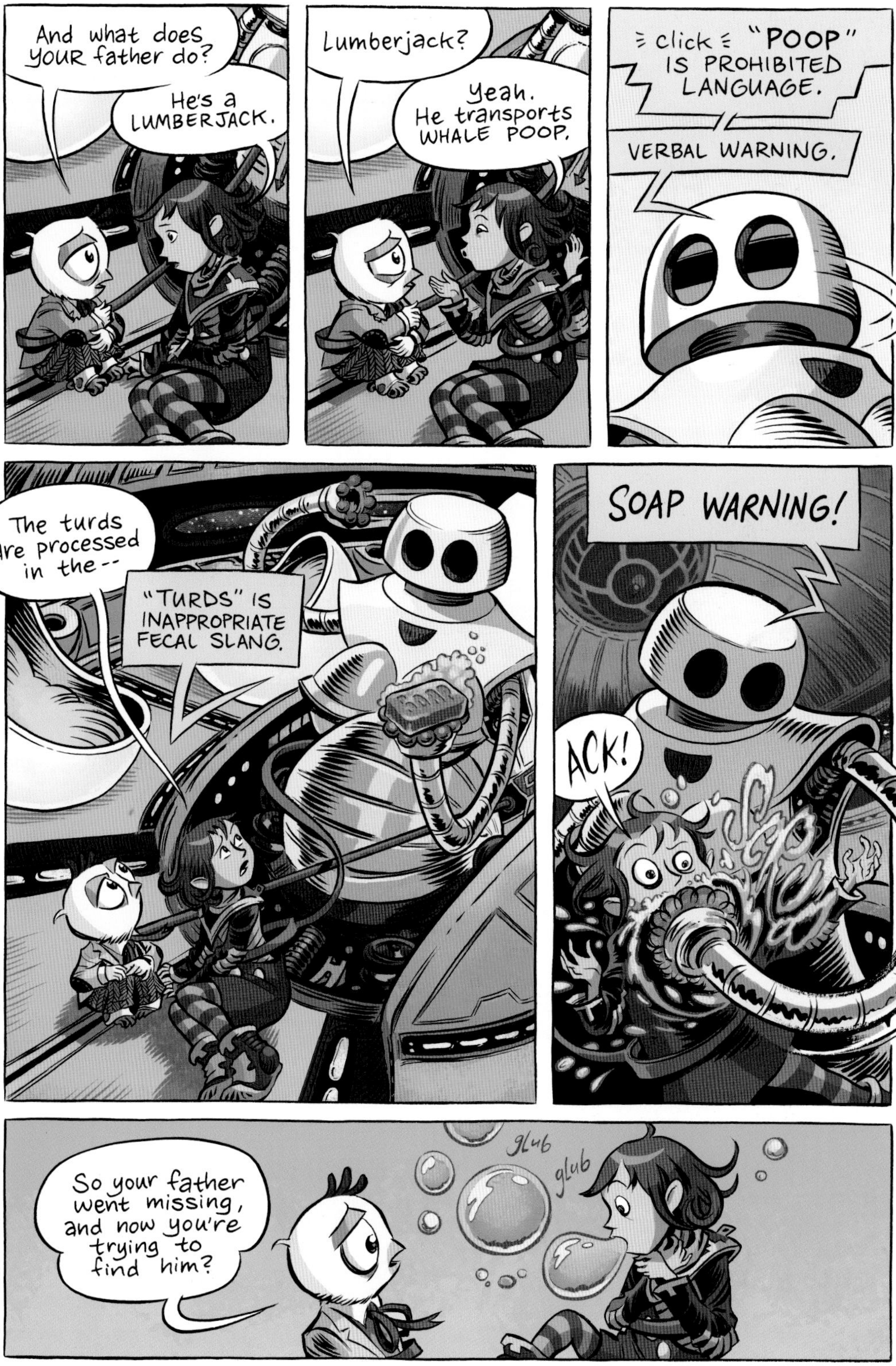

And what does YOUR father do?
He's a LUMBERJACK.
Lumberjack?
Yeah. He transports WHALE POOP.
click "POOP" IS PROHIBITED LANGUAGE.
VERBAL WARNING.
The turds are processed in the--
"TURDS" IS INAPPROPRIATE FECAL SLANG.
SOAP
SOAP WARNING!
ACK!
glub
glub
So your father went missing, and now you're trying to find him?

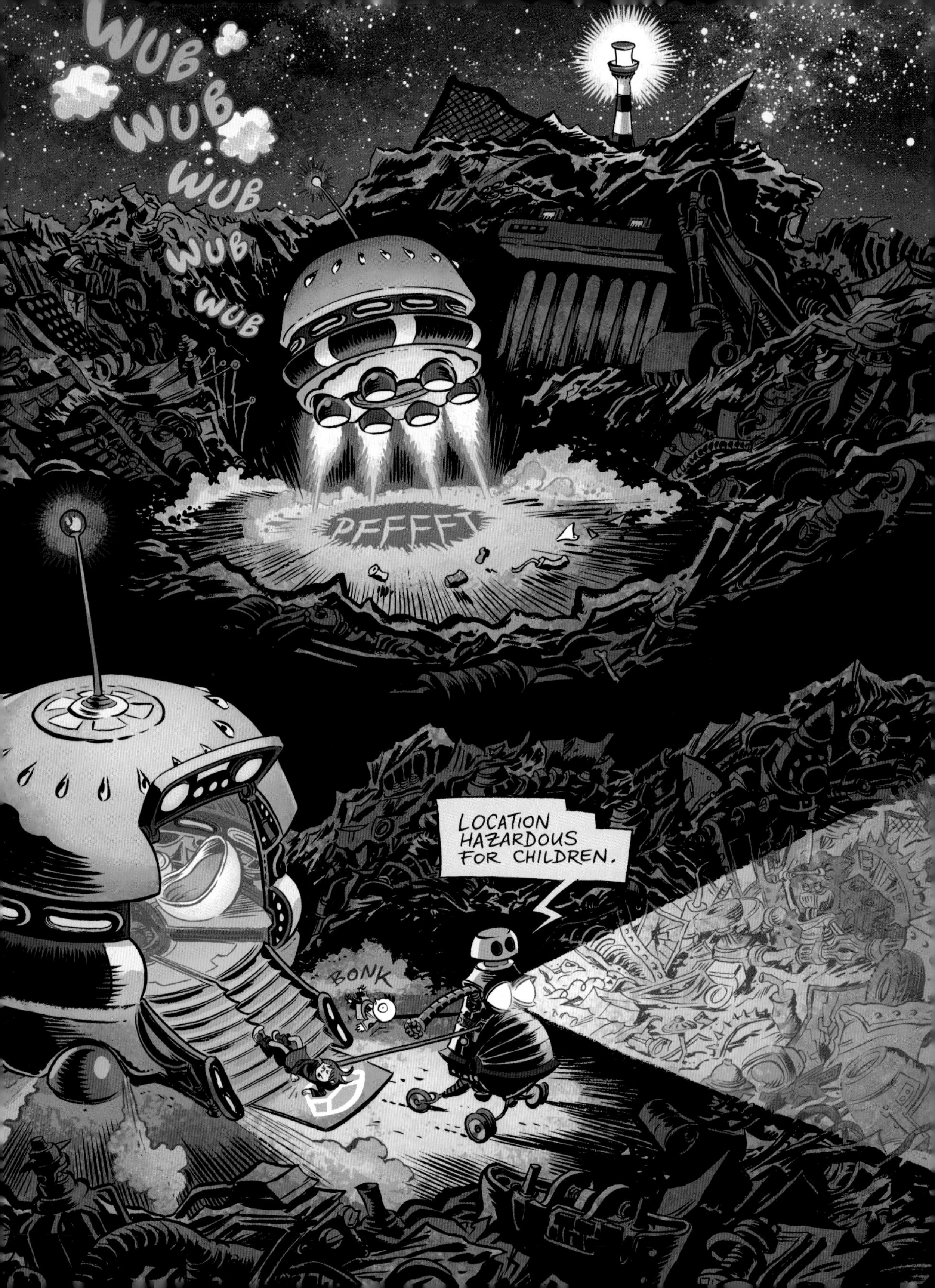
WUB WUB WUB WUB WUB
PFFFFT
LOCATION HAZARDOUS FOR CHILDREN.
BONK

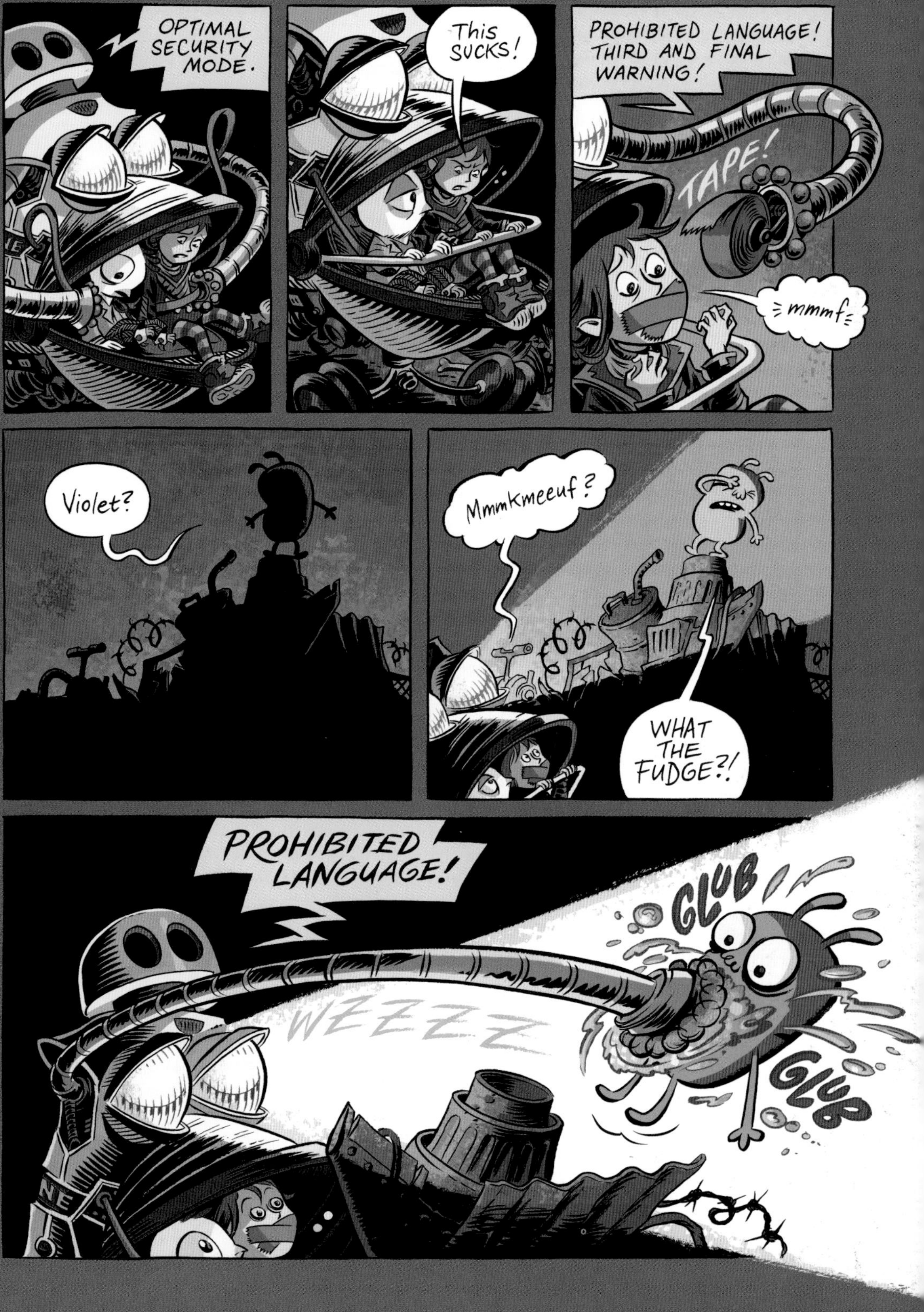
OPTIMAL SECURITY MODE.
This SUCKS!
PROHIBITED LANGUAGE! THIRD AND FINAL WARNING!
TAPE!
mmmf
Violet?
Mmmkmeeuf?
WHAT THE FUDGE?!
PROHIBITED LANGUAGE!
WZZZZ
GLUB
GLUB

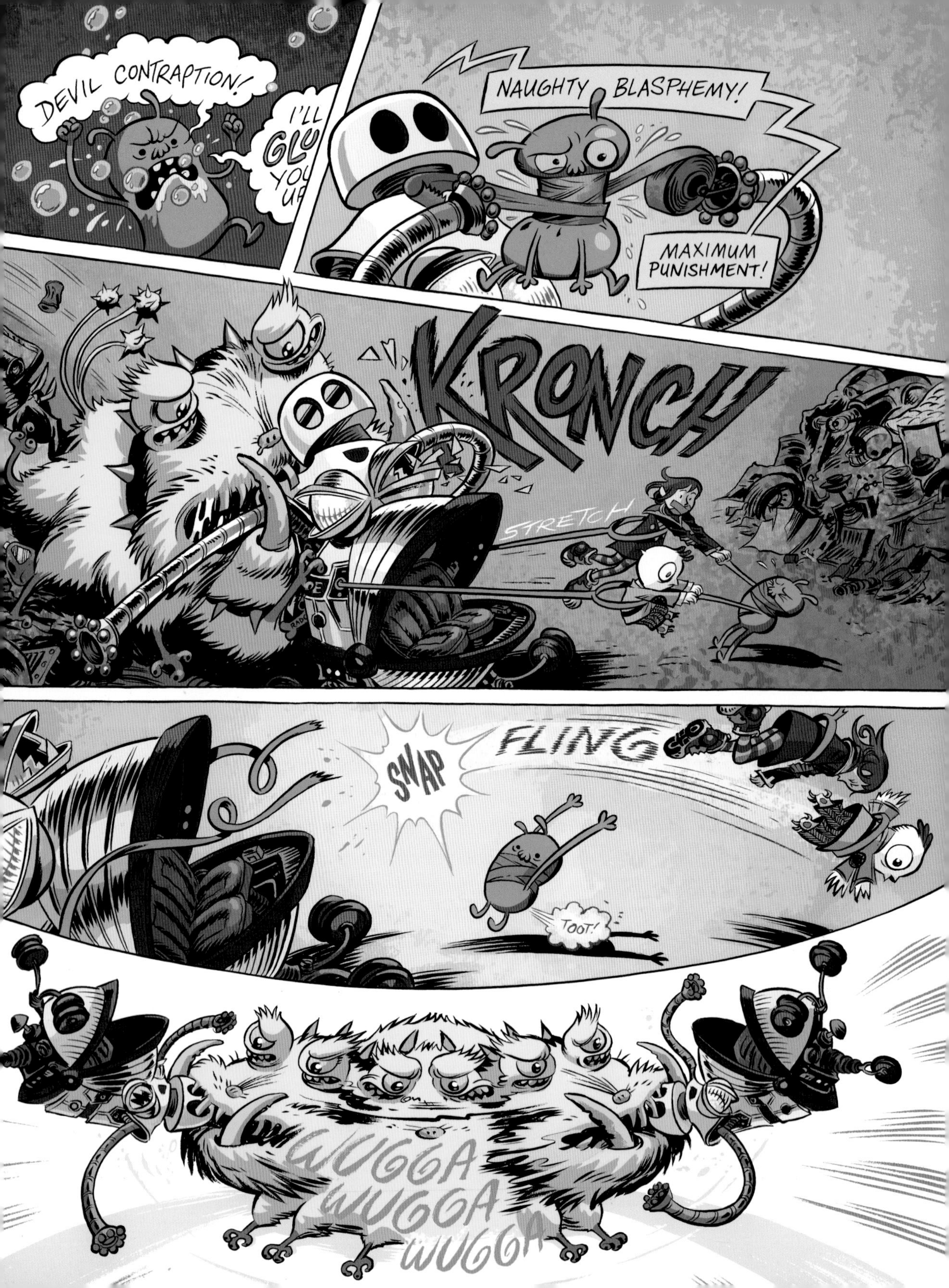
DEVIL CONTRAPTION!
I'LL GLU YOU UP
NAUGHTY BLASPHEMY!
MAXIMUM PUNISHMENT!
KRONCH
STRETCH
SNAP
FLING
TOOT!
WUGGA WUGGA WUGGA

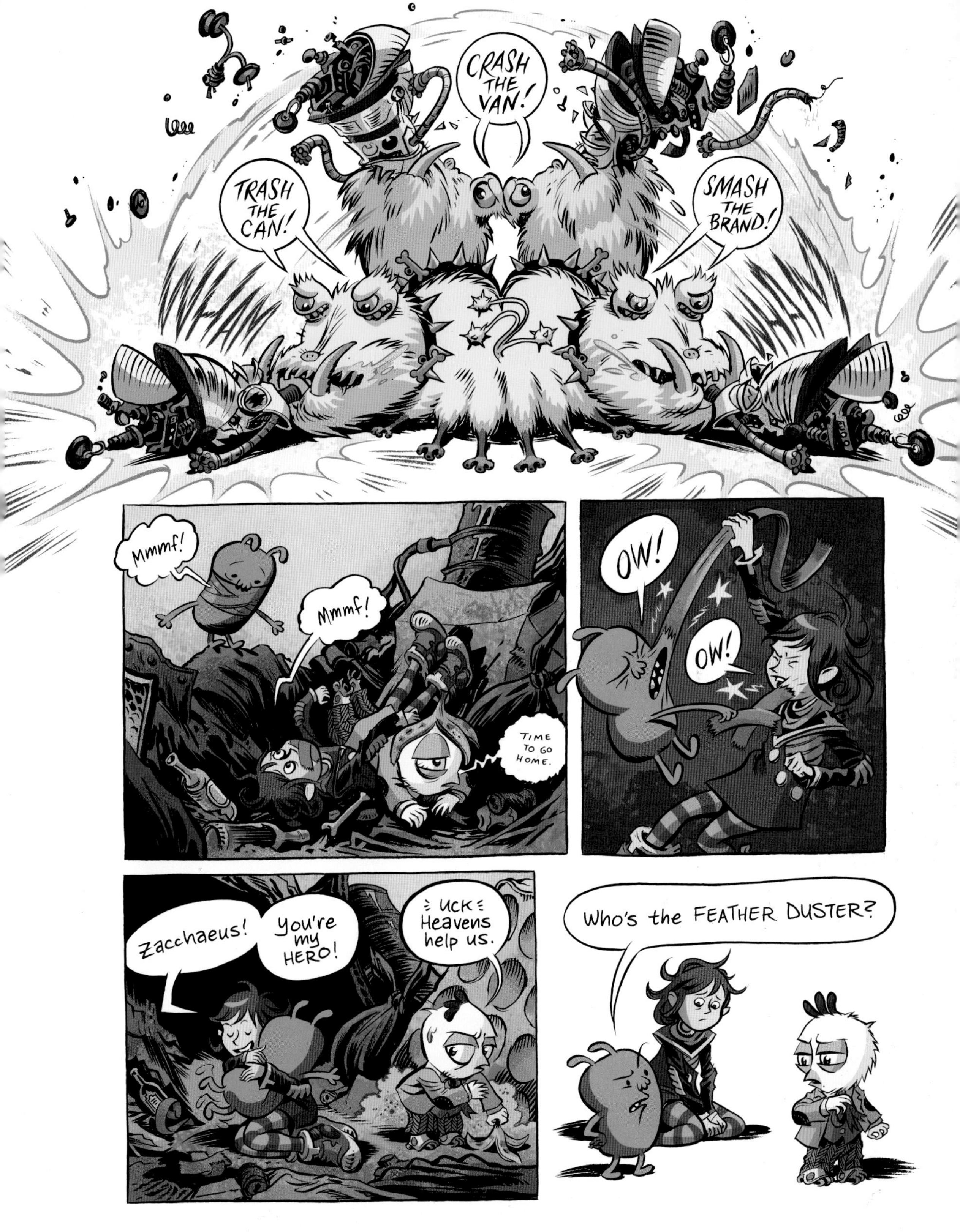
TRASH THE CAN!
CRASH THE VAN!
SMASH THE BRAND!
Mmmf!
Mmmf!
TIME TO GO HOME.
OW!
OW!
Zacchaeus!
You're my HERO!
UCK Heavens help us.
Who's the FEATHER DUSTER?

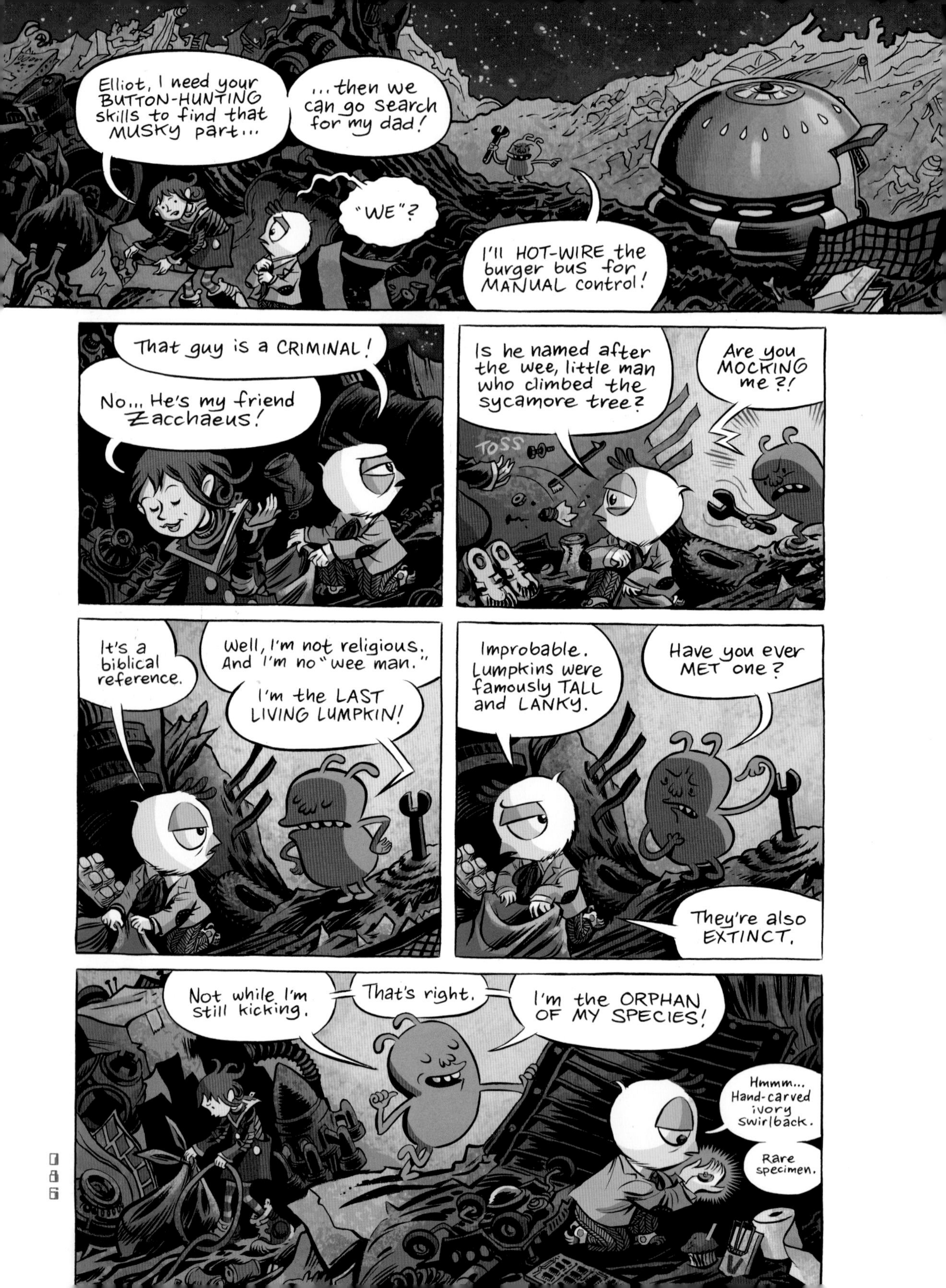

Elliot, I need your BUTTON-HUNTING skills to find that MUSKY part...
...then we can go search for my dad!
"WE"?
I'll HOT-WIRE the burger bus for MANUAL control!
That guy is a CRIMINAL!
No... He's my friend Zacchaeus!
Is he named after the wee, little man who climbed the sycamore tree?
TOSS
Are you MOCKING me?!
It's a biblical reference.
Well, I'm not religious. And I'm no "wee man."
I'm the LAST LIVING LUMPKIN!
Improbable. Lumpkins were famously TALL and LANKY.
Have you ever MET one?
They're also EXTINCT.
Not while I'm still kicking.
That's right.
I'm the ORPHAN OF MY SPECIES!
Hmmm... Hand-carved ivory swirlback.
Rare specimen.

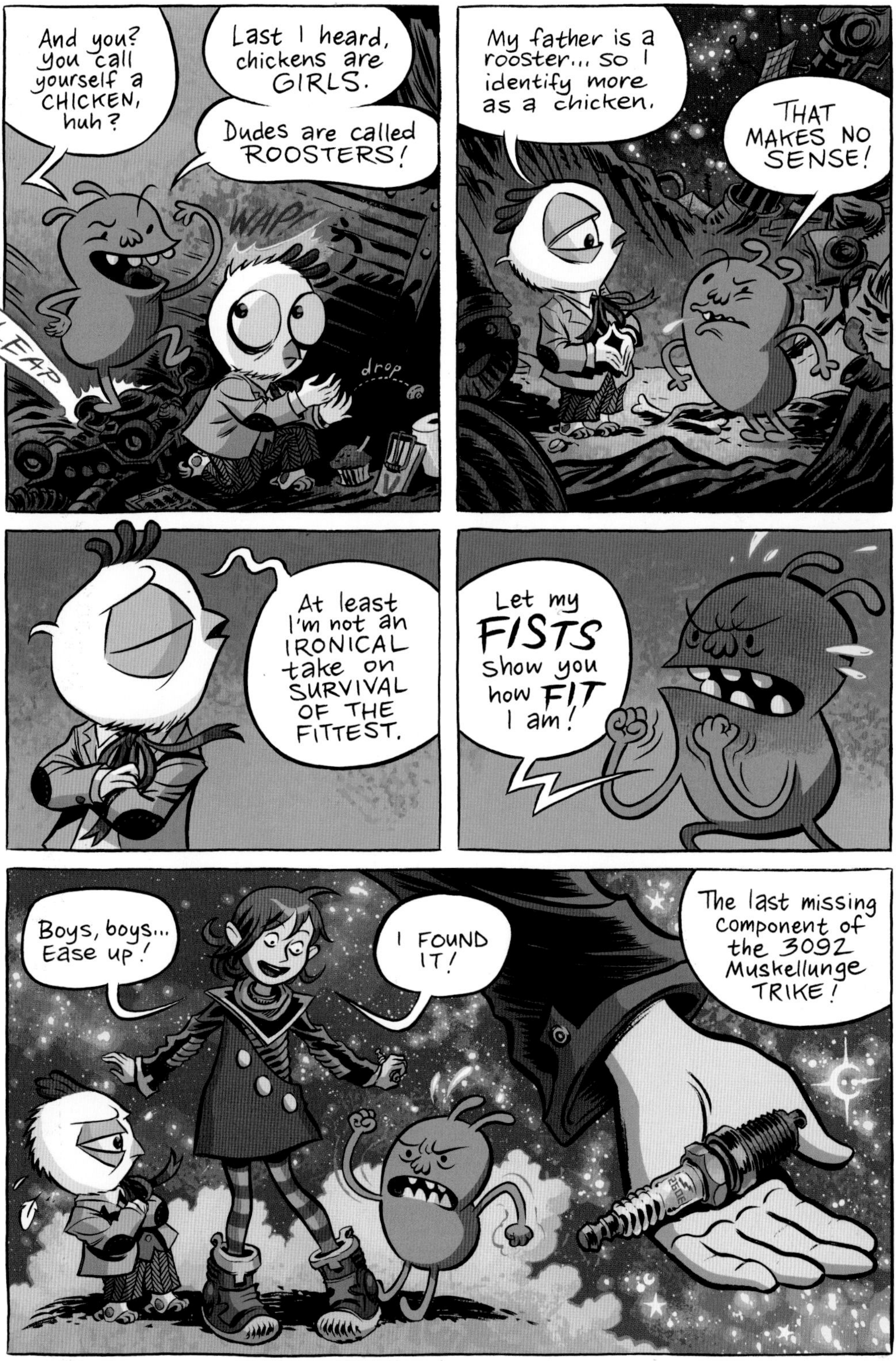

And you? You call yourself a CHICKEN, huh?
Last I heard, chickens are GIRLS.
Dudes are called ROOSTERS!
WAP!
LEAP
drop
My father is a rooster... so I identify more as a chicken.
THAT MAKES NO SENSE!
At least I'm not an IRONICAL take on SURVIVAL OF THE FITTEST.
Let my FISTS show you how FIT I am!
Boys, boys... Ease up!
I FOUND IT!
The last missing component of the 3092 Muskellunge TRIKE!

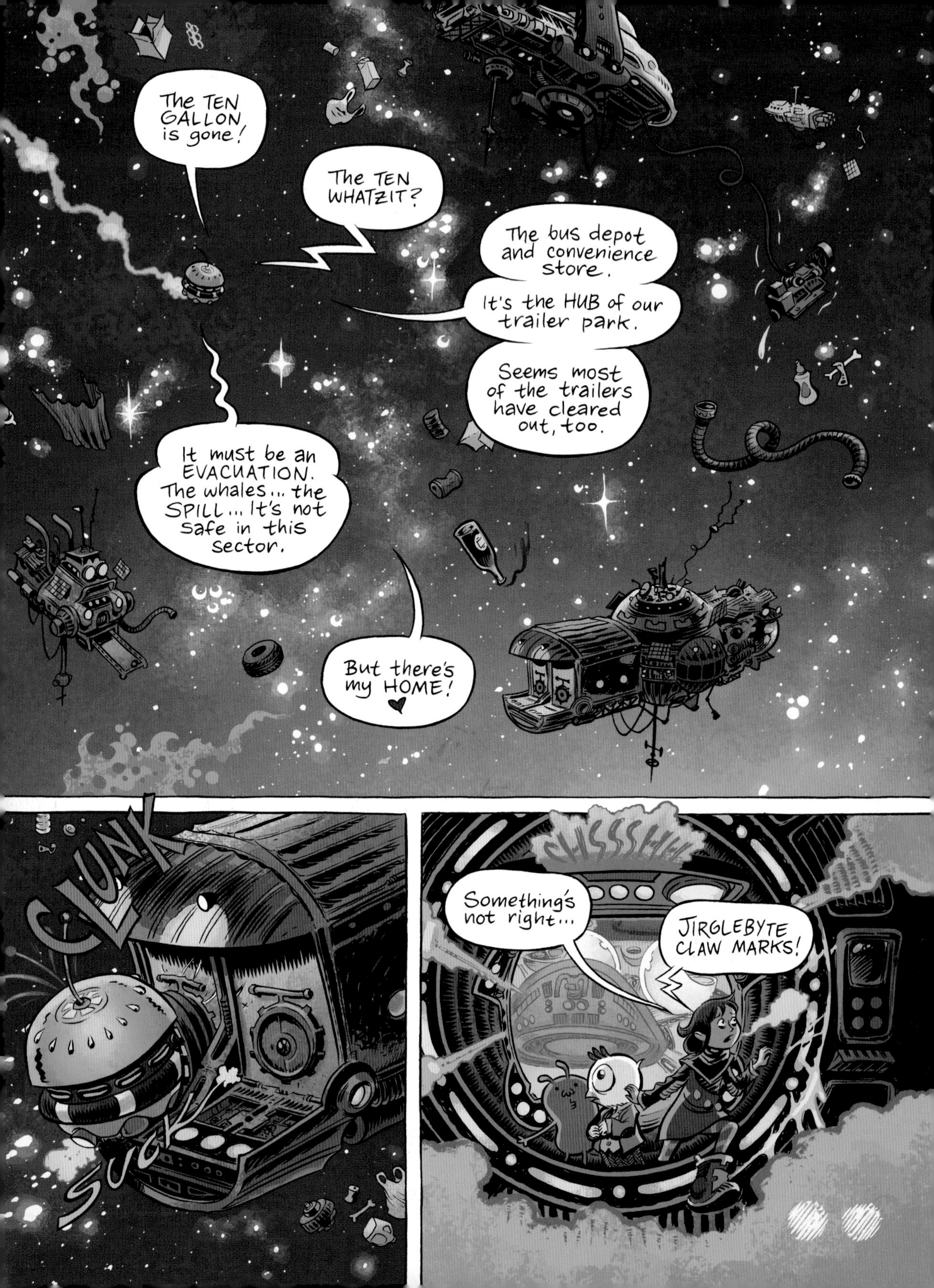
The TEN GALLON is gone!
The TEN WHATZIT?
The bus depot and convenience store.
It's the HUB of our trailer park.
Seems most of the trailers have cleared out, too.
It must be an EVACUATION. The whales... the SPILL... It's not safe in this sector.
But there's my HOME!
CLUNK
SUCK
CHSSSHH
Something's not right...
JIRGLEBYTE CLAW MARKS!

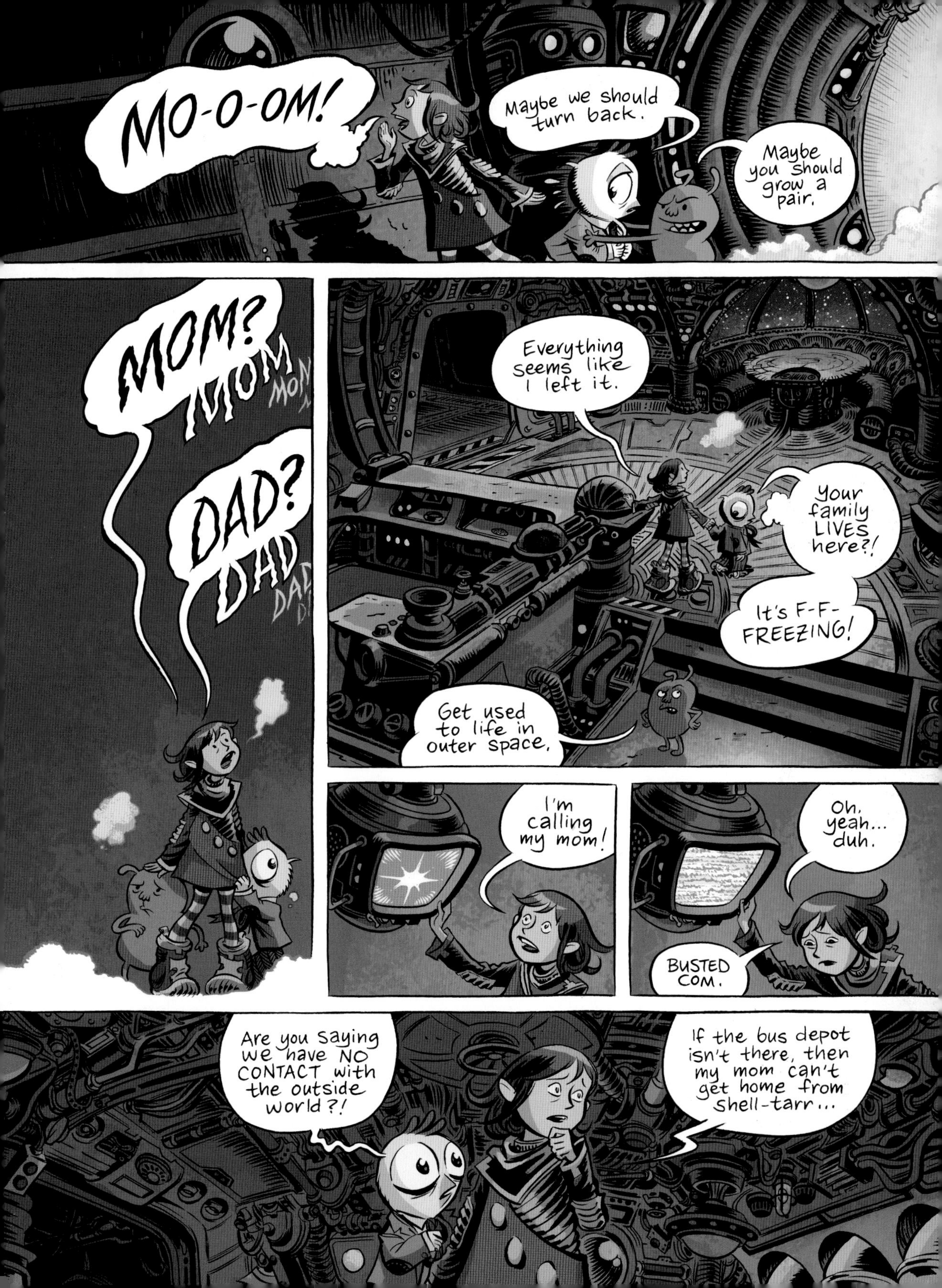
MO-O-OM!
Maybe we should turn back.
Maybe you should grow a pair.
MOM? MOM MOM
DAD? DAD DAD
Everything seems like I left it.
Your family LIVES here?!
It's F-F-FREEZING!
Get used to life in outer space.
I'm calling my mom!
Oh, yeah... duh.
BUSTED COM.
Are you saying we have NO CONTACT with the outside world?!
If the bus depot isn't there, then my mom can't get home from Shell-tarr...

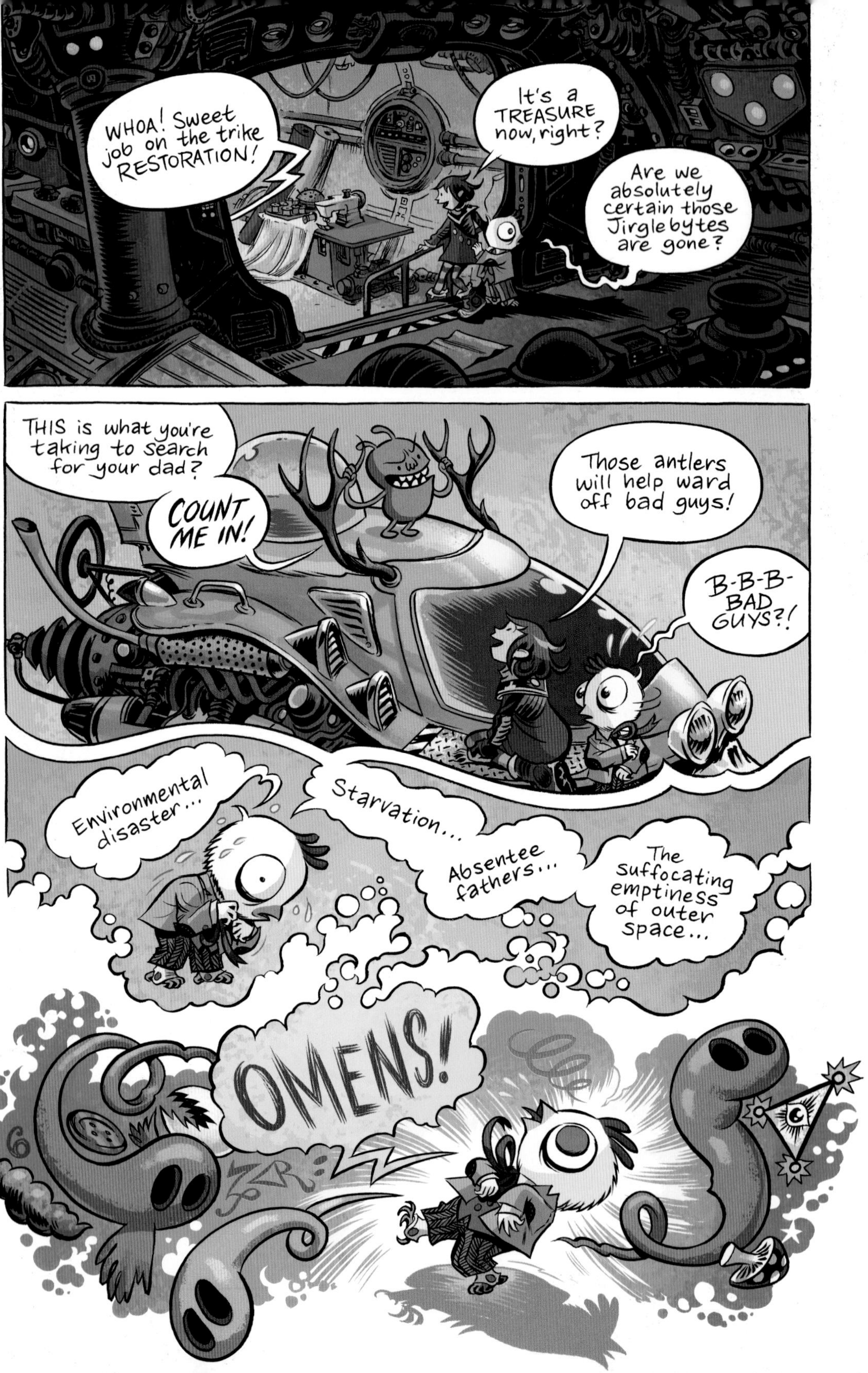

WHOA! Sweet job on the trike RESTORATION!
It's a TREASURE now, right?
Are we absolutely certain those Jirglebytes are gone?
THIS is what you're taking to search for your dad?
COUNT ME IN!
Those antlers will help ward off bad guys!
B-B-B-BAD GUYS?!
Environmental disaster...
Starvation...
Absentee fathers...
The suffocating emptiness of outer space...
OMENS!

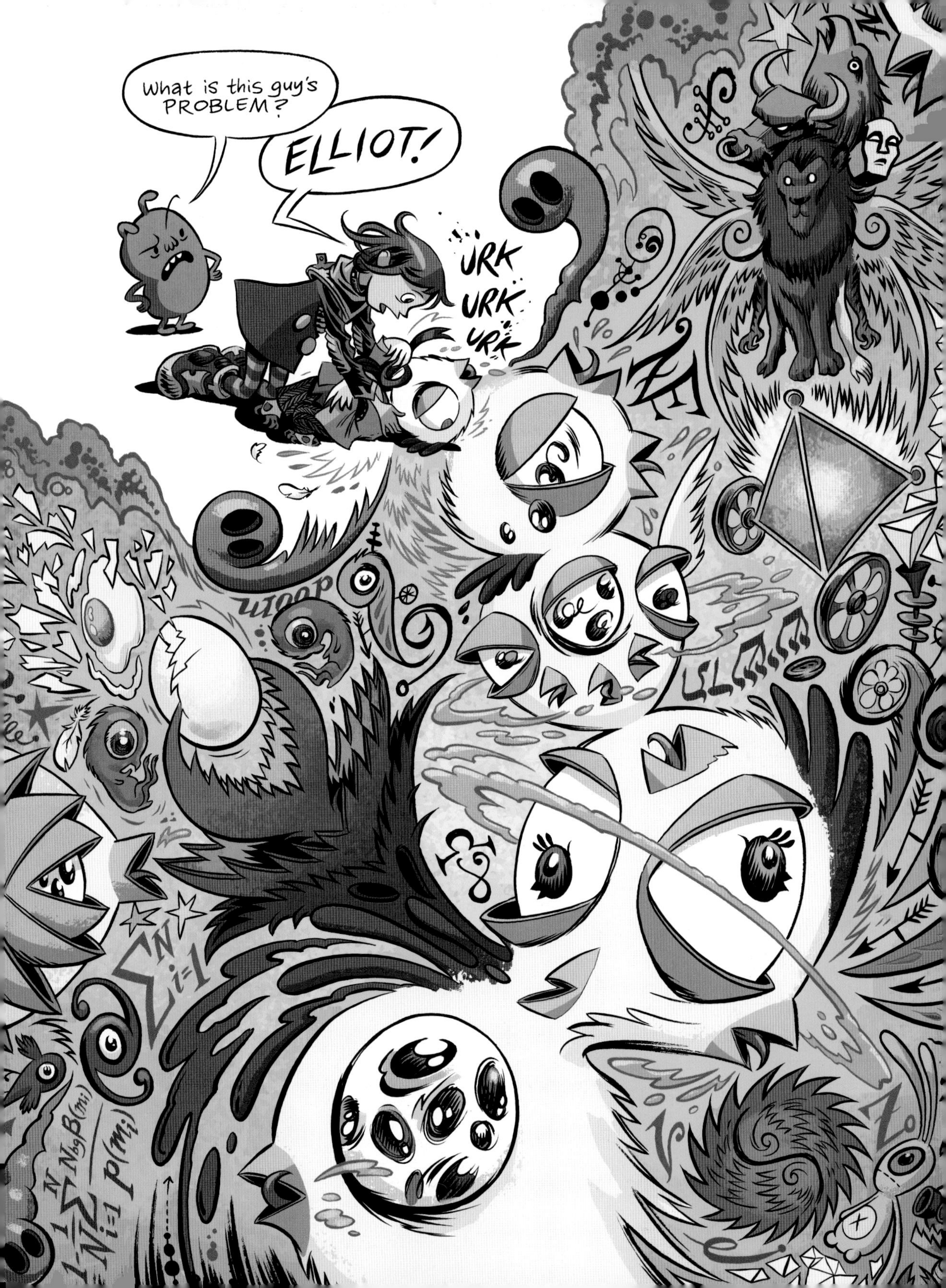
What is this guy's PROBLEM?
ELLIOT!
URK
URK
URK

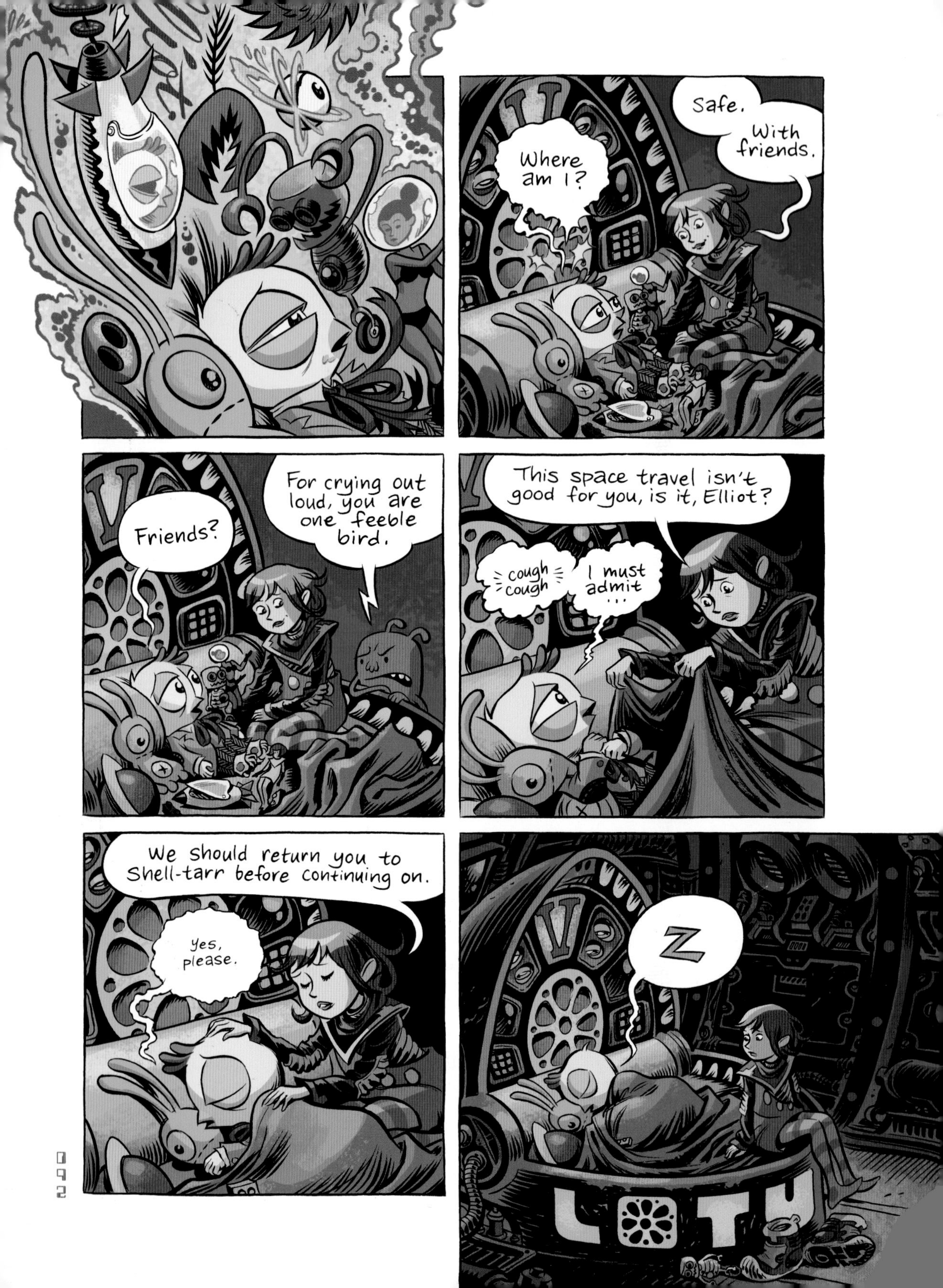
Where am I?
Safe.
With friends.
Friends?
For crying out loud, you are one feeble bird.
This space travel isn't good for you, is it, Elliot?
cough cough
I must admit . . .
We should return you to Shell-tarr before continuing on.
yes, please.
Z

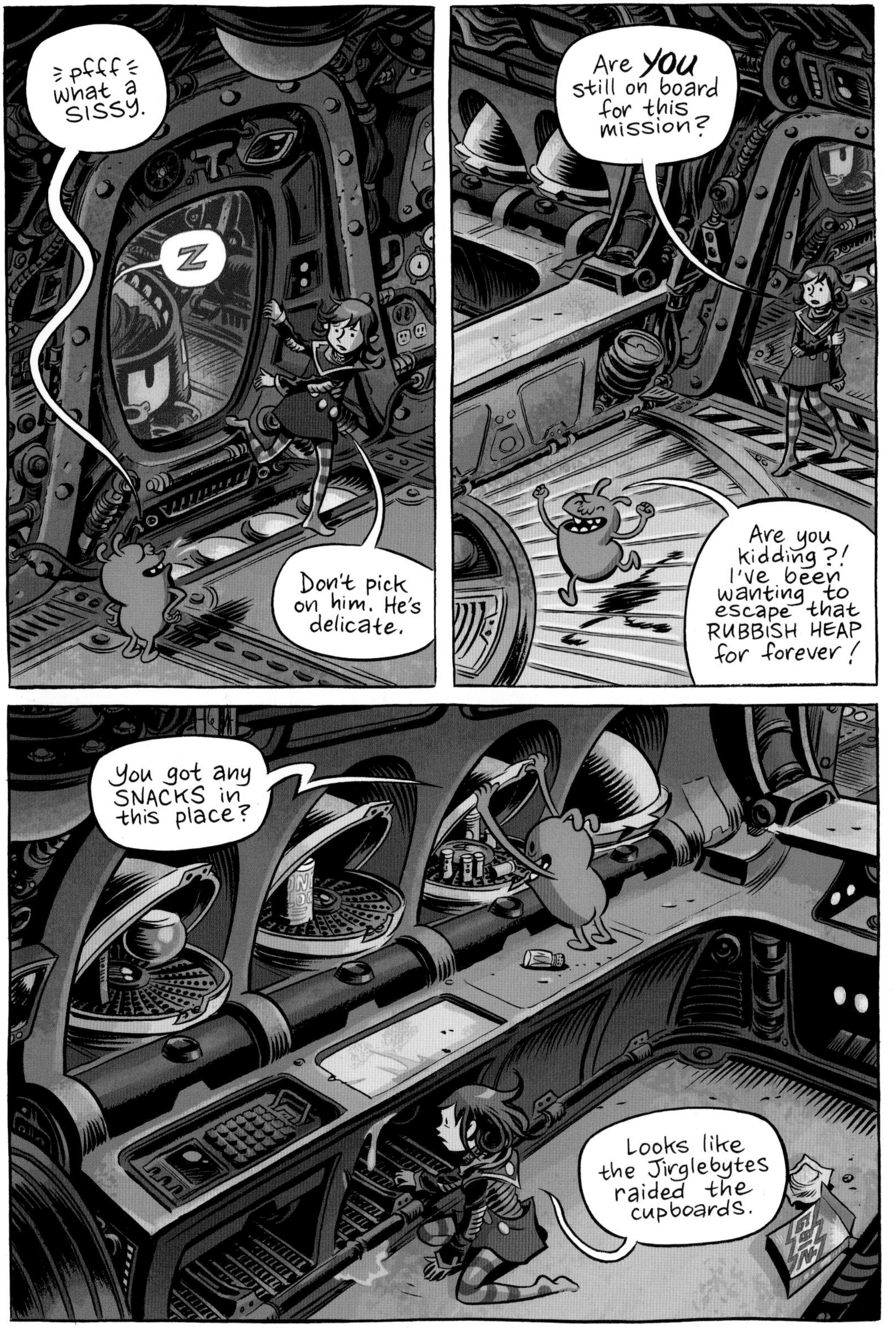

pfff what a SISSY.
Z
Don't pick on him. He's delicate.
Are YOU still on board for this mission?
Are you kidding?! I've been wanting to escape that RUBBISH HEAP for forever!
You got any SNACKS in this place?
Looks like the Jirglebytes raided the cupboards.

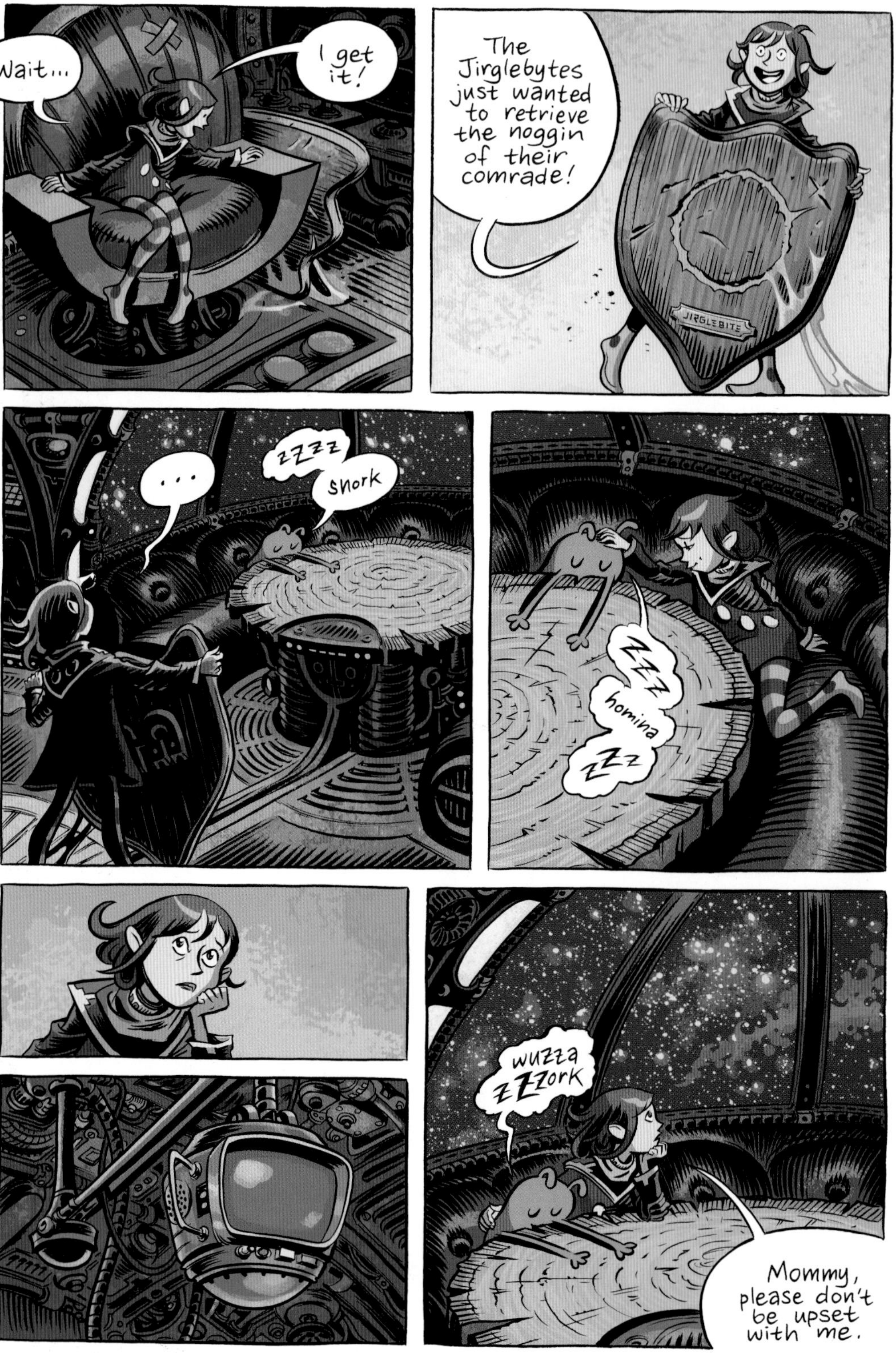
Wait...
I get it!
The Jirglebytes just wanted to retrieve the noggin of their comrade!
JIRGLEBITE
...
ZZZZ
shork
ZZZ
homina
ZZZ
wuzza
ZZZork
Mommy, please don't be upset with me.

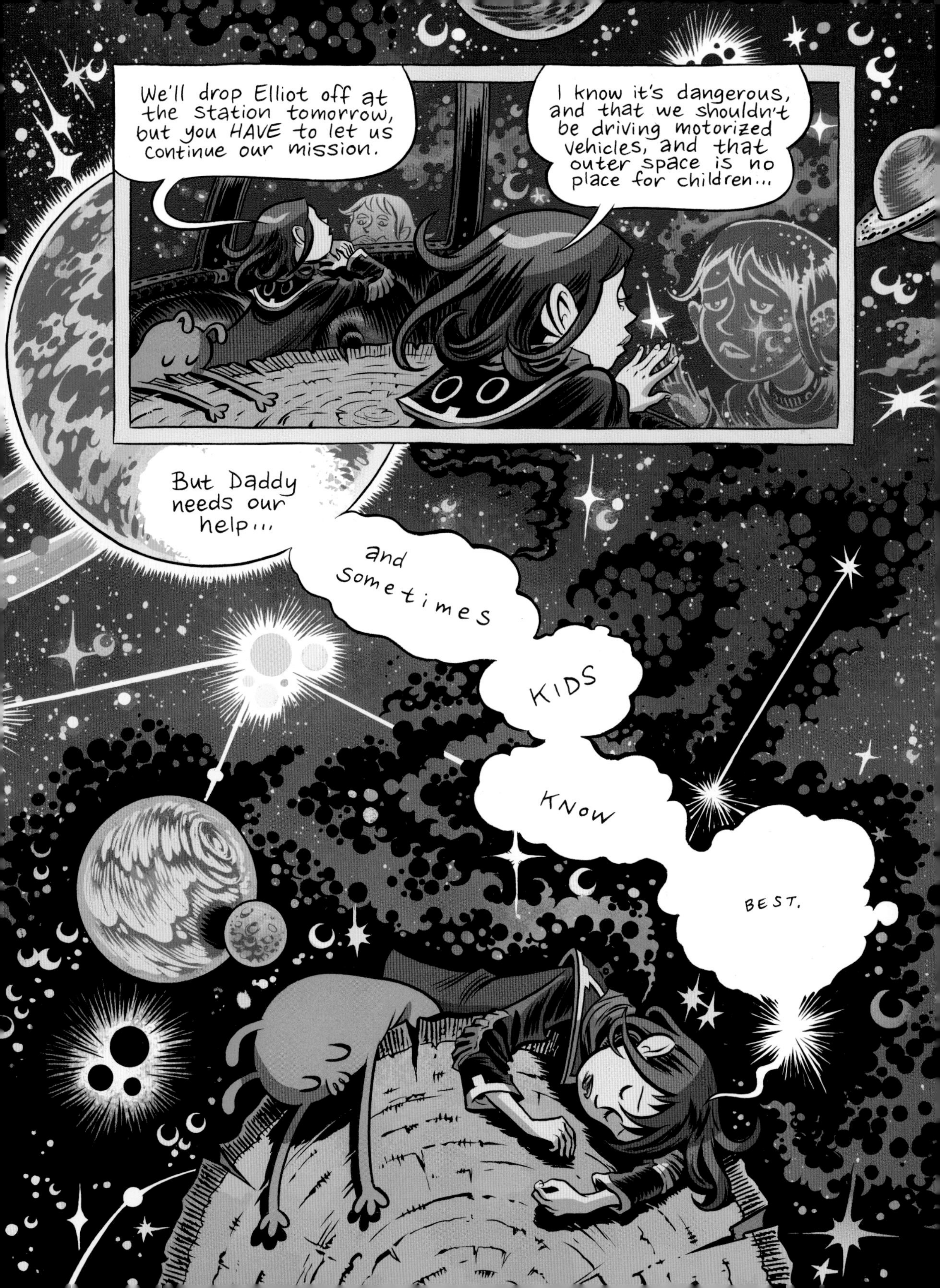
We'll drop Elliot off at the station tomorrow, but you HAVE to let us continue our mission.
I know it's dangerous, and that we shouldn't be driving motorized vehicles, and that outer space is no place for children...
But Daddy needs our help...
and sometimes
KIDS
KNOW
BEST.

03

MAG/
GYRO
NAV\

MAGNITUDES:

TRIPLE
THREAT

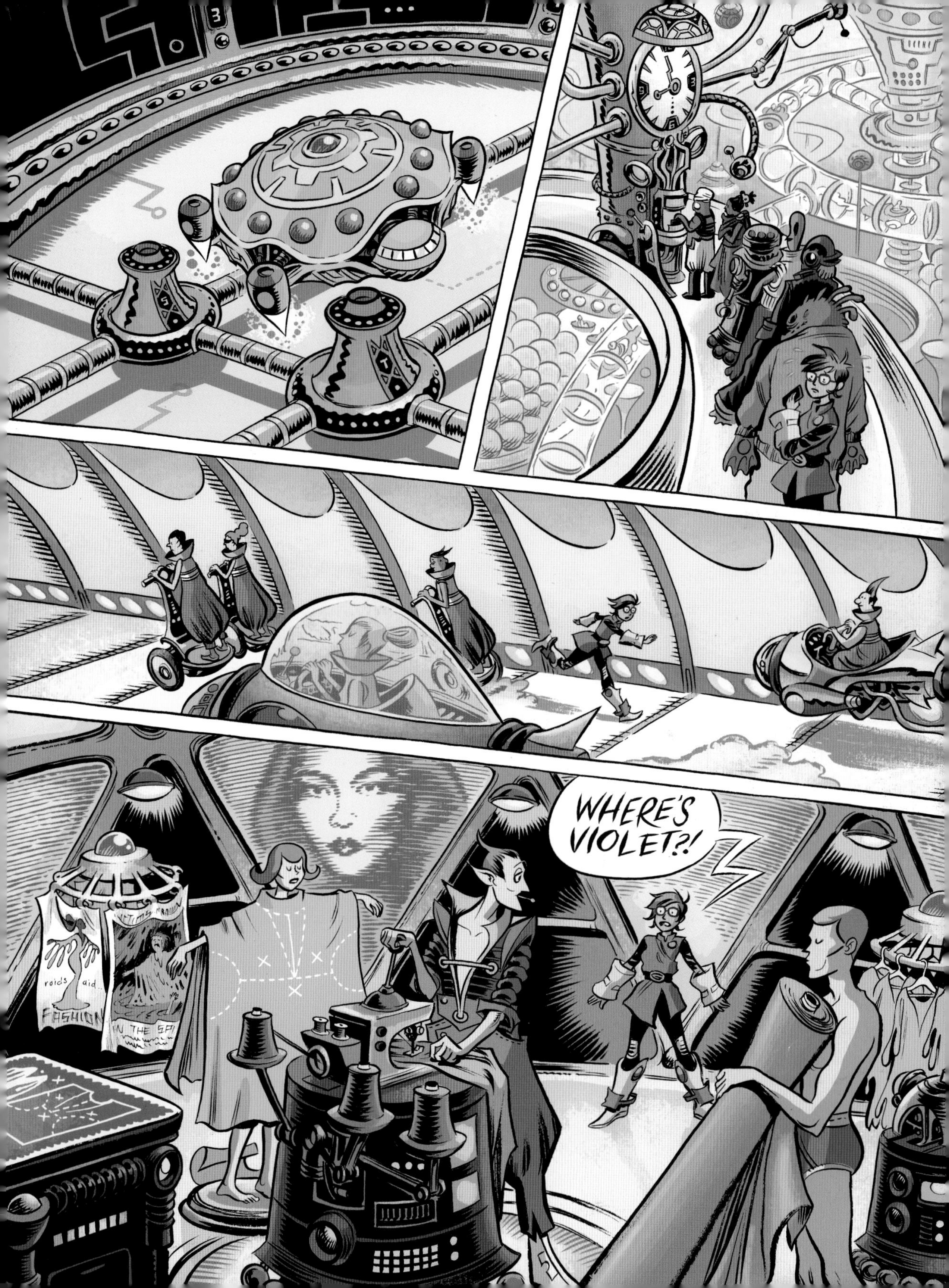
WHERE'S VIOLET?!

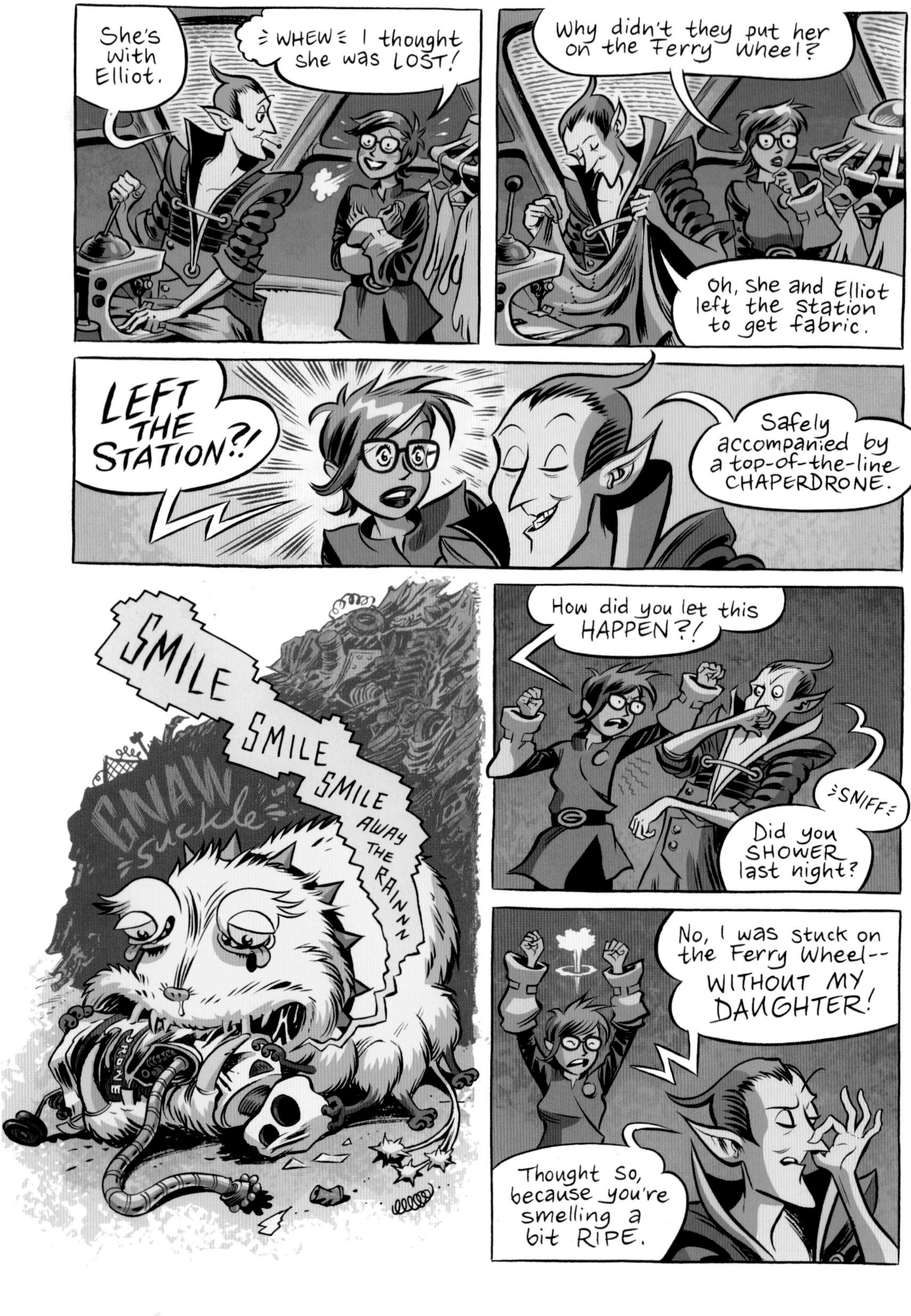

She's with Elliot.
≡WHEW≡ I thought she was LOST!
Why didn't they put her on the Ferry Wheel?
Oh, she and Elliot left the station to get fabric.
LEFT THE STATION?!
Safely accompanied by a top-of-the-line CHAPERDRONE.
SMILE SMILE SMILE AWAY THE RAINNN
GNAW suckle
DRONE
How did you let this HAPPEN?!
≡SNIFF≡
Did you SHOWER last night?
No, I was stuck on the Ferry Wheel-- WITHOUT MY DAUGHTER!
Thought so, because you're smelling a bit RIPE.

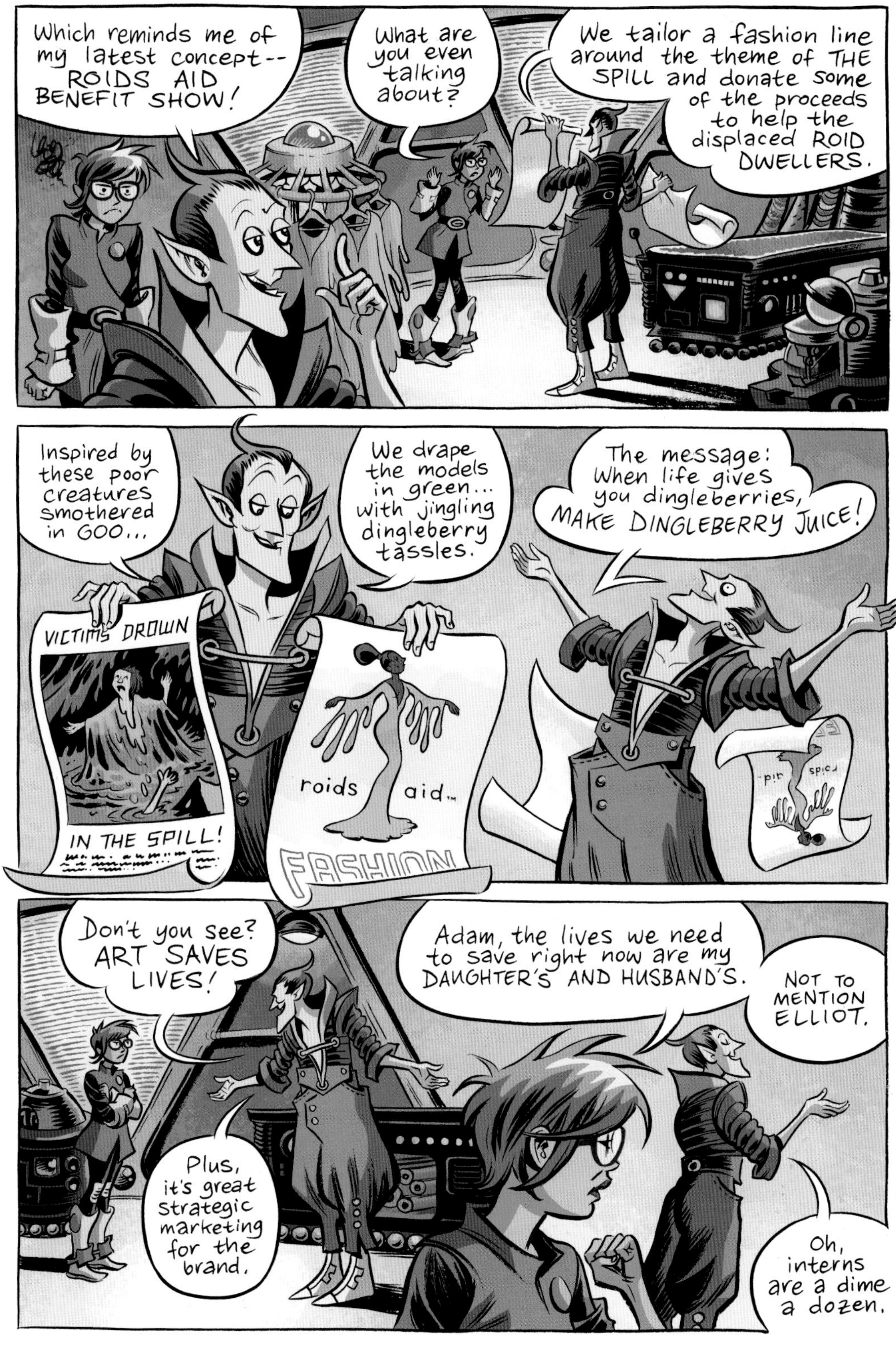
Which reminds me of my latest concept-- ROIDS AID BENEFIT SHOW!
What are you even talking about?
We tailor a fashion line around the theme of THE SPILL and donate some of the proceeds to help the displaced ROID DWELLERS.
Inspired by these poor creatures smothered in GOO...
We drape the models in green... with jingling dingleberry tassles.
The message: When life gives you dingleberries, MAKE DINGLEBERRY JUICE!
VICTIMS DROWN
IN THE SPILL!
roids aid™
FASHION
Don't you see? ART SAVES LIVES!
Plus, it's great strategic marketing for the brand.
Adam, the lives we need to save right now are my DAUGHTER'S AND HUSBAND'S.
NOT TO MENTION ELLIOT.
Oh, interns are a dime a dozen.

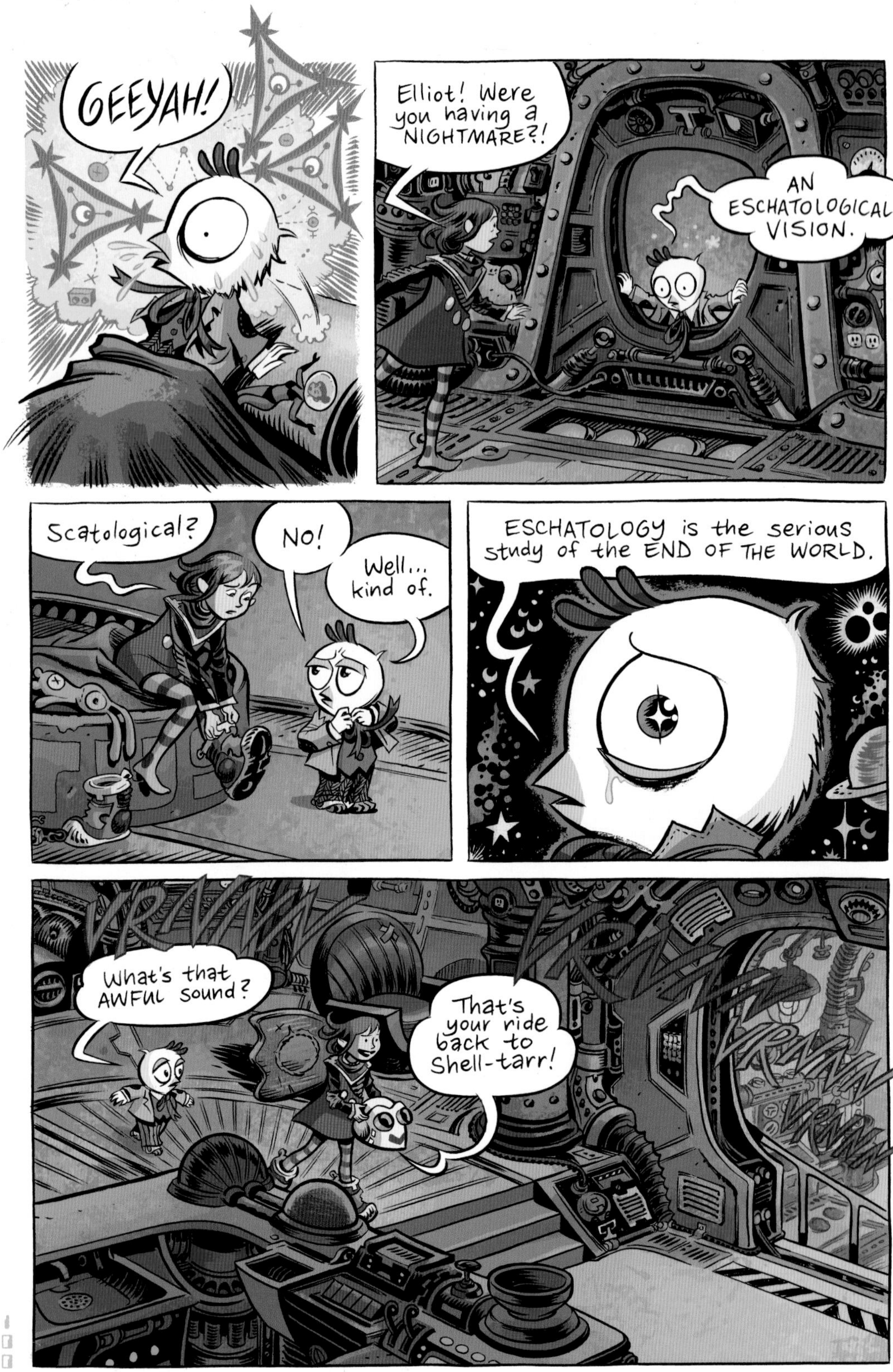
GEEYAH!
Elliot! Were you having a NIGHTMARE?!
AN ESCHATOLOGICAL VISION.
Scatological?
NO!
Well... kind of.
ESCHATOLOGY is the serious study of the END OF THE WORLD.
What's that AWFUL sound?
That's your ride back to Shell-tarr!

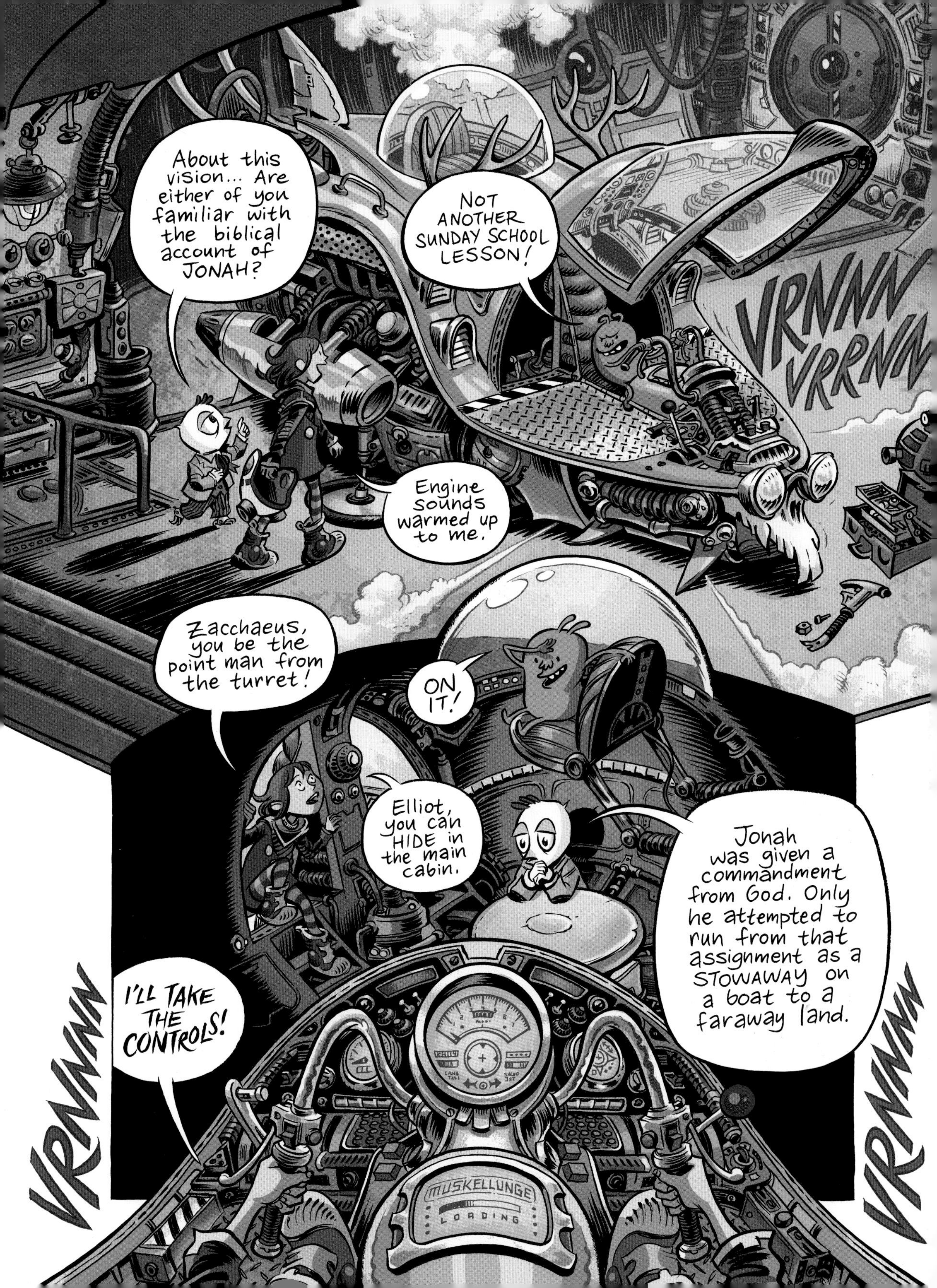

About this vision... Are either of you familiar with the biblical account of JONAH?
NOT ANOTHER SUNDAY SCHOOL LESSON!
VRNNN VRRNN
Engine sounds warmed up to me.
Zacchaeus, you be the point man from the turret!
ON IT!
Elliot, you can HIDE in the main cabin.
Jonah was given a commandment from God. Only he attempted to run from that assignment as a STOWAWAY on a boat to a faraway land.
I'LL TAKE THE CONTROLS!
VRNNNN
VRNNNN
MUSKELLUNGE
LOADING

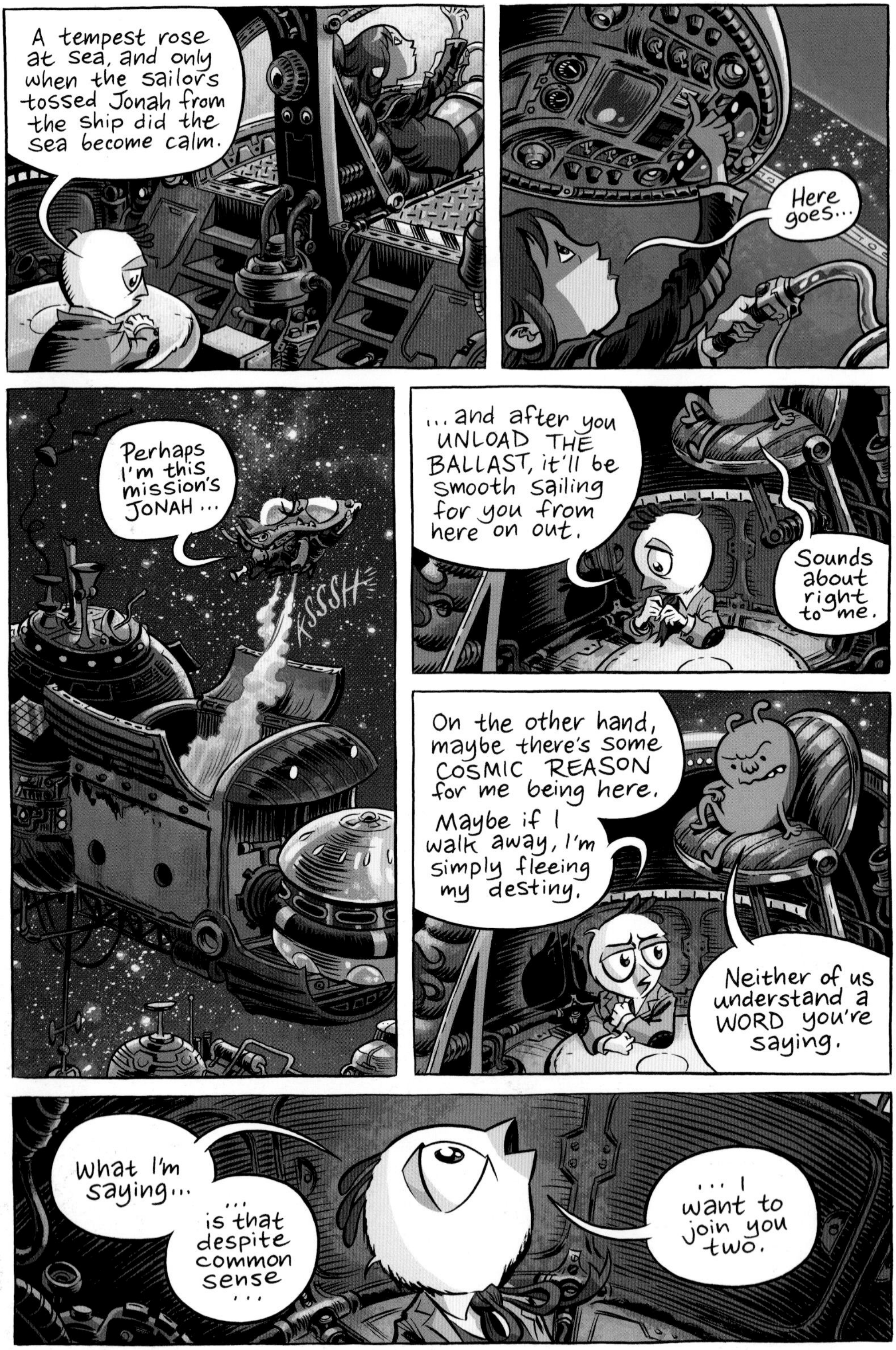
A tempest rose at sea, and only when the sailors tossed Jonah from the ship did the sea become calm.
Here goes...
Perhaps I'm this mission's JONAH...
KSSSH
...and after you UNLOAD THE BALLAST, it'll be smooth sailing for you from here on out.
Sounds about right to me.
On the other hand, maybe there's some COSMIC REASON for me being here.
Maybe if I walk away, I'm simply fleeing my destiny.
Neither of us understand a WORD you're saying.
What I'm saying...
...is that despite common sense...
...I want to join you two.

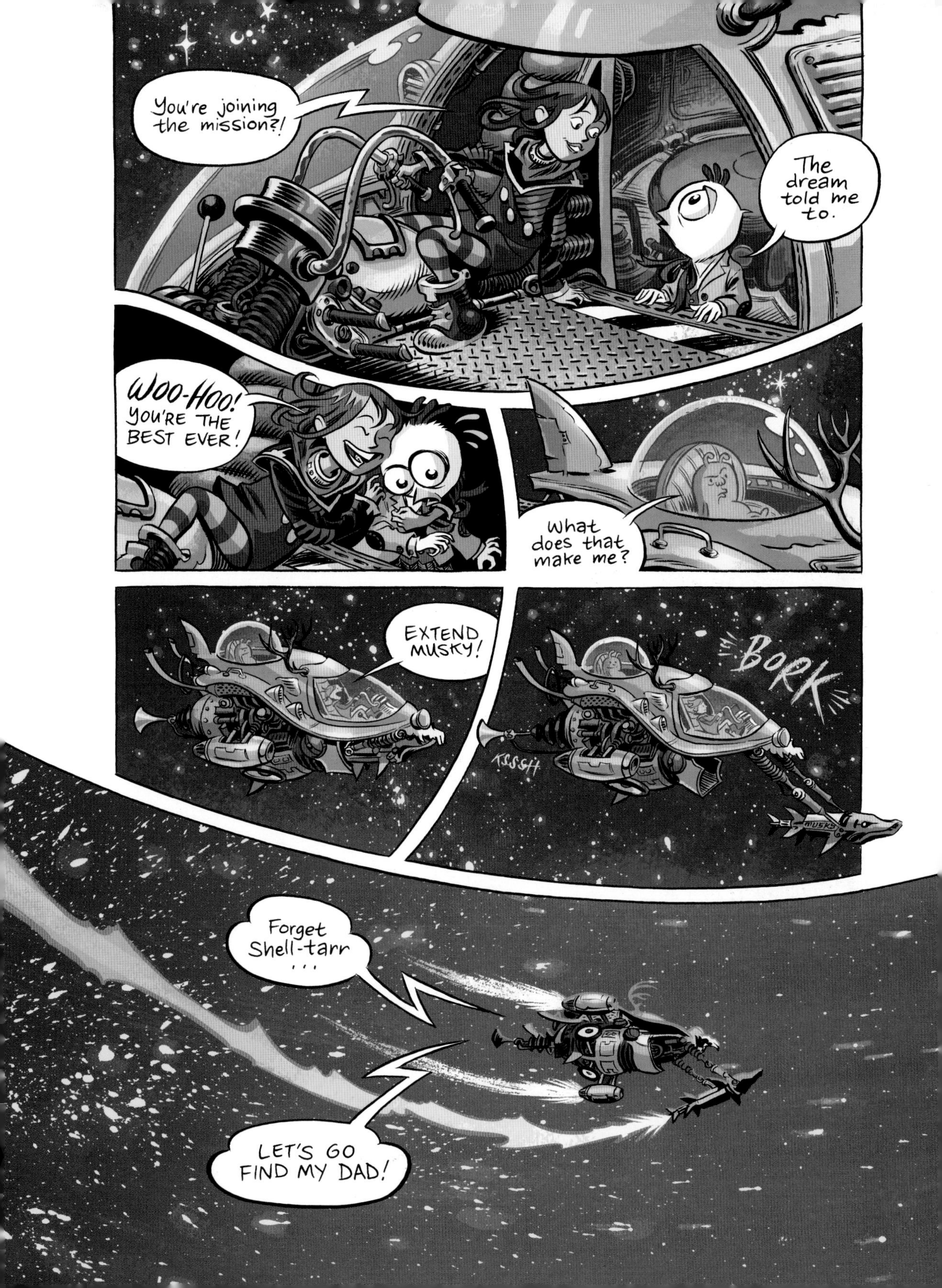

You're joining the mission?!
The dream told me to.
WOO-HOO! YOU'RE THE BEST EVER!
What does that make me?
EXTEND MUSKY!
BORK
KSSSH
MUSKY
Forget Shell-tarr . . .
LET'S GO FIND MY DAD!

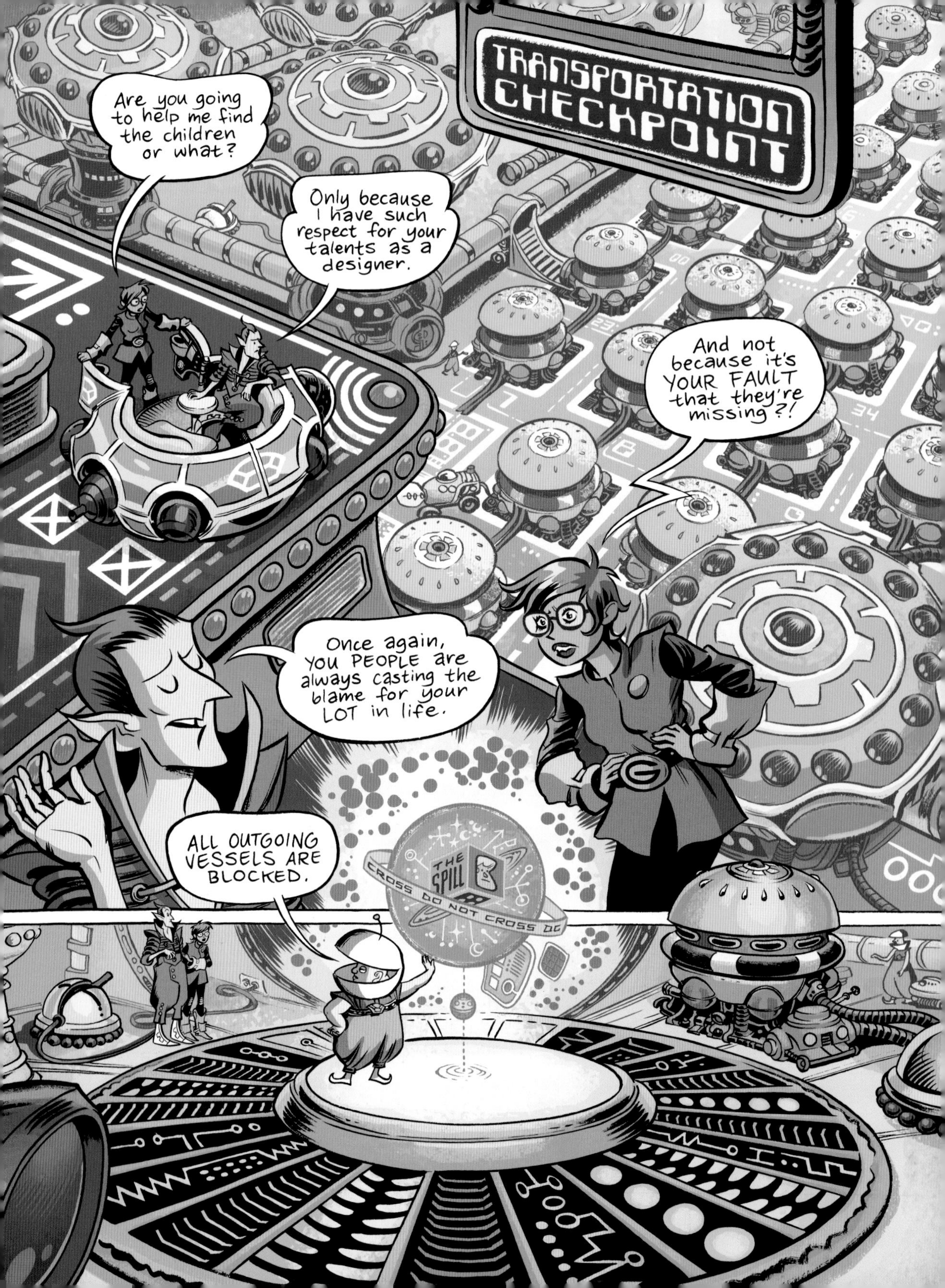
TRANSPORTATION CHECKPOINT
Are you going to help me find the children or what?
Only because I have such respect for your talents as a designer.
And not because it's YOUR FAULT that they're missing?!
Once again, YOU PEOPLE are always casting the blame for your LOT in life.
ALL OUTGOING VESSELS ARE BLOCKED.
THE SPILL
CROSS DO NOT CROSS DO NOT CROSS DO

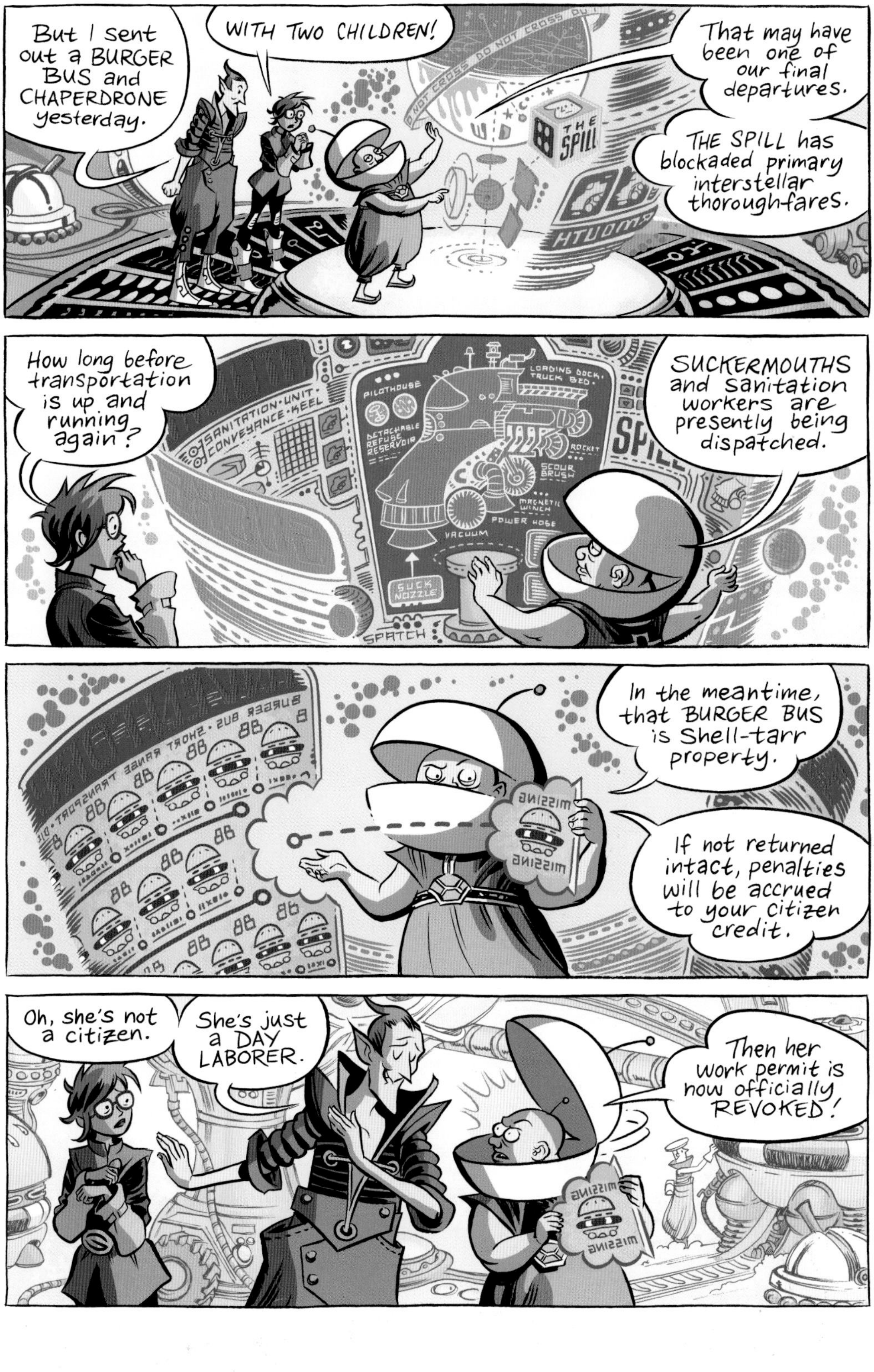
But I sent out a BURGER BUS and CHAPERDRONE yesterday.
WITH TWO CHILDREN!
That may have been one of our final departures.
THE SPILL has blockaded primary interstellar thoroughfares.
THE SPILL
How long before transportation is up and running again?
SUCKERMOUTHS and sanitation workers are presently being dispatched.
PILOTHOUSE
LOADING DOCK TRUCK BED
DETACHABLE REFUSE RESERVOIR
ROCKET
SCOUR BRUSH
MAGNETIC WINCH
POWER HOSE
VACUUM
SUCK NOZZLE
SANITATION UNIT CONVEYANCE KEEL
SPATCH
In the meantime, that BURGER BUS is Shell-tarr property.
If not returned intact, penalties will be accrued to your citizen credit.
Oh, she's not a citizen.
She's just a DAY LABORER.
Then her work permit is now officially REVOKED!

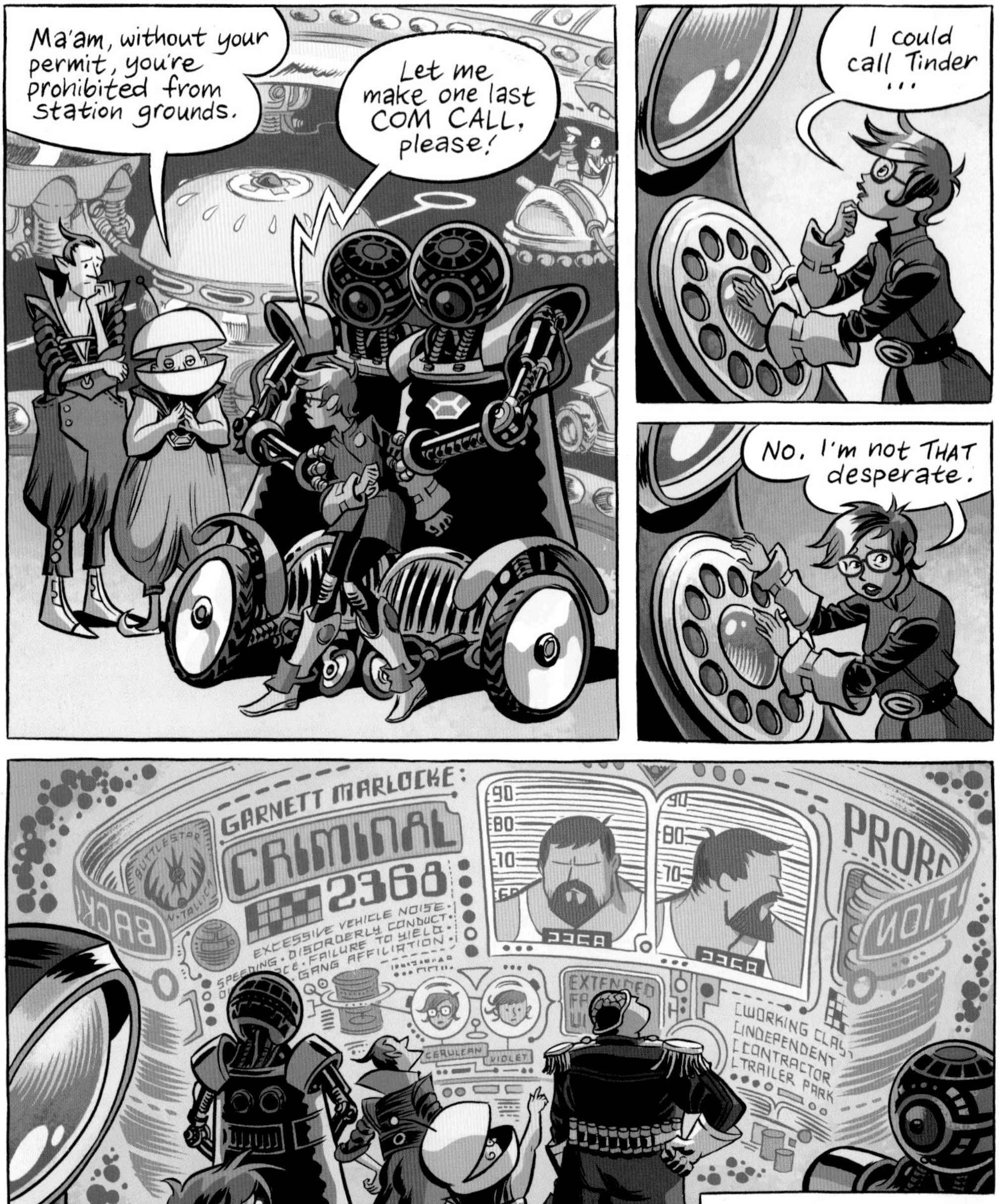

Ma'am, without your permit, you're prohibited from station grounds.
Let me make one last COM CALL, please!
I could call Tinder ...
No. I'm not THAT desperate.
GARNETT MARLOCKE:
CRIMINAL
2368
EXCESSIVE VEHICLE NOISE
DISORDERLY CONDUCT
FAILURE TO YIELD
GANG AFFILIATION
CERULEAN
VIOLET
INDEPENDENT
CONTRACTOR
TRAILER PARK
I AM that desperate.

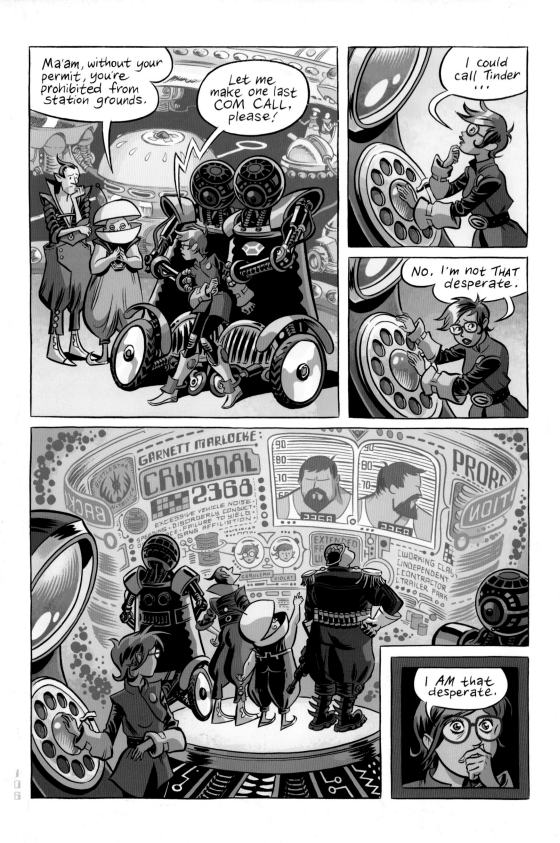

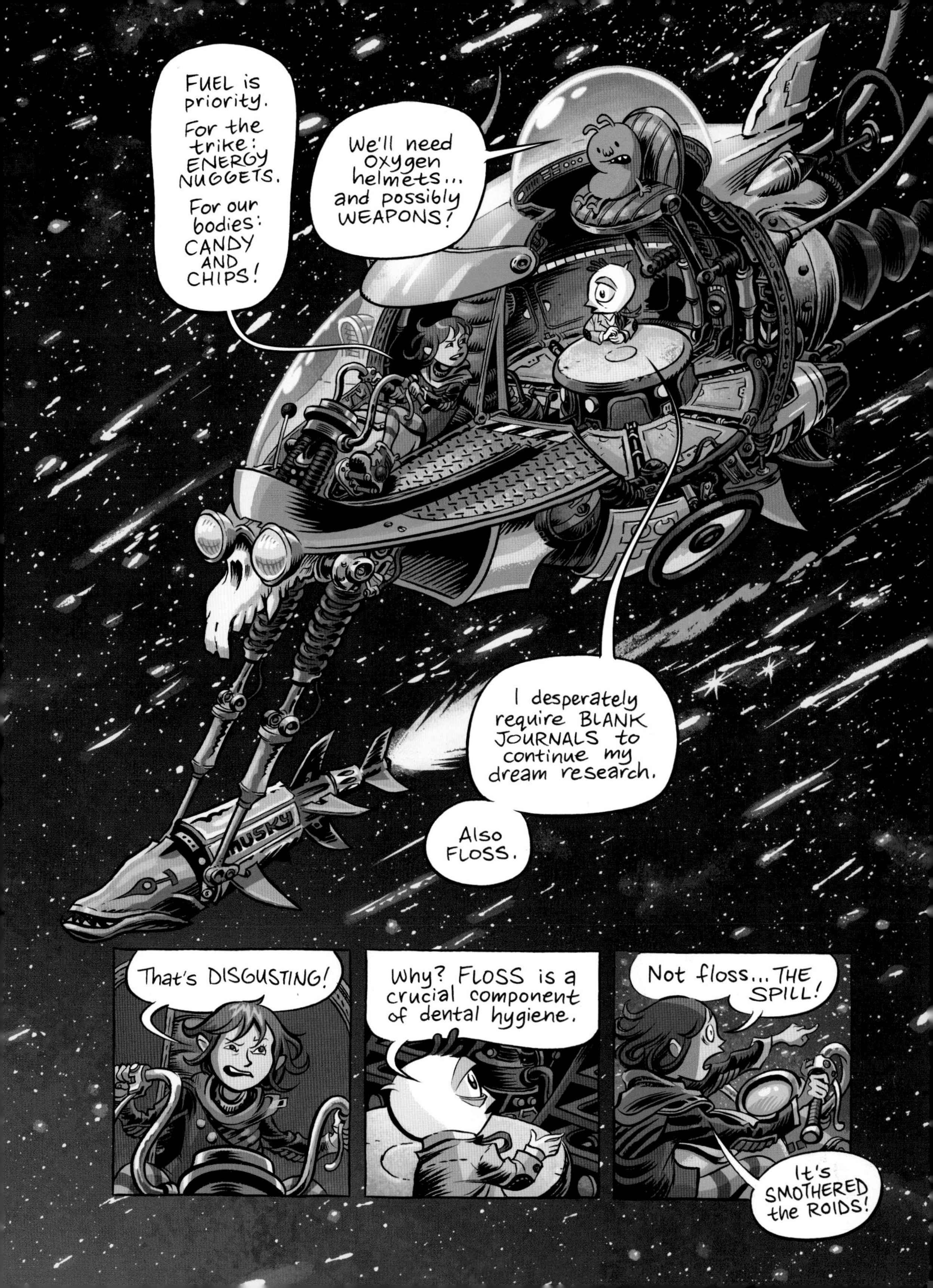
FUEL is priority.
For the trike: ENERGY NUGGETS.
For our bodies: CANDY AND CHIPS!
We'll need oxygen helmets... and possibly WEAPONS!
I desperately require BLANK JOURNALS to continue my dream research.
Also FLOSS.
That's DISGUSTING!
Why? FLOSS is a crucial component of dental hygiene.
Not floss... THE SPILL!
It's SMOTHERED the ROIDS!

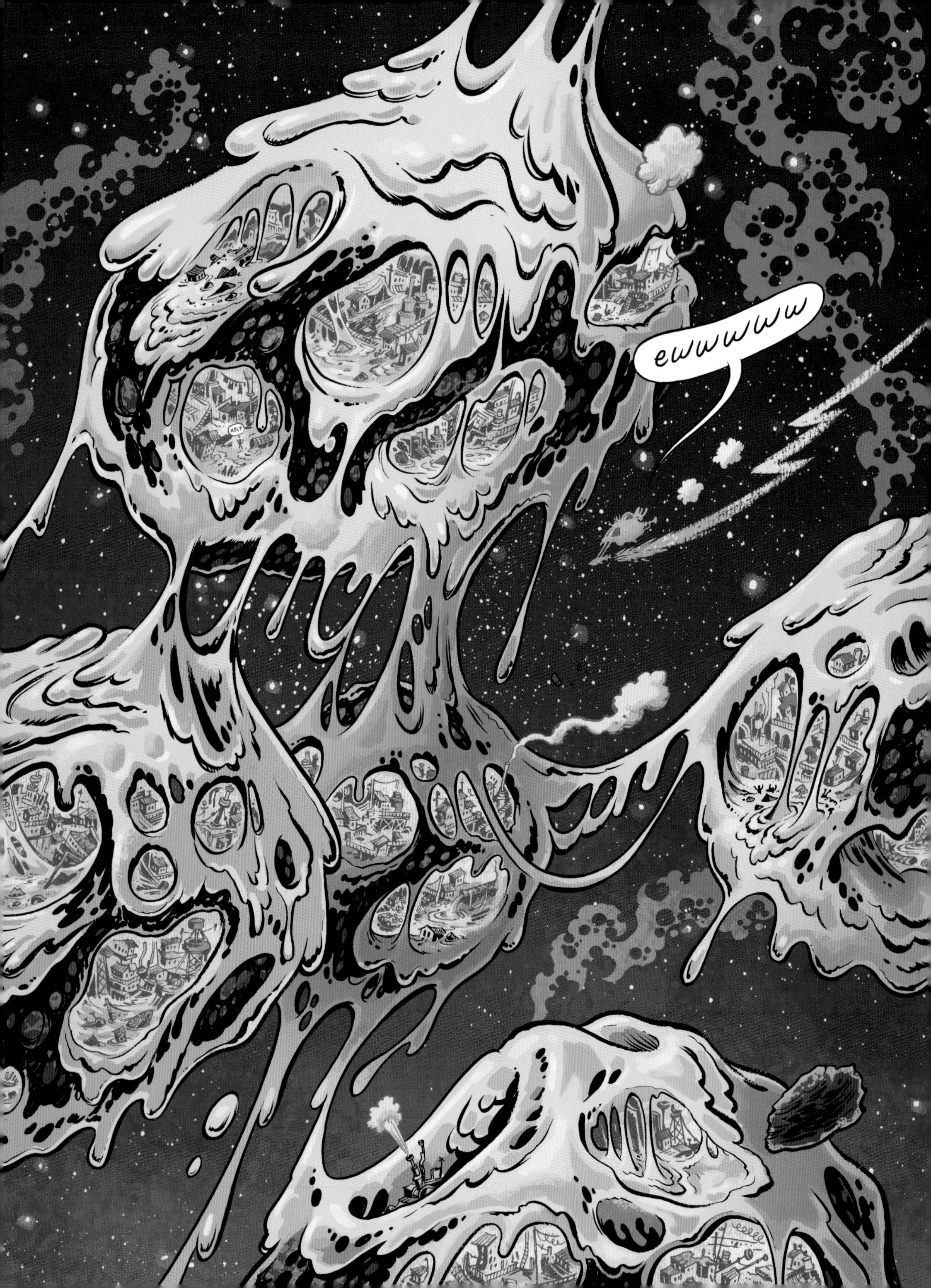
HELP
ewwwww

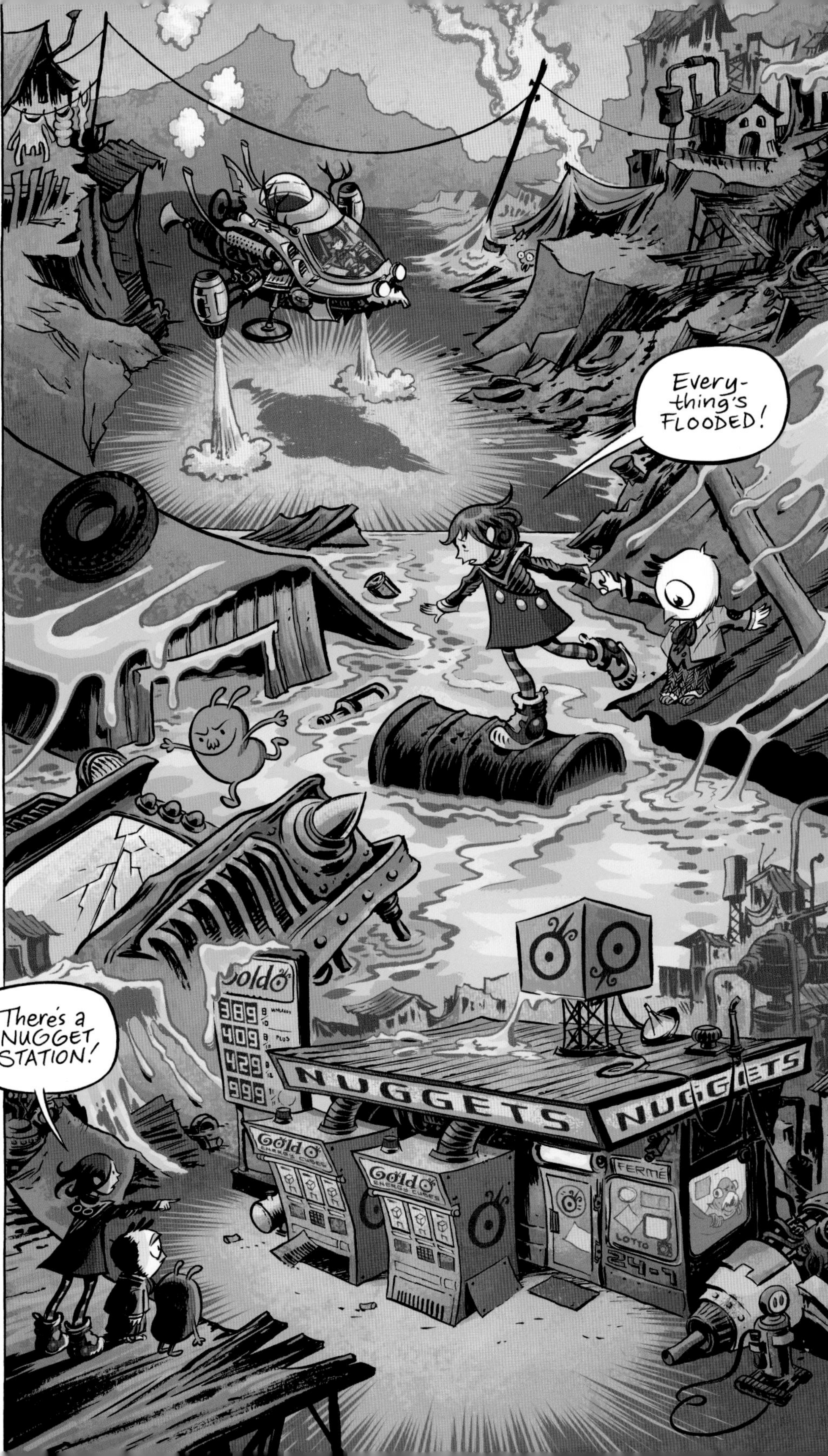
Every-
thing's
FLOODED!
There's a
NUGGET
STATION!
NUGGETS
NUGGETS
FERMÉ
LOTTO
24-7

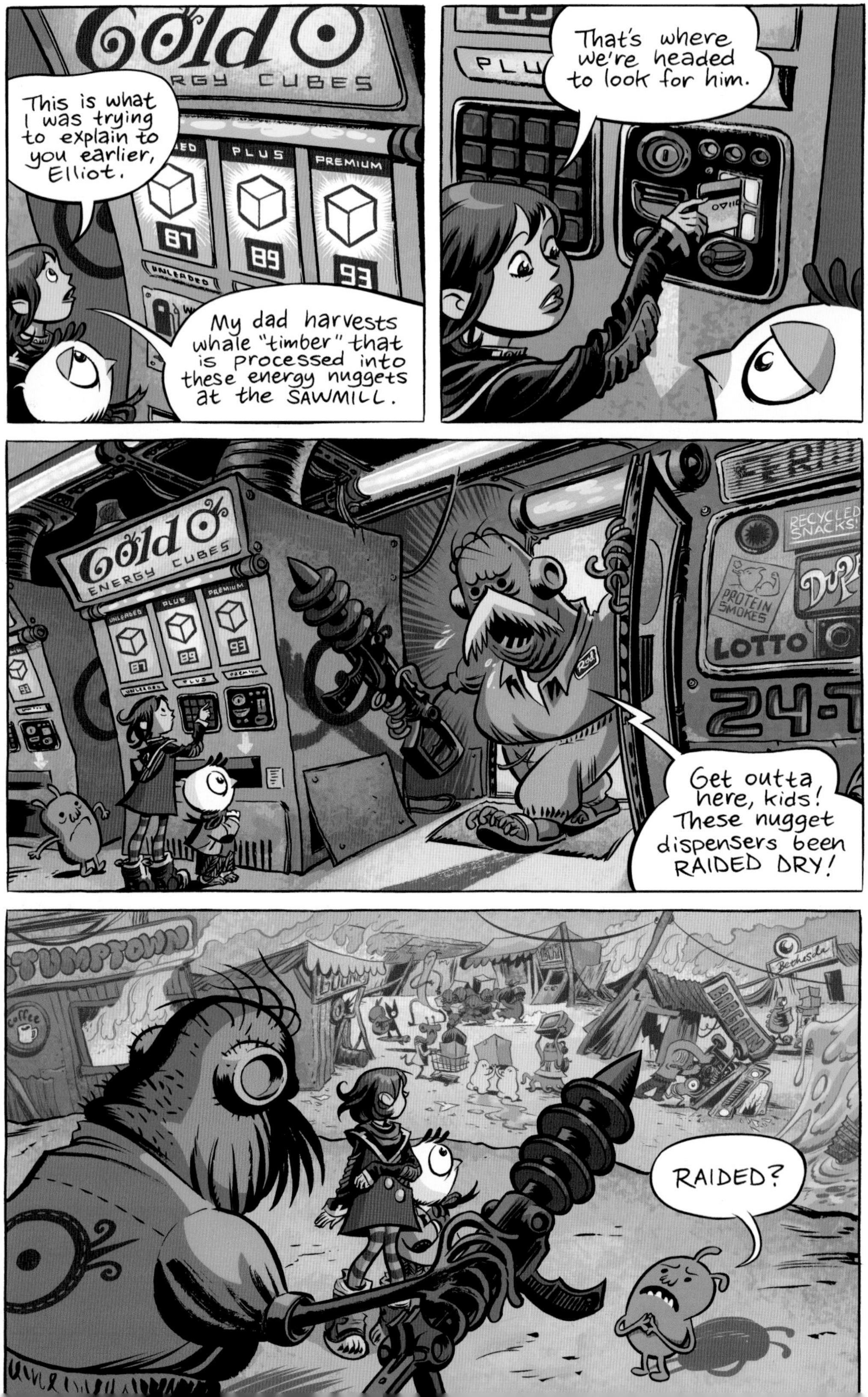
Gold
ENERGY CUBES
This is what I was trying to explain to you earlier, Elliot.
PLUS
PREMIUM
87
89
93
UNLEADED
My dad harvests whale "timber" that is processed into these energy nuggets at the SAWMILL.
That's where we're headed to look for him.
Gold
ENERGY CUBES
RECYCLED SNACKS!
PROTEIN SMOKES
LOTTO
Get outta here, kids! These nugget dispensers been RAIDED DRY!
STUMPTOWN
Coffee
RAIDED?

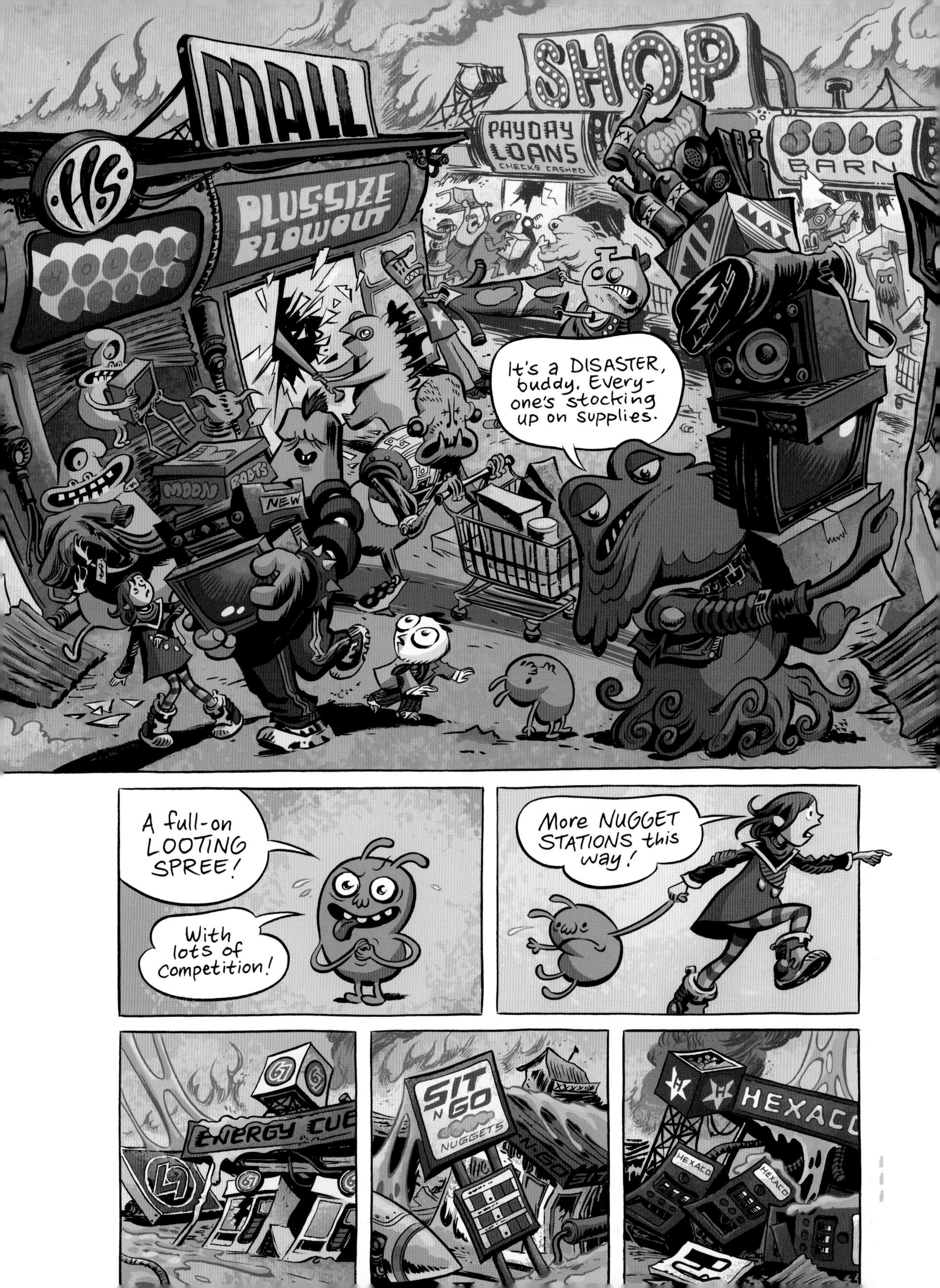
MALL
SHOP
PAYDAY LOANS CHECKS CASHED
SALE BARN
PLUS-SIZE BLOWOUT
MOON BOOTS
NEW
It's a DISASTER, buddy. Everyone's stocking up on supplies.
A full-on LOOTING SPREE!
With lots of Competition!
More NUGGET STATIONS this way!
ENERGY CUE
SIT N GO NUGGETS
HEXACO
HEXACO
HEXACO

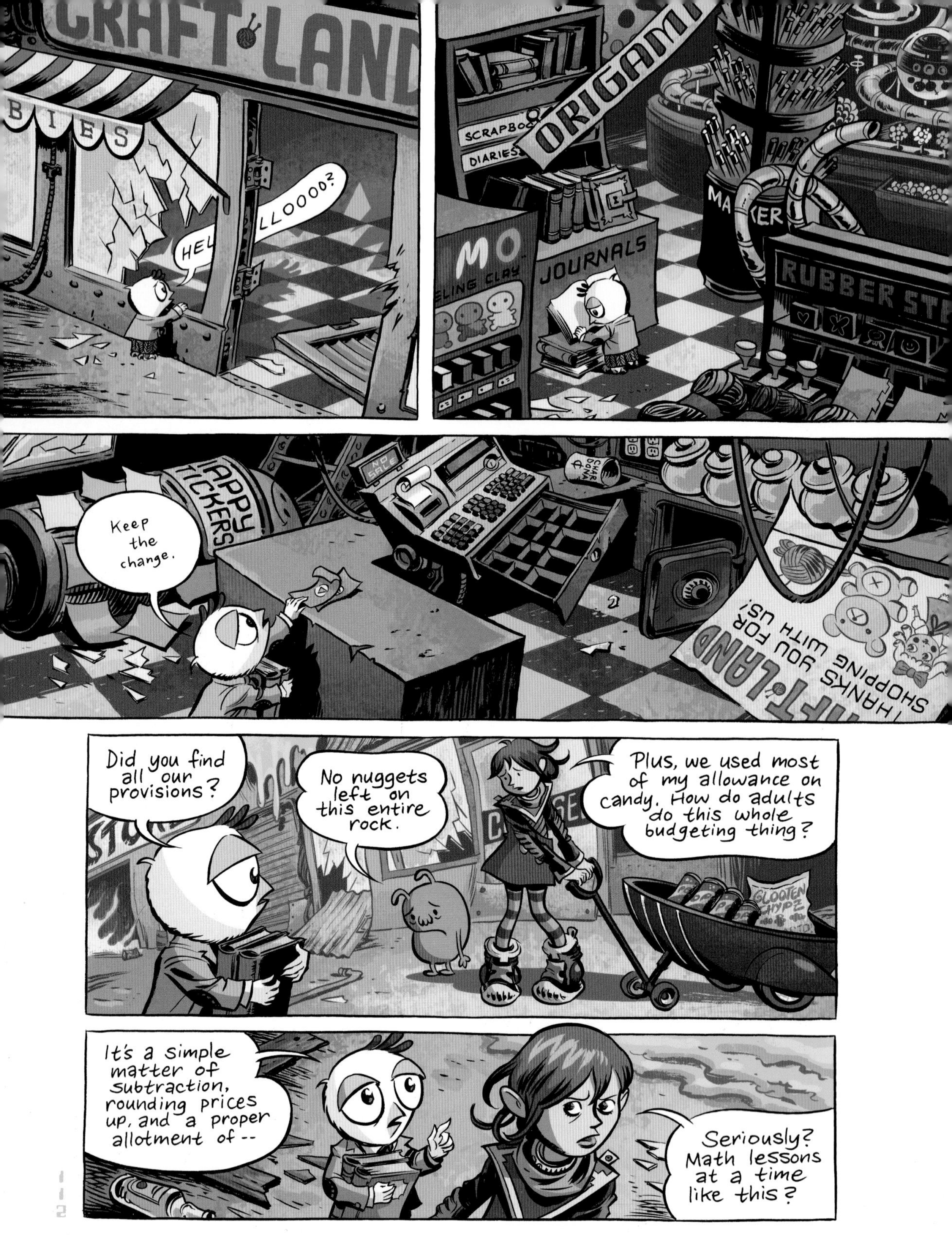
CRAFT LAND
BIES
HELLOOOO?
ORIGAMI
SCRAPBO
DIARIES
JOURNALS
MO
ELING CLAY
MA KER
RUBBER ST
NO SALE
APPY TICKERS
Keep the change.
THANKS YOU FOR SHOPPING WITH US!
Did you find all our provisions?
No nuggets left on this entire rock.
Plus, we used most of my allowance on candy. How do adults do this whole budgeting thing?
GLOOTEN CHYPZ
It's a simple matter of subtraction, rounding prices up, and a proper allotment of --
Seriously? Math lessons at a time like this?

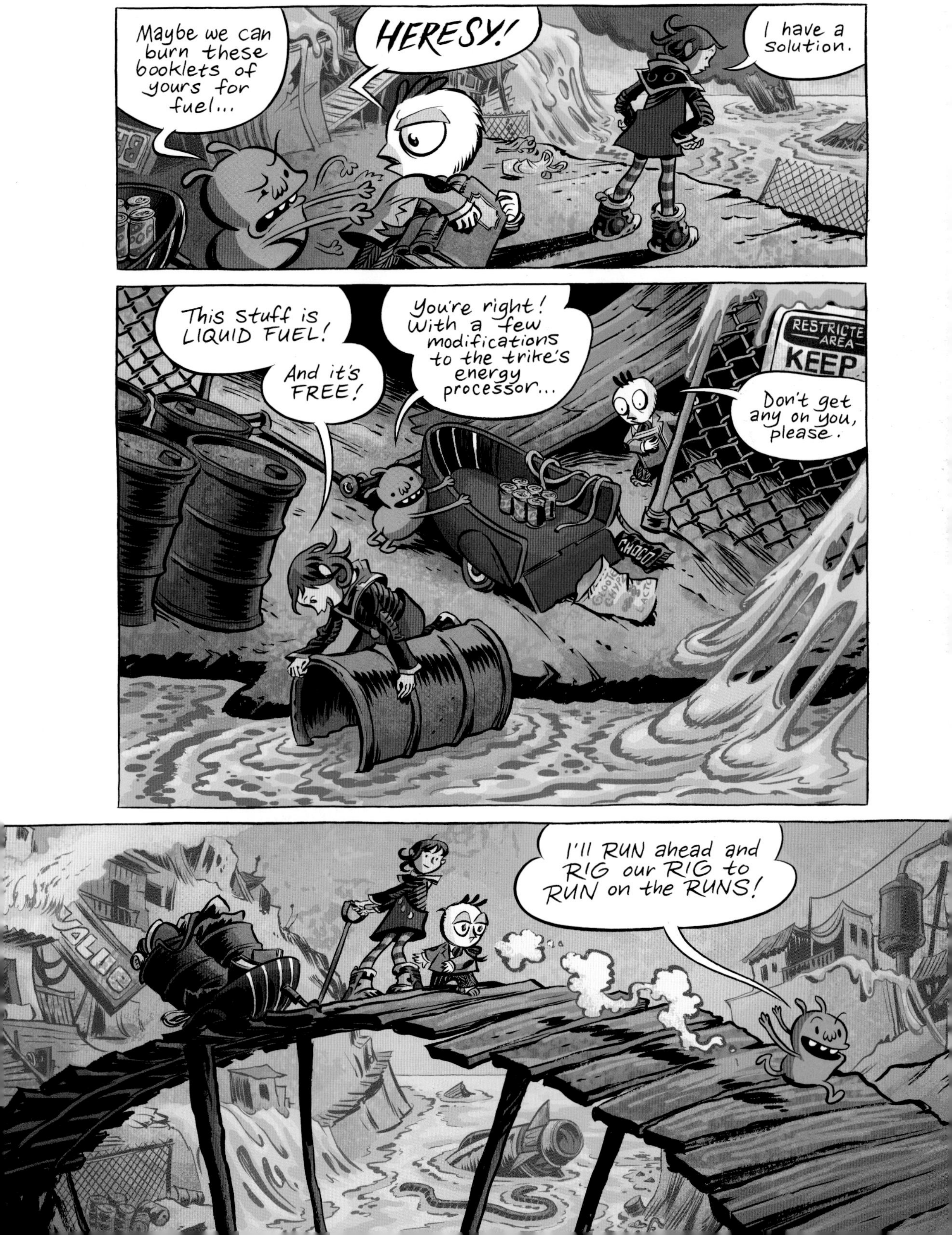
Maybe we can burn these booklets of yours for fuel...
HERESY!
I have a solution.
This stuff is LIQUID FUEL!
And it's FREE!
You're right! With a few modifications to the trike's energy processor...
RESTRICTED AREA
KEEP
Don't get any on you, please.
CHOCO
I'll RUN ahead and RIG our RIG to RUN on the RUNS!

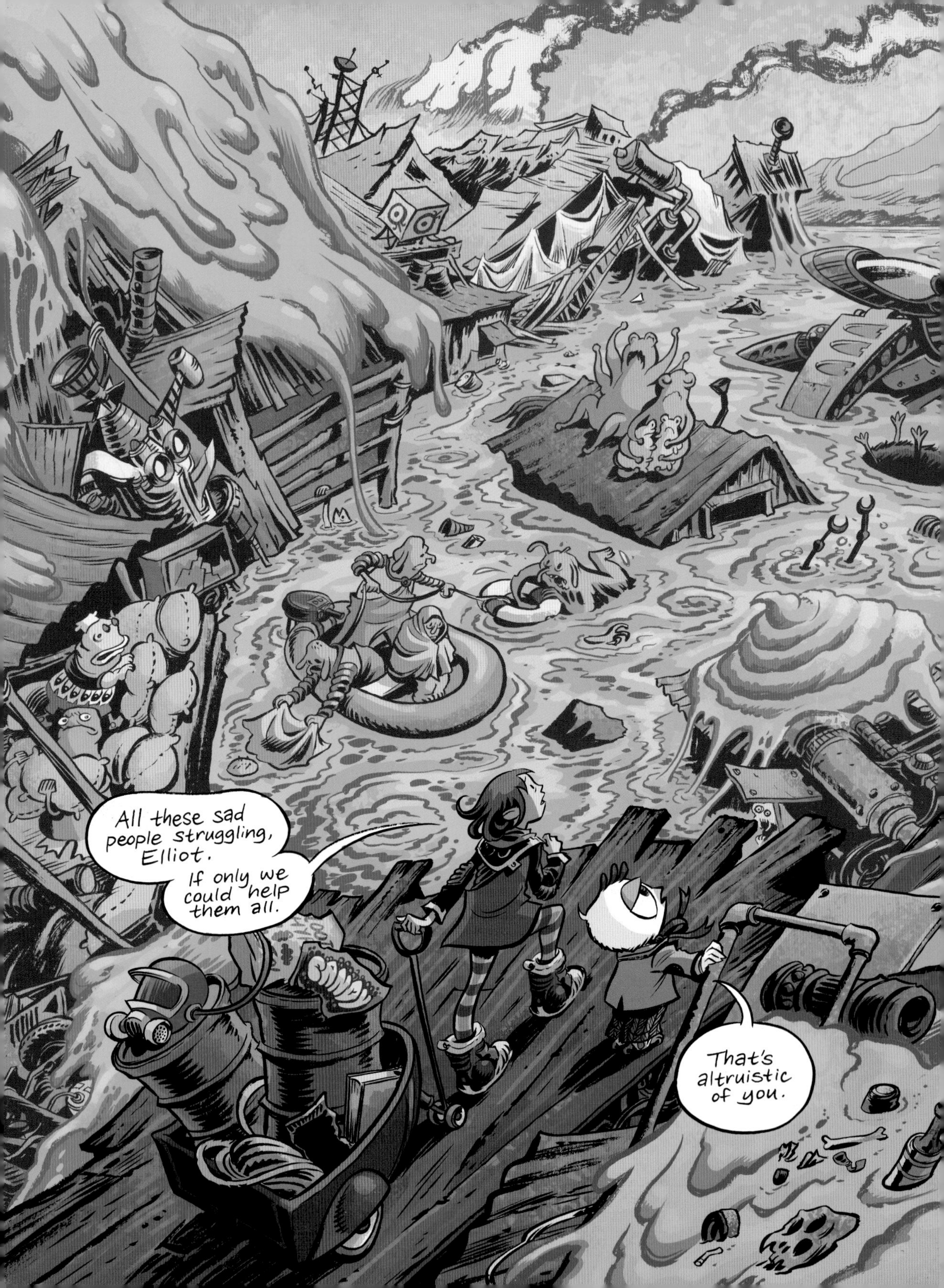
All these sad people struggling, Elliot.
If only we could help them all.
That's altruistic of you.

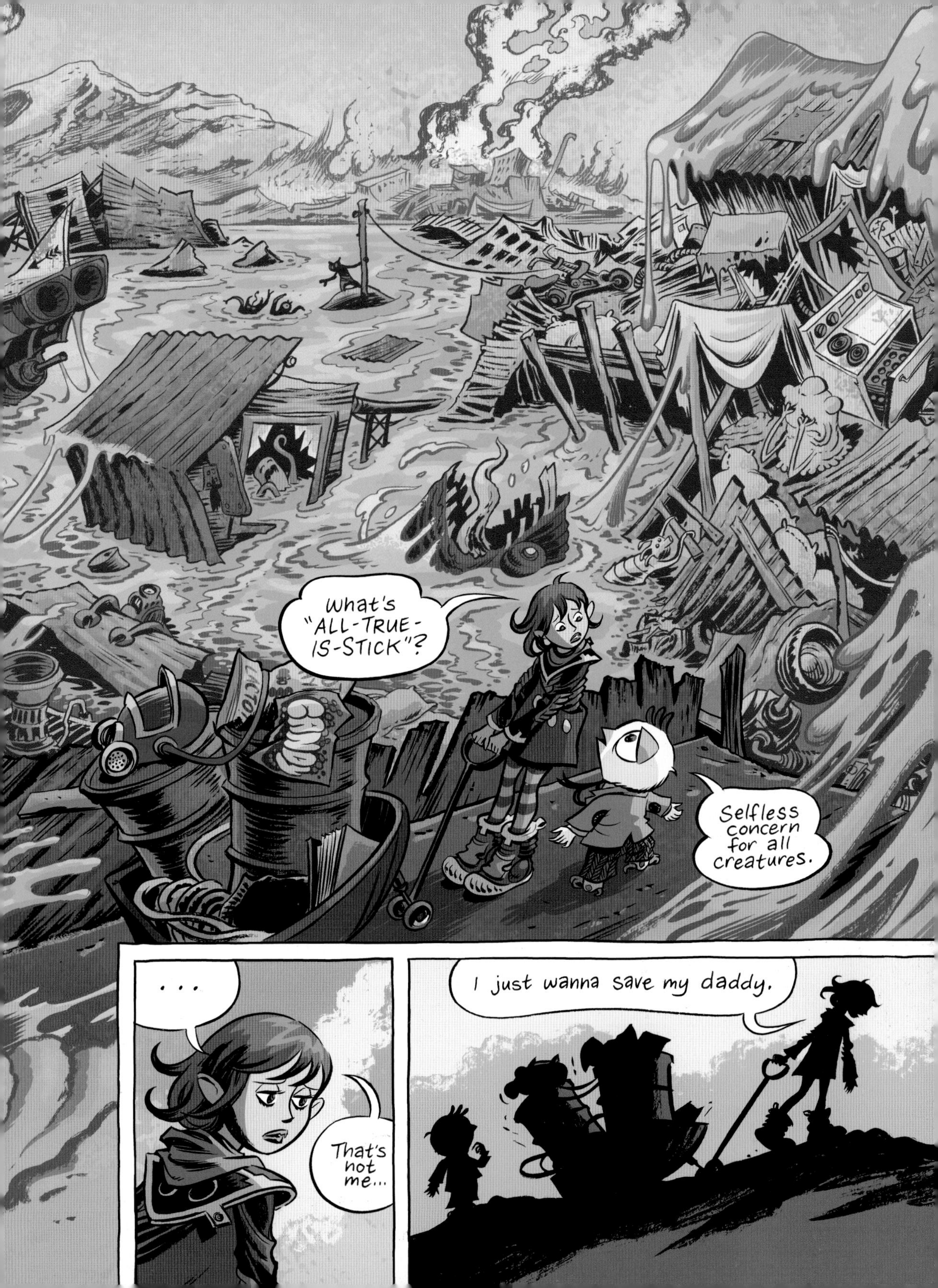
What's "ALL-TRUE-IS-STICK"?
Selfless concern for all creatures.
...
That's not me...
I just wanna save my daddy.

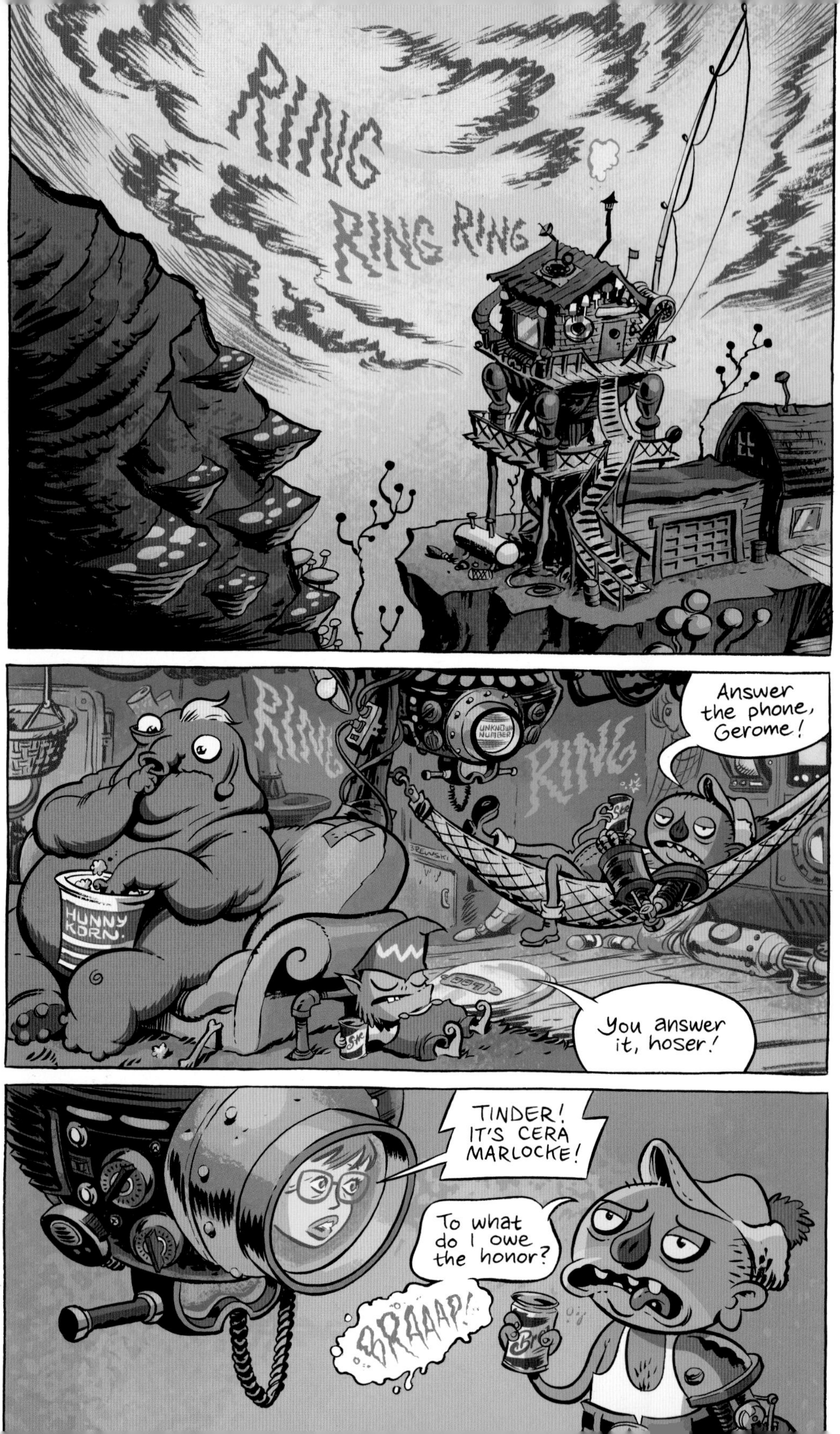
RING
RING RING
RING
RING
UNKNOWN NUMBER
Answer the phone, Gerome!
HUNNY KORN.
You answer it, hoser!
TINDER! IT'S CERA MARLOCKE!
To what do I owe the honor?
BRAAAP!

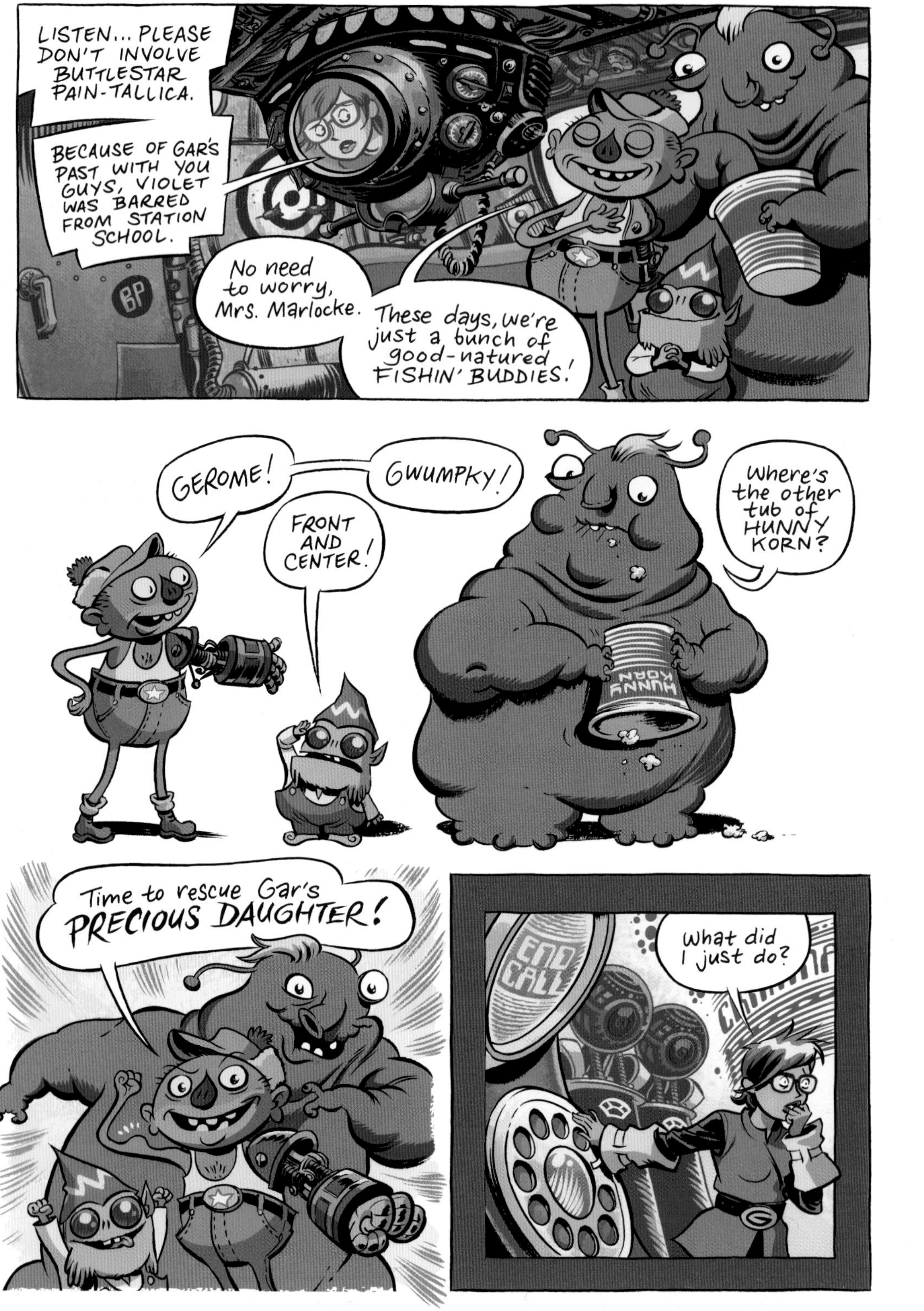
LISTEN... PLEASE DON'T INVOLVE BUTTLESTAR PAIN-TALLICA.
BECAUSE OF GAR'S PAST WITH YOU GUYS, VIOLET WAS BARRED FROM STATION SCHOOL.
No need to worry, Mrs. Marlocke.
These days, we're just a bunch of good-natured FISHIN' BUDDIES!
GEROME!
GWUMPKY!
FRONT AND CENTER!
Where's the other tub of HUNNY KORN?
HUNNY KORN
Time to rescue Gar's PRECIOUS DAUGHTER!
What did I just do?

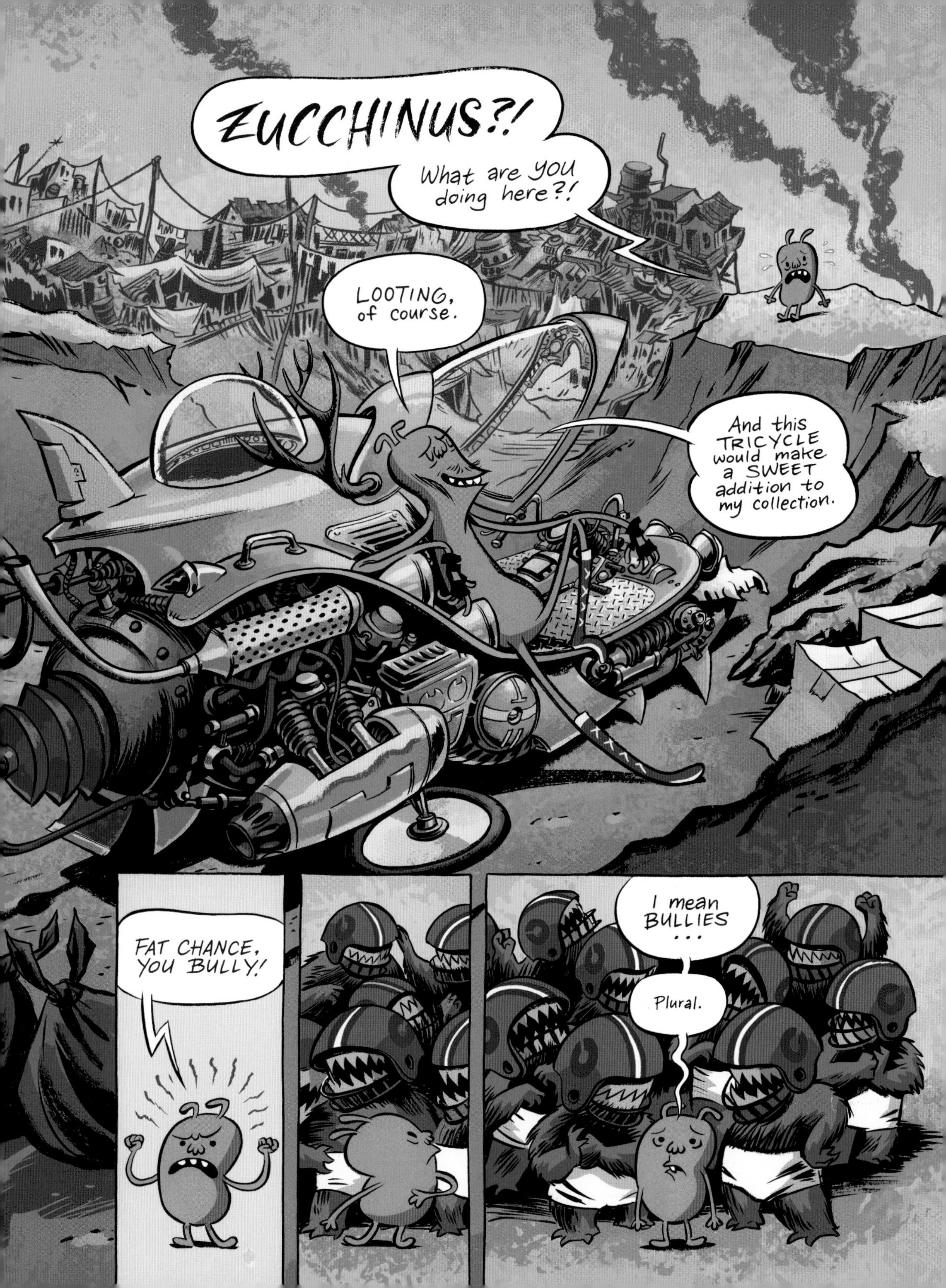
ZUCCHINUS?!
What are YOU doing here?!
LOOTING, of course.
And this TRICYCLE would make a SWEET addition to my collection.
FAT CHANCE, YOU BULLY!
I mean BULLIES . . .
Plural.

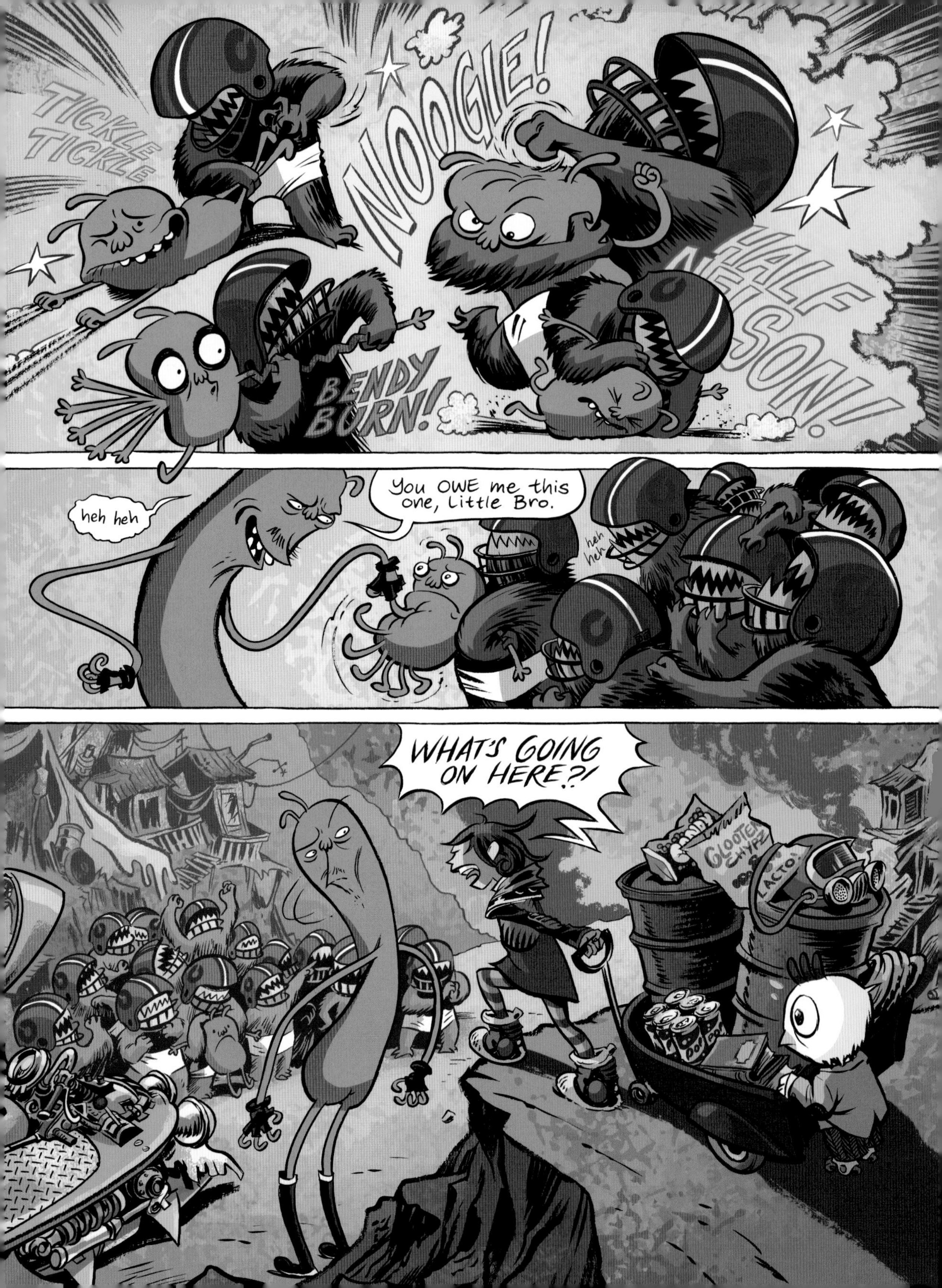
TICKLE TICKLE
NOOGIE!
HALF NELSON!
BENDY BURN!
heh heh
You OWE me this one, Little Bro.
heh heh
WHAT'S GOING ON HERE?!
GLOOTEN CHYPZ
LACTO

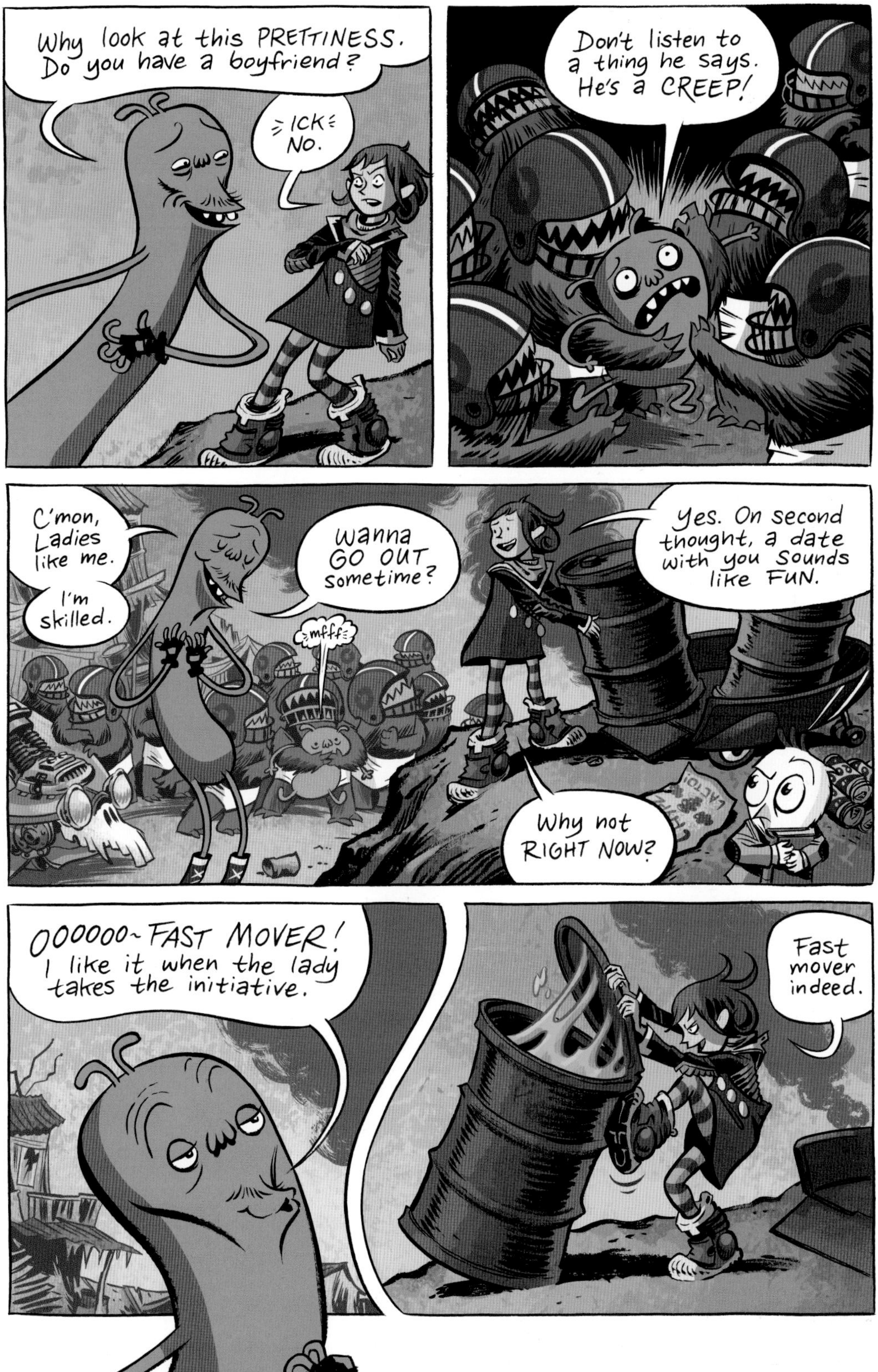
Why look at this PRETTINESS. Do you have a boyfriend?
ICK NO.
Don't listen to a thing he says. He's a CREEP!
C'mon, Ladies like me.
I'm skilled.
Wanna GO OUT sometime?
mfff
Yes. On second thought, a date with you sounds like FUN.
Why not RIGHT NOW?
OOOOOO~FAST MOVER! I like it when the lady takes the initiative.
Fast mover indeed.

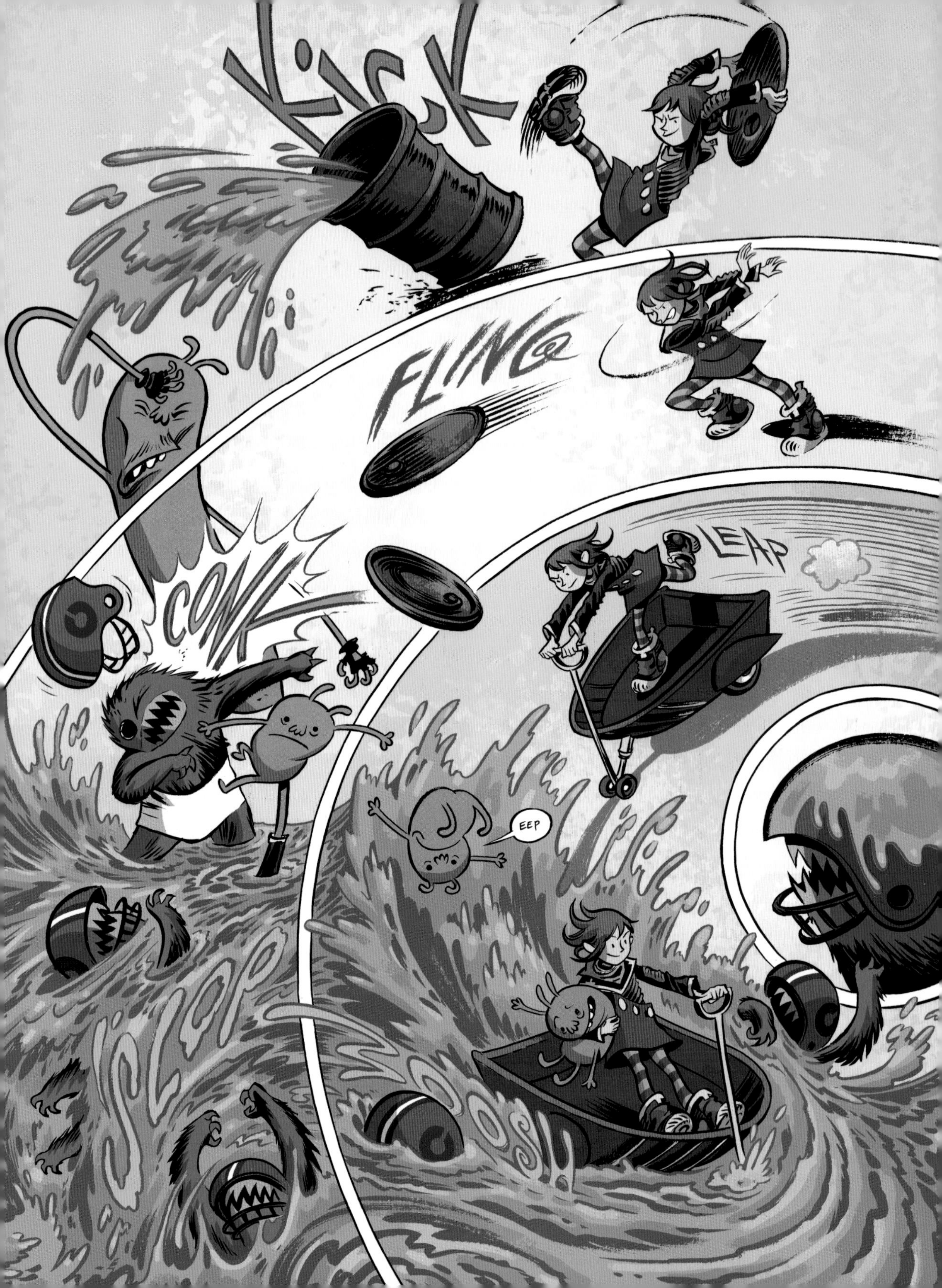
KICK
FLING
CONK
LEAP
EEP
SCOOP
SWOOSH

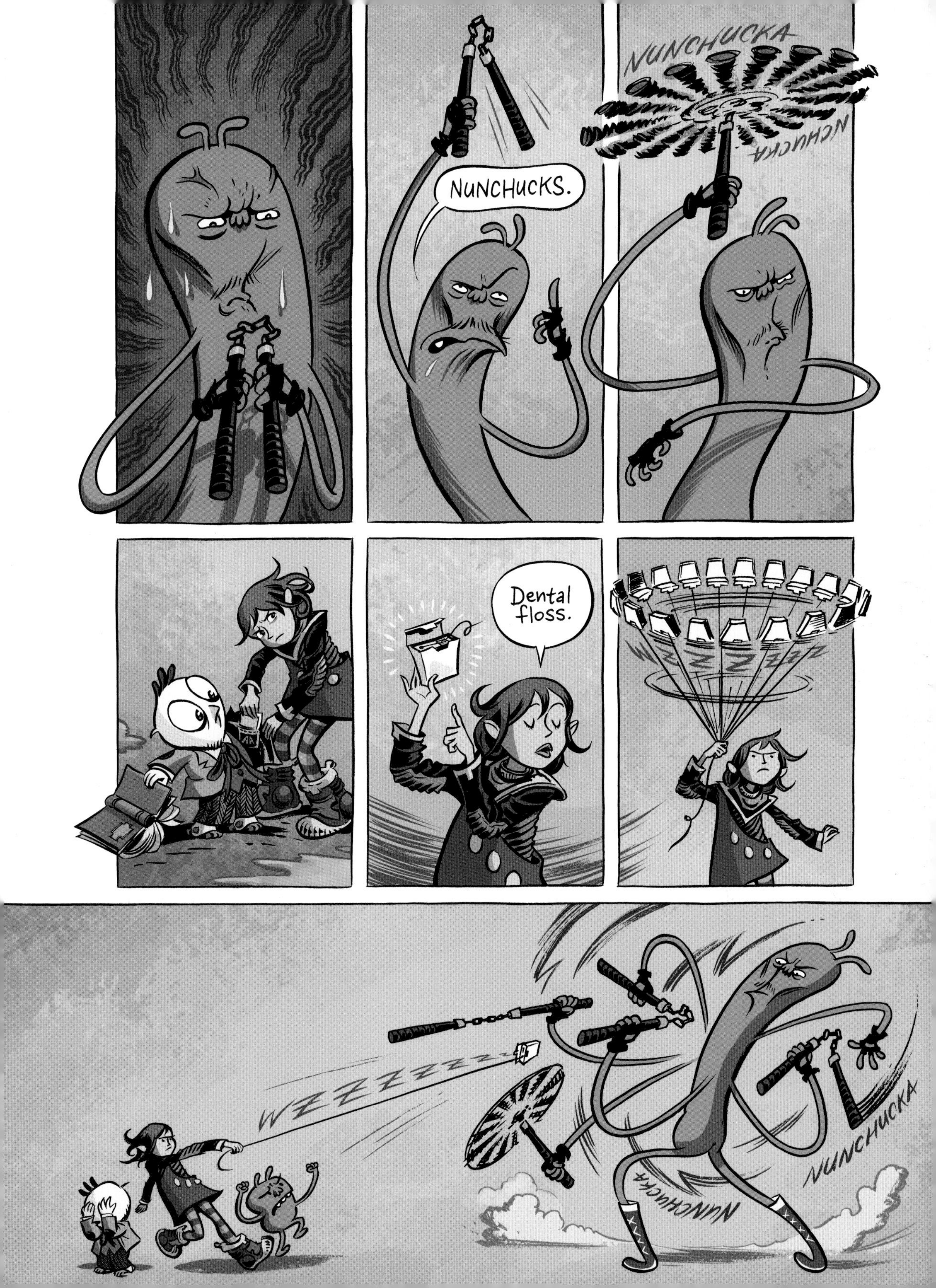

NUNCHUCKS.
NUNCHUCKA
NCHUCKA
Dental floss.
WZZZZZZZZZZ
NUNCHUCKA
NUNCHUCKA
NUNCHUCKA

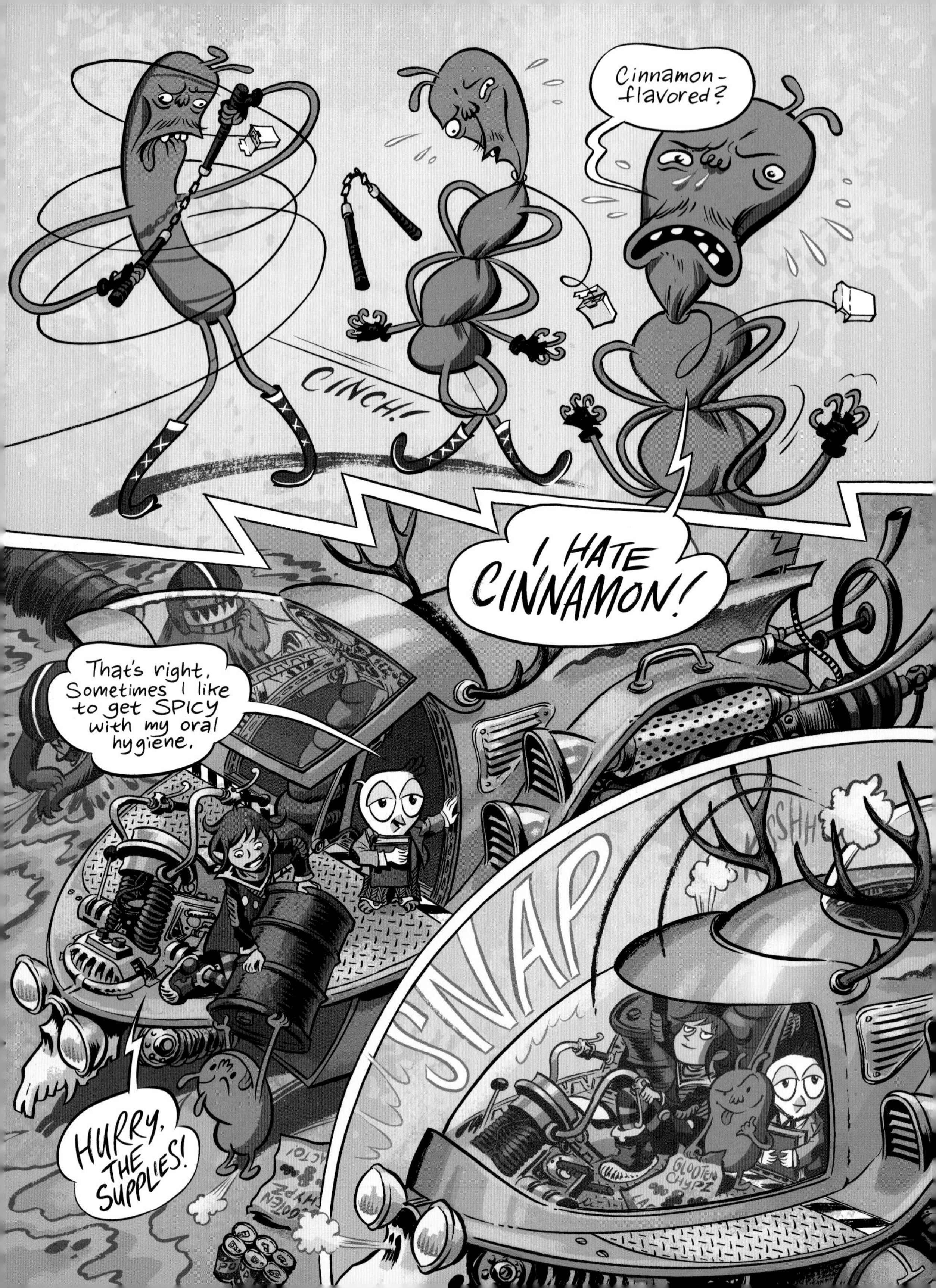
Cinnamon-flavored?
CINCH!
I HATE CINNAMON!
That's right. Sometimes I like to get SPICY with my oral hygiene.
HURRY, THE SUPPLIES!
SNAP
KSSHHH
GLOOTEN CHYPZ

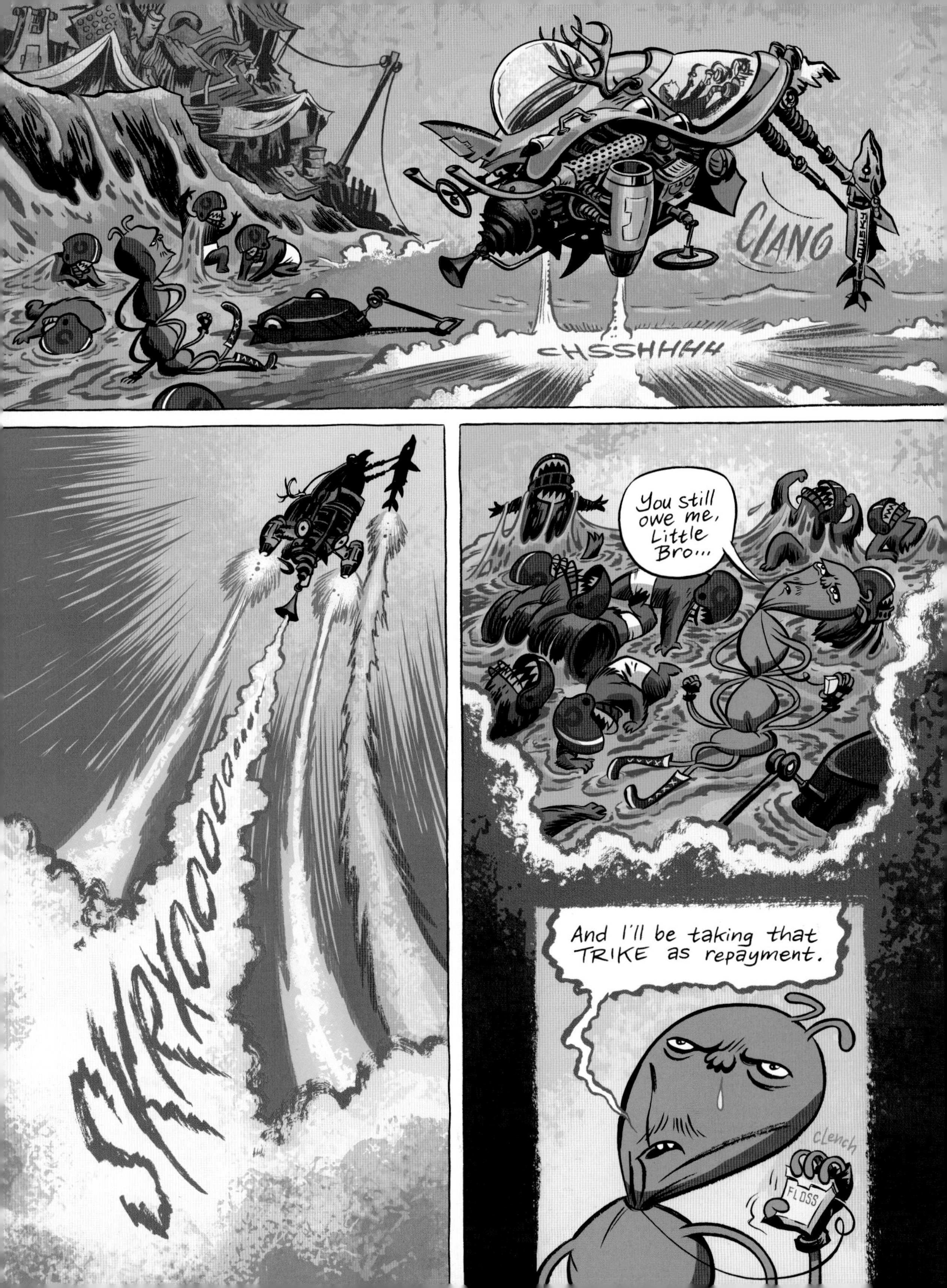
CLANG
CHSSHHHH
SHHOOOOOOO
You still owe me, Little Bro...
And I'll be taking that TRIKE as repayment.
Clench
FLOSS

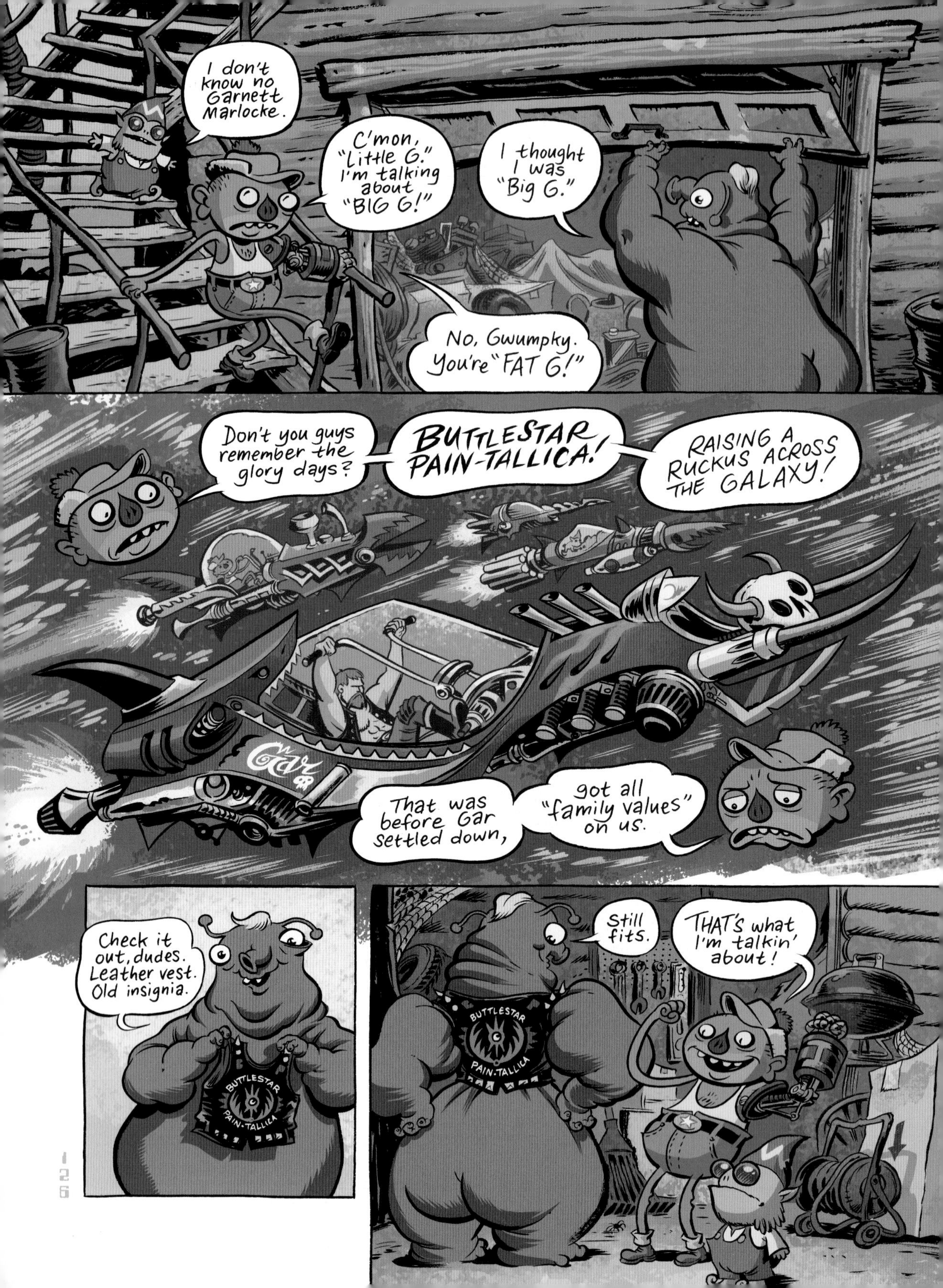
I don't know no Garnett Marlocke.
C'mon, "Little G." I'm talking about "BIG G!"
I thought I was "Big G."
No, Gwumpky. You're "FAT G!"
Don't you guys remember the glory days?
BUTTLESTAR PAIN-TALLICA!
RAISING A RUCKUS ACROSS THE GALAXY!
That was before Gar settled down,
got all "family values" on us.
Check it out, dudes. Leather vest. Old insignia.
BUTTLESTAR PAIN-TALLICA
Still fits.
THAT'S what I'm talkin' about!
BUTTLESTAR PAIN-TALLICA

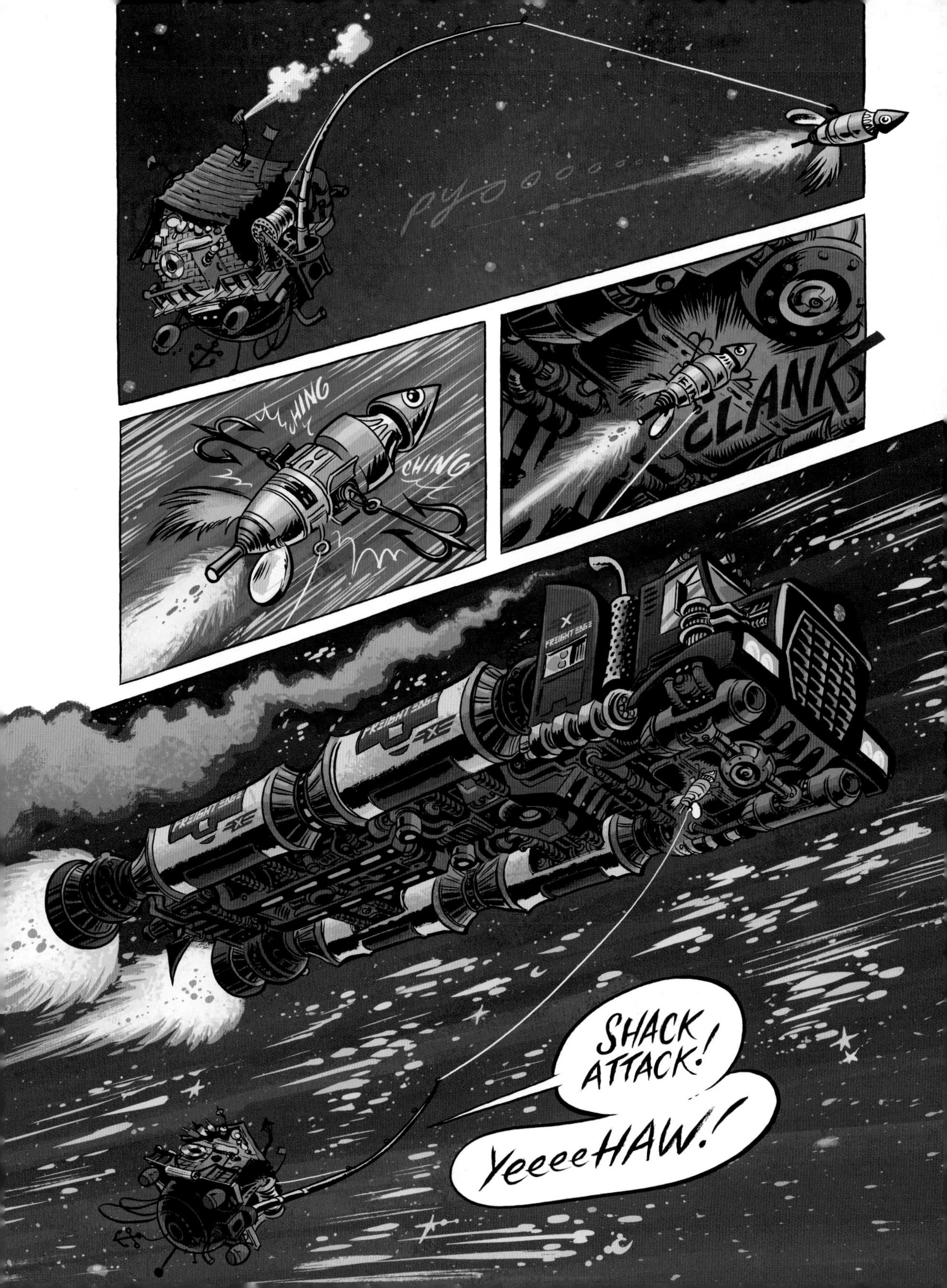
pyoooooo
CHING
CHING
CLANK
FREIGHT EDGE
SHACK ATTACK!
YeeeeHAW!

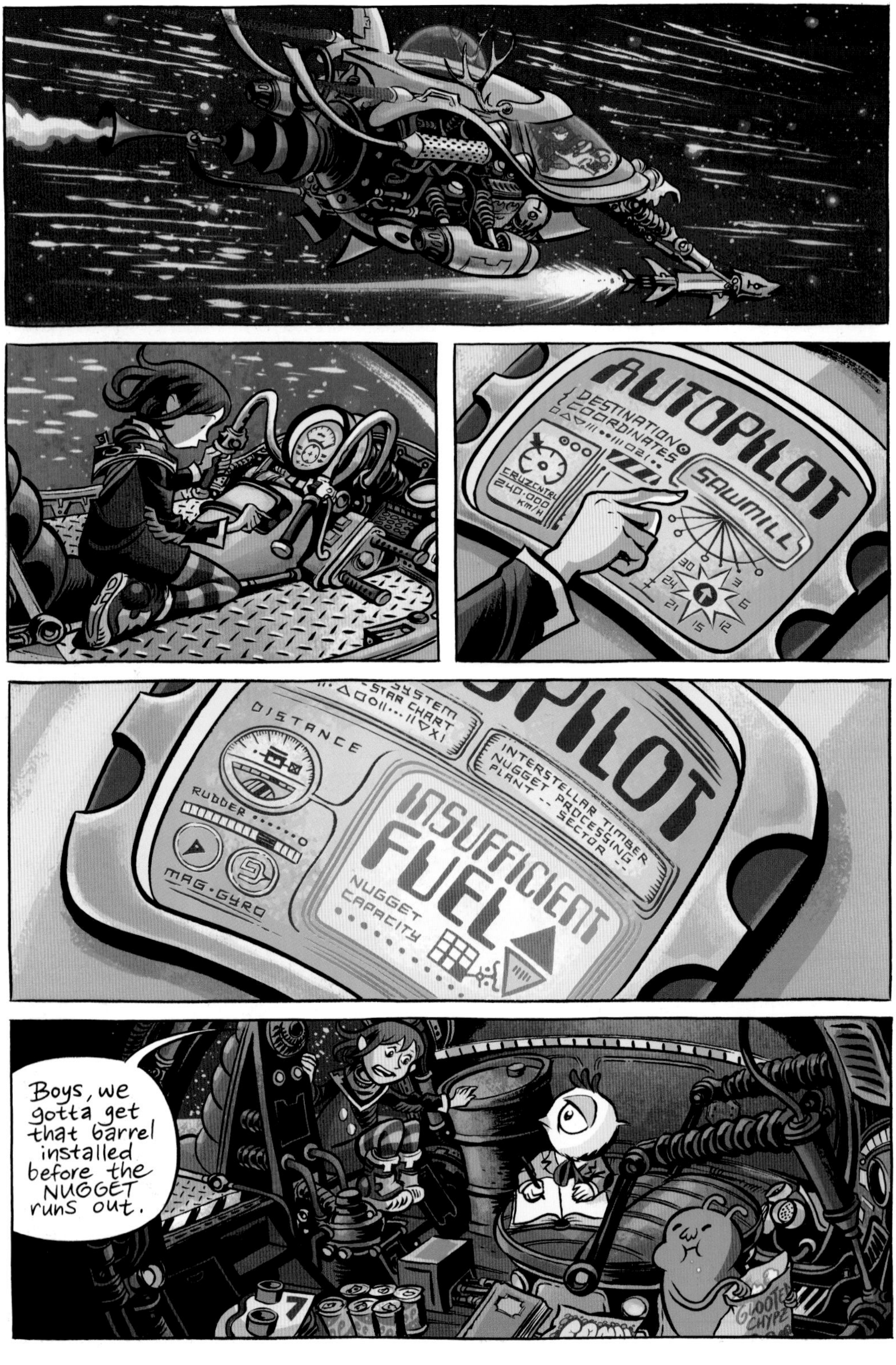
AUTOPILOT
DESTINATION COORDINATES
CRUZCNTRL 240.000 KM/H
SAWMILL
STAR CHART
SYSTEM
DISTANCE
RUDDER
MAG-GYRO
INTERSTELLAR TIMBER NUGGET PROCESSING PLANT -- SECTOR --
INSUFFICIENT FUEL
NUGGET CAPACITY
Boys, we gotta get that barrel installed before the NUGGET runs out.
GLOOTED CHYPZ

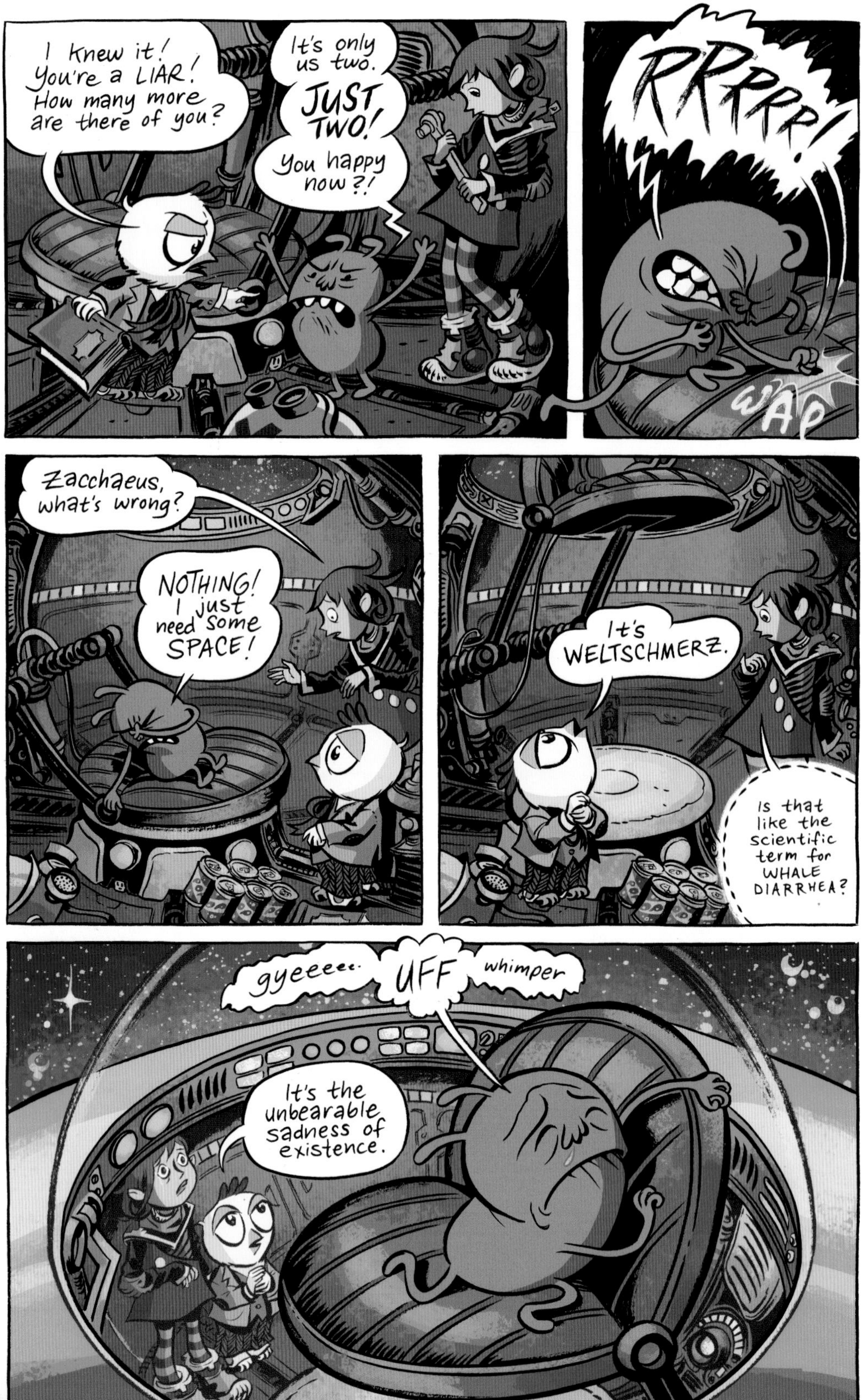
I knew it! You're a LIAR! How many more are there of you?
It's only us two. JUST TWO! You happy now?!
RRRRR!
WAP
Zacchaeus, what's wrong?
NOTHING! I just need some SPACE!
It's WELTSCHMERZ.
Is that like the scientific term for WHALE DIARRHEA?
gyeeee..
UFF
whimper
It's the unbearable sadness of existence.

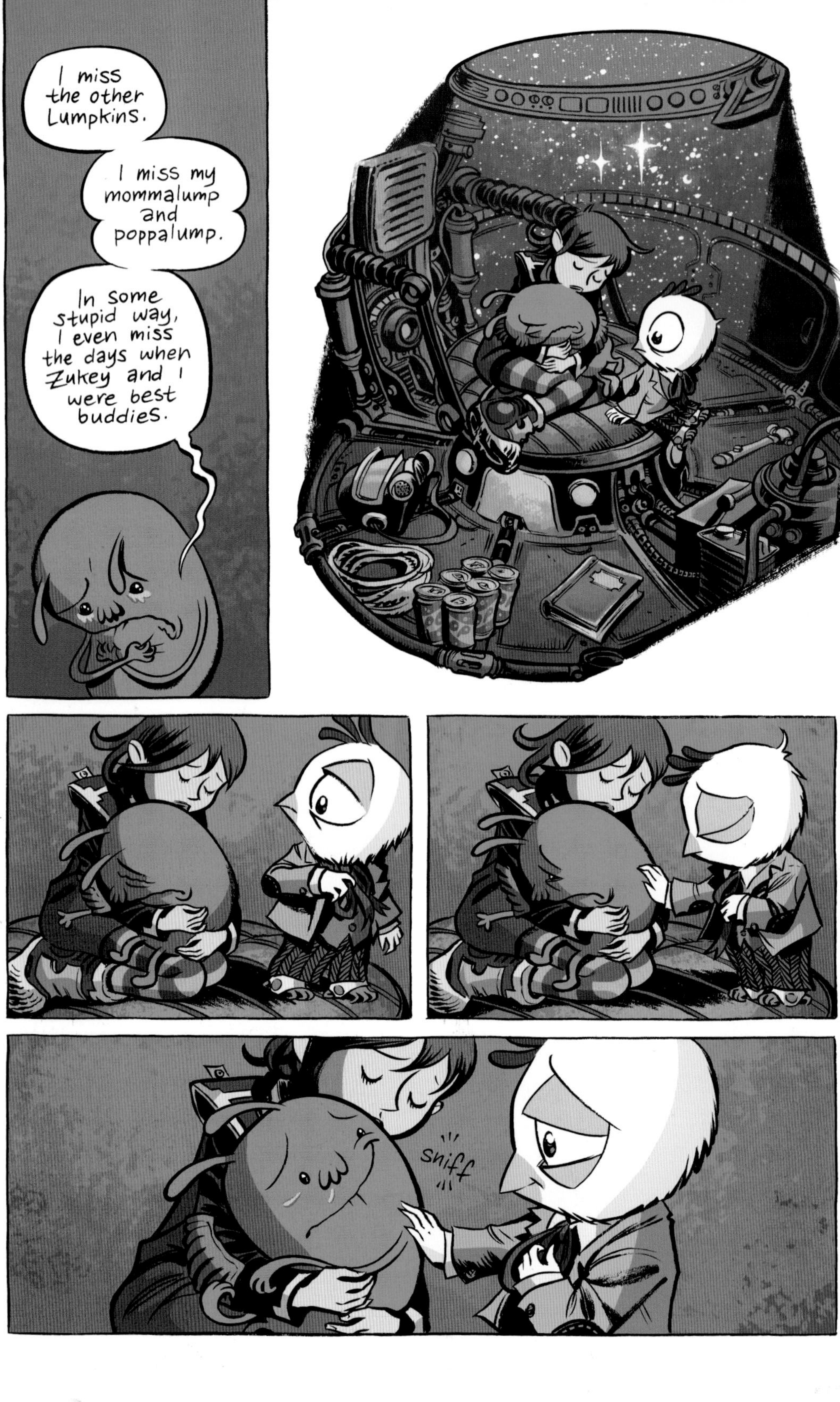

I miss the other Lumpkins.
I miss my mommalump and poppalump.
In some stupid way, I even miss the days when Zukey and I were best buddies.
sniff

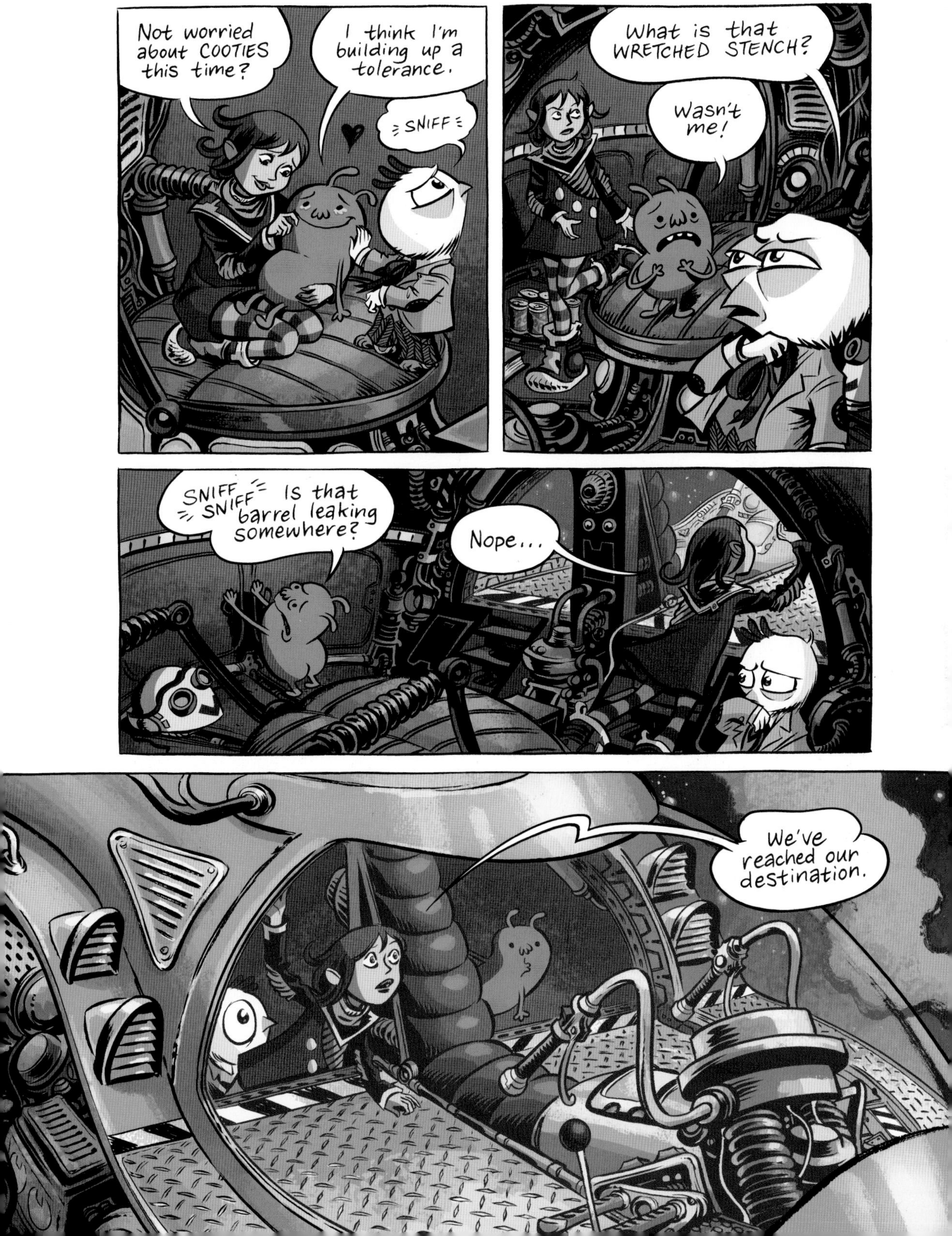
Not worried about COOTIES this time?
I think I'm building up a tolerance.
SNIFF
What is that WRETCHED STENCH?
Wasn't me!
SNIFF SNIFF Is that barrel leaking somewhere?
Nope...
We've reached our destination.

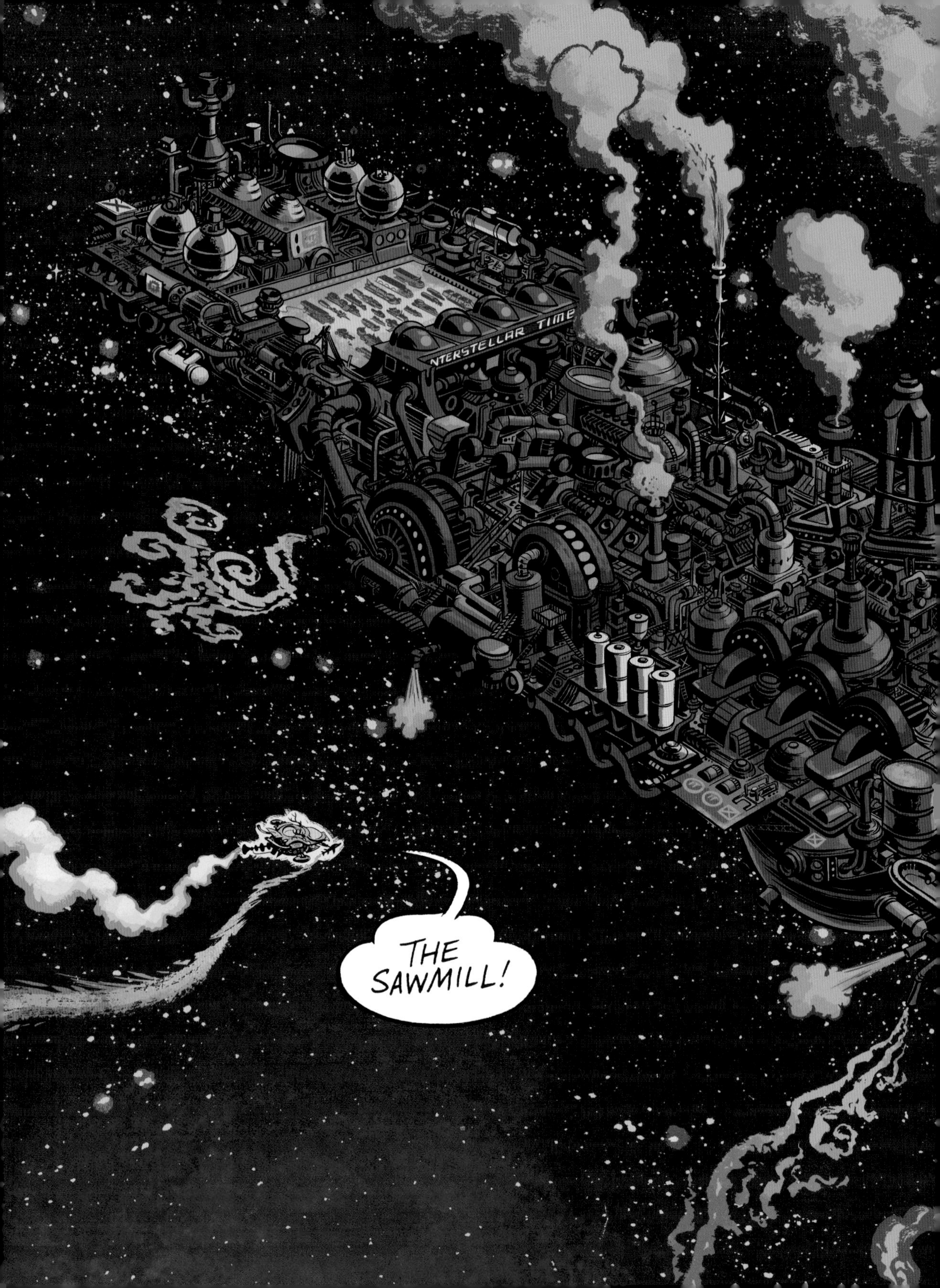
NTERSTELLAR TIME
THE SAWMILL!

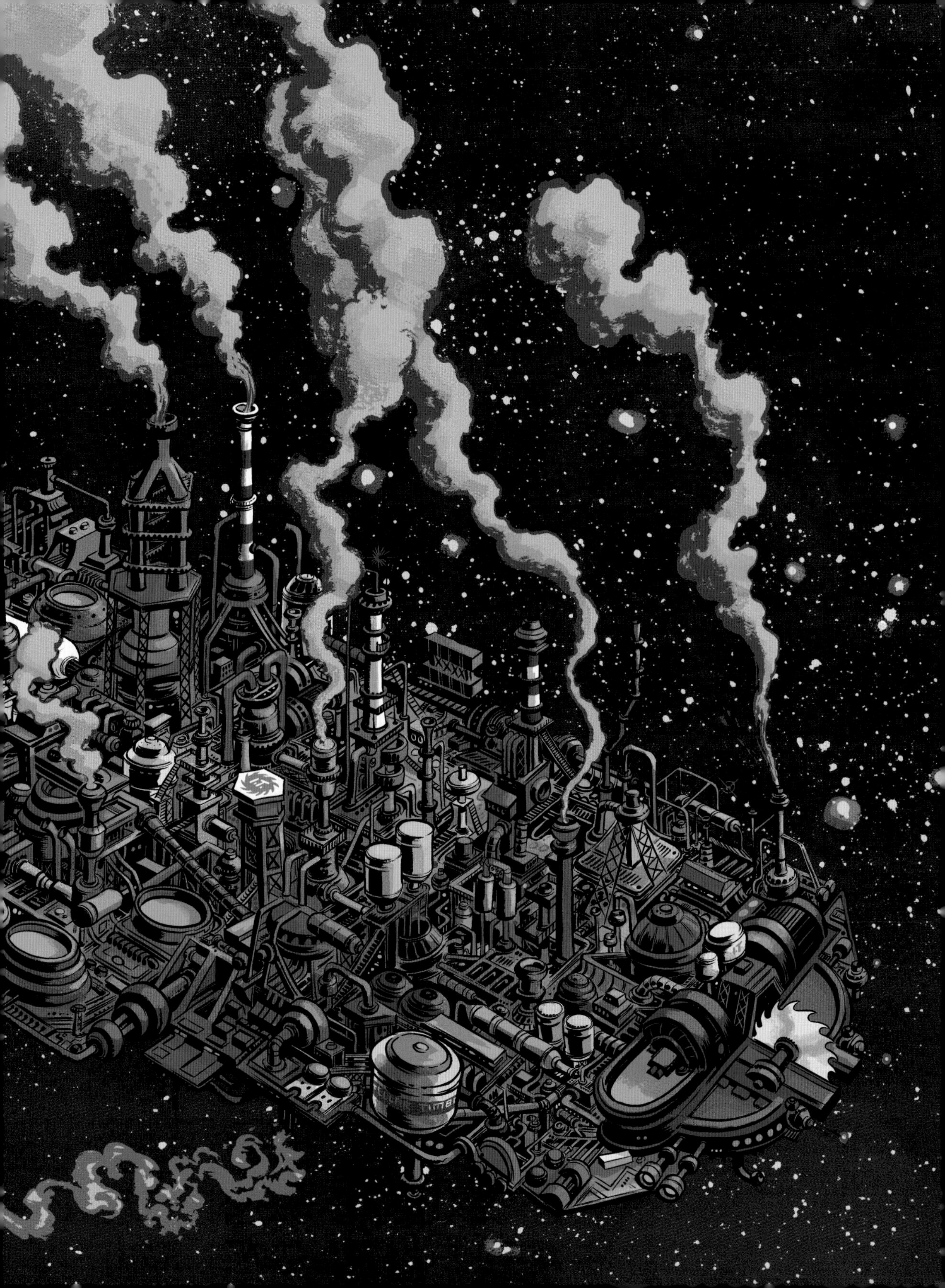

04
Occupational Hazard

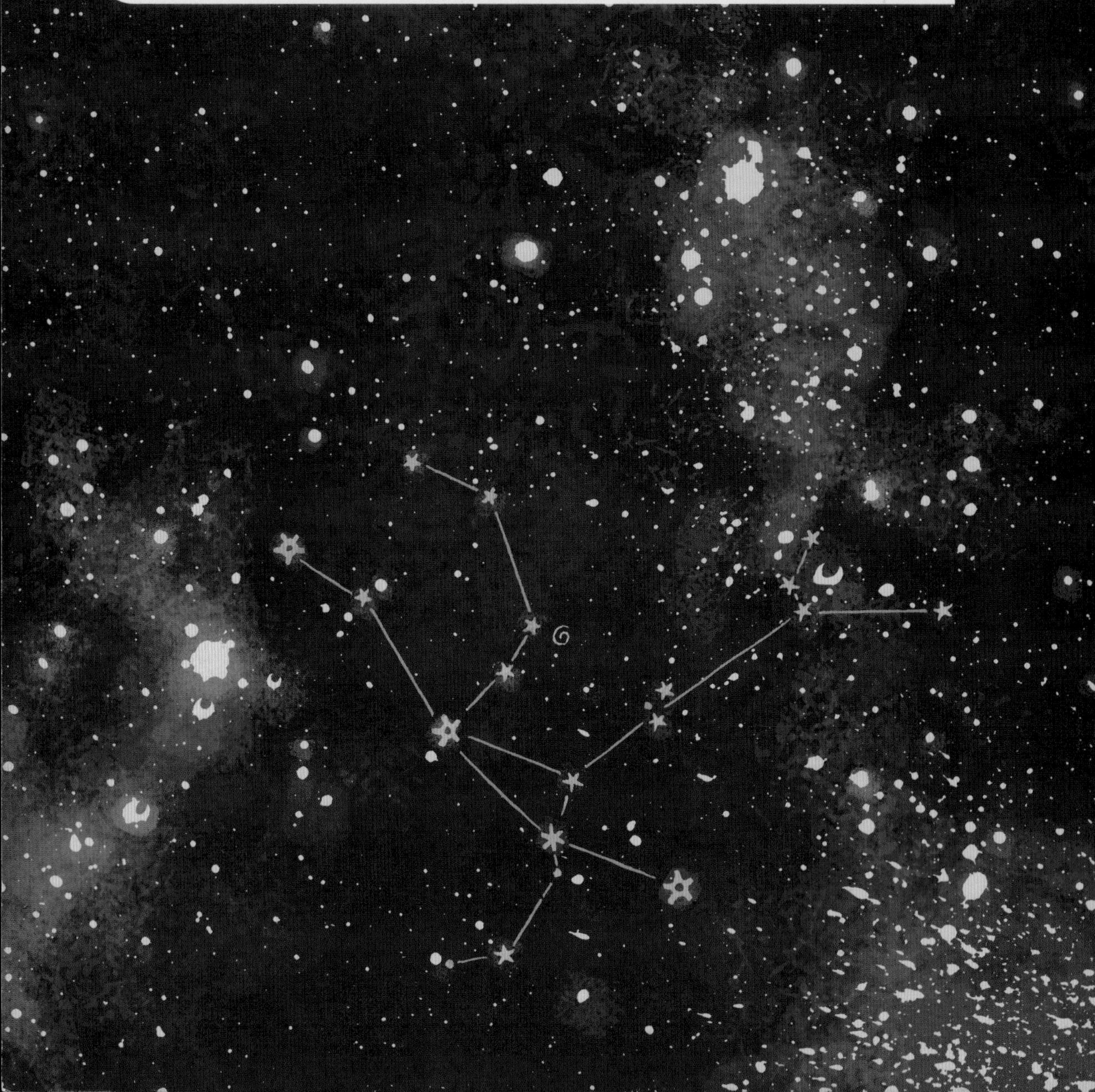

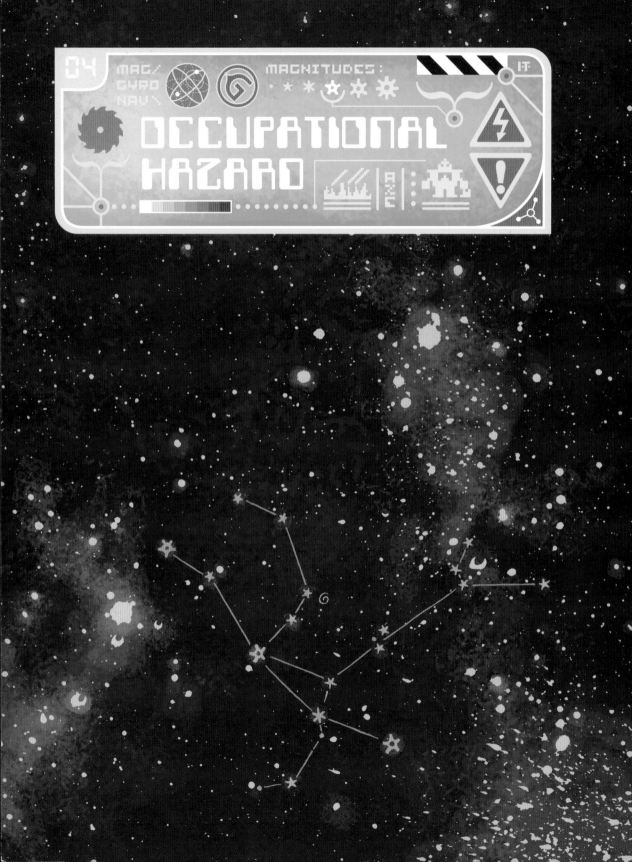

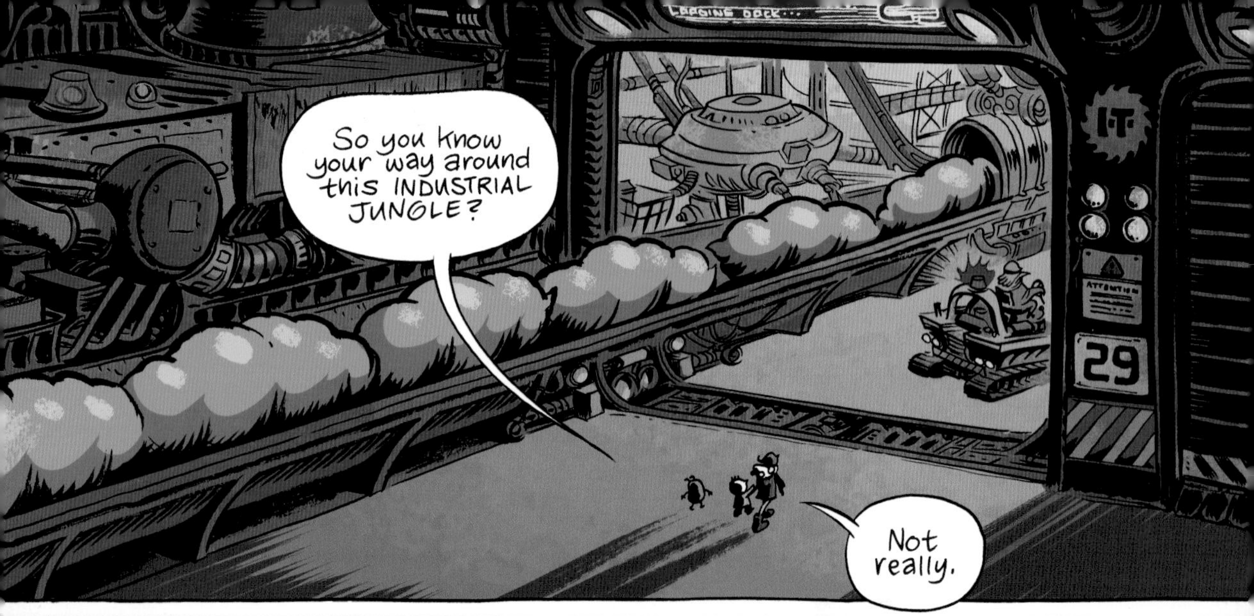
29
So you know your way around this INDUSTRIAL JUNGLE?
Not really.

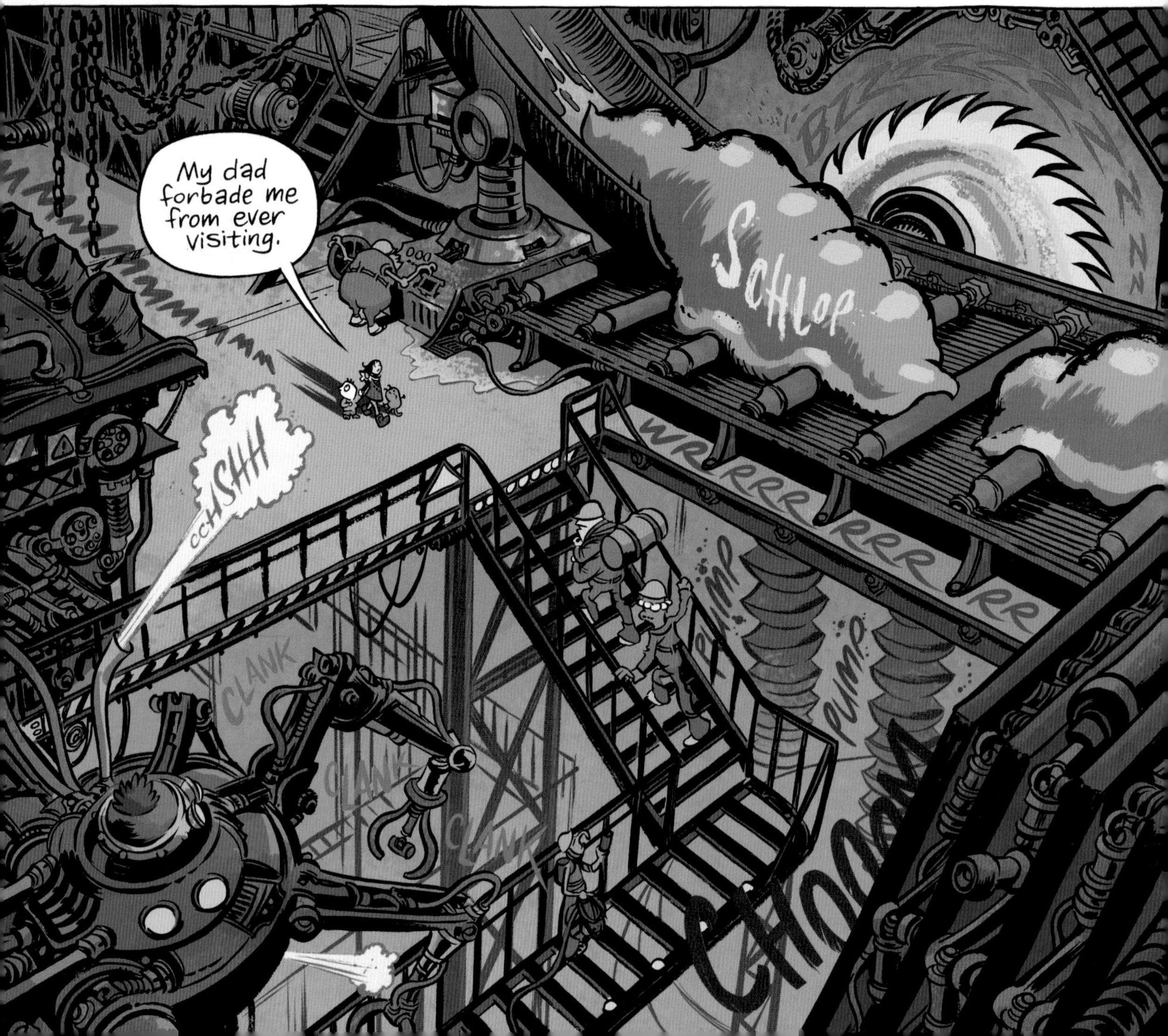
My dad forbade me from ever visiting.
SCHLOP
CCHSHH
PUMP
PUMP
CLANK
CLANK
CLANK

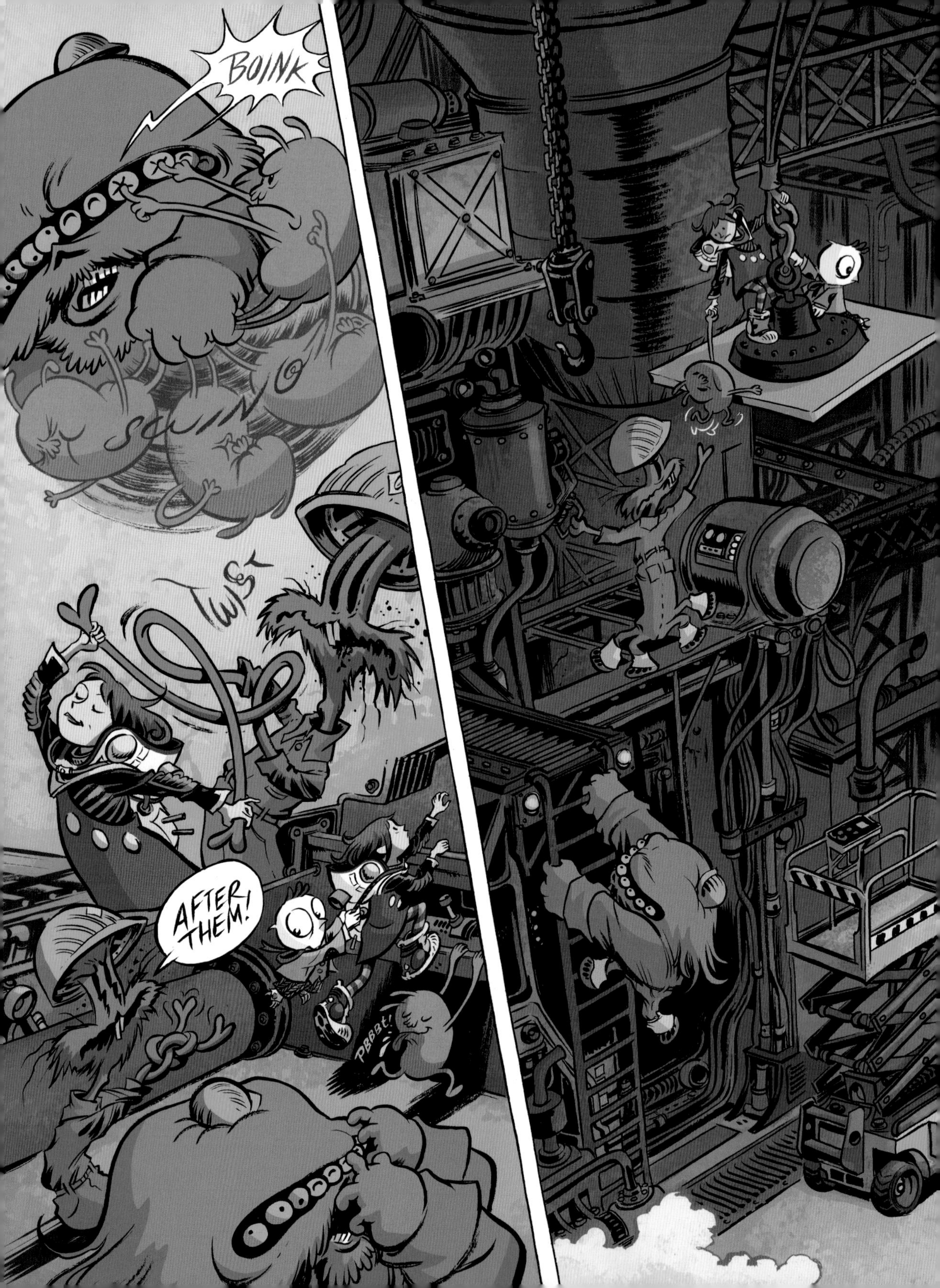
BOINK
TWIST
AFTER THEM!
PBBBt!

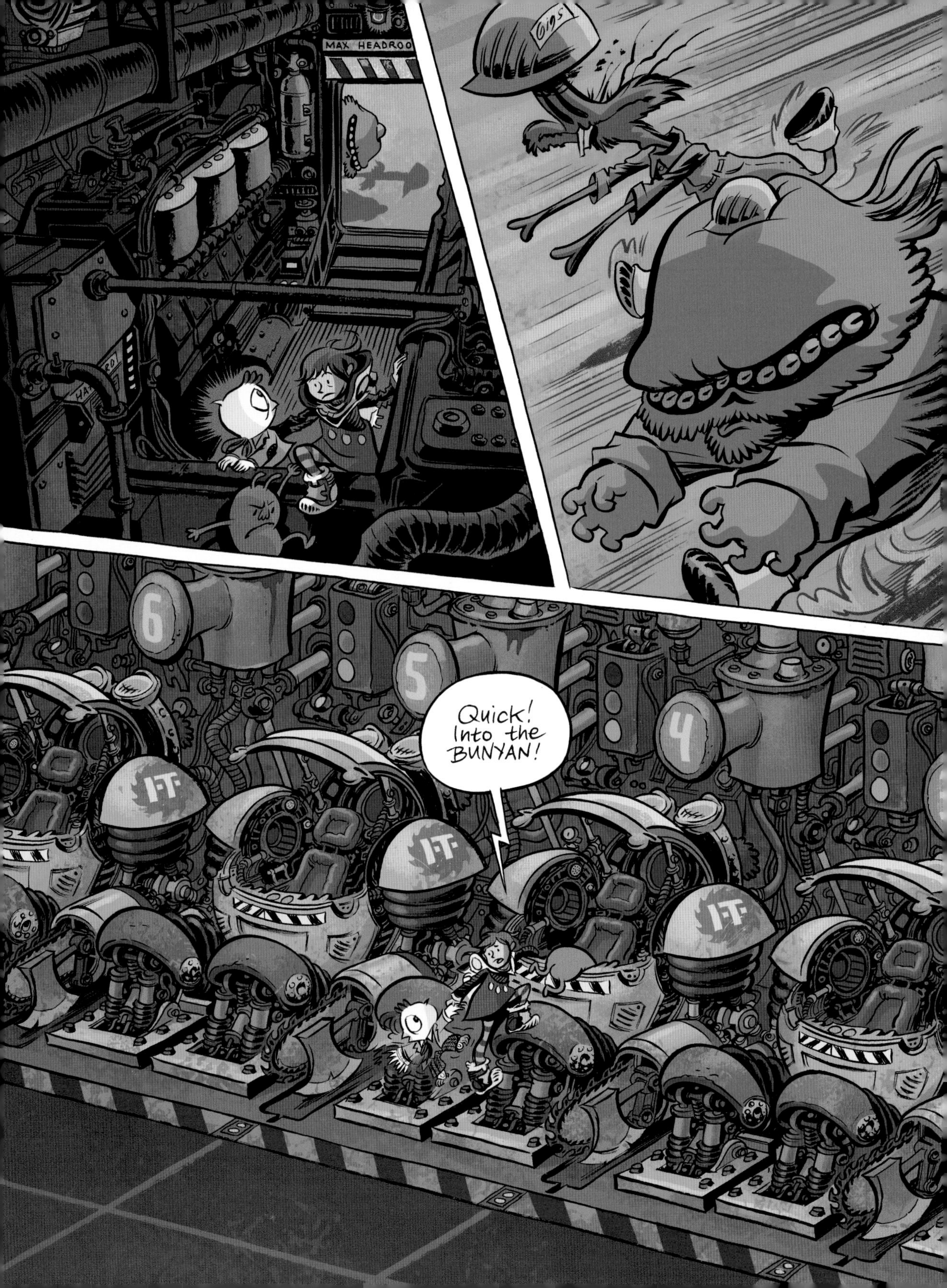
Quick! Into the BUNYAN!

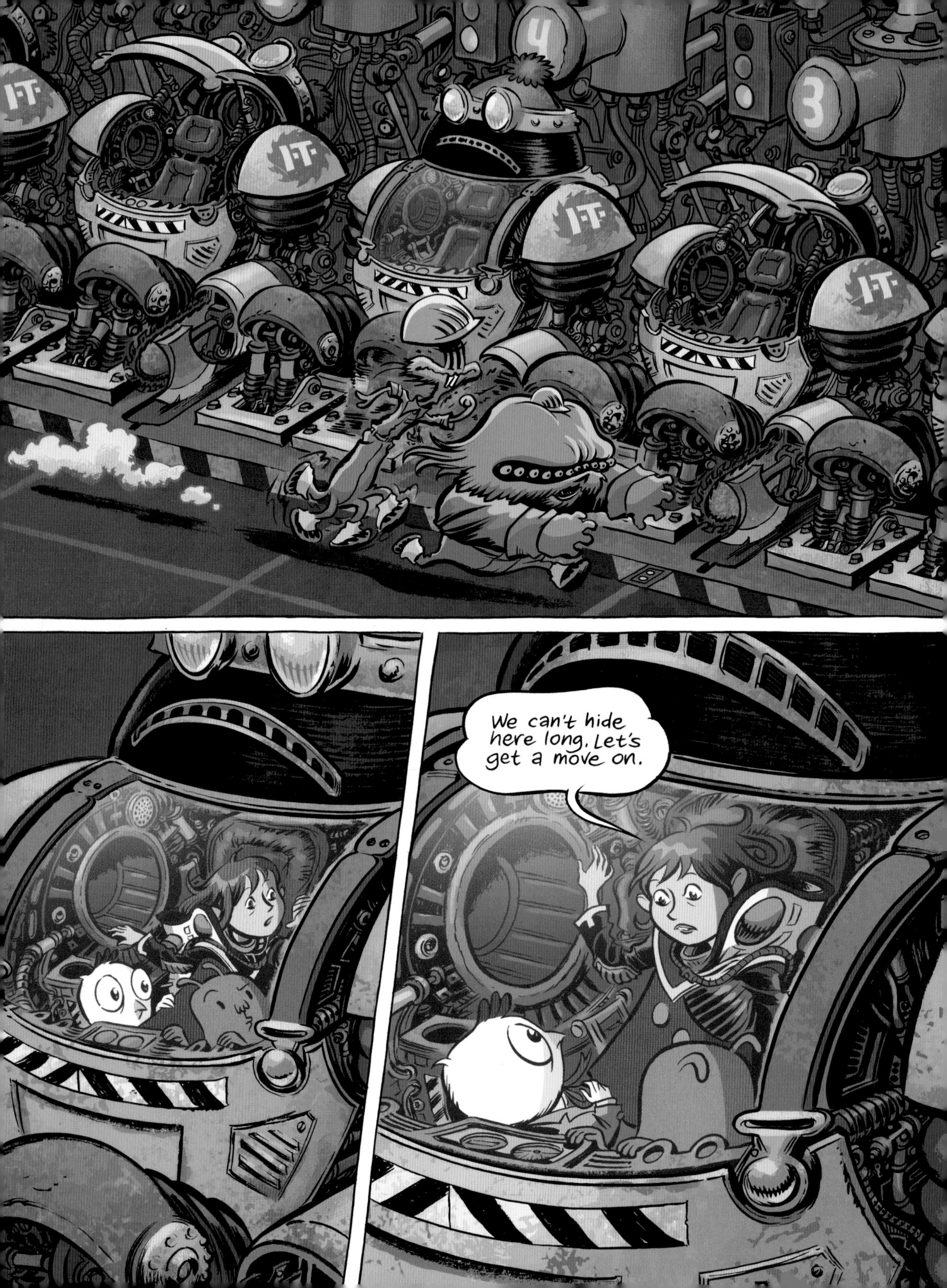
We can't hide here long. Let's get a move on.

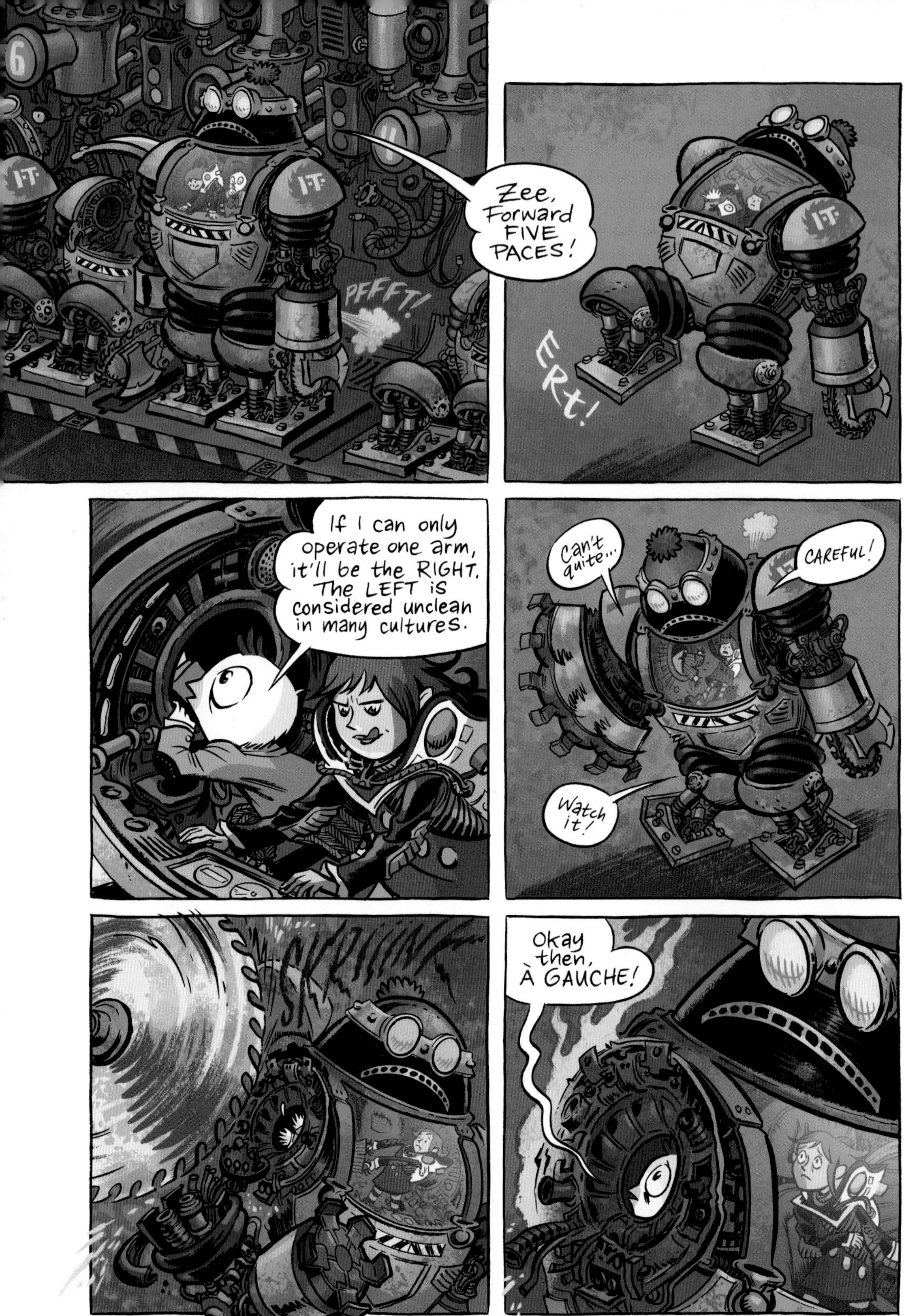

6
Zee, Forward FIVE PACES!
PFFFT!
ERt!
If I can only operate one arm, it'll be the RIGHT. The LEFT is considered unclean in many cultures.
Can't quite...
CAREFUL!
Watch it!
SKRZINK
Okay then, À GAUCHE!

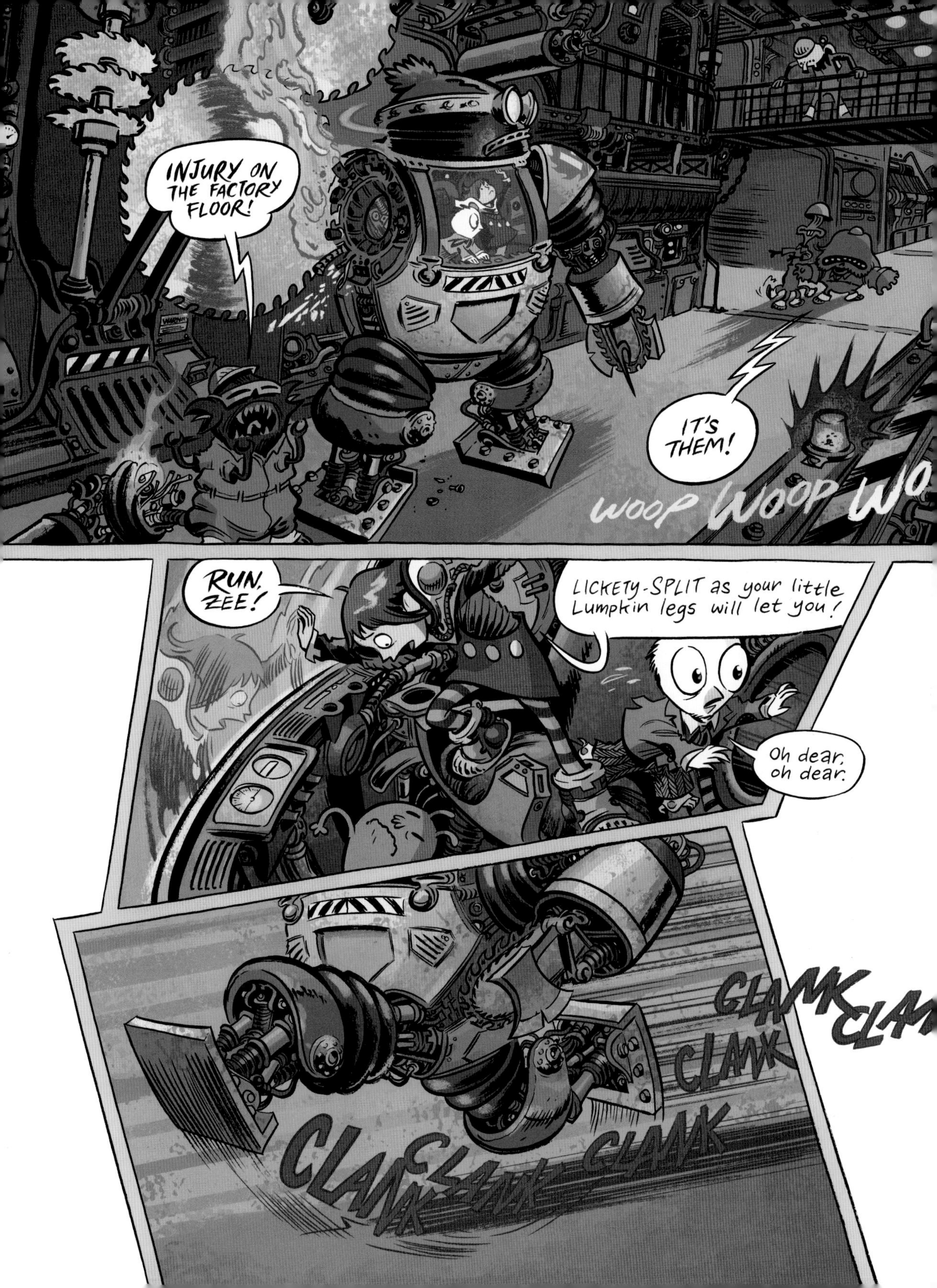
INJURY ON THE FACTORY FLOOR!
IT'S THEM!
WOOP WOOP WO
RUN, ZEE!
LICKETY-SPLIT as your little Lumpkin legs will let you!
Oh dear, oh dear.
CLANK CLANK
CLANK
CLANK CLANK
CLANK

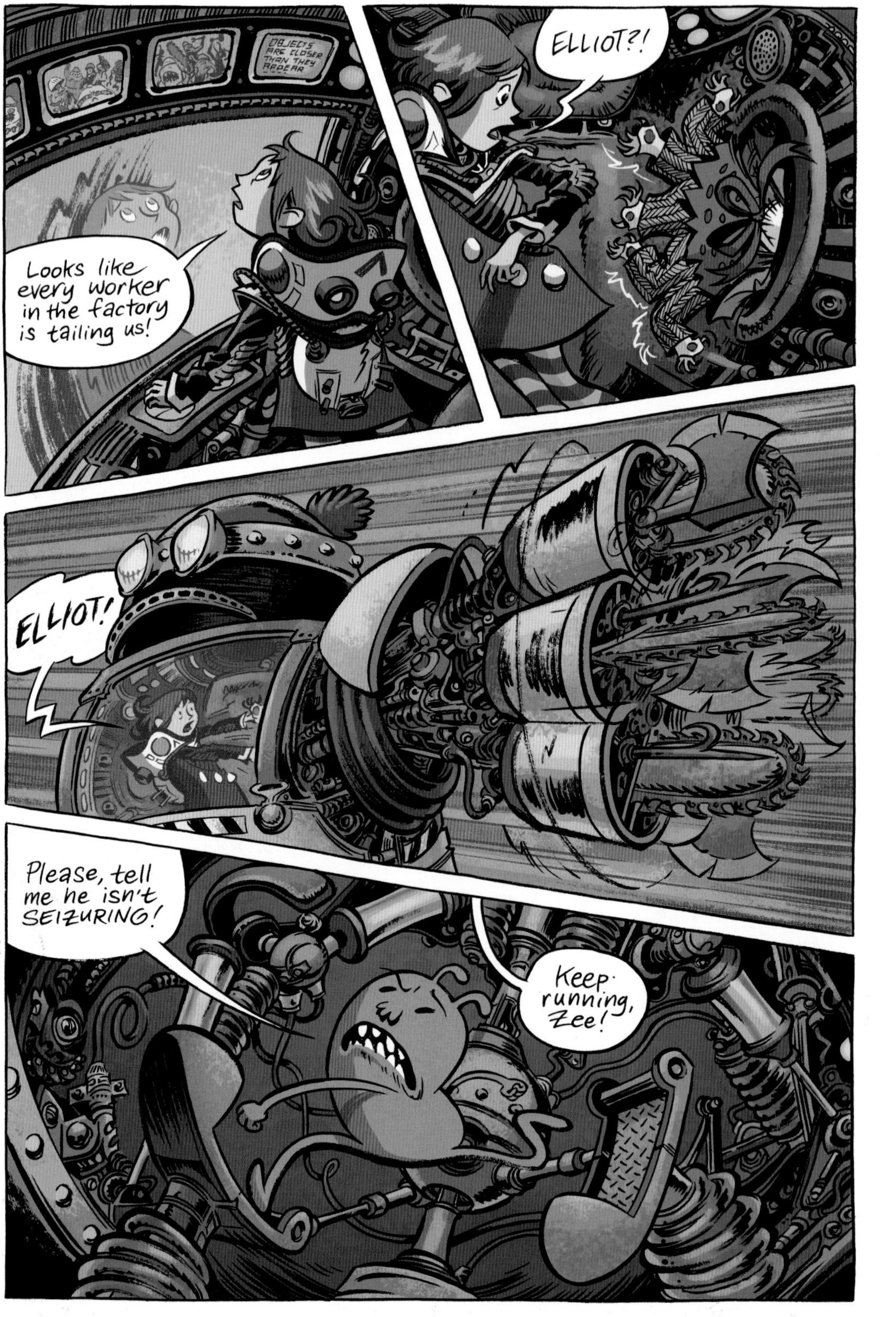
OBJECTS ARE CLOSER THAN THEY APPEAR
Looks like every worker in the factory is tailing us!
ELLIOT?!
ELLIOT!
Please, tell me he isn't SEIZURING!
Keep running, Zee!

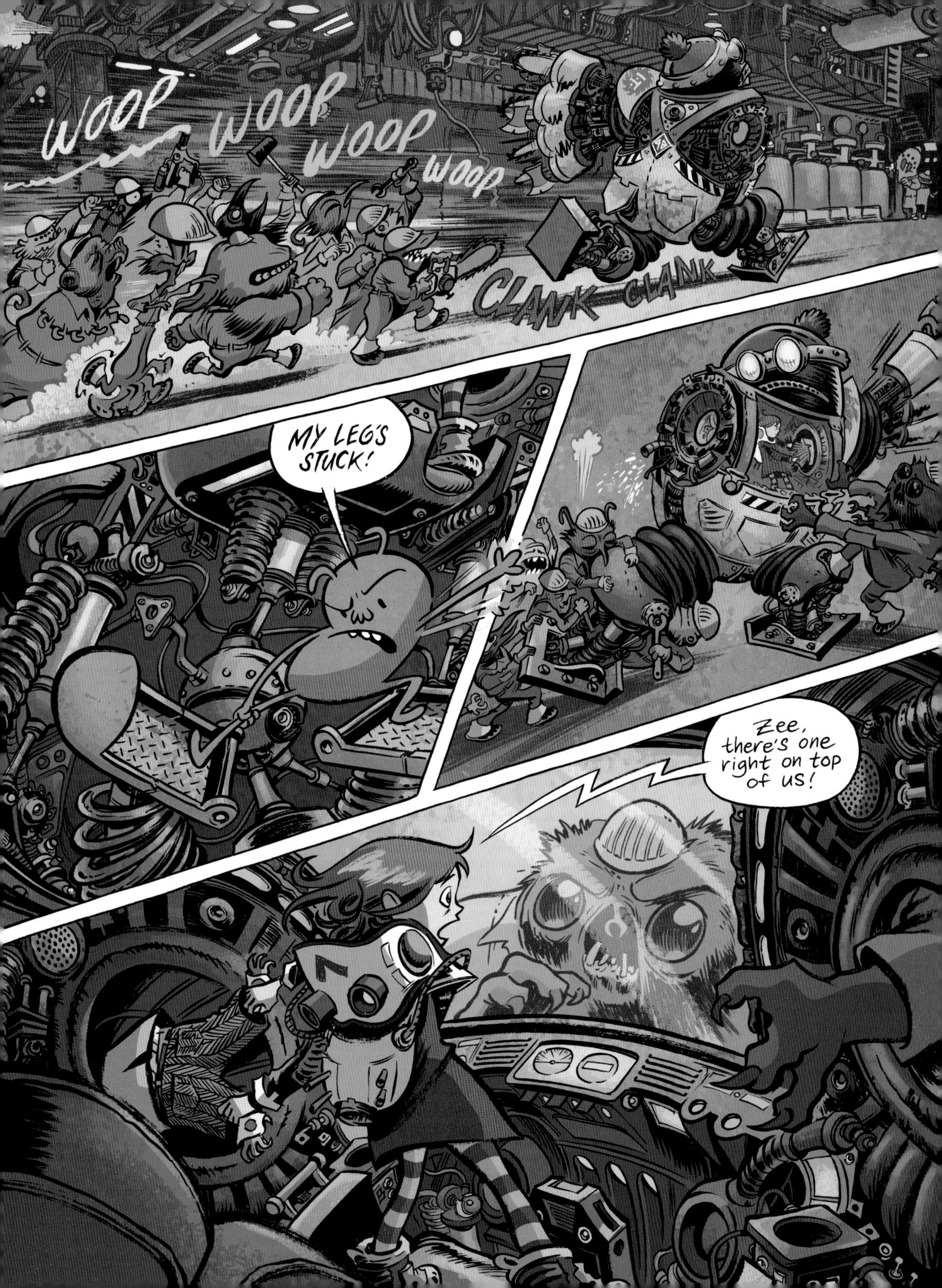
WOOP WOOP WOOP WOOP
CLANK CLANK
MY LEG'S STUCK!
Zee, there's one right on top of us!

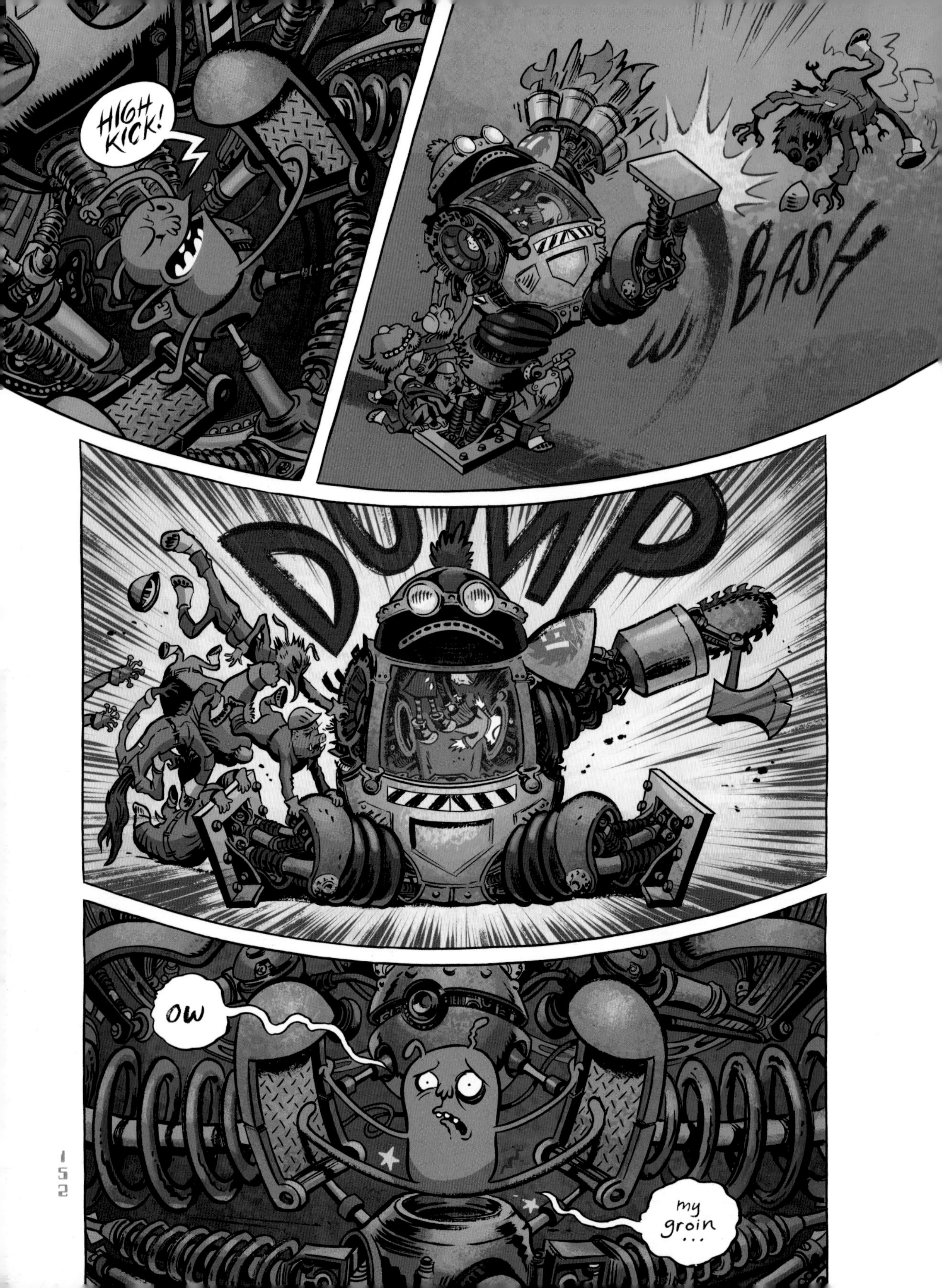
HIGH KICK!
BASH
DUMP
OW
my groin . . .

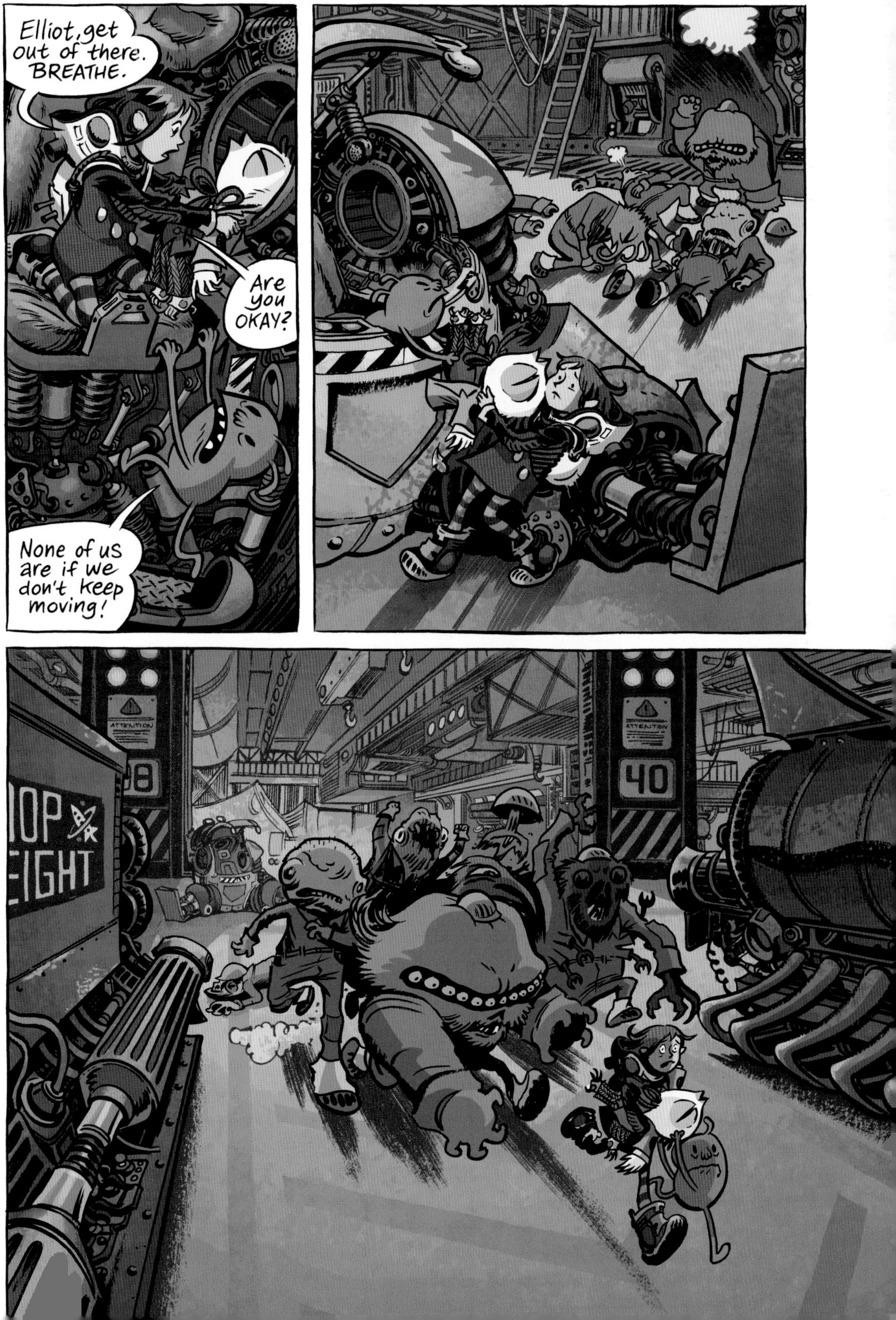
Elliot, get out of there. BREATHE.
Are you OKAY?
None of us are if we don't keep moving!
40

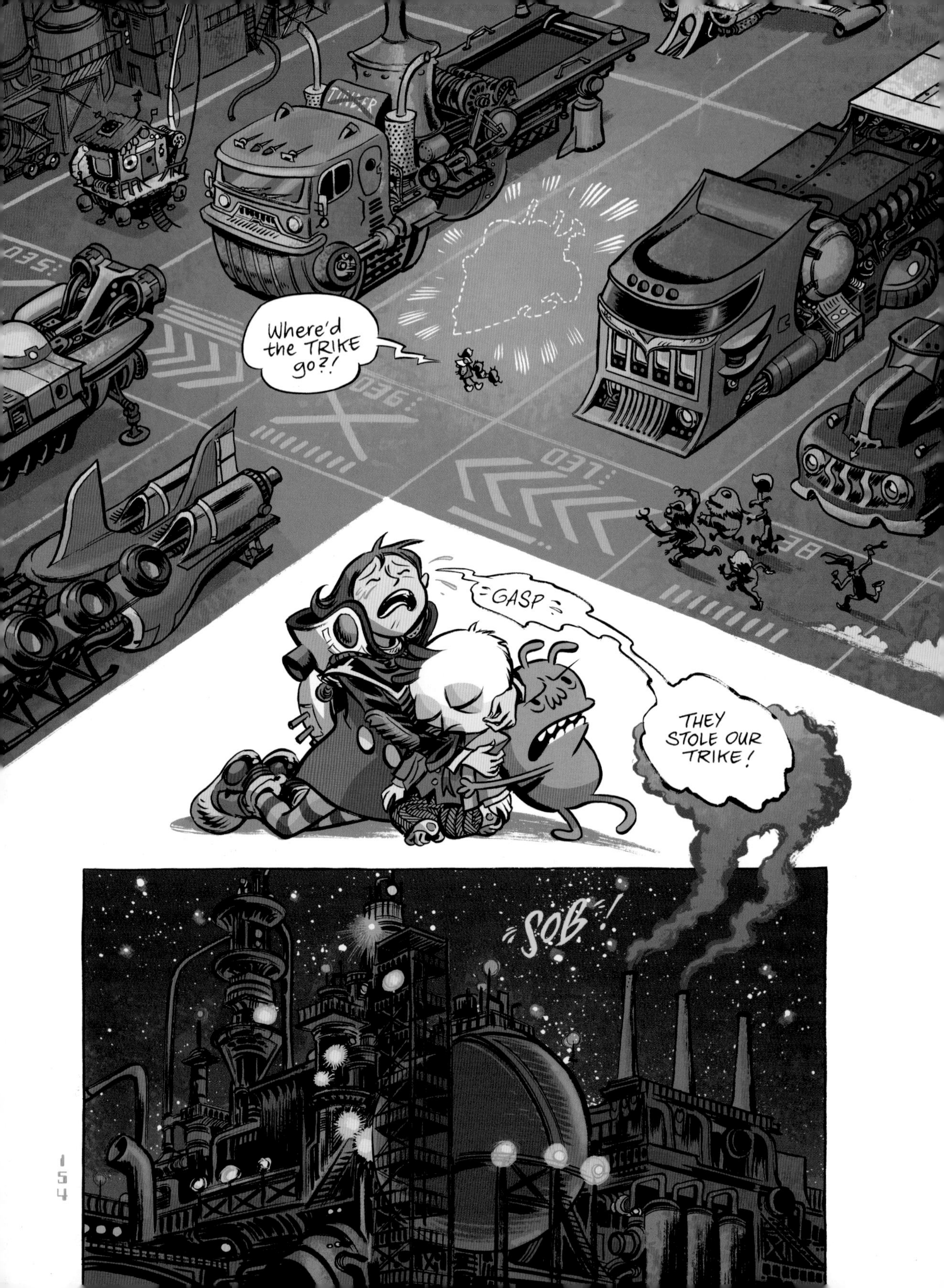
Where'd the TRIKE go?!
GASP
THEY STOLE OUR TRIKE!
SOB!

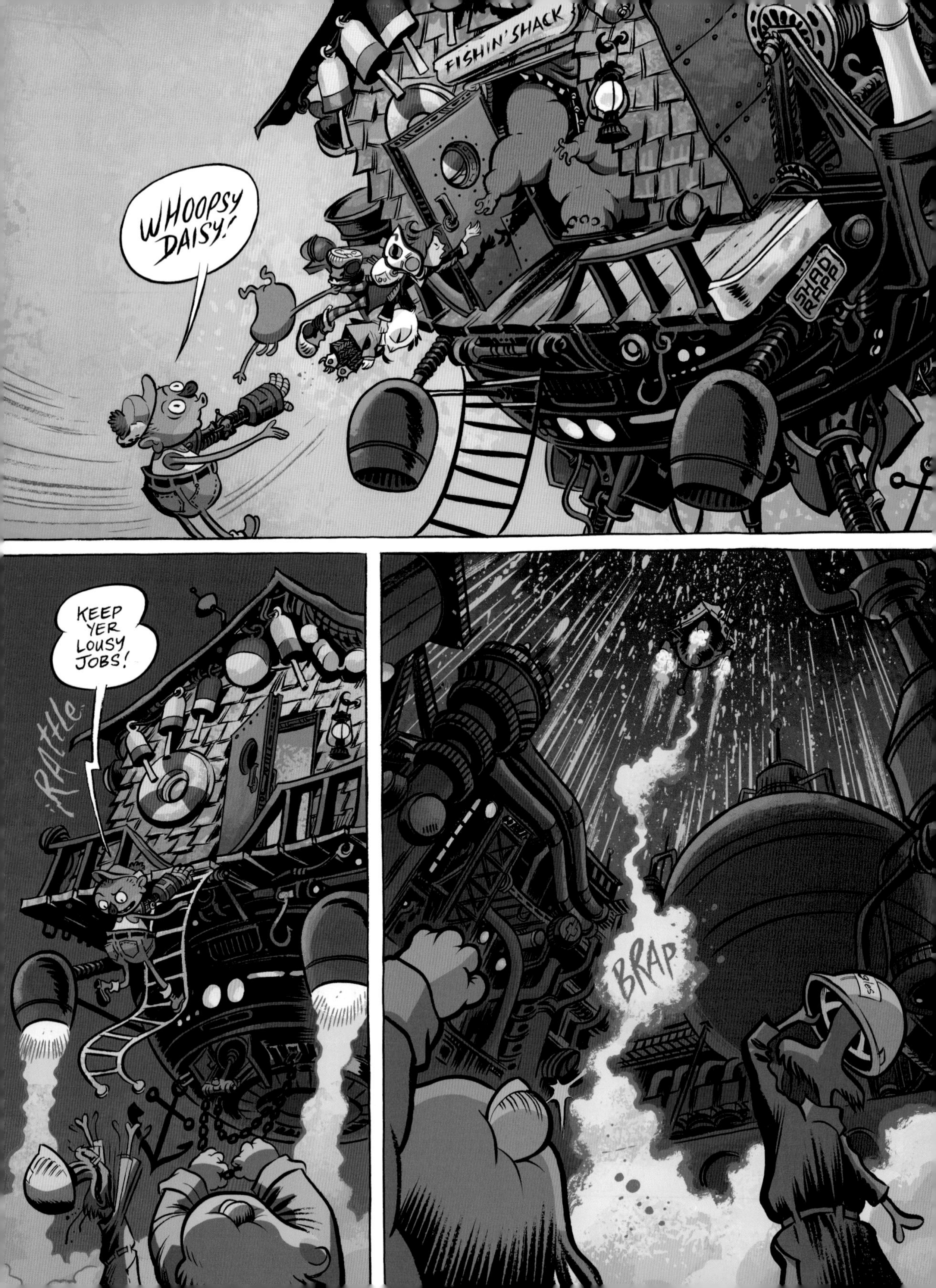
FISHIN' SHACK
WHOOPSY DAISY!
SHAD RAPP
KEEP YER LOUSY JOBS!
RATTLE
BRAP

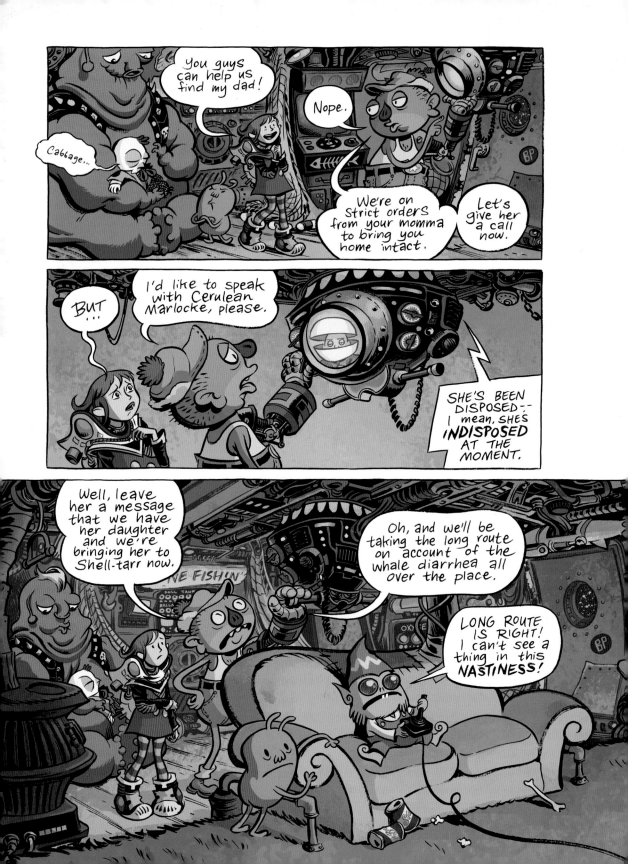

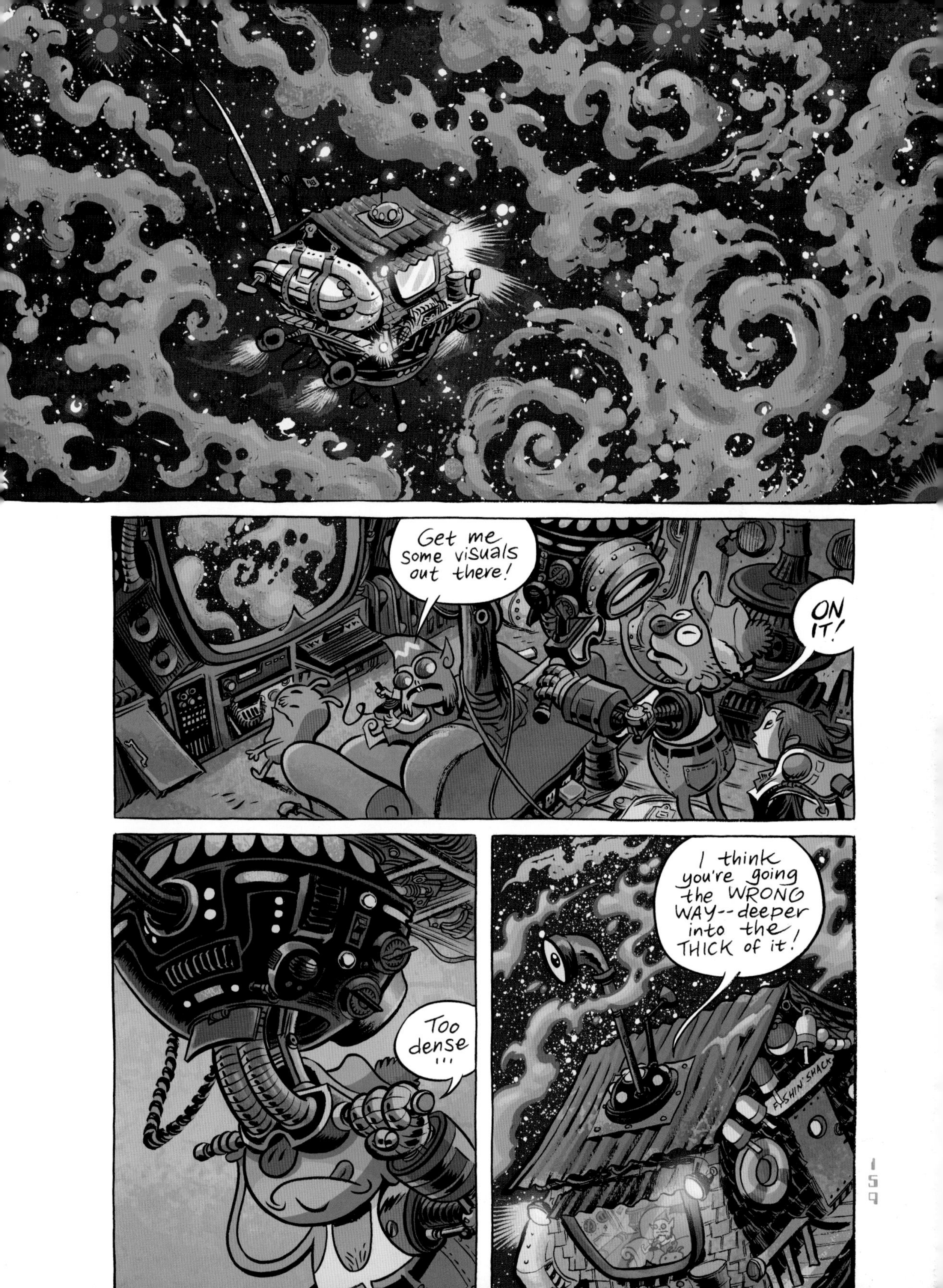
Get me some visuals out there!
ON IT!
Too dense ...
I think you're going the WRONG WAY--deeper into the THICK of it!
FISHIN' SHACK

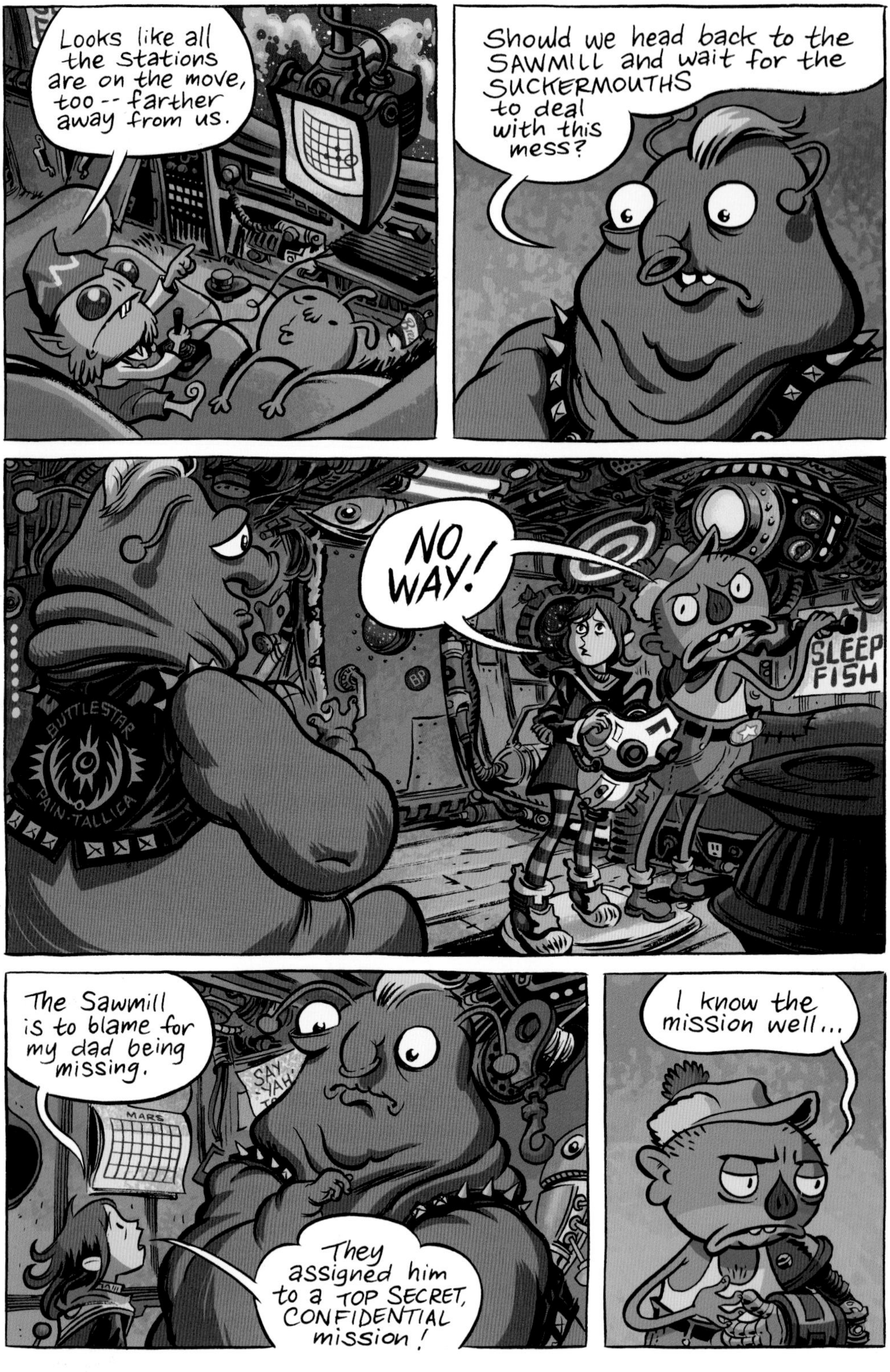
Looks like all the stations are on the move, too -- farther away from us.
Should we head back to the SAWMILL and wait for the SUCKERMOUTHS to deal with this mess?
NO WAY!
SLEEP FISH
BUTTLESTAR
PAIN-TALLICA
BP
The Sawmill is to blame for my dad being missing.
MARS
They assigned him to a TOP SECRET, CONFIDENTIAL mission!
I know the mission well...

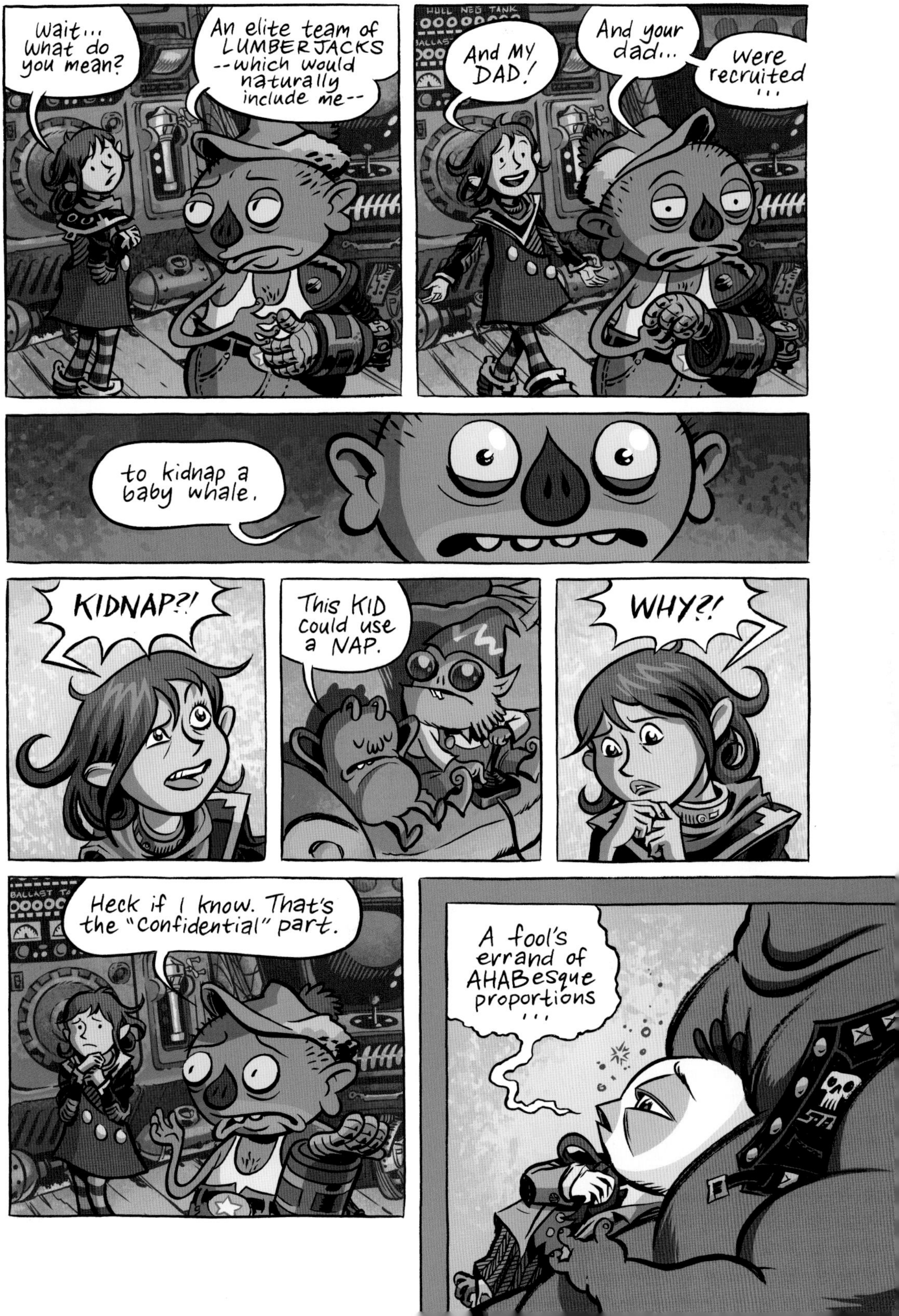
Wait... what do you mean?
An elite team of LUMBERJACKS --which would naturally include me--
HULL NEG TANK
BALLAST
And MY DAD!
And your dad...
were recruited ...
to kidnap a baby whale.
KIDNAP?!
This KID could use a NAP.
WHY?!
BALLAST TA
Heck if I know. That's the "Confidential" part.
A fool's errand of AHABesque proportions ...

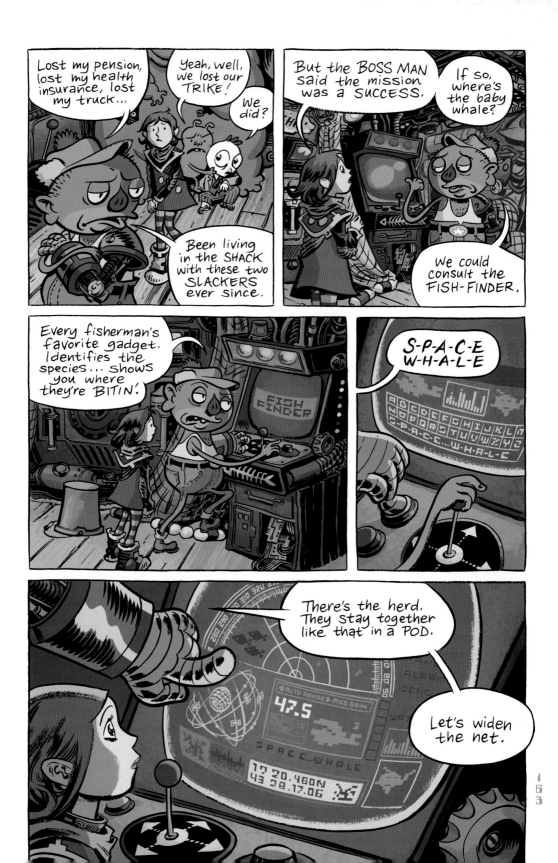

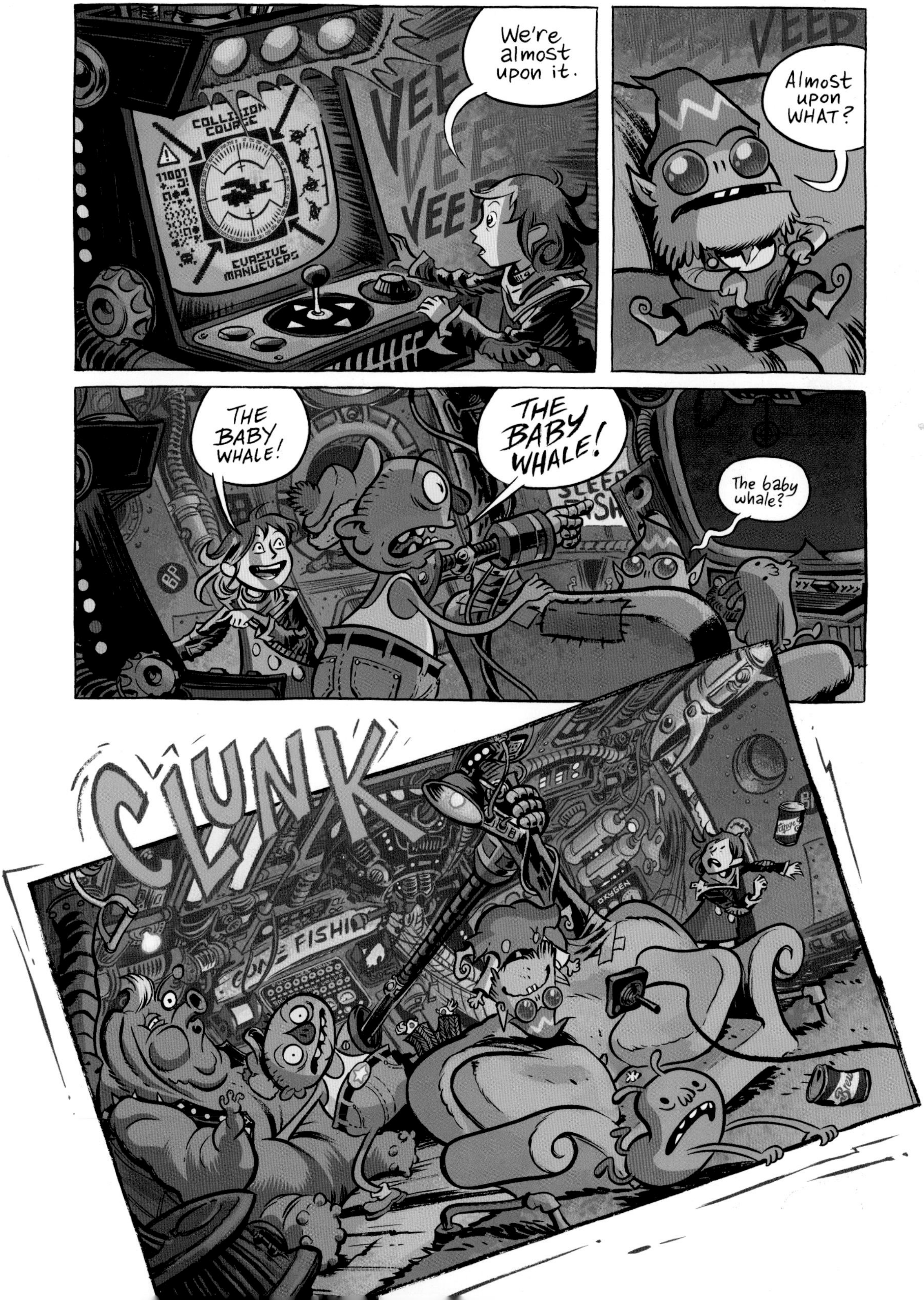
We're almost upon it.
Almost upon WHAT?
THE BABY WHALE!
THE BABY WHALE!
The baby whale?
CLUNK

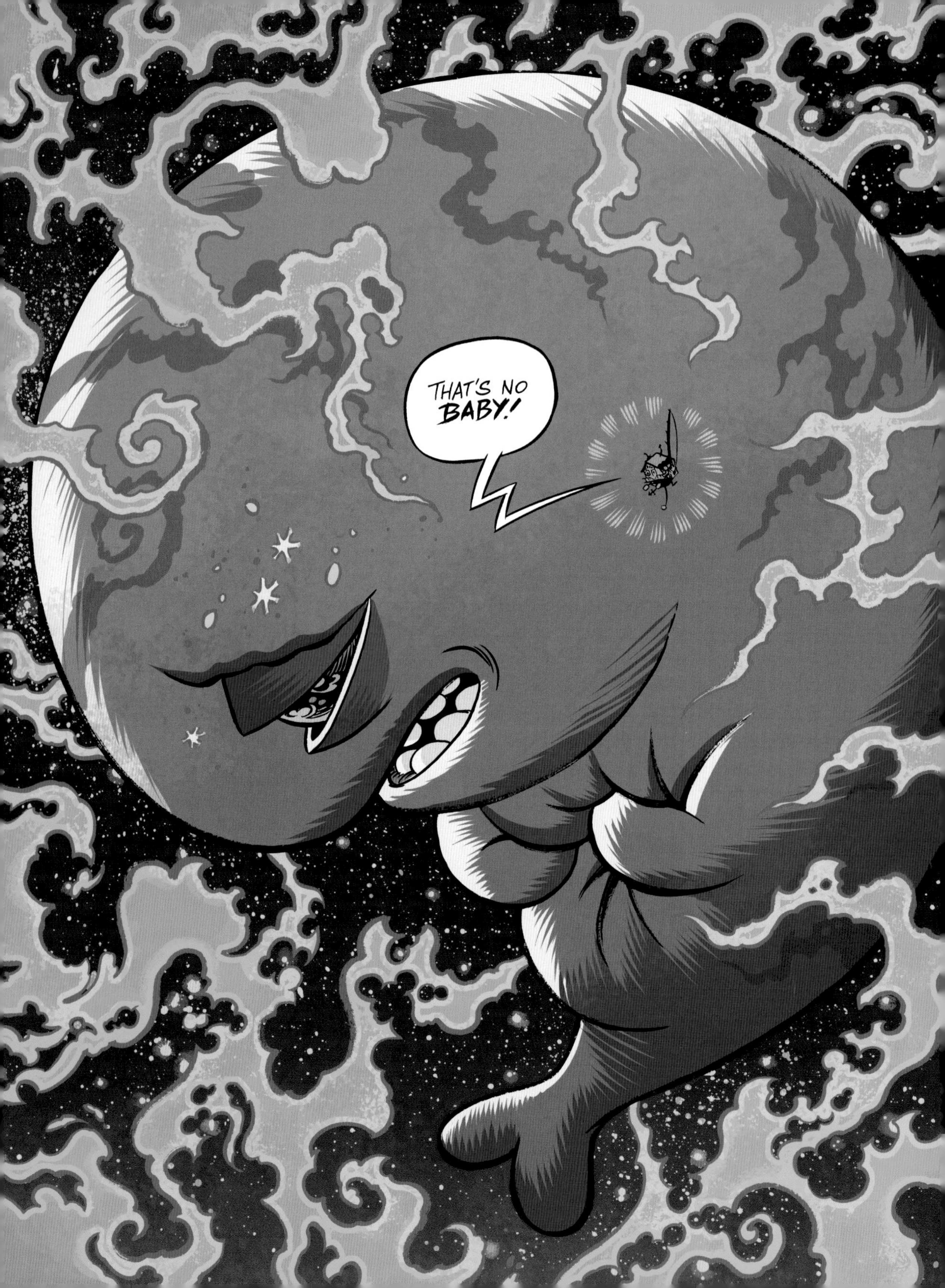
THAT'S NO BABY!

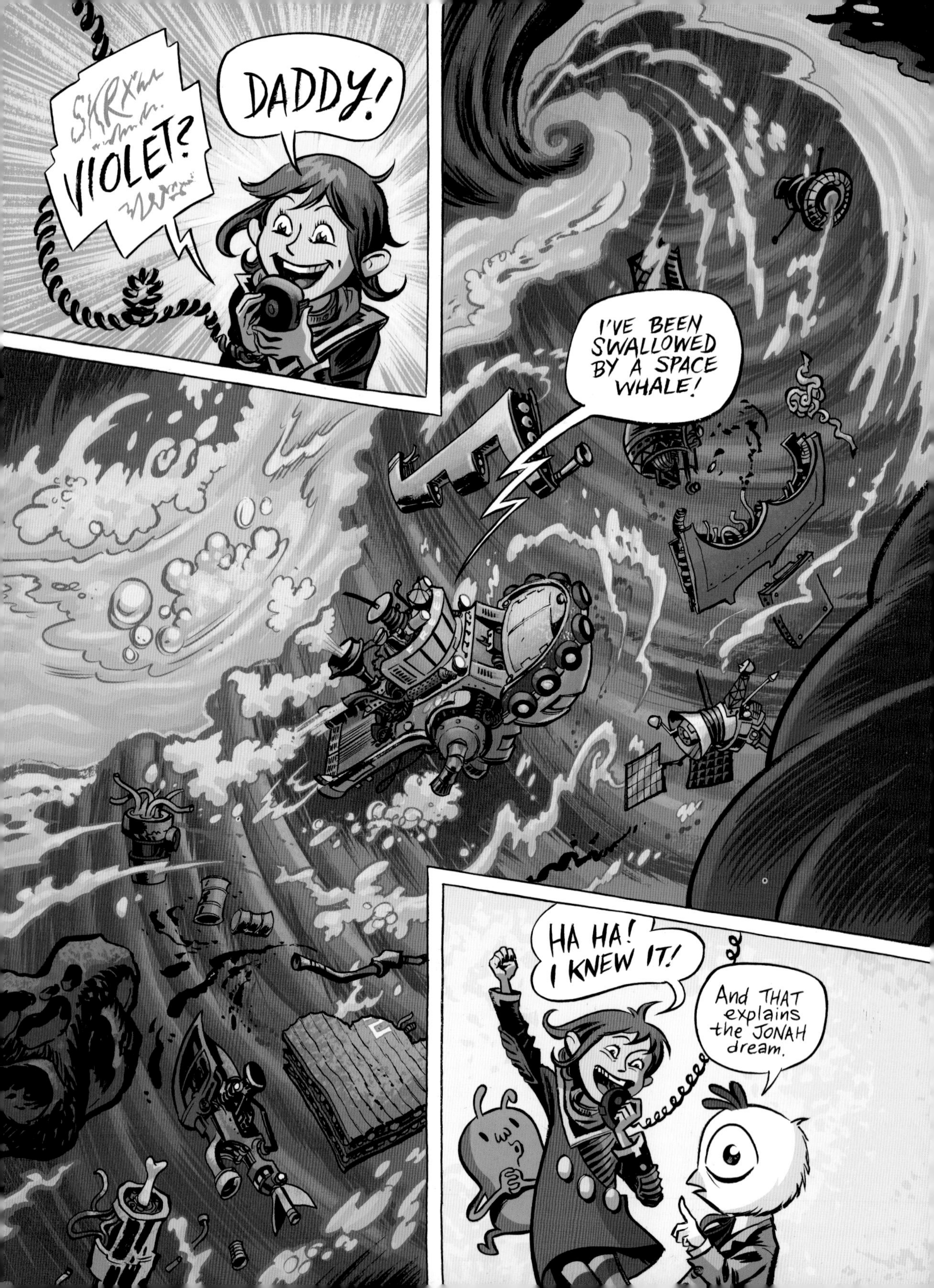
SKR
VIOLET?
DADDY!
I'VE BEEN SWALLOWED BY A SPACE WHALE!
HA HA! I KNEW IT!
And THAT explains the JONAH dream.

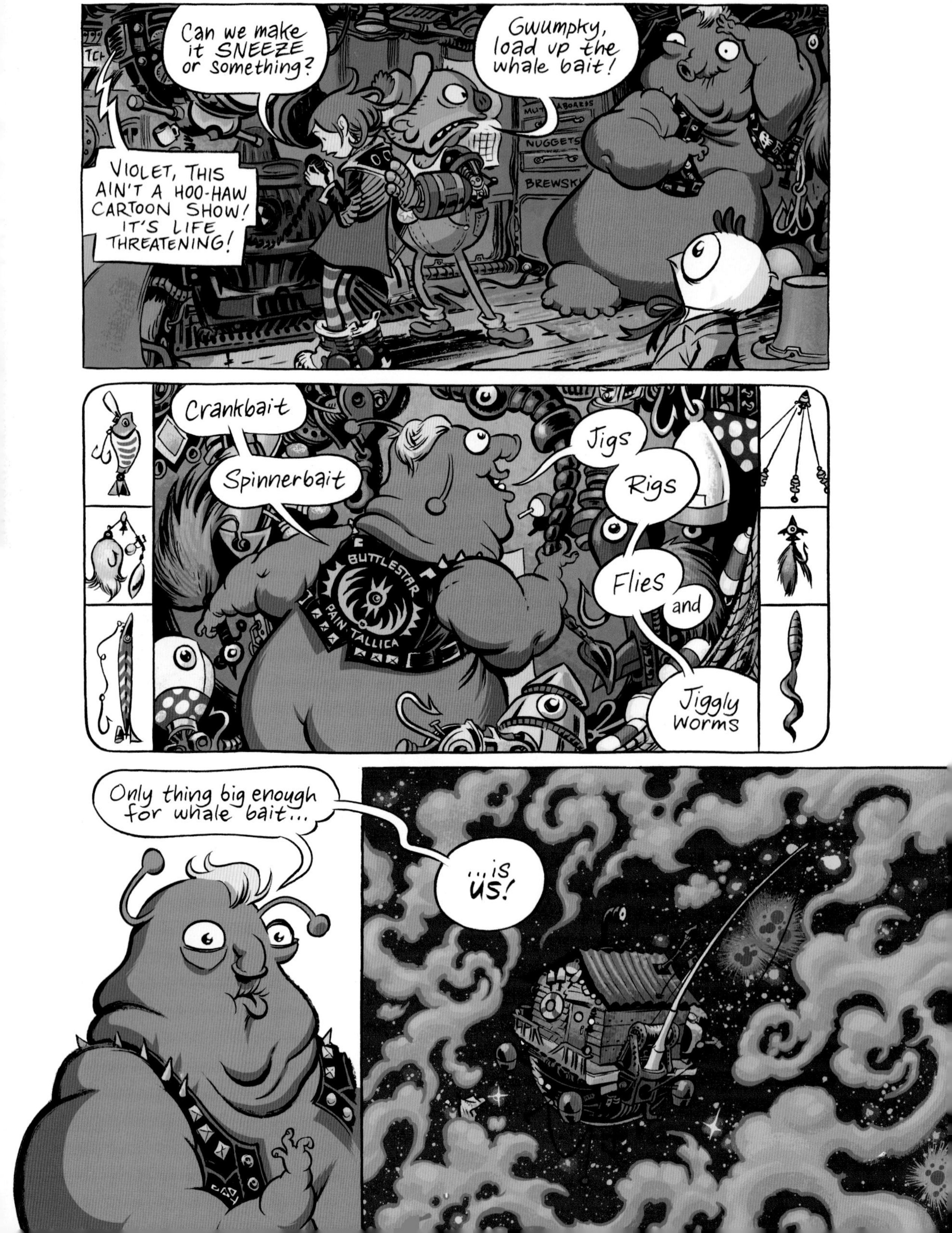
Can we make it SNEEZE or something?
Gwumpky, load up the whale bait!
VIOLET, THIS AIN'T A HOO-HAW CARTOON SHOW! IT'S LIFE THREATENING!
NUGGETS
BREWSKI
Crankbait
Spinnerbait
Jigs
Rigs
Flies
and
Jiggly worms
BUTTLESTAR PAIN-TALLICA
Only thing big enough for whale bait...
...is US!

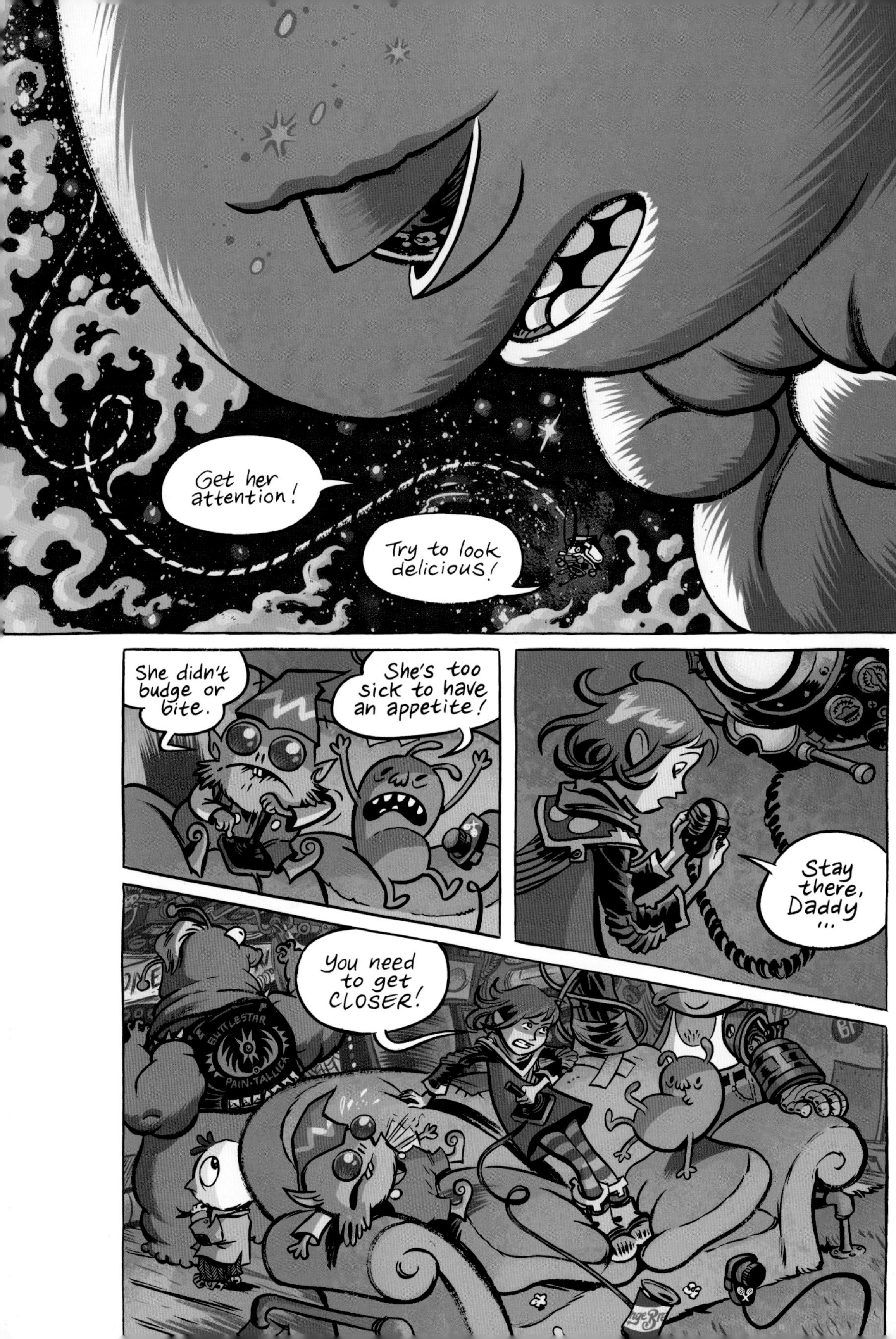
Get her attention!
Try to look delicious!
She didn't budge or bite.
She's too sick to have an appetite!
Stay there, Daddy ...
You need to get CLOSER!

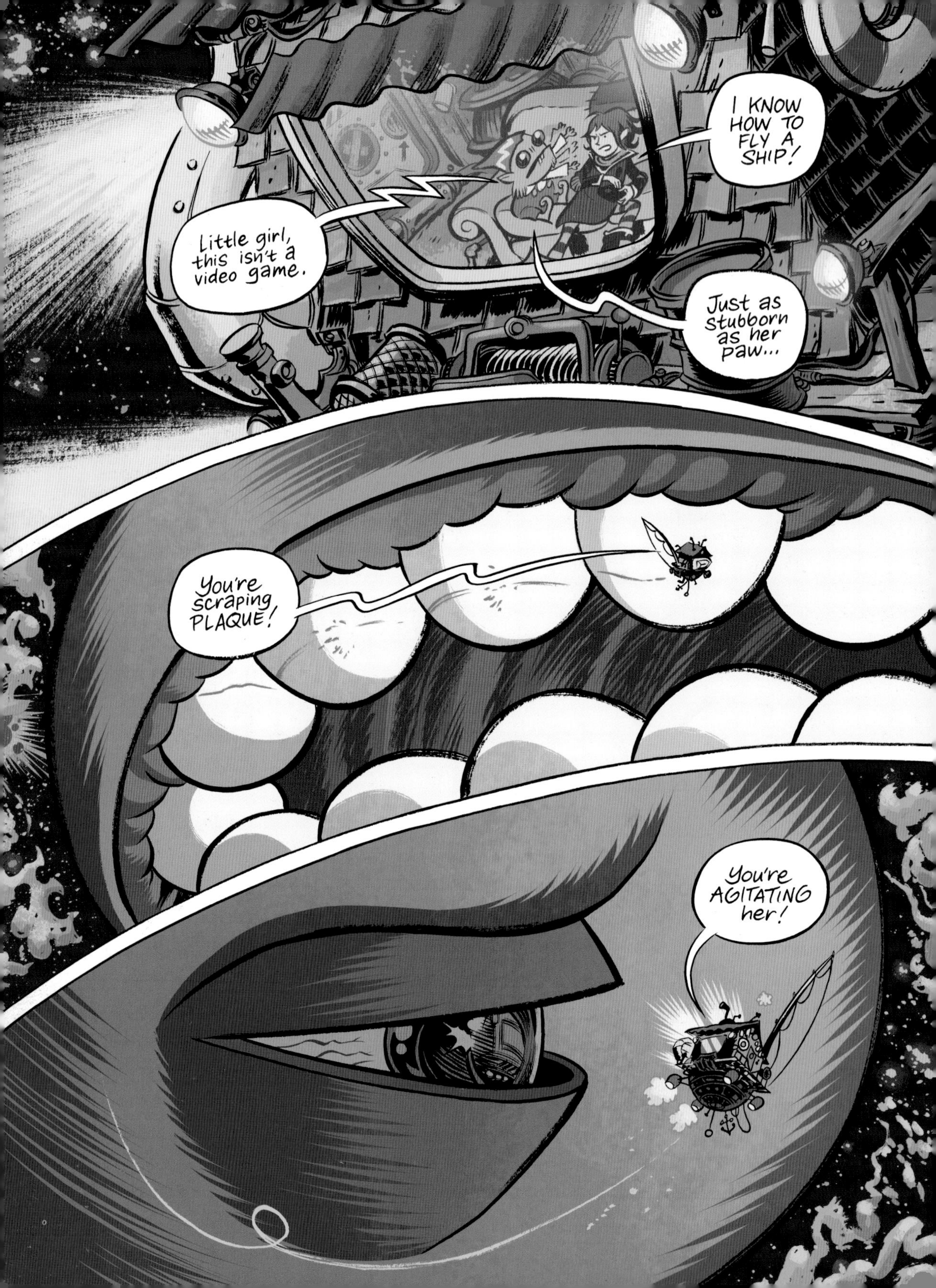
I KNOW HOW TO FLY A SHIP!
Little girl, this isn't a video game.
Just as stubborn as her paw...
You're scraping PLAQUE!
You're AGITATING her!

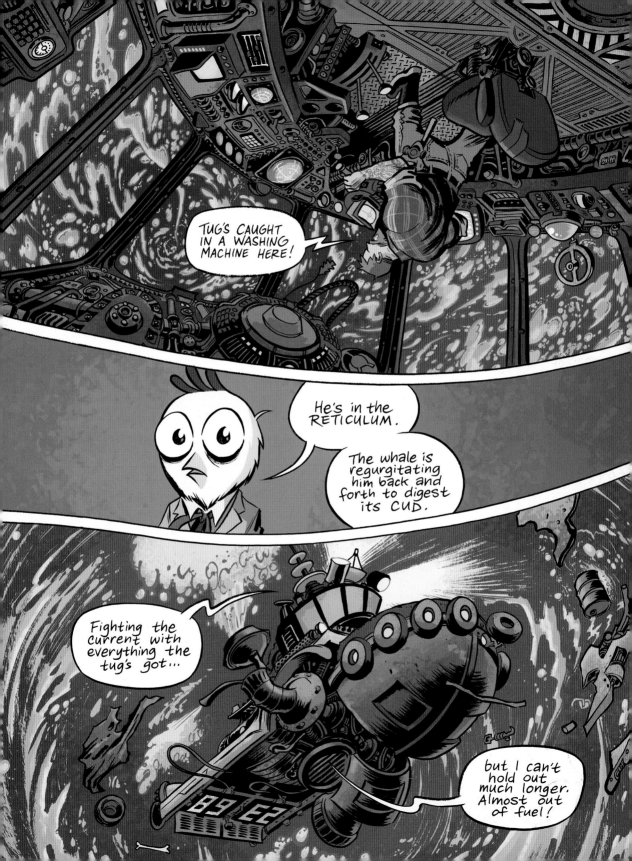

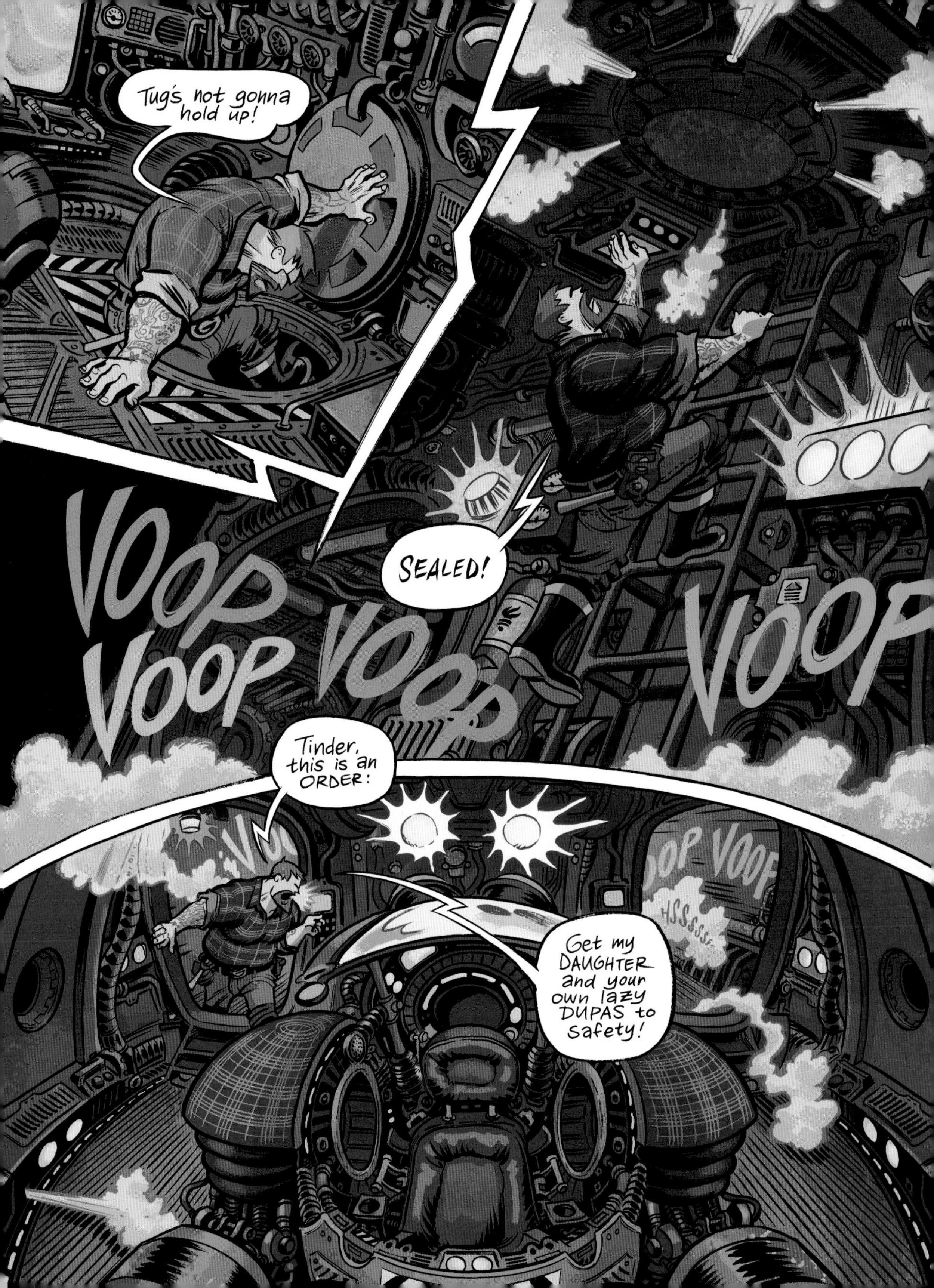
Tug's not gonna hold up!
SEALED!
VOOP VOOP VOOP VOOP
Tinder, this is an ORDER:
Get my DAUGHTER and your own lazy DUPAS to safety!

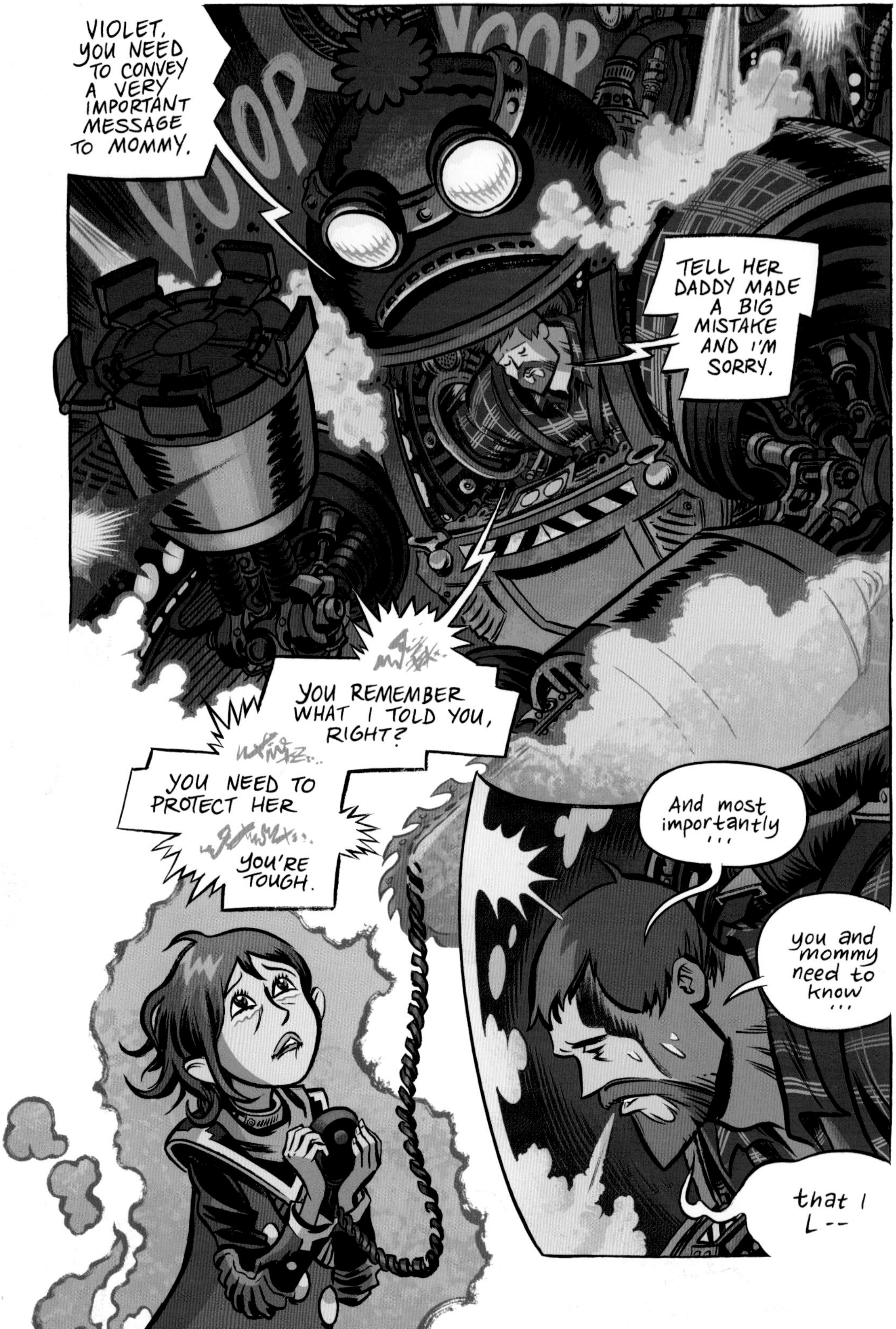
VOOP VOOP
VIOLET, YOU NEED TO CONVEY A VERY IMPORTANT MESSAGE TO MOMMY.
TELL HER DADDY MADE A BIG MISTAKE AND I'M SORRY.
YOU REMEMBER WHAT I TOLD YOU, RIGHT?
YOU NEED TO PROTECT HER
YOU'RE TOUGH.
And most importantly ...
you and mommy need to know ...
that I L--

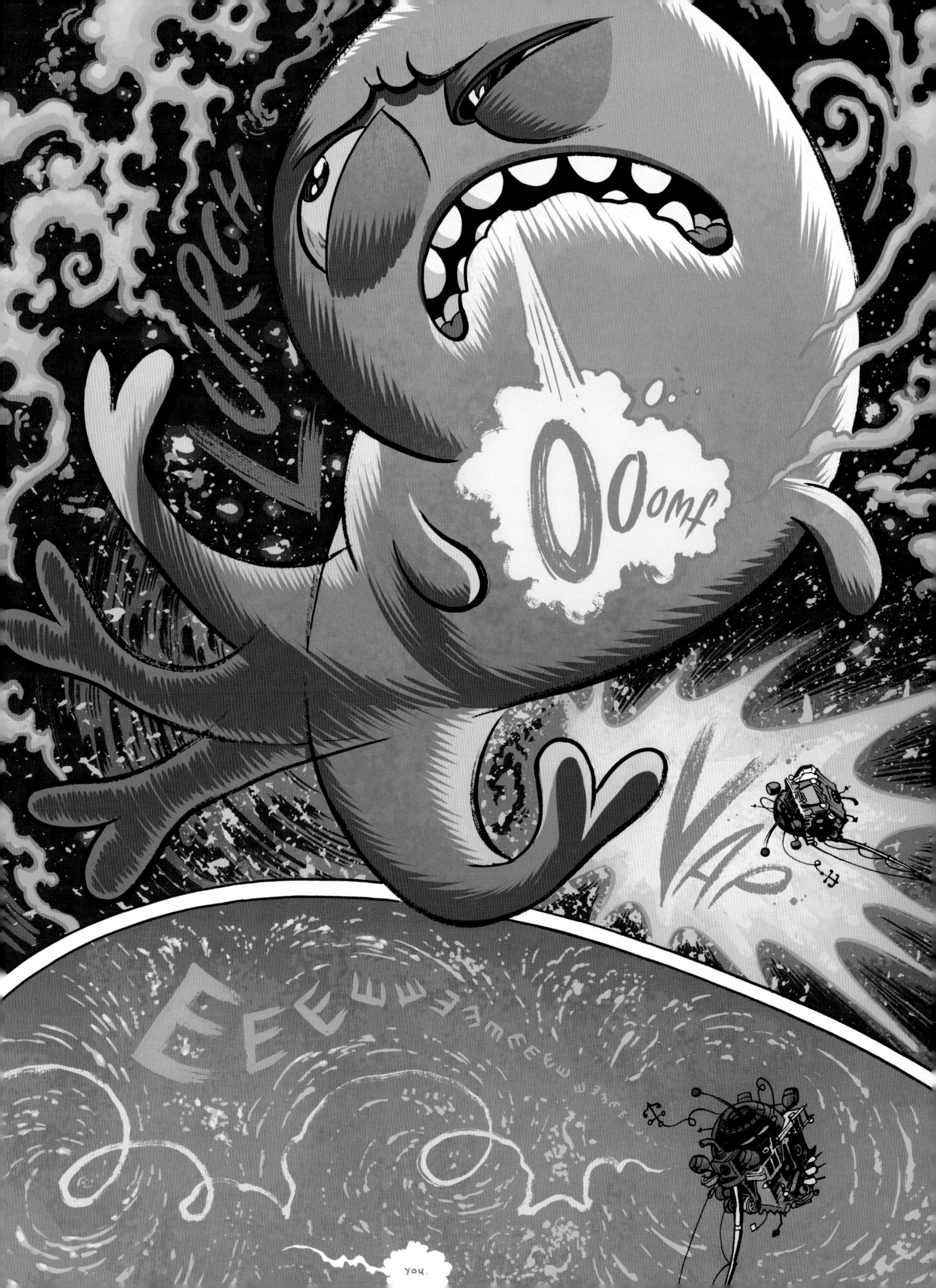
Ooomf
YOU.

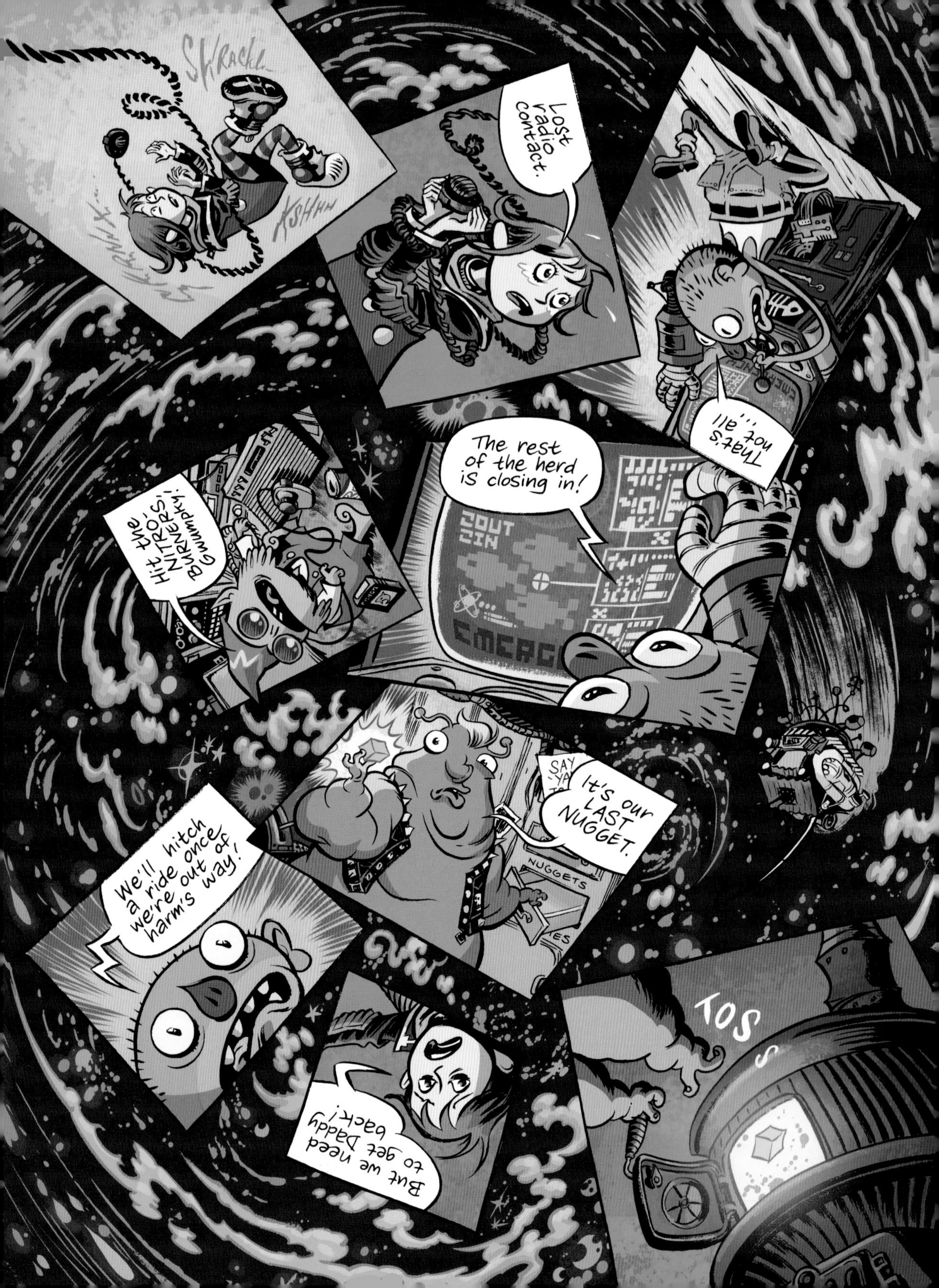
SKRACKL
KSHHH
Lost radio contact.
That's not all...
The rest of the herd is closing in!
Hit the NITROS, BURNERPY, GWUMPKY!
It's our LAST NUGGET.
NUGGETS
We'll hitch a ride once we're out of harm's way!
But we need to get Daddy back!
TOSS

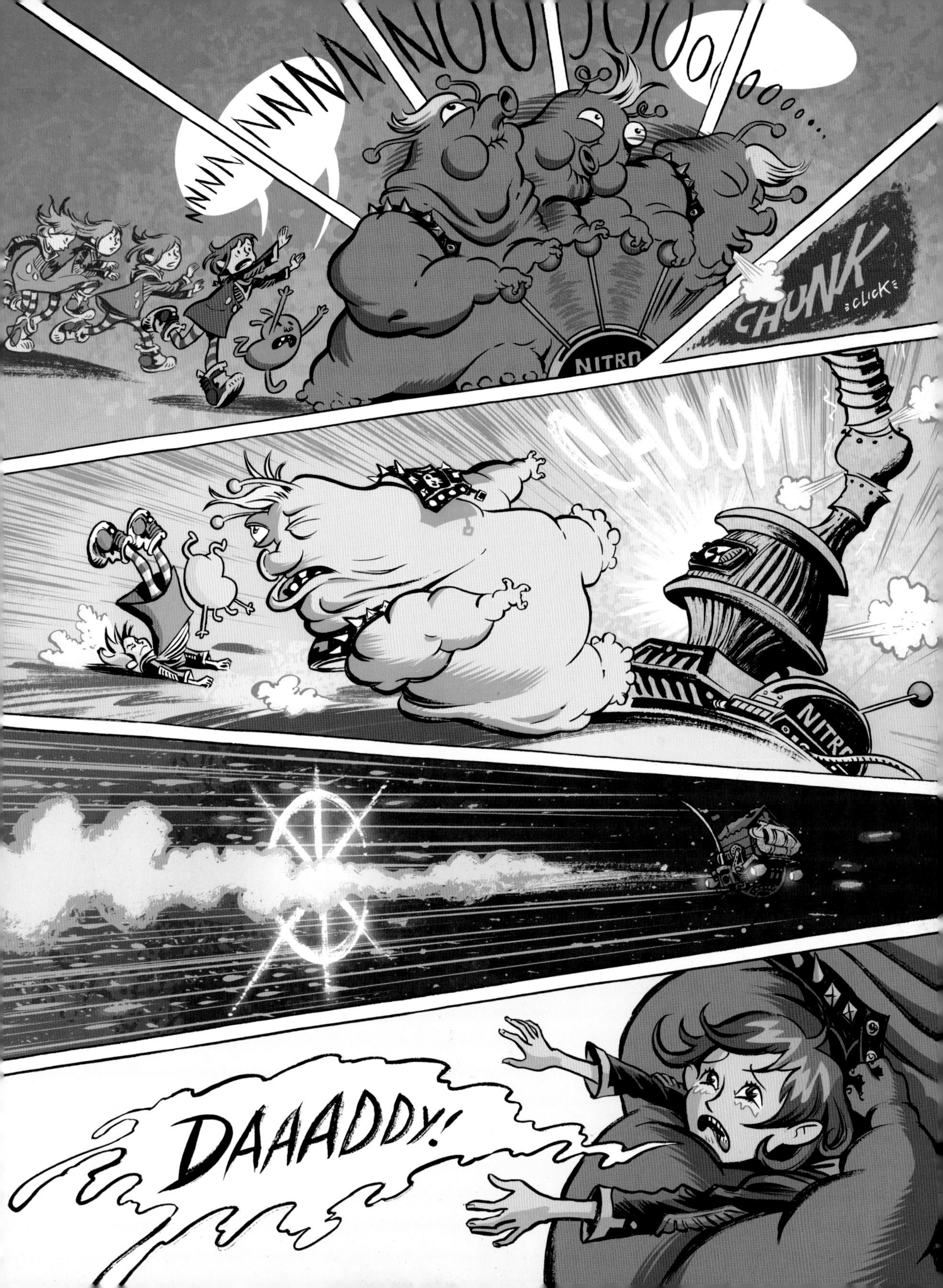
NNNNNNNNNNOOOOOOoooooo...
CHUNK
CLICK
NITRO
CHOOM
NITRO
DAAADDY!

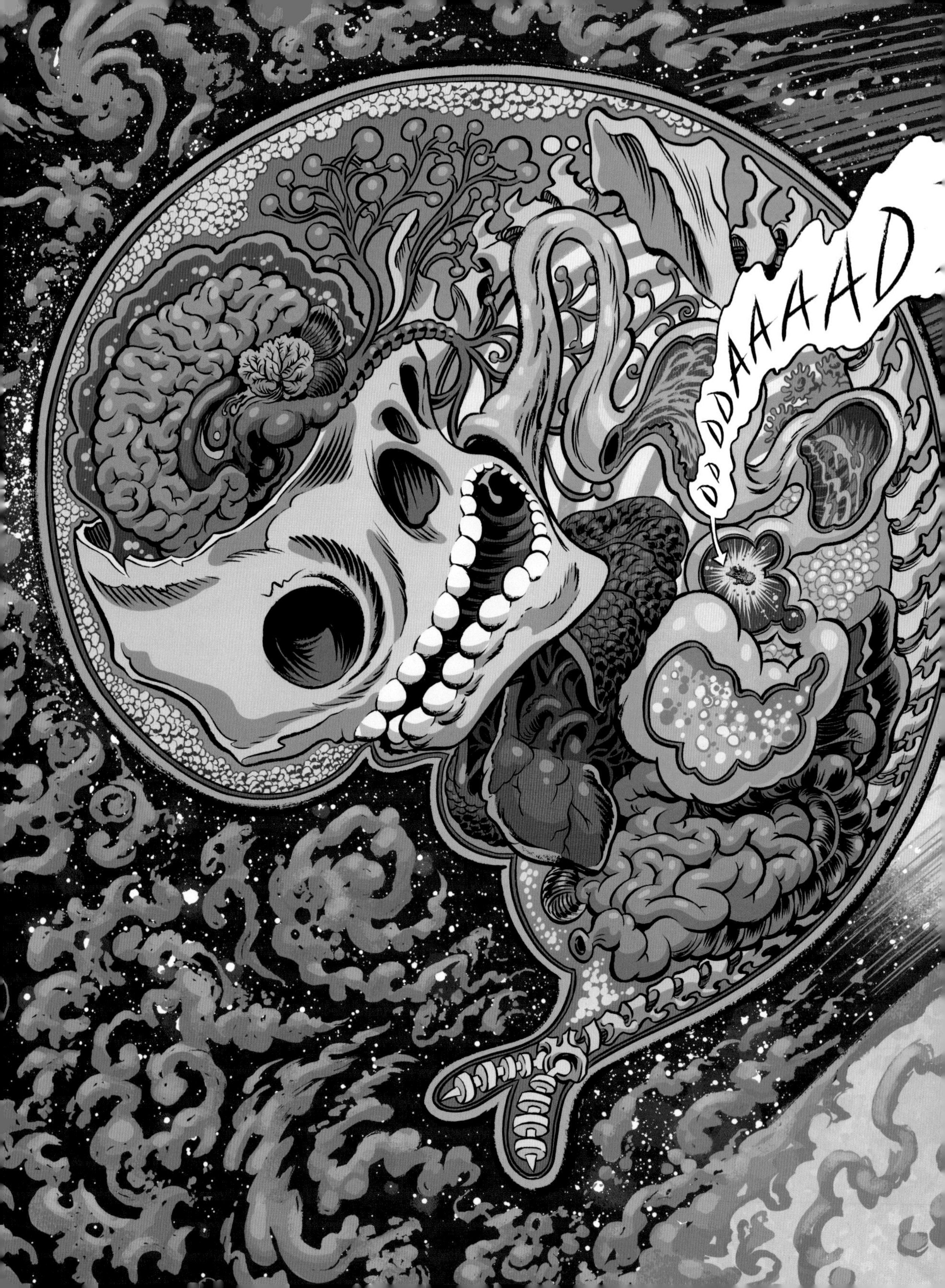
DDDDAAAAD

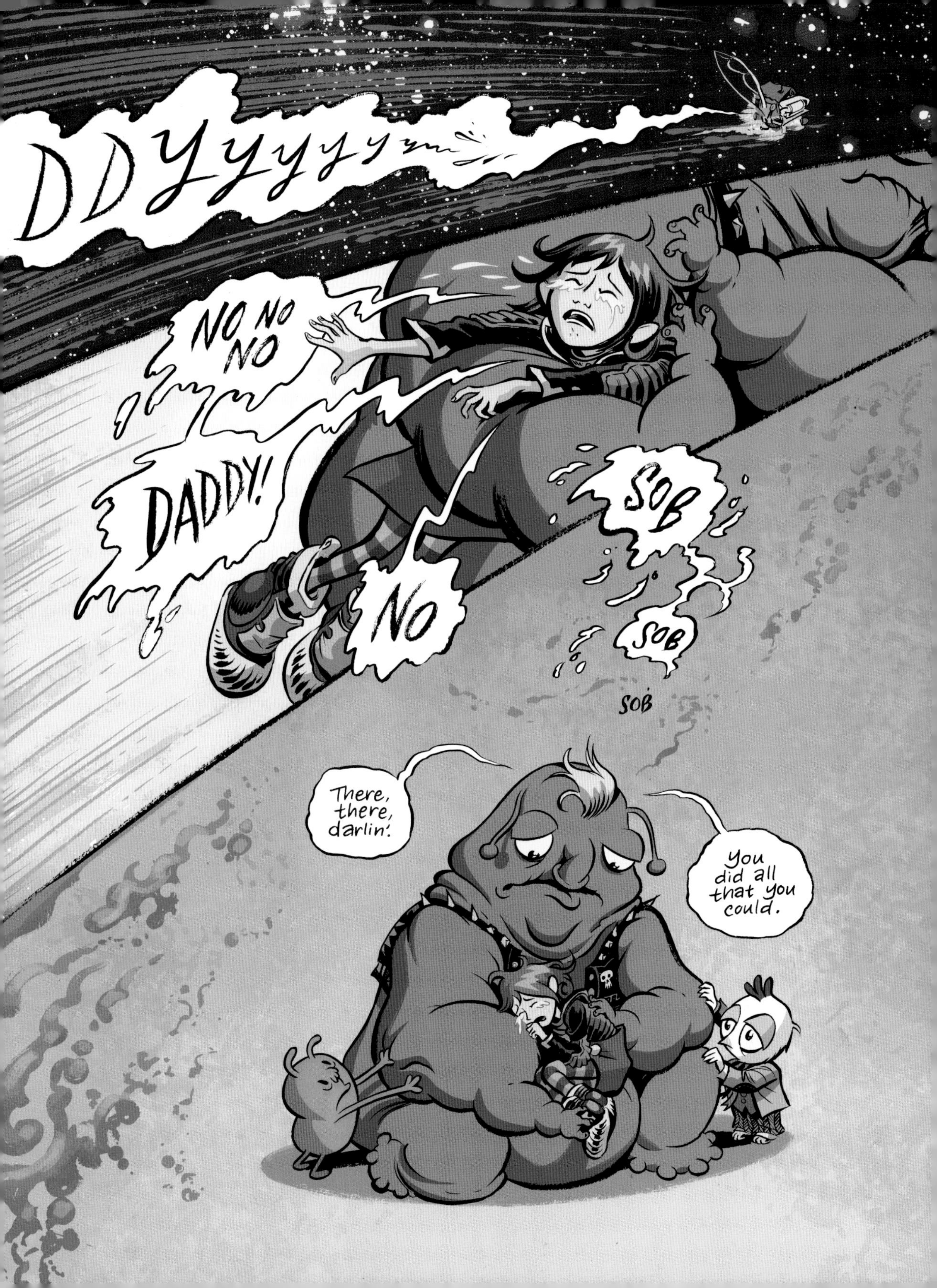
DDYyyyyyy
NO NO NO
DADDY!
NO
SOB
SOB
SOB
There, there, darlin'.
You did all that you could.

05

BAIT & SWITCH

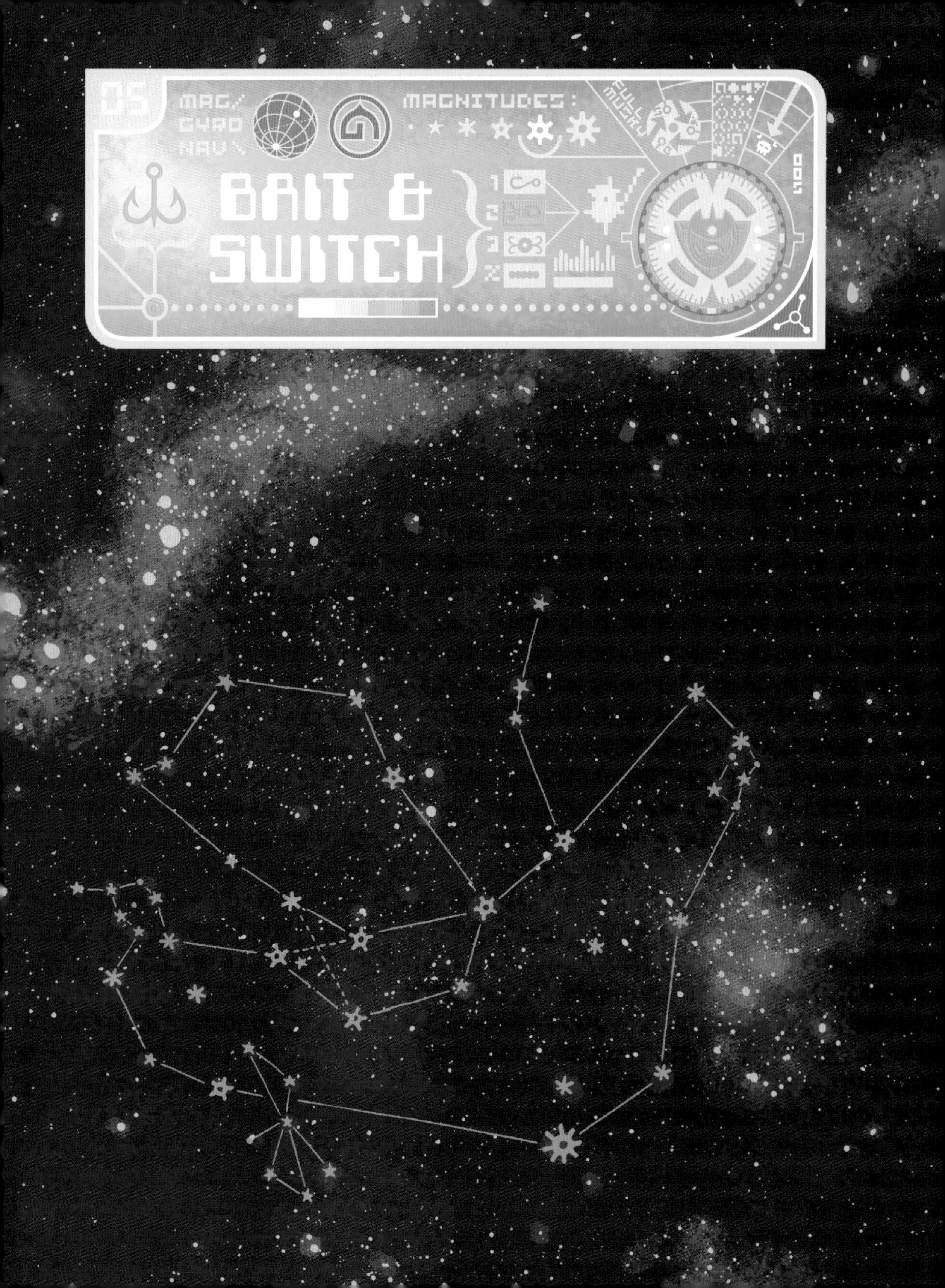

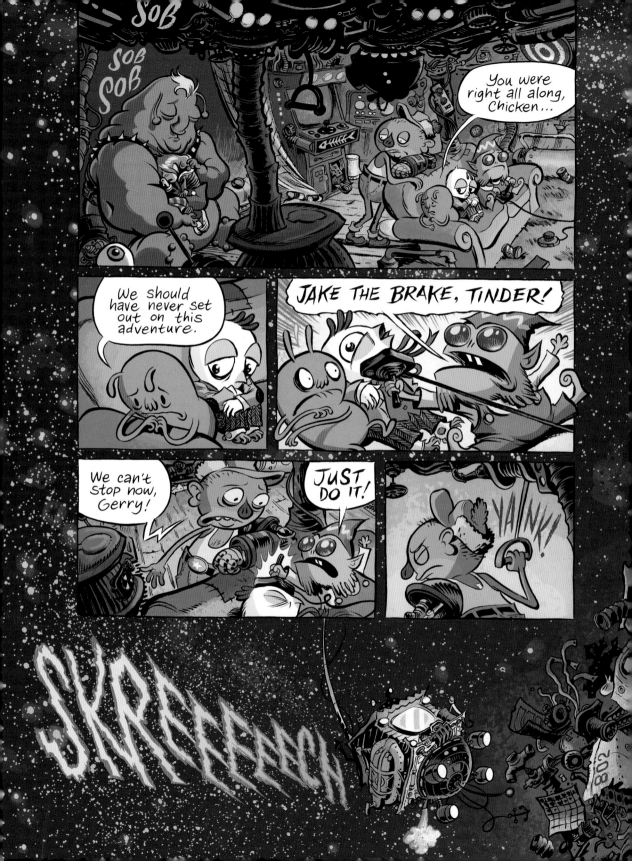

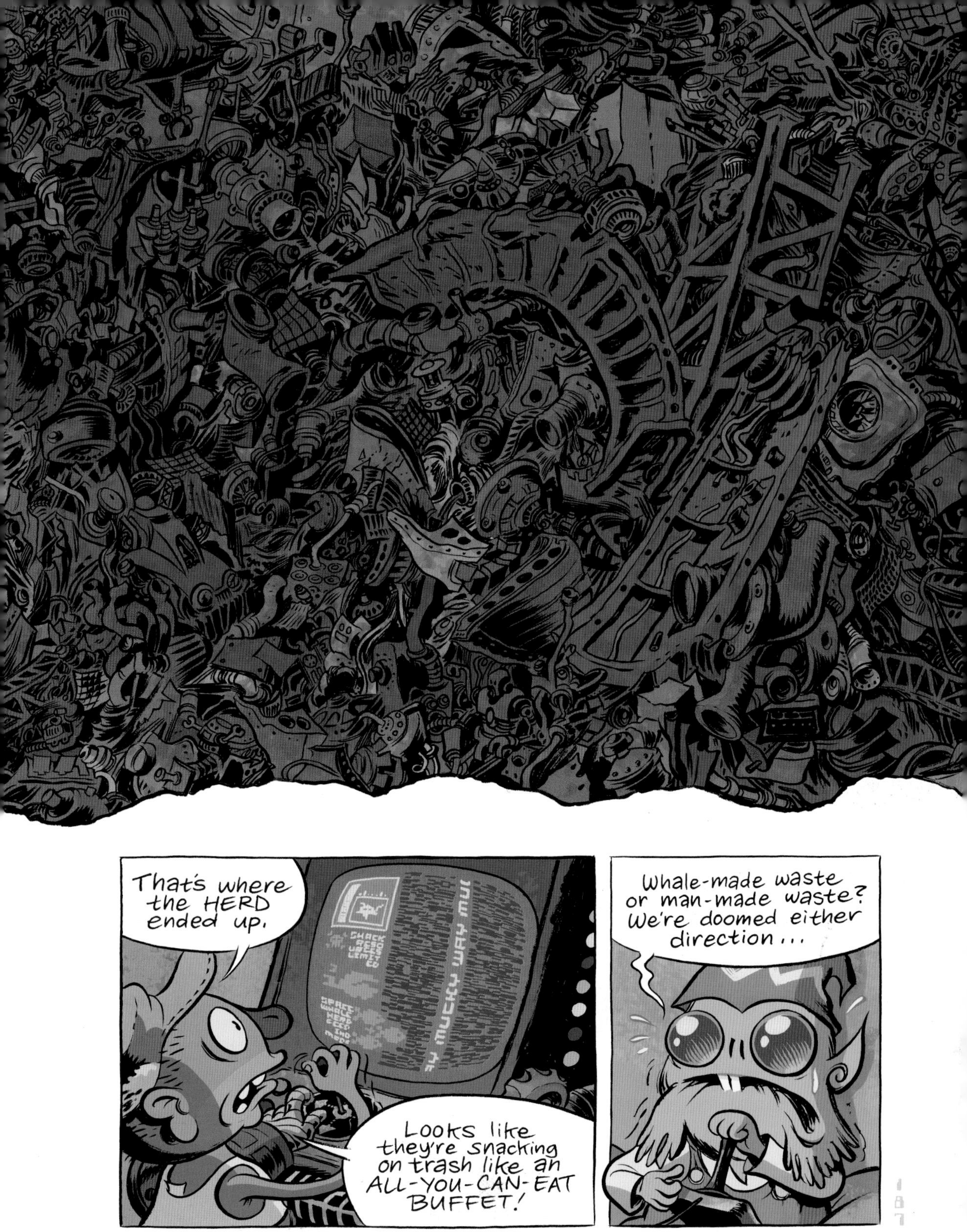

That's where the HERD ended up.
Looks like they're snacking on trash like an ALL-YOU-CAN-EAT BUFFET!
Whale-made waste or man-made waste? We're doomed either direction...

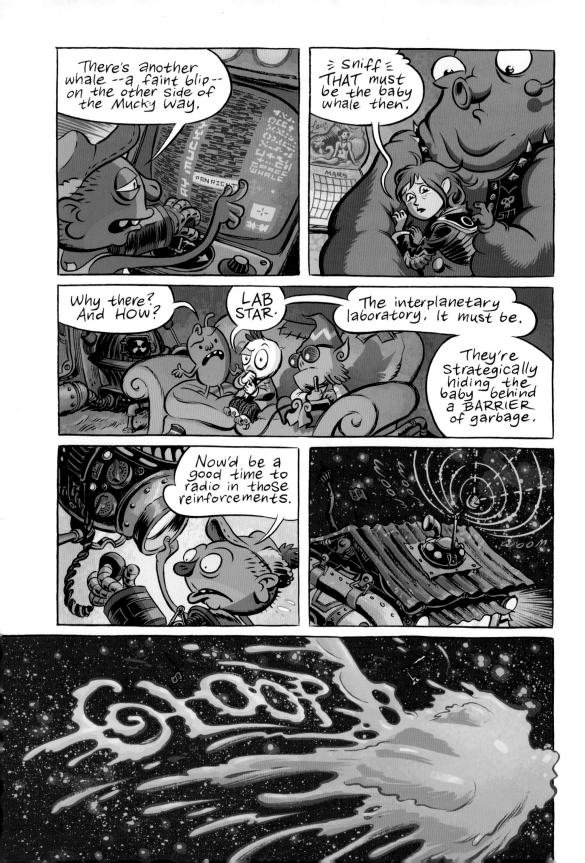

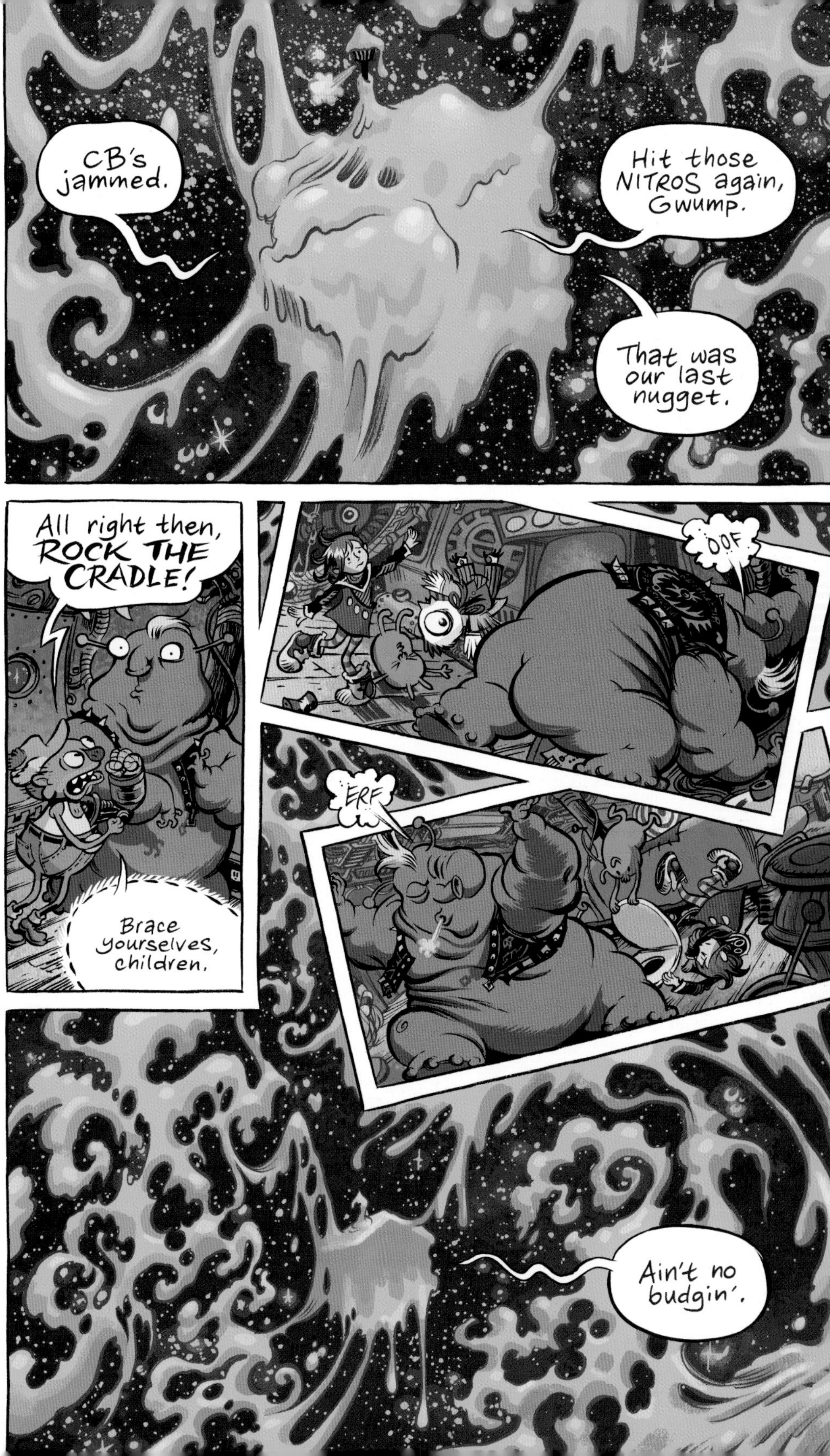
CB's jammed.
Hit those NITROS again, Gwump.
That was our last nugget.
All right then, ROCK THE CRADLE!
Brace yourselves, children.
OOF
ERF
Ain't no budgin'.

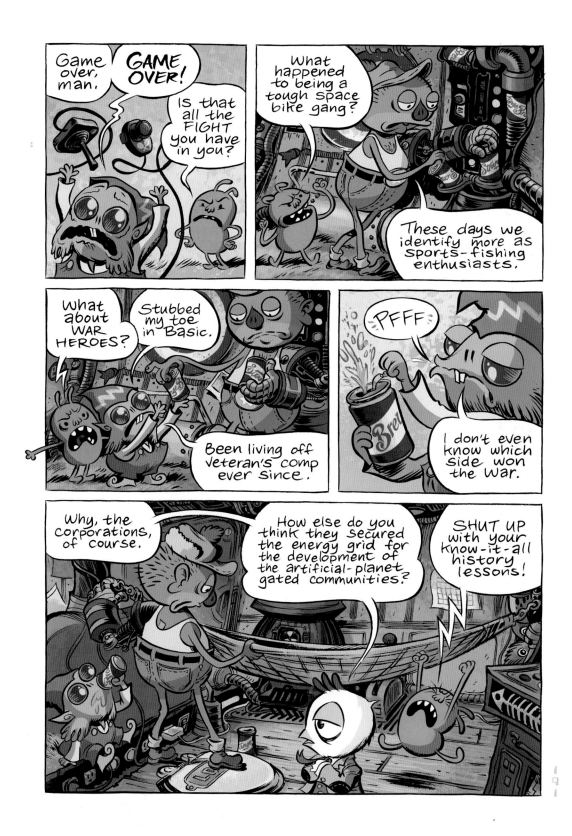

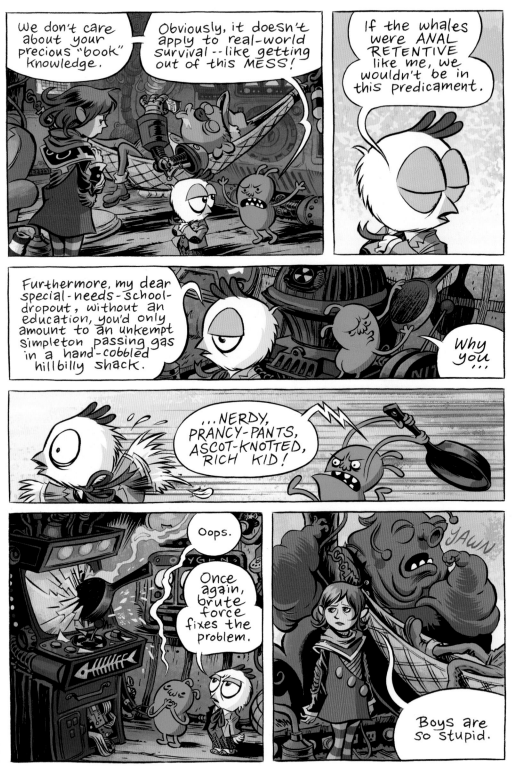

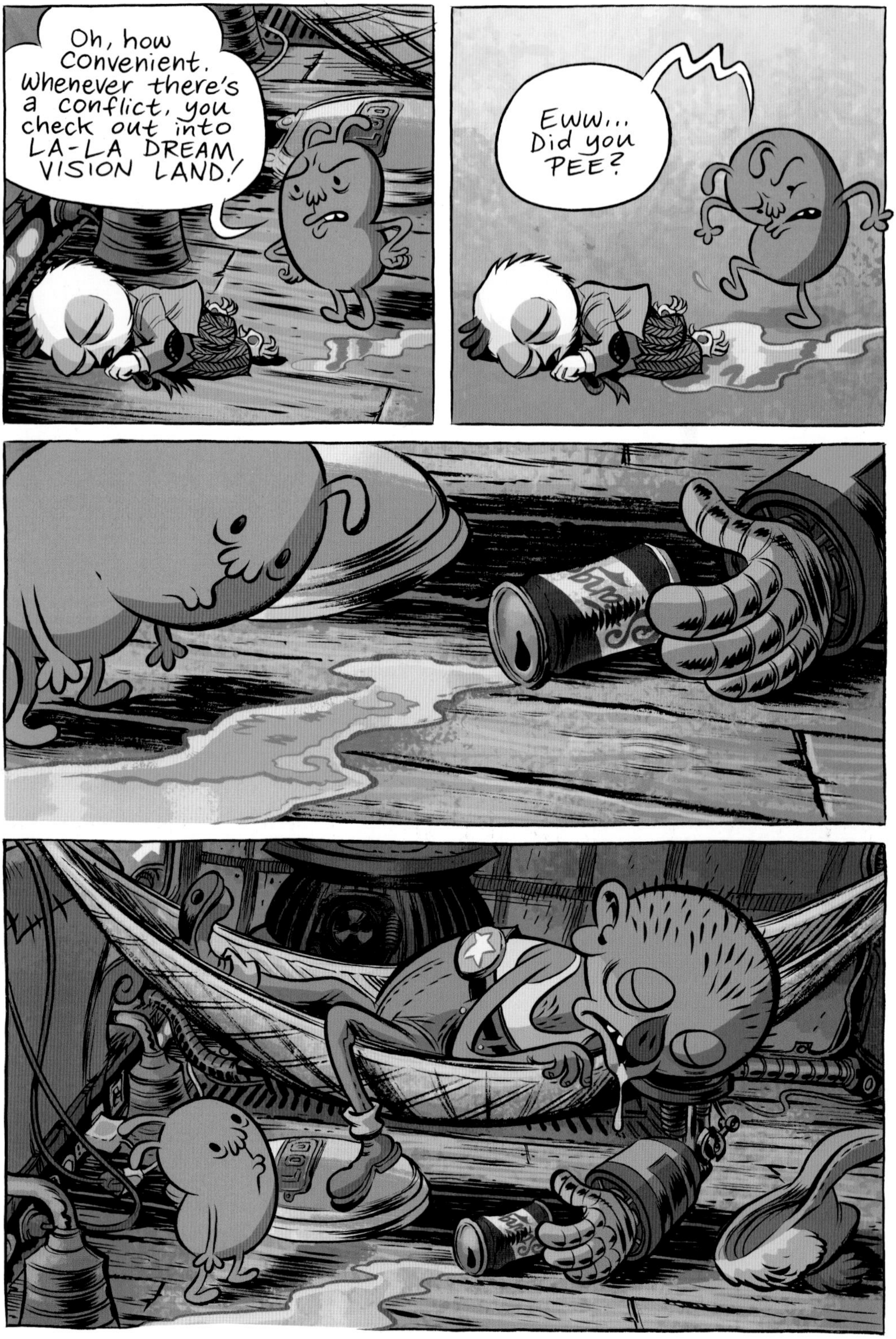
Oh, how Convenient. Whenever there's a conflict, you check out into LA-LA DREAM VISION LAND!
Eww... Did you PEE?

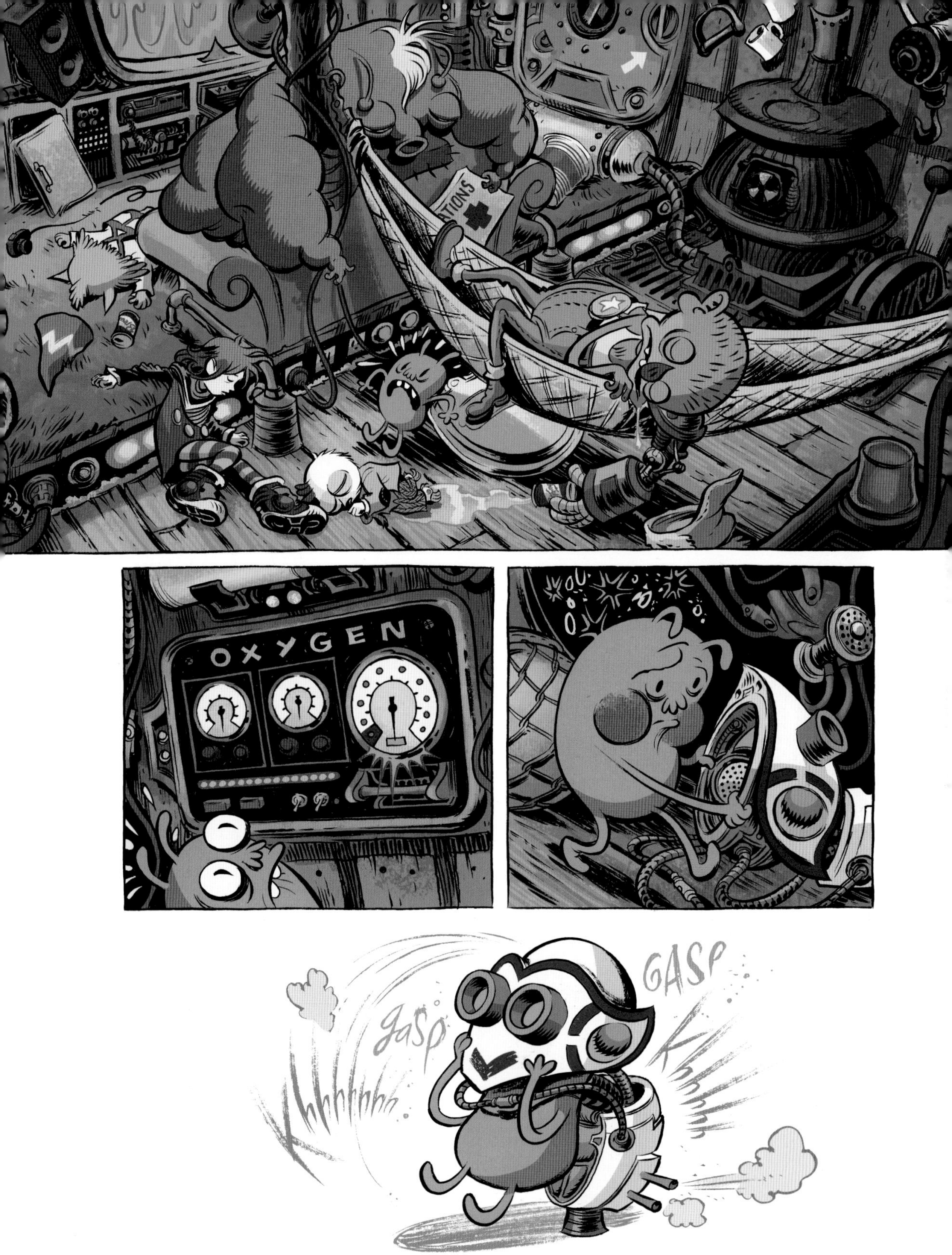
NITRO
OXYGEN
gasp
Khhhhhhhh
GASP
Khhhhhh

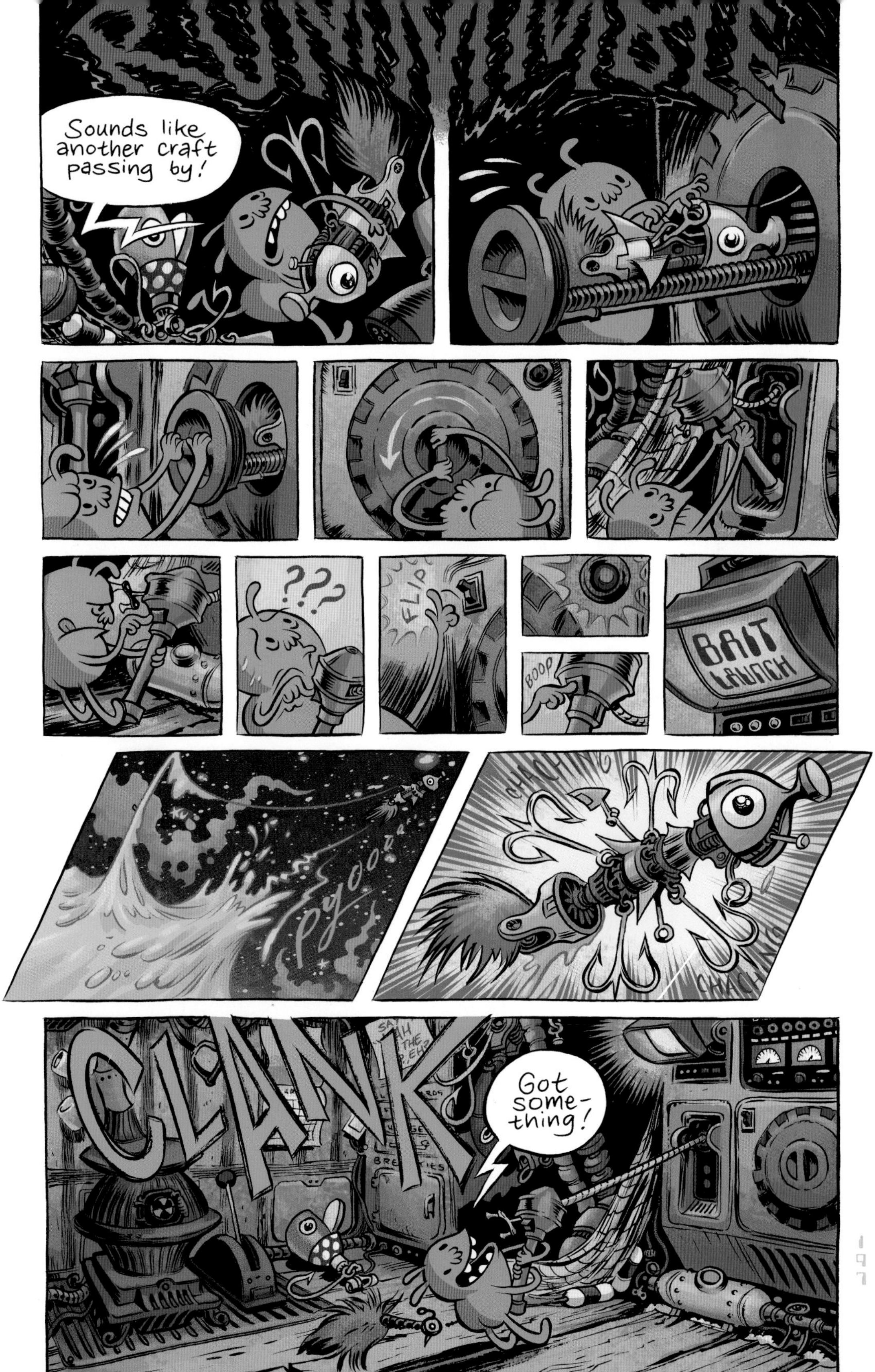
Sounds like another craft passing by!
???
FLIP
BOOP
BAIT LAUNCH
CLANK
Got some-thing!

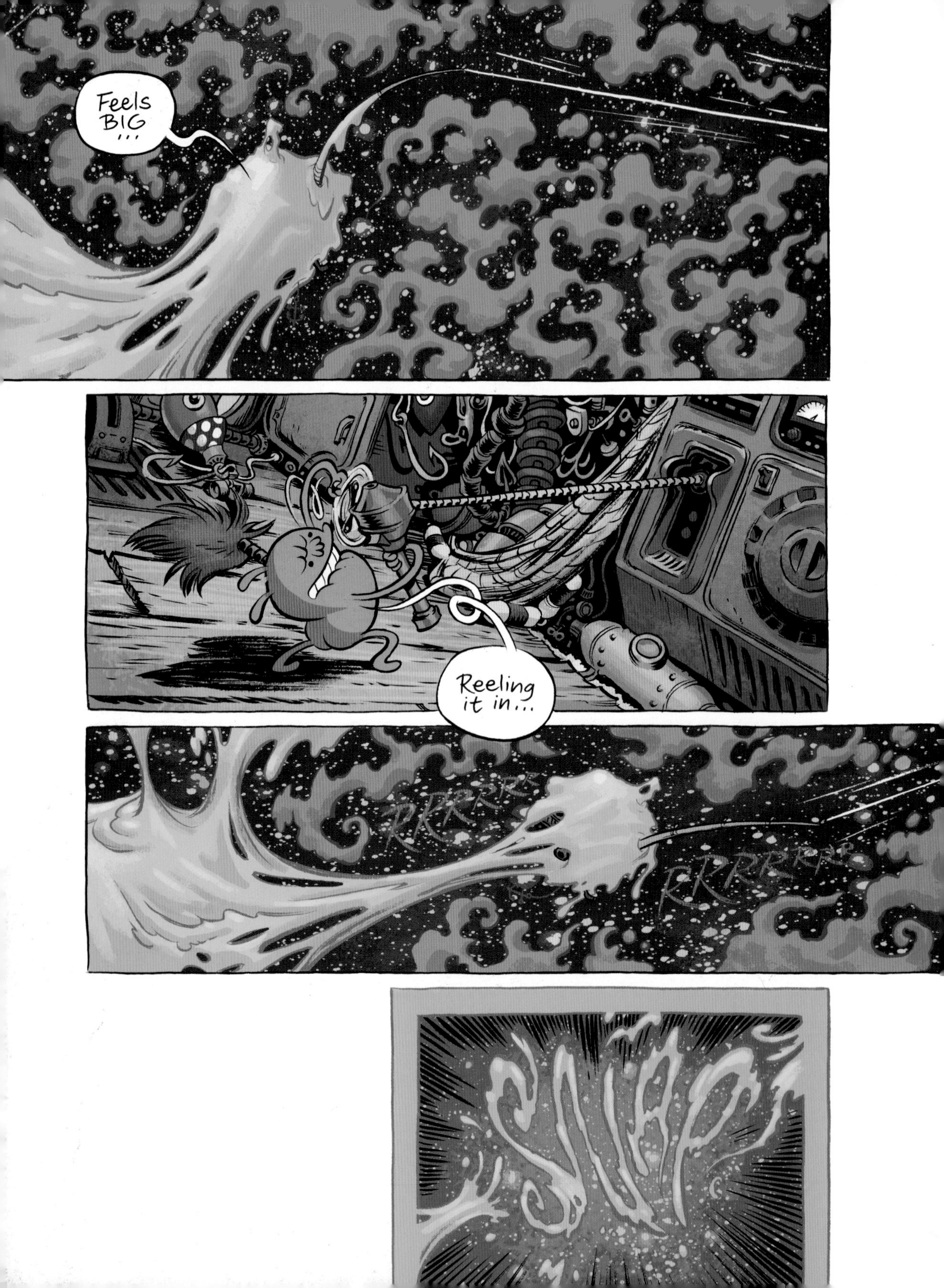

Feels BIG...
Reeling it in...
RRRRRR
RRRRRRRR
SNAP

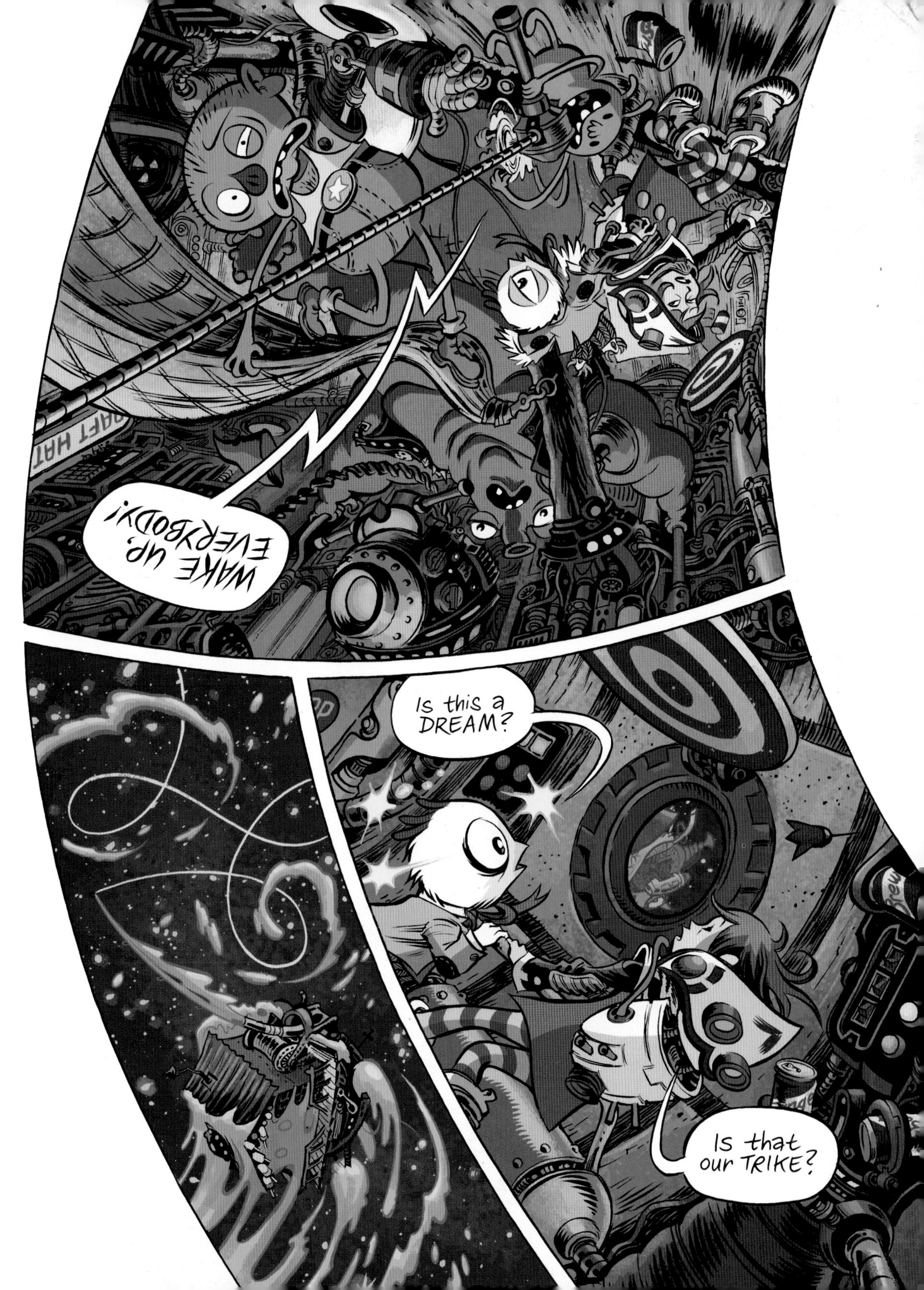
WAKE UP, EVERYBODY!
Is this a DREAM?
Is that our TRIKE?

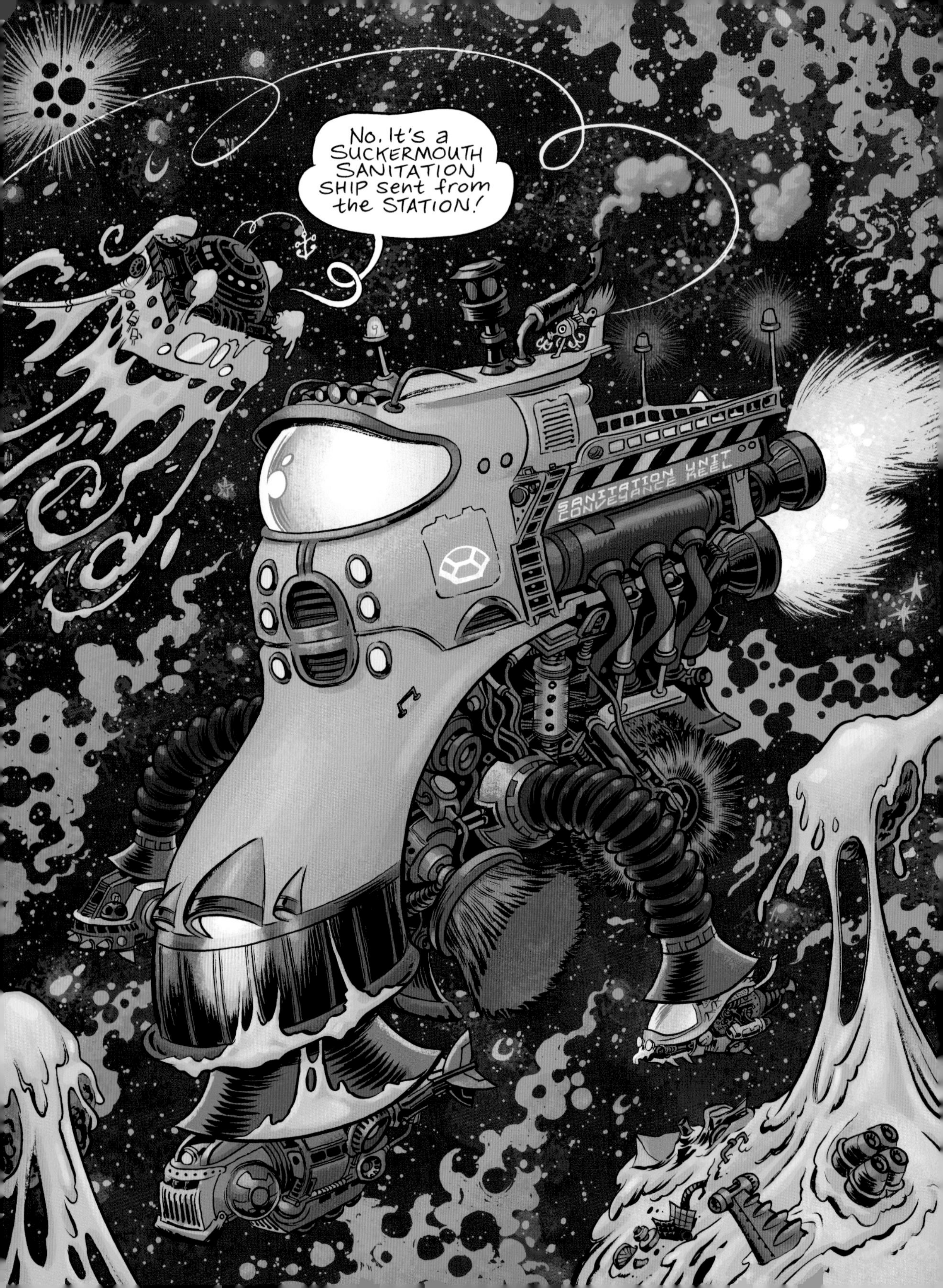
No. It's a SUCKERMOUTH SANITATION SHIP sent from the STATION!
SANITATION UNIT
CONVEYANCE KEEL

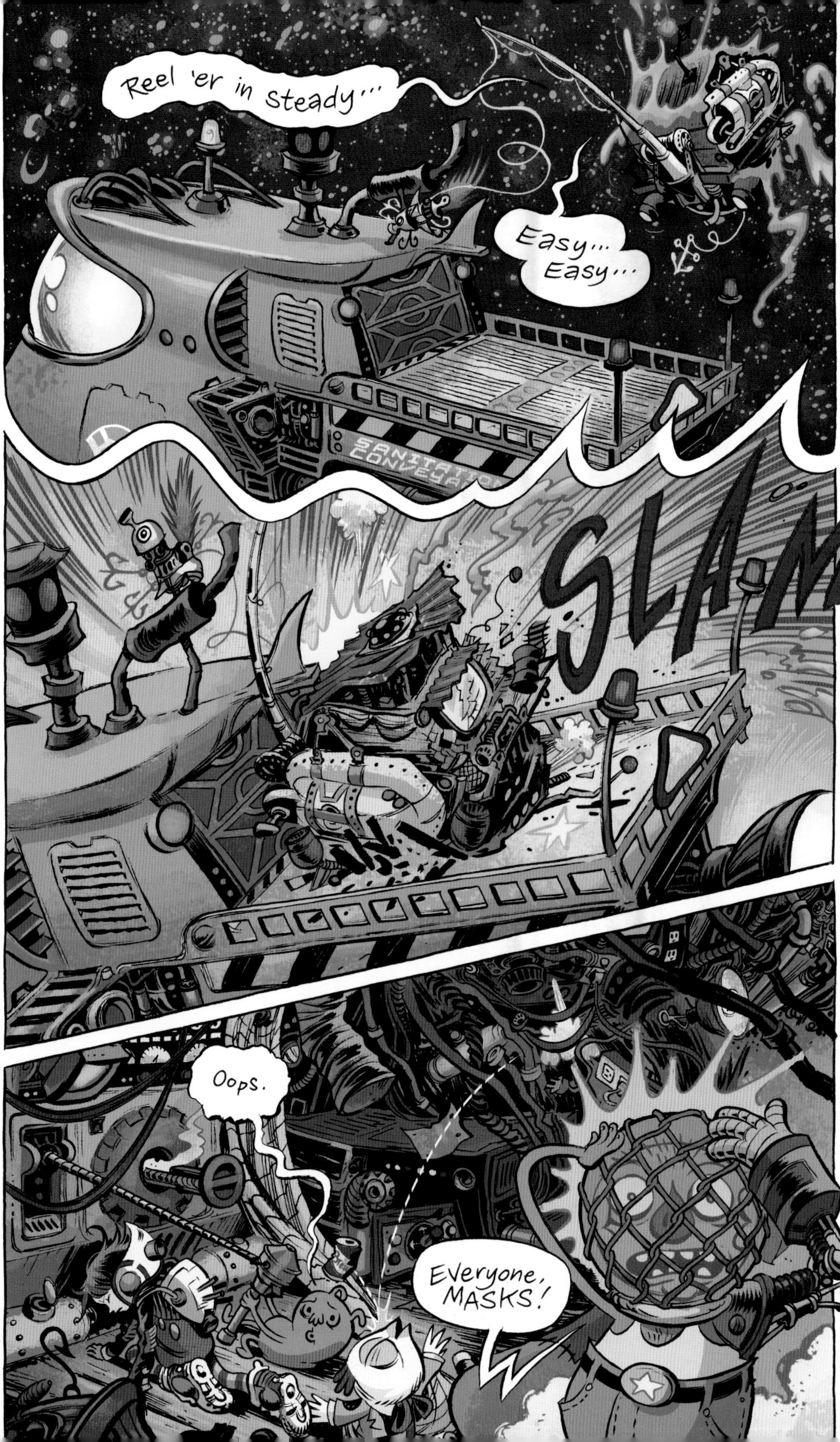
Reel 'er in steady...
Easy... Easy...
SANITATION CONVEYA
SLAM
Oops.
Everyone, MASKS!

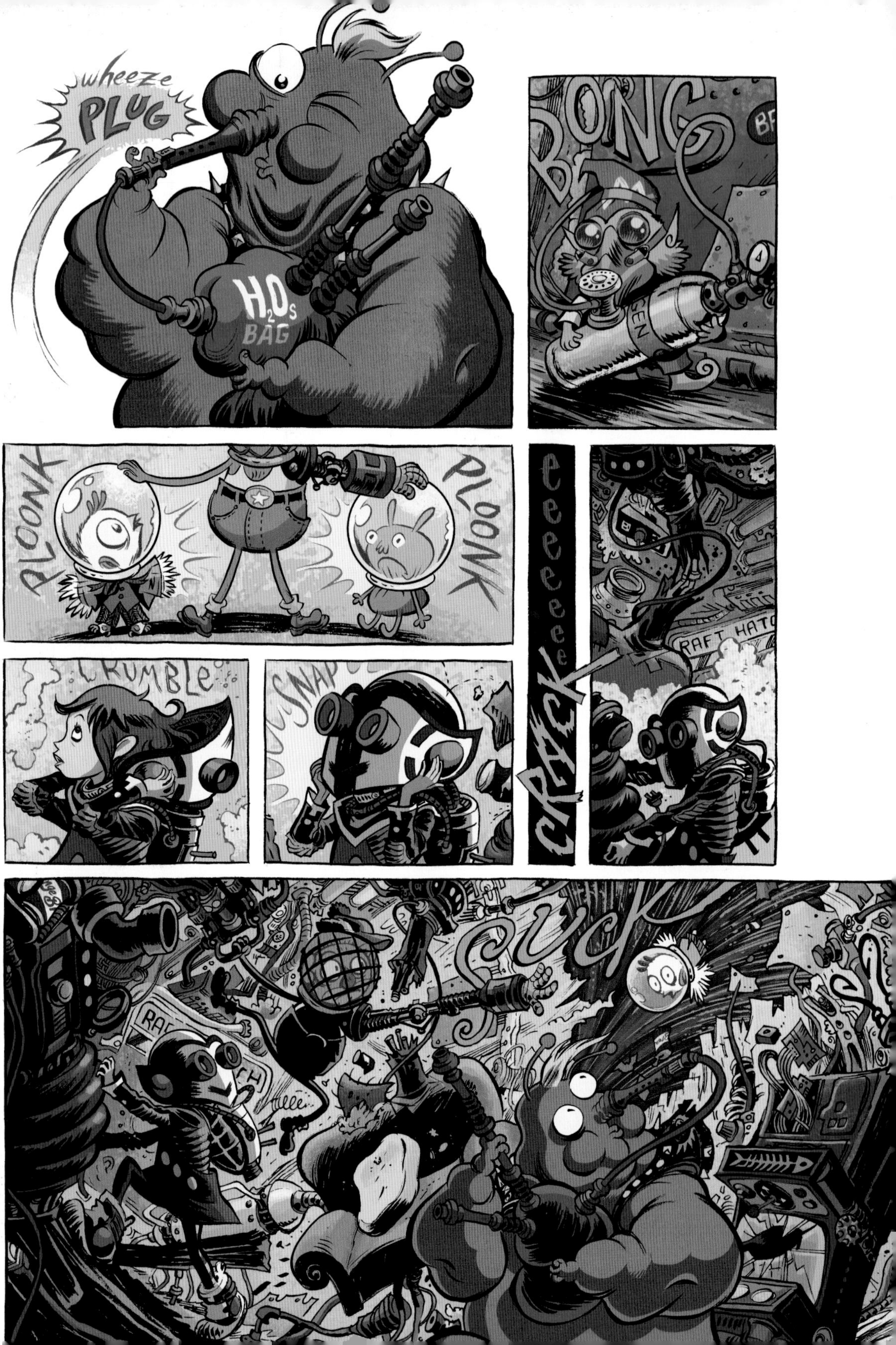
wheeze
PLUG
H2OS
BAG
BONG
PLOONK
PLOONK
eeeeeee
CRACK
RAFT HATC
CRUMBLE
SNAP
wheee

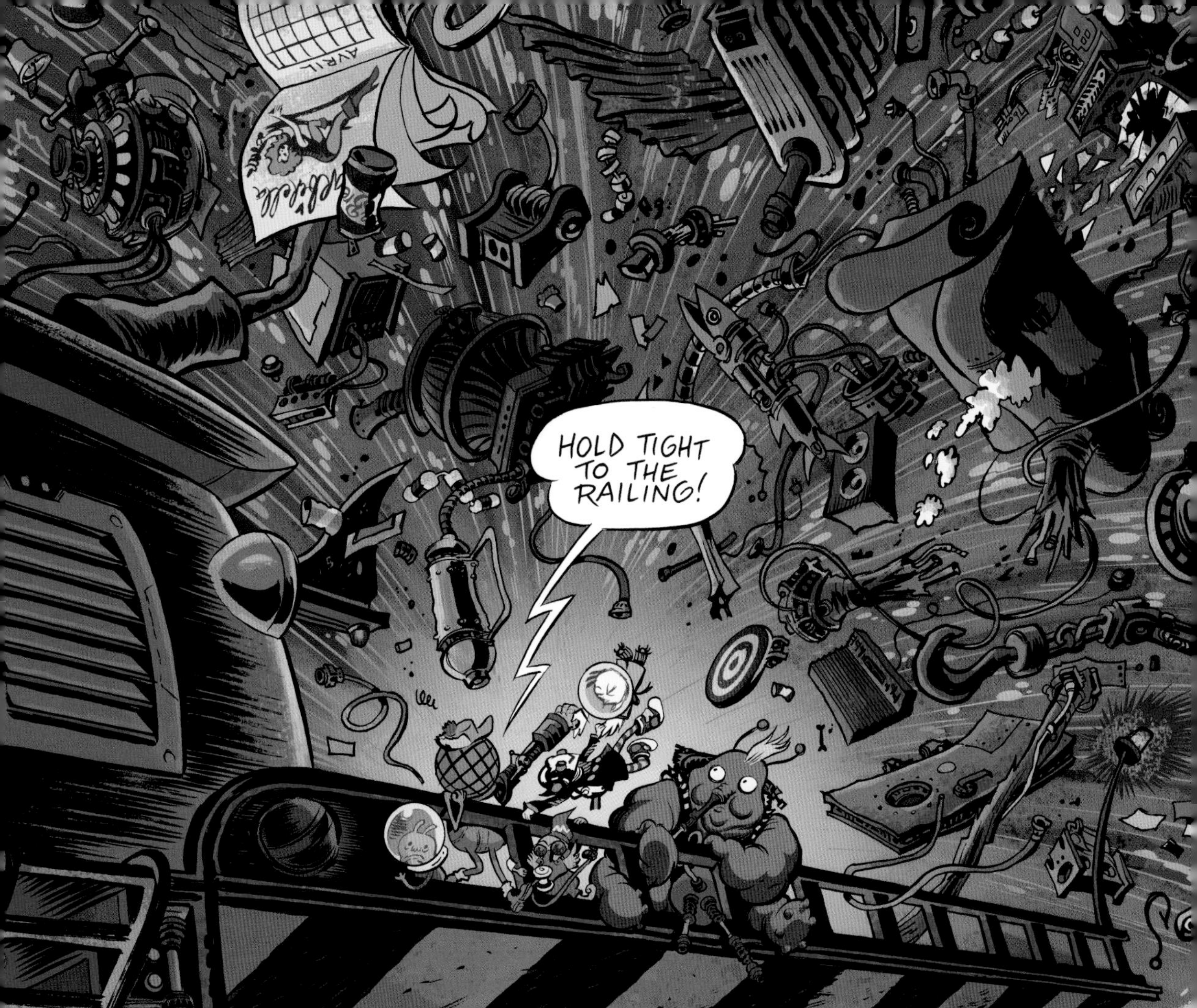
AVRIL
HOLD TIGHT TO THE RAILING!

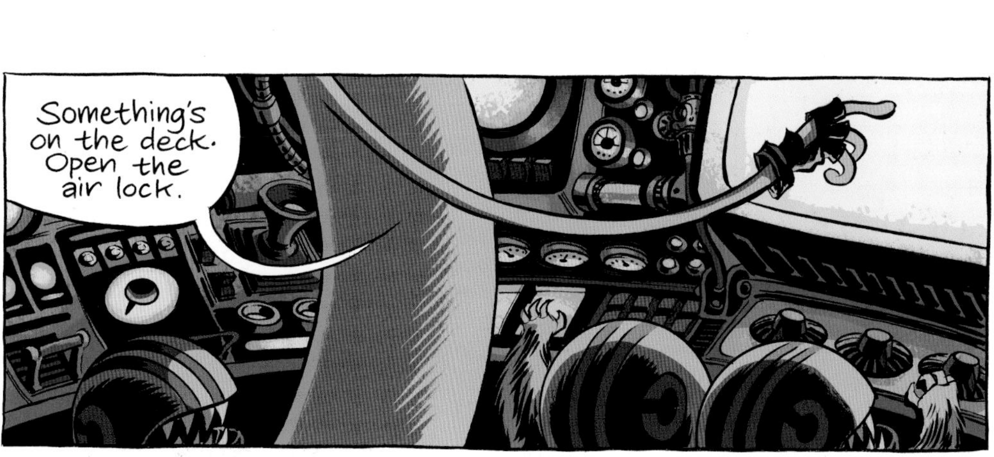
Something's on the deck. Open the air lock.

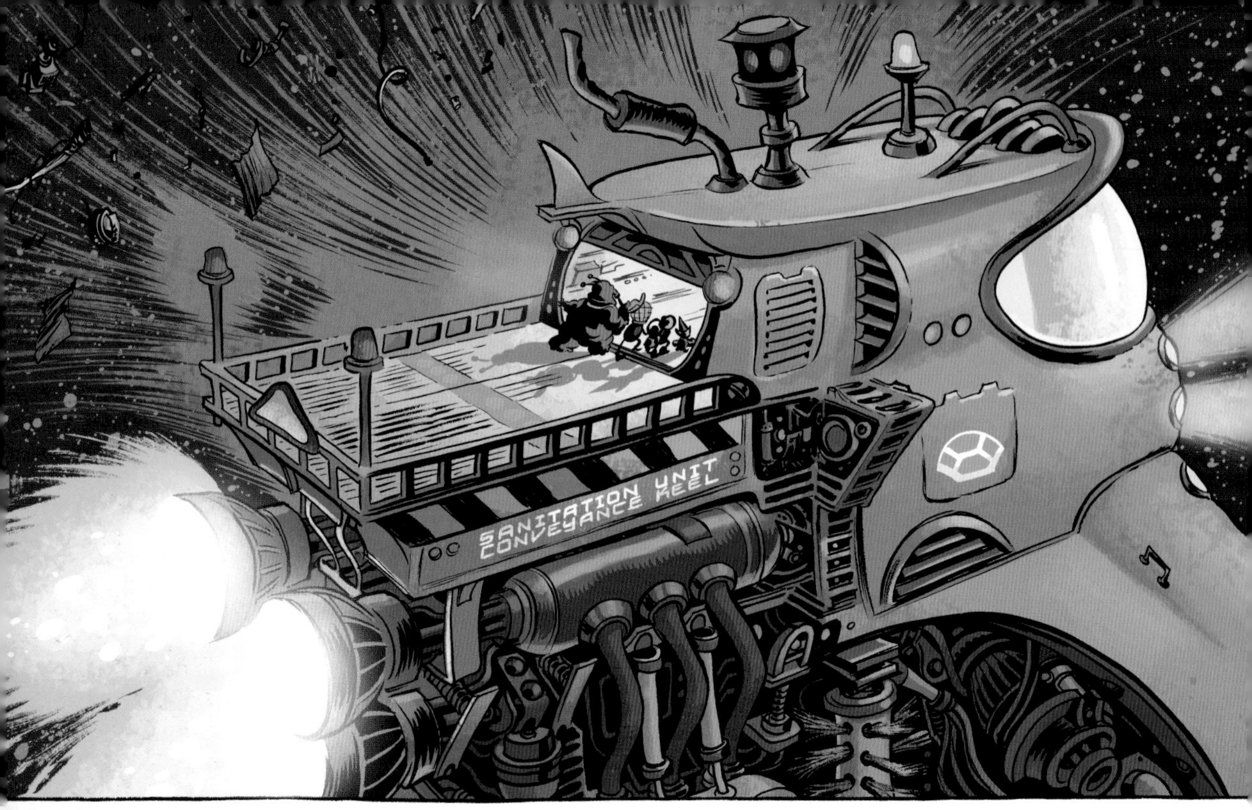

SANITATION UNIT
CONVEYANCE KEEL

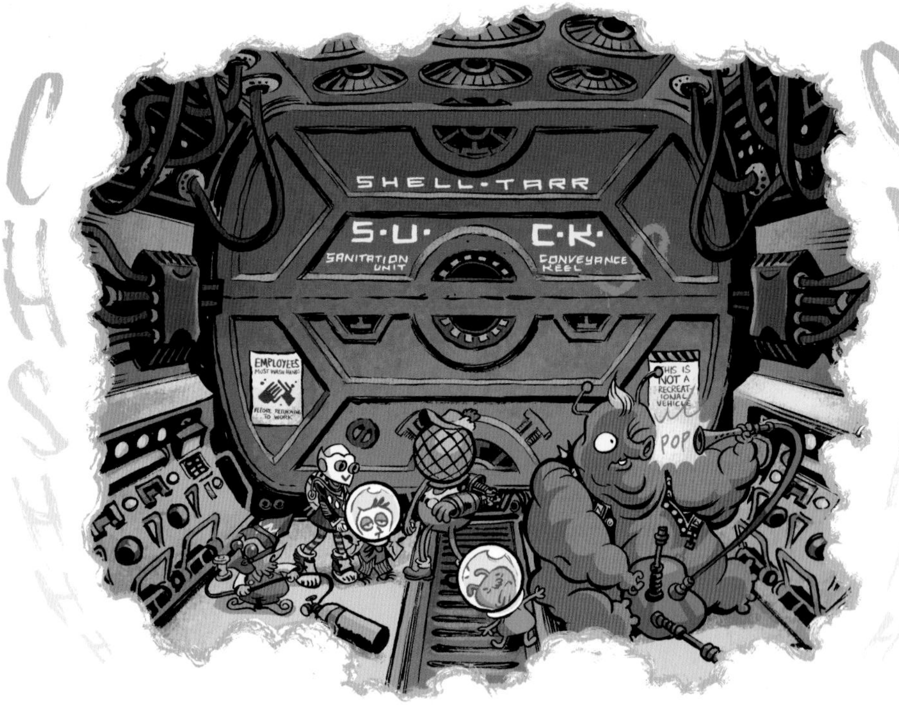

CHSH
SHELL-TARR
S·U· C·K·
SANITATION UNIT
CONVEYANCE KEEL
EMPLOYEES MUST WASH HANDS BEFORE RETURNING TO WORK
THIS IS NOT A RECREATIONAL VEHICLE
POP
CHSH

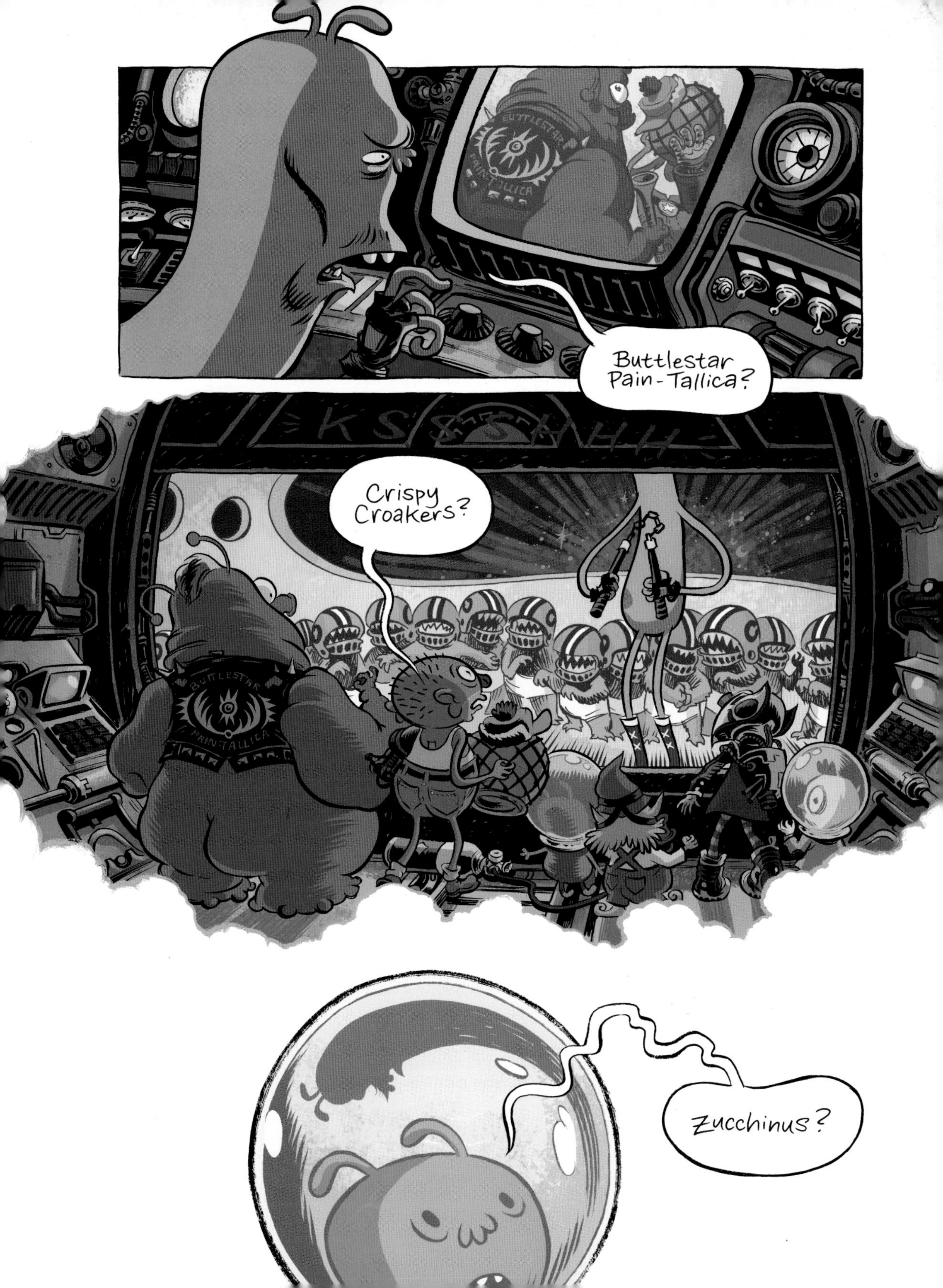

Buttlestar Pain-Tallica?
Crispy Croakers?
Zucchinus?

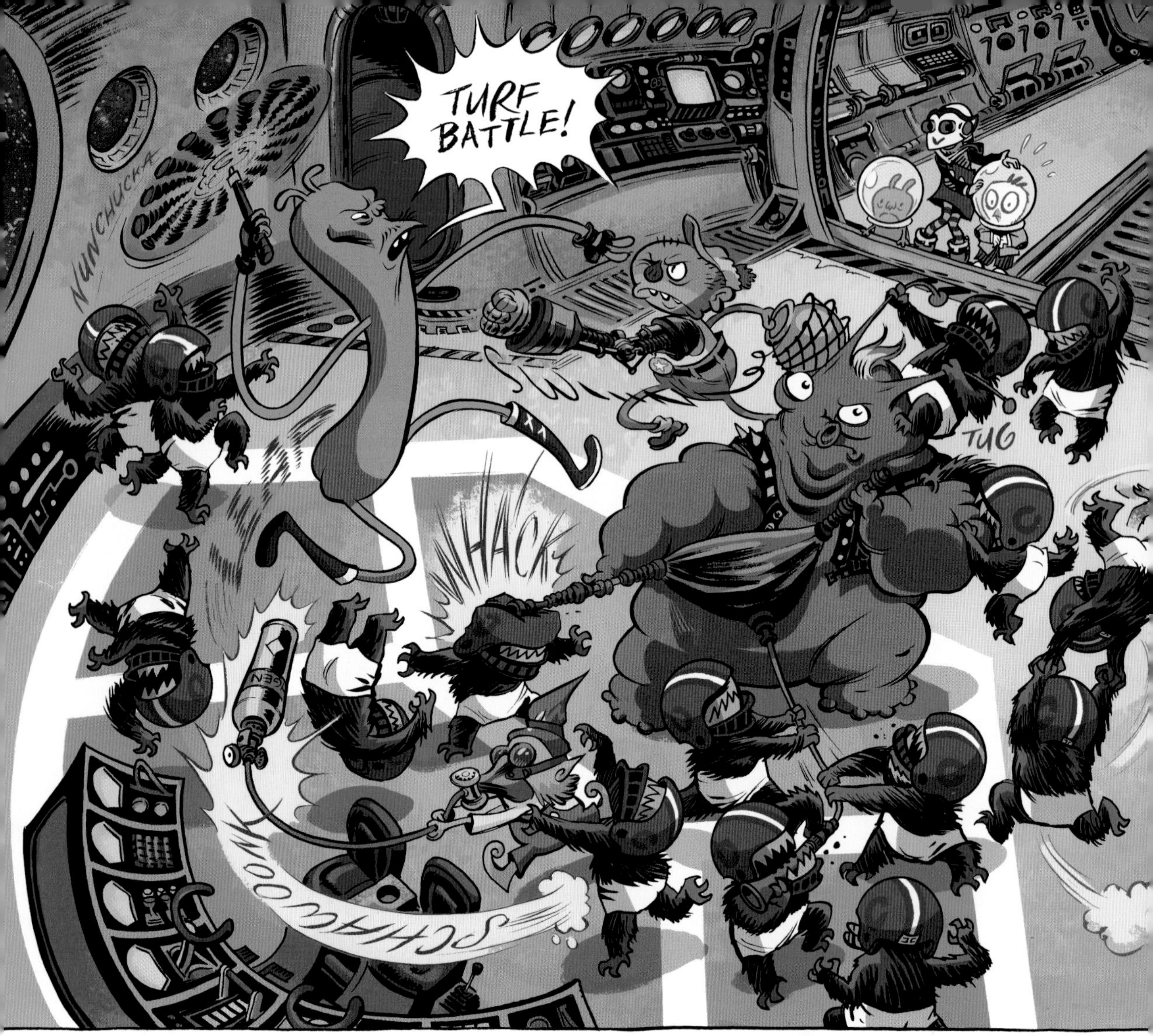
NUNCHUCKA
TURF BATTLE!
TUG
WHACK
SPCHWOOOOM

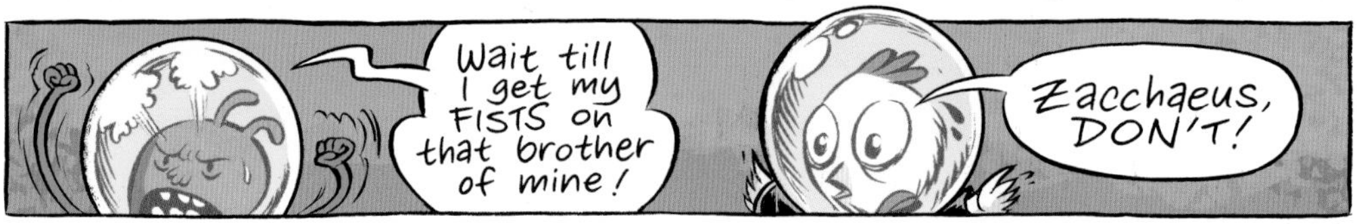
Wait till I get my FISTS on that brother of mine!
Zacchaeus, DON'T!

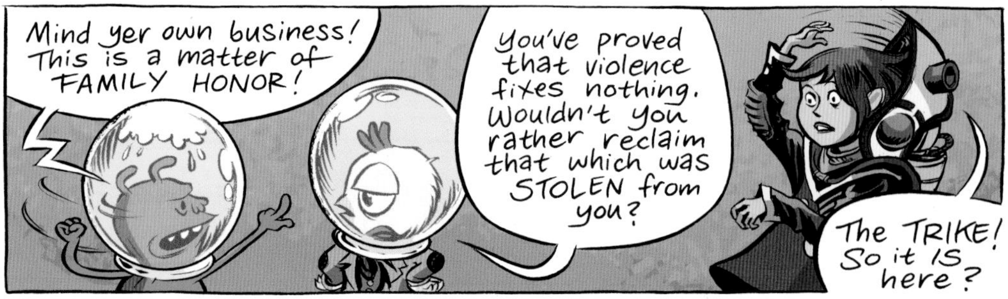
Mind yer own business! This is a matter of FAMILY HONOR!
You've proved that violence fixes nothing. Wouldn't you rather reclaim that which was STOLEN from you?
The TRIKE! So it IS here?

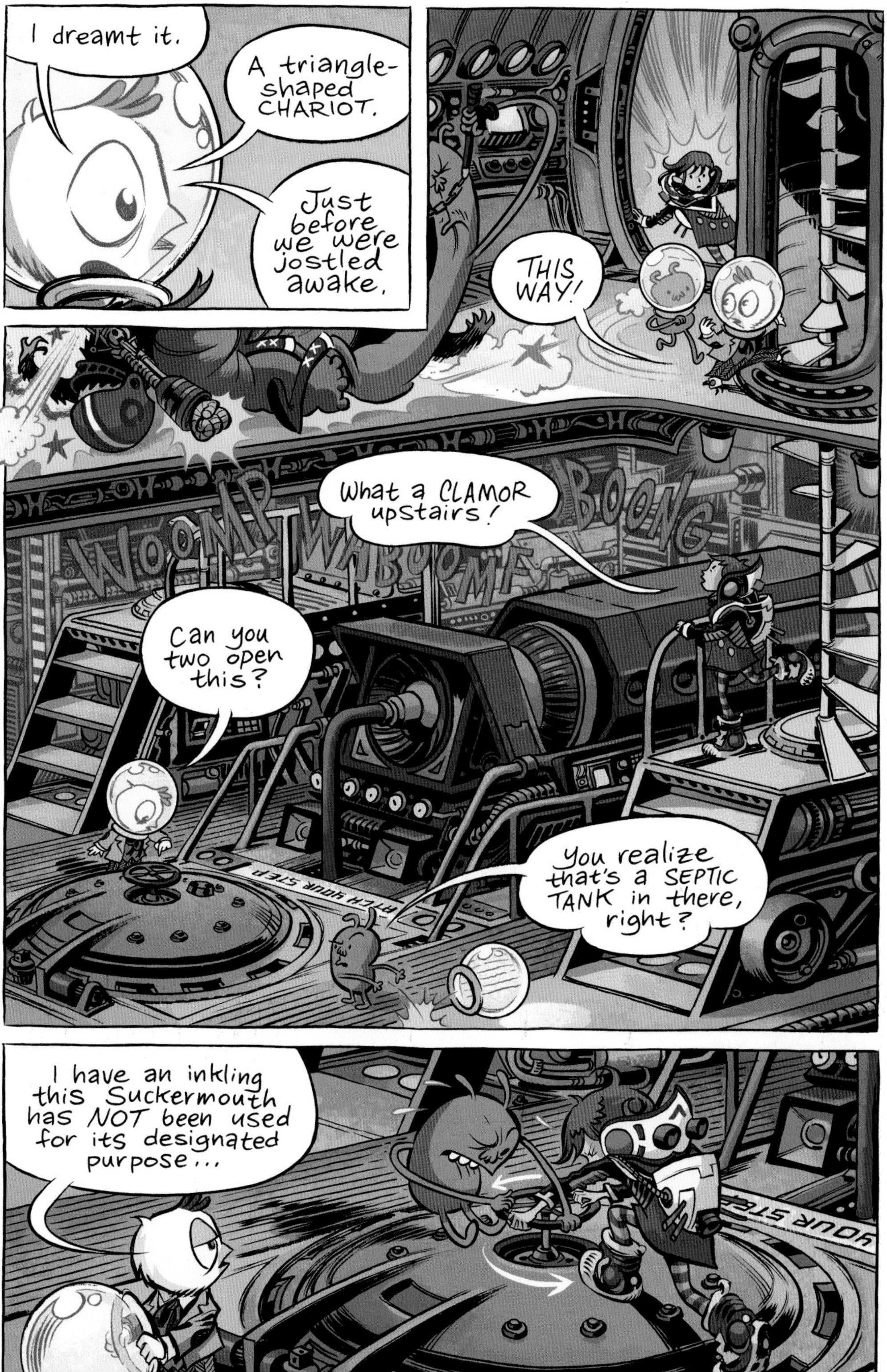

I dreamt it.
A triangle-shaped CHARIOT.
Just before we were jostled awake.
THIS WAY!
WOOMP
WABOOMF
BOONG
What a CLAMOR upstairs!
Can you two open this?
You realize that's a SEPTIC TANK in there, right?
I have an inkling this Suckermouth has NOT been used for its designated purpose...

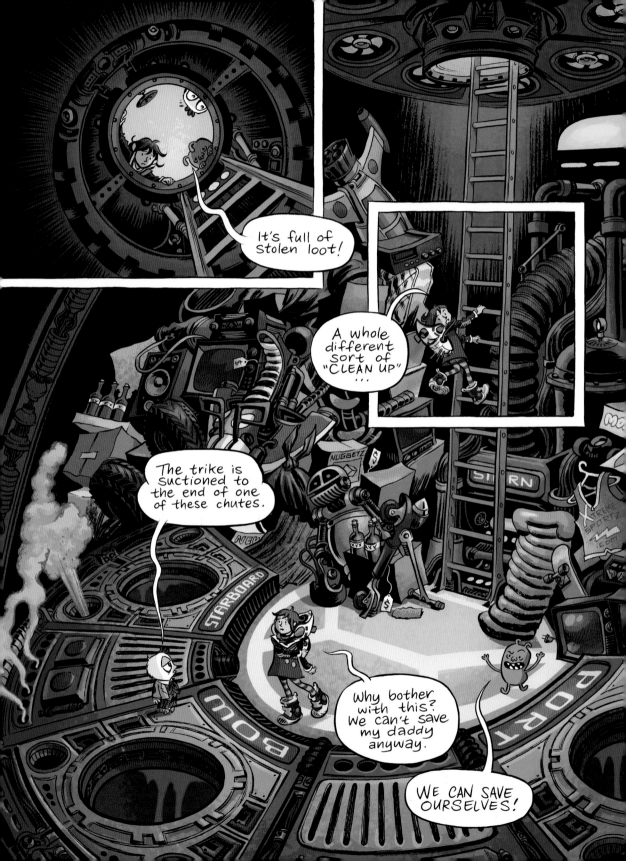

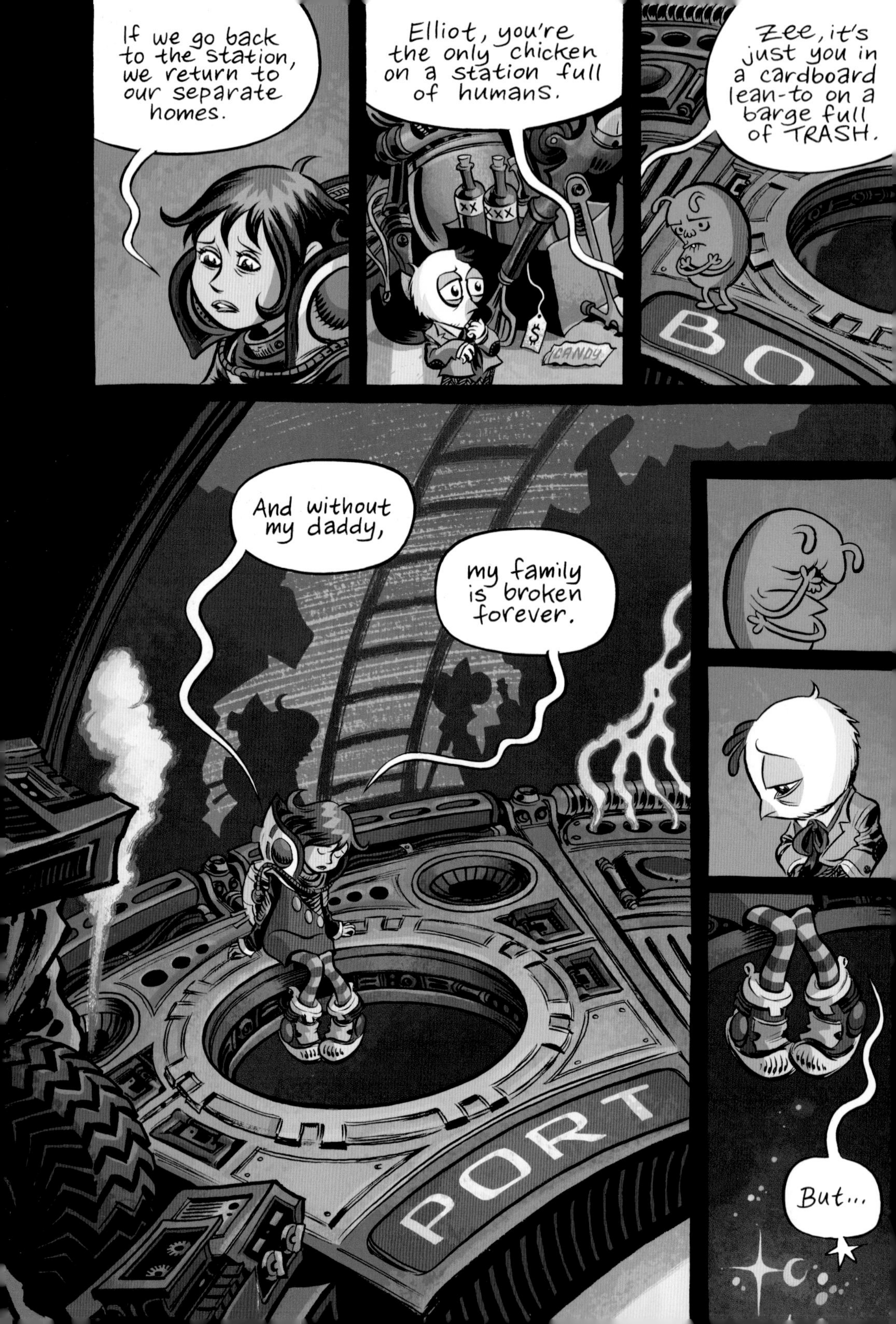
If we go back to the station, we return to our separate homes.
Elliot, you're the only chicken on a station full of humans.
CANDY
Zee, it's just you in a cardboard lean-to on a barge full of TRASH.
BO
And without my daddy,
my family is broken forever.
PORT
But...

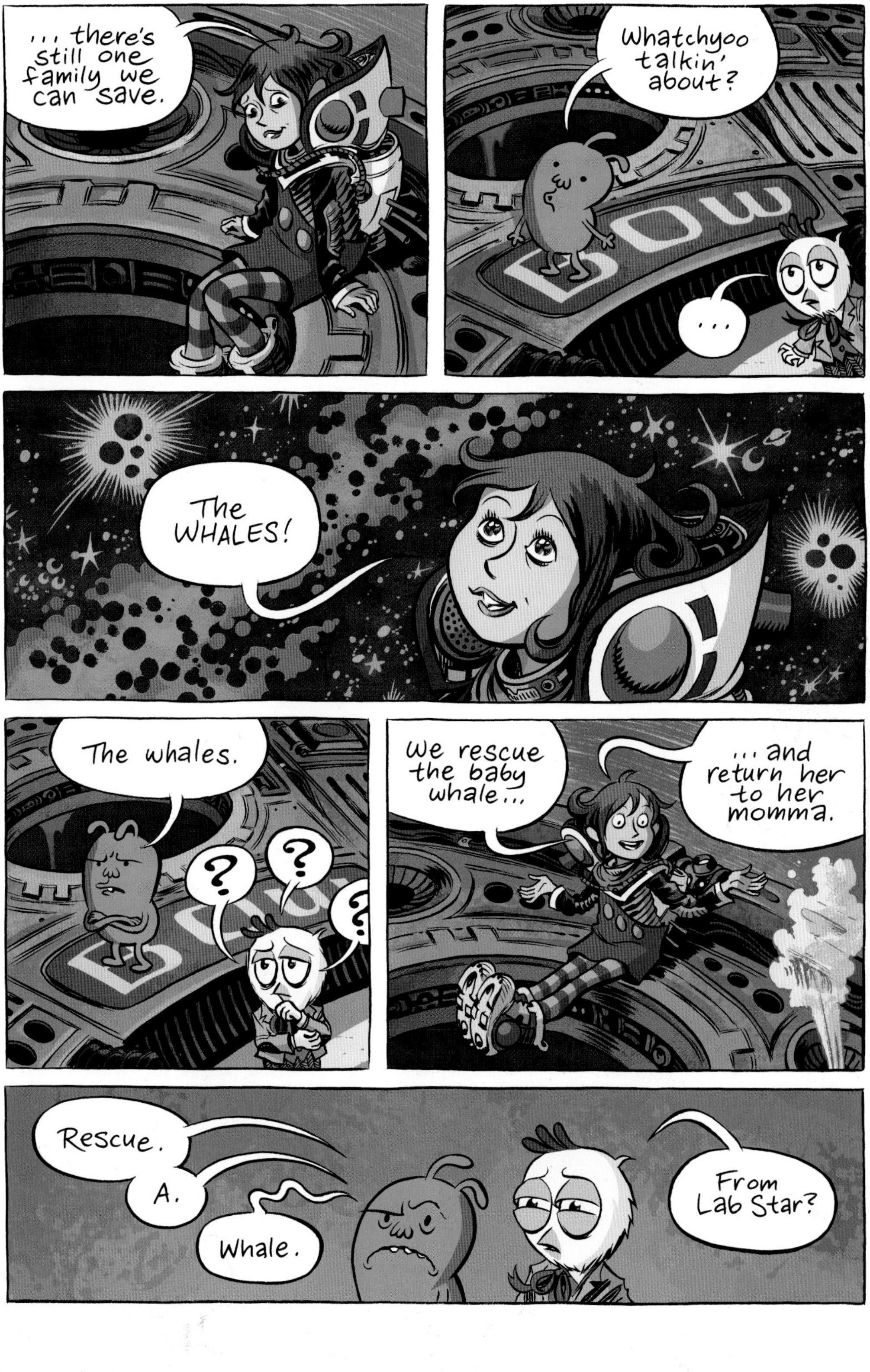

...there's still one family we can save.
Whatchyoo talkin' about?
...
The WHALES!
The whales.
?
?
?
We rescue the baby whale...
...and return her to her momma.
Rescue.
A.
Whale.
From Lab Star?

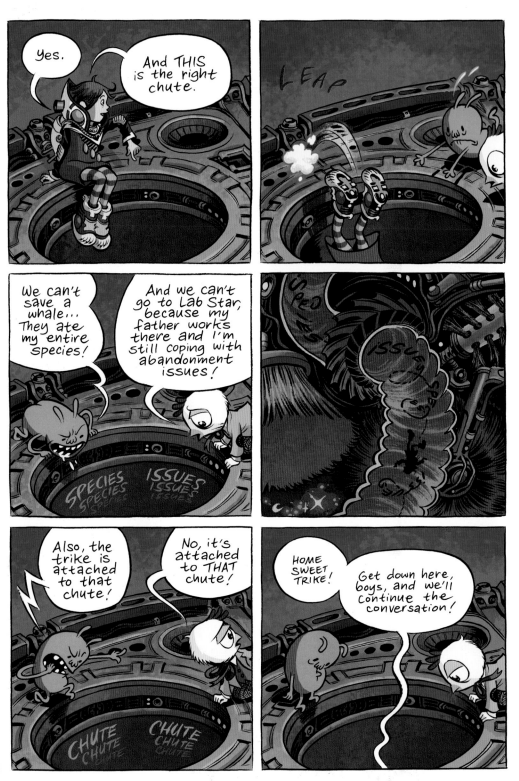

2
1
2

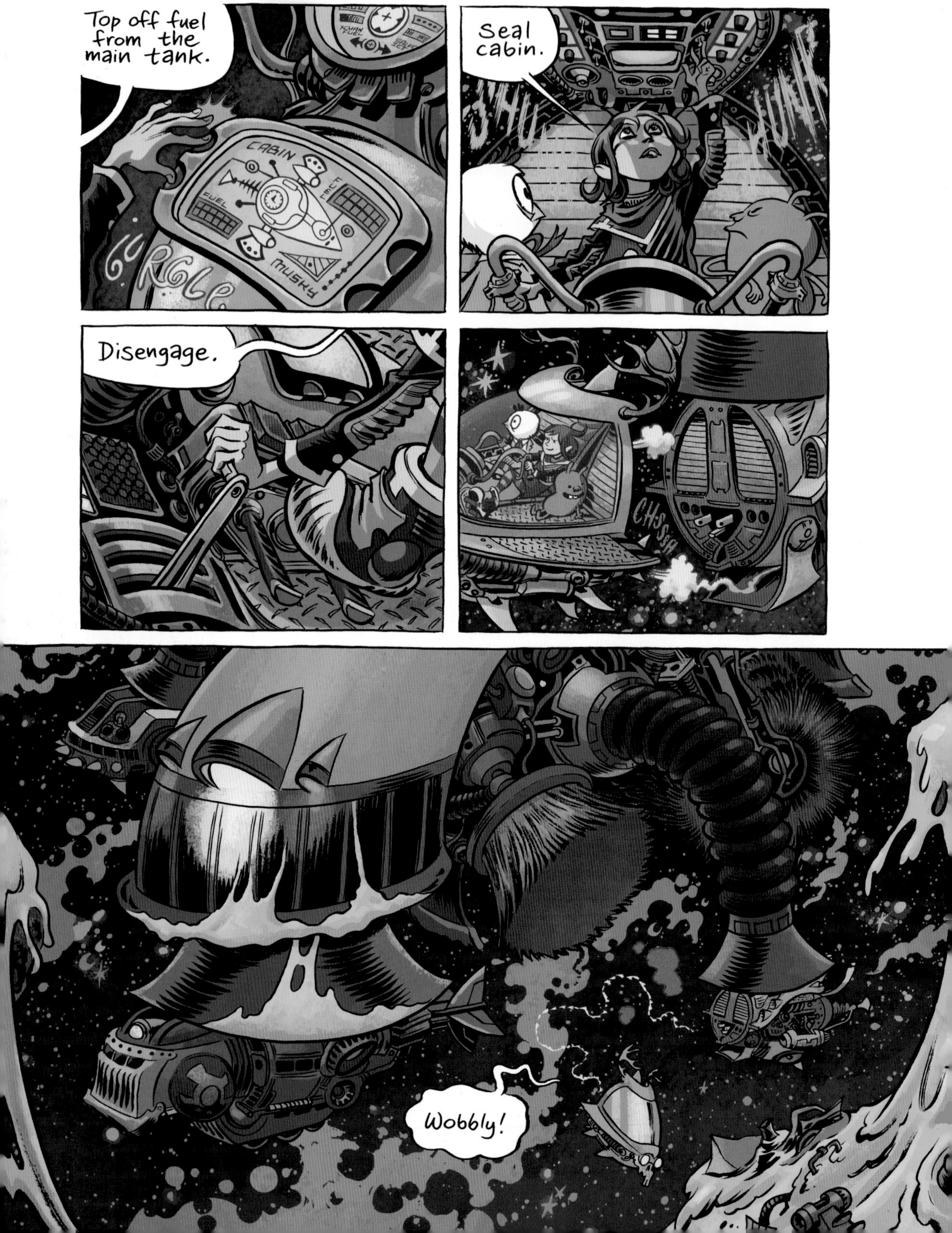
Top off fuel from the main tank.
CABIN
FUEL
MUSKY
GURGLE
Seal cabin.
Disengage.
Wobbly!

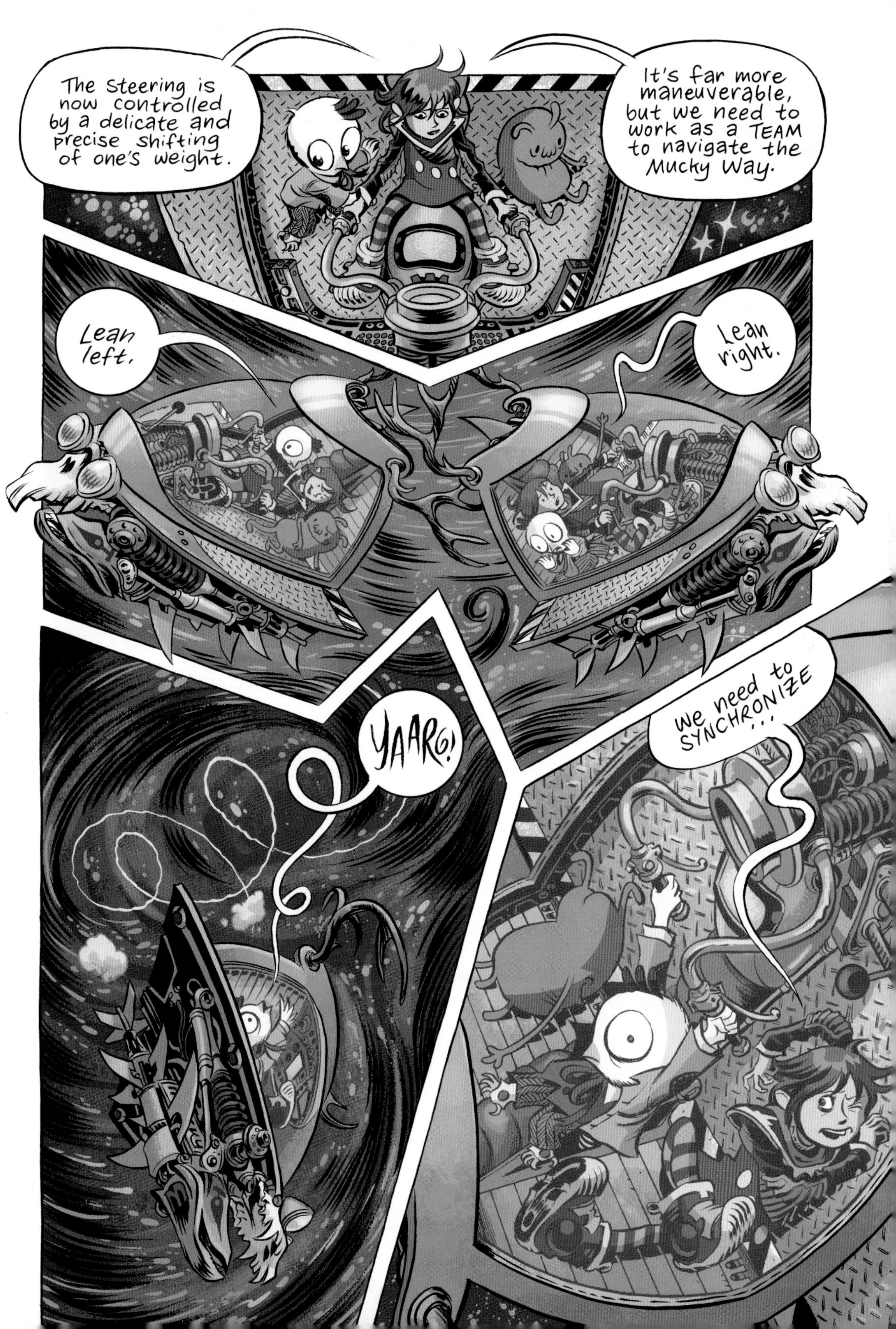
The Steering is now controlled by a delicate and precise shifting of one's weight.
It's far more maneuverable, but we need to work as a TEAM to navigate the Mucky Way.
Lean left.
Lean right.
YAARG!
We need to SYNCHRONIZE...

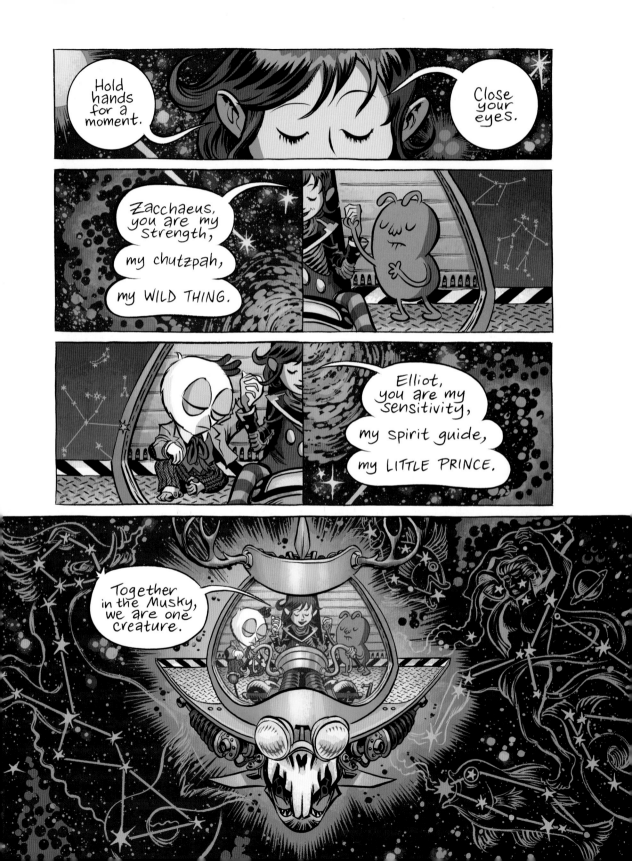

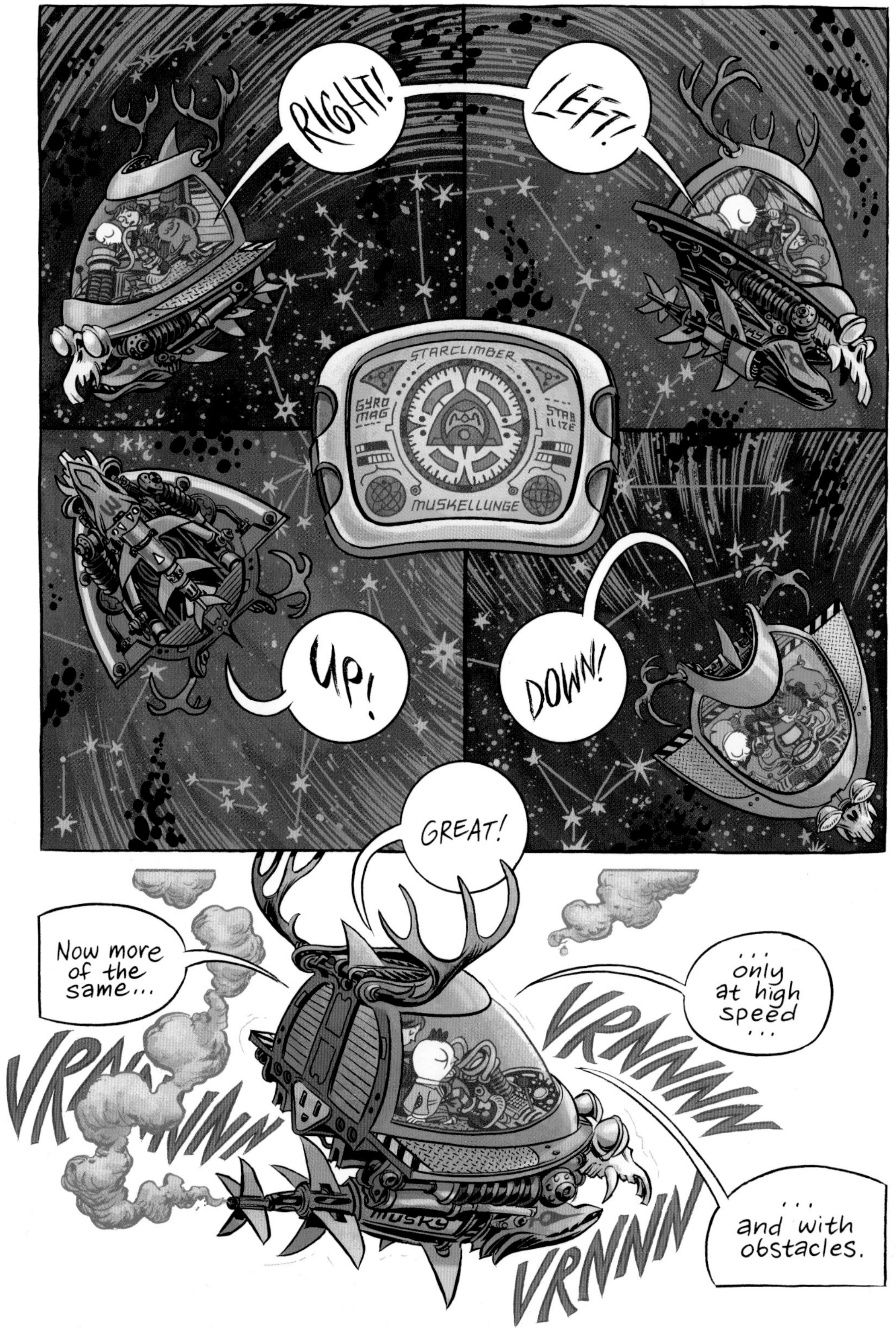
RIGHT!
LEFT!
STARCLIMBER
GYRO MAG
STAB ILIZE
MUSKELLUNGE
UP!
DOWN!
GREAT!
Now more of the same...
...only at high speed...
VRNNNNN
VRNNNNN
...and with obstacles.
VRNNNN
MUSKY

06

MAG/
GYRO
NAV

MAGNITUDES:

RED SHELL,
BLUE BLOOD

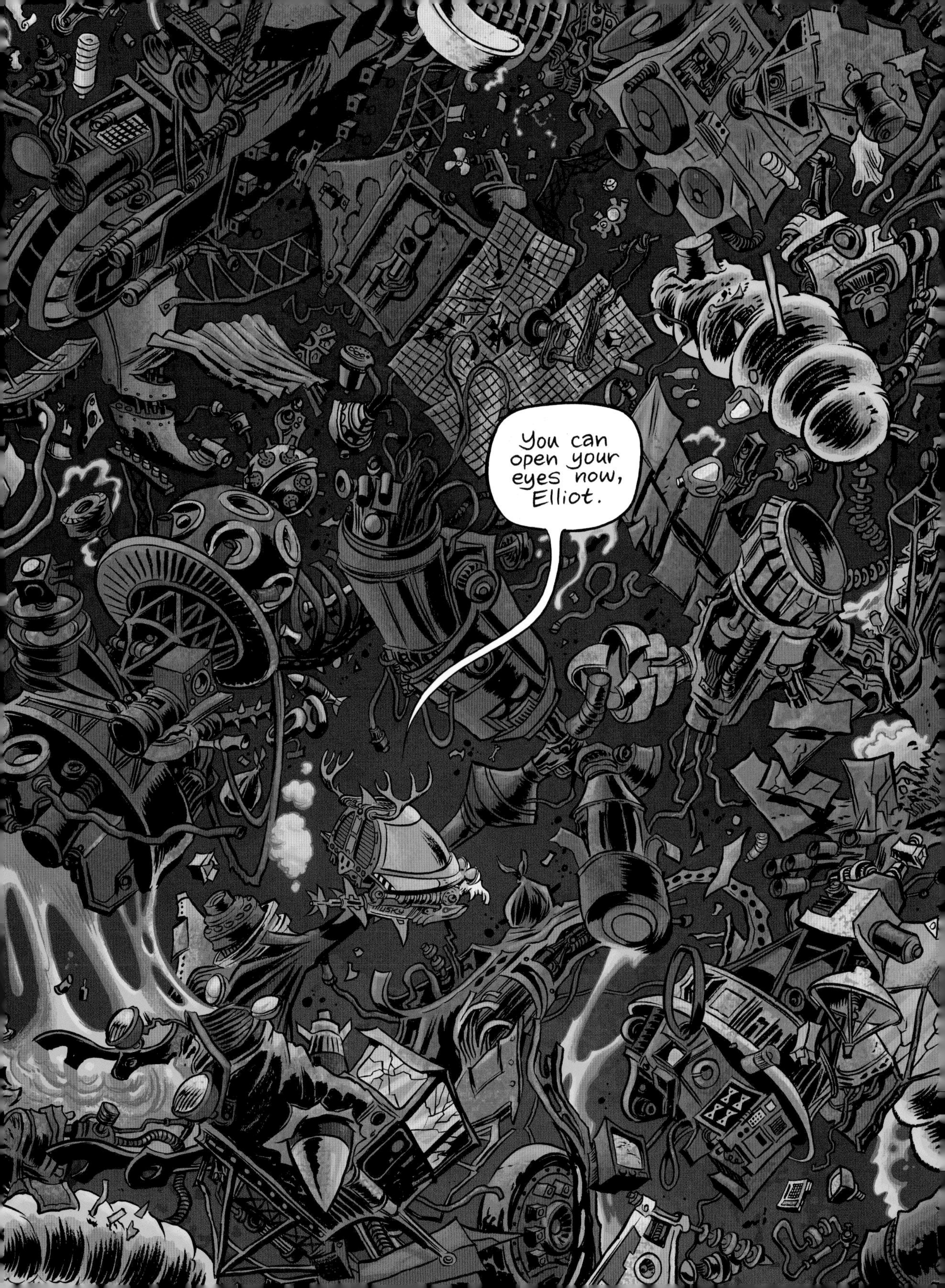
You can open your eyes now, Elliot.

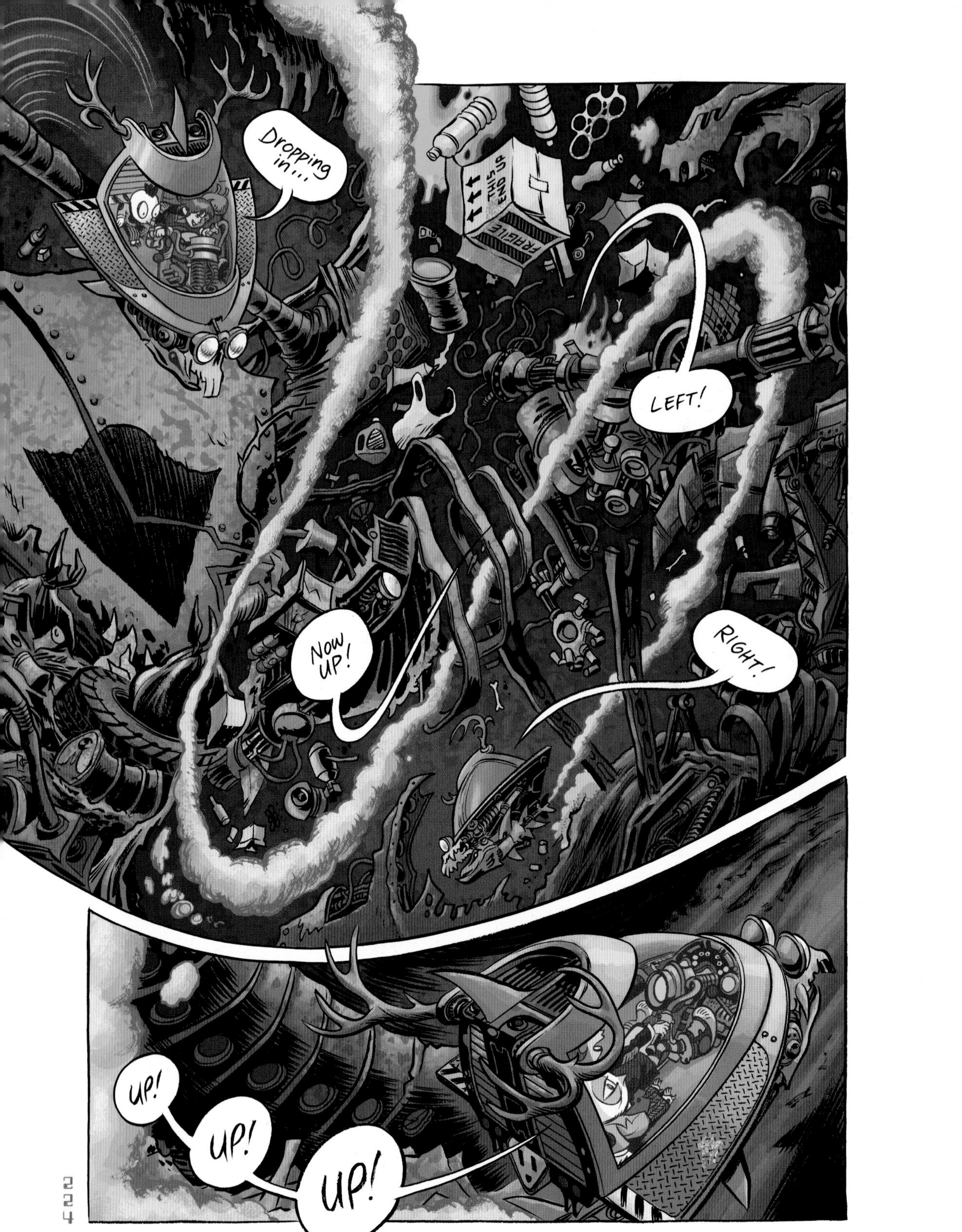
Dropping in...
THIS END UP
FRAGILE
LEFT!
Now UP!
RIGHT!
UP!
UP!
UP!

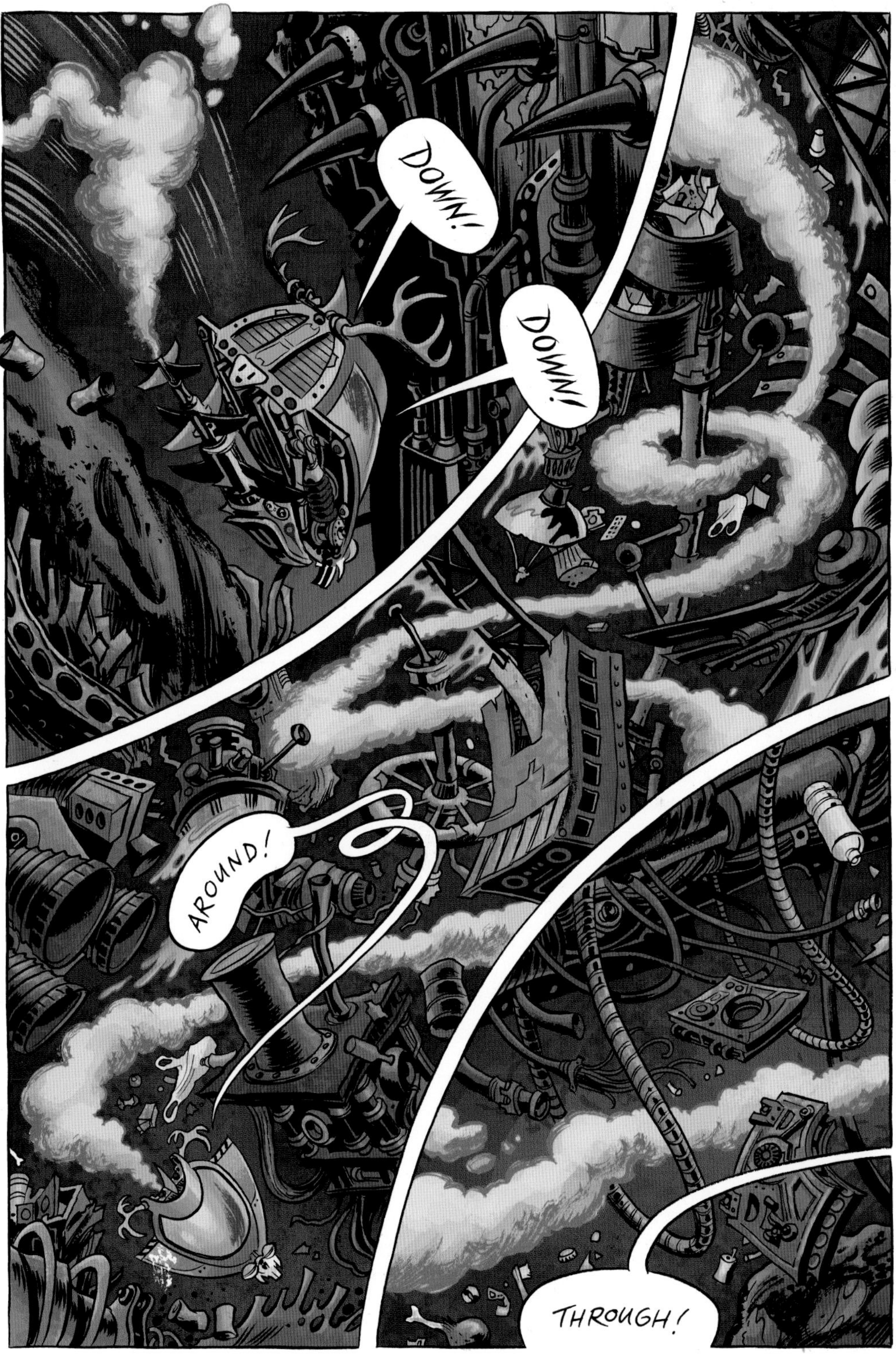
DOWN!
DOWN!
AROUND!
THROUGH!

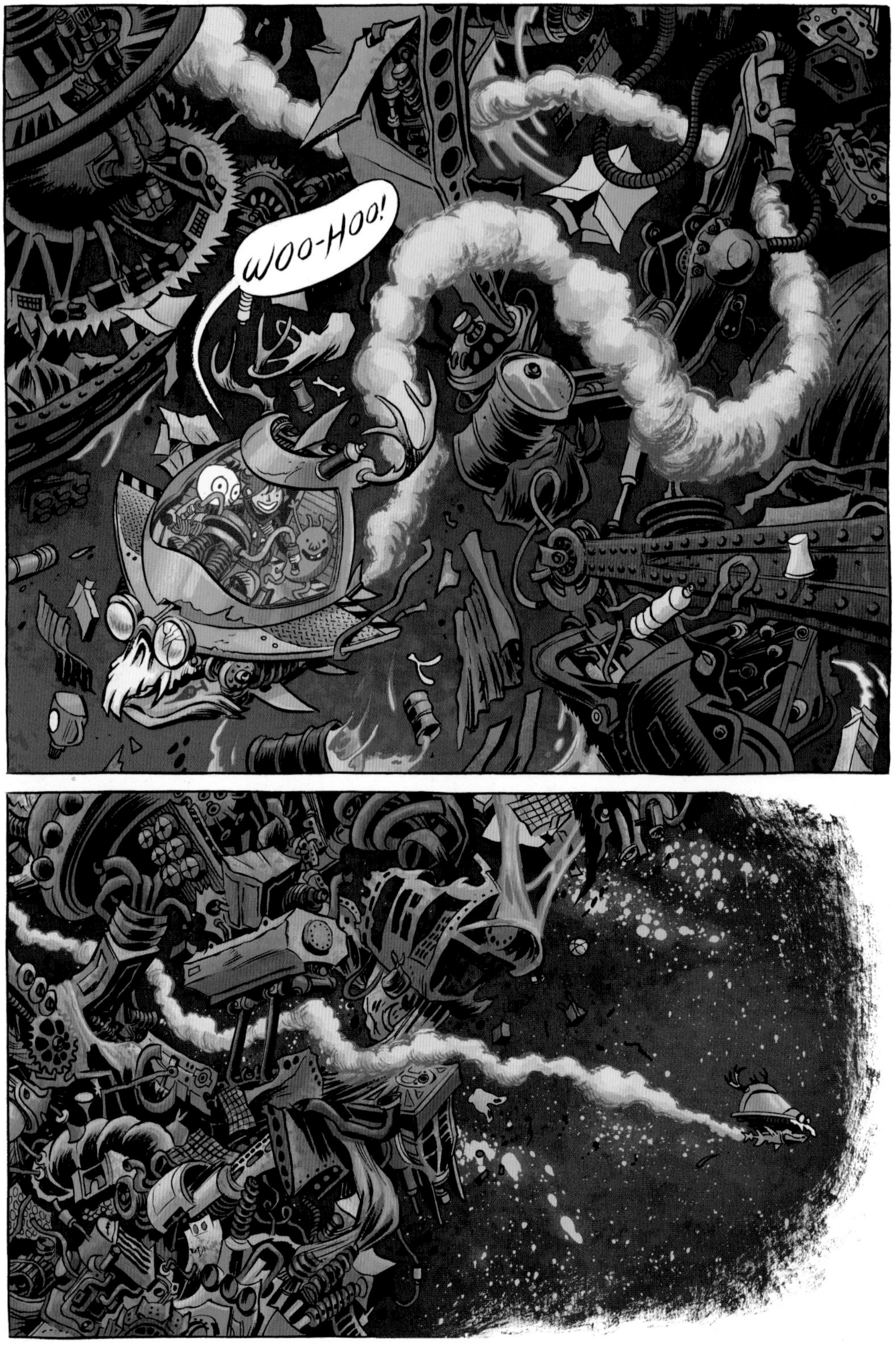
WOO-HOO!

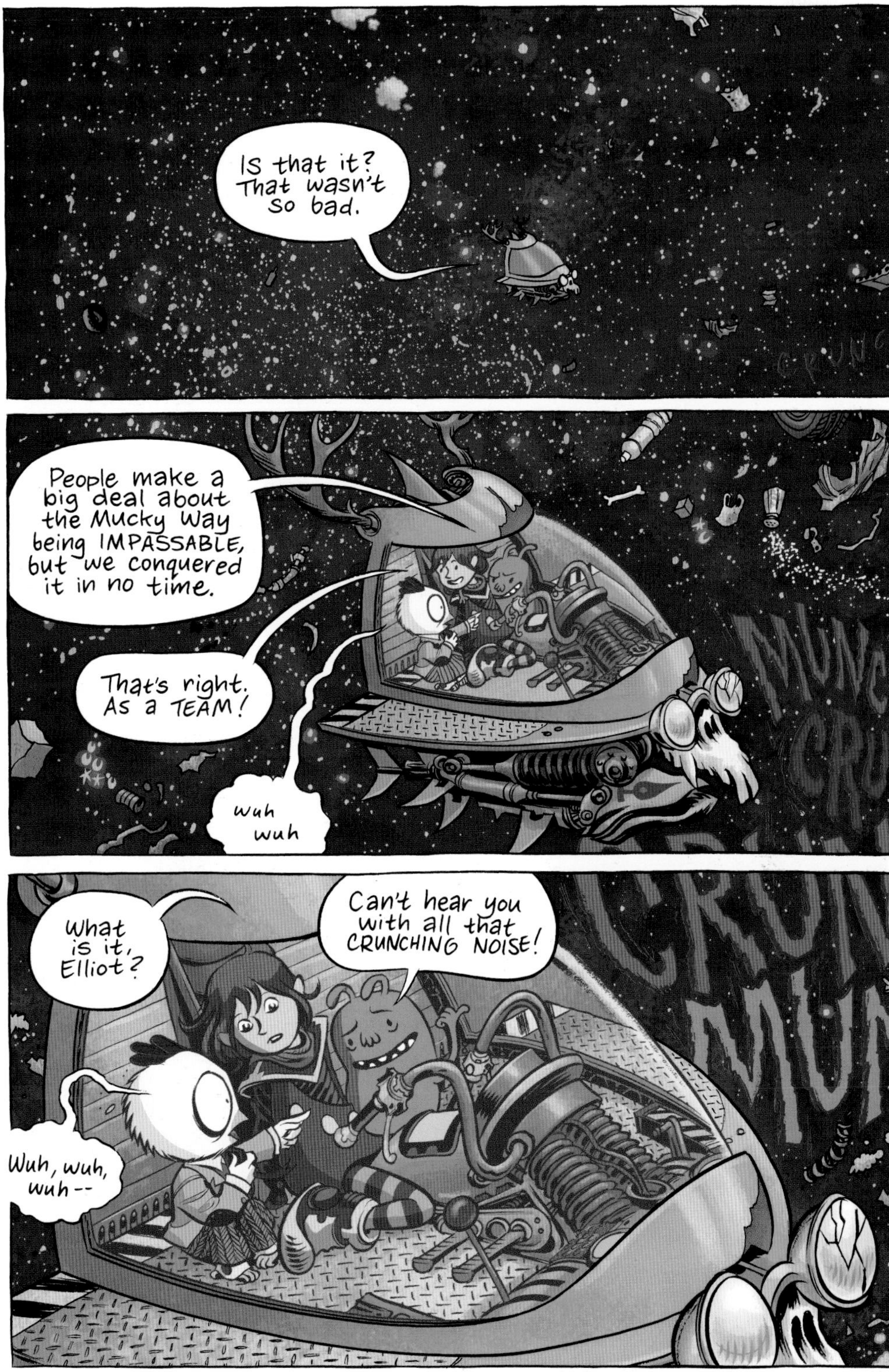

Is that it? That wasn't so bad.
CRUNCH
People make a big deal about the Mucky Way being IMPASSABLE, but we conquered it in no time.
That's right. As a TEAM!
wuh wuh
What is it, Elliot?
Can't hear you with all that CRUNCHING NOISE!
Wuh, wuh, wuh--

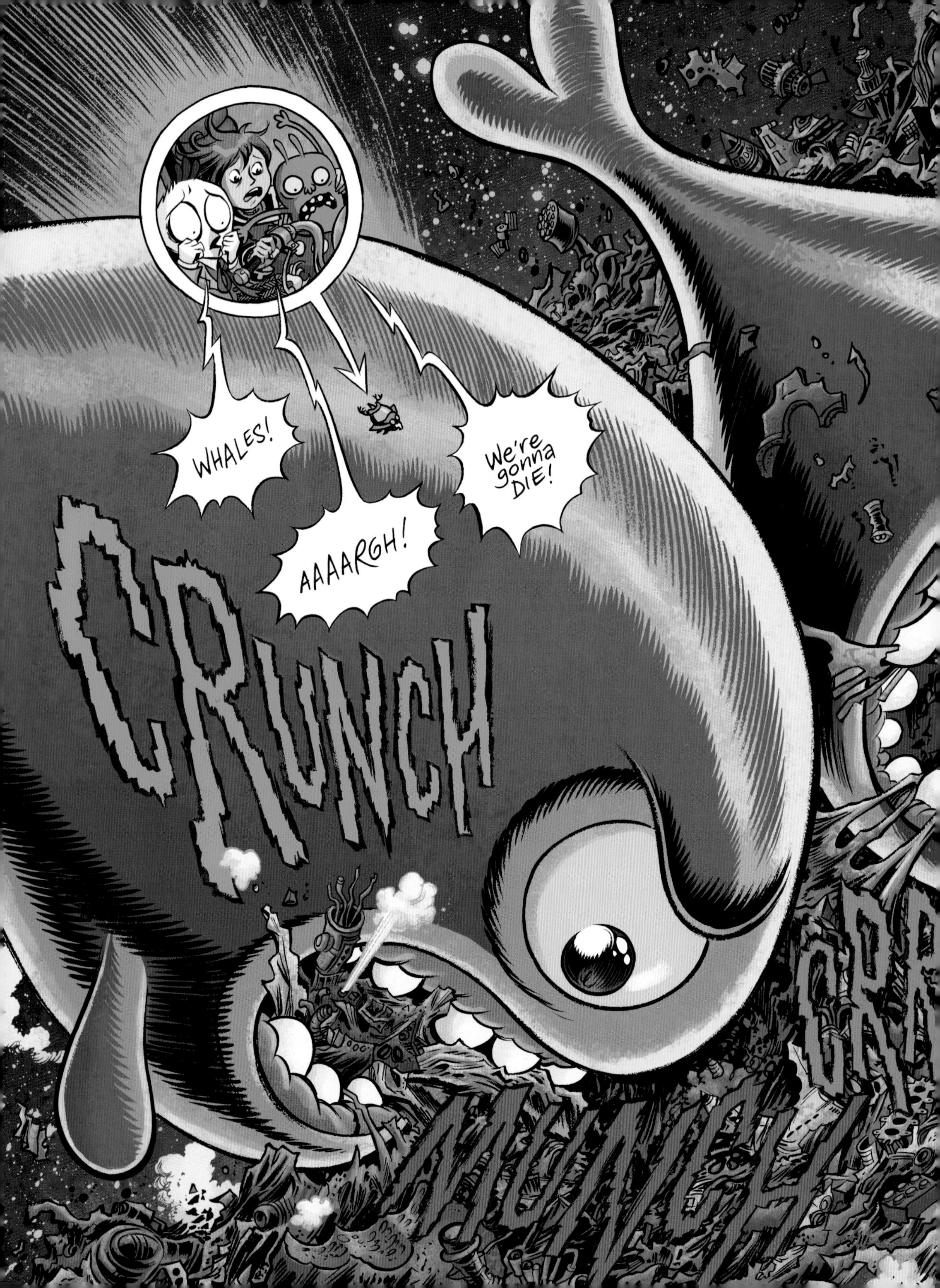
WHALES!
AAAARGH!
We're gonna DIE!
CRUNCH

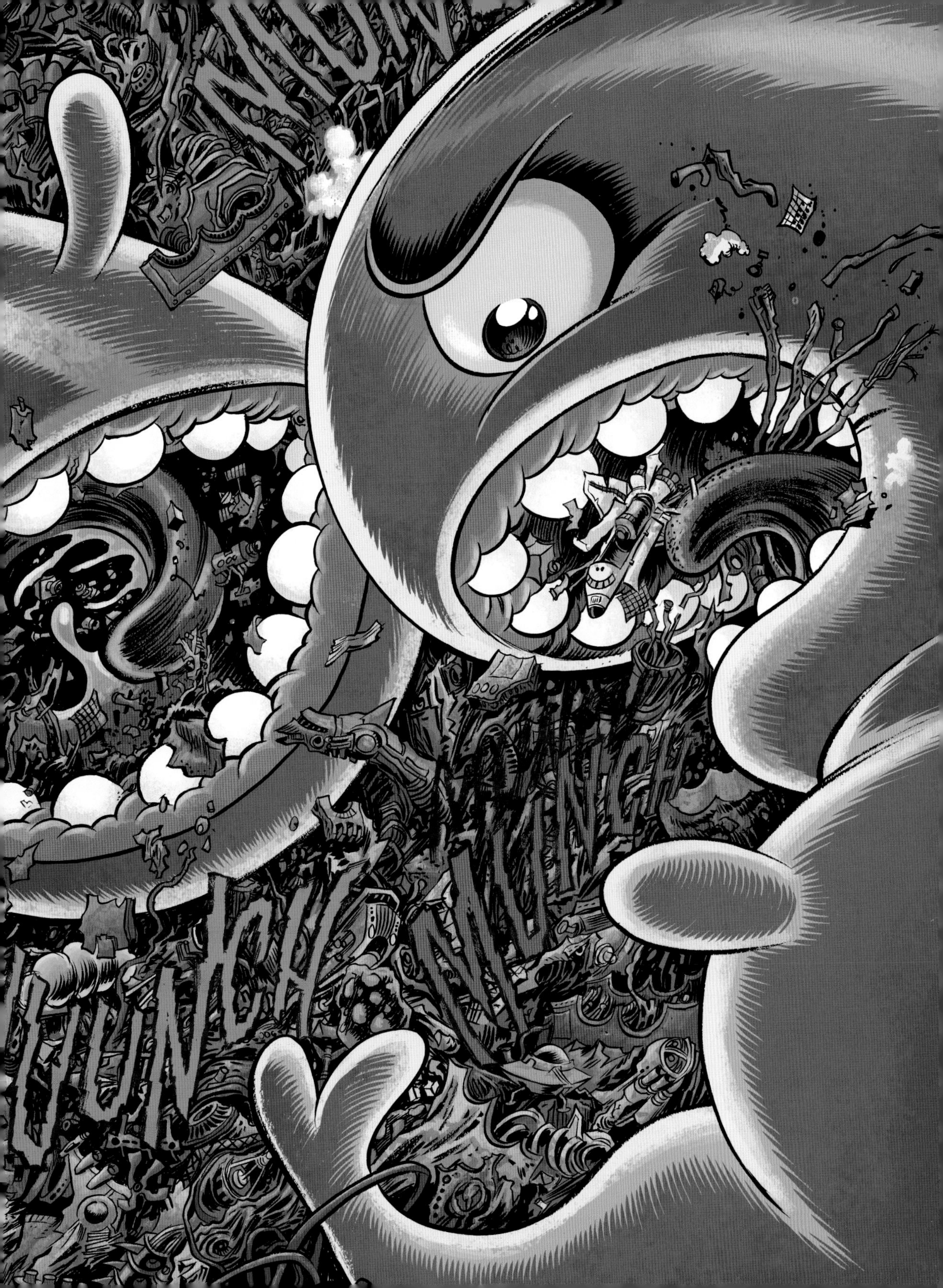
MUNCH
MUNCH

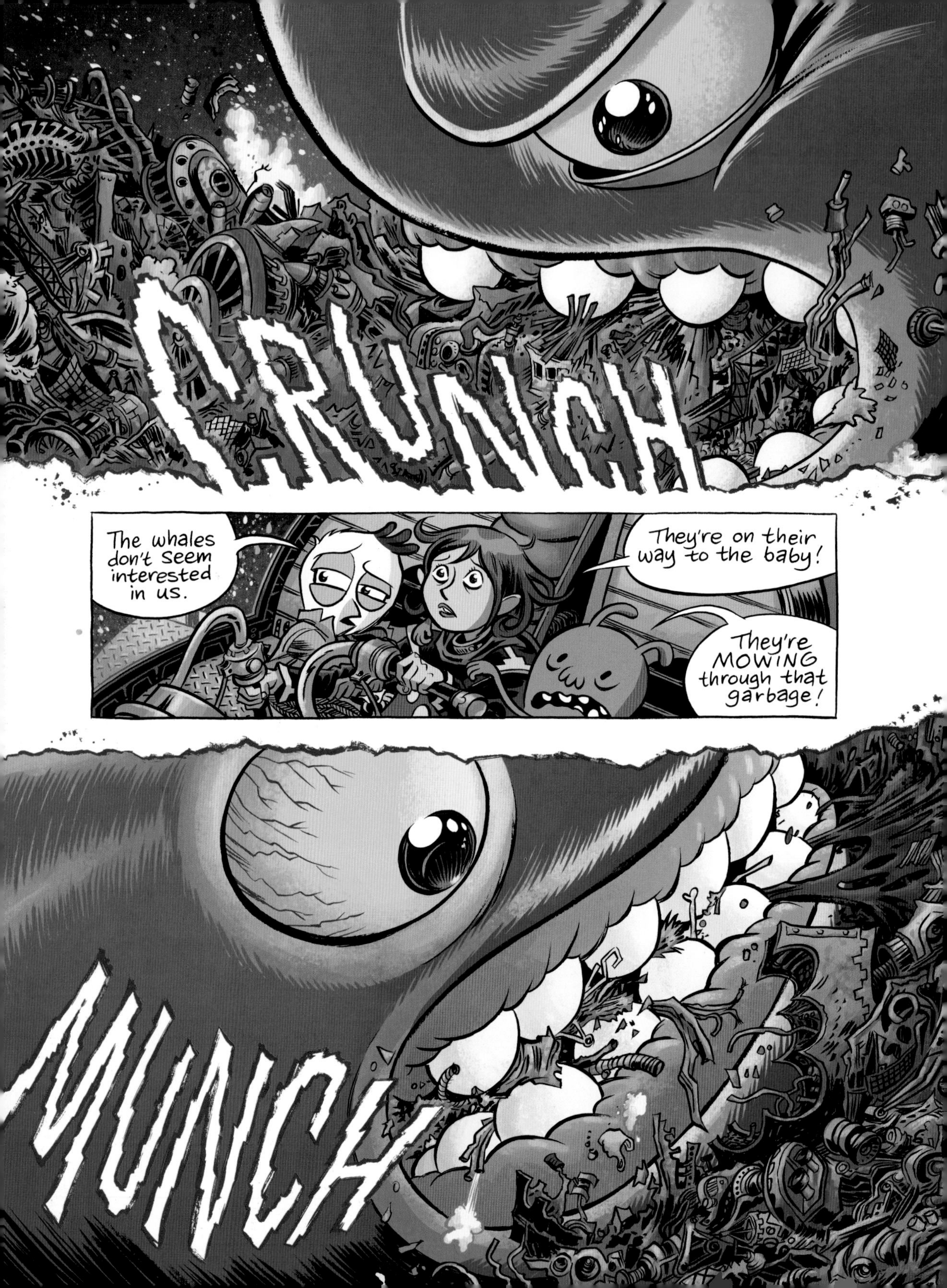
CRUNCH
The whales don't seem interested in us.
They're on their way to the baby!
They're MOWING through that garbage!
MUNCH

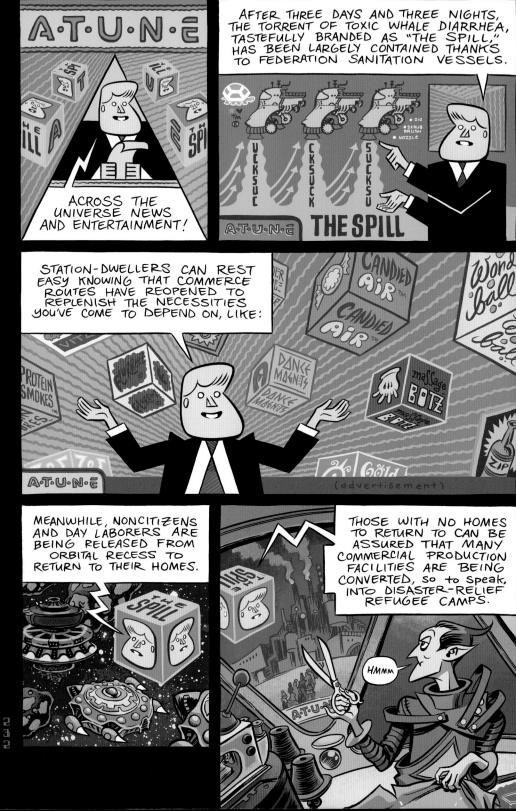

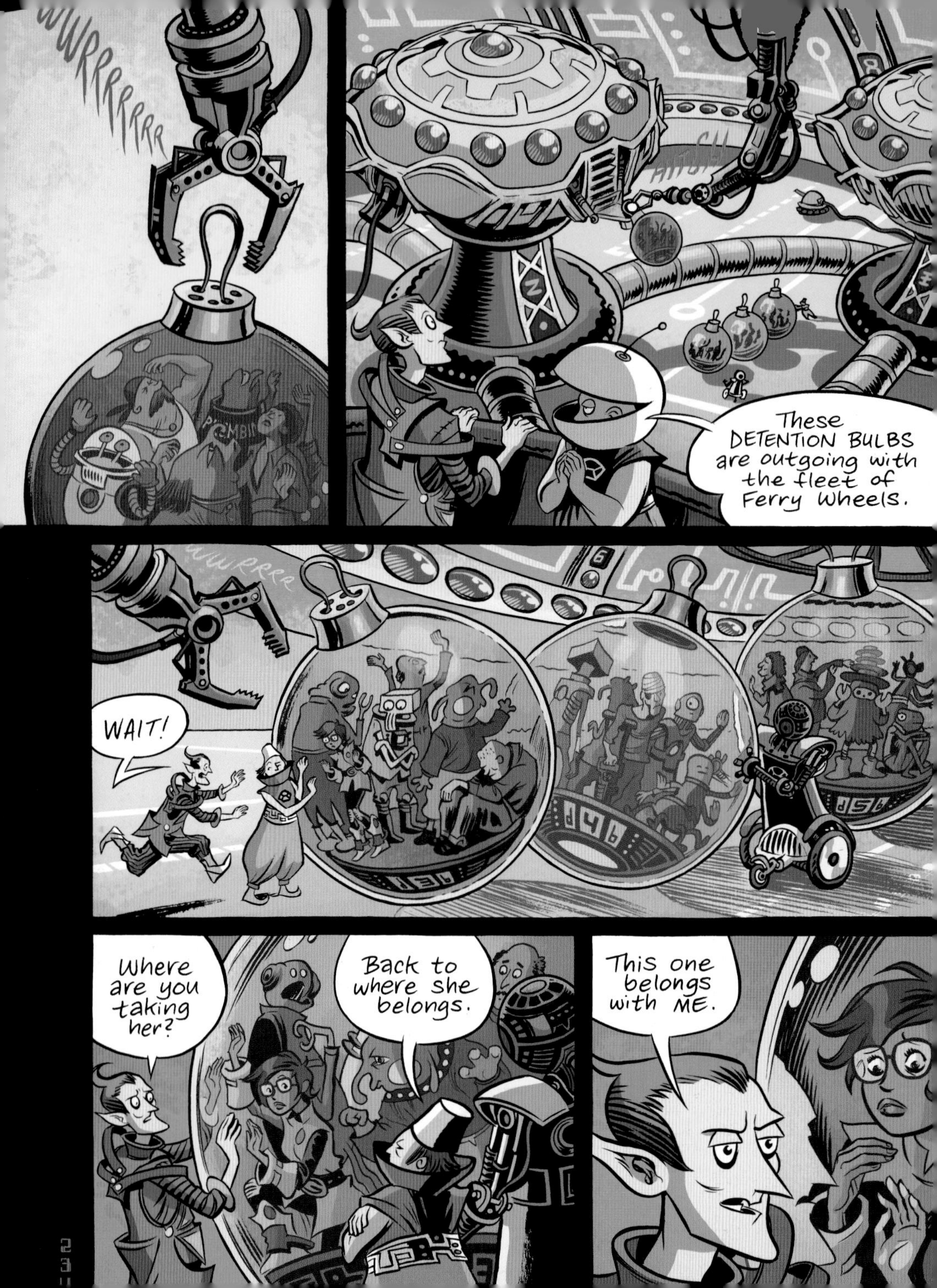
These DETENTION BULBS are outgoing with the fleet of Ferry Wheels.
WAIT!
Where are you taking her?
Back to where she belongs.
This one belongs with ME.

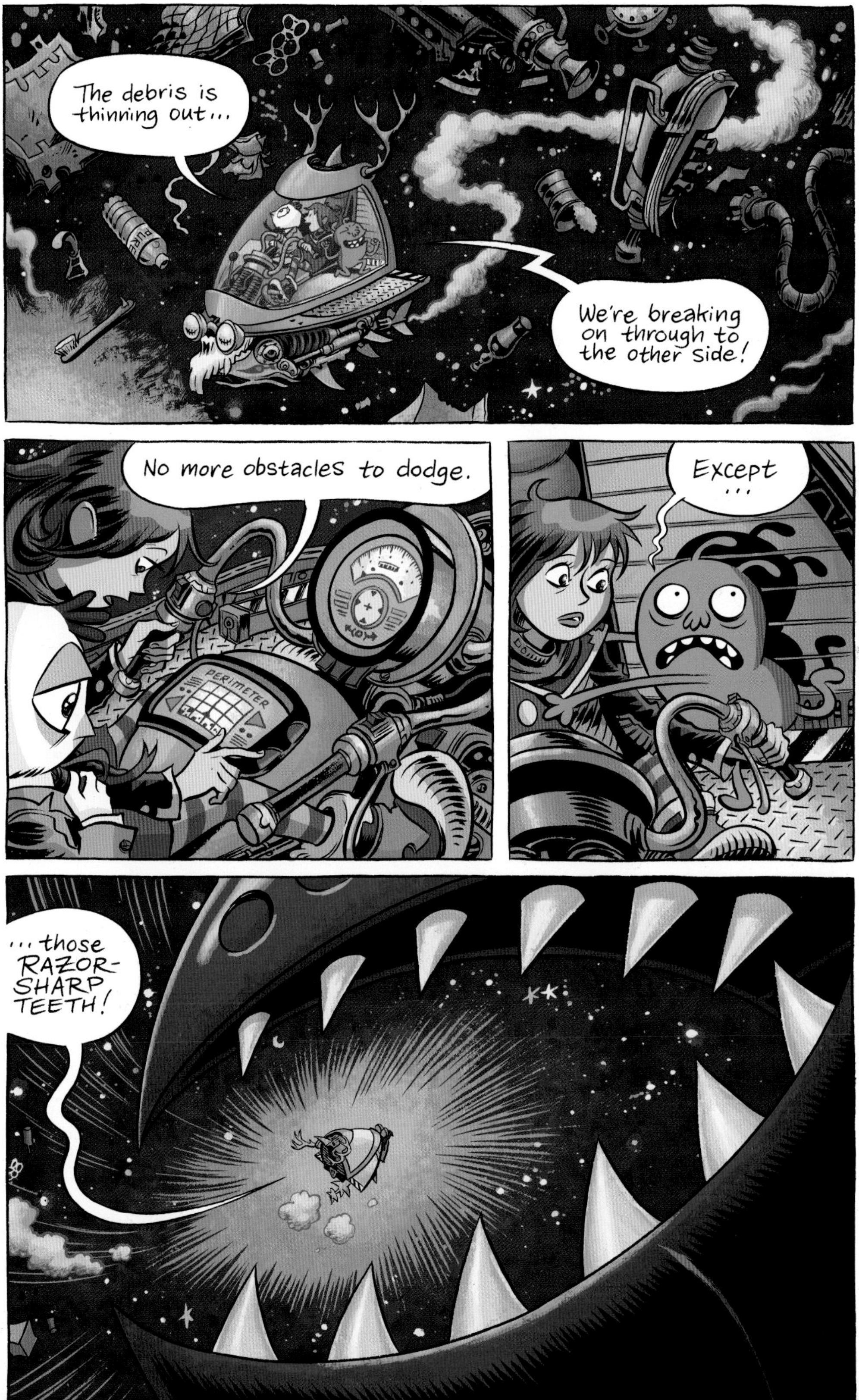

The debris is thinning out...
We're breaking on through to the other side!
No more obstacles to dodge.
PERIMETER
Except ...
... those RAZOR-SHARP TEETH!

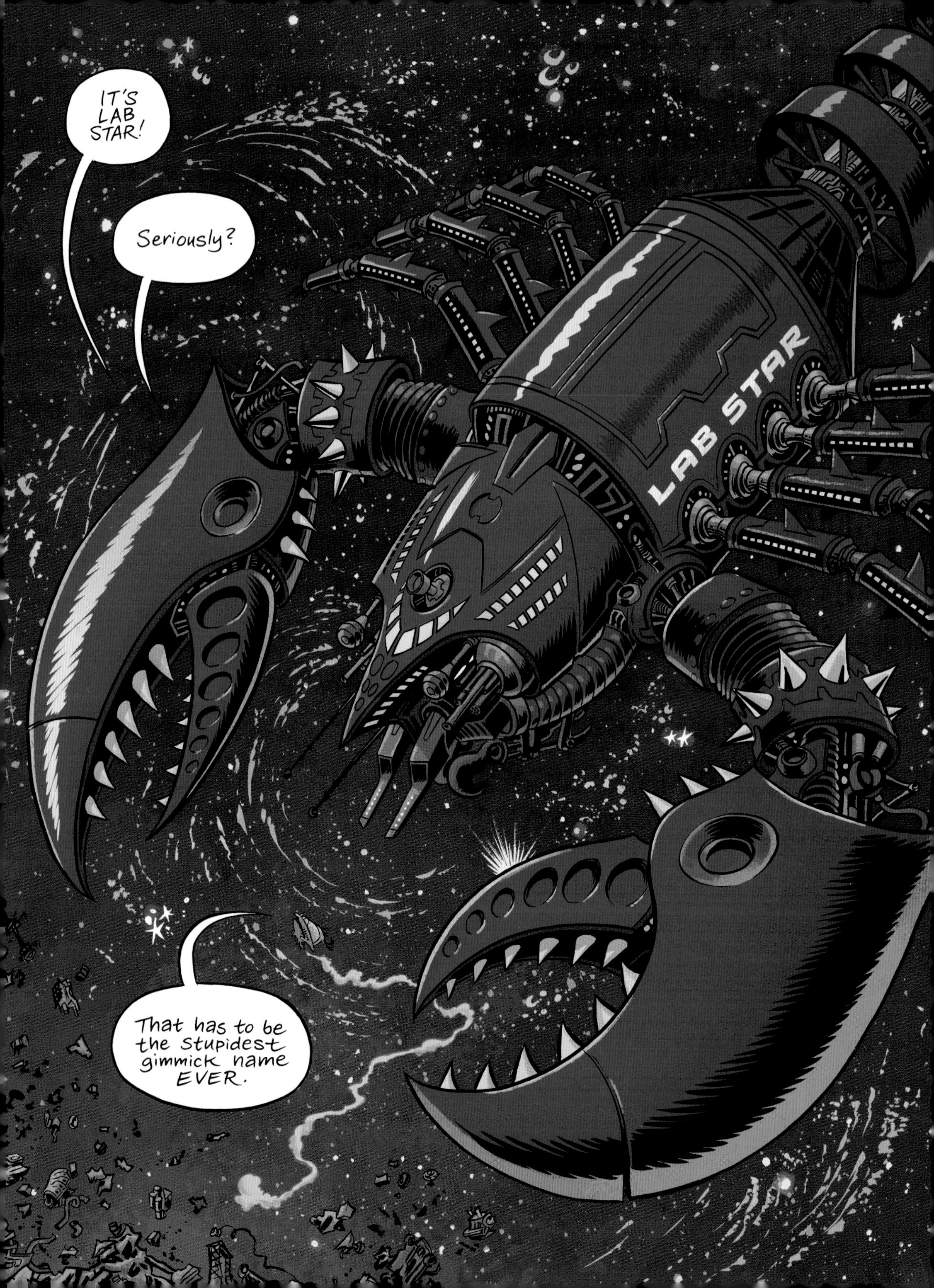
IT'S LAB STAR!
Seriously?
LAB STAR
That has to be the stupidest gimmick name EVER.

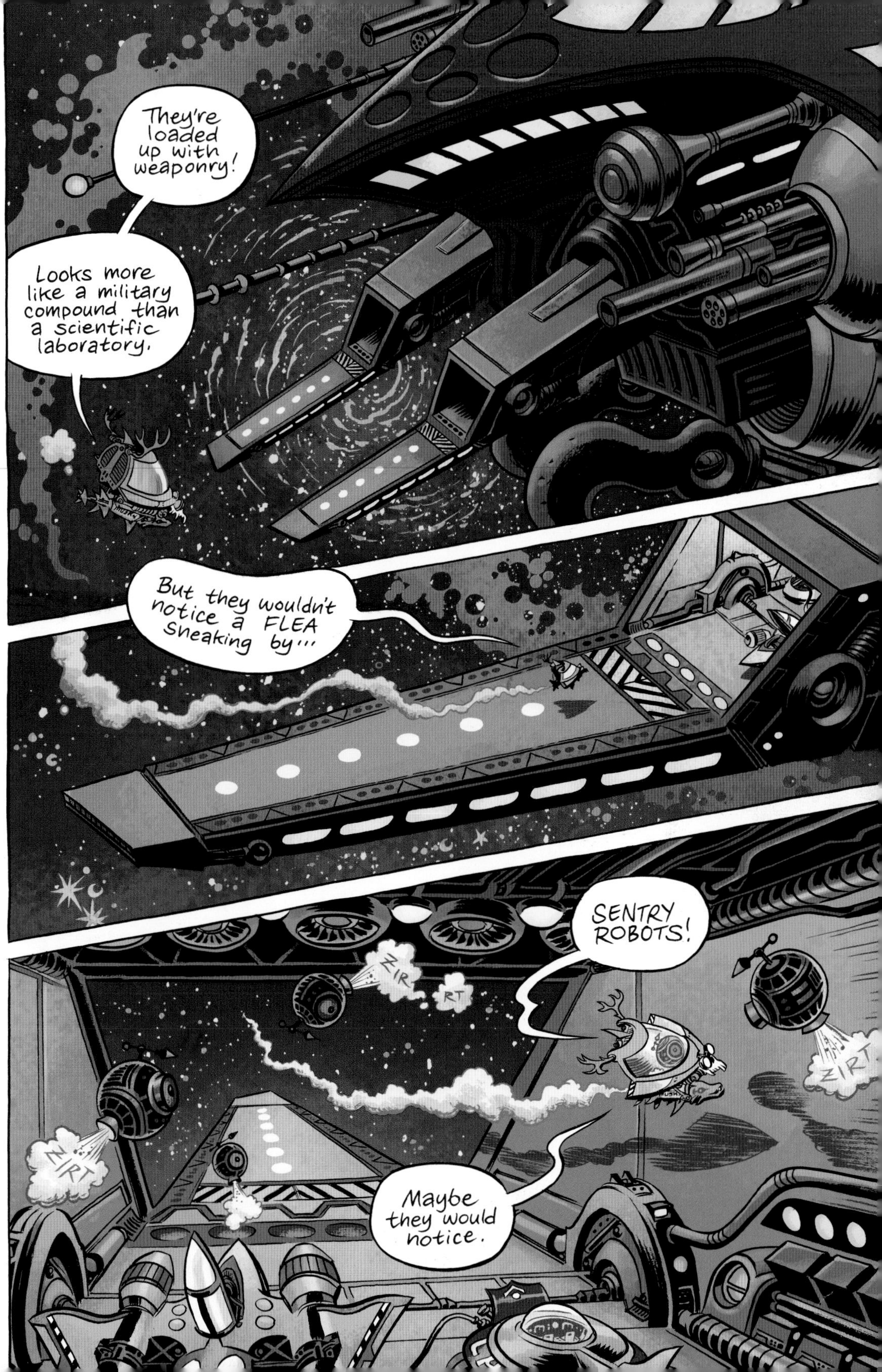
They're loaded up with weaponry!
Looks more like a military compound than a scientific laboratory.
But they wouldn't notice a FLEA sneaking by...
SENTRY ROBOTS!
ZIRT
RT
ZIRT
ZIRT
Maybe they would notice.

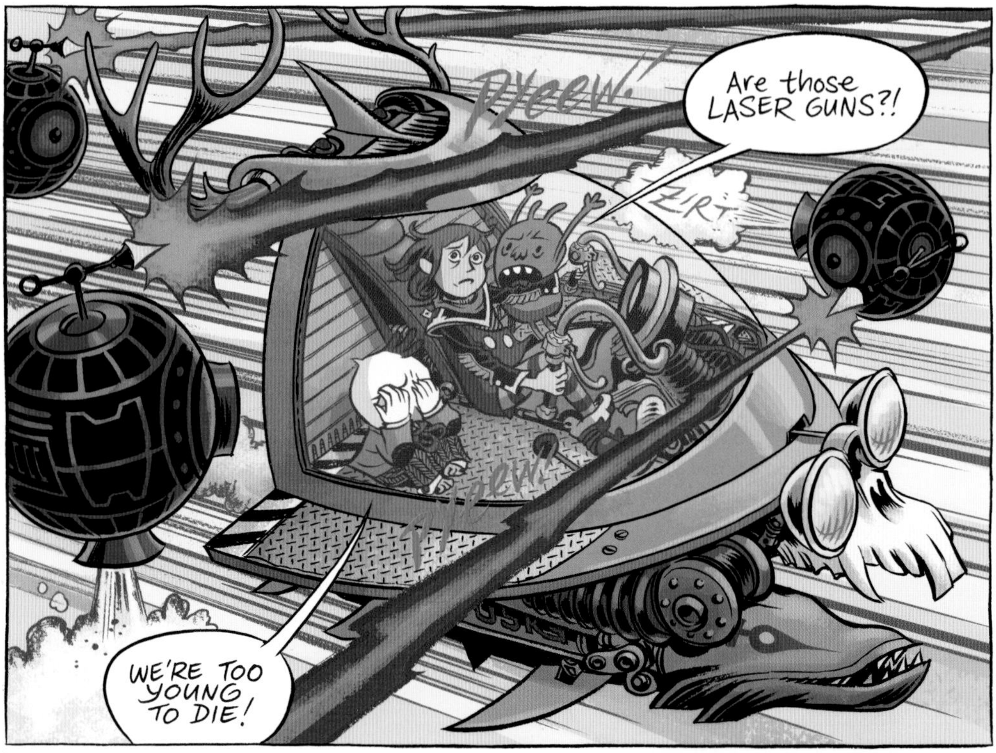
DYEEW!
Are those LASER GUNS?!
ZIRT
PYEEW!
WE'RE TOO YOUNG TO DIE!

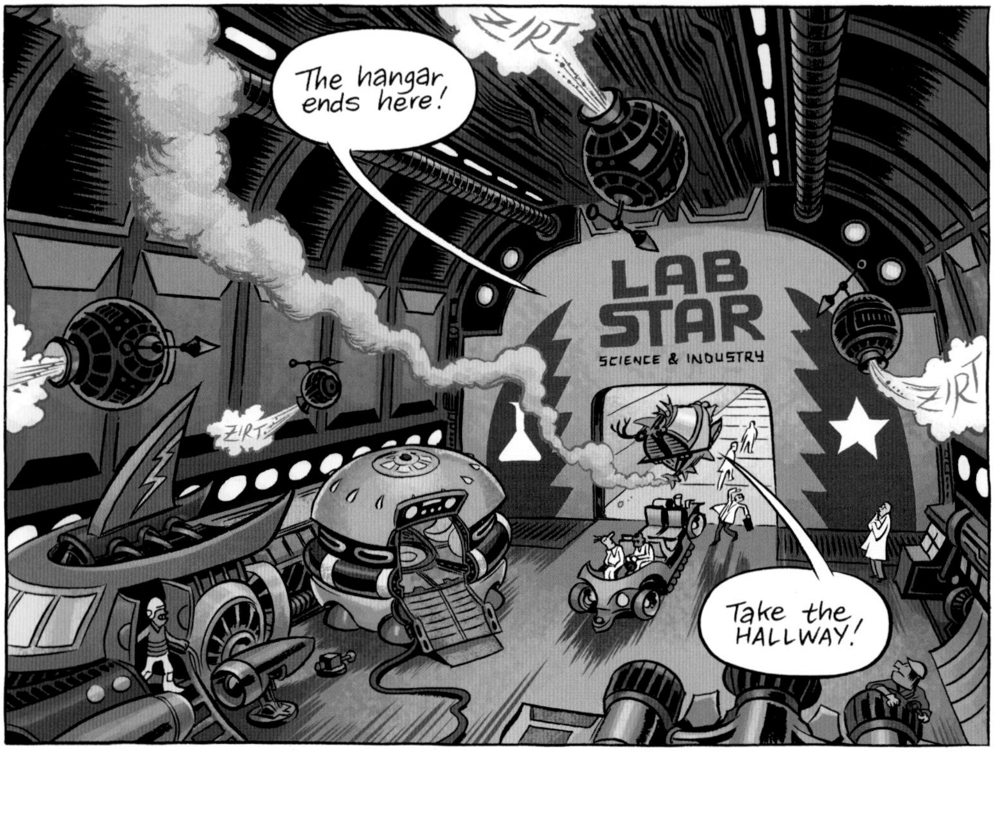
ZIRT
The hangar ends here!
LAB STAR
SCIENCE & INDUSTRY
ZIRT
ZIRT
Take the HALLWAY!

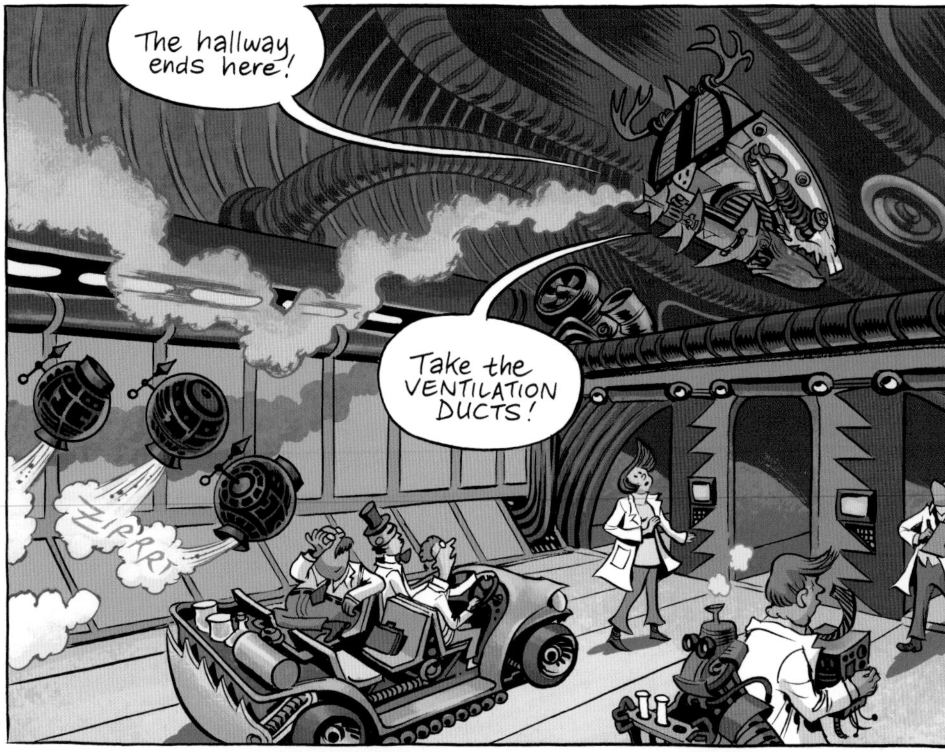
The hallway ends here!
Take the VENTILATION DUCTS!
ZIPRRT

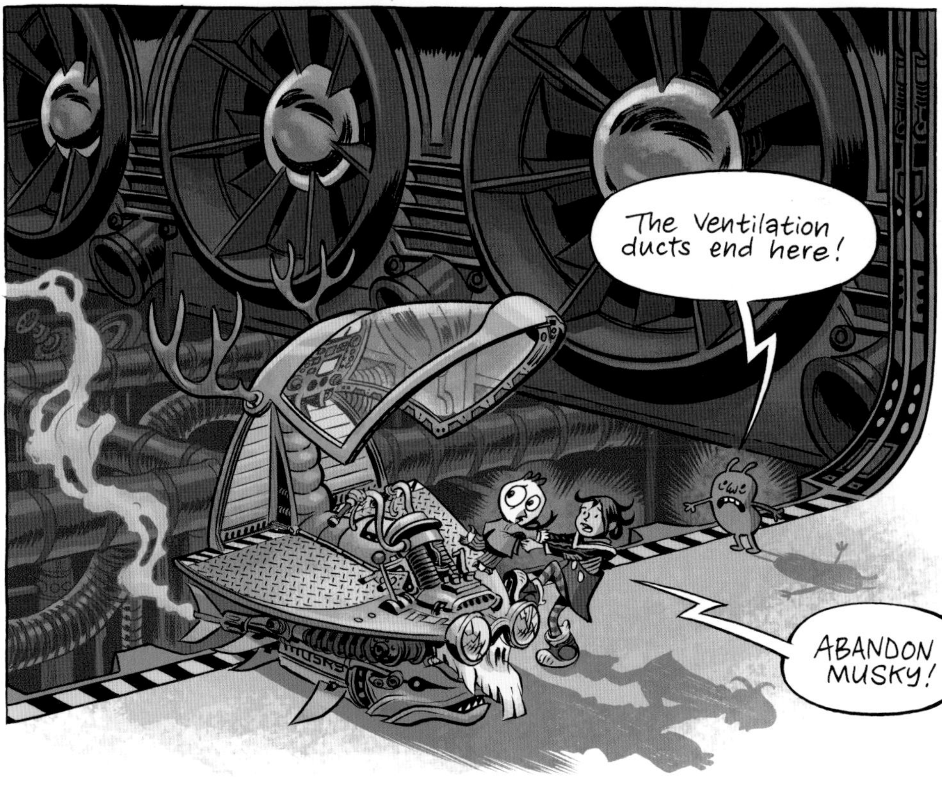
The Ventilation ducts end here!
ABANDON MUSKY!

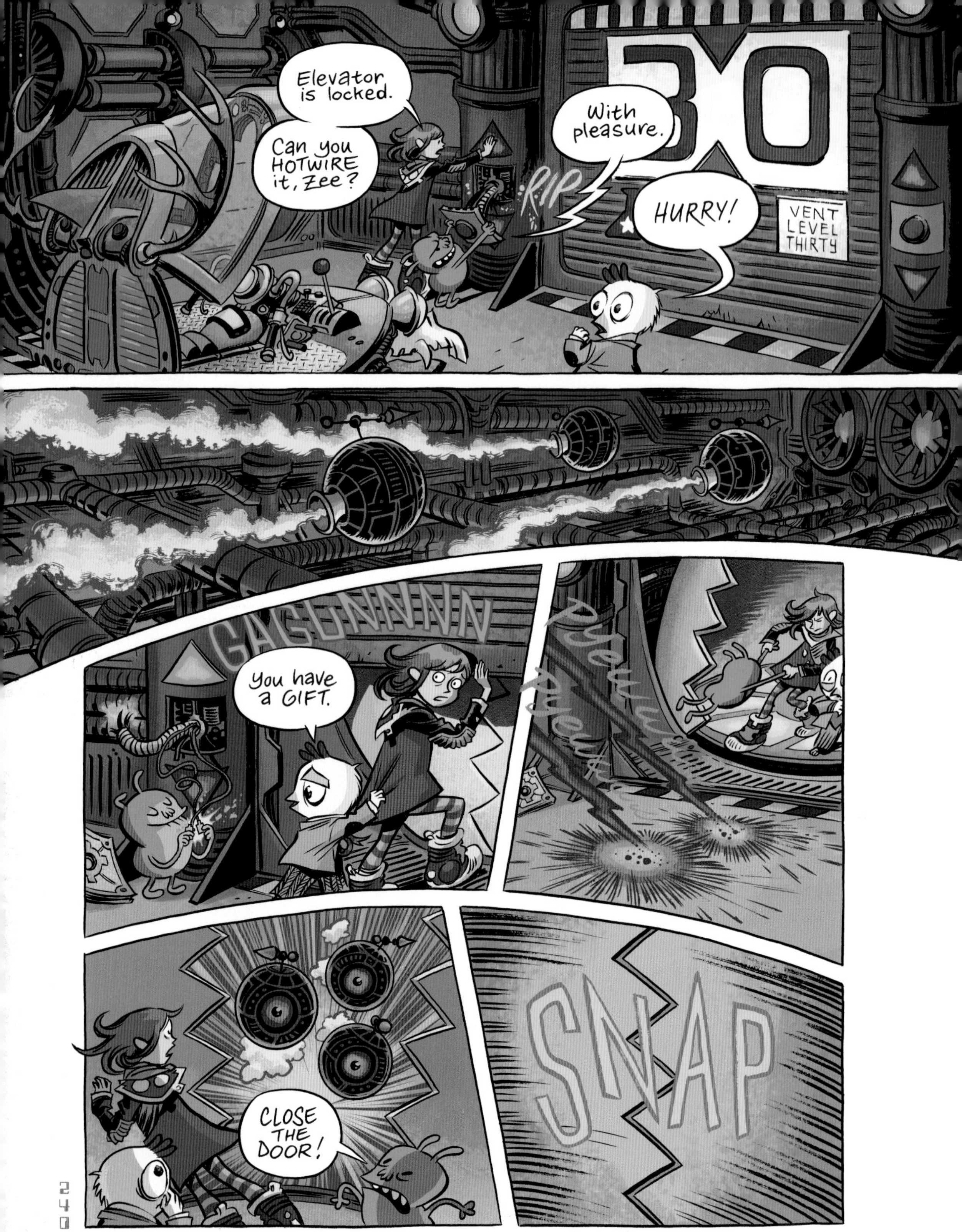
30
Elevator is locked.
Can you HOTWIRE it, Zee?
With pleasure.
RIP
HURRY!
VENT LEVEL THIRTY
GAGUNNNNN
You have a GIFT.
CLOSE THE DOOR!
SNAP

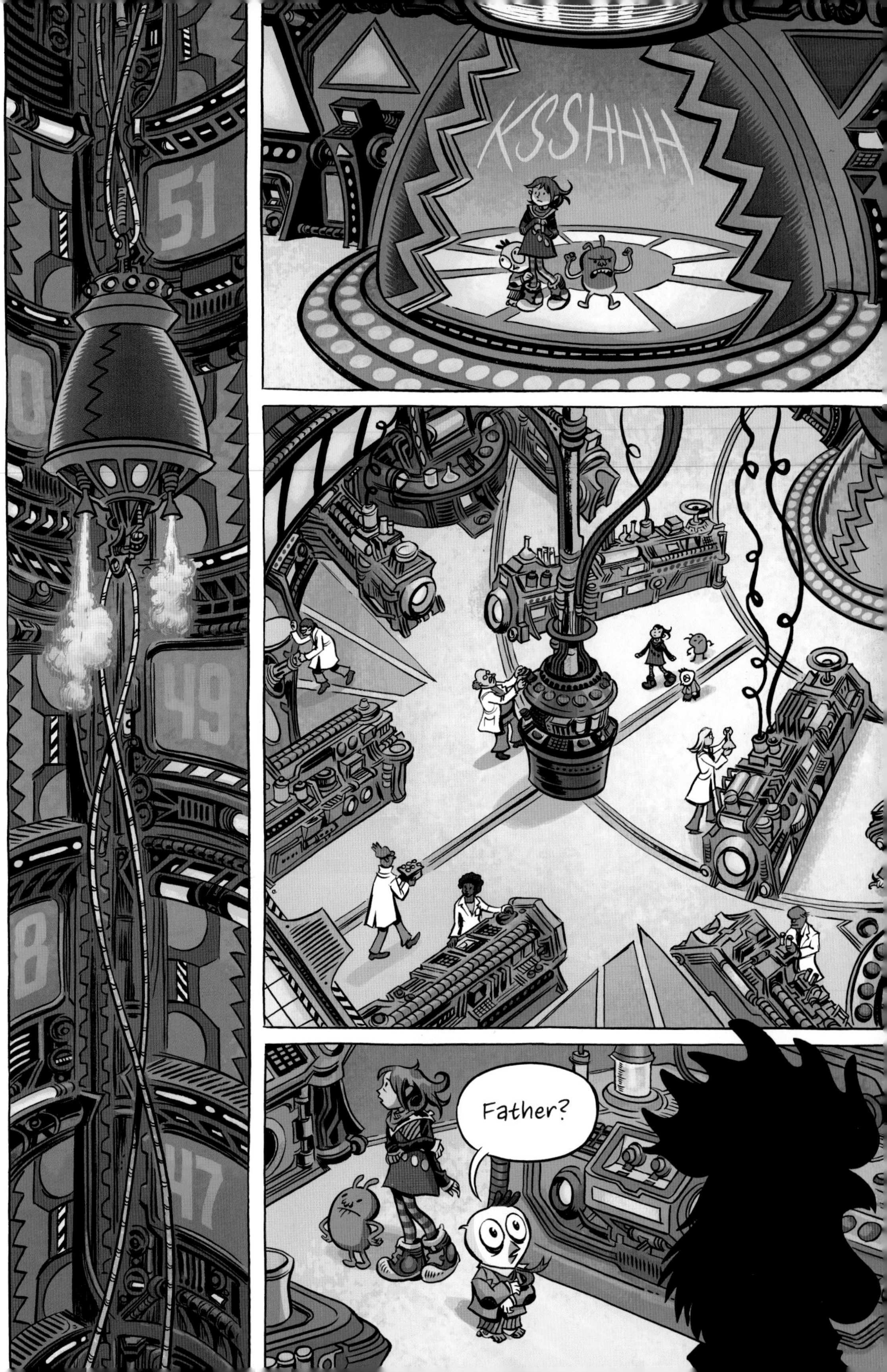
51
49
47
KSSHHH
Father?

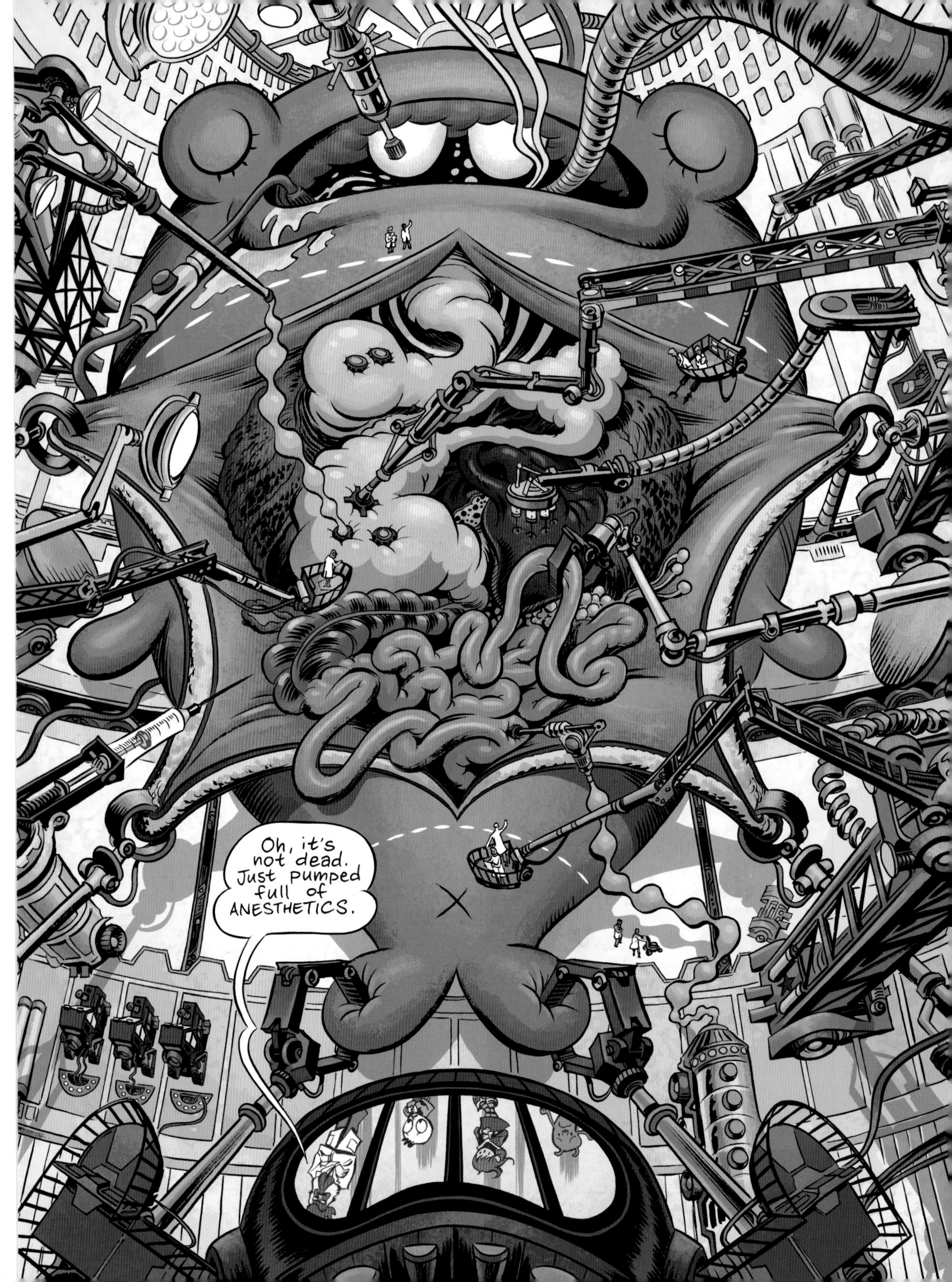
Oh, it's not dead. Just pumped full of ANESTHETICS.

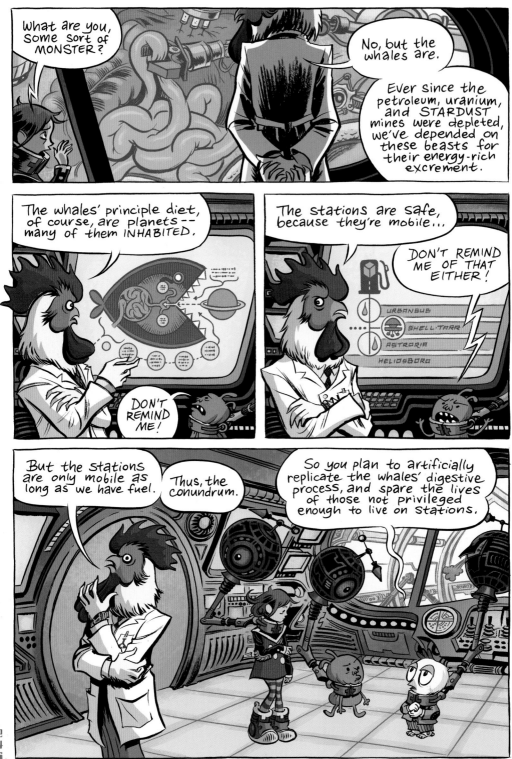

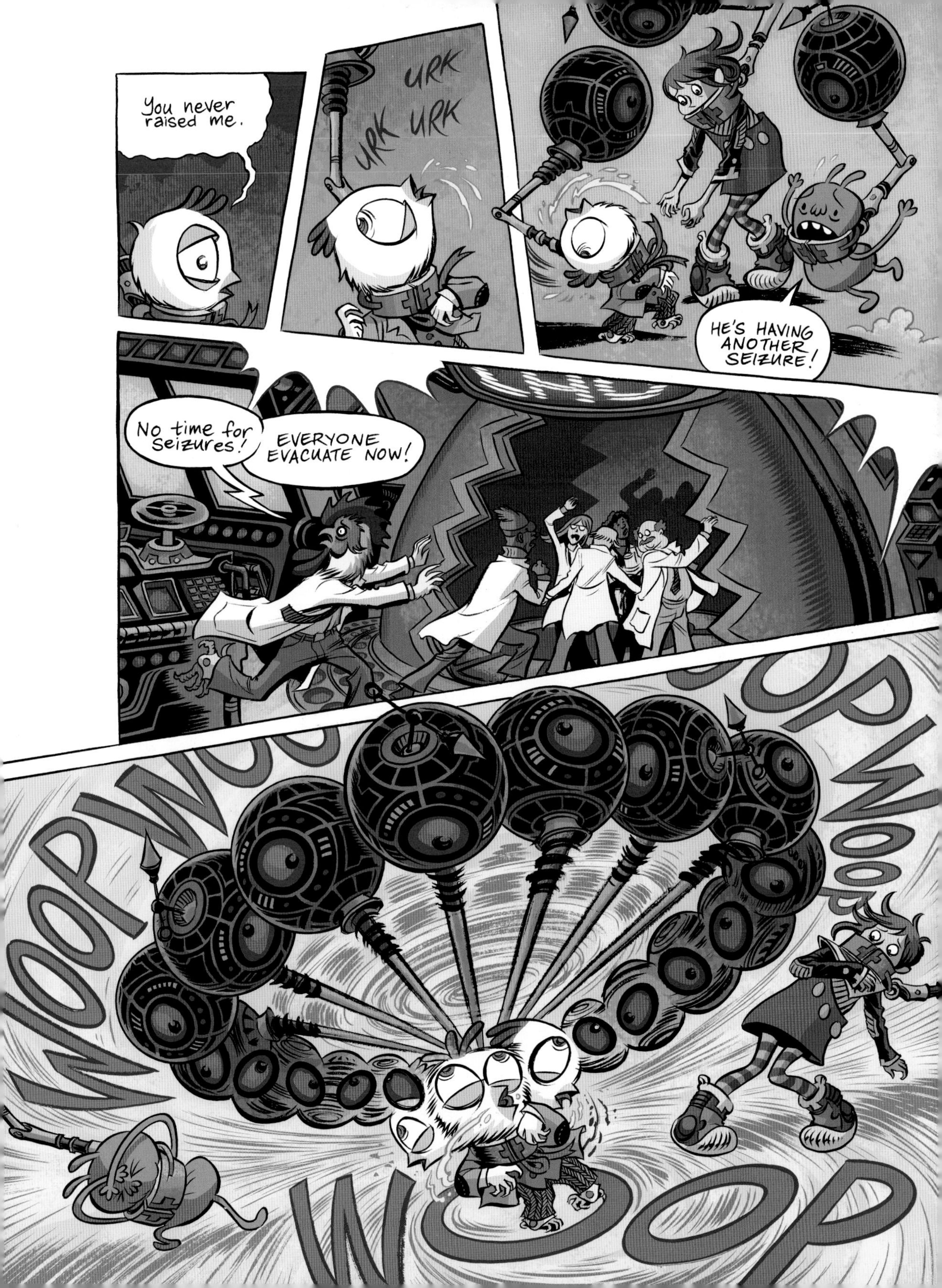
You never raised me.
URK
URK URK
HE'S HAVING ANOTHER SEIZURE!
No time for seizures!
EVERYONE EVACUATE NOW!
WOOP WOOP WOOP WOOP
WOOP

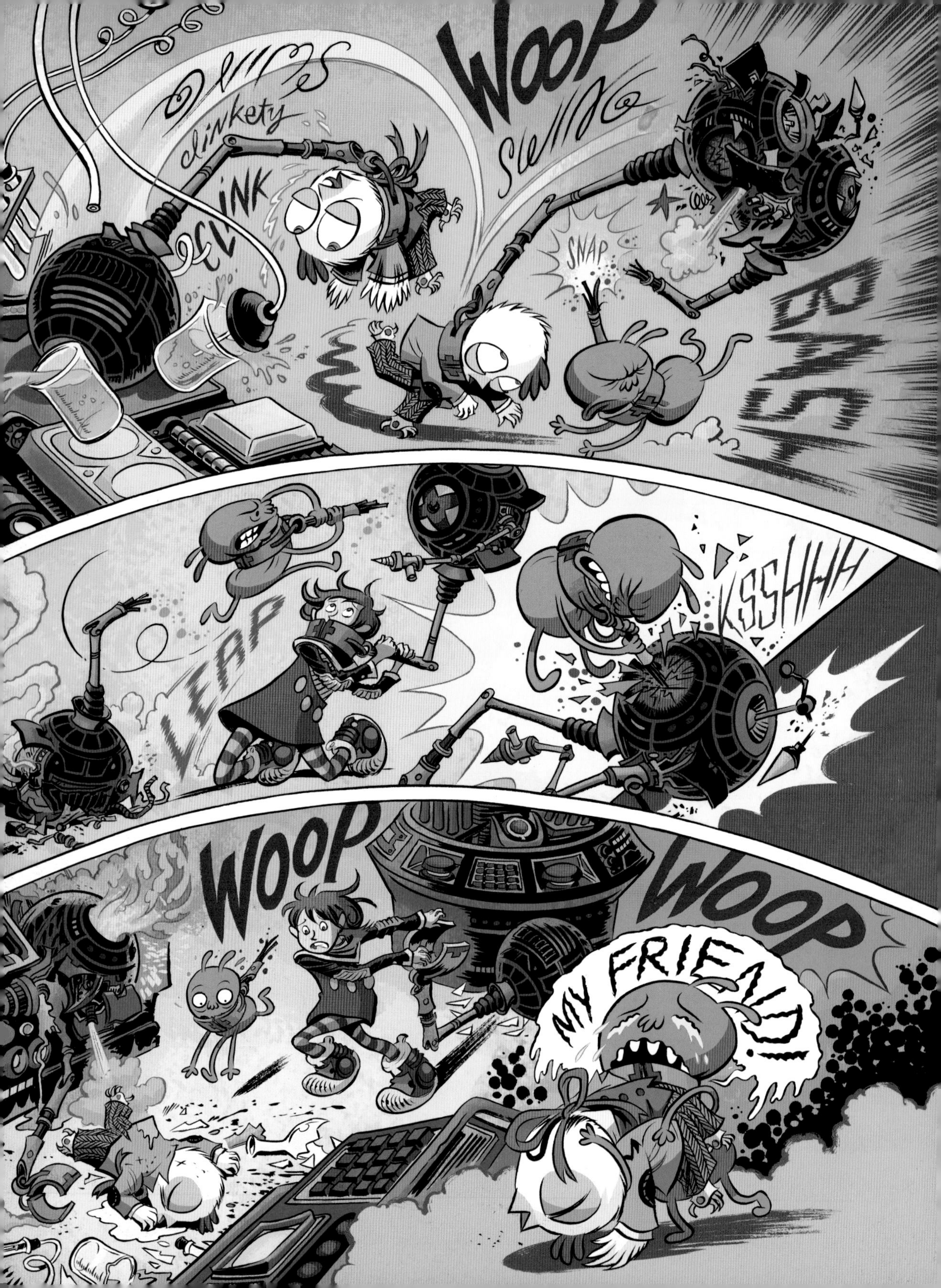

WOOP
clinkety
CLINK
SNAP
BASH
LEAP
KSSHHH
WOOP
WOOP
MY FRIEND!

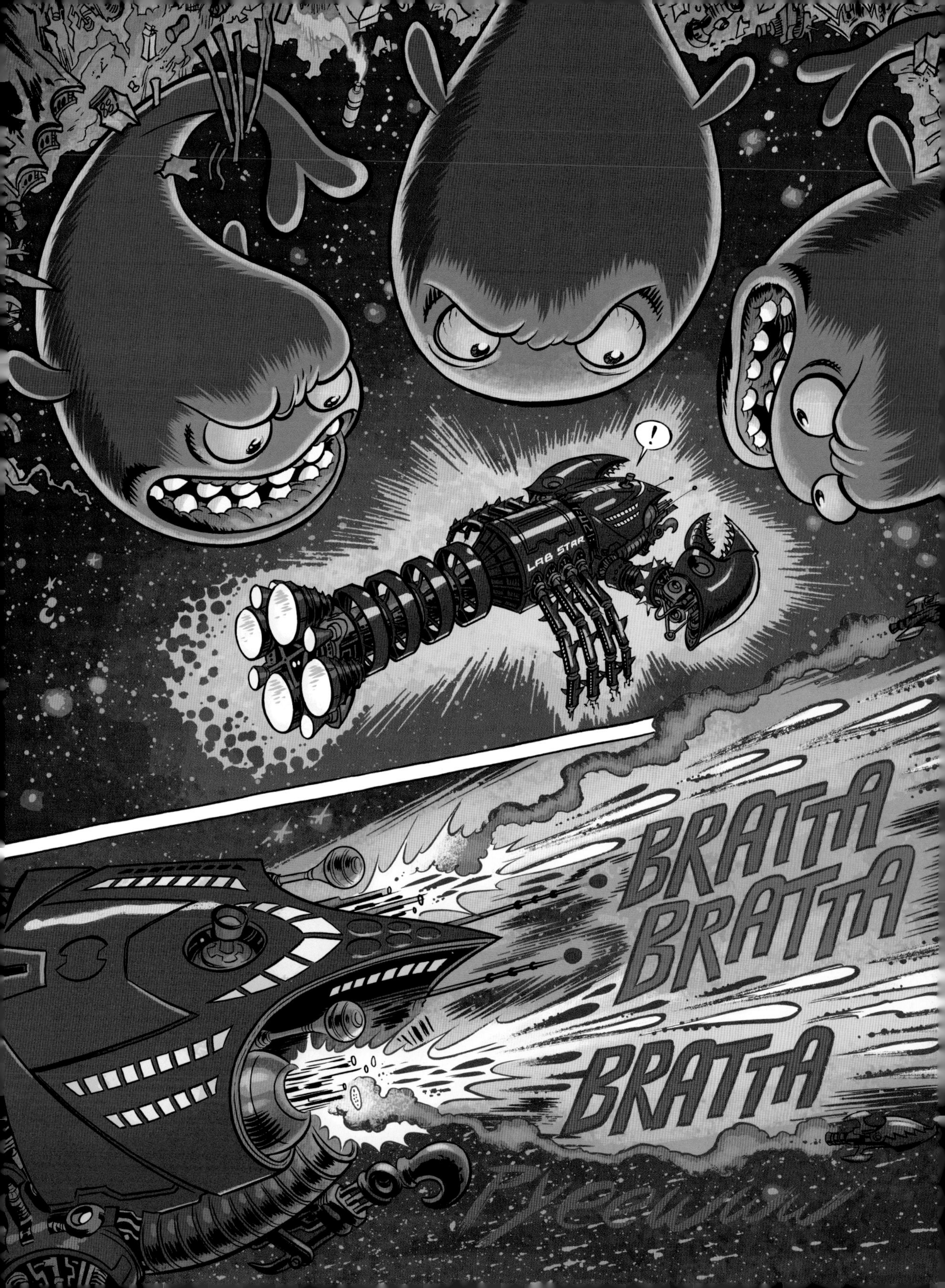
!
LAB STAR
BRATTA
BRATTA
BRATTA

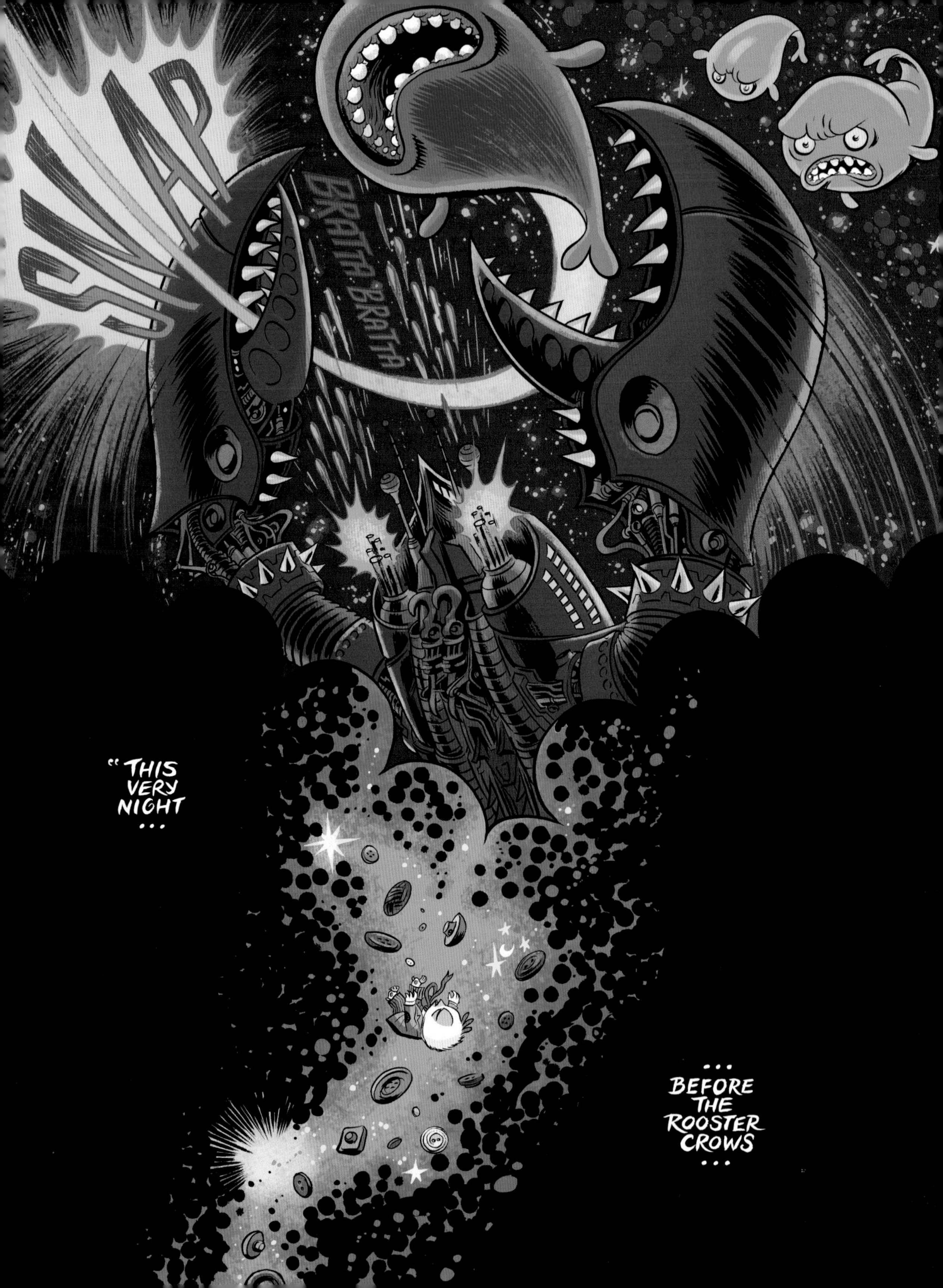
SNAP
BRATTA BRATTA BRATTA
"THIS VERY NIGHT . . .
. . . BEFORE THE ROOSTER CROWS . . .

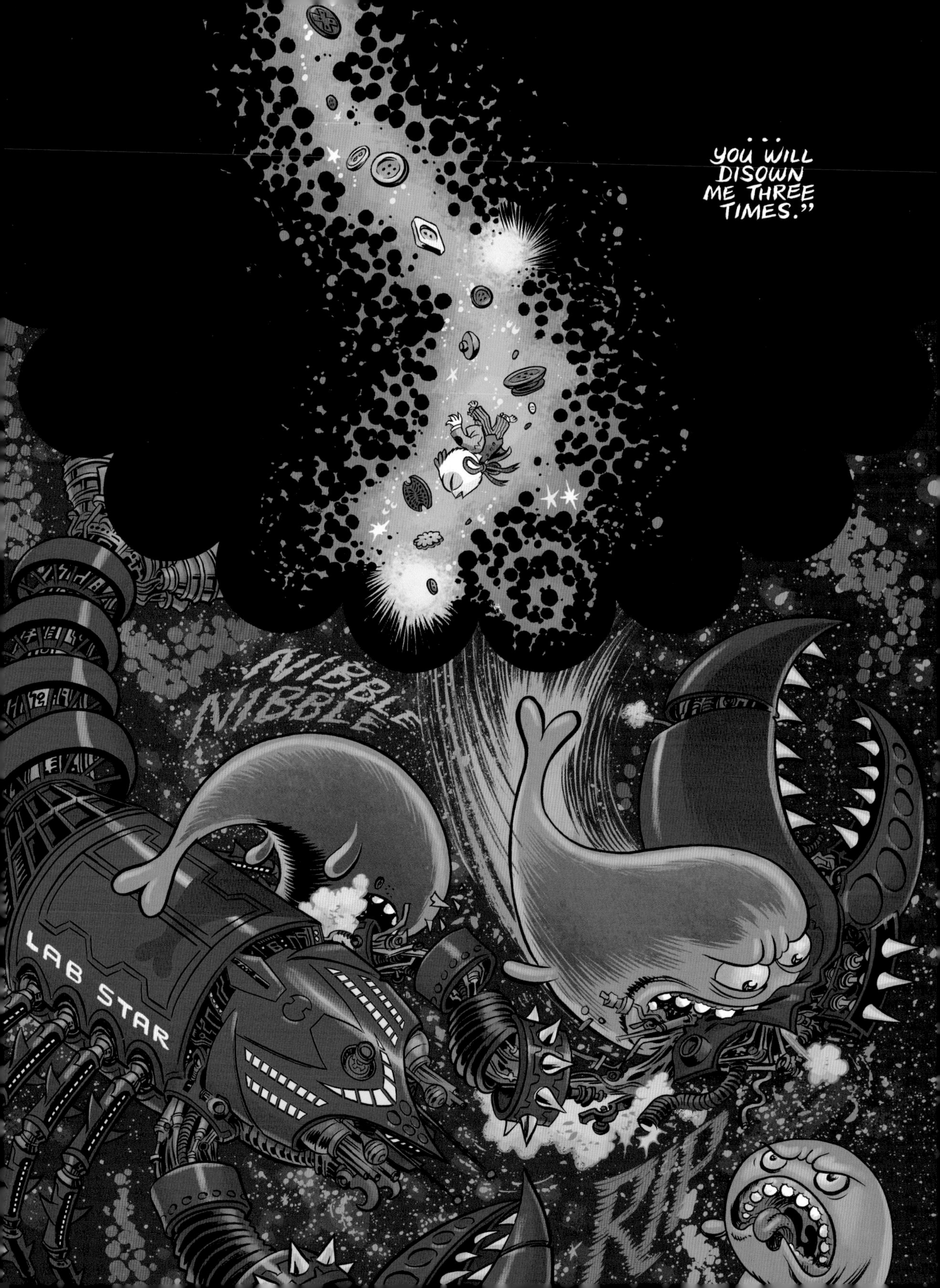
. . . YOU WILL DISOWN ME THREE TIMES."
NIBBLE NIBBLE
LAB STAR

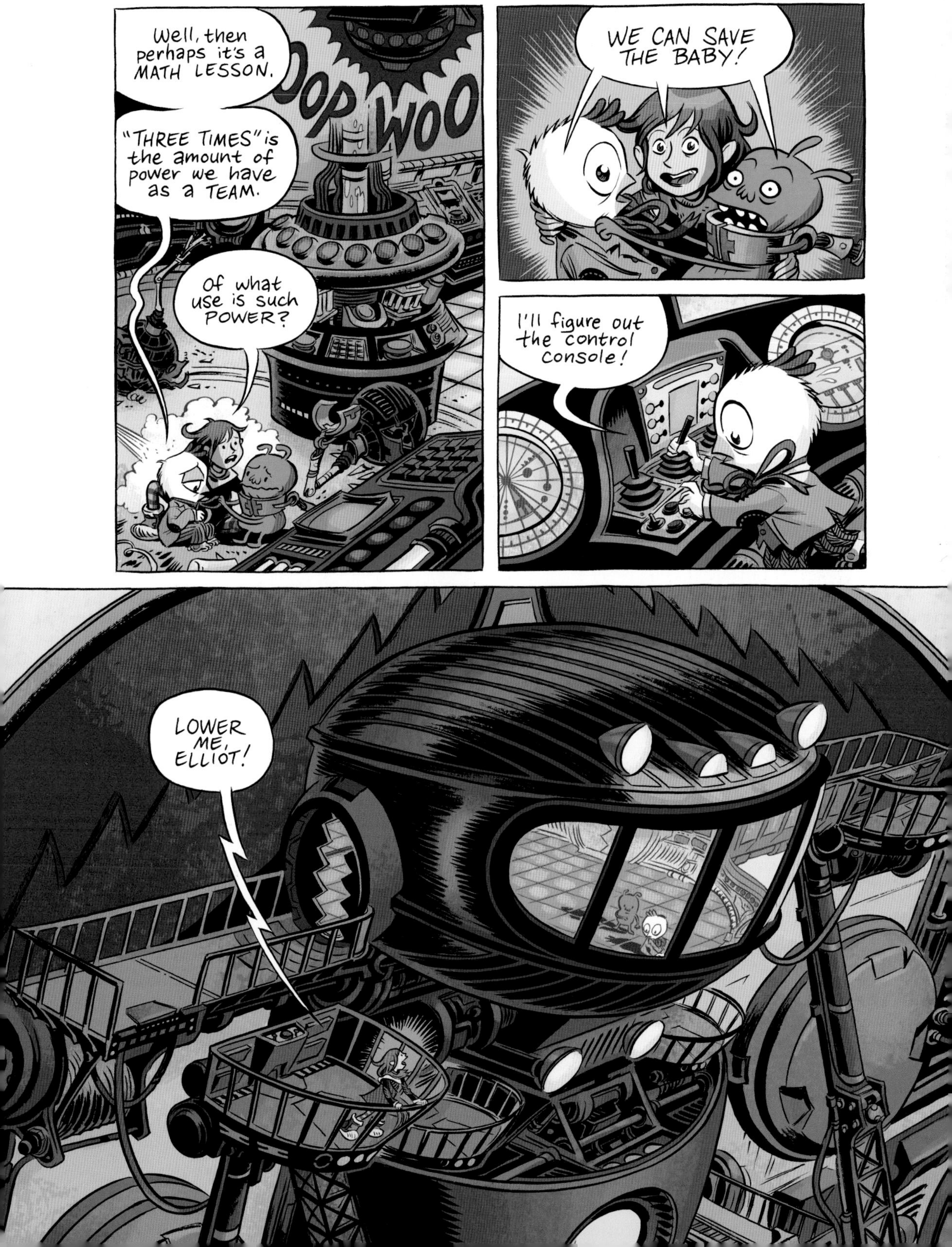
Well, then perhaps it's a MATH LESSON.
WOOP WOO
"THREE TIMES" is the amount of power we have as a TEAM.
Of what use is such POWER?
WE CAN SAVE THE BABY!
I'll figure out the control console!
LOWER ME, ELLIOT!

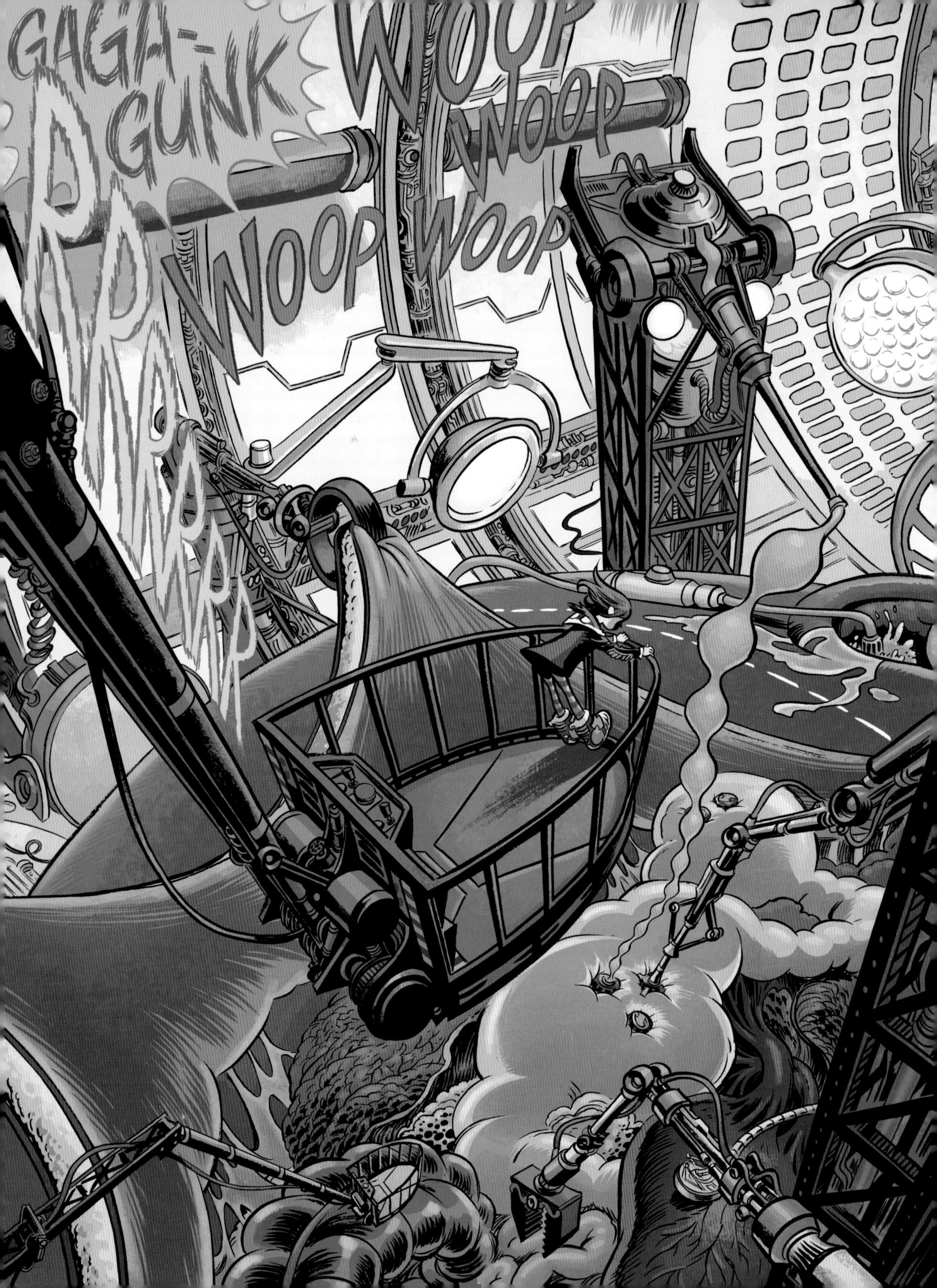
GAGA-GUNK
WOOP
WOOP
WOOP WOOP
RRRRRRR

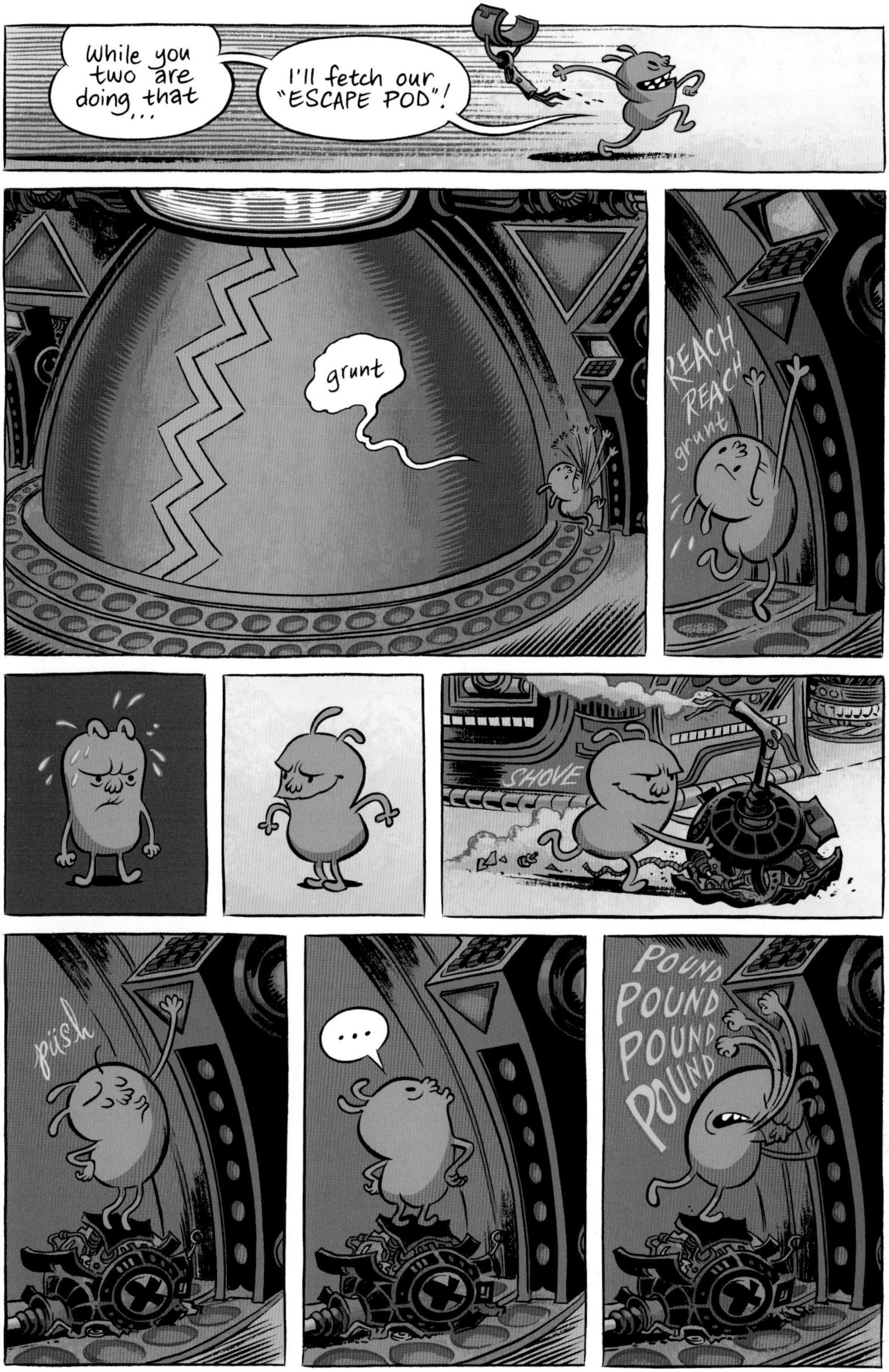
While you two are doing that...
I'll fetch our "ESCAPE POD"!
grunt
REACH
REACH
grunt
SHOVE
püsh
...
POUND
POUND
POUND
POUND

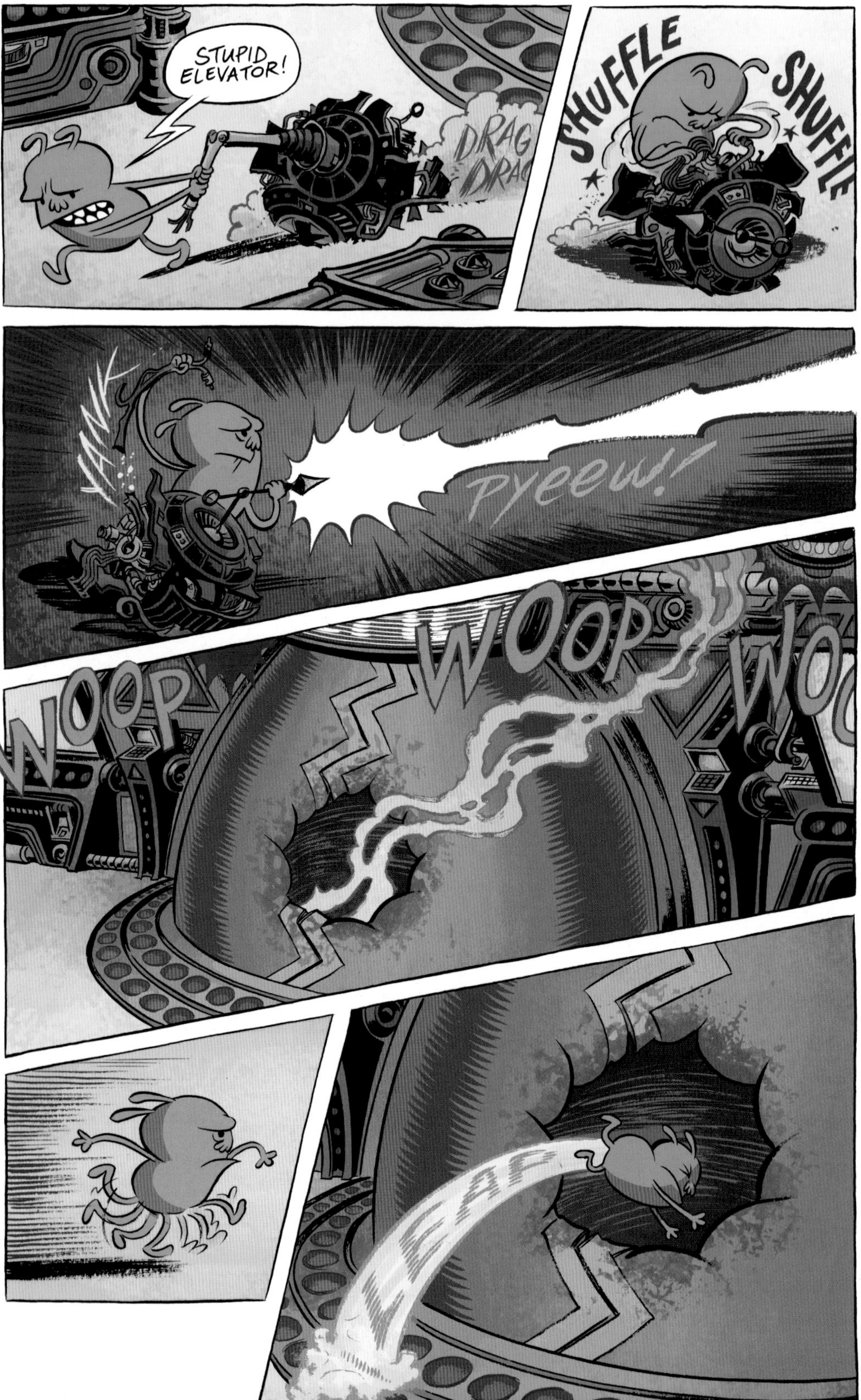
STUPID ELEVATOR!
DRAG
SHUFFLE
SHUFFLE
YANK
pyeew!
WOOP
WOOP
LEAP

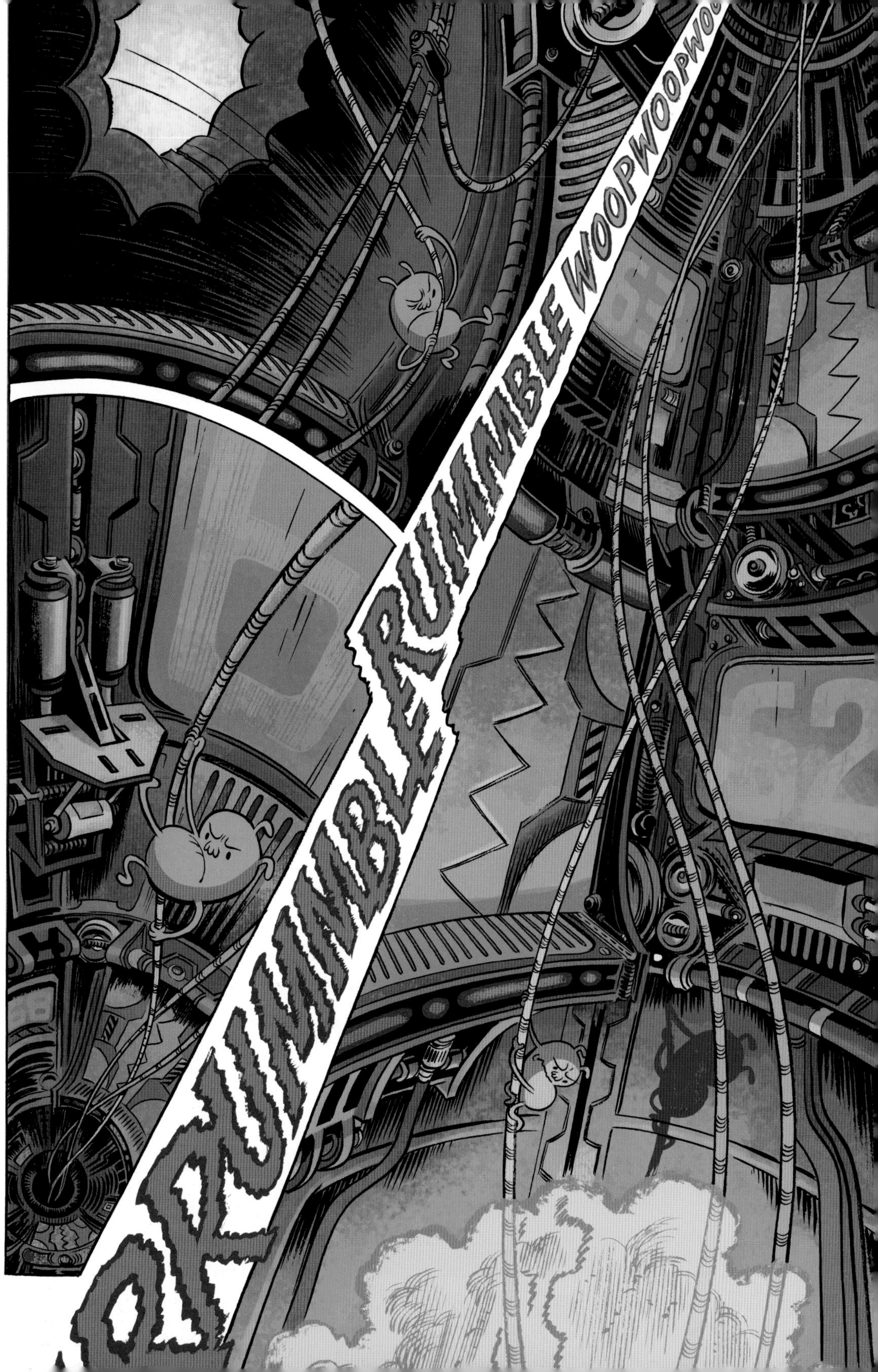
RRUMMBLERUMMBLE
WOOPWOOPWOO

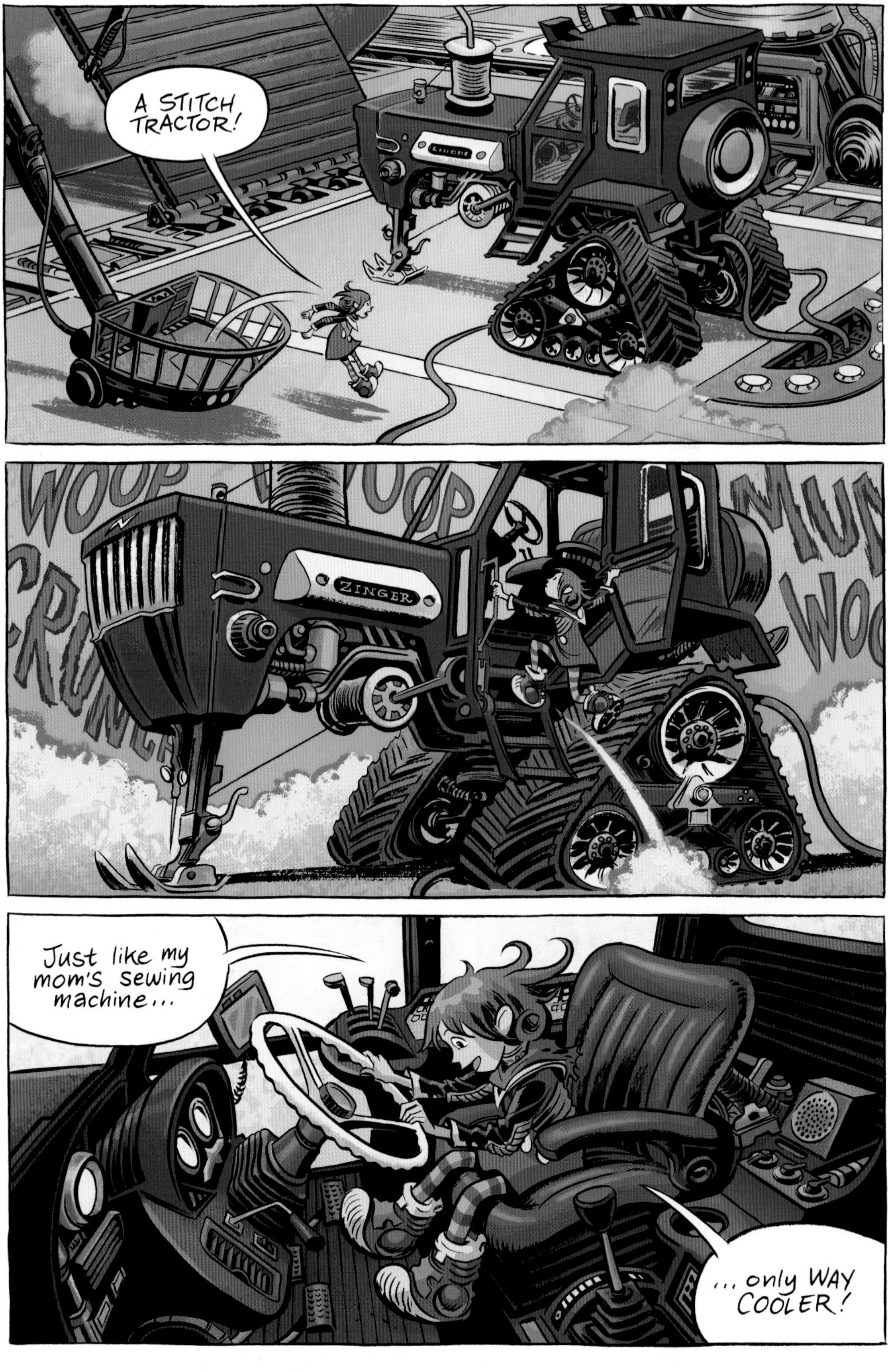
A STITCH TRACTOR!
WOOP
ZINGER
Just like my mom's sewing machine...
...only WAY COOLER!

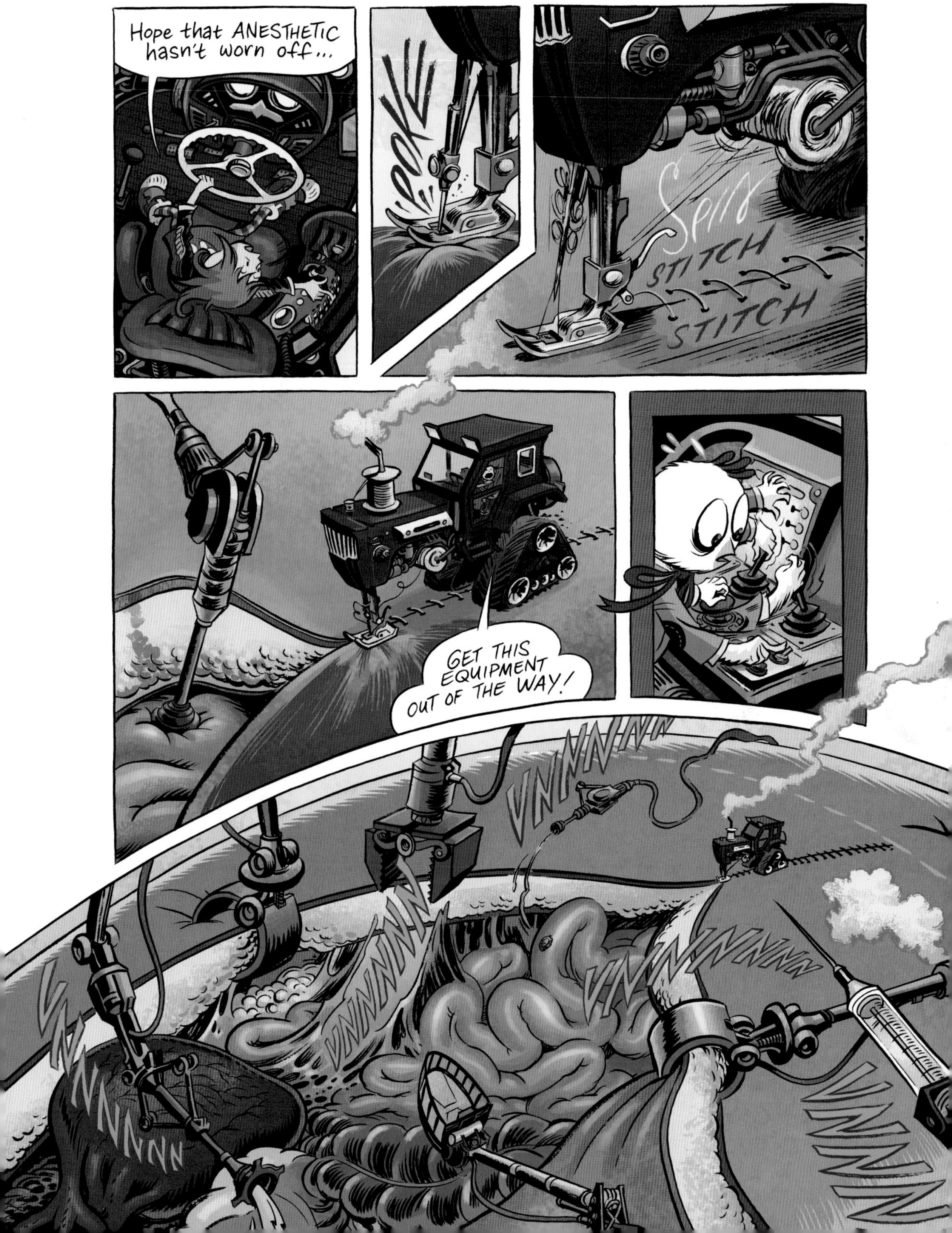
Hope that ANESTHETIC hasn't worn off...
POKE
Spin
STITCH
STITCH
GET THIS EQUIPMENT OUT OF THE WAY!
VNNNNNN
VNNNNNN
VNNNNNN
VNNNNNNNN
VNNNNNNN
VNNNNNNN

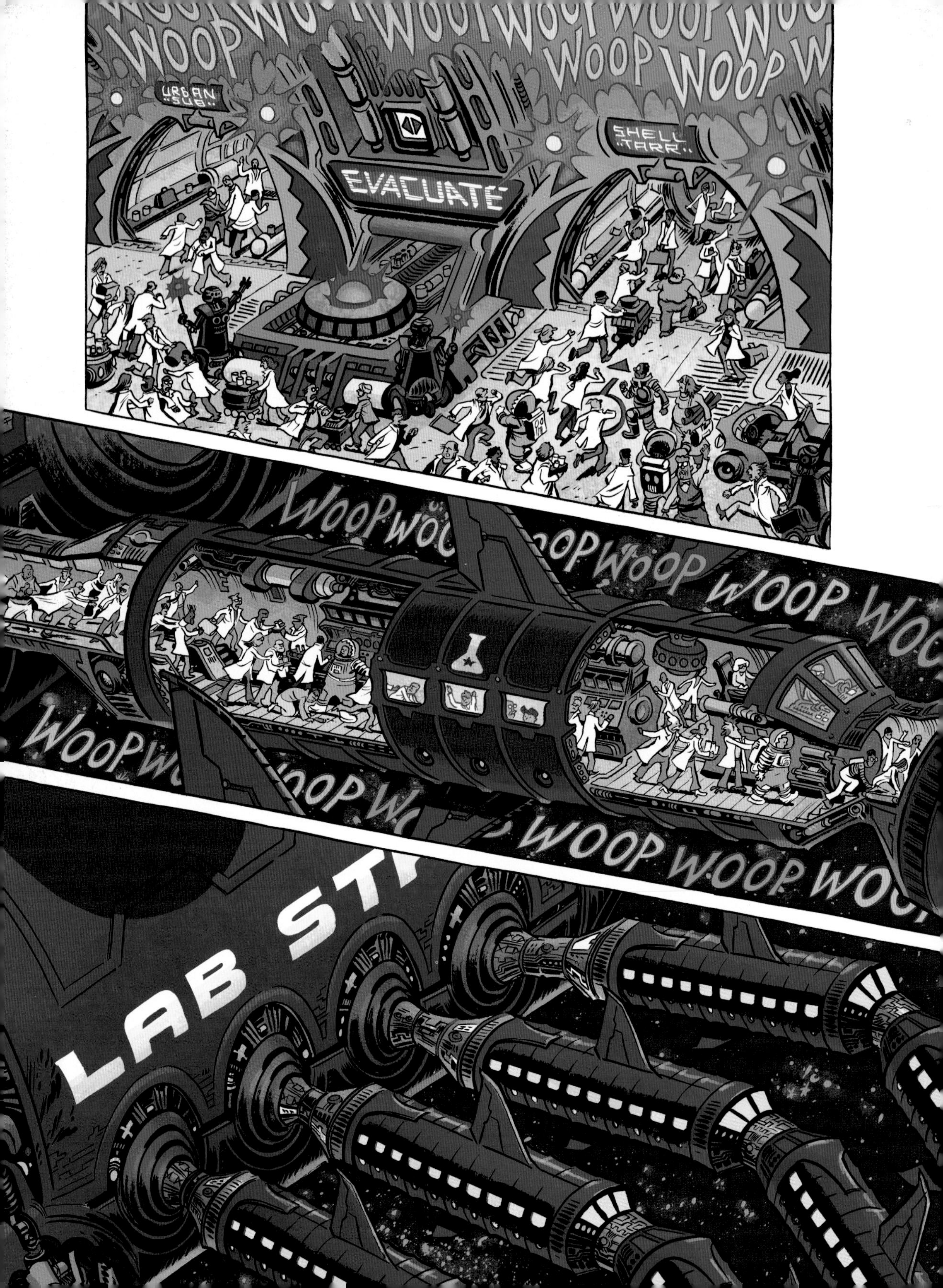
WOOP WOOP WOOP WOOP
WOOP WOOP
URBAN SUB
SHELL TARR
EVACUATE
WOOP WOOP WOOP WOOP WOOP WOO
WOOP WOOP
WOOP WOOP WOOP WOO
LAB ST

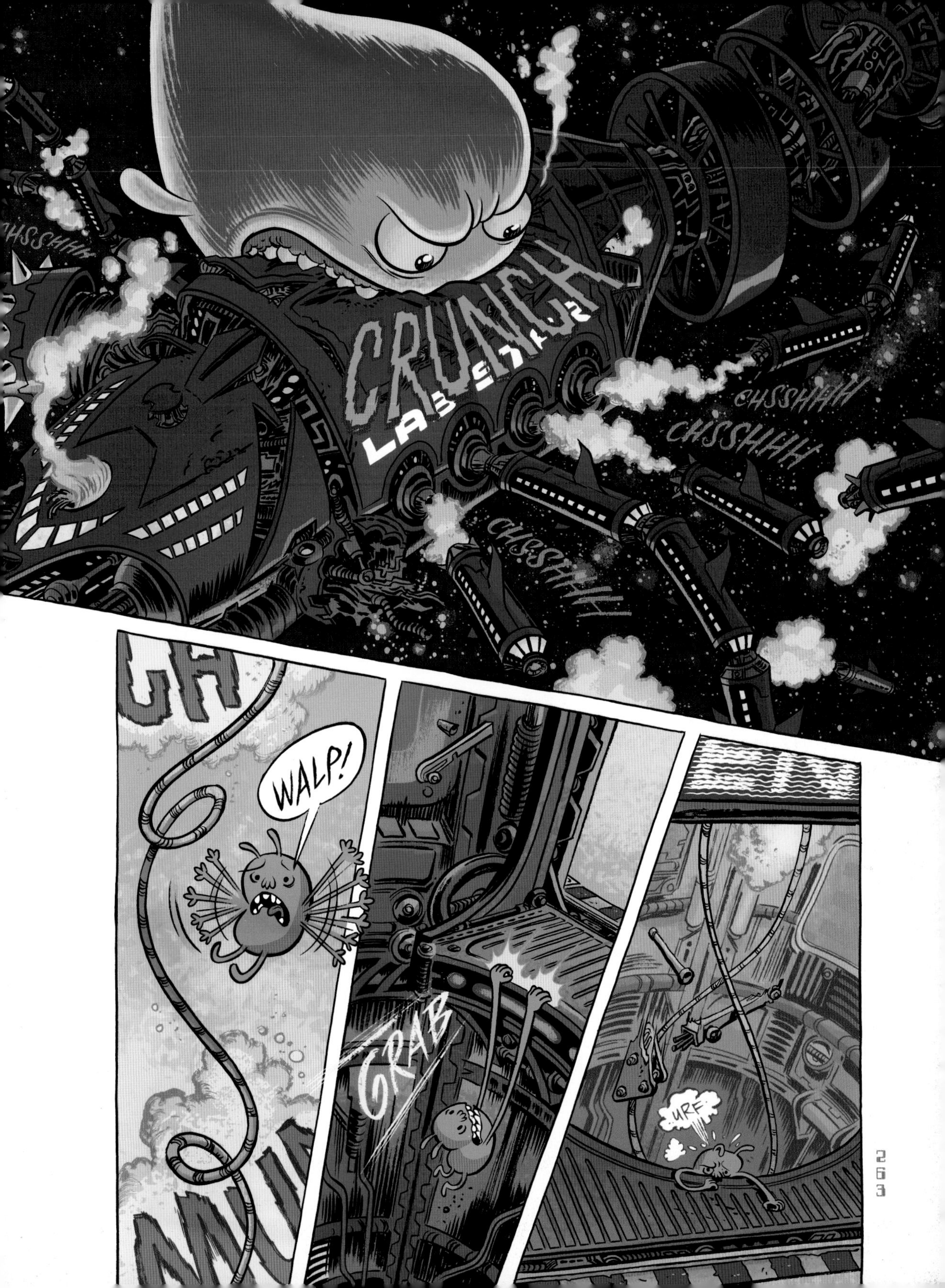
CHSSHHH
CRUNCH
CHSSHHH
CHSSHHH
CHSSHHH
WALP!
GRAB
URF

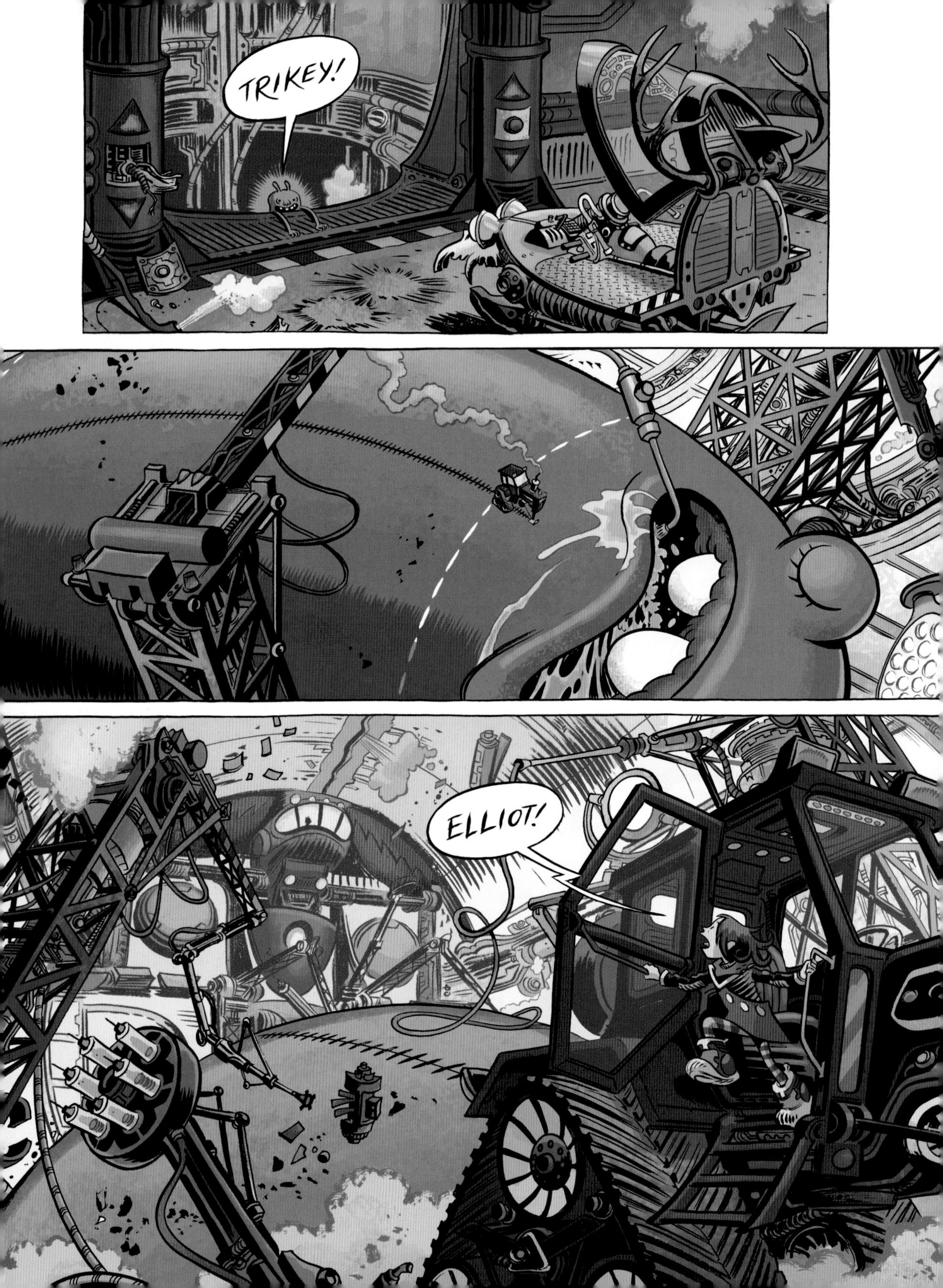
TRIKEY!
ELLIOT!

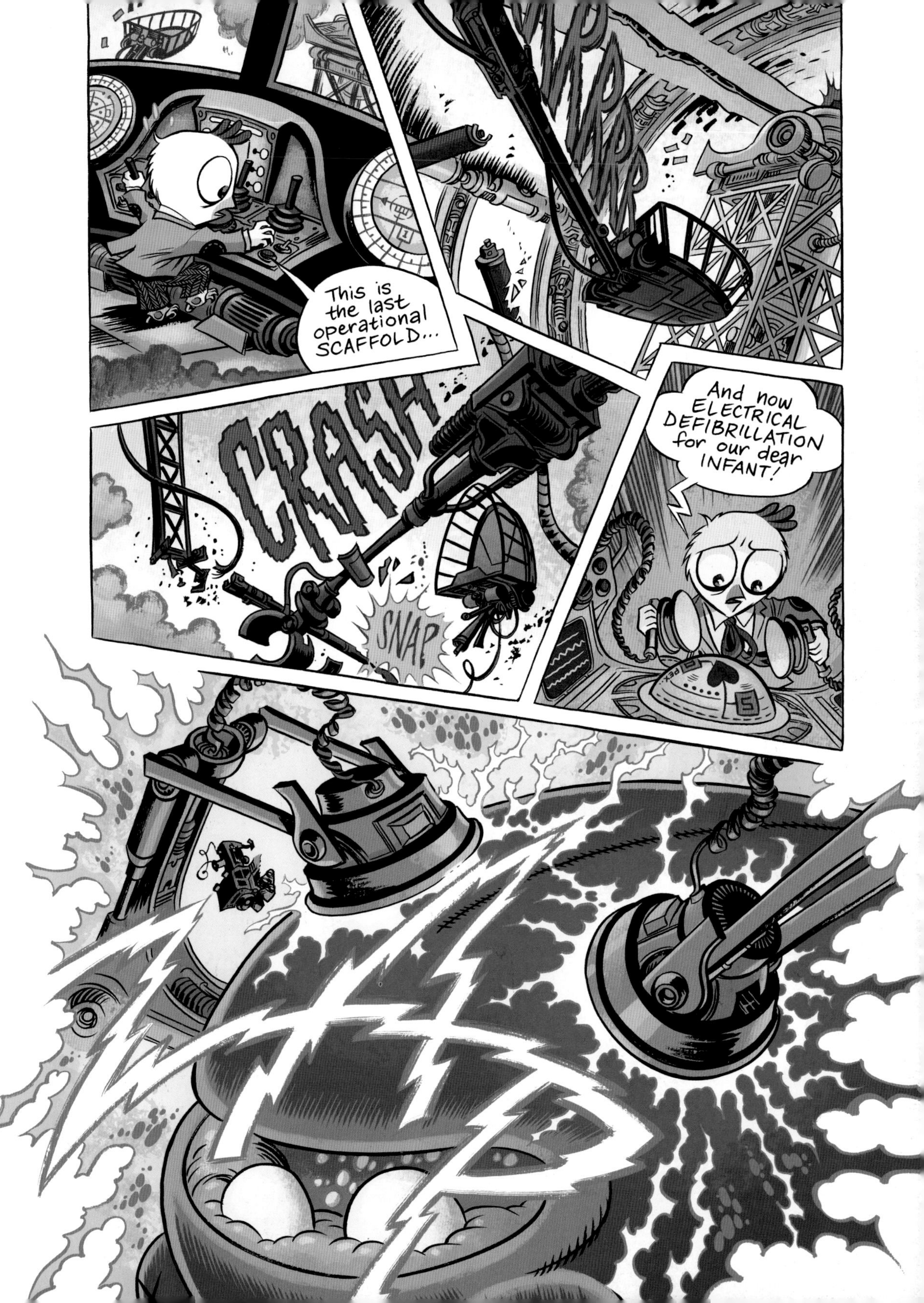
This is the last operational SCAFFOLD...
CRASH
SNAP
And now ELECTRICAL DEFIBRILLATION for our dear INFANT!

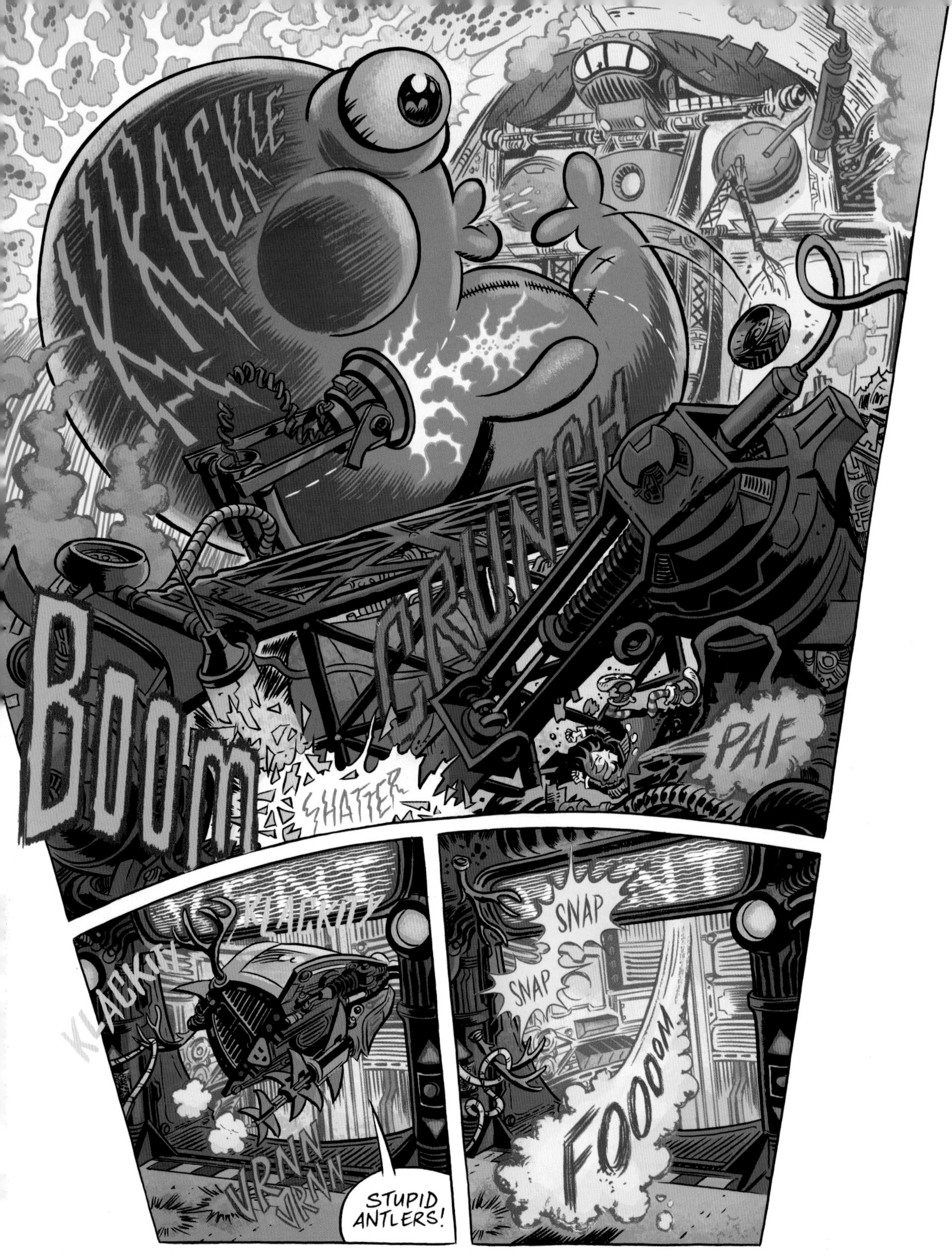
KRACKLE
CRUNCH
BOOM
SHATTER
PAF
KLACKITY KLACKITY
VRNN VRNN
STUPID ANTLERS!
SNAP SNAP
FOOOOOM

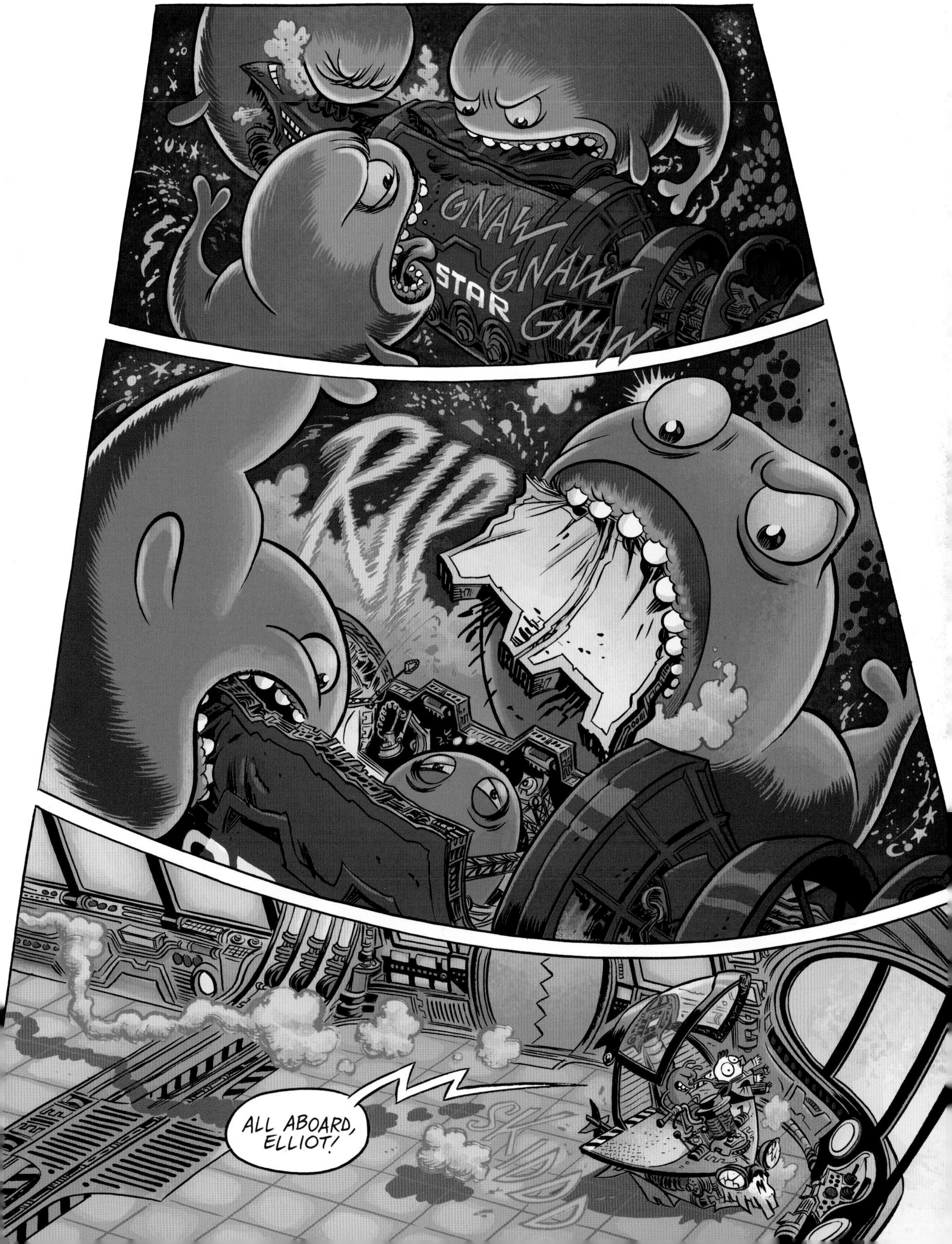
GNAW
GNAW
GNAW
STAR
RIP
ALL ABOARD, ELLIOT!

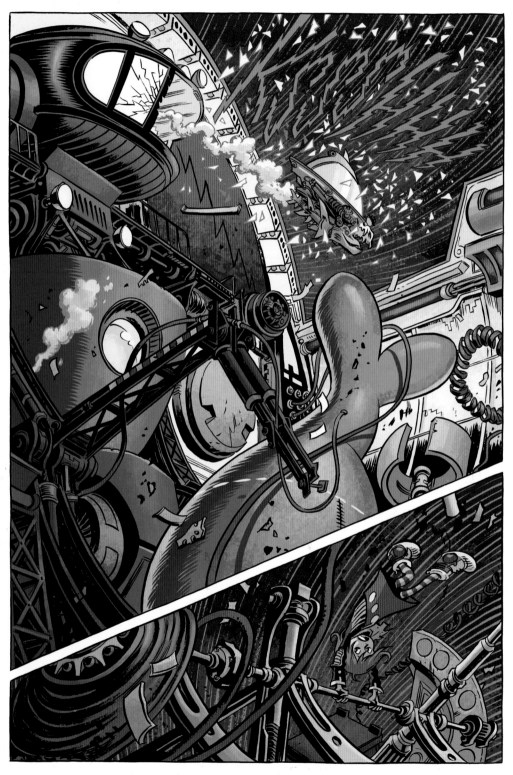

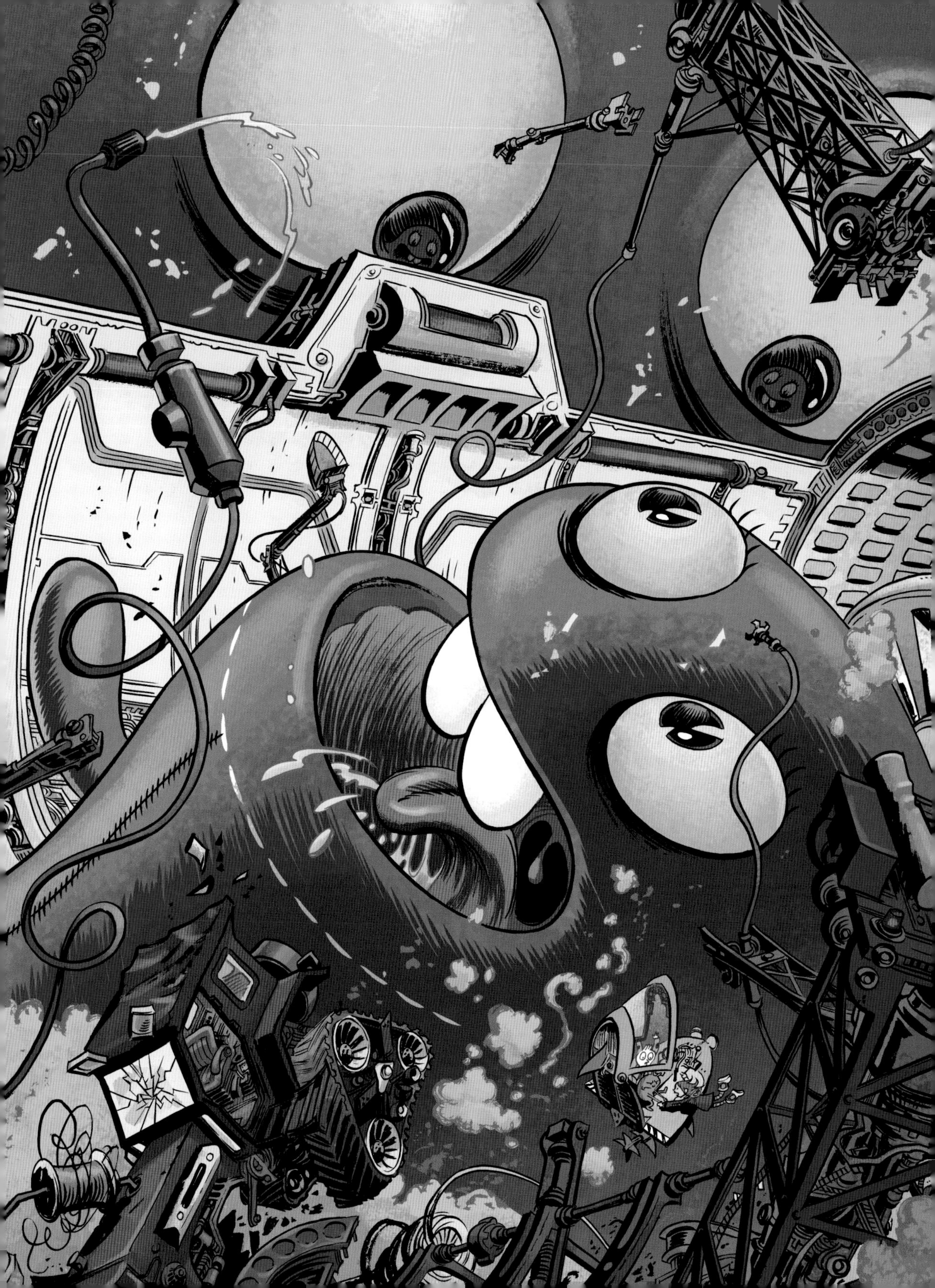
MOON

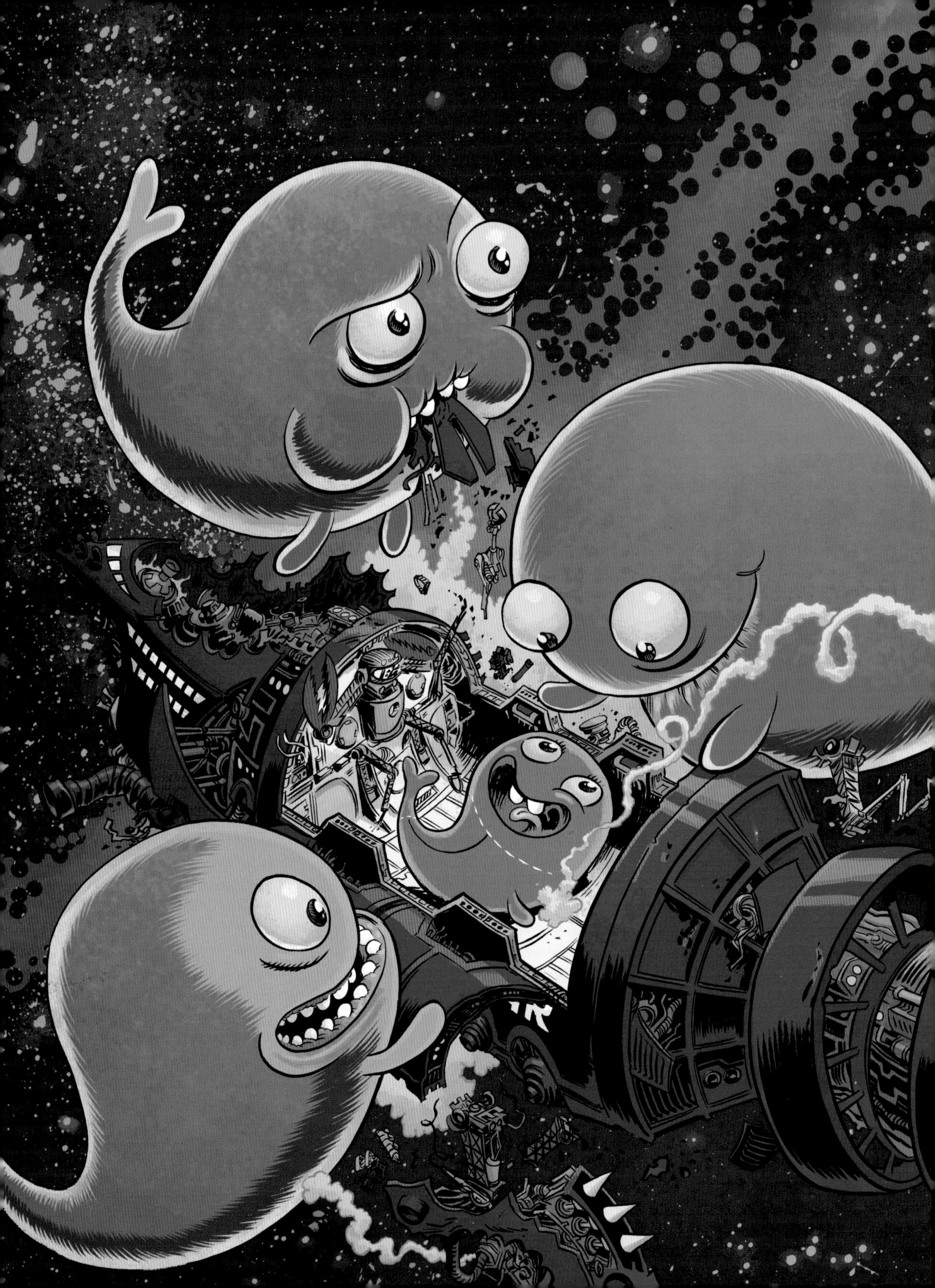

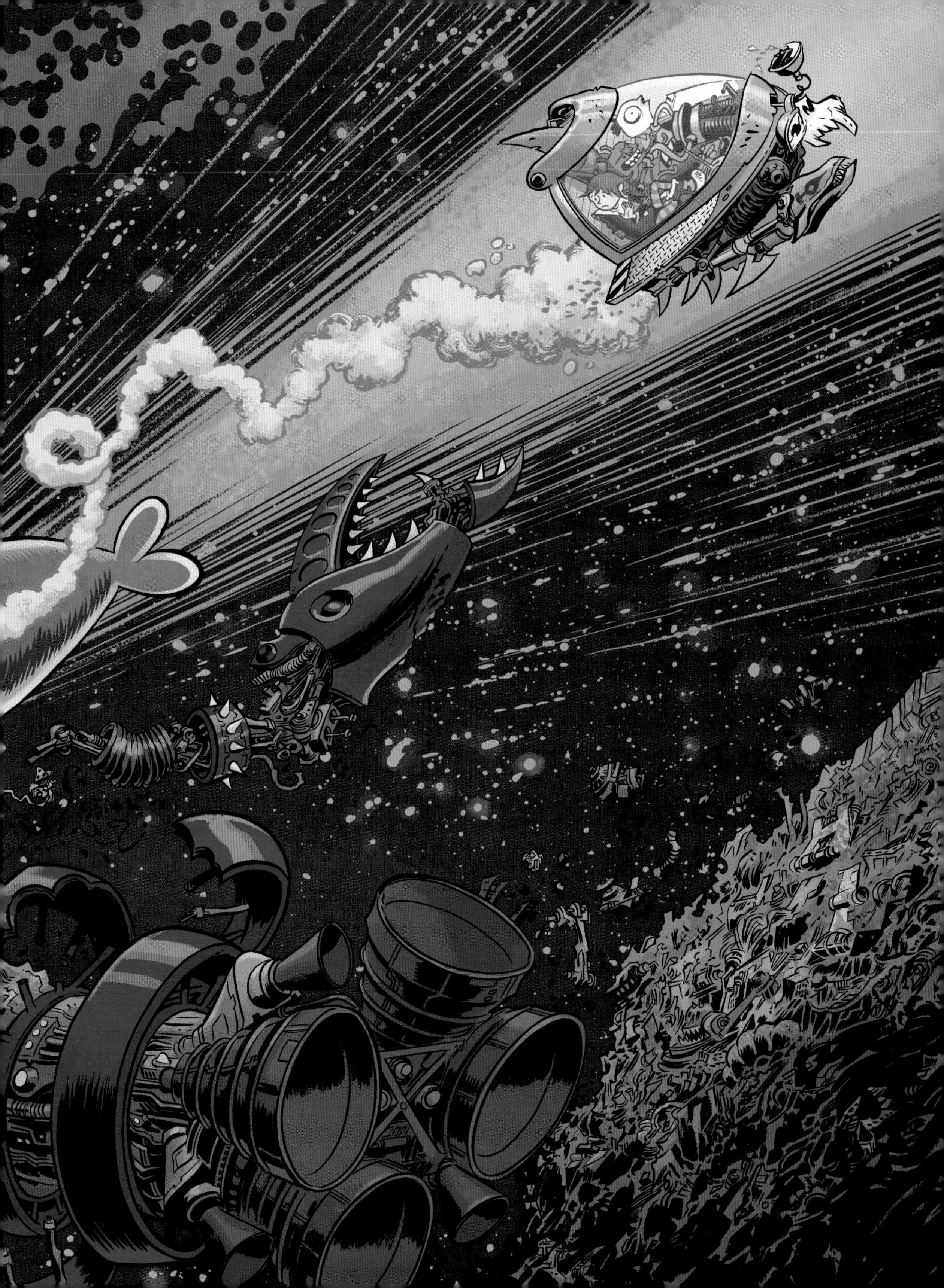

07 MAG/
    GYRO
    NAV

MAGNITUDES:

RUDDER

001

FIN OR
FLUKE?

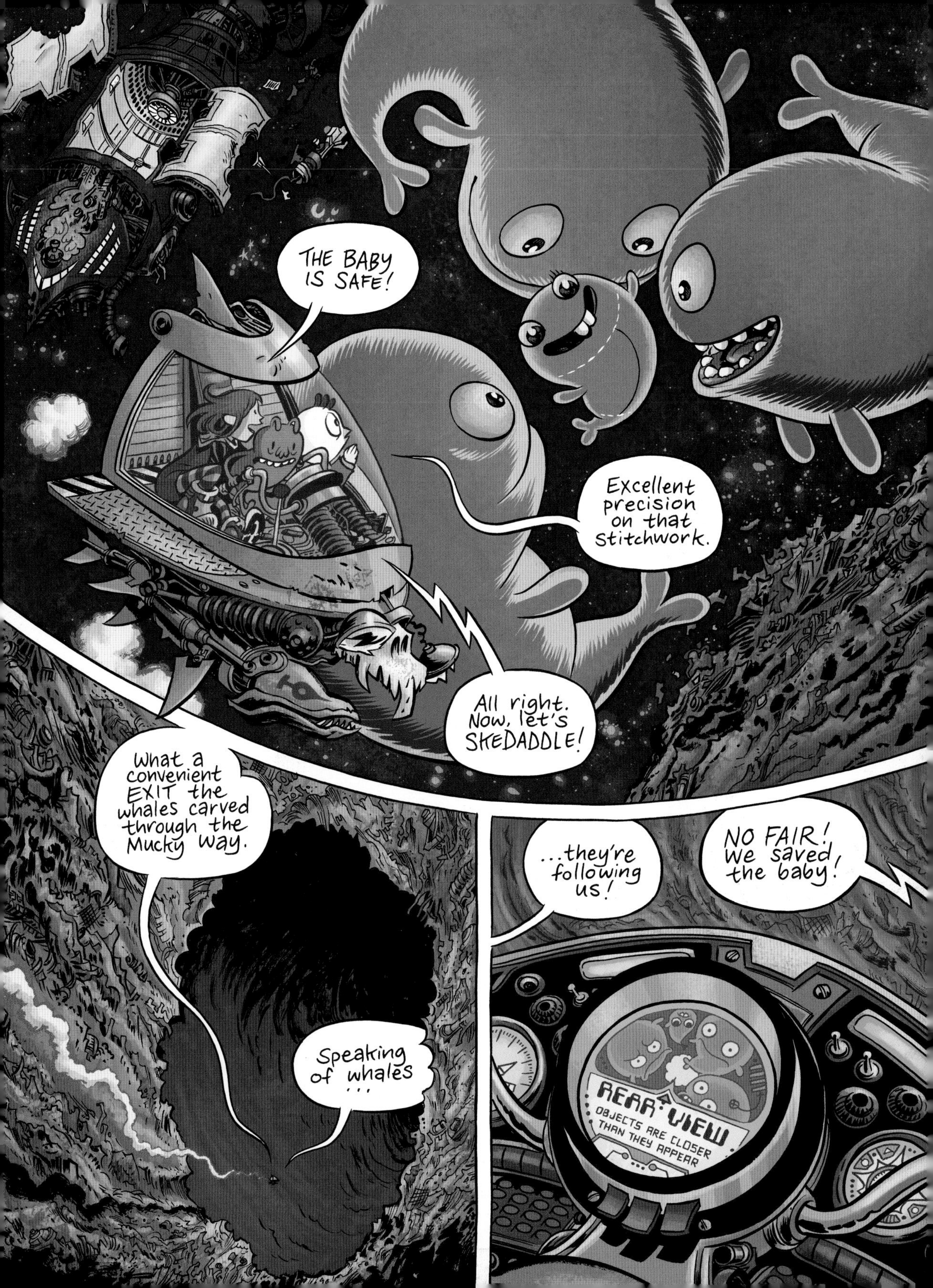
THE BABY IS SAFE!
Excellent precision on that stitchwork.
All right. Now, let's SKEDADDLE!
What a convenient EXIT the whales carved through the Mucky Way.
Speaking of whales ...
...they're following us!
NO FAIR! We saved the baby!
REAR VIEW
OBJECTS ARE CLOSER THAN THEY APPEAR

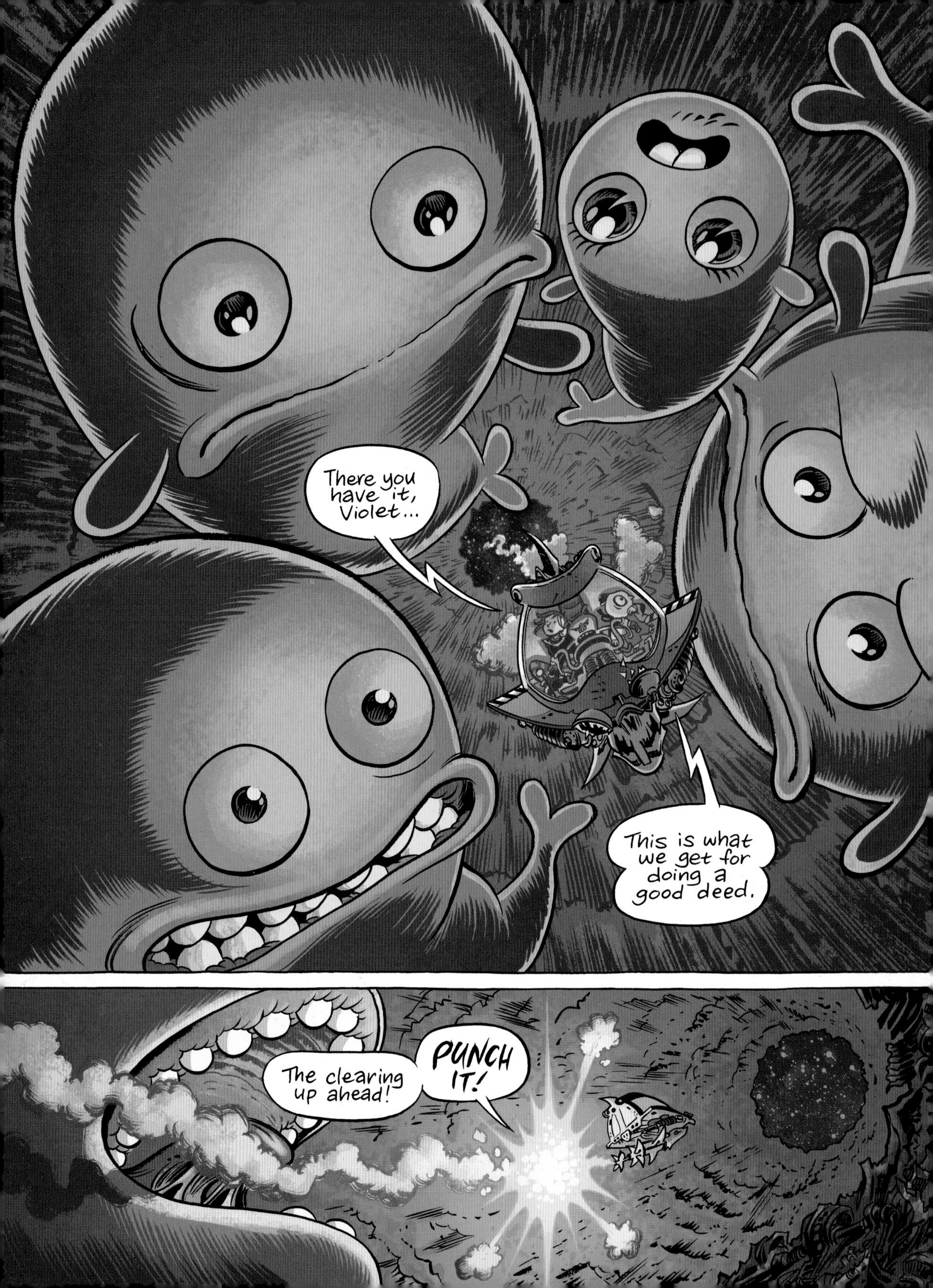
There you have it, Violet...
This is what we get for doing a good deed.
The clearing up ahead!
PUNCH IT!

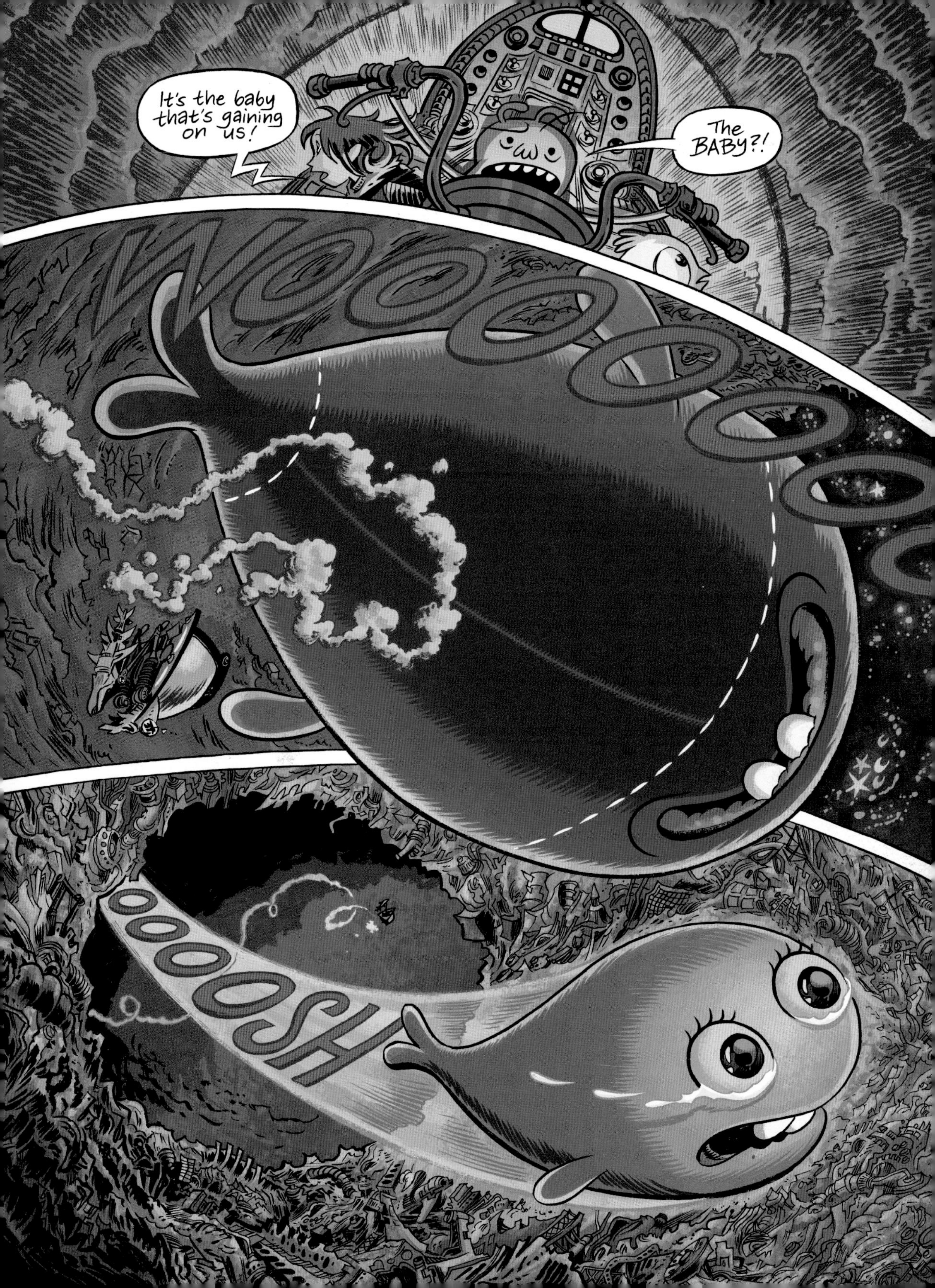
It's the baby that's gaining on us!
The BABY?!
WOOOOOOOOOOOOOOOOOSH

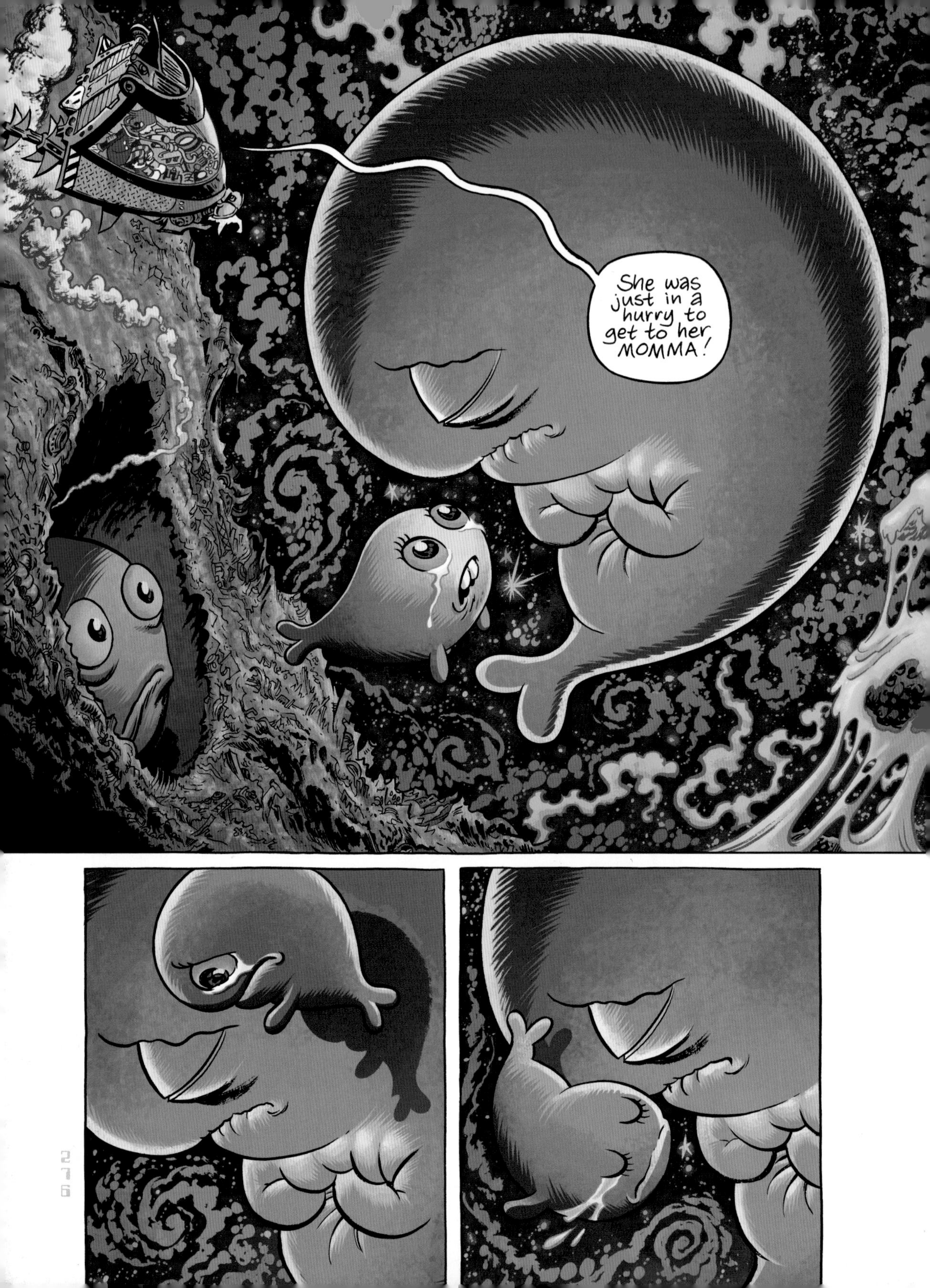
She was just in a hurry to get to her, MOMMA!

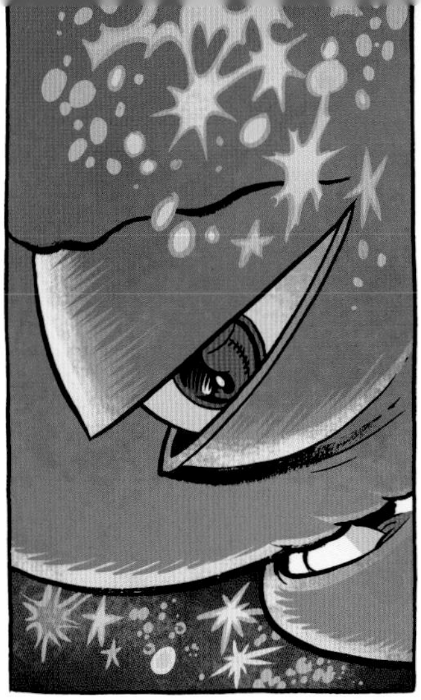
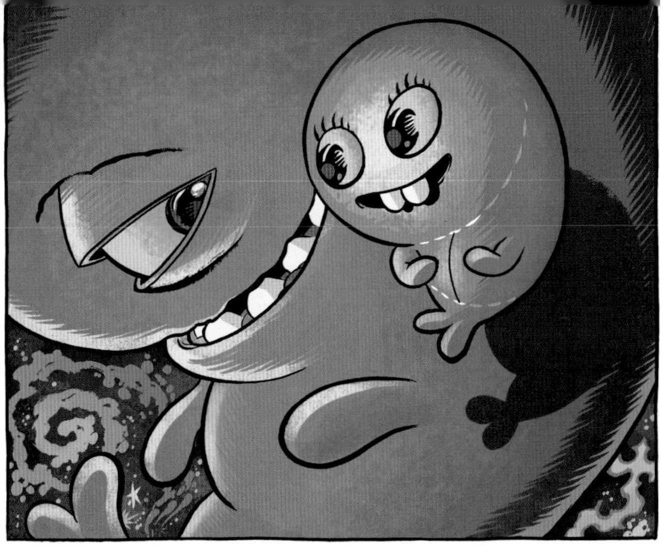
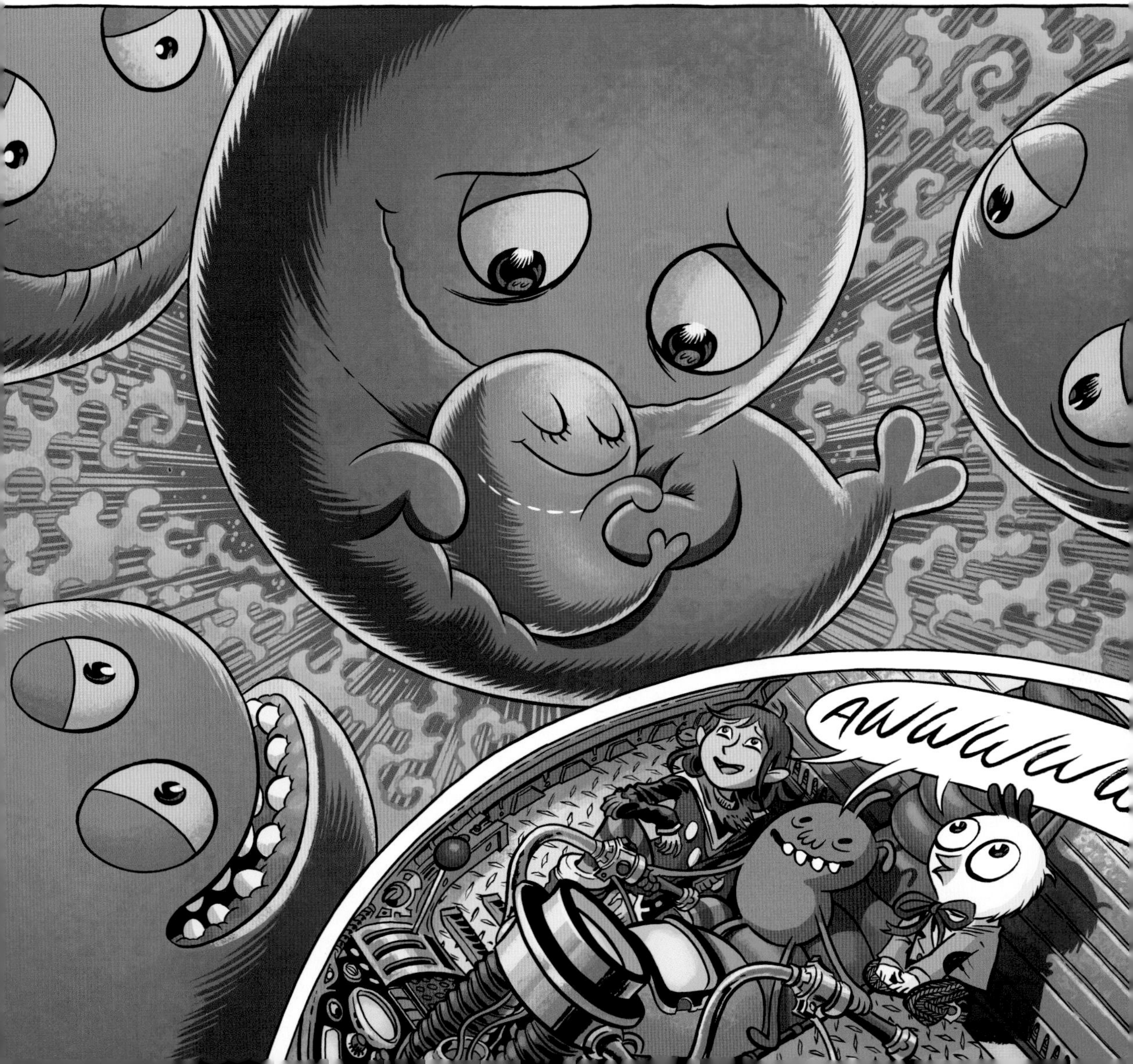
AWWWWW

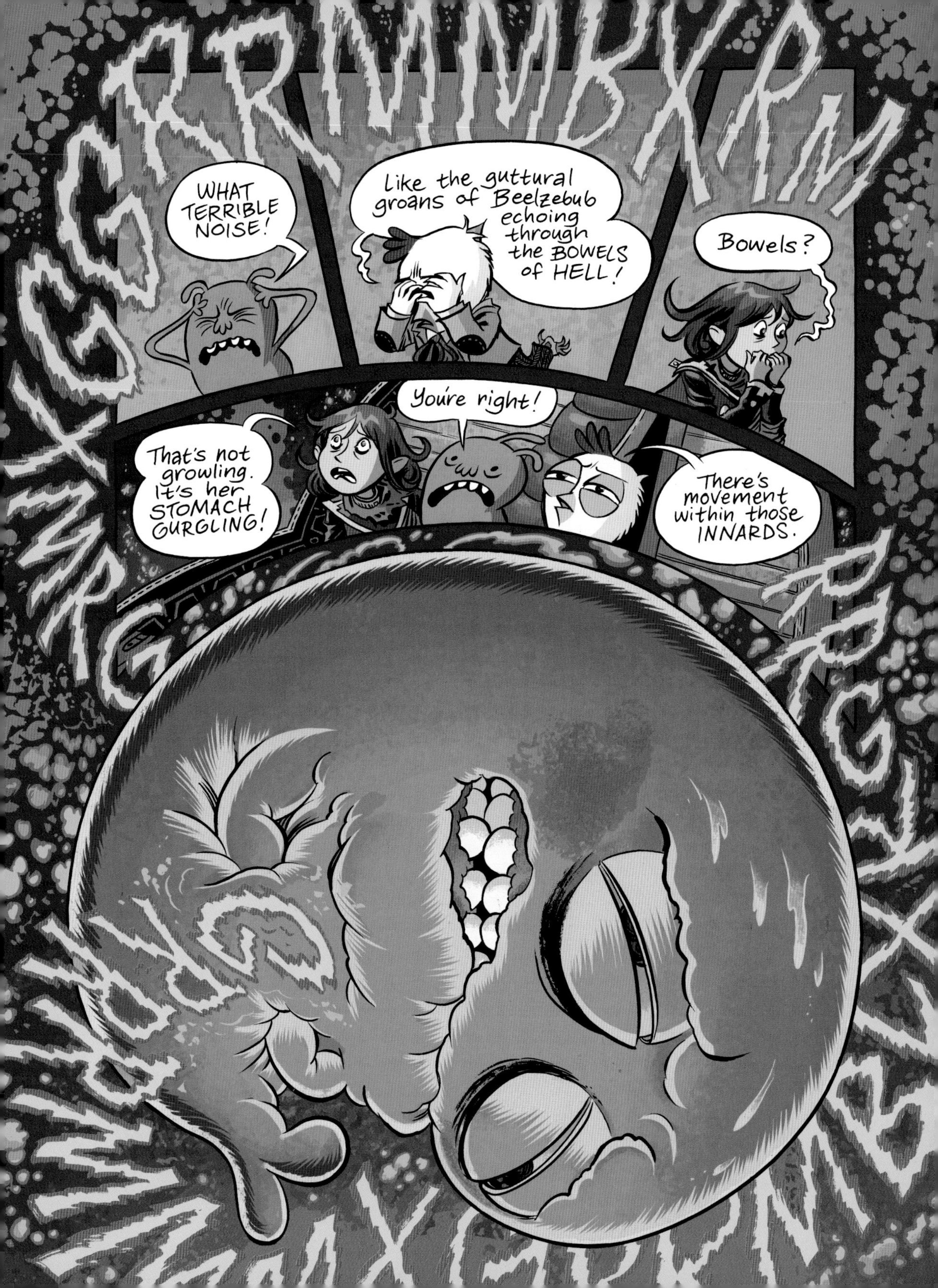
WHAT TERRIBLE NOISE!
Like the guttural groans of Beelzebub echoing through the BOWELS of HELL!
Bowels?
That's not growling. It's her STOMACH GURGLING!
You're right!
There's movement within those INNARDS.

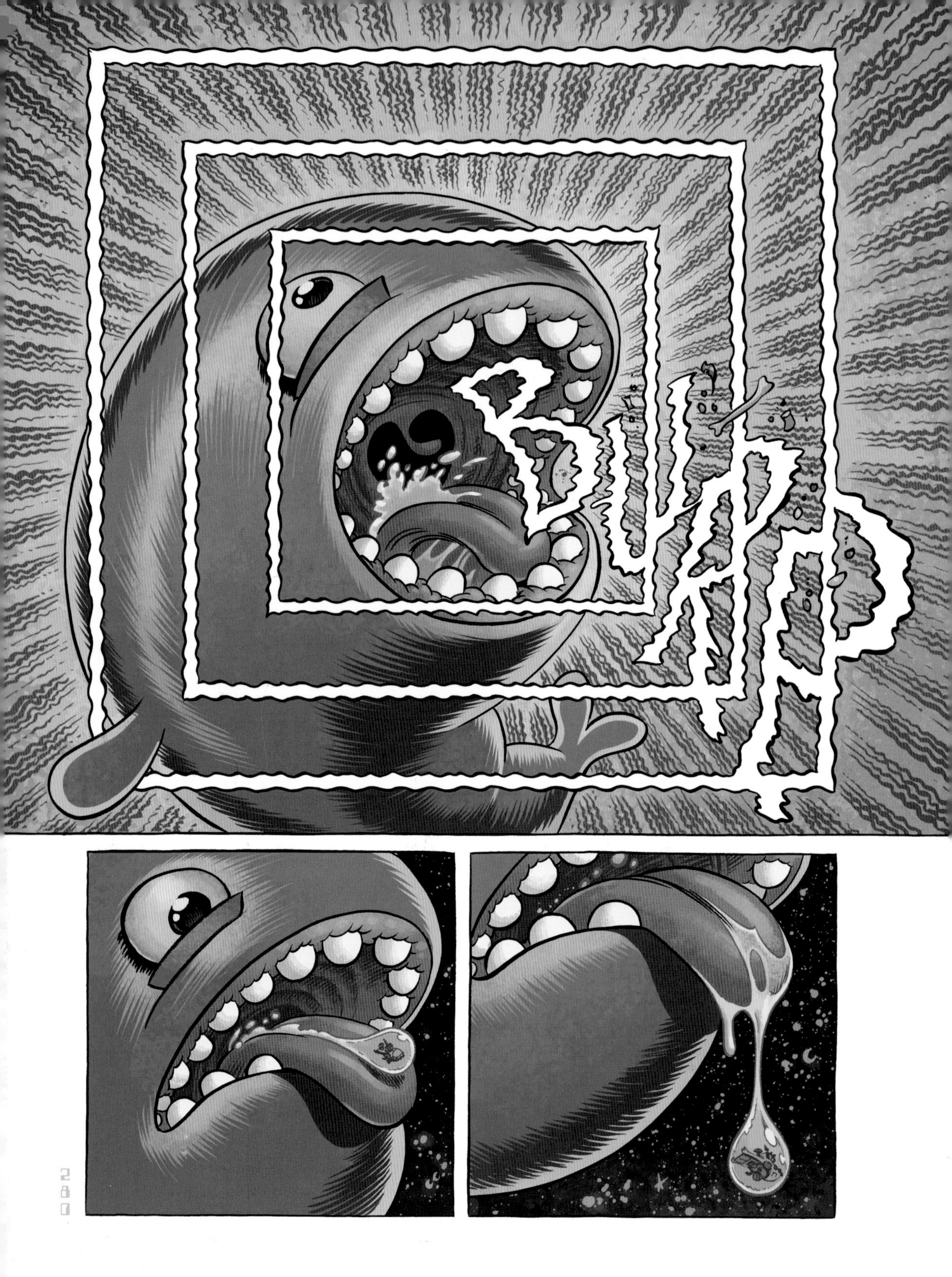
BURP

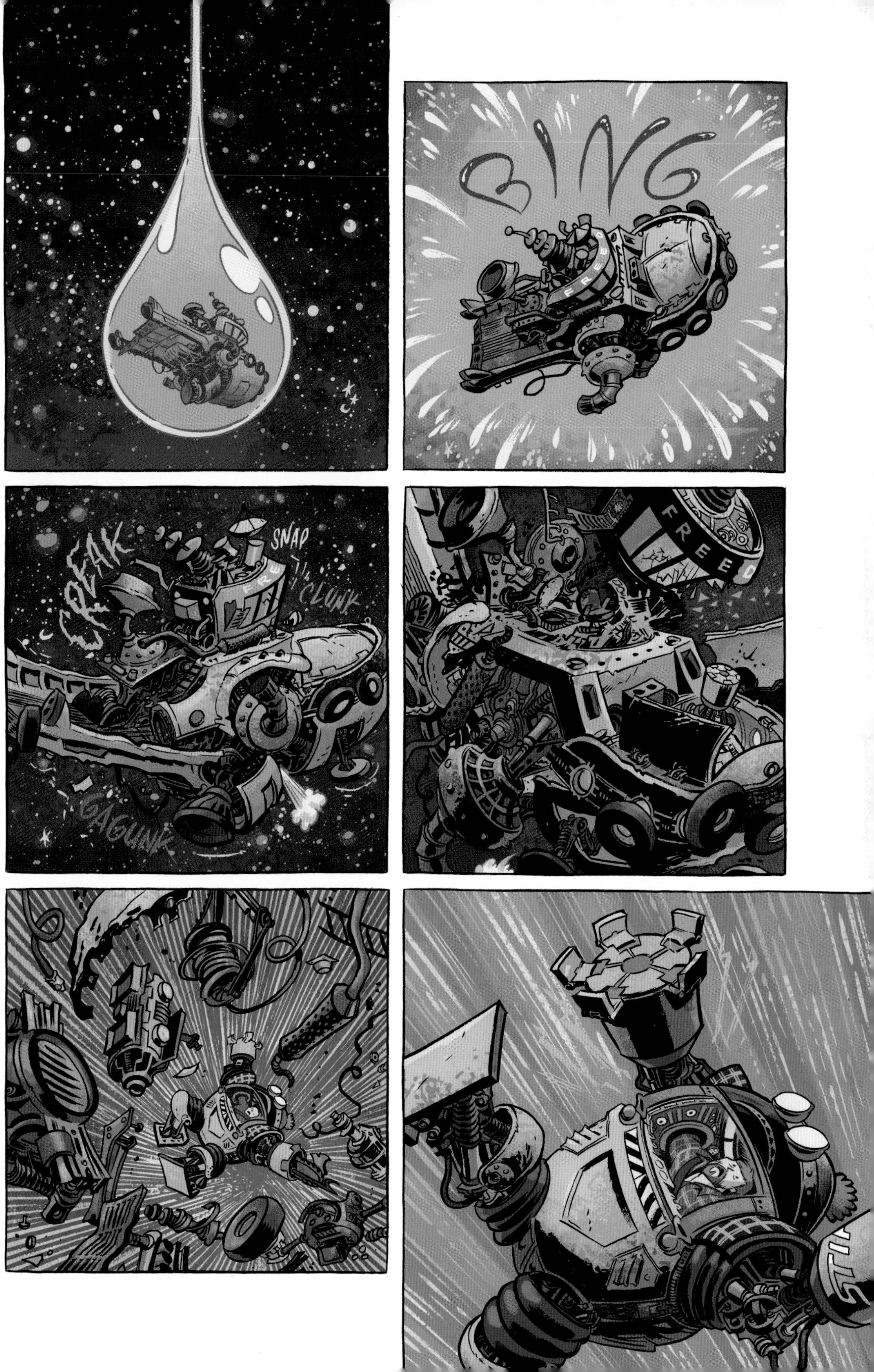
BING
FREED
CREAK
SNAP
FRE
CLUNK
GAGUNK
FREED

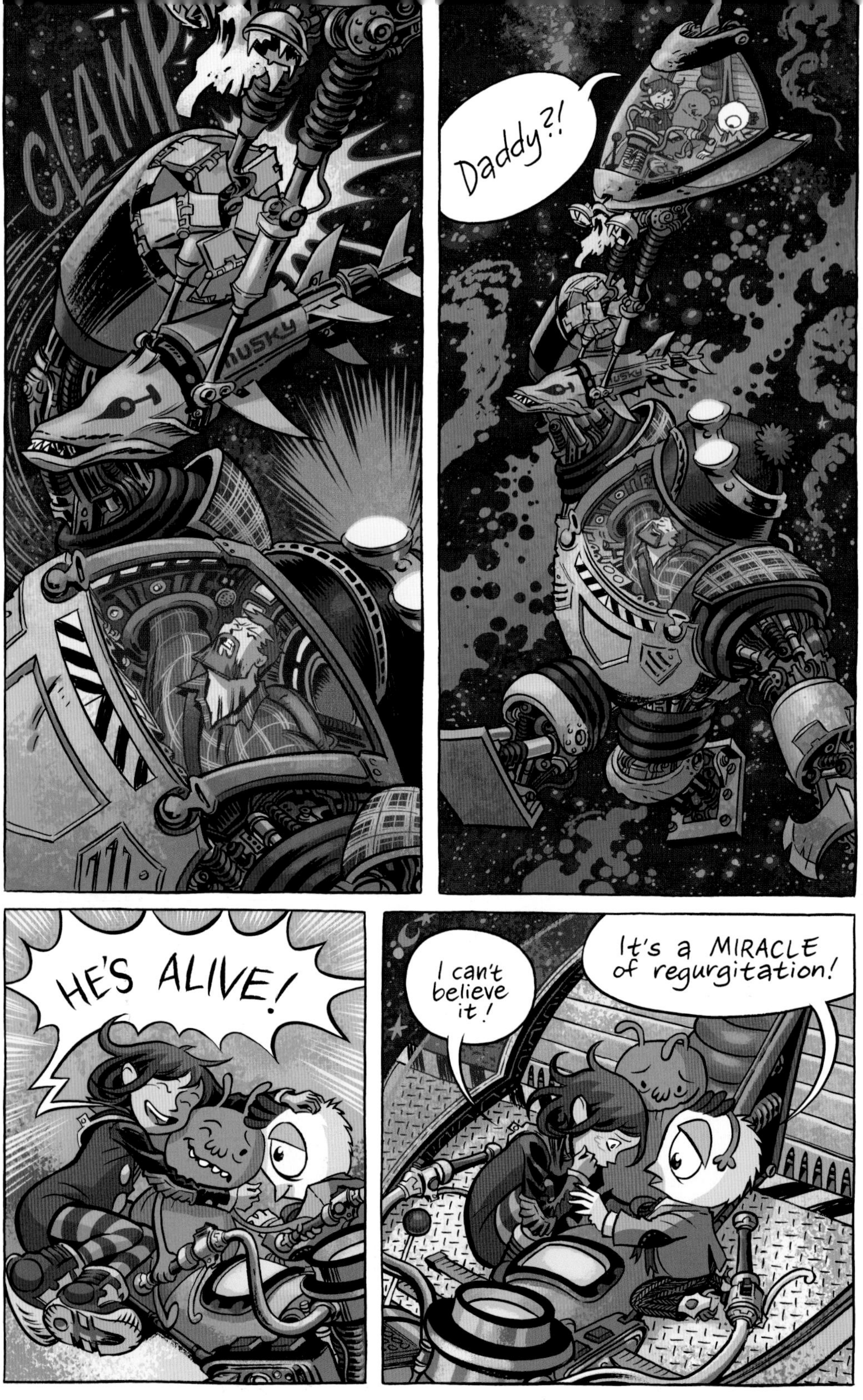
CLAMP
MUSKY
Daddy?!
HE'S ALIVE!
I can't believe it!
It's a MIRACLE of regurgitation!

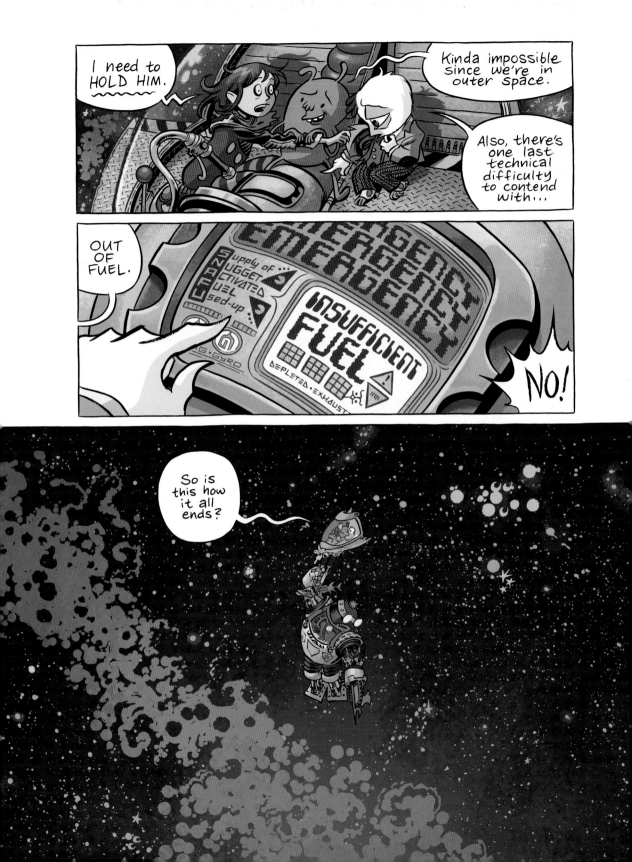

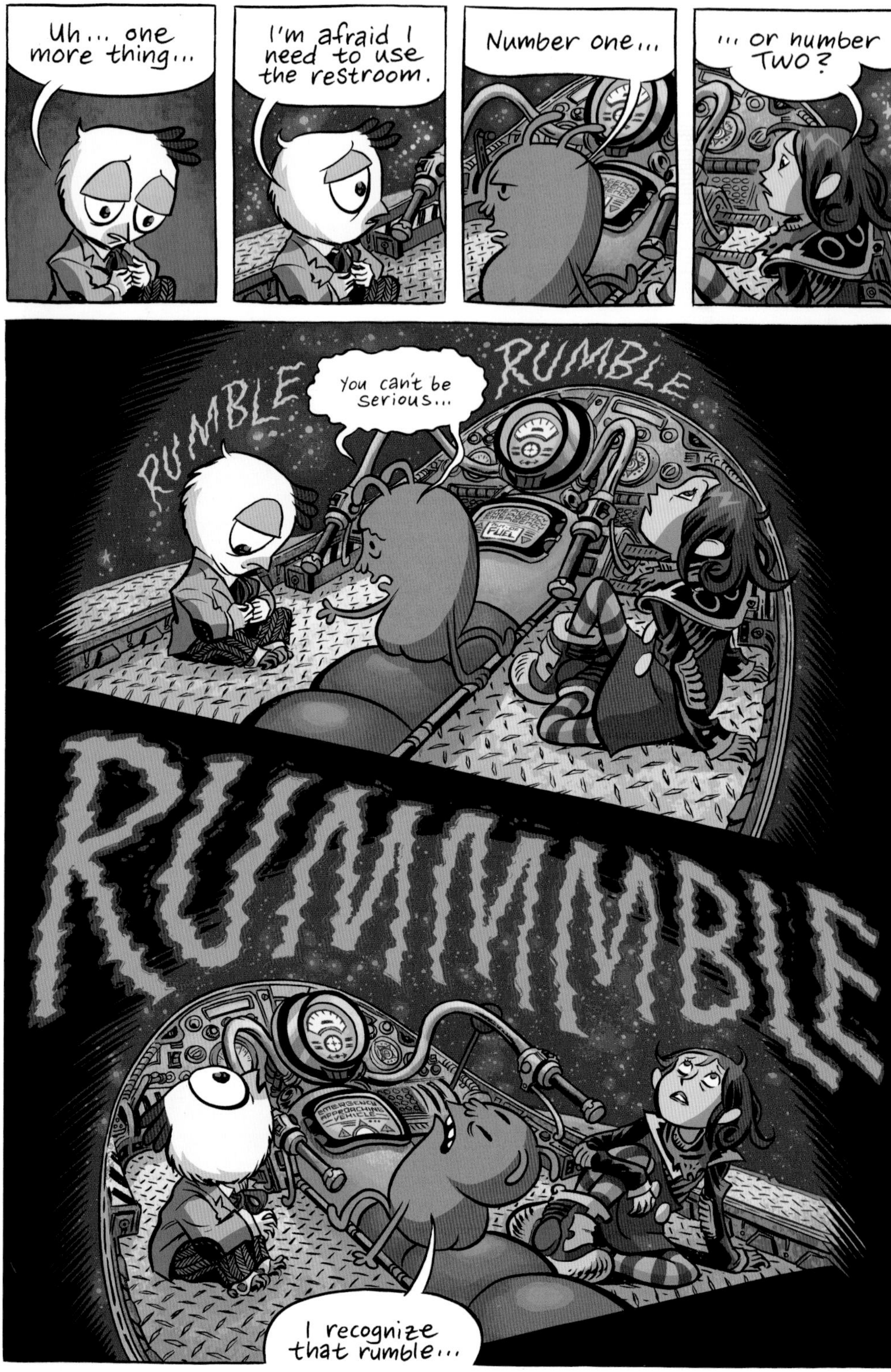
Uh... one more thing...
I'm afraid I need to use the restroom.
Number one...
... or number TWO?
RUMBLE
You can't be serious...
RUMBLE
FUEL
RUMMMBLE
EMERGENCY APPROACHING VEHICLE
I recognize that rumble...

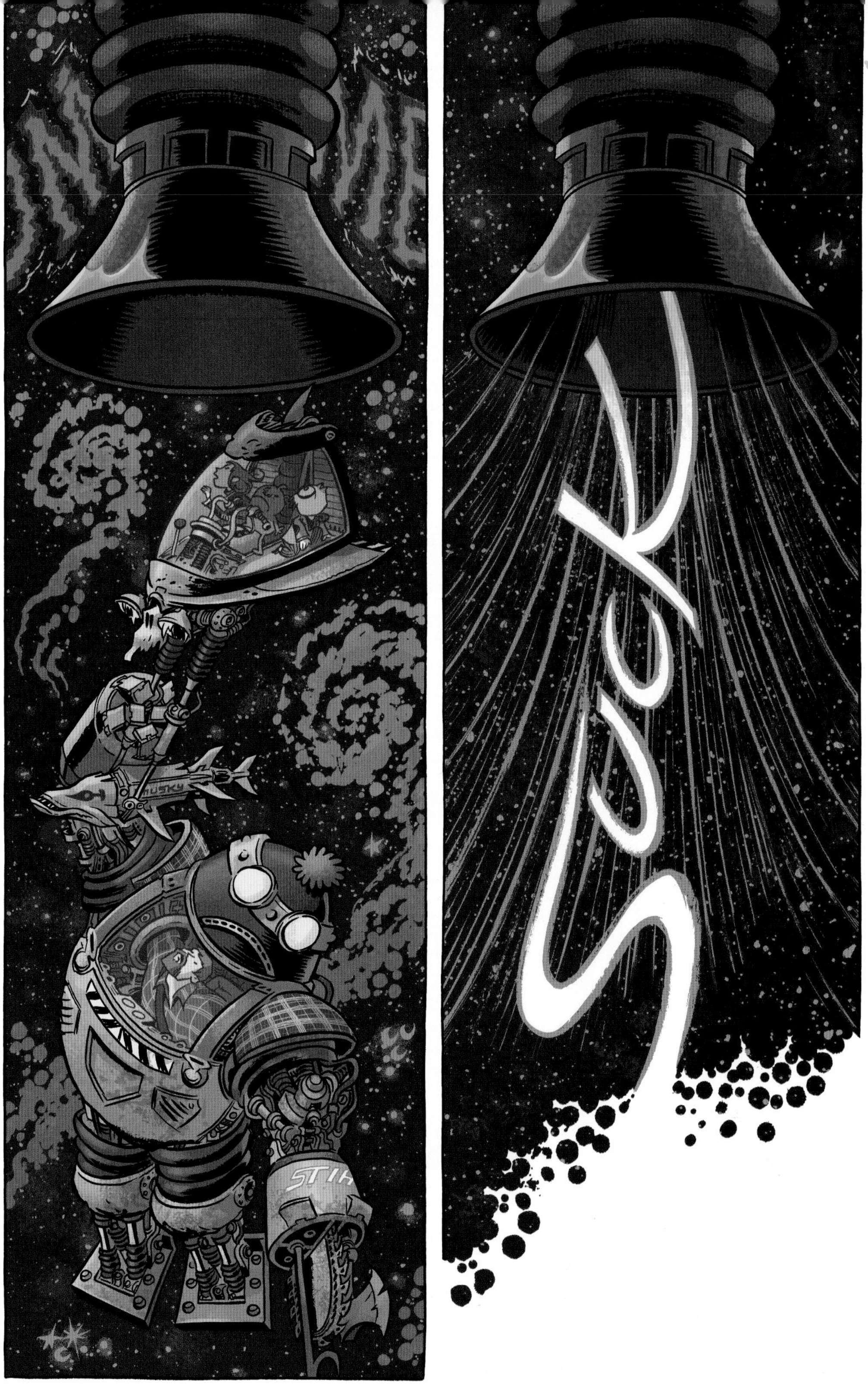
Suck

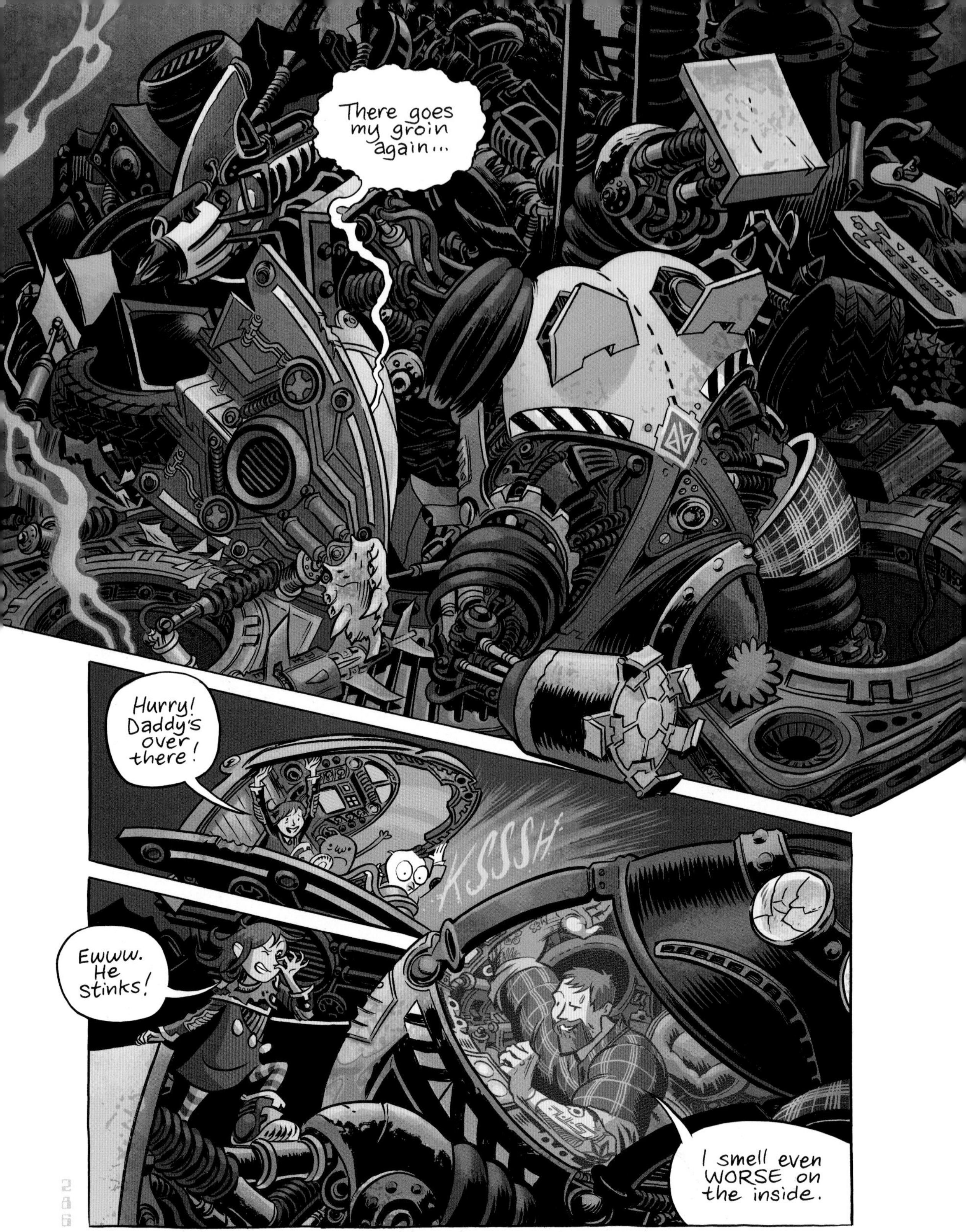
There goes my groin again...
Hurry! Daddy's over there!
KSSSH
Ewww. He stinks!
I smell even WORSE on the inside.

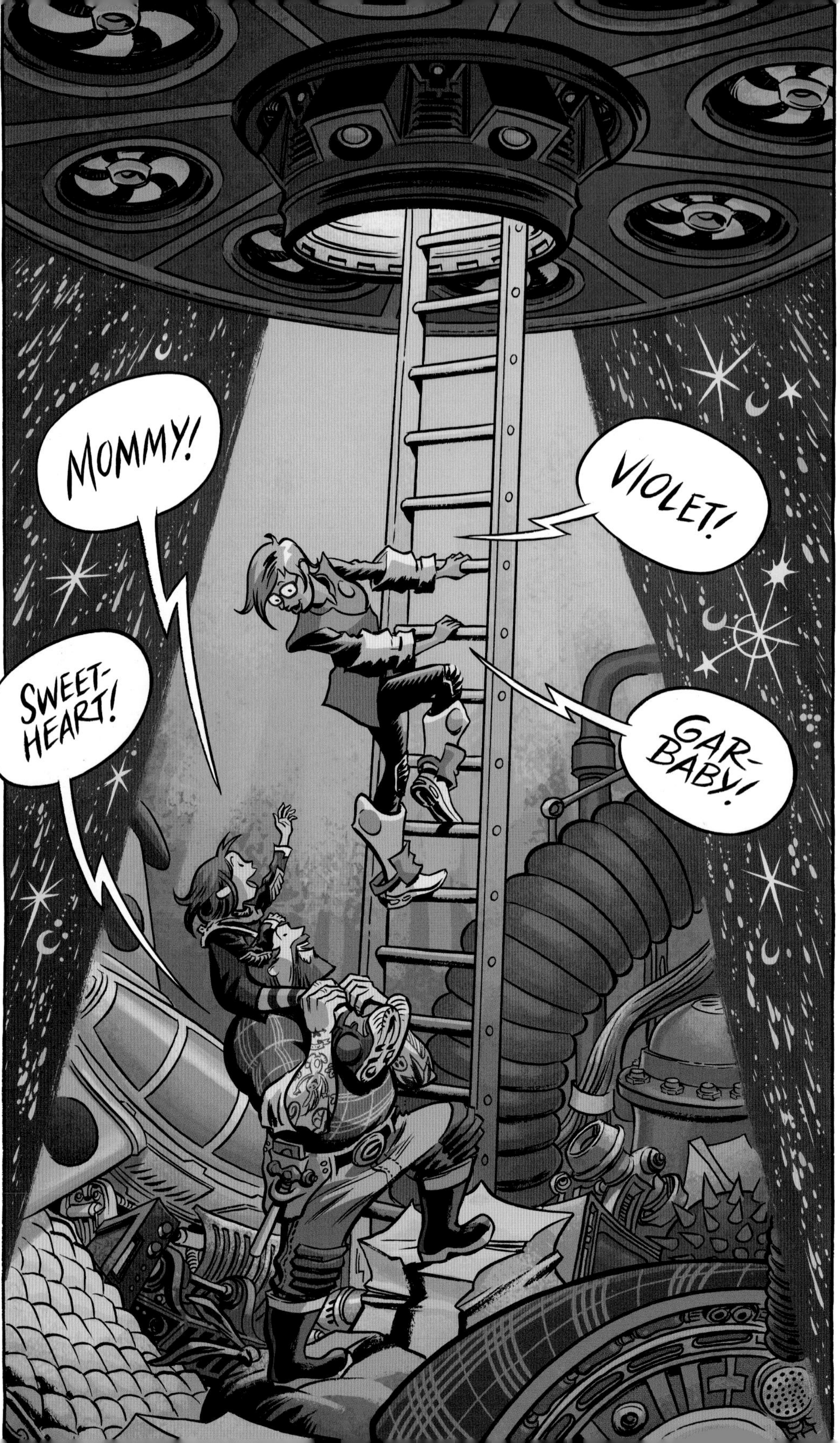
MOMMY!
VIOLET!
SWEET-HEART!
GAR-BABY!

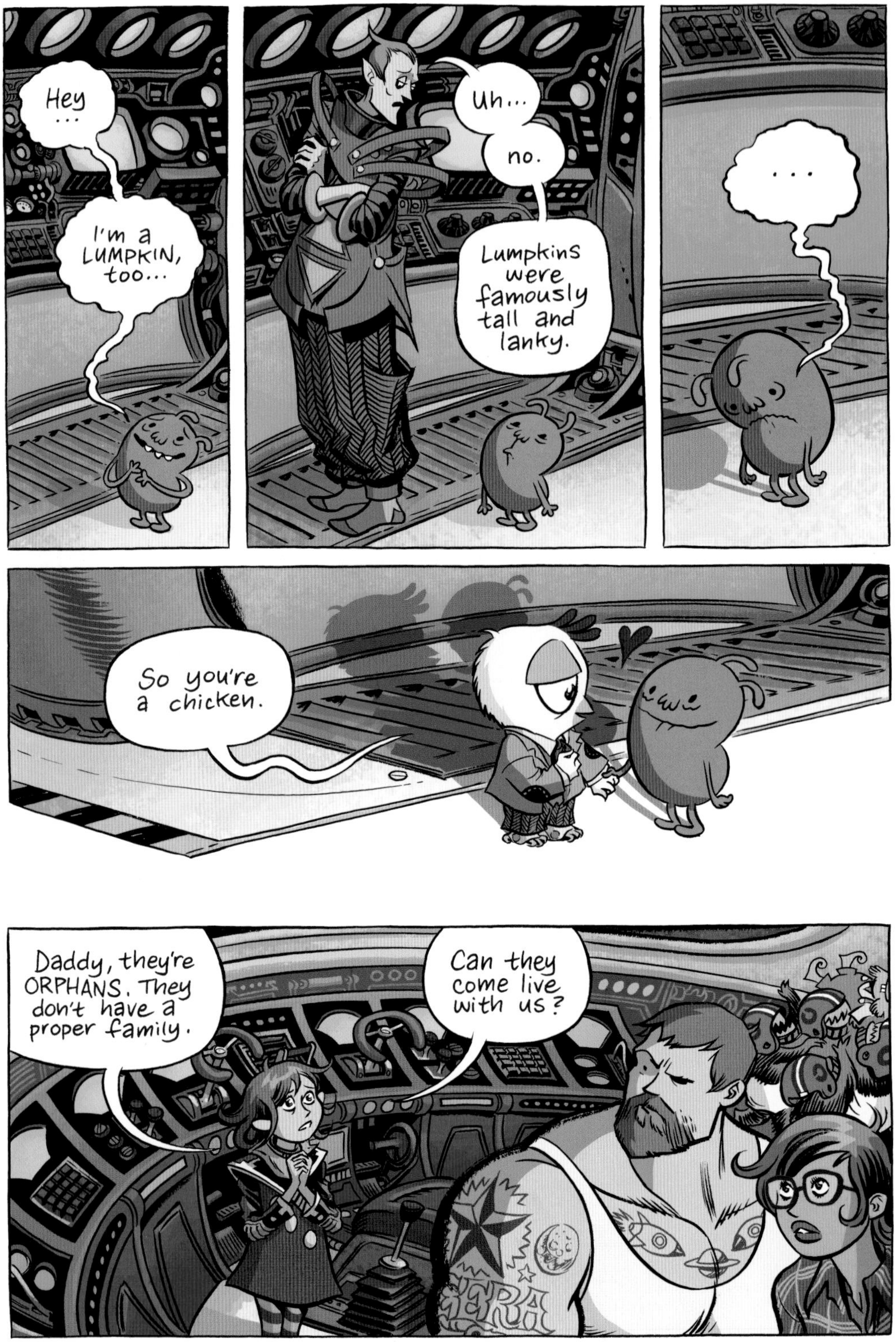
Hey ...
I'm a LUMPKIN, too...
Uh...
no.
Lumpkins were famously tall and lanky.
...
So you're a chicken.
Daddy, they're ORPHANS. They don't have a proper family.
Can they come live with us?

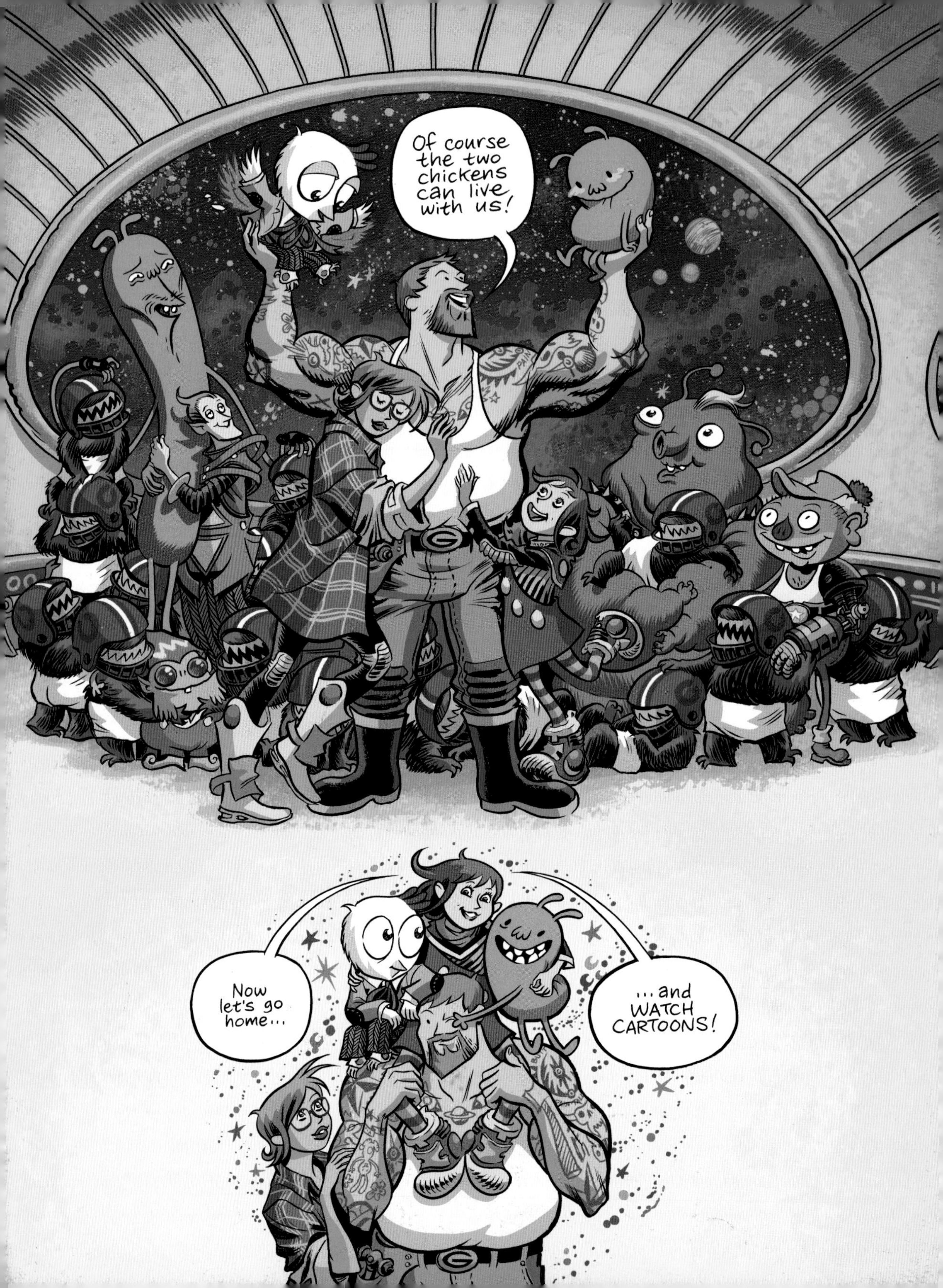
Of course the two chickens can live with us!
Now let's go home...
...and WATCH CARTOONS!

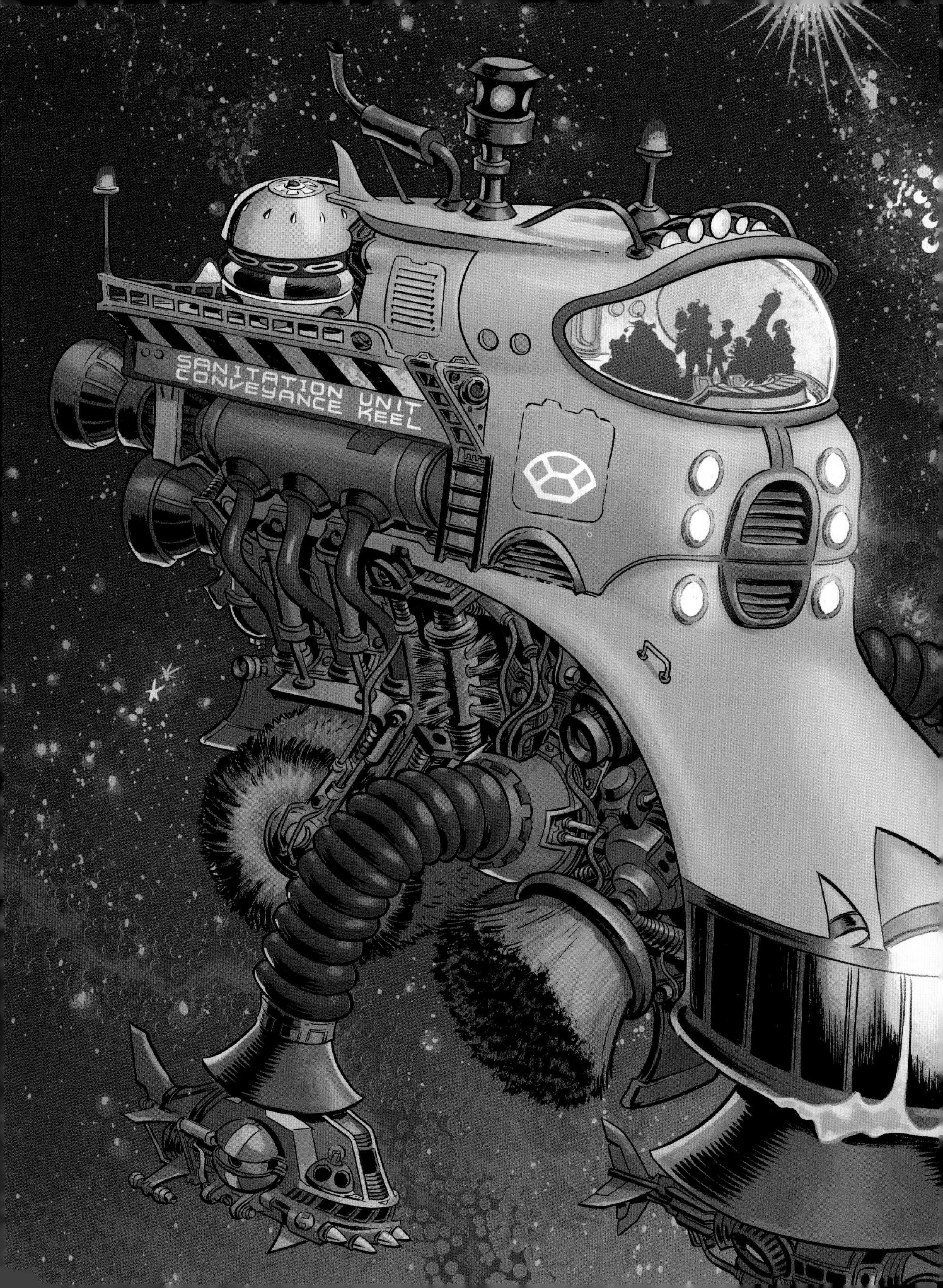
SANITATION UNIT
CONVEYANCE KEEL

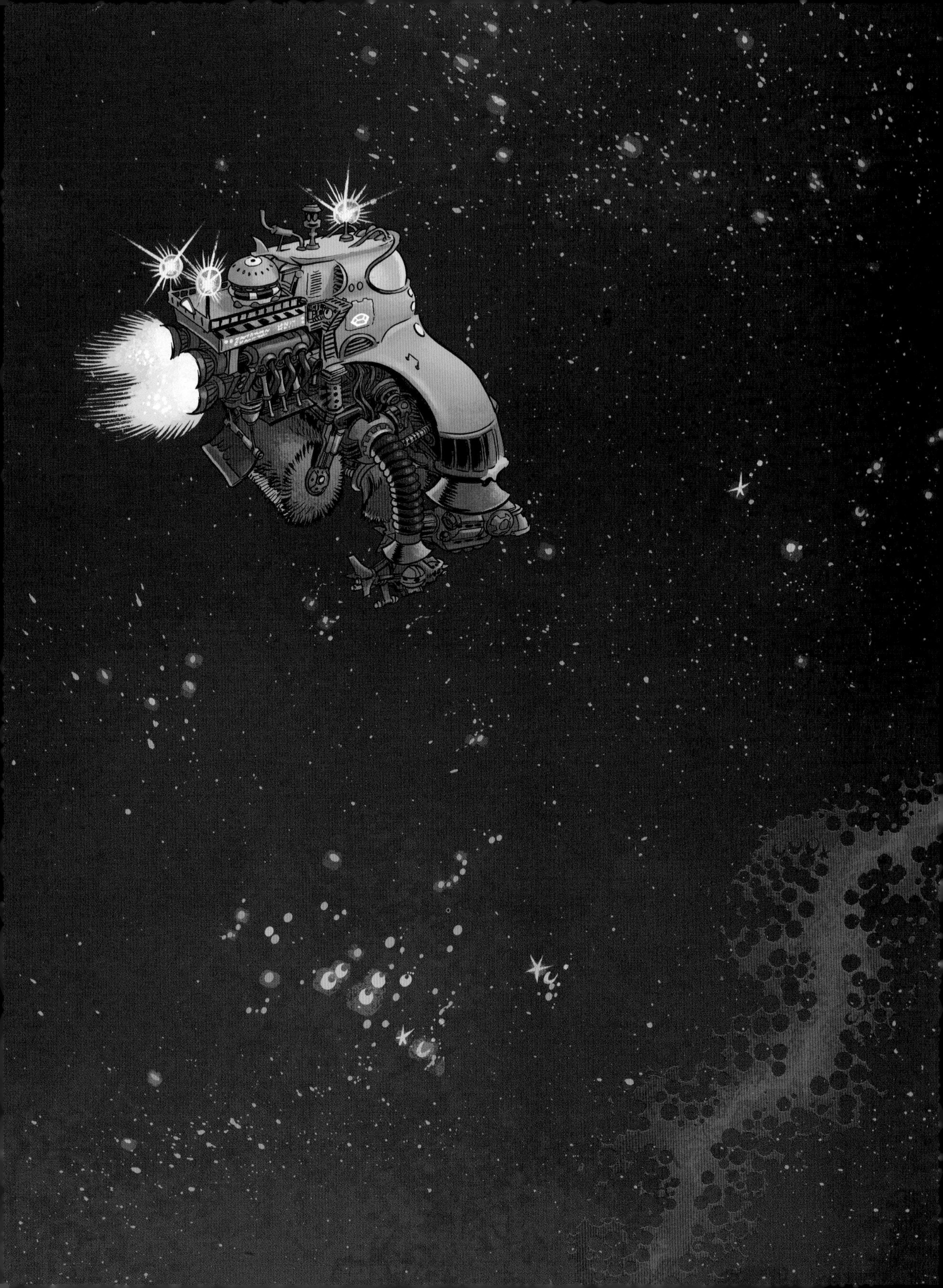

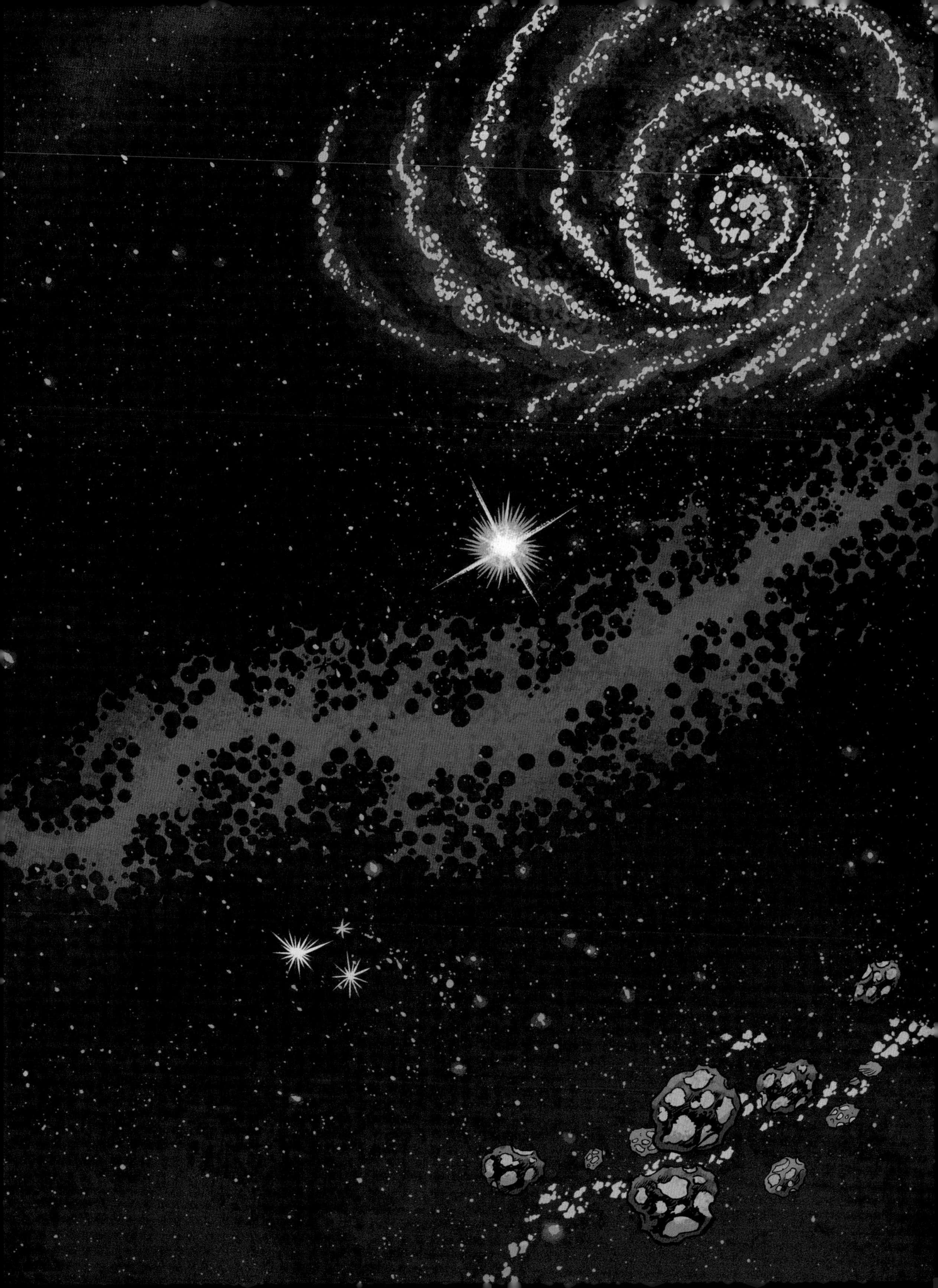

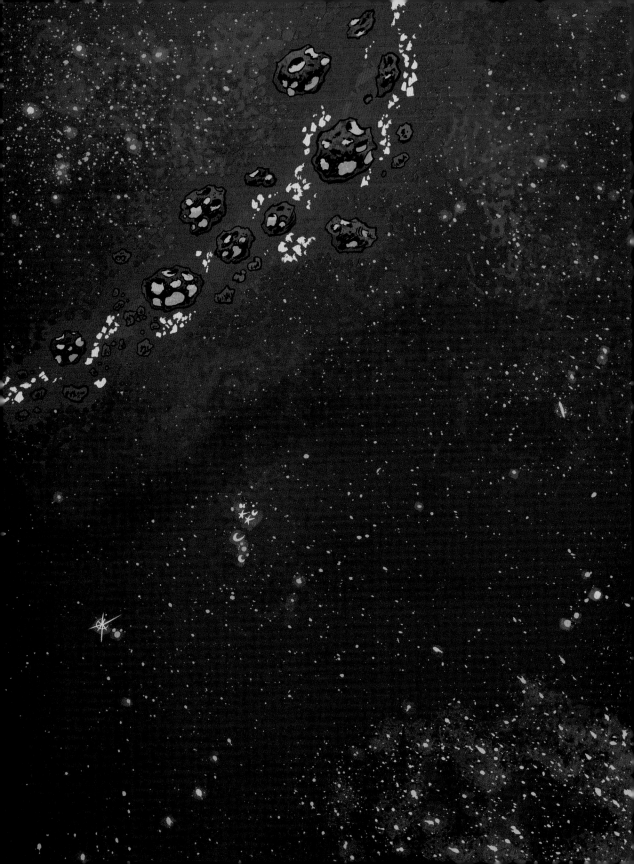

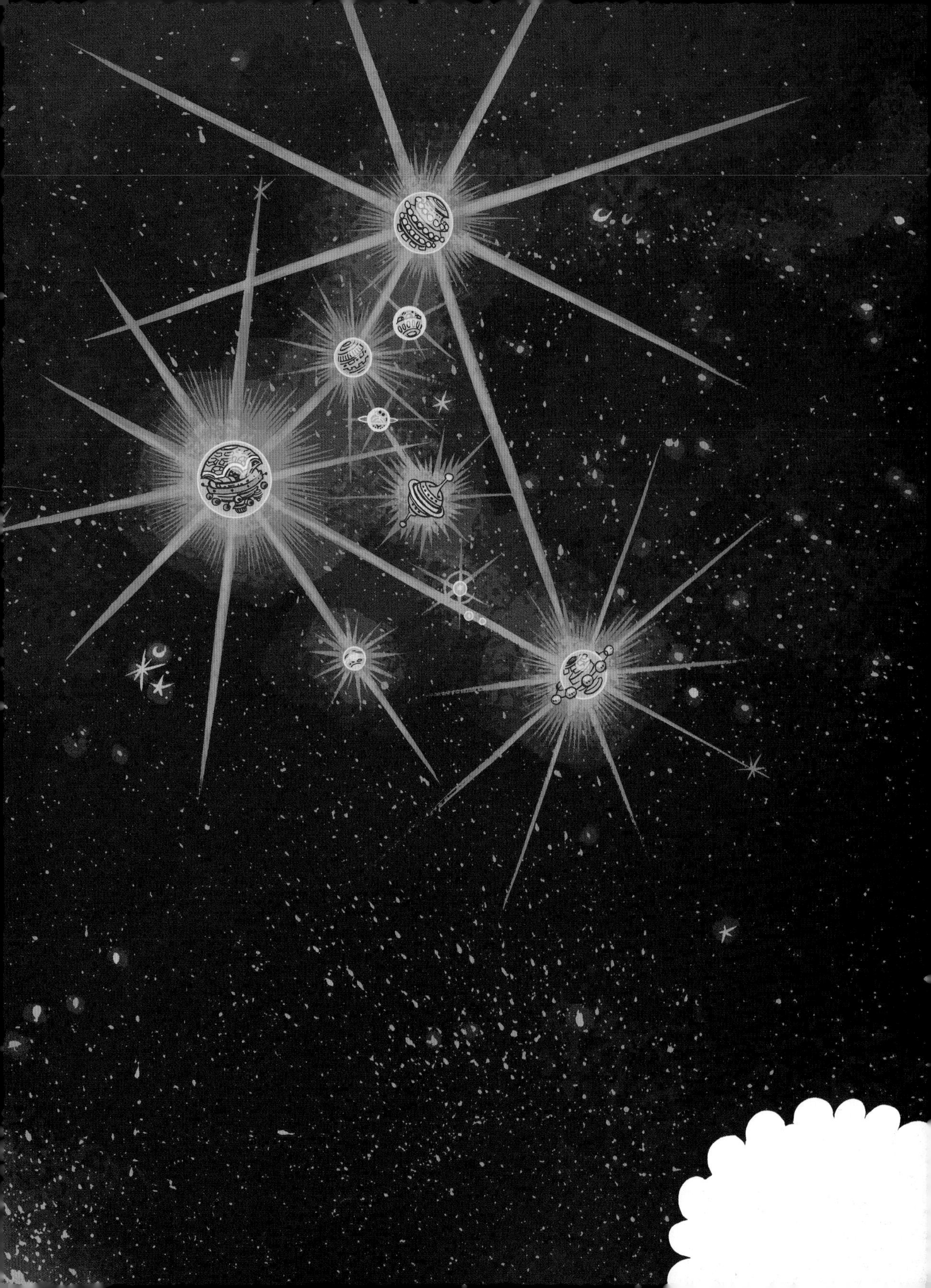

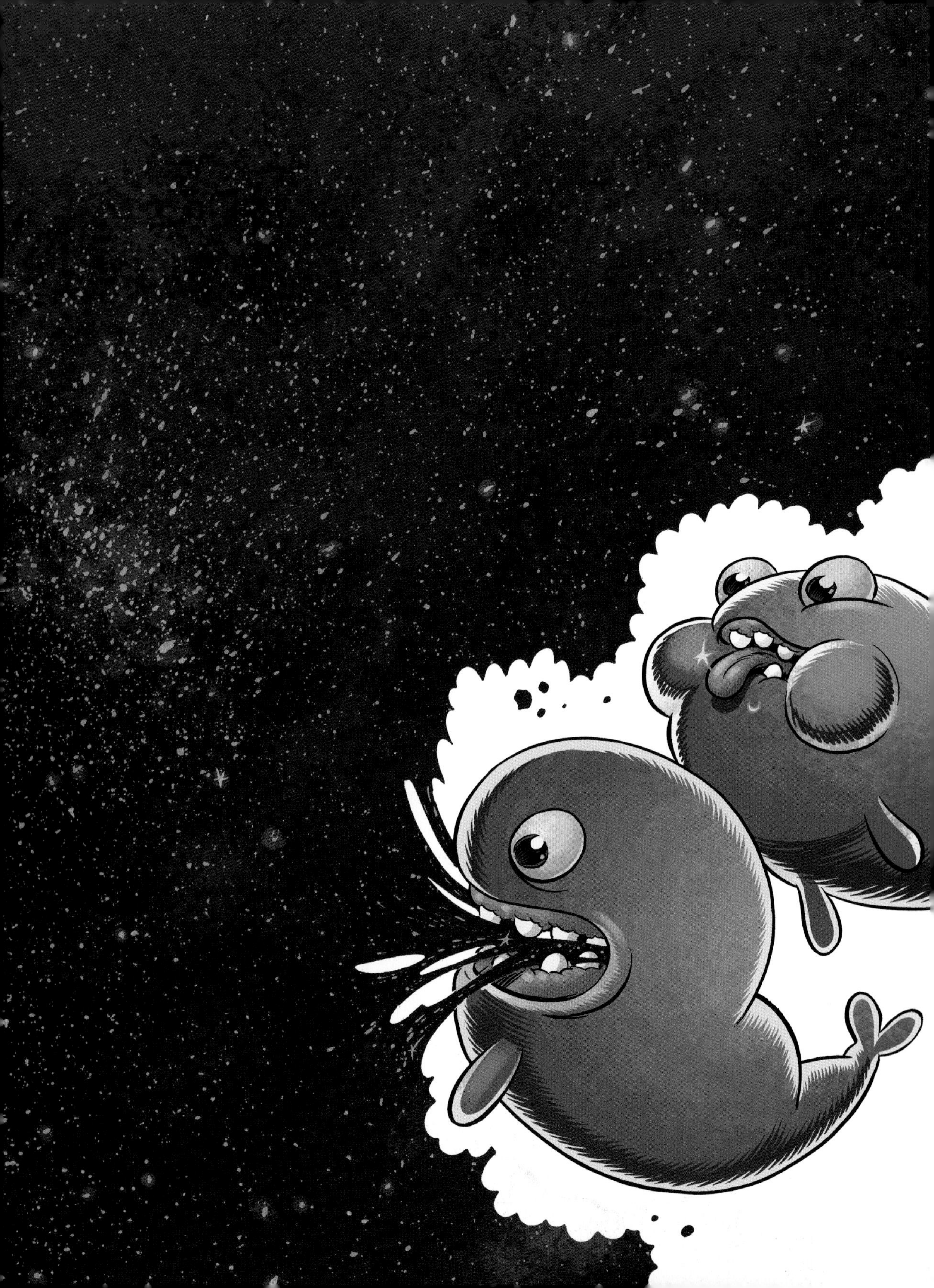

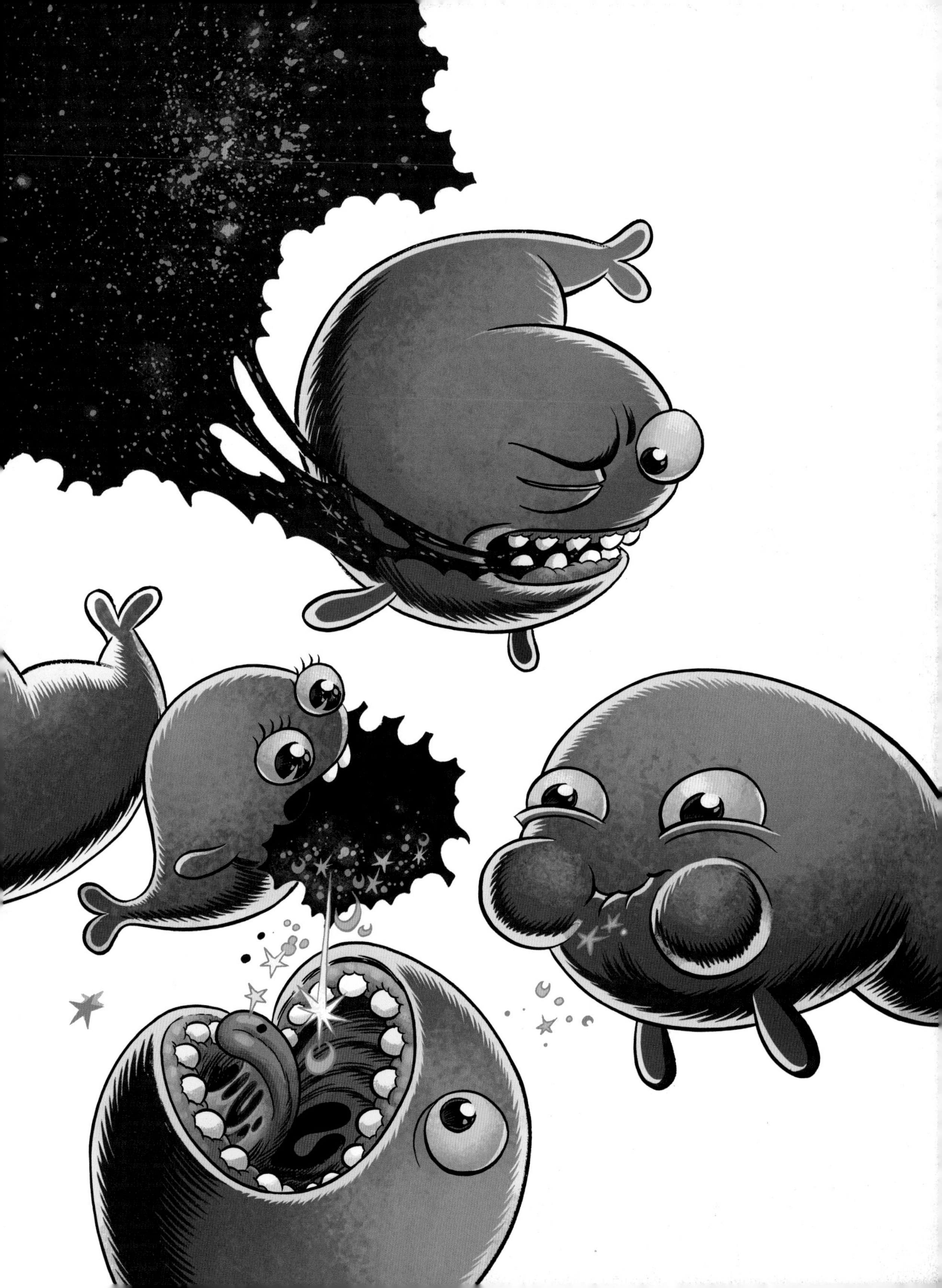

fin.

epilogue

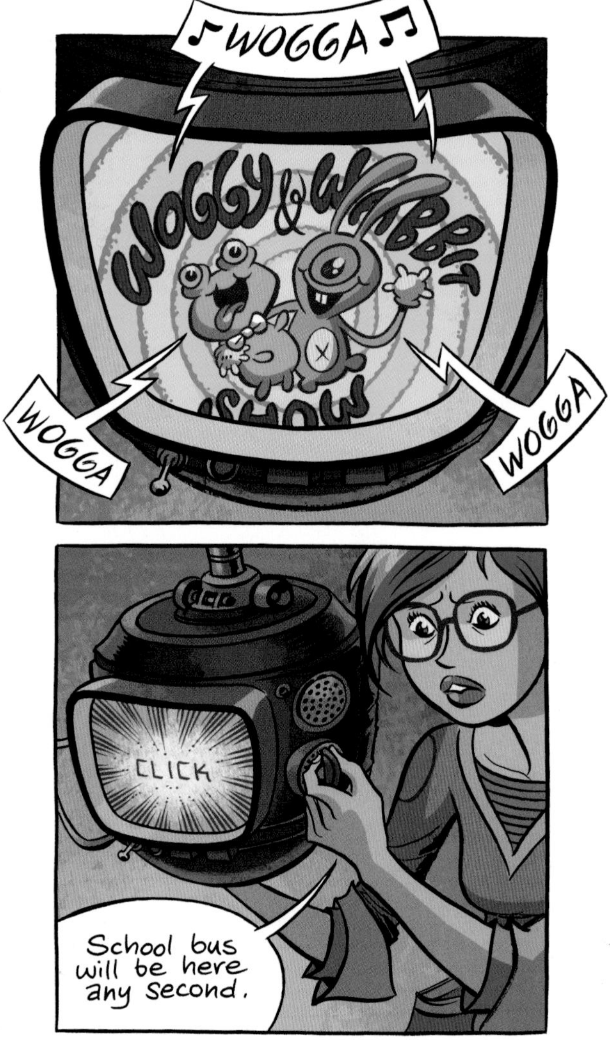
WOGGA
WOGGY & WABBIT SHOW
WOGGA
WOGGA
CLICK
School bus will be here any second.

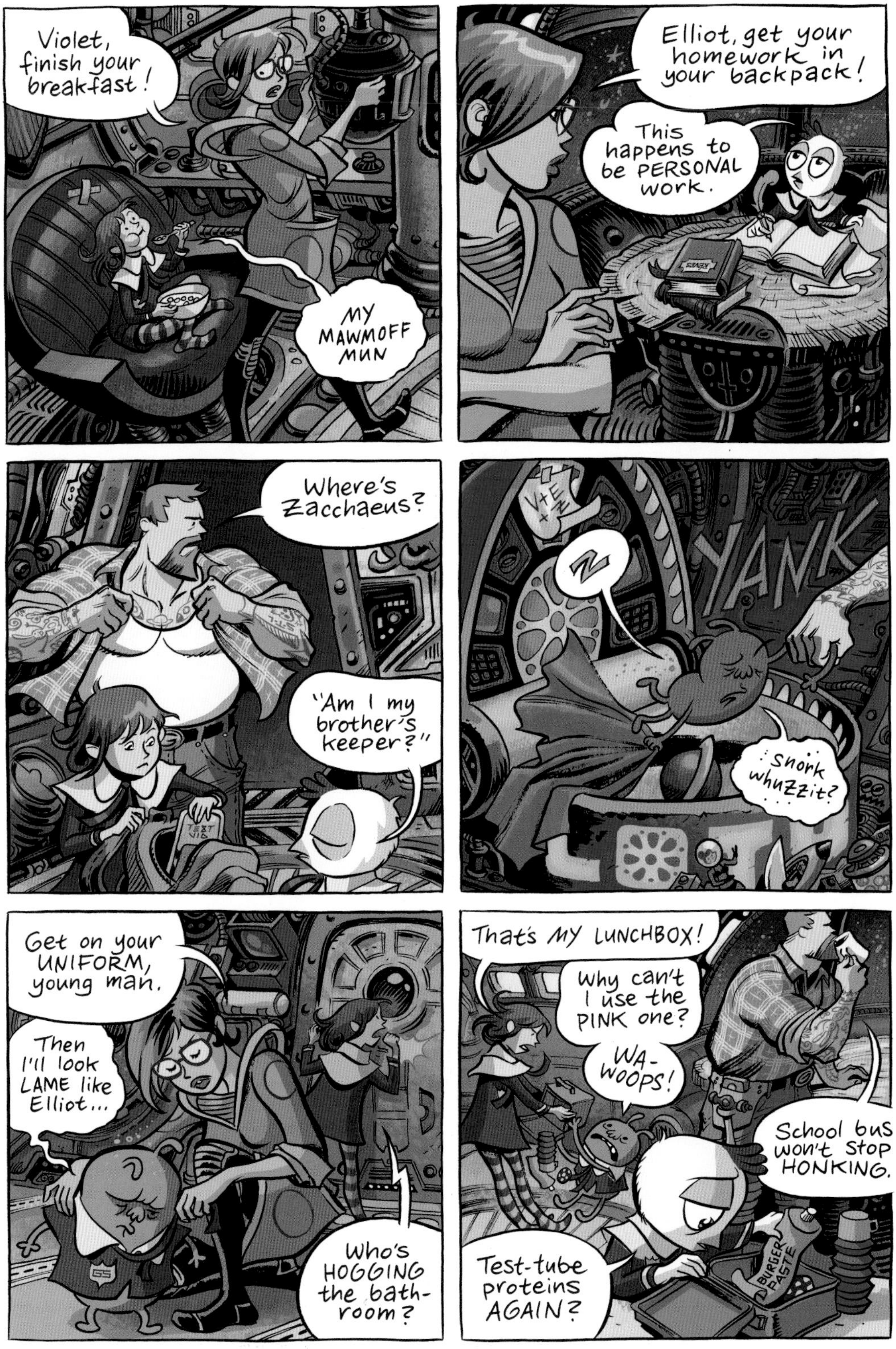
Violet, finish your breakfast!
MY MAWMOFF MUN
Elliot, get your homework in your backpack!
This happens to be PERSONAL work.
Where's Zacchaeus?
"Am I my brother's keeper?"
YANK
Z
: snork whuzzit? :
Get on your UNIFORM, young man.
Then I'll look LAME like Elliot...
Who's HOGGING the bath-room?
That's MY LUNCHBOX!
Why can't I use the PINK one?
WA-WOOPS!
School bus won't stop HONKING.
Test-tube proteins AGAIN?
BURGER PASTE

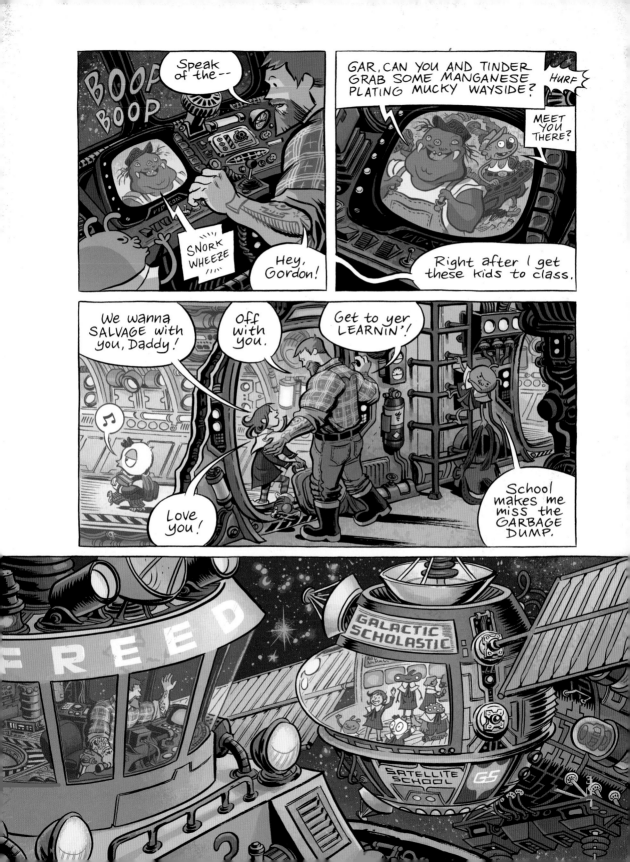

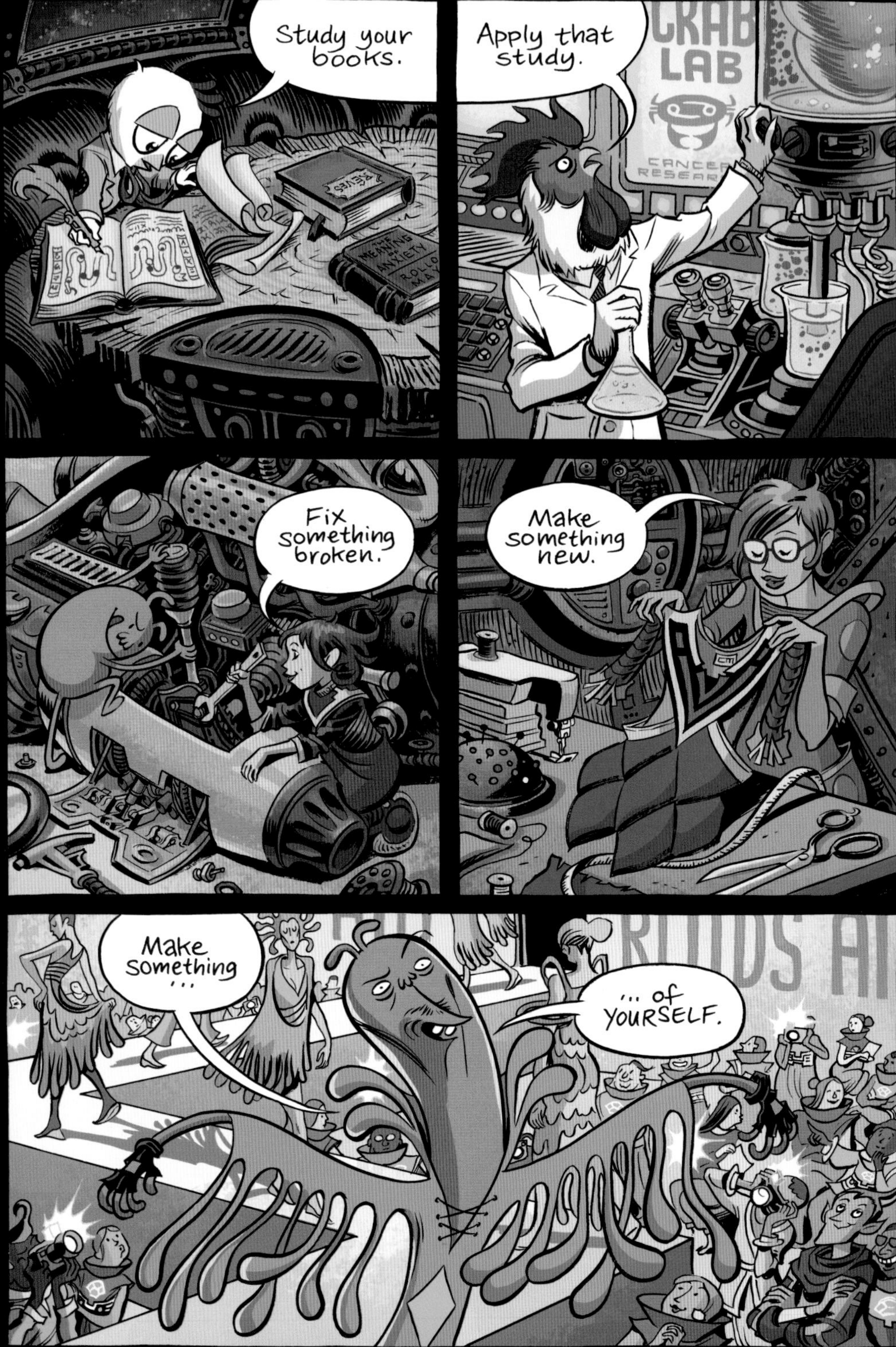
Study your books.
THE MEANING OF ANXIETY
Apply that study.
CRAB LAB
Fix something broken.
Make something new.
Make something ...
... of YOURSELF.

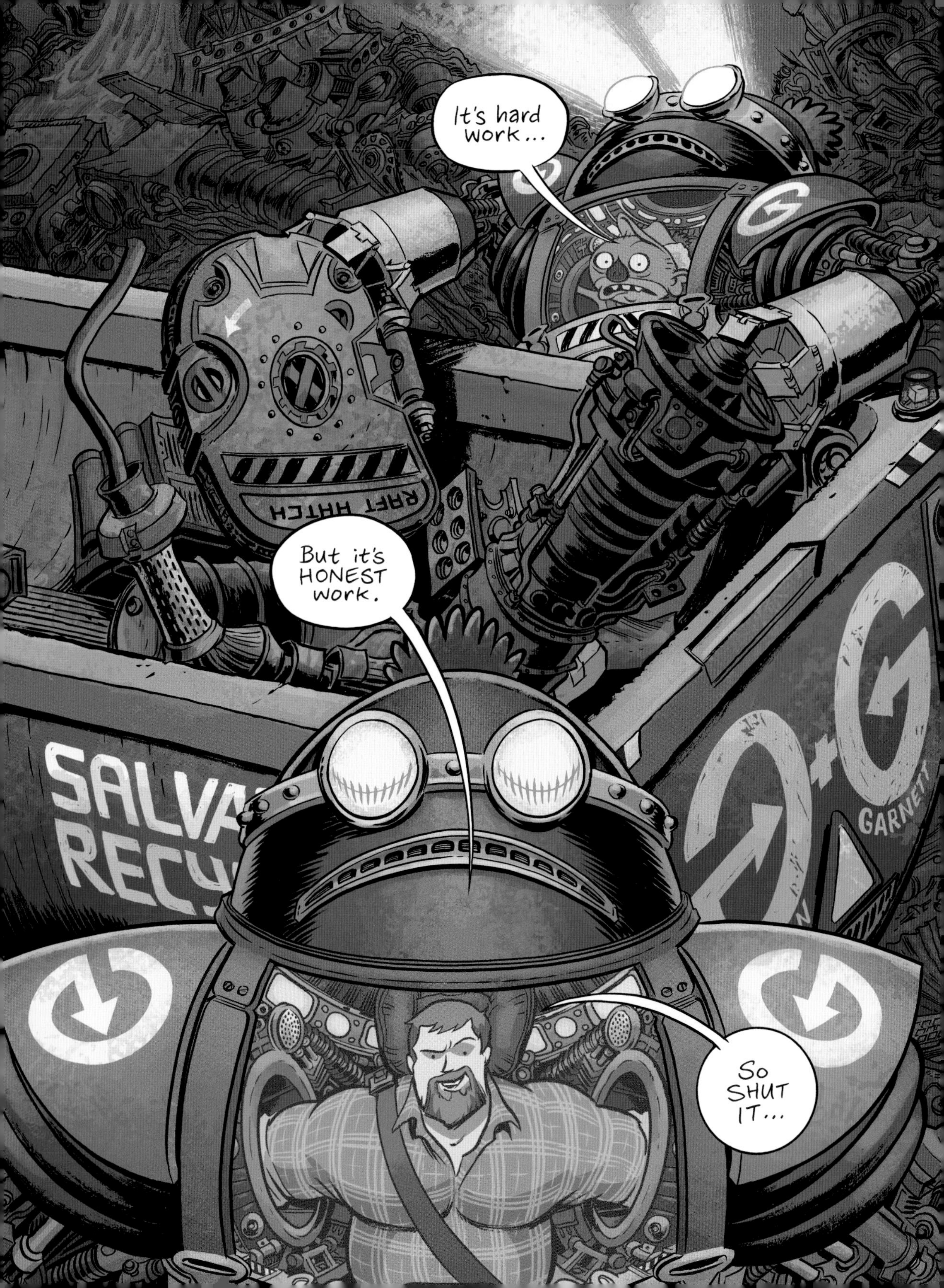
It's hard work...
RAFT HATCH
But it's HONEST work.
GARNETT
So SHUT IT...

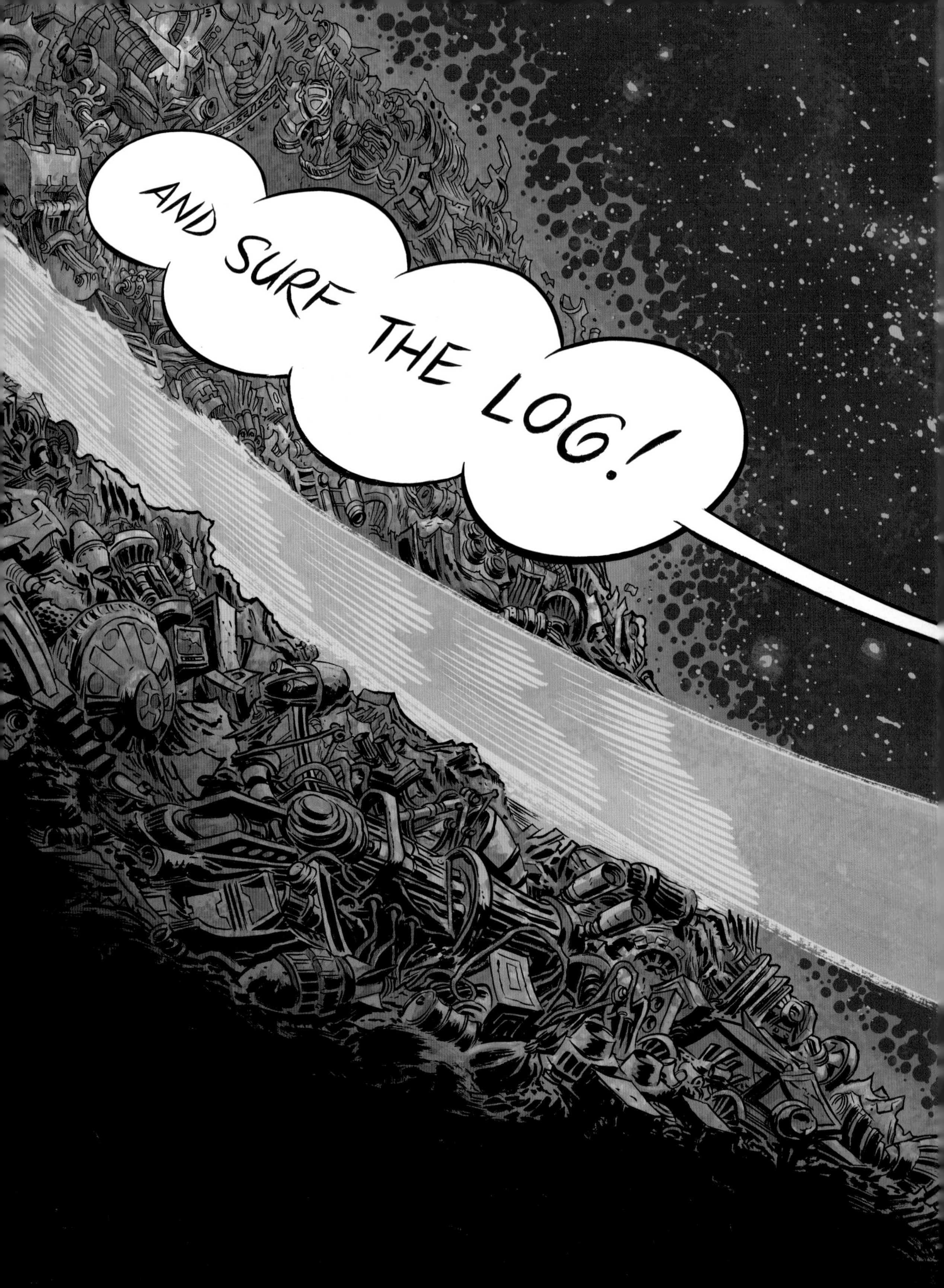
AND SURF THE LOG!

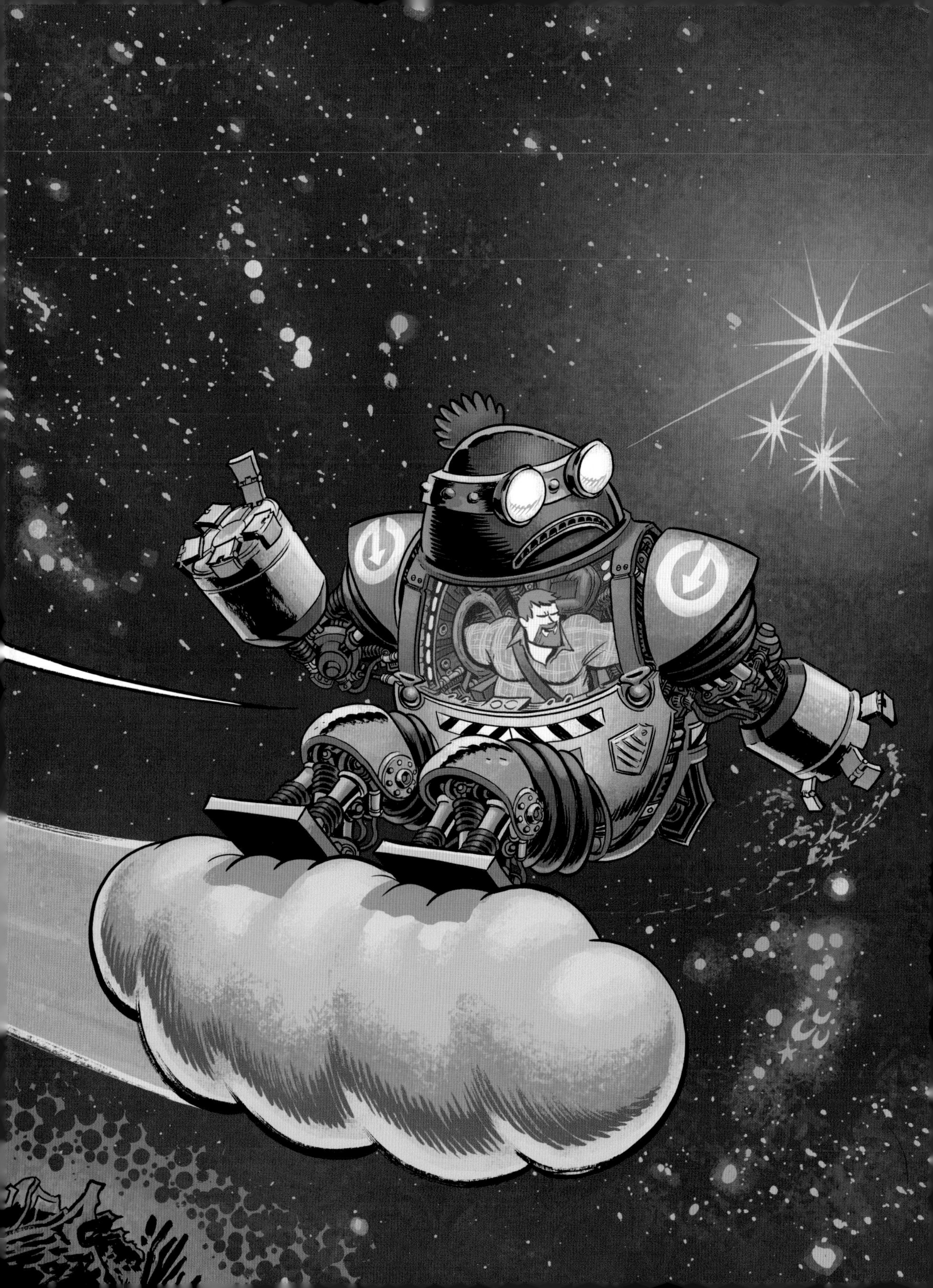

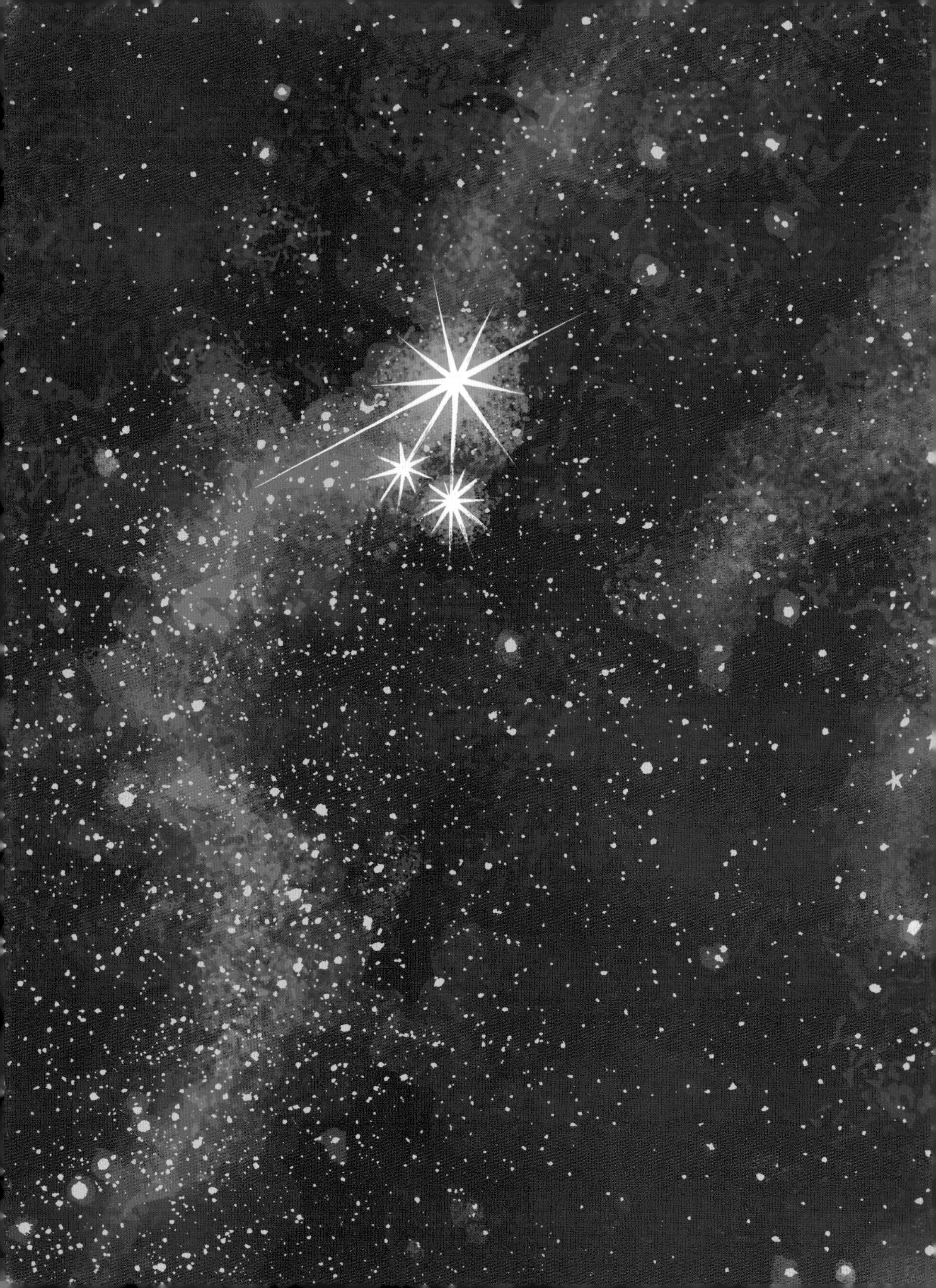

THANKS TO...

Violet, Azure, and Dan, for being the inspiration.

Lily Mason, Stella Sablan, and Joy Wurz, for their girl-hero expertise.

Adam Arnold, for his namesake, and Jeremy Tinder, for his likeness.

Jeffrey Alden, Lucie Bonvalet, Pegi Christensen, Chris Duffy, Alessandro Ferrari, Justin Harris, Georgia Hussey, Rebecca & Brian Hahn, David Naimon, and Ami & Jon Thompson, for being first readers.

Joshin Yamada, for the photos; Timothy Arp, for the spaceship model; Jon Thompson and Bolster, for the video.

Dave Stewart, for brilliant coloring and plenty of patience.

Phil Falco, Adam Rau, David Saylor, and the entire Scholastic team, for believing in the project.

PJ Mark, for being an amazing agent, along with Cecile Barendsma and Marya Spence.

My dear friends and family, for their constant encouragement.

You readers, who stick along for the ride.

And finally Sierra Hahn, for looking after my neurotic Elliot side and my impulsive Zacchaeus side. Also, for being the love of my life.

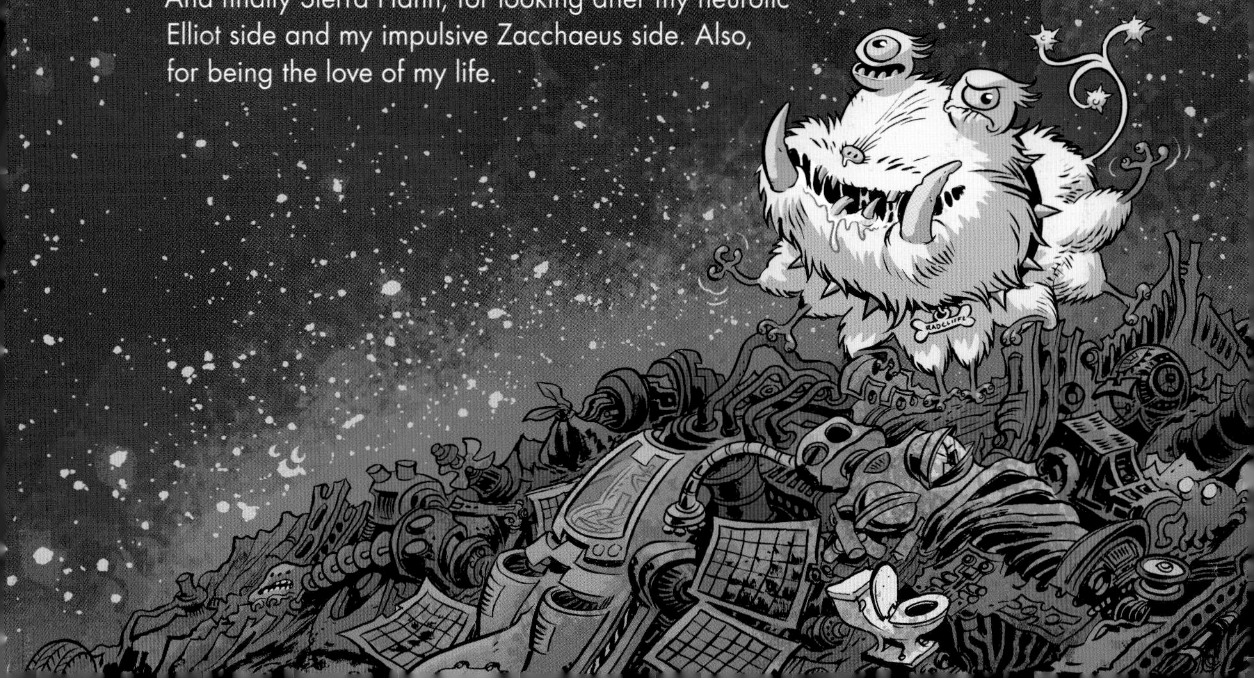

CRAIG THOMPSON

is an award-winning graphic novelist best known for his books *Good-bye, Chunky Rice*; *Blankets*; *Carnet de Voyage*; and *Habibi*. He has received three Eisner Awards, four Harvey Awards, and two Ignatz Awards. Craig lives in Los Angeles, California.

DAVE STEWART is an eight-time Eisner Award–winning colorist best known for his work at Dark Horse Comics, DC Comics, and Marvel Comics.

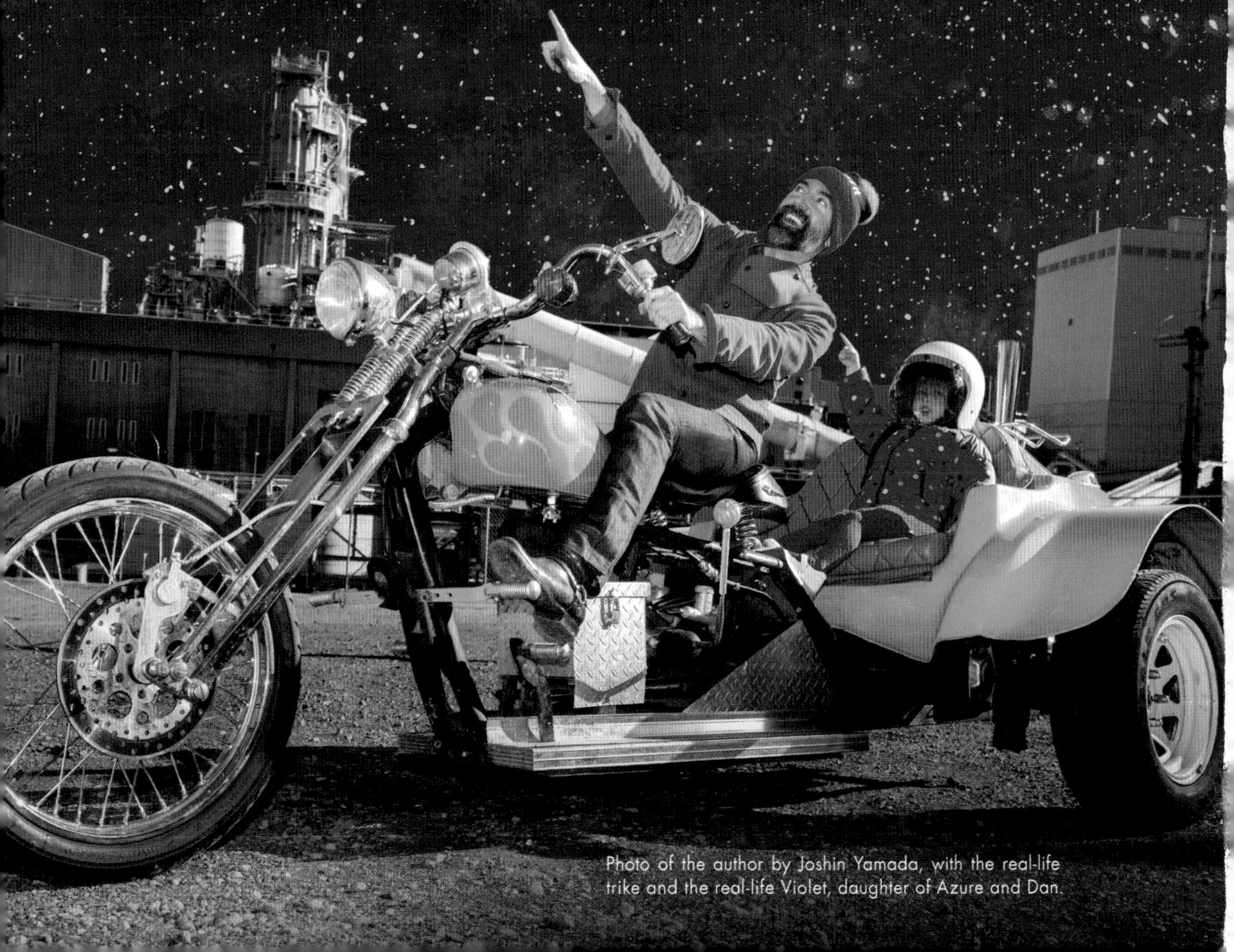

Photo of the author by Joshin Yamada, with the real-life trike and the real-life Violet, daughter of Azure and Dan.